Shiver the Moon

The Chain of Living Fire: Book 1

Phillip M. Locey

Elisahd Books

DURHAM, NORTH CAROLINA

Phillip M. Locey/Elisahd Books
5 Waterview Ct
Durham, North Carolina 27703
www.elisahdbooks.com

Publisher's Note: This is a work of fiction. Names, characters, places, and incidents are a product of the author's imagination. Locales and public names are sometimes used for atmospheric purposes. Any resemblance to actual people, living or dead, or to businesses, companies, events, institutions, or locales is completely coincidental.

Book Layout © 2017 BookDesignTemplates.com
Cover Art by Soheil Toosi
Interior Map by Cornelia Yoder (www.corneliayoder.com)

Shiver the Moon / Phillip M. Locey. -- 1st ed.
ISBN 978-1-947579-04-0

This book is dedicated to the members of Durham Voices
who helped make this book a reality:
JQ Abbey, Jeremy Cribb, Rachel Hamm, Hannah Phoenix,
Jenn Robinson, and Ken Wetherington.

Thanks to the multitudes who gave support along the way.

*"The gods of our past will come haunting soon;
Let tremble the earth and shiver the moon."*

–SEER OF CRIOC

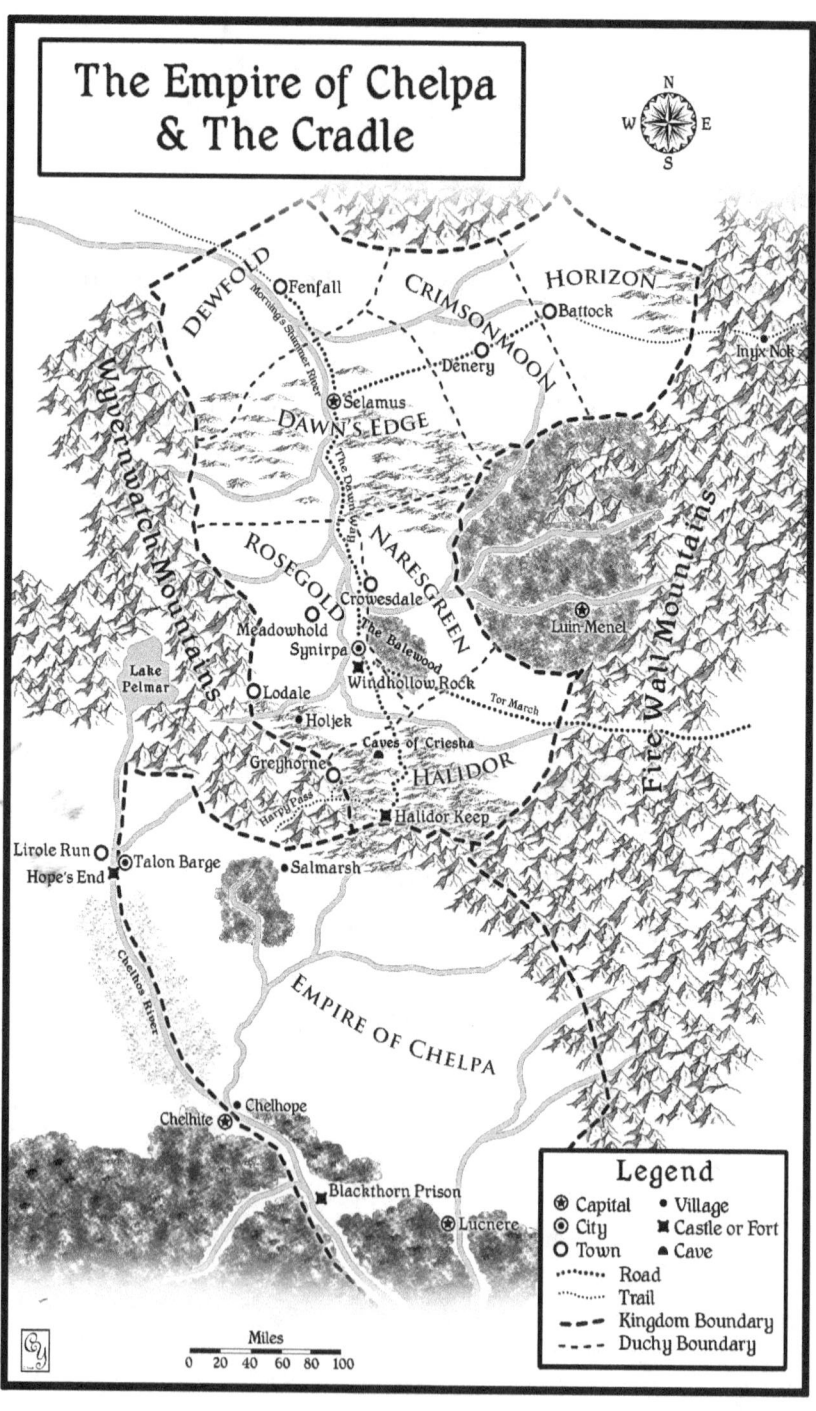

The Empire of Chelpa & The Cradle

Contents

Escape from Blackthorn..I

The Lure of Battle 19

A Motley Crew 30

Assassinating the Crown 48

Expanding the Empire 70

Reality in Dreams 82

Not Alone 99

Shared Enemies 116

After a Long Climb..136

Finding the Lessons 161

Caught on the Road 177

Giving In 193

Redirection 222

The Birth of Fire..239

Talon Barge 258

Only as Good as the Armor 279

Hope's End..297

Calling Up the Storm..323

Assault on Blackthorn..354

Spoils of Victory 378

Touch of the Moon..398

The Miracle at Windhollow Rock..423

Growing the Banner...450

Gods and Men...467

Decisions of the Heart 488

Nothing Can Last...521

Matters of Trust 546

Haunt of the Bone Man..568

Call to Arms...596

The Defense of Windhollow 623

A Deeper Darkness 651

The Battle of Naresgreen...681

Forging a New Order..714

Epilogue 724

Chapter 1

Escape from Blackthorn

Rogan was nearly close enough to taste his freedom, but that wasn't making the climb any easier. Sweat dripped down his face, stinging as it fell from his chin to the wound on his left bicep. Progress up the shaft was labored and too slow for his liking. He only hoped he could reach the top before his body yielded to exhaustion or the guards tracked him down. He doubted they would let him merely remain a prisoner after what he had done.

One painstaking move at a time, he tucked his legs as far back as he could, feet pressed flat against the dark, unforgiving stone. His arms were buttressed against opposite sides of the shaft, their strength the only thing preventing him from slipping back to where he started. There was nothing to hold on to. With only four body lengths to go, he wondered whether his struggle would all be for nothing. His arms were on fire, his sweat making the surface ever more slick. Rogan briefly wondered if he could use the length of rope he'd coiled around his body to help his predicament, but quickly realized the tight quarters would not allow him to even get it off his shoulder. No, he would just have to press on.

He slid upward another body length and felt a sharp pain as an uneven piece of masonry cut through his shirt and into the flesh of his back. Suddenly, raised voices echoed up the chute; they must have discovered the guard's body. He was sure they would track him down any moment. With new vigor, born from panic, Rogan tucked his legs again and pushed. The pain in his arm and back stung anew with the effort, but it did not match his resolve. He *would* get out of this prison alive. He would complete his bargain with the cloaked man, exact vengeance, and be truly free once more.

Rogan had been presented with this opportunity only an hour ago, after languishing in Blackthorn prison for three years. His sentence for treason came down without even the pretense of a trial, though he didn't expect otherwise from this regime. He prepared for execution – that had been the price of treason in times past. Then he learned what was more important than the death of traitors, and what was worse. The King-priest needed more labor to mine the precious uril-chent ore from beneath Blackthorn. Only recently discovered alongside known deposits of copper and gold, the veins of this unique mineral radiated dangerous energies. Hundreds of miners afflicted by a strange sickness had died before the threat was discovered. The worked uril-chent alloy it yielded was extraordinary, however; the King-priest horded it, judging it worth the cost in lives.

Although Rogan had been a well-respected baron under the previous ruler, he was targeted for it by the other prisoners. His background prepared him all the same, for he mastered the politics of the prison with the quickness of necessity, only his own hands and wits fending off its brutality. Despite his adeptness, he never once felt safe during the past three years. There were simply too many unpredictable elements down in the pits.

Working the mines was exhausting labor – swinging pick-axes and hammers, loading sacks and carts of ore – and exposure to the uril-chent often left him nauseous and debilitated by headaches. During his time at Blackthorn, Rogan assumed the outside world had forgotten him, and was glad for it. He did not need reminders of what he had lost, and he never received visitors, sympathetic or otherwise, until this afternoon.

The day began as usual – a meager breakfast before being led into the mines beneath the bowels of the prison-fortress. He hauled carts of ore for a few hours before being summoned above. Suspicious, but not unhappy for the reprieve, he was escorted to the surface levels, then down a hallway to a plain, stone-walled room with a thick, iron door. Once the pair of guards unbound his wrists, they took positions flanking it.

A rough, wooden table and two chairs were the only furniture; he was ordered to sit. Another man sat across the table wearing a dark, crimson cloak bearing the new royal insignia – a charred skull, bleeding from the eye sockets, wearing a wreath of thorns. It was also the emblem of Gholdur the Tyrant, the god from which Ebon Khorel, the new King-priest, supposedly drew power and offered allegiance.

The man at the table did not give his name, only identifying himself as the Royal Inquisitor. Another figure loomed in the corner of the room – a silent, still form, draped in a black, hooded cloak, with shadow hanging heavily upon him.

The Inquisitor interrogated Rogan for almost an hour, remaining vague while probing for information about a plot against the King-priest's agents. The man seemed sure that Rogan, being a traitor himself, had illicit contacts in the outside realm threatening the interests of the king. Most of the people Rogan once associated with had already been arrested, but he intentionally prolonged the questioning, hoping the Inquisitor would slip into telling him some shred of useful information. In the end the whole exchange proved fruitless, as neither party revealed anything insightful. Finally, with a glance over his shoulder, the Royal Inquisitor and guards left the room, shutting the door behind them.

Rogan was confused, though his heart beat rapidly. He was alone in a room, hands unbound, with a frail-looking man; though for all he knew this was Death himself, visiting. Rogan waited, watching the figure as violent scenarios ran through his mind. The hooded form watched him as well, perhaps sizing him up, perhaps staring into his soul. After several silent moments he stepped forward and sat in the chair vacated by the Inquisitor. With a sinister, almost hissing voice, he simply stated, "I have a proposition for you." Rogan was too unnerved to speak, allowing the figure to continue. "I know you hate thisss place, and I know you don't belong here."

Rogan glanced from side to side, eyes narrowed with distrust, looking to see if anyone might be listening. "What do you know of me?" he spat through gritted teeth.

"Do not be upssset, Baron Rogan. I am here to offer you a chance to not only leave thisss place, but to get what it isss you want most of all."

"No one can give me that." His voice trailed off as he conjured thoughts of his wife and child.

The cloaked figure seemed to ponder his statement for a moment before continuing with a more sympathetic tone. "Perhaps that is ssso. I can give you the opportunity to escape, and a chance for you to do something that sserves usss both... killing the King." He paused to let the request sink in. "Are you interesssted?"

Surely this was a trick. Rogan still roasted with thoughts of vengeance, his time in prison acting like coals added to the fire of his fury. But surely... "It cannot be done, Ebon Khorel is too mighty. He has already weeded out the strongest who would oppose him, and his god grants him powers greater than the Shapers of old."

"Too mighty for a coup, perhapsss. But thiss will be an assssassination. And you will lead it."

The eagerness in the figure's voice sounded genuine to Rogan, but what did this stranger have to gain from the King-priest's death, and what association with the Inquisitor allowed him access to Blackthorn prisoners in the first place? Though it sounded like an impossible task, what did Rogan have to lose? He was already a convicted traitor who could be executed on a whim, so he could fathom no reason for this to be a trick. And there were a thousand possible reasons to want Ebon Khorel's reign ended. He was a tyrant, after all, and many had suffered since his ascendancy. Rogan's life in this place was a waste, and when it came down to it, he did not need to know his prospective patron's motives – his own vengeance would do.

"So, how do I get out of here?" he gestured to the stone walls around him.

"Firsst, sswear to do this thing; then I will tell you."

Even though it seemed a goal destined to fail, Rogan knew he couldn't pass up any good chance to get out of Blackthorn, even if he died in the attempt. "If you help me get out of this place, I swear to do what I can to kill the King."

"That iss enough," the figure nodded. "I know you are a man of your word. Lissten carefully. It has been arranged for one of the furnaces to run cold for an hour. Thisss time, unfortunately, has already begun. Down thiss hall to the east, there is a chimney chute with a sssmall door for wassste. It won't be eassy, but you can use it to climb to the roof. The hallway should be unguarded for now, but there are, of coursse, patrols. The last door on the left isss unlocked. There iss rope and a knife for you, along with a map. Oncce outside the prison, follow the map to a cave. There will be more ssuppliess, along with others to help you ssucceed."

"Others? Other prisoners?" Rogan didn't like the thought of trusting people he didn't know, especially if they had spent time in Blackthorn.

"Yesss. They have their chance to escape, even as you have yourss. Each has ssomething to offer the cause, and you may need them all for their skillss, I think." The cloaked figure stood and made his way to the door. "Time iss short, Baron Rogan. Give me a few momentss before you go. I will assure no guardss linger about. I will be watching your progresss with interesst. May your godss be with you."

With a slight nod of his head the figure turned and, with obvious effort, opened the heavy door. Rogan never did see his face, and the wisp of black cloth was soon gone, leaving him wondering if it was all a dream. The rush he felt suggested otherwise. He forced himself to calm down, breathe deeply, and count to a hundred.

Then, after a silent oath to do whatever it took, he cracked the door and peered to either side of the hallway. It seemed deserted. Soft steps, like those he took to sneak around the castle as a child, spying on banquets and balls while he was supposed to be asleep, led him silently down the hall. He could see the chimney chute at its end, where another hallway cut across his. Rogan's head swiveled, making sure no one was alert to his presence. He reached the door and found it unlocked just as the figure promised. Rogan shut it behind him before taking stock of his new surroundings.

It was a small, dark room, lit by a single candle. Upon a wooden table were the objects he expected: fifty feet of coiled rope, a piece of rolled parchment – which he quickly unrolled to reveal the crucial map – and a sheathed dagger.

As he drew the dagger to inspect it, the room grew dimmer. The candle was still burning, but it was as if the blade was absorbing its light. Black and sharp, it gave way to a handle of cold, dark stone. The weapon was quite unusual. A thought suddenly struck him – perhaps it was made of the same uril-chent he had been mining the past three years. The handle looked like it, and the metal of the blade could have been an uril-chent alloy.

Sure enough, when he sheathed the blade the light returned to normal. Rogan wondered what other properties the alloy might have, but had to shelve such thoughts for later. He loosened his belt and attached the sheath to it, tucked the map underneath, and slung the rope over his head and across his torso. He blew out the candle before sneaking back into the hall.

Another twenty paces brought him to the chimney. Once he forced open the small, iron door he realized how awkward it would be to maneuver inside the chute. As he ducked his head in to look both up and down, the prospects seemed grim. There was nothing to help gain purchase – no ledges, no handholds. It became painfully apparent the length of rope would be no help here. Twisting his body to the correct orientation alone would be a feat. It was a long fifty feet up to the small patch of grey sky beckoning from above. Better get to work, he thought.

"You there, don't move!"

Rogan had just enough time to get his head out of the shaft before a guard was thrusting a fist to his gut, knocking the wind from his lungs and bringing him to his knees. It hurt like hell and Rogan gasped for breath, but fortunately the guard's attack left him off-balance. With a quick spin, Rogan used his leg to sweep the guard's feet, toppling him. A light *chink* sounded as the metal studs on his leather armor met the cold, stone floor. Rogan crawled away to gain space and forced himself to stand.

"Now you've done it, maggot! You've earned yourself a proper lashing." Rogan heard true disgust in the man's voice, though he had never met him. The guard also managed to stand, pulling a wooden rod with a small iron head from his belt. He showed no intention of taking Rogan gently.

But Rogan did not intend to be taken at all, not with a real chance to escape this damned place. He crouched in a defensive posture, arms bent, ready to deflect any blows he could not evade. In his youth, Rogan always enjoyed combat lessons, and as an adult, continued honing the skills his noble upbringing had bought him. He had practiced against the sons of other nobles: swords, knives, archery, unarmed fighting, and even mounted combat. The aristocracy could always be called into military service at the behest of the king, and his father wanted him well prepared. Working in the mines had kept his muscles active, and he hoped his old lessons would be enough to overcome this prison guard, whose features had taken an astonishing turn toward savagery.

The guard lunged forward, wailing away with his club, unconcerned that his blows might shatter the escaping prisoner's skull. But his rage destabilized him. Rogan grasped the guard's wrist with his left hand, and slammed his right elbow violently against his attacker's chin. With a cracking sound, a few of the guard's teeth fell to the floor. The hand wielding the club went limp and dropped the weapon as the guard staggered back against the wall.

Rogan steadied himself and stared at his opponent, preparing for another rush. He wasn't disappointed. This time, though, as the guard started to swing his fist in a right hook, he quickly raised it inside and grasped Rogan's throat. Rogan grabbed the man's wrist with both hands and twisted his own body around, forcing the guard's release.

A sharp pain erupted in Rogan's left side. From somewhere unnoticed, the guard had drawn a knife and plunged it into his lower back. Something deeper than flesh had been punctured, and as the knife withdrew, he felt his lifeblood following.

Panic shot through after the pain, and then a strange calm took over as he realized and accepted this was a fatal wound. Yet as quickly as this acceptance came, it vanished in a new wash of anger. Rogan slumped forward, but refused to give in to this man, who suddenly represented the three years lost in this prison – and the evil behind his family being taken from him.

His back still to his attacker, Rogan drew his own dagger, blade down, and spun as he raised his arm. The weapon was sharp and struck true. The blade sliced easily through the guard's throat; a surprised look barely had time to register across his pale face, made paler as blood spilled from the wound.

Rogan was stunned too, as a surge of warmth passed from the weapon through his arm and across his entire body. His side prickled uncomfortably, and when he reached for the hole in his shirt his hand came away red with blood, but could find no wound. It was as if the puncture had instantly closed itself, leaving him free of pain. Remembering where he was, he quickly wiped the blood off his hand onto the guard's sleeve. Intending to clean his weapon next, he found no trace of blood on it. Perhaps it absorbed more than just light. Sheathing his dagger, Rogan returned to the small shaft door and put his energy toward squeezing his lithe frame into the cramped space.

In a quick succession of controlled movements – tuck, slide, reach – Rogan willed himself up the remaining length of the shaft. Surely the guards below would inform their fellows of his whereabouts within minutes. Finally, his arms reached over the lip of the chimney and he hoisted his exhausted body over the ledge.

The afternoon was quickly fading, though his first taste of fresh air in three years invigorated him. Everything was alive. The wind carried heavy smells of the surrounding jungle, a pungent mix of aromas still preferable to the stale earthiness of the mines. The croaking of hundreds of frogs and insects was likewise a welcome exchange for the constant ringing of metal on stone. He hoped he could cover enough ground for the approaching darkness and thick shadows of the jungle to hide him.

But, getting down was going to be a messy business. Blackthorn had once been a huge fortress, built on a strategic summit overlooking the Chelhos River. Through constant warring over the past decades, the Empire of Chelpa had expanded its territory until Blackthorn was no longer near the frontier, and the citadel had been converted to a prison. To the west, a steep trail led down to the docks where Blackthorn received all its incoming supplies – and free labor. A moat of slimy swamp sludge surrounded the prison, and beyond that, on all sides except the west, where a steep cliff dropped down to the river, a gradual slope of sharp and irregular rock threatened to break the ankles and shred the feet of anyone who did not travel on the solitary, northbound road. Where the rocks finally gave way to softer ground was a field of sparse vegetation, choked by thick layers of dark, thorny briars, for which the place had earned its name. Finally, beyond that, a couple hundred yards from where Rogan now crouched, was the inviting darkness of the dense jungle. Although dangerous in its own right, he wouldn't start to feel safe until he reached it.

Rogan had to be both quick and careful; there were sentries on the battlements. They hadn't noticed him yet, but it was only a matter of time until the general alarm was raised. He had to get at least far enough down the wall to jump before they either peppered him with arrows or managed to cut the rope he was preparing for descent.

Staying close to the chimney to shield himself from the lookouts, Rogan tossed a length of rope around it and quickly tied a serviceable knot. He was about to tie the other end around his waist when the clamor of bells rang from the inner courtyard. No time now. He moved to the edge of the roof, casting the rope over before rappelling down the side of Blackthorn. He would have given a good night's sleep for a pair of thick gloves, though as it turned out, he ended with rope burns on his hands and still came up two body-lengths short. He yearned to take the cordage with him but knew that if he didn't move rapidly, no amount of future usefulness would bear him any fruit.

Rogan dropped the remaining distance into the muck of the moat. Slimy vegetation clung to him as he swam to the rocky shore, too focused to think about what horrid things might be living in the cesspit. The alarm bells, now a thick mass of stone away, were muffled enough that he could hear the hounds barking. Weary arms lifted his fatigued body out of the moat, and as he made his way through the field of rough rocks, gave thanks that at least the terrain prevented a pursuit from horseback.

He turned just in time to see a pack of large hunting dogs rounding the corner from the north side of the prison. The animals, hungry for the chase, did not seem pleased with the sharp, broken ground between them and their prey. No sooner had Rogan turned back to picking out his own path than an arrow passed over his shoulder and shattered against a stone. He had to find cover soon. He crossed a couple of gaps where the rocks dropped off with two quick leaps, nearly losing his balance and plummeting into the space between. Combined with the slope of the terrain, he hoped these would give the hounds problems. Another near-miss from a barbed arrow later, he was crouched behind a boulder big enough to give him temporary cover from the archers.

How was he going to make his way across the expanse of briars while under fire and pursuit? Rogan cursed the fact he hadn't thought of these details during his incarceration. Sweat dripped into his eyes and his pulse beat in his ears. The dogs would navigate the small channels soon enough. Rogan drew his dagger in preparation, and was startled again as the light around him dimmed, leaving a sphere of twilight shadow.

The baying of the closing dogs made him unsure of exactly what it was he heard – a song of some sort, haunting and alien, but at the same time beautiful. From the direction of the jungle it carried on the wind, sweet and forbidding, holding a power that seemed to take grip from the inside. To his amazement, the thick bed of thorns just paces from him peeled back to form a path, too narrow to notice from a distance, but perhaps just wide enough for him to escape. For all his wonderment, Rogan had time for naught but acceptance, and with a deep breath made a dash for the fortunate gap. The briars continued to part before him, closing again just after he passed. All the while, the haunting tune stayed with him, its source remaining just beyond reach.

Occasional arrows whisked toward him, but the thick thorns caught them in their tangled mass. Within moments Rogan was through the hazardous field, and the enchanted melody broke off to fade on the wind. Looking back he couldn't even see the dogs – the thorns were so thick – but he heard their angry, yelping complaints at being cheated from their hunt. When he sheathed his dagger it was still dim, the sun gifting its final rays of the day. As he slipped into the shade of the thick trees, Rogan knew the hardest part was behind him. Blackthorn's isolation and unforgiving terrain were now his boons, for it would take a hunting party some time to go all the way around and approach his position from the north. This part of the rainforest was trackless, and he had no doubt he could stay ahead of guards forced to travel on foot.

As soon as he felt a safe distance from the prison, Rogan took out the map tucked in his belt and unrolled it. There was scarcely light to read by, but he wanted an idea of his heading before looking for a place to spend the night. A cave was marked as his destination, and it appeared to be some miles to the northeast. He rolled the parchment closed and put it away. He would make his way there in the morning, but in a roundabout way. Rogan did not want to head there straight off as it would bring him closer to settled patches of jungle, increasing the chance he would be seen before reaching the cave. He could only wonder what awaited, but found himself willing to trust the dark conspirator. Some sort of magic was in play – this much he realized already. First the uril-chent dagger, then the song clearing the thorns. Rogan didn't know who or what was behind either, let alone the assassination plot he had agreed to participate in. No, to lead. Whoever it was obviously had influence beyond mere political persuasion. Perhaps even enough to get the deed done.

Rogan walked until near-dark, but couldn't afford the luxury of a fire. Since he missed supper and had no rations to quell the grumbling of his stomach, the best thing was to find somewhere to sleep and start fresh in the morning. He found a likely spot, settling at the base of a large tree further sheltered by a gentle rise of nearby earth. Weariness overtook him as soon as he was off his feet. The trials of the day left him bone-tired, and even amongst the strange sounds of the jungle, sleep quickly claimed him.

Rogan woke gradually, his first morning in three years not started with the clanging of metal on metal. A snake, green and brown as the leaves and the earth, crept its way down his shoulder, curiously sniffing the air with its frenetic tongue. He watched, motionless, as it continued a slow path down his leg and onto the ground.

Once his heartbeat returned to normal, the acute realization that he was absolutely famished set in. With a deep sigh he rose and checked his map in the new light of morning. If everything went well, Rogan guessed he might make the cave by that afternoon. Hopefully a meal of some sort would be waiting for him there, or he would have to go hunting.

Hunting – he had enjoyed the sport immensely in his old life. Chasing wild boar, and then later in the season, vibrant, long-antlered deer, used to occupy much of his leisure time. The smell of the woods, the galloping of his horse, and stories of his fellow huntsmen were all things he took for granted, yet lost in one hellish night three years ago that still haunted his dreams.

He was returning one evening on horseback from a ride in the hills, full of his own thoughts. Several of his friends who dared to defy the King-priest set a plan in motion to overthrow their cruel Lord, and tonight was the night. Although he sympathized with them, Rogan could not take part. He just had too much to lose. His young wife, Riah – the center of his world

– had recently given birth to their first son. They were the air he breathed, and he would not put them at risk for the sake of dangerous politics, however just.

He didn't realize danger might find them anyway, until he heard Riah's screams. Shrill and piercing, they were punctuated by dreadful sobbing, before picking up again. Rogan seemed to be moving through quicksand as he dismounted and ran through the open door of his house. As soon as he entered, black-clothed men hiding on either side of the doorway seized him, and with alarming proficiency, bound his arms to his side. He struggled, but his legs were kicked out from under him and he fell painfully to his knees. His captors deftly tied his wrists and ankles, then raised his head by a handful of hair to watch what was happening to his wife.

His curses were cut off by shock and rage so overwhelming it baffled his senses. She was bent over the low table where she kept her pottery collection, face pressed by a heavy hand against its polished surface. The pottery was spread across the room in shards. Riah's screams had stopped, but tears streamed down her face as her eyes met his. Her body lunged harshly against the table, in time with the thrusts of the man behind her. Her lips mouthed the words "I'm sorry," though no sound escaped.

Finally, Rogan's rage found expression. He howled so loudly that, to his own ears, it seemed to come from someone else. He smashed his head against the man to his right, but was struck by a skull-jarring blow, and everything went black.

The smell of smoke brought him back for a moment. He was being carried like a sack of meal into the courtyard. His house was on fire, and he could not see his wife. He was deposited into the back of a wagon, and noticed a black dagger tattooed on the back of the neck of the man who put him there. He had just enough time to worry for his son's safety before passing back into a thick darkness.

Rogan shuddered as he shook off his thoughts. The time for justice would come soon enough. First, he had to make it to the cave without getting caught. He headed for a stream marked on his map, thinking to relieve his thirst before cutting north. The rest of the day became a wash of navigating the thick jungle growth, finding ways around obstacles with no visible paths. At last, exhausted as the light softened with the sun's decline, Rogan burrowed into the leaf litter of the jungle floor and fell into an uneasy sleep.

Within an hour after starting off the next morning, Rogan was sure he must be close. He checked his map again when a voice from up ahead nearly made him jump out of his boots.

"That'll be far enough," it informed Rogan. A man dressed in black, with a dark cloth covering his mouth and nose, stood atop a capsized tree trunk, aiming a crossbow at him. "What are you doing in these parts, stranger?"

Chapter 2

The Lure of Battle

His father's firm hand gently jostled Jaiden's head from side to side, rousing him from sleep. "Come, son. Get some breakfast, then it's time to see your Papa off."

Opening his eyes, the room was nearly as dim as with them shut. It couldn't be much past dawn. Jaiden grudgingly climbed down from the stiff bunk above his father's with sloth-like deliberateness. It always took a few moments in the morning before he was ready to move at regular speed.

Their home was near the base of the Fifth Hill of the metropolis of Selamus – a modest home incomparable to the splendorous mansions further up the hill. Composed of two small rooms, Jaiden only had to share the abode with his father, who was off fighting half the time, so it would be unfair to call it cramped. A professional mercenary, Wendell Luminere often commented on the foolishness of extravagance when Jaiden complained about what they didn't have.

"There's food in your belly, no?" That was always his closing argument, and one Jaiden had yet to penetrate. Though far from being a wealthy man, Jaiden loved and looked up to his father. He did the best he could with the skills he had to provide for his son – and could certainly wield a sword.

As long as Jaiden could remember, he had been fascinated by his father's adeptness with a blade. He spent countless childhood hours watching quietly while his father sparred with other soldiers or honed his craft. When Jaiden turned ten he was taught how to care for the weapon, oiling the steel to keep it free from rust, and sharpening the blade to keep it lethal.

Once he had earned the trust that came with practiced responsibility, his father gave him weekly lessons, and allowed Jaiden to practice on his own on the rare occasions the sword was free. Over the last three years of strict training, Jaiden had come to respect that sword nearly as much as his father.

Jaiden slogged over to the table in what served as both the kitchen and common room, pulling out one of the cracked, wooden chairs that always seemed to find a way to give him splinters. A bowl of porridge waited for him, though his father had not. He was scooping the remnants of his portion into his mouth just as Jaiden dipped his wooden spoon into the lumpy concoction. At least it was still warm.

"I may be gone for a while this time, Jaid, so I left what silver I could spare in the chest. You remember where the key is?"

Jaiden nodded, his mouth full.

"Good. If you run out, Pendarin said he could use help bringing in his mid-season harvest, so see him if you need work. Probably ought to anyway to keep yourself occupied and out of trouble. I don't want you spending too much time with those boys from the Nest, huh?" He paused a moment until Jaiden made eye contact. "Most of them are on their way to picking pockets if they're not there already. You're better than that, right?"

Jaiden nodded again.

"That's right. You keep up with your swordplay, and maybe you'll end up in the Prince's Guard one day."

"But how am I going to practice when you're gone, Papa? I need a sword of my own." Jaiden raised his eyebrows, hoping this was the time his father relented to his repeated plea. A tight-lipped "Hmmm," was all he got, however.

Jaiden finished his porridge while his father left the table and gathered the supplies for his journey. Jaiden was used to being alone. His mother died shortly after he was born, leaving him without siblings, and his father was off fighting in skirmishes for weeks or months at a time. When he was younger, that meant being dropped off to stay with friends of his father. More recently, depending on the campaign and the associated danger, he would sometimes get to tag along to the initial encampments. Jaiden loved that.

Nothing quite compared to the smell of a hundred campfires and the songs of courage men sang to convince themselves they too would be brave when the moment of truth arrived. There were always opportunities to get some sparring in with the younger soldiers as well, or their sons with similar circumstances. Story-telling, horses, men in fancy armor, the silent shroud of impending danger lingering over everything – all of it a real-life fairy tale.

This new excursion didn't offer such opportunity. "Who are you fighting this time, Papa?" Jaiden asked as he stood and cleared their bowls from the table. He remembered, of course, but liked hearing about his father's enemies as much as possible, each detail feeding his imagination when he'd pretend to battle them later. His father didn't know, but almost every day he was gone to battle, Jaiden defeated the same opponent over and over – it helped him feel connected.

"I'm going south, past the boundaries of the Cradle, too far for you to join me. The self-proclaimed 'Empire' of Chelpa is trying to spread beyond the jungles again. This time is different, though. Their new king is supposedly some fanatical zealot who worships one of the old gods." Jaiden's father stopped talking to heft his bulging pack over his shoulders and across his back.

"You've fought against Chelpians before, haven't you?" Formerly vanquished foes made for more reassuring opponents in Jaiden's eyes.

"Yes, years ago. They have long been aggressors toward their neighbors." He placed his hands atop Jaiden's shoulders and looked him squarely in the eyes. "Son, I know some of your friends must give you a hard time about me being a sword for hire." He laughed grimly, possibly remembering an insult from his past. "Some may think the Grey Wastes of Limbo are lined with souls like mine, devoid of loyalty. I want to make sure you know the truth. It's important to me."

Jaiden got an uneasy feeling in his stomach. His father had left on missions numerous times before, but this time there was too much talking. Jaiden didn't blink and nodded slightly to indicate his attention, suddenly scared at the possibility of silence.

"I take money for my services, of course I do; a man has to earn a wage. But what most don't realize is that I don't always work for the side offering the largest coin purse. A man gets to choose what he fights for, and will always have to live with that decision, whatever the payoff."

Jaiden nodded his understanding and his father withdrew his hands, putting them to work tightening the straps of his pack. "Minor lords constantly squabble for the pettiest reasons, son. Usually a victory means very little to anyone not directly involved." His attention returned to Jaiden, who was still soaking up every word. "However, every so often a conflict arises that could shape the world around us for years to come. There is evil in the world, after all, and sometimes it bears a clear standard."

"Is this such a fight?" Jaiden asked, barely able to get the words out.

His father's lips tightened as he nodded. "I believe so. The stories I've heard about this King-priest... they're not even fit for a winter evening. He thrives on fear, and despair follows in his wake. He has to be stopped, and if it's not now, it will only become harder to do so."

"I understand, Papa."

His father clicked his tongue and ruffled Jaiden's hair. "You'll be fine. Remember to visit Pendarin, and remember what I taught you about borrowing—"

"Better to go without than owe a favor."

"That's my boy. We're free people, Jaid, and debts are a restriction of freedom. Honest work for honest pay – don't take anything up front if you can help it." His father looked over his shoulder out the ever-lightening window. "It's time for me to go. Be good."

After an uncertain pause, Jaiden stepped forward and embraced his father. "Come back with stories," he muttered, his face pressed sideways against his father's arm. He felt a hand in his hair once again, and the pressure of his father's chest expanding with a deep breath.

"You know I will," he said, before giving a brief squeeze and separating.

A thought surged past the early-morning fog in Jaiden's head, reminding him of something important. "Oh, Papa, before you leave..." He ran back to his bunk and retrieved a small item from underneath his pillow. "I made this for you," he said, holding out a carved piece of light-colored wood.

"You made this?" his father replied, accepting the polished figurine in his calloused palm and lifting it for inspection.

Jaiden shrugged. "I thought of mom and how you always say her spirit is protecting me like a shield, even though I can't see her. I thought maybe my spirit could watch over you too, if you keep this with you."

His father stared silently at the carved shield, running his thumb across its smooth surface as his eyes clouded up.

Jaiden didn't know how to interpret his father's speechlessness. "Do you like it? I worked on it a while, but I know I'm still not very good yet. I put my initials on the bottom so you'd know I made it."

"It's perfect, son," his father finally answered, though his words were soft. "I'll keep it close by." After a brief pause he blinked hard twice, sniffed, and spoke with his usual, clear tone. "Farewell, Jaiden." Without another word he turned and opened the door, stepping out and letting too much of the morning chill in before he closed it. Then, he was gone.

Jaiden sighed and decided to climb back into bed to get warm. He didn't feel like venturing out and finding his friends just yet. Lying on his stomach, he closed his eyes, settling into the idea he was going to be on his own again, this time for probably quite a while. It bothered him to think too far ahead, so he let his mind drift over the possibilities of his first free afternoon while he skirted along the blurry line of consciousness, before eventually falling asleep.

Suddenly, the eye not smashed against his pillow opened. Jaiden was not aware of why it did so, but the light filtering through the dirty windows was noticeably brighter, and clearly within his line of vision was his father's sword, propped up in its scabbard in the far corner of the room. He blinked purposefully in case his waking mind was playing tricks, but the weapon remained when he reopened his eyes.

Jaiden pushed himself up from the mattress and scurried down from his bunk, quickly covering the width of their meager quarters. He lifted the weapon with care, his hand slipping around the comfortable curve of its handle. How could his father have left without his sword? There was no way he would have forgotten it. Jaiden' mind skimmed back over the morning's conversation, trying to remember any ignored indicators that would explain such a choice. He had hinted at wanting his own weapon to practice with, but that was nearly a daily occurrence. Perhaps his father's patron was wealthy enough to supply all his mercenaries with arms? That must be it.

Lifting the hilt a few inches, Jaiden basked in the sight and sound of the steel coming free of its cocoon. It was a glorious moment, full of promise, and he never tired of it. He let the blade slide back down and smiled. Jaiden knew how he would be spending the afternoon. He made a silent vow to master every fighting technique he could manage by the time his father returned.

Three months passed quickly without his father around, and Jaiden had all but run out of the silver saved up for his absence. Pendarin's harvest came in weeks ago, but Jaiden found more pressing things to do at the time than plucking vegetables from their stalks. He spent hours every day practicing with his father's sword, and felt his improvement worth a tighter belly.

Jaiden held out hope his father would return before the situation turned drastic, but a creeping notion he would be on his own for a while was gaining strength. This feeling, along with the steady rumbling of his stomach, led him to the First Hill Market. Scores of merchants displayed their wares for potential customers, and the milling bodies created the right amount of chaos for pickpockets to thrive.

Food was his first concern, though he had friends making a nice profit from lifting coin purses and fencing small, precious objects. They had been recruiting Jaiden on and off for seasons, though the temptation was more easily fought off when his father was around. While on his own, immersion in his training was the only thing working to keep him honest.

Yet, here he was, shadowing the stalls and carts of the vendors like a half-dozen other urchins, looking for a chance to lift what he needed. Though it was clear why he was at the market – it wasn't as if the First Hill was near any of his usual haunts – Jaiden still wasn't fully committed. He knew his Papa would disapprove, and thoughts of the lecture he'd receive if his father ever learned of such a devolvement battled with the persistent persuasion of his peers and the gnawing hunger, which were more immediate.

Jaiden tried to appear casual while strolling into the section of the market designated for southern goods. He circled displays of colorful, exotic fruits, promising both sustenance and sweetness. Watching the merchants with occasional sideways glances, waiting for an opportunity and the courage to seize it, he feigned interest in a collection of trinkets stacked on a terrace of wooden shelves on an adjacent cart.

His fingers touched a familiar object while his attention was still focused on the fruit vendor. Jaiden's heart skipped a beat when he turned and saw that the object his palm had settled upon was none other than the carving he had given his father on the morning he left. He lifted the figurine from its shelf to inspect it closer.

The top of the shield had picked up a nick in its travels, but the unicorn's head carved into its surface was the same. Tilting the figurine to expose its base, Jaiden's stomach tightened even further when his initials confirmed his handiwork past any doubt.

"Where did you get this?" he demanded of the merchant, a wiry man with skin the darker hue of the jungles.

The man squinted and shrugged his shoulders, "All of my wares come from Chelpa. It is nice work, but I will make you a deal – one of your Duke's silver coins."

"I made this!" Jaiden hissed back, anger unsuspectingly taking hold. His head swiveled as he looked for nearby guards, and noticing none, he suddenly bolted into the maze of the busy marketplace.

Cries for justice rose behind him, but Jaiden ran without looking back, ducking around wagons and pavilions until he left the market far in his wake. As he ran, tears sprung from his eyes, washed away by the wind as he fled down the slope of the First Hill. Once he reached the valley he finally stopped to catch his breath, but grief caught up with him and an uncontrolled sobbing stole it again.

His father was dead – he felt it in his bones. No reports of the campaign had reached this far north yet, but he knew his Papa would never have parted willingly from this gift, from the last thing his son had shared with him.

Jaiden wiped his eyes and struggled to calm his seizing chest; such a reaction was unbecoming for a warrior. He thought back to his father's sword. Was it possible he left it for Jaiden on purpose, knowing he was unlikely to return? He clenched his fists, nearly snapping the carving in two. He made a silent vow to take vengeance on the armies of Chelpa, if it was the last thing he did.

Chapter 3

A Motley Crew

Rogan wondered if he had come so far only to be caught, or if this lean man with the raspy voice was one of the other escapees. "I am a hungry man, who has traveled a long way." As he spoke he twisted his right arm, revealing the raised tattoo branded into his forearm: a skull wearing a crown of thorns, weeping tears of blood – the mark put on every prisoner of Blackthorn.

The other man seemed to recognize this, and lowered his crossbow. "Aye, so you're him," he said, matter-of-factly, shifting his arm to reveal his own brand. "Well, come get some breakfast." He turned and bounded from the log with feline grace. "We were only waiting one more night for you, you know. Good thing you showed up during the day, too. This place is near-impossible to find by starlight." Rogan followed the man in a winding path around some broad-leafed trees, and over a rise. He noticed a second tattoo on the back of the man's neck: a dagger, blade down, from which fell a single drop of blood – the mark of the Blood-tear Brotherhood. An elite group of assassins and spies loyal to the King-priest, the Brotherhood perpetrated the vilest tasks of the Empire. The men who raped his wife bore the same mark. Rogan fought to subdue the sudden wrenching of his stomach. At the top of the rise the ground dropped away quickly, revealing the mouth of a surprisingly deep cave. Small stone steps descended steeply to the entrance. Two other men, silhouetted by candlelight, sat on rocks within.

Well, not men exactly, he noticed as he drew closer. One was a hulking, hairy mass with feral features. As he spotted Rogan his face lit up in a toothy grin, revealing two over-sized, tusk-like incisors that protruded over his bottom lip. "Welcome, comrade. Name's Groscil." He reached out his huge paw-like hand in greeting. Rogan took it, somewhat alarmed at Groscil's size, but mostly caught off-guard by his ebullient nature.

"Call me..." he paused, surveying the group of criminals before him, then took a chance, "Rogan."

"*That's Baron Rogan, isn't it?*" The voice was clear and almost musical, but he did not hear it with his ears. It was as if he thought the question himself. He turned to the cave's other occupant. To his surprise, it was a Damper. How could the serene voice in his head belong to that... creature?

Frail and misshapen, Dampers were a strange race kept as slaves in the uril-chent mines. Their skin was cold and black as coal, gnarled like knots in an oak tree, and oozed thick, sticky mucus. Slim hands ended in extraordinarily long and slender fingers. With joints allowing their extremities to move in any direction, their limbs often bent at strange angles. Dampers bodies held little symmetry, and were too weak to lift or dig, yet somehow absorbed the harmful energies emanating from the ore. Prisoners had gotten sick from working in the mines until the Dampers were brought in, though they didn't seem to have problems being near the ore themselves. Still, other prisoners hated them because their weakness meant no labor, and the guards hated them because they couldn't stand much punishment without dying. Everyone hated them for their grotesqueness. Rogan had never known one to speak, and assumed they could not.

"I'm sorry; I suppose telepathy can be a bit unnerving at first," it added, likely reading the astonishment on Rogan's face.

"I trust from that look Creepy L'Fingers there has introduced himself," the man with the crossbow stated as he slung it over his shoulder. The cloth obscuring most of his face also muffled his voice. The eyes were dark and sure, taking note of everything. "I guess that leaves me then, eh? I'm Yennic. As much as I hate to break up these touching introductions, are you going to tell us what the plan is?"

"The plan?" Rogan asked, still distracted by the voice entering his mind.

"Yes, the plan; the assassination. We were told you would be leading this little expedition, and that if we did our jobs, we would be allowed to remain free."

Rogan sighed. "I haven't come up with a plan yet. All my energy has been spent escaping alive and finding this place." He tried to quell his annoyance of their expectations. Starting off with animosity was unproductive. "I suppose, if I'm the leader, I'll need to take stock of our supplies and the group's abilities. What do we have here?"

Groscil shuffled over to where sacks of various items had already been rummaged through and laid out. He gestured toward the pile with a sweep of his arm, as if presenting a valuable treasure or important diplomat. "At your service, sir." The politeness of his manner belied the deep, menacing voice behind it. Rogan assumed Groscil couldn't help it, though it could've been the creature's disturbing attempt at sarcasm.

There were rations of bread and cured meats, as well as full waterskins for each of them. Rogan couldn't help himself and immediately took a long drink. The cold water revitalized him. Red cloaks were folded and stacked, each emblazoned with the Imperial insignia. No doubt they would help avert trouble from the public, and maybe more official personnel, if they could avoid in-depth interactions. Finally, he came to the weapons. He had already seen Yennic's crossbow, and here was a case of quarrels for it, though some had already been claimed. He inspected one of the bolts more closely, noticing it was tipped in a greenish substance – probably poison of some sort. Whether they had come prepared, or this was Yennic's doing, he didn't care to speculate. Two long swords in scabbards leaned against a rock, though a quick check revealed they were made of steel and not fashioned of the same uril-chent alloy as his dagger.

Finally, Rogan noticed a rolled-up piece of parchment, which he carried to the edge of the cave for better light. On one side was a map, showing the best route from the cave to the King-priest's citadel in Lucnere. The other side contained script, written in a language Rogan had not seen since his studies as a youth. The words were penned in a complexly beautiful hand, in ancient Thurese no less – a dead language of the people who first migrated to the region from beyond the Fire-Wall Mountains. Their enigmatic patron had certainly done his research, for it was unlikely another reader would have been tutored in their distant ancestor's script. Rogan wondered how much of his past was known. Was it the same for the others? He did his best to decipher the text, his Thurese admittedly rusty.

"Baron Rogan, congratulations on making it this far; it means your escape went well, and my part of the bargain has been fulfilled. I trust you are now ready to perform yours. You know from acute experience that Ebon Khorel is a tyrant whose rule has crushed the spirit and lives of many in Chelpa. He does as he wishes, and those who serve him abuse his subjects daily in his name. His regime must come to an end if anything here is to be good again. It is time for justice, time for vengeance, time for a new King. You need not know who I am, only what I want, which I trust is the same as you. Ebon Khorel will be out of the palace and vulnerable while performing the Ritual of the Black Sun on Midsummer. His power is great, so you must be resourceful. You have no doubt assessed the skills of your new companions; they

were chosen carefully. As for the Damper, you will need him close if the King-priest calls down divine power against you. You will be watched, so please do not think too hard on giving up. There would be harsh consequences if you were to do so, though it's not what either of us wants. If you are victorious, there will be grand opportunities for you in the new order. Good luck to us, Kingmakers all."

The intricate seal at the bottom of the letter was not one Rogan recognized. Midsummer – that only gave them two days. Two days to devise and execute a plot against the most powerful regent in living memory. He was hardly likely to succeed, but what if he did? In his heart, Rogan knew his reasons were selfish. Part of him died when his wife and newborn son were lost, leaving a hole all too easily filled with hate. Rogan often dreamed of killing those who had wronged him, feeling their warm blood cool on his bare hands. Sometimes they weren't dreams at all, but visions that came while he toiled endless hours in the mines beneath the bleak, prison fortress. Apart from the personal satisfaction, a regime change would benefit his country in innumerable ways. The oppression, constant warmongering, and cruelty perpetrated by Ebon Khorel destroyed the morale and culled the sons of too many families.

"So what does it say, mate?" Yennic questioned.

"It says we have to be in Lucnere in two days, and that we are being watched to make sure we carry out our mission."

"Two days – is that all, then?" Yennic stood with most of his weight on one leg, and his crossbow slung over the opposite shoulder.

"Yes, the King-priest will be performing a ritual at Midsummer; that's our opportunity. Our benefactors seem to know a good deal about us, and I suppose I shall have to trust that. There'll be time to learn about your strengths as we travel." Rogan rolled up the parchment, adding, "We should wear these royal cloaks over our clothes. They may not be enough to fool seasoned guards, but should at least keep the general population at bay. Come along then." He snagged a length of jerky before checking the ascending sun to get his bearings. "Groscil, grab these supplies, will you?"

"Is it better to be thought of as Royal Inquisitors or escaped criminals?" Groscil mused while slinging the heaviest pack of gear over a broad shoulder.

"What about Stinky L'Slimeface, there?" Yennic nodded in the Damper's direction as he secured one of the red cloaks over his shoulders. "I think he might stand out even a bit more than 'ol tree-legs there. A half-orc as a Royal bodyguard – that might pass. But a gods-forsaken stinking Damper – not likely."

Rogan watched as the Damper turned its gaze upon Yennic, and wondered what thoughts he might be projecting. If he had words to share Rogan couldn't tell, and no other response was evident.

"We'll keep out of sight as much as possible, and if we're confronted, pretend he's a prisoner." The presence of a Damper might be enough to keep anyone from approaching them in the first place, Rogan thought. "Now, let's to it."

The four unlikely companions headed northeast. Yennic scouted ahead of the others, staying mostly beyond sight, but dropping back occasionally to re-establish visual contact. Rogan meant to speak with each of them during the trip to assess their skills, but he was already getting a picture of what Yennic brought to the table. Despite his coarseness and sarcastic wit, he had a way of remaining unseen until desired. A few hours into the trip, when Rogan decided to stop for a rest and bite to eat, Yennic returned with a wild rabbit already in hand, no doubt brought down with an accurate shot from his crossbow. He tossed the hare directly to Groscil, who gave a horrifying, appreciative grin before tearing into the raw meat with his tusk-like teeth.

Rogan and Yennic both opted for the prepared rations they'd brought, but the Damper sat quietly to the side, not eating a single bite. Rogan took advantage of the break to question Groscil.

"So what's your story, if you don't mind me asking?"

"Not much to tell, Baron. Same story as anyone been in Blackthorn, I wager."

"Well, you are a half-orc, right? There must at least be a story there?"

"I suppose, though I don't rightly know that one." Groscil paused to take an enormous swig from his waterskin. "Never met my parents, Baron. I got teased plenty when I was younger – being the only child with tusks an' all."

"Ah, they was just jealous, mate," Yennic chimed in and Groscil gave a toothy grin, acknowledging some shared joke between them.

"I'd wager you're right," Groscil responded, stroking the tuft of rough hair on his chin in mock contemplation. "Anyhow, that all stopped soon as I got big."

"And when was that, age three?" Yennic snorted. "You probably came out of the womb half-way to humongous."

"If you must know, I was somewhat of a late-bloomer, like an Autumn Flame or Turtleweed," Groscil responded.

Yennic gave a short-lived laugh, "Did I hear you right, mate? You just compare yourself to a delicate flower?"

"So what landed you in the mines, then?" Rogan tried to steer the conversation back on target, while sounding casual. He sensed honesty from the half-orc, but didn't want to trust too much until he knew more.

"Well, I don't really like to talk about it much, Baron, if you'll forgive me." Groscil's expression became suddenly sullen.

"He killed a man." Both their heads snapped toward Yennic, who nonchalantly scraped mud from his boot heel with a stick. "He killed a man, no different than any of us...well maybe not Darky L'Melody over there. Of course, I killed lots of men, but that's not the point. You couldn't throw a stone in Blackthorn and not hit a killer. It's not like most of us didn't deserve to be there, but not this chap." He discarded his soiled branch and lowered his foot to the ground. "The big brute's just got more strength than he knows how to manage sometimes, and his *crime* was no crime at all. It was an accident, a bar-fight-gone-bad. He was actually trying to break things up, though you can guess how far that story went with the Inquisitor, with this one being three hundred pounds of vicious, toothy muscle."

"Is that it, then?" Rogan asked Groscil, who avoided his gaze. "You killed a man by accident, and it landed you in Blackthorn?" It was important for Rogan to know, so he could best choose what roles each would play in their upcoming plot. He also felt some pity for the half-breed – even more evidence of the injustice of the King-priest's regime.

"I suppose that's the way of it, Baron. Things happen when the pints start piling up, eh? But don't feel sorry for me. I did kill a man who didn't deserve it, and there's a price to pay for that. But I reckon, what with the hell that goes on in them mines, I've just about paid my debt. So, here I am."

"I don't think it's the killing that makes a man bad, Groscil." Rogan's comment drew a rise from one of Groscil's bushy eyebrows. "If you want my opinion, it's the callousness of the deed, or the cruelty behind it that tells the tale of a man's soul."

"And I suppose that means my soul's as black as my mask, if I get you right," Yennic contributed. "Look," he added casually, "I am what the world made me. I don't ask your forgiveness, nor anyone else's, for that."

"What the world *made* you?" Rogan's voice rose a notch. "The world has given *me* more sorrow than a man like you can understand, but it is not the world I blame. My revenge shall be kept for those who have wronged me, not delivered indiscriminately, for that is the way of the Tyrant and his Brotherhood!" Rogan realized he was yelling and took a moment to regain his calm before continuing almost in a whisper, "The world doesn't make you who you are; it merely provides the opportunities for you to show it."

They finished their meal in silence, and were soon back on their way. The closest human dwellings were still a day away, beyond the jungle. They spent the night in darkness, unwilling to risk fire as they drew nearer to civilization. Rogan lay on his back, staring up at the constellations, thinking of his wife and son and wondering why his life had to change so drastically. Destiny was either a cruel matron, or her benevolence was too complicated for him to comprehend. Sleep would not come, though he was tired, so he set to figuring out how to get close to Ebon Khorel.

The next morning Rogan woke with a start; he couldn't remember falling asleep. He thought he heard the fleeting notes of an enchanting melody, but couldn't be sure if they were anything more than the echoes of a dream. He felt refreshed, however, and pleased to find the others already packed and ready. According to the map, he calculated they would reach Lucnere later that day. Rogan hoped enough daylight would remain to scout the grounds where the Black Sun ritual would take place.

Checking the contents of his traveling pack, he noticed the Damper sat quietly on his own, perhaps twenty paces away. That seemed to be the way of things; it was obvious Yennic, and to a certain degree Groscil, was unnerved by his presence. Actually, Yennic seemed to loathe the creature, though Rogan could not recall a single story of a Damper causing harm to anyone. With a few exceptions, he barely noticed them in the mines. They were present so the other prisoners could work, but they never spoke, never harassed anyone, and never caused any problems as far as he knew. That wasn't to say they never received their share of punishment. The guards seemed to erupt in anger around them sometimes, for no apparent reason.

Rogan remembered one day while in the mines, seeing a crowd on the verge of frenzy, all roaring and cheering encouragement. Drawing closer, he saw a guard fiercely whipping a Damper. A spike had been driven through one of its hands, nailing it to the rock of the cavern. Weak as it was, it had no chance of breaking free. The strokes of the lash were so harsh that depressions were scored into the soft, wet flesh of the Damper. It did not cry out or show any emotion Rogan could recognize, yet each peeling crack of the whip against its skin was followed by a sound like a soft note, broken off in mid-song. Rogan could never decide whether the creature was somehow able to remain sublime in the face of great cruelty, or just lacked the capacity to express the pain it felt. Eventually, a prisoner joined in. He picked up an iron shovel and speared the Damper's thin, black leg. The head, blunt from overuse, still had no problem passing right through. At that point Rogan abandoned the crowd, hoping death came soon after to end the creature's suffering.

"We have all felt much pain." The voice in his head was soft and gentle as a lullaby. The Damper was standing only a few yards away. *"My kind has been through much – as have you, perhaps?"*

"What do you know of my pain?" Rogan said harshly, unsure why he felt defensive. Was it a natural response to the intrusion of hearing this voice in his mind?

"Nothing in particular; I did not mean to offend. I just sense you carry much pain with you."

For all the melody in that voice, Rogan was still unnerved by the proximity of the grotesque, oozing body accompanying it. It almost made him nauseous. "I'm sorry," he offered, "but I don't really know anything about your kind. Do you have a story you would like to share?" Even while asking, he silently hoped the Damper would choose to keep to itself.

"My story is one of woe, Lord Rogan, and not one many are inclined to believe." The voice in his head went quiet, but the Damper continued to stare at Rogan, as if evaluating him. *"Perhaps that does not matter, in the end. Perhaps the telling alone serves some purpose. I can see you are anxious to begin our travels, however, so I shall tell it as we walk."*

"Agreed." Rogan was thankful he didn't have to endure that stare for the duration of the Damper's personal history. The heavy sounds of the jungle, insects and frogs communicating in summer melodies, filled the silence before the Damper actually began.

"We were not always as you see us now, my kind. This body I inhabit is part of a curse – punishment for a crime I will not try to explain. We were once Aasimar, immortal beings living in a realm beyond this world.

"Memories are a strange thing, my friend. When we were cast down, inheriting these weak and hideous bodies, our memories were taken as well. Only a distinct impression that we had lost remained. We were sure we didn't belong here, but couldn't remember where we were from. We were isolated, full of misery. All we knew was that it hadn't always been so. Though as cruel and total as our punishment seemed to be in those early days, Rogan, it got worse. All who saw us were frightened and repelled, until it became clear how physically weak we were. Ebon Khorel sent his soldiers to round us up, and we have been captives ever since."

Rogan watched the Damper walking ahead, but he had no need to look back as he talked.

"Being sent to the uril-chent mines was surely the work of fate. Though you rightfully think of them as the pits of hell, that is where our rebirth began. The energies that harm and eventually kill your kind are absorbed by whatever remnants of divinity still reside within us. Some of this, you already know. But our secret, what none save us knows, is the effect those energies have on our memories. As time passes and our exposure continues, we remember more. The memories come faster to some than others.

"Before our fall we would sing – beautiful songs." The voice in Rogan's head took on a wistful tone, as if transitioning to pleasant memories. *"There was movement, grace, life – power – in those songs. But the songs themselves were forgotten. Our lives here were designed precisely to remind us of everything we had lost. In that way, the memories add to our curse. Before, we only knew that we had lost, but not what we had lost. That knowledge haunts and torments us more than the cruelty we face at the hands of your people."*

Although there was no judgment in that last statement, Rogan felt the impact of it. He had long considered himself a man apart from those the Damper was talking about, but he also realized from the Damper's perspective, they were likely the same. Feeling uncomfortable, Rogan cleared his throat, but continued listening. Incredible as it sounded, he couldn't deny the story felt like truth.

"And yet, the songs too return. What began as fleeting traces of notes in the recesses of our minds have grown into melodies, and as they come back to us, so does our ability to use their magic."

"So that is what I heard before?" Rogan interjected. "When I was escaping, it was you who made a path through the thorns?"

The Damper answered with a nod. Rogan's mind flooded with the possibilities. "What else can you do with these songs? Is that why you were picked to come on this mission?"

"*Unfortunately, my songs are still incomplete. Some are just fragments, really, and the memories along with them. I am not sure what use my melodies can be to you. This body, my body, is still so weak. I am here, I think, to absorb the divine power the King-priest might call down against you.*"

A flatness to this last statement caught Rogan's attention. It was the first time anything the Damper had said felt like a lie. Even so, Rogan didn't press the issue. He had enough to consider, wondering how best to utilize the Damper during the assassination attempt. Although not strictly requested of him, Rogan decided to keep the Damper's secret. The only ones he had to share it with were a pair of criminals, or perhaps the King-priest himself. His thoughts occupied him for hours as they wound their way through the rich green of the rainforest, fording several small streams, to avoid the denser marshland.

A sudden bird-call from Yennic put Rogan on alert. He crouched and quickly made his way to where his scout stood behind a thick tree trunk, using it for cover. The canopy and undergrowth had gradually become sparser, and here they ended. Beyond Yennic the ground sloped downward, nothing but lush grass covering the hill. Where the ground leveled out again, perhaps a hundred paces from the tree-line, stood a small farmhouse. A slow curl of grey smoke rose from its stone chimney. Beyond, the landscape was peppered with houses and cottages. Time had come for their reemergence into civilization.

They could perhaps hope to be stealthy, making their way to the capital by darting from house to house, or hiding in the jungle and taking a longer route. But he knew they simply didn't have the time, not if they were going to reach the King-priest's citadel with hopes of even meager preparation. No, they would walk down to the road minding their own business, and hope anyone who saw them would mind theirs as well. He was counting on the sheer presence of the bulky Groscil being enough to discourage any questions, even if someone bothered to wonder why a half-orc was wearing the robes of the crown.

Standing behind the last of the trees, Rogan realized the other three were looking to him. He asked Groscil to get out the rope, then turned to the Damper. "I'm sorry, but we're going to need to bind your hands. It'll look better if you appear to be our prisoner." The Damper said nothing, but quietly placed his wrists together and stretched out his arms. They were black, sticky, and covered with scars. Rogan tried to keep his hands steady as he tied knots around them, guilt rising through his core.

"What's the plan, then?" Yennic finally asked.

"Well," Rogan pointed down the hill, "I can see by the direction of the road that it probably leads to Lucnere, so we're going to take it. I'll travel in front alongside Groscil, and lead the Damper. You follow a few paces behind and watch our backs. It probably wouldn't hurt to show off that crossbow."

Rogan was expecting some sort of resistance, though he wasn't sure why. Perhaps because if he were following someone, he'd hope they had a better plan than that. But with no dissent he nodded, took the end of the rope, and stepped onto the open expanse of green ahead.

He didn't detect anyone about, at least until they reached the first farmhouse. There, Rogan heard the sounds of people through an open window, talking and preparing for the midday meal.

"Psst!"

Rogan turned, visually following the direction of Yennic's nod. Thirty paces away, in the shadow of an open barn, a large wooden wagon was already hitched to a pair of horses. It was partially loaded with what appeared to be baskets of vegetables, though a heavy tarpaulin was thrown over most.

Rogan didn't like the thought of stealing from innocent farmers, but he looked at his crew and knew this wouldn't be his last harsh decision; they were, after all, planning an assassination. His own sense of morality, however distasteful to subdue, would have to be retired for the length of this mission.

He nodded and they made their way as inconspicuously as possible to the barn, where they boarded the wagon. "Groscil, cover the Damper and ride in back with him. And untie him, please. Yennic and I will drive the horses." They moved quickly, as if they had worked together and done such things a dozen times before. Within moments, Rogan gave the reins a snap and the horses pulled onto the wide, packed-earth road.

The door to the farmhouse suddenly flew open and a middle-aged man with a heavy beard hustled into the yard. He carried a long, wooden staff, which he raised to threaten them. "Hey! Just what do you—" the question cut off mid-yell, and the staff resigned.

Yennic's crossbow was pointed directly at the man's heart, but Rogan wondered if it wasn't the cloaks they wore that stayed his protests. People expected to lose things at the hands of those in service to the crown.

Chapter 4

Assassinating the Crown

The wagon clicked along at a pleasant speed. The horses were well-kept and familiar with the route. Lucnere came into view as the sun was beginning its fatal dip below the horizon. Rogan knew it made little difference that the light was fading. The streets were paved with obsidian, and many of the buildings were constructed of the same black stone. Smoke from numerous blacksmiths and armorers filled the sky, signs of a kingdom perpetually preparing for war. Neighboring countries feared remained on edge because of it.

Using his backward logic, Ebon Khorel used this fear to justify being ready to launch a campaign at a moment's notice.

Things had been bad for a generation – crops struggling and outside trade nearly cut off. They were made even worse when the King-priest came to power and mandated worship of Gholdur the Tyrant, one of the absent gods from an earlier age. Whether or not they believed, his newfound followers used Gholdur to justify absolute control and a disdain for empathy. In his name the spirits of the people were suffocated. A jest arose amongst the more rebellious nobles that even the official flower changed to the black rose.

Given the hour, it became obvious night would be fully upon them by the time they reached the palace. Rogan considered seeking sanctuary at the manor of one of the nobles he knew before going to prison, but dismissed the idea. How could he possibly trust anyone he hadn't seen in years? He had to remember he was an outlaw in a kingdom that punished without mercy. He couldn't put such friends in danger, should they prove to still be friends.

They couldn't risk staying at an inn either – not while pretending to be officers of the Royal Inquisitor, and certainly not with a Damper. A deserted street or building close enough to scout the palace would have to do.

As the wagon rolled up to the southern gate of the walled city, Rogan suddenly panicked. The armed guards stationed at the entrance were checking papers and collecting silver from a line of wagons ahead of them. Of course there was a tax; he chided himself for not considering this earlier. He had been so focused on the idea of actually killing the King-priest that he ignored the details of making it into the city. It appeared their mission would fail before he even set eyes on Ebon Khorel. The red and black cloaks may have dissuaded a rural farmer from interfering, but gate soldiers were another matter. He wasn't sure what other form of identification a true Inquisitor would have.

Rogan averted his eyes from the guards as they drew closer, his mind scurrying for solutions. Yennic's hurried, sideways glances suggested he had become aware of the situation as well.

"Any ideas?" the slim assassin whispered.

Only one more wagon lay ahead of them, and the driver was already reaching for his coin purse. If Rogan had any money, the situation wouldn't have been so bad. He was sure the gate guard was probably accustomed to being bribed, but he had nothing to offer save a heap of vegetables, and was about to be caught impersonating an officer of the crown.

Yennic reached slowly for his crossbow and gently set a bolt in front of the already drawn twine. "I could take him down; just say the word."

Rogan shook his head as the guard called to him in a weary tone. He wondered if the Damper had a song to get them through this pinch.

"Well, gents, looks like you just made it. Gate closes at sundown, you know."

That voice... Rogan recognized it immediately, though he hadn't heard it in years. It belonged to a man named Merrick, Rogan's trusted bodyguard in his previous life. He counted Merrick a friend back then, and just as importantly now, a man whose discretion could be relied upon. Deciding to trust him once more, Rogan turned to allow Merrick a clear look at his face.

"And how much is the toll, my good man?" Rogan held his breath after asking, hoping his instincts would not betray him.

"The same as always, sir. That'll be..." Merrick faced Rogan directly and saw the familiar, hopeful eyes staring back at him. He muttered an oath under his breath, and time froze for Rogan as he watched his once-friend contemplating his next move. Merrick's eyes shifted to the half-orc sitting in back of the partly-covered vegetable cart before returning to the visage of his former lord. "Of course, no tax for the House of the Inquisitor on official business," he finally replied, loud enough for his fellow guards to hear. "Move it on through."

Rogan released his breath and managed a slight nod before snapping the reins to get the wagon started. He heard Yennic exhale as well, and caught him relaxing the hold on his crossbow.

As a former baron, Rogan had made several trips to the capital, and once inside the gates, the geography came back rapidly. He bypassed the familiar taverns, continuing closer to the palace until he found what he was looking for. Deep into the merchant district they came upon a warehouse gutted by fire. Timbers hung at odd angles and the earth was covered with a thick layer of ash and soot. Behind the lot ran an alleyway and, at least in what tiny light remained of the fading day, the area looked deserted. The spot would do nicely.

Once the wagon came to a stop, Rogan handed the reins to Yennic and thankfully stepped down onto the solid, unmoving ground. With deft fingers he unclasped his cloak and twirled it from his shoulders onto the wooden board that had been his seat for the better part of the day. He could see Yennic was about to ask a question and did his best to head it off.

"I've got some scouting to do. I may still have a few contacts I can get information from without drawing too much attention. I'm going to need to know more about this ritual tomorrow and see where it's being held with my own eyes before I can decide on the best course of action."

"Well," Groscil put in as he drew the tarp back from the Damper, "there's plenty here to snack on." The half-orc picked up a long, green cucumber and snapped half of it off in one chomp.

"Right, like I haven't heard you eating the whole ride up here, muscles." Yennic looked at the Damper, then to Groscil, and shook his head. "And what are we supposed to do in the meantime, mate? Weave a tapestry?" Yennic stood, his lean figure growing even taller as he stretched his cramped legs.

"You can do as you like, I suppose," Rogan answered. "Just don't get noticed. I should be back in a few hours. You might want to get whatever sleep you're able." Rogan set off the direction they had come, toward the more-populated city streets.

"Oh yeah, right. 'Don't get noticed,' he says. Pretty bloody impossible with these two, now itn't it?" Yennic raised his voice just loud enough so Rogan could hear, but the baron merely shrugged in response, not bothering to turn around.

Dawn was less than an hour away when Rogan returned. The others were lying across the wagon, still awake.

"Is everyone ready to move? I want to be in position before sunrise." Rogan's voice was a touch more than a whisper.

"Ahhh." Groscil smacked his lips before giving a throaty sigh. "I thought you'd never get back, Baron. You know, patience has never really been one of my strengths."

"Excellent trait for a man in prison, eh?" Yennic sat up and within seconds had all his gear strapped and slung in place. "Somebody give Drowsy L'Gooey a kick, would ya?"

"*I am ready.*" The response surprised them all and was followed by a sweet melody that drizzled over them like a refreshing spring rain, washing the exhaustion of their sleepless night from mind and body. The singing did not last long, but Rogan could actually feel his anxiety dissipate, evaporating on the wind with the remnants of the last note. The Damper stared directly at him, giving the impression the next words were for his mind alone, "*It is a day of days.*"

After he and Groscil fastened the longswords to their belts, Rogan instructed them to leave the cloaks behind. "With pleasure," Yennic said, tossing his into the wagon before spitting on the ground.

"We've got some ground to cover, so I'll fill you in as we walk," Rogan said. "The bad news is the ceremony is performed indoors, so there's no chance of just a simple, straight shot."

Yennic groaned his disappointment. "And the good news?"

"I still think a well-placed bolt by surprise is the best chance we have. How potent is that poison, Yennic?"

"A clean shot – it'll get the job done. I'd wager even *this* horse wouldn't last two minutes," Yennic jested as he nudged Groscil.

His pride settled Rogan's speculation about who was responsible for the toxin.

"More bad news; the King-priest never appears in public without wearing full armor. Do you think that crossbow can penetrate plate mail?" Rogan supposed it could, but wanted to test Yennic's confidence in his role.

"All armor's got weak spots, sir."

It was the first time Rogan had heard Yennic sound sincerely respectful. "Good," he continued. "Then you'll have to find them. There's a bell tower outside the building where the ritual's taking place, overlooking a huge sundial in the courtyard. A sentry rings out the hours, so you'll have to take care of him once we get there. We'll wait for the new watch to start at dawn."

"We're going to need to give Ebon Khorel a reason to go out in that courtyard. That's where you come in, Groscil." The half-orc nodded silently. "There's a half-dozen guards within shouting distance of the sundial. I know it's dangerous, but I need you to pick a fight with them. Make it loud. Keep them occupied long enough to raise the alarm, then retreat if you can. We don't care about the guards, so don't get yourself killed.

"By all accounts the King-priest enjoys inflicting pain and might be tempted outside by the promise of delivering some upon those who dare interrupt him. The Damper and I will sneak inside and watch as we can; we'll have to deal with him if he doesn't take the bait. In his mind he's the divine vessel of his god and impervious to normal threats; we shall become an extraordinary one. "

By the time Rogan explained the plan they were almost to the bell tower, and cock crows were rising from the city's outlying farms. "All right, there it is." Rogan pointed out the tower. "And there's the morning shift. Sorry Groscil, but there's more waiting to do. The ritual won't begin for some hours, so you'll have to stay out of sight until you get the signal. Yennic, once you take position, you'll have to ring out the hours on schedule. When he rings out the noon hour, Groscil, do... what you do."

Rogan looked into each of their faces. He had only known them a couple of days and here he was, feeling as though he was saying farewell to two longtime friends. He didn't even like Yennic that much when he thought about it, yet he understood him, somehow, rough edges and all. "Does everyone follow?" he said, suddenly struggling with tightness in his throat.

"Well, you kind of skipped the part where we all meet up for an ale afterwards and tell our sides of the story." Groscil gave a big, toothy grin, and Rogan helplessly cracked a smile as well.

"Anywhere you like, big guy." Rogan clasped his oversized shoulder as he added, "And the ale's on me."

"Yeah, with what coin?" Yennic contested. "We're free after this, right?" he called as Rogan and the Damper started to walk away.

Rogan swallowed through the lump in his throat. "That's right. I'm sure our patron has agents who will relay the completion of our task, if he's not watching himself. I believe we'll have no more to fear after today... assuming we succeed."

Yennic simply nodded, and Rogan turned to take the Damper to a place where they could hide for a few hours. He was sure they could all sense the weight of the moment upon them, but what could they do but try? Dying in the pursuit of freedom couldn't be held as folly, when the alternative was a lifetime inside Blackthorn.

The priesthood of Gholdur favored darkness, which worked to the would-be assassins' advantage. Aided by a song of concealment the Damper draped over them, they had little problem sneaking through a side portal into the dimly lit temple. The building was a domed hemisphere, made of the black rock favored in Lucnere. It stretched to a height of forty feet at the apex, and was cleverly constructed so the support pillars left the middle of the floor open. These columns were half-again as wide as a man from shoulder-to-shoulder, carved with the likenesses of gargoyles and other monstrous, obsidian shapes. Rogan's contact had referred to the temple as the "Skull Dome," with open disgust.

In the center of the floor was an altar and Rogan could see, even from a distance, the dark stains on its surface. The smell of decay lingered in the stale air. Three steps led down from the central platform in each cardinal direction, and rows of long, wooden benches extended beyond. At each corner of the altar stood a tall, brass spire, tipped by a lit candle. A hole, perhaps an arm's length across, lay at the peak of the dome, allowing a meager beam of sunlight to enter the dreary structure. It shone down upon the altar when the sun was overhead, immediately drawing the attention of anyone who entered.

Weary from his long night of scouting, despite the Damper's previous revitalizing song, Rogan eventually drifted off, concealed behind one of the large, gargoyled pillars. Just before the noon hour the Damper nudged him to alertness. It was the first time the creature initiated contact, and Rogan's shoulder prickled with a deep chill for several seconds after the touching ceased. Startled, he followed the Damper's gaze to the other side of the temple.

A procession of six, black-robed men appeared from the direction of the palace, holding lit candles before them. Their hands were the only skin visible, as hoods concealed their faces in shadow. They took places on the floor below the raised altar, nearly encircling it in a wide crescent. In their wake, the King-priest entered.

Tall and completely encased in a suit of black plate armor, his was a commanding presence. The mail was perfectly fitted so as not to hamper movement. Its shoulder and knee guards were crafted in the likeness of horrible skulls wearing crowns of thick thorns. The King-priest wore a full helm, whose front was fashioned to appear like the gaping maw of some feral beast, lined with sharp teeth. From the sides of the helm sprang curved horns of ebony. In place of a scepter, the King-priest carried a long-hafted mace of black metal, whose head sprouted a dozen sharp spikes.

A few steps behind him followed a second man, who appeared to be the King-priest's personal bodyguard. He wore a chain hauberk without sleeves, leaving his muscular shoulders and arms visible. Covering his head was a helm crafted to look like a spider – holes for vision and breathing peeked out from between eight spindly legs. He carried a sharp, double-bladed axe in his right hand.

When the King-priest neared the altar, Rogan watched the candles dim considerably, as if his presence drained the light from the room. Remembering his own dagger, he realized Ebon Khorel's armor or mace must also be crafted of uril-chent alloy. He propped the latter against the altar, then raised an arm to begin the ritual.

As he had done the last six hours, Yennic rang the bell in his tower as the shadow of the sun dial reached the next notch in the stone. The difference was that this ring was accompanied by a surge of adrenaline, as he anticipated making his most prestigious kill – Ebon Khorel, his one-time employer. His crossbow lay loaded at his feet. He made sure its quarrel had an ample coating of his special poison. No harm in over-doing it, he thought. Now, he had only to wait for Groscil to lure out their prey, and make sure his one shot counted.

At the sound of the signal, Groscil made his move. After some scouting of his own the past few hours, he knew the best escape routes and had already overpowered some of the lone, imtermediate sentries to clear the way. The numbers in the courtyard, however, were still not in his favor. Surprise would help even the odds, but after that initial stealth the plan called for him to become as openly threatening as possible.

Everything was backwards from how he had enviosned it. He wanted his life back, yes, and this task would help him earn that. Still, he couldn't ignore the fact that these guards were just doing their job. They were not evil men as far as he knew, and it was a shame either of them had to die. There was no turning back now, though.

He started with the pair of guards stationed at the gate across from the temple. Groscil lurked in the shadows of one of the stone towers to which the gate hinged. With quickness belying his size, he leapt upon the guards, seizing each of their heads in his massive, taloned hands. He smashed them together, only their metal-capped helms preventing one skull from crushing another. While the guards were stunned, Groscil snatched a glaive from one of their grasps. Using the pole arm's shaft, he struck them behind their knees, collapsing them to the ground. After a moment of hesitation he drove the blade into the upper thigh of each, wounding them enough to reduce them to crawling, limiting their threat.

The deed done, Groscil turned his attention to the pair guarding the doors of the Skull Dome. They spotted him across the courtyard and readied their glaives, but did not leave their post. As Groscil charged, they called out to the tower guard to sound the alarm.

Yennic took advantage of the opportunity. "Look out!" he answered. "There're more of them coming from the south." Then he rang the hour bell over and over, until he thought he might become deaf.

The ritual of the Midnight Sun was not a lengthy one. The priests around the altar each recited a prayer to Gholdur in turn, then blew out their candles. Ebon Khorel stood at the altar, waiting for the last to finish. His lone bodyguard stood in the ever-thickening shadows of one of the large pillars. As the final priest extinguished his flame, the King-priest lifted his arms in preparation to speak.

He was interrupted by the sound of shouting from outside. Rogan's ears strained to catch any words, but they were too muffled. The shouts were quickly overcome by the vigorous clanging of the alarm bell. Rogan's hand closed around the hilt of his dagger as he turned to see what the King-priest would do next.

Unwilling to halt the ritual, Ebon Khorel merely turned his head toward his bodyguard and bellowed through his great helm, "Settle it." The man in the shadows answered with a simple nod, and crossed the floor to the double doors leading outside. The ringing of the bell had ceased by the time he swung the doors open, though there was still plenty of shouting. A bright square of sunlight pierced the room, and Rogan was relieved to make out the resonant snarling of a certain half-orc before the light and shouting were snuffed by the slamming of the door.

The King-priest waited for silence to reclaim the room before continuing. Some design of his helmet amplified his voice, leaving it deep and menacing, even in prayer. "My dread Lord Gholdur, you show us the path to might and cleanse the world through your hatred. In darkness we prepare for your coming, and through your favor we fulfill our destiny to rule over the weak. Today, on Midsummer, we blot out the sun and dwell in darkness, as shall the whole world upon your return."

One at a time, the light of the four candles surrounding the altar turned from yellow to dark blue as the King-priest stretched his hand in their direction. Then he clasped his hands together and slowly drew them apart. In the space between, growing with the distance of his palms, was a disc of solid shadow. Once he had broadened his reach beyond the width of his shoulders, Ebon Khorel threw the disc upward. Straight and swift it rose until it had sealed the hole in the ceiling, completely blocking out the sun.

The candles bathed the King-priest in their ghoulish blue hue, causing him to appear even more sinister in his elaborate armor. The priests once again filed in procession toward the palace, Ebon Khorel at their rear.

Outside, the courtyard was chaos. Once the alarm sounded and the fighting began, merchants and bystanders scurried to get themselves and their wares out of harm's way. Yennic knelt down and picked up his crossbow, resting it on the rail of the tower enclosure, aimed at the doorway of the Skull Dome. "Come on, don't make me wait, you treacherous bastard."

For all his good intentions, Groscil still had orc-blood running through his veins, and knew how to fight. Even as he charged the guards, howling like a frenzied berserker, he prepared his next move. Seeing they were holding their ground and setting their polearms to impale him, Groscil pulled up short. A sweeping swing of his weapon cleft the wooden shaft of one guard's glaive, striking the second with a loud *thwack*.

With his superior strength, Groscil bore down on his weapon, pinning his enemy's blade to the ground. For a moment, nobody moved. The guard struggled in vain to raise his weapon, but Groscil held firm. The half-orc broke into a tusk-revealing grin just as the door behind the guards opened. While Groscil was momentarily distracted, the empty-handed guard gave a shout and brought a heavy boot down upon his shaft, snapping it in two.

Yennic almost pulled his trigger, but was able to hold back when he saw the new combatant was not the King-priest. Uvar, Ebon Khorel's personal bodyguard, had joined the fray. Yennic knew from experience the odds had shifted against them.

"To the Hells with this!" Yennic declared. He wasn't about to see Groscil, his long-time prison-mate and only friend, slain for what was plainly becoming a useless distraction. Rogan would have to take care of the King-priest himself. Then, just as he lined up his shot, Yennic heard the chanting from the other side of the courtyard.

With viper-strike reflexes he shifted his crossbow and let the poisoned bolt fly. Its course was true, silencing the War-priest in a choking gargle of agony as it pierced his neck. It was still a heartbeat too late; the god-bestowed curse had been invoked.

Just as Groscil drew his sword from its scabbard, he heard a clap of thunder and his vision went dark. A wave of unrepentant nausea rose within him and he collapsed to the ground, vomiting the remains of what would be his last meal.

Yennic saw Uvar raise his head toward the bell tower, and though his eyes were hidden underneath his spider-like helm,

Yennic knew the look it concealed – one of pure hatred, born of a desire to inflict the greatest pain possible.

"No!" Yennic screamed. With no time to reload his crossbow, he dropped it and scrambled down the ladder, jumping the final body length. As Groscil, blind and defenseless, wretched the contents from his stomach, the King-priest's bodyguard lifted his axe and brought it swooshing down upon the half-orc's exposed neck. His head landed with a damp thump in the pool of vomit.

Yennic charged the guards that arrived with the fallen War-priest, though he had no weapon. Surprised by his brashness, they were slow to set their pole arms, and left them too high. Yennic somersaulted beneath their blades to the outside of the rightmost guard. As his momentum carried him past the guard's hip, he reached out and pulled the short sword from his belt. The blade was made for thrusting and Yennic used it so, driving underneath the back of his enemy's breastplate. That guard crumpled in a heap, and the one beside him dropped his glaive to draw his own sword, realizing close combat was inevitable.

Yennic spotted Uvar fast approaching out of the corner of his eye, and knew he had to act fast. He purposefully thrust forward and to his left, wide enough so the guard easily dodged by pulling back his right side. This, however, put Yennic beyond the guard's reach, and created more than enough of an opening for a former member of the blood-tear brotherhood. Yennic reversed the grip on his own sword and plunged it sideways into the guard's neck, killing him before his body slumped to the ground.

Yennic had just enough time to pick up his victim's sword and back away before the King-priest's bodyguard tried to level him with a mighty swing of his axe. Against another opponent, Yennic would have liked his odds – two quick blades against a man with a larger, slower weapon – but Uvar was rightfully feared. He wielded his axe with a fluidity that belied the rage behind it. He was strong as well; Yennic had once seen him sunder a man's shield while swinging his axe one-handed.

Uvar approached slowly, whirling his axe in a figure-eight pattern. Yennic was nearly mesmerized, so graceful was the motion, but he focused on finding a weakness to exploit.

He had no idea who shot him in the back, or from where. The impact caused Yennic to stumble forward, and the loss of balance was the only opportunity Uvar needed. His axe plunged down across Yennic's shoulder, its weight cleaving through muscle and bone as easily as a pudding. Yennic only had time to think of Groscil's head falling from his body before the world went black.

It was now or never, Rogan thought. The King-priest was walking past his hiding place in the shadows, and in a moment more he would be back in the palace, out of reach. And yet, Rogan hesitated. Was it fear, uncertainty, hopelessness? He owed it to his murdered wife and son to act. He owed it to Groscil and Yennic, who were playing their part out in the courtyard. Rogan looked at the Damper, barely visible in the pale blue light; he owed it to him too, for all the suffering his kind had seen at the hands of men. All this Rogan knew, but his feet still dragged like they were made of lead.

Then he heard the singing. It broke out in a clear and crystalline voice beside him, and although he didn't know the language of the song he understood its meaning – it was a song of courage, urging him to action. The priests heard it as well, and to a man they turned and stared, frozen by the realization of interlopers in their church.

With sudden determination Rogan drew his dagger and stepped out from behind the pillar, ready to pounce. The King-priest reacted by raising his left arm skyward and extending his mace in Rogan's direction. Upon chanting a few words, shrouded by the Damper's song, a column of red-gold fire roared downward from the ceiling above Rogan's head, threatening to engulf him. At the last moment the column curved to strike the Damper instead, outlining his dark body in a wreath of bright flame.

The singing ceased, and the lesser priests fled toward the palace. Rogan looked at the Damper in amazement, and though he appeared stunned by the blast, he still lived. The King-priest, however, didn't hesitate.

"Mornus alto!" he cried, thrusting his open palm in Rogan's direction. Three blade-like shards of crackling blue energy, the same color as the distorted candlelight, shot forth, but again swerved to strike the Damper. This time, Rogan didn't wait to count his blessings. He closed the distance quickly and slashed at the King-priest's leg, trying to stay clear of his mace. Ebon Khorel appeared startled by his charge and was slow to react.

The dagger found its mark, but glanced off his armor with an impotent *clang*.

Perhaps spurred by this impudent assault, the King-priest abandoned magic for his mace. He swung two-handed at Rogan, who barely managed to back out of reach. "Your Damper won't save you from this," he mocked in a bellowing voice. "I am your doom!"

Rogan fought to stay calm, but couldn't imagine how to penetrate that armor with his small blade. If he could wrestle the helmet off, maybe he could slice his throat? Just as the thought crossed his mind he saw his opening. The King-priest took a step back and lowered his weapon to chant again.

"Illian turong!"

Rogan dove forward as the King-priest spoke, encircling his neck with his arms. Shockingly, Rogan passed through the King-priest as if he were no more substantial than shadow. His amazement, though, was soon drowned out by pain.

He actually heard the muted crunching of his vertebrae being smashed before he felt it. Rogan fell face-first to the ground, spasms of fire surging through his upper body. He tried to roll over, but his limbs resisted. Resigned, he waited to be put out of his misery.

Instead he heard music – beautiful music – a song much like the Damper's from before, but accompanied by an entire chorus of voices. Its harmonies rose and fell like the eternal rolling of waves toward the shore. Wrapped in its comfort, he could taste its sweetness, and Rogan could not help but weep for joy, his own pain forgotten. A white light filled the room and

Rogan felt a soft breeze upon his skin, as if he were lying at peace in a spring-touched meadow.

Abruptly the music was gone and Rogan felt his body being moved. Once on his back he could see that the disc of shadow previously blocking the sun had melted away. Above him crouched a beautiful creature, an angel perhaps, flawless and feather-winged with iridescent, pearl-white skin.

"Rogan, my friend." The voice in his head was melodious and familiar. *"You are hurt; the blood of life leaves you."*

"No." He hoped he spoke the truth – that the joy of the music had repaired his injury. Yet, Rogan felt the pain creeping back, and neither his arms nor legs responded to his urgings. "What has happened?"

"I owe you an explanation, I realize, but I have also realized a great many things and must be brief, for you are not safe here. The power I absorbed from the King-priest's channeling revealed the Song of Redemption to me, as I hoped. Rogan, this body before you is my true form. Recovering this elusive memory was my true goal through all of this. I am sorry to have deceived you so. When I put my plan in motion, I didn't think much about leaving a group of criminals to a cruel fate. After all, it seemed little next to the cruelty my kind has been subjected to."

"*Your* plan?" Rogan was awash in confusion.

"Yesss, my friend." The creature spoke from his lips, and Rogan heard with his ears and not just his mind. "Your tongue wasss not eassy to masster." Rogan's eyes widened at the sound of this voice, and the Aasimar returned to speaking telepathically. *"I meant to serve the greater good by learning the Song of Redemption and teaching it to my brethren. But I now also remember the path we took to our fall, and realize there is no greater good. There is merely good... and evil. I have done evil to you and the others, Rogan. They are falling,"* the Aasimar lifted his eyes in the direction of the courtyard, *"and I cannot save them. But I can save you."*

"What of the King-priest?" Rogan blurted, though he had many questions he could not find words for.

"He fled when he saw my transformation, but he may return with others. Do not think on his destruction now, Rogan; there will be time for that later. Here, hold your dagger." The Aasimar placed the uril-chent blade in Rogan's hand, and helped tighten his fingers around it. *"I wish I had a song to remedy this, but my life-blood shall have to suffice."* With that he tilted Rogan's arm upward and held it firm, the dagger's tip inches from his heart.

"What are you doing?" Rogan cried, horrified by the creature's apparent intentions.

"There is no time, friend. The bodyguard returns. Do not despair; although this body allows me to remain here, my spirit is free, and will return to Mount Celestia. You do not destroy me... although I would have liked to stay and teach the others. Still," the Aasimar gave a smile full of solace, *"Fate will run its course for all things. Take heart in that."*

The words spoken, he let his body sink onto the dagger. Rogan felt warmth surge from the weapon, down his arm and into his back, healing him. A few breaths later he could move again on his own and looked to the Aasimar, but there was no life left in him. He thought he saw a tiny globe of white light ascend from the body and escape through the hole in the ceiling, but couldn't be sure it was real.

A rage welled within and Rogan longed to go after the King-priest, for the world seemed made of injustice. He agreed with the Aasimar's words, however – there would have to be another day for vengeance. He knew there were others who longed for it, and he would search until he found them. Rogan made a silent vow to unite them, and return one day to make it right.

He crept out the side door they entered through, just as Uvar returned to find the curious, winged body slumped on the Skull Dome floor. Rogan kept to the back alleys and avenues as best he could while making his way to the stolen wagon. He would find a way to help the other Dampers, he decided – help them remember their former glory, and set them free. Once they had their songs, perhaps true justice could be done, and a new age ushered in.

Chapter 5

Expanding the Empire

Jaiden Luminere fastened his baldric as he pushed his way through the mass of soldiers huddled inside Halidor Keep. Twelve miles on foot in the last three hours brought him just in time for his first battle, and the glory awaiting him. Though most of those gathered were the Duke's own men, Jaiden answered the general call-to-arms issued throughout the province. Rumors had reached most corners of the Cradle, luring him toward the oncoming doom from the south, and the supposed return of the Dread Tyrant, Gholdur.

As Jaiden pushed up the winding stairs toward the outer wall of the southern battlement, he adjusted his tunic and nestled an iron cap over his thick, dark hair. He muttered insincere apologies as he forced his way to the edge of the wall and looked outward.

The vista was spectacular. At seventeen, his young eyes, closely mirroring the tint of the afternoon sky, had rarely seen such a view. Mountains rose steeply from eastern and western sides of Halidor Keep, which was strategically nestled at the base of two ranges. A brisk wind cooled the sweat from Jaiden's skin, and the rocky plane to the south seemed to stretch on forever. The Duke's flag whipped in the wind from atop a turret, practically the only sound to be heard as the entire Keep held its collective breath.

A galloping horse and rider cut toward the stronghold from the horizon – a scout, carrying news of the enemy's numbers as they marched north to lay siege. Jaiden could see the tension in the rigid postures of his fellow soldiers as they awaited the tidings. Did no one else relish the promise of approaching battle? He'd travelled far from home for a chance to finally use his swordsmanship for something other than performance.

Even so, the Duke's coin wouldn't hurt. These past few years of fending for himself were difficult. His father never returned from the campaign against Chelpa, and the streets of Selamus were fraught with temptations and their own kind of danger. Money hadn't come easily, since he was too focused on perfecting his swordsmanship to learn a viable trade.

What's more, Jaiden was selective about taking assignments. Not owing fealty to any lord himself, Jaiden's dad taught him to choose sides with care. "You can't escape yourself," he'd say. "Silver might keep you fed, but you still have to wake up every morning and live with the decisions you've made." Jaiden was certain his choice to face his father's final enemy was one he would not regret.

Once the scout finally entered the keep and dismounted, the news he brought spread through the ranks of the assembled defenders like wildfire. Outnumbering them at least five-to-one, the army of Chelpa was superior in more than just size. Their infantry was better armed and outfitted, for war was the modern birthright of every able-bodied Chelpian man.

Furthermore, the King-priest employed beast-masters who trained exotic and devastating creatures. Jaiden reasoned their true value was more likely demoralization of foes than tactical combat, but even more potent was the Blood Tear Brotherhood: a team of elite spies and assassins who studied the deadly arts and coated the tips of their weapons with poison.

Finally, there was the King-priest himself. Ebon Khorel relished riding into battle at the head of his cavalry, and he was enveloped by the Dread Tyrant's devilry. His armor was reportedly crafted of powerful uril-chent alloy, which the King-priest coveted. It was hard enough to shatter steel blades, and absorbed light. The world dimmed wherever he rode, and tales of his invulnerability spread in his wake.

Jaiden didn't care about any of it. He grew up in the shadow of his father, dragged from one conflict to another, his Papa's sword his favorite plaything. Endless hours of practice had earned him quite a reputation.

He could whip a blade from one hand to another, behind his back and over his head, like a juggling magician performing sleight-of-hand to mesmerize a crowd. But his talent wasn't merely for display; Jaiden Luminere's father had taught him fighting techniques from several different cultures. Since his fourteenth summer, he'd defeated every man who tried him in single combat.

Fear of a fight might paralyze some of the soldiers around him, but Jaiden was not afflicted. He waited impatiently along the battlements of Fortress Halidor, looking forward to repaying the enemy who had taken the only person he cared about. The upcoming battle held more significance than his personal grudge, he knew.

The Empire of Chelpa was expanding under the reign of the King-priest. The Northern Provinces shared a similar culture and a desire to remain free, but were no longer unified by leadership. They'd heard of the oppression choking Ebon Khorel's kingdom, and feared its spread to their lands.

The Keep stood as a gateway into those lands, and if it fell they would be vulnerable to the insistent march of the King-priest. Knowing the strategic importance of his territory, the Duke of Halidor put out a plea for other Dukes to send troops – few had come. Halidor resorted to hiring what mercenaries he could beyond his own mustered forces, but Jaiden was a rare nugget among a scattering of false gold.

There was naught to do now but hold out as best they could, short of surrendering straight away and hoping for mercy. Mercy, however, was not something the King-priest of Chelpa was known for. Tales of other engagements already circulated amongst the soldiers, echoing of cruelty and a distinct lack of quarter given.

It seemed Ebon Khorel was not only interested in defeating his opponents, but in making the idea of standing against him so harrowing others wouldn't dare. His cavalry rode down any who sought retreat, and his soldiers speared the fallen to make sure they never arose again. He fed live prisoners to the charges of his beast-masters, and employed torture without a second thought to squeeze out useful information.

Jaiden tapped his finger on the hilt of his sword, scanning the horizon for his promised enemy. Though he'd participated in a few skirmishes, this was his first real battle. He hoped too much time wouldn't be wasted on siege engines and archery; he wanted to see the eyes of the men he bested, and lose count as they fell to his whirling blade. That was going to be hard to do from the battlement – unless they brought ladders, of course. The thought kept him optimistic.

A great cloud of dust finally arose in the south at the edge of sight. Carrion birds circled and cawed above it, anticipating carnage in the wake of Chelpa's hordes. The afternoon was late, but the sun still reflected off the angled slopes of the Wyvernwatch Mountains to the west. It did little to warm the air. Spring arrived a couple of weeks ago, only to seemingly retreat the last few days, revealing the last of winter's cold.

The minutes stretched out as the enemy advanced, but slowly Jaiden began to distinguish individual bodies amongst the mass. A line of cavalry on black horses flared across the front boundary of marching troops, spearheaded by Ebon Khorel himself, clad in his black, uril-chent-forged armor.

This is real, Jaiden thought – his chance had finally come. He almost missed that chance altogether as a boulder crashed against the stone of Halidor Keep, exploding into fragments only a few feet below him on the outer wall. Jaiden ducked reflexively as the floor beneath him shook; he had not seen the trebuchets approaching from the flank.

As the battering began, a boastful roar rose up from the enemy, as if the outcome was but a formality – they had not failed a test yet. The plight of the forces inside Halidor was exacerbated by their complete lack of siege craft. Not a single engineer was present, let alone a catapult or mounted ballista with which to retaliate.

Shot after shot came from the Chelpian machines, slamming rock against stone in a primal battle of supreme stubbornness. Eventually, however, the toll of the onslaught rendered itself in deep cracks throughout the keep's foundation. Groaning and crumbling of the mortar followed, setting off a panic amongst the defenders.

"We can't just sit here waiting to be pounded into dust," the soldier to Jaiden's left protested.

"You're right. I'm not dying a coward's death," Jaiden replied. He unslung the shield from his back and strapped it to his forearm, then shouted as he pushed his way down the stairs to the inner courtyard, "Come, brothers, I'm taking the fight to them. Who's with me?"

A surge of hurrahs ensued, bolstered when Jaiden convinced the guards at the front gate to swing the doors open. The enthusiasm was loud enough to drown out the Duke's commands to halt, and within moments the soldiers of Halidor flooded across the uneven, stony field toward their invaders.

The engineers ceased their bombardment as the King-priest raised his mace and circled it in the air, signaling his troops to charge. The horses surged ahead of the trailing foot soldiers, gaining speed to mow down their earthbound opposition. Jaiden halted the Halidor advance, seeing no need to wear themselves out when their enemy was closing the distance on their own. He recalled what his father had shown him about fighting mounted opponents.

A steed's forward momentum limits lateral movement, which, along with the angle-limitations of the weapon-wielding rider, creates the best advantage for a more agile combatant on foot. Jaiden lifted the hilt of his longsword above his waist, and steadied the top of his shield a shade below eye level. He stood calmly, parallel to the nearest oncoming horse, and focused on the clip-clopping rhythm of the animal's hooves. He timed its strides, intuiting the number of paces it would take to reach him. Jaiden took another half-step forward to maximize his balance advantage against the rider, who was already lowering his lance to skewer him.

At precisely the correct moment Jaiden lunged to his left, out of range of the rider's weapon. As his attacker moved past, Jaiden tilted his sword outward, allowing the inertia of the steed to create all the force necessary to puncture the protective links of his enemy's hauberk. His blade sliced through the rider's side just above his hip, a bleeding wound that would lead to death.

However, Jaiden's leap brought him too close to the next horse in line, and though it trailed its neighbor slightly, the creature's flank collided hard into Jaiden's shield, spinning him to the ground. Lucky not to get trampled, by the time Jaiden regained his feet and wits, the cavalry had pushed past and the infantry quickly closed toward him.

With no fear for his own safety, Jaiden waded into the fray, his sword spinning and cutting, his shield blocking blows. Foe after foe fell before him, broken and bleeding. As his years of training took control, Jaiden lost all measure of the growing distance between himself and his allies.

Oncoming warriors began giving a wide berth to the deadly whirlwind, circling around until he was surrounded. Jaiden was soon deep into enemy lines, and as he searched for another soldier to strike, his head snapped around at the sound of an echoing, gurgling roar.

The roar Jaiden heard was not actually echoing, he realized, despite the nearby rising cliffs. In truth it was five roars, one from each of the ferocious heads of a mighty hydra. Its bulging, lizard-like body shifted from green to gray as it lumbered forward in search of prey. It must have broken free from one of the beast-masters, and men scattered ahead of it, unconcerned that doing so might put them in peril from human enemies.

Jaiden's mindset didn't allow for retreat, though the hungry beast was nearly three times his height when rearing its long, sinuous necks. He evaded the first two snaps of fanged maws with inspiring agility, but the hydra's heads worked together, each aware of the other. Just as Jaiden side-stepped the second head, a third reached from behind and snagged his shield-arm in its jaws.

The frame of the shield kept his arm from being snapped clean off, but it bent under the crushing pressure. Jaiden, strapped to it, was effectively immobilized. A fourth head lunged to bite into his right leg, its sharp teeth puncturing leather and flesh. His sword swung quickly in response, cutting deeply into the monster's nose.

The jaws released his leg, though the mouth holding his shield yanked back with incredible force before letting go, flinging Jaiden through the air in an uncontrolled spin. Sky and earth alternated rapidly in his vision, and all he could do was stretch his limbs, hoping to land on his feet.

His back, though, came down first with a crack. His neck whipped from the impact, smacking his skull against the stony ground, painting everything in silent darkness.

Jaiden's eyes shot open as a spark of pain brought him back to consciousness. The back of his head throbbed, but his wrists and shoulder sockets screamed as his arms were pulled tightly away from his body. His right leg felt as if it were on fire. Night had fallen, and the air was cold and dark. Armored men stood over him, their grim features exaggerated in the flickering torchlight. One form looked like a horrid, black spider had enveloped his head, though his pain left Jaiden uncertain.

He was tied to a makeshift wooden frame, and the cords around his wrist bit into his skin as they stretched him nearly to the point of breaking. A tall figure clad in black, metal armor joined the gathering above him, before dropping to one knee. His face was obscured by a fearsome, bestial helm, and a hum filled Jaiden's ears as if the very air surrounding this dark figure vibrated with power.

"What is your name, soldier?" The man's voice sounded deep and hollow from within his horned helmet.

"Jaiden," he responded through clenched teeth as he strained to pull his arms inward. "Jaiden Luminere," he added, figuring his enemies might as well have his full name. He wanted them to know precisely who was going to exact revenge on them, once he found a way free of this mess.

A cold, metal gauntlet gripped Jaiden's right arm and moved along it, testing the tautness of his extended muscles. "One of my captains reported that you acquitted yourself quite well on the battlefield today. What is your rank in this... army?" The last word was drawn out with clear disdain.

"No rank; I'm a soldier-for-hire." Jaiden paused, but ultimately couldn't resist. "That was still enough to best twenty of your men before your beast arrived. He probably spared twenty more." Jaiden would have boasted further, but his waning endurance made it difficult to craft insults.

"Is that so?" the metallic voice responded. The armored figure moved his hand to the exposed wound in Jaiden's leg. He pressed his finger into one of the hydra's teeth marks, bypassing the severed muscle tissue and driving straight to the bone.

Jaiden howled at the intrusion.

"You wouldn't lie to me, would you, Jaiden Luminere?"

"I'm not lying!" Jaiden screamed, involuntary tears rolling down his cheeks.

"Good," the hollow voice receded as the man stood and turned his back. After muttering briefly, the man turned again and Jaiden could see, through the distortion of unfallen tears, the palm of his left hand glowing with an ice-blue aura. The man knelt once more, his hand hovering over Jaiden's bare chest. The menacing hum in Jaiden's ears grew louder.

"Do you know who has captured you?"

Jaiden shook his head from side-to-side, teeth clenched in pain.

"I am Ebon Khorel, mouth of The Most Potent and Dread Tyrant, Gholdur. His power assures my victory, and if you don't tell me what I ask to know, that power is the last thing you shall feel in this world."

Jaiden searched the faces of the other men standing over him for sympathy, but found none.

Ebon Khorel continued, "There may have been a strange creature among the visitors to this keep the last several days. Do you know of whom I speak?"

Jaiden tried to follow what the King-priest was saying, but nothing registered beyond the panic that his life was about to be extinguished. He reluctantly shook his head, knowing the consequence of doing so was more pain. Ebon Khorel pressed his glowing hand upon Jaiden's chest, and a sharp pulse of agony wracked his body. His eyes rolled upward, and his vision was obscured by an intruding white light.

"His body is not unlike a man's, but feathery wings protrude from his back," the King-priest continued. "He is not easy to miss, and may call himself, 'Aasimar'. Tell me where he is or what direction he was heading, and you shall feel no more."

"Please," Jaiden whimpered, "I know nothing of such a creature, I swear." Jaiden's pain allowed him to show momentary weakness, but he quickly blinked the tears from his eyes and regained his defiance. "Even if I did know, tyrant," he spat, "the Ninth Hell would claim me before I told you anything!"

"You disappoint me, Jaiden. Talented warriors are useful, but you are either lying or indeed, ignorant. Either way, you shall never raise a sword against me again." Ebon Khorel touched Jaiden's chest again, and once more, pain surged through him. This time bile rose into his throat, and Jaiden had to turn his head sideways to avoid choking on his own vomit.

The King-priest stood, and Jaiden, teetering on the verge of consciousness, managed to catch only a few more sentences.

"I must find the Aasimar, Uvar," he said to the man with the spider's head. "I don't doubt he was here – next time, bring me a more pliant prisoner. I will continue north, along the road. Resistance should be minimal this far from Selamus. Head west with the Blood-tear Brotherhood and send your report if you pick up the trail."

Though more was said, Jaiden could no longer hold on. His determination spent, he slipped from the waking world, unsure he would ever return, and happy for it.

Chapter 6

Reality in Dreams

Jaiden looked down to find himself knee-deep in mist, which extended in all directions. The air was calm around him, though the brilliant, star-studded canopy of the night sky hung tantalizingly close overhead. Was he standing among the clouds?

He looked at his wrists in wonder, grasping them one at a time, unable to find any trace of injury. Likewise, his leg showed no signs of damage. The question of his whereabouts was just solidifying in his mind when a serene, alluring, female voice answered it.

"You are safe in my realm, Jaiden Luminere."

Jaiden swiveled left and right, looking for the source of the voice, which seemed to surround him. "And who are you, exactly?" he asked, hoping a response would grant him another chance at locating the speaker. This might be a trick of the King-priest to extract more information.

"I am Criesha. Your people once called me 'Goddess of the Moons and Magic.' The night sky and dreams of men are my provinces, though the latter I have not visited in ages."

This time the words came only from ahead, and when Jaiden looked forward once more he saw a woman of unearthly beauty walking toward him down a mist-enveloped slope. Her ebony hair was drawn above her shoulders with strings of silver and moonstones, and her luminescent skin gave off the slightest green hue. She was dressed in a diaphanous gown of deeper green with accents of royal blue. It shimmered as her body swayed, yet was insubstantial enough that the light of her bare skin could be seen through it.

"So, this is a dream, then?" Jaiden asked, his eyes lingering on a dominion usually reserved for his imagination. The prospect appeared more plausible to him than the alternative; still, her presence felt distinctly more real than any dream.

"Yes, and no," the woman responded. "You are in a dream of sorts, though not one of your own making. I brought you here for a purpose." She drew within an arms-length, and all Jaiden's senses felt heightened to extraordinary awareness. He experienced more vigor in her proximity than any time in his normal life. The sensation was truly astounding.

"And what purpose is that? Criesha, was it? Will I be staying?" Jaiden certainly hoped the answer to his last question was yes, if only for a while longer. Her presence was intoxicating.

"Only to introduce myself to you; for now, Jaiden, that is enough. There are others working on my behalf, but I wanted to grant you this visit to prove I am real."

"Real? But didn't you say yourself, this is all a dream?"

"You may find the line between the two not as certain as you think," she smiled. "I am sorry for the difficulty of the road ahead, Jaiden, but you will ultimately have the choosing of where that road leads. All I seek at the moment is a bit of your trust." One of Criesha's eyebrows arched as she awaited his response.

Jaiden shrugged. "Sure, why not?" What harm was there in trusting a dream? Especially one so astonishingly beautiful.

"Good. Now if you would, please close your eyes."

Jaiden did as asked. He felt warmth upon his forehead and the gentle pressing of soft lips. When he opened his eyes, however, the night sky was no longer above him. There was harsh light, and he blinked several times, fighting it off. The pain had returned – his head and chest throbbed, his arms and leg stung.

A woman with dark hair looked down on him, but her face was obscured in shadow. "This one's alive," she said, though her foreign accent didn't belong to the woman of his dream.

His eyes shut again, hoping the pain would ease if he gave himself over to the other world. Nothing. He beckoned that realm with all his desire, but instead felt the tug on his arms relent as the cords around his wrists were cut. His body was lifted, but he didn't bother opening his eyes, unwilling to acknowledge this agonizing reality.

After a few moments, Jaiden felt the cushion of soft cloth against his back. He dared to open his eyes again. It was darker – he was in some sort of enclosure that blocked the sun. This time, a man's face looked down upon him. Framed by a coif of chainmail from which strands of blonde hair protruded, it held weary, compassionate turquoise eyes that darted about as they considered Jaiden's condition.

"Welcome back, my friend. Criesha be praised; life is not through with you yet, it seems." He added a smile, and Jaiden felt the warmth of strong, rough hands clasping his.

"Where am I?" Jaiden asked. He was riding upon a sea of uncertainty, rising and falling from peace to suffering under the influence of secret tides.

"You are still at Halidor Keep, where you fell in service to the Duke, it seems. I am Sir Amurel Golddrake, Master of the Order of the Rising Moon. We have been riding for days, hoping to make the Keep before the battle, but were delayed. You seem to be the only northern survivor of this annihilation. Unless others fled."

Sir Golddrake pulled back the coif from his head, revealing thick locks of flaxen hair, befitting his surname. He wore the full plate armor of a land-owning knight, beneath a pristine, white tabard. Emblazoned in purple across his chest was the image of a crescent moon. "We have not, for instance, found the body of the Duke nearby; though it is quite possible he would have been taken as a prisoner by Chelpa."

Memories of the King-priest's withering touch flooded back; had it been real, or just a nightmare? Jaiden remembered walking amidst the night sky, talking to a strikingly beautiful woman. That seemed substantial enough at the time, but now the truth was trying to reveal itself through his body – his chest, head, and leg all spoke of it.

"My mistress, Criesha, told me I would find you here, though I'm sorry it wasn't sooner," Sir Golddrake continued, assessing his condition.

Criesha – that name was familiar, Jaiden thought. Yes, that was what the raven-haired woman from his dream called herself. Was she real, after all, if this other man had spoken to her?

"You know of Criesha?" Jaiden asked, hoping conversation might distract him from the pain.

Sir Golddrake raised an eyebrow at Jaiden's question, as if it were a jest, or he was being tested. "Yes, she is my guiding light. As I said before, I founded the Order of the Rising Moon, and Criesha told me I'd find someone here who would help our cause. I'm guessing by your resilience, and the fact you must have fought bravely and not fled in the face of such overwhelming odds, that you are him. I will pray on it later, of course, but I feel in my bones you are the one she spoke of.

"She also led me to this... said it would be of particular value to you."

Jaiden's eyes grew wide as the blonde knight presented the hilt of his father's sword, no doubt scavenged from the bones of the battlefield.

"But tell me..." Sir Golddrake held out his palm in invitation.

"Jaiden. Jaiden Luminere," he said, forcing his name past the rising lump in his throat. He hadn't dared to hope his familial blade might be recovered.

"Tell me, Jaiden, how is it you have come to know our goddess, if you don't mind my question? I have never met a man who already shared my faith."

"Goddess?" Jaiden coughed, nearly choking on his own spit. Was this knight a lunatic? "How can that be so? The gods are only legend – they don't truly exist."

"Ah, but they do, my friend." Sir Golddrake's posture slackened, and Jaiden guessed trying to convince the uninitiated was a familiar role. "It is true they have been absent a very long time, but that is changing. We will speak more of this later, however. I do not wish to overwhelm you with too much at once. For now, get your rest. The physicians are eager to begin tending to you, and I should not impede them too long. I wanted to meet you, though, before riding on.

"I am leaving my very able companion, Saffron min Furasi, in charge of your care. We shall speak again in a few days, once you've mended further."

Sir Amurel Golddrake stood to take his leave, and Jaiden noticed as he did so, it was with a pronounced limp. The lower half of his right leg jutted outward at an awkward angle, leaving it a couple inches short of the ground when the knight stood erect.

As he left the tent, two men in gray, hooded robes replaced him. They began dressing Jaiden's wounds with bandages that quickly dyed red with his blood. Jaiden closed his eyes and gritted his teeth while his discomfort deepened.

Unsure of how much time had passed, Jaiden remained cautious about deciding he was awake and not dead. His stomach grumbled – between it and his parched mouth, he finally felt assured he was no longer dreaming. While passing in and out of consciousness, none of his dreams were accompanied by the harshness of his unfortunate conditions.

He was still in a tent, but alone. His cot was soaked with sweat from the fever he developed fighting the infection of his injuries. A single oil lamp, standing on a leveled tree stump, cast a dim halo, and he could hear laughter, along with the faintest bits of lyre music, rising and falling outside.

Jaiden raised his hands to his head to find it wrapped in bandages. He sat up and groaned; both his chest and injured leg protested the movement. Looking at his torso, he saw a patch of black skin near his heart, as if the area were scorched by fire. His lower half was covered by a woolen blanket.

Summoning what courage he could manage, he lifted the edge of the blanket just enough to peek at his leg. His entire thigh, from knee to groin, was wrapped in white bandages and he let out a sigh, replacing the blanket. Though not likely to admit it, Jaiden was grateful the damage was hidden, awful as it felt.

His attention returned to discovering his surroundings, and his nose led his eyes to a bowl of steaming broth, set on a second stump in the shadow of the lamp. Thankfully, it was within reach. Jaiden didn't bother using the wooden spoon to ladle his meal, pouring the contents directly into his mouth. His throat was dry and a fierce hunger ravaged his belly, both of which were remedied by the thick broth. Bittersweet with healing herbs, he swallowed so quickly it burnt the roof of his mouth.

With the immediate need for sustenance subdued, he listened more closely to the music wafting on an otherwise hollow breeze. It was stirring, as if the notes sang of bravery, though there was no voice accompanying them. He wiped the slurped remains from his chin and gripped the cot on either side of his waist. Time to give standing a try, he thought.

As Jaiden's right knee started to bend, the resulting pressure on his thigh evoked a cry of pain, loud as a battle-charge, and the music stopped. The conversation outside trailed to a halt.

Jaiden settled back into the sagging curve of coarse cloth, wincing. A few breaths later the flap to his tent whisked back and a dark-haired woman, her face obscured by a silk veil, entered. Her long-lashed, obsidian eyes remained starkly visible, and her locks were gathered into a single braid that disappeared behind bare shoulders.

"You are awake," she said, stopping just short of Jaiden's cot, where she positioned and took a seat on a severed section of cedar log. She pressed the back of her hand to his forehead, beaded with sweat. "Good, your fever has broken."

"I'm alive, but I feel like the Abyss." Jaiden tried to sit a little straighter, hoping to appear tall.

"That doesn't surprise me," she said. "It looks like a horned demon has been gnawing on your leg. You're lucky not to have lost it altogether." The woman gathered a bowl of water and white cloth, then nodded for permission to inspect his wounds.

Jaiden gave consent with the extension of his palm, and braced for more pain. He didn't want to appear weak in front of a woman. "My name is Jaiden Luminere, what's yours?"

"Saffron min Furasi." Her eyes seemed to smile as she considered his bare physique, but he couldn't be sure what her mouth was doing. "This will hurt."

Saffron peeled back the blanket covering his lower half, reaching over his lap to lift the bandages that clung to his leg. He winced and tensed his arms, which shook as she began prodding and applying a poultice. Unable to look, he lifted his eyes upward to trace creases of shadow in the roof of the tent.

"The bone is broken, that will take two moons to heal," Saffron shared, matter-of-factly. "Some of the muscle is also gone, and that—"

"Your accent is unfamiliar to me, where are you from?" Jaiden interrupted, the tent folds failing to provide adequate distraction from the pain. He struggled to hold the tears welling in his eyes from falling, but they could only be held in check for so long.

Saffron paused, then played along. "I am a musician from the Emirate of Begnasharan. I was on my way to Selamus with my sister when our caravan was attacked by the Chelpians."

Thankfully, she finished her ministrations and started rewrapping bandages. Jaiden quickly wiped the wetness from his eyes before leveling his chin, hoping she didn't notice.

"You're Begnari? I've never met anyone from that far west. My father told me a man could travel for four days and see nothing but sand. What's it like? You have beautiful eyes."

His last comment drew a turn of Saffron's head, catching his eyes as they lingered too long on her breasts. "Well, it looks like at least something down here is working properly." Saffron raised her forearm from his lap, allowing the rise of his erection to push against his undergarments.

She delicately replaced the blanket over Jaiden's lap. His face grew warm and he couldn't find any words as she stood up and gathered his empty bowl. "A surgeon should arrive in camp tomorrow, and he will evaluate your injuries with more skill than I possess. Amurel should not be much longer, either, and he'll undoubtedly have some plan for you, too. Sleep well, Jaiden Luminere."

Jaiden was still breathing in the lingering traces of her perfume when four men wearing white tabards entered the tent. They carried straw-stuffed bedrolls and threadbare blankets, laughing at a shared joke. One of them nodded in recognition of Jaiden's presence, but the others didn't seem to notice. They unrolled their mats beside one another on the open ground near the middle of the tent.

Jaiden wouldn't have known whether he'd been sharing this tent all along, but he couldn't help feeling intruded upon now. Given the severity of his injuries, all he wanted was solitude. Sinking lower in his cot, he thought if perhaps he could only fall asleep quickly he might dream of Criesha again, and his pain would be forgotten. Instead, he lay awake for hours, suffering the snoring of his neighbors and striving to ignore the throbbing heat and itching under his bandages.

Longing for a distraction, he peeked over to make sure his tentmates were asleep before sliding his blanket down past his groin. Jaiden closed his eyes and thought of Saffron dressing his wound. Then, using his own hand, he thought of hers moving higher into his lap and stimulating him. He imagined he could hear lyre music playing while he watched the curve of her breasts heave beneath her clothes as they both grew more excited. His breath shallowed and his heartbeat quickened. Finally, he softly grunted his release and was able to attain repose.

A cock crowed somewhere nearby, outside the tent, startling Jaiden awake. He was in the midst of dreaming, but couldn't remember the details. He found waking up to be the worst part of the day, as it only reminded him of his pain and predicament.

Saffron entered as he was rinsing and presented him with a sturdy crutch, carved from cedar. He noticed her veil was still in place, but her thick, sable hair was damp and unwound. It cascaded over her shoulders to the middle of her breasts, where Jaiden's eye lingered as he remembered his late-night diversion.

"Come, if you want breakfast. You'll have to start fending for yourself." She turned and exited without waiting for him, emphasizing her point about self-reliance.

Jaiden found loose breeches and a simple gray tunic left on the stump beside his cot. He struggled to dress, as every movement brought pain with it. The other soldiers sharing his tent were long-gone, so there was no one to help him, and it took several minutes before he emerged from the flap of his canvas sanctuary.

Saffron was there to greet him, however, skillfully weaving her hair back into a single braid. She'd fitted a brightly colored flower, magenta and yellow, into the strands behind her ear and began walking as she spoke. "Over here are the water basins – these two for washing, the other for drawing drinking water. Rations are spread on the westernmost table at dawn and dusk – if you want to eat anything between meals, you'll have to provide for yourself. Wait too long, the food will be gone and you'll go hungry. Sleeping in can be a hazard around here, for more than one reason."

Jaiden was only half-listening to his guide, the bulk of his concentration split between awkwardly following with his crutch, and watching the sway of Saffron's hips as she moved.

"When you're mended," she continued, "should you choose to stay, you'll be expected to contribute to the chores: gathering wood, cooking, packing the wagons, you get the point. The Order won't abide laziness." She turned to look at Jaiden as she made this final statement to ensure it was received.

His brow was moist with the effort of keeping up, and the scorched region around his heart throbbed. "May we sit for a moment, miss?" he asked, short of breath.

Saffron's tone softened, and her eyes widened. "Certainly. I am sorry if I have rushed your recovery. Amurel tells me often I could benefit from more patience."

Jaiden labored to seat himself on a pine bench at an empty mess table. Around the camp, men were busy cutting wood, packing their horses, sharpening the tools of war. Looking about, Jaiden could not find anyone simply idle. Discipline reigned.

"Amurel is the leader of this camp?"

Saffron nodded as she also sat.

"Is he nobility?"

"He is – was – a landed noble," Saffron amended. "He has no siblings, and when his parents died, Sir Golddrake sold his ancestral holdings for supplies and a charter from the Prince to create the Order of the Rising Moon. This," she gestured to the camp around them, "is his dream."

"Order of the Rising Moon, huh? Yes, these are clearly fighting men." Jaiden took note that nearly everyone in the yard wore some degree of armor. "The Duke of Halidor certainly could've used them."

Saffron shook her head from side to side. "We tried to reach your battle, but from what I've seen since, it is probably best we did not. Amurel is proud, but he does not yet have the numbers to directly face the armies of the Dread Tyrant."

"Begging your pardon, but I'm a single man and I was faring well against those same troops. What does a woman and a foreigner know of such matters, anyway?"

Saffron's eyes narrowed, but she didn't back away. "Typical. You were beaten to the edge of death, but it is I who know nothing of warfare? Where I am from, Jaiden Luminere, women share the dangers of battle with our men, who are grateful for it. You would be lucky to live long enough to learn this lesson." Saffron stood.

"I'm sorry, I didn't mean to offend you. Please, don't leave." He truly didn't want her to. "The flower in your hair is beautiful. What kind is it?"

"If you didn't mean to offend, you chose your words poorly, master Luminere." Saffron stared at him hotly for a long breath, then softened her eyes. "I will forgive you because of your ordeal. Did you see the one who did this to you?" she gestured toward him, but could've meant any number of things.

"It was a beast brought me down; a beast with many heads. But Ebon Khorel saw me afterwards." Jaiden's hand rose to his chest at the memory.

"You were face-to-face with the King-priest?" Saffron drew closer.

"Well, I was tied up, like you found me. He questioned me – wanted to know if I'd seen a winged man, or something crazy like that."

"A winged man?"

"That's all I remember." Seeing her interest, Jaiden altered his tone. "Would you like to go back to my tent and talk about it a little more?"

"Hmm," she leaned back. "Rest while you can, Jaiden. We rarely stay encamped more than a week, and will be on the move when Sir Golddrake returns, I imagine. When the surgeon arrives, I will send him to your tent." She stood, but spoke again before leaving.

"It's a zinnia." Saffron must've seen the confusion on Jaiden's face. "The flower. It symbolizes thoughtfulness for an absent friend. I wear it for my sister."

Jaiden watched as Saffron's braid snapped behind her like a whip of fire. She took meaningful strides toward a large tent at the center of camp, and didn't look back. He had his work cut out for him, no doubt. With a deep breath and the somber realization of the discomfort to come, Jaiden stood and limped back to his cot, foregoing breakfast altogether.

Jaiden's stomach had spent the afternoon grumbling its displeasure, when a middle-aged man wearing a tight, leather jerkin entered the tent. A pack hung by his side from one shoulder, and a trimmed beard with ample gray framed his face.

"Greetings, young sir. I'm finishing my rounds, but was told to pay special attention to you."

Jaiden sat up in his cot, wincing at the movement, but anxious to get an accurate prognosis for when he might be able to continue the fight against Ebon Khorel.

"You must be the surgeon. Thank you for seeing me, Master...?"

"Kimbrel," the elder man finished. "And no need for thanks – Sir Golddrake pays me good coin to tend his wounded. Now, let's take a look at your injuries, shall we? I'll require you to disrobe." The surgeon opened his satchel and removed several instruments while Jaiden obeyed.

Jaiden tried to imagine once again walking amongst the clouds of the night sky, hoping to summon the goddess whose presence so soothed him, as the surgeon investigated the wounds on both his leg and chest. His efforts were in vain and he couldn't help groaning at the surgeon's invasions, each instance drawing concerned looks from Master Kimbrel.

"You can put your clothes back on. I'll summon the Mistress so I don't have to repeat myself." When he returned, Saffron was with him, still carrying her spear and shield from sparring practice.

"Young man," he began, looking straight into Jaiden's eyes, "I want you first to be aware how close to death you came. Had the angle of the teeth that impaled you been ever-so-slightly different, they would have severed an artery, and you would've bled to death on the spot. Your leg bone is broken, but it's already been set," he glanced at Saffron, "and fairly well, I might add. It should mend in a matter of months, if you stay off it."

Jaiden nodded. A few months was a long time, but he could endure.

"However," Master Kimbrel continued, "it probably won't do you any good. Much of the muscle is simply gone, and though it's not imperative I remove your right leg completely, I'm afraid I may as well. It's going to be useless to you and cumbersome to carry, and another infection could be fatal."

The bearded man's lips kept moving, but Jaiden no longer heard any words. Everything was muted, as if he were underwater.

"—I've never seen anything quite like it. I'm certain the heart is damaged, but to what extent, I can't tell without examining the tissue underneath. If you were my boy, I'd tell you to avoid anything that might cause undue strain."

"Jaiden, are you all right?" Saffron asked, genuine concern reflected in her eyes as a trickle of blood started leaking from one of his nostrils.

"Get out! No one is taking my leg!" He waved his arms wildly as if fighting off an unseen ghost.

Saffron dropped her spear. "Jaiden, calm down, no one's here to hurt you."

He tried to rise, but grasped his chest as a surge of pain shot through it, almost as if the surgeon's words chose that moment to bloom truth. It was too much. Why did they bother saving him in the first place?

The surgeon stepped forward to offer stability, but all Jaiden could see was a man coming to make sure he never walked again. He lunged to avoid him, but succeeded in falling off his cot onto the dirt floor. Saffron dropped to her knees and cradled his head in her hands, speaking softly, but his nose continued to bleed, followed by eyes rolling upward as Jaiden lapsed out of consciousness.

Chapter 7

Not Alone

Amurel Golddrake's agents had spent six weeks following leads about a community ripe for revolution. If his newer information was correct, there was no time to lose.

Such thoughts occupied his mind as he returned to his own camp, but he was also eager to learn more about the young warrior Criesha had guided him to. She often visited Amurel's dreams, appearing as a pale green moonbeam, illuminating the path she desired for him. Such intervention brought him solace, and his faith was unwavering.

"Hail, Lady Saffron." The Begnari woman approached him on horseback, flanked by an initiate of the Order. She had become something of an unofficial lieutenant since the day he'd freed her from a Chelpian slave caravan.

Saffron raised her palm in greeting. "Happy returns, Sir Golddrake. I trust your mission went well?" She tugged gently on the reins and halted her horse, allowing Amurel to finish his approach, in deference to his authority.

He nodded. "There is much to tell. Find Orestes and bring him to my tent. Sir Kilborn and I will join you for council shortly. First, though, I shall speak with our newest patient. How is Master Luminere faring?"

Saffron pursed her lips and her posture slackened. "He is having some difficulty with his new condition – and I with him. He is stubborn as a kank at a watering hole, Amurel. Perhaps you will have more success consoling him." Her eyes slipped to his malformed right leg.

"Until council then, Lady Saffron." Amurel bowed before nudging the reins and clicking his heels gently to his horse's flank. He made his way to Jaiden's tent, where an attendant tried to assist him from the saddle. Amurel waved him off. "My horse needs attention, squire, not I."

He removed his gauntlets and limped to the entrance flap, then took a breath and straightened his posture before whisking it back. Sure enough, Jaiden Luminere was reclining in the same spot Amurel had left him. "Ho, friend. You seem to be as immovable as Mount Massither. Perhaps we should pluck you down before the gates the next time we are besieged – we shall outlast the enemy a fortnight at least."

Jaiden sat up straighter upon being addressed, though he was unsure of the identity of the knight speaking to him. He had not held a conversation with anyone for two days, not since the doctor, and was suspicious this man might be coming to execute the surgeon's orders. "What do you want with me?"

"Relax, Jaiden." Sir Golddrake pulled a section of log beside the dirty cot and sat, before removing his helm and sliding the coif back from his head.

Upon seeing his golden mane, Jaiden recognized the leader of the Order, and eased a little. He imagined such an important man would not be singlehandedly implementing any surgeries.

"Sir Golddrake, I was unaware you'd returned."

"I only just arrived. You were my first concern."

"Have I earned a reputation already?" Jaiden teased, while knowing it would be well-deserved. He hadn't been easy to get along with, and his refusals to give or receive help had worn the patience of those around him.

"I'm not sure what you mean, my friend. I wanted to see and hear from you, first-hand, how your recovery has progressed."

"Progressed?" Jaiden felt his frustration rising again. "Well, I'm stuck in this cot for most of the day. My leg is broken, and the surgeon wants to saw it off altogether." Despite his intention to challenge, Jaiden's eyes couldn't maintain contact with the calm gaze of Sir Golddrake. Realizing he wasn't being judged, he sighed and spoke more softly. "I feel useless. I'm a swordsman in a camp of soldiers, yet I'm useless."

Sir Golddrake lifted his chin for a moment in consideration before speaking. "I was brought into this life a cripple. The midwife told my mother I had turned in the womb, and nothing could be done. If not a nobleman's heir, I probably would have been left to perish.

"There were certainly times in my youth I felt sorry for myself, Jaiden, but you can't let that kind of thinking seize you, or you *will* become useless. Years ago, when my parents died, I knew I must find a way to contribute to the Golddrake legacy.

"Nothing came easily, but I dedicated myself to equestrian pursuits. My own legs wouldn't get me far, so I learned to use my steed as a living extension of my desire. Once I mastered riding, I practiced doing everything from horseback: combat, falconry, even eating. You can't imagine how perilous it is to ladle soup from the saddle without spilling every last drop."

Jaiden raised his eyebrows at the last image. "I am not a rich man, Sir. There is no way I could afford such a talented and patient horse."

"My point, lad, is that nothing is impossible if we search hard enough for a way – and are open when the way reveals itself." Sir Golddrake paused, seeming to weigh the possible impact of his next statement. "Criesha has plans for you, I feel it. Would you consider joining my Order and staying on under my tutelage?"

"I don't know." Jaiden had the impression of being led into some sort of trap. What would he do in such a group? Sir Golddrake believed in things he could not see; Jaiden believed only in himself and the transcendence of sharp steel. There was always a cost involved with choices like these. He'd learned this lesson from his father: nothing was free unless you took it. "How would I serve with only one good leg?"

"Give it time and we will find a way, together." Sir Golddrake waited until Jaiden nodded his agreement, then smiled and lightly swatted Jaiden's feet with his gauntlets as he stood.

"Sir Golddrake, why do you serve Criesha? I mean, if she's real, what is it about her you find worthy of worship?"

Sir Golddrake didn't seem to expect such a question, and considered his answer carefully. "Have you ever heard stories of the green moon, the larger of the twins?"

Jaiden shook his head, none coming to mind.

"Legend has it the Eladrin named it Criesha, believing that was where the soul of the goddess rested. Criesha controls the flow of all natural magic – it grows and ebbs with the faces of the moon. Magic is all around us, Jaiden: in the music of the waterfall, the wisdom of the oak, the strength of the mountain. I believe it is important for us to honor this magic, protect its sanctuaries, and prepare ourselves to be better instruments of its power.

"My goddess has shown me that the way to do so is by being courageous, honorable, loyal, generous, and obedient. Natural magic is the path to our better selves. Dominion and suffering stifles it, Jaiden. This is why Ebon Khorel must be stopped, beyond the obvious need to end his cruelty.

"We will be breaking camp on the morrow. I shall ride with the cavalry across the border into Chelpa – we have a mission to perform there. You can accompany the support troops to the town of Greyhorne, further north, to resupply and await our return."

"May I go with you?" Jaiden asked. He knew it a foolish request, but longed to be part of the action.

"I am sorry, but it would be too dangerous for you. You've got healing to do, and we must be fleet to succeed. Lady Saffron will be accompanying me, but find Lieutenant Orestes in the morning, and he'll get you sorted out."

Sir Golddrake was almost to the exit when Jaiden asked one final question of him. "Will you teach me to ride like you?"

Sir Golddrake stopped, though didn't turn to face his inquisitor. "If Criesha wills it." He lifted the tent flap with his left hand, and carrying his purple-plumed helmet in the other, limped back toward his horse.

By the time Amurel reached his own tent and retired his stallion, Bastion, for the evening, his council was assembled and waiting. Maps of Halidor and the adjacent provinces were spread across the table that dominated the pavilion. Though he was Master of the Order of the Rising Moon, his accoutrements were only slightly more grandiose than his followers'. Amurel had no desire to set himself apart in such fashion. His tent was larger out of necessity, and his polished armor suggested familial wealth, but he ate the same food and slept on a simple bed.

His inner-circle consisted of three members; he trusted and was grateful for each. Sir Geldrick Kilborn came from a noble family, knew Amurel's father, and had been instrumental in negotiating the creation of his Order with the Prince of Dawn's Edge. Lord Kilborn kept watch over Amurel since his parents' deaths, though the man never dishonored him by claiming so.

He always rode into conflicts at his Master's side, and showed no qualms about following Amurel's lead, though he was older and just as highborn.

Orestes was a fighting man with a knack for organization. A longtime man-at-arms under the Golddrakes, he knew more about the upkeep of the Order than even Amurel, and served as his chief lieutenant. He dispersed orders to the troops, kept everyone on task, and arranged for the company to be resupplied when necessary.

Then, there was Saffron min Furasi. She was a foreigner, and Amurel had not known her long, yet he could not escape the secret truth he knew from the moment he emancipated her – he would gladly give his life for hers. She was a unique woman, and he didn't know a man among the Order who would claim to have seen her equal.

She spoke with a tongue as sharp as her mind; she grasped and assimilated new concepts almost instantly. Saffron's talent for musical arrangement seemed to spill over into tactics of all sorts. Her native people trained her with horse and spear, and she fought with a western style that perplexed many of the soldiers she now taught, giving her advantage in battle. Consisting of graceful movement so quick she seemed to strike from two places at once, she called it the *Ghostwind*.

Amurel suspected she served him out of a sense of indebtedness, yet he held no sense she owed him anything. He was aware she used her high position to search for her captive sister, but did not mind. He saw how Saffron burned with disgust for the King-priest, and could count on her loyalty as long as he was their common enemy.

"I am sorry if you've been waiting long," Amurel apologized. "I wanted to speak with the survivor of the Halidor massacre."

"Hmm, it was that," Sir Kilborn agreed. "It seems like this King-priest is just as happy to slaughter his enemies as rule them. No wonder the free provinces are nervous. Did this survivor have any useful intelligence on the enemy?"

"Unfortunately, no," Saffron interjected. "He was badly injured, and though interrogated by Ebon Khorel himself, he knows little, and has not been particularly helpful."

Amurel glanced at Saffron, taking note to discuss their patient further, in private. "Even so, I feel Criesha has delivered him for a purpose. The matter at hand, however, is a discussion of our next mission. It's difficult to understand a man like Ebon Khorel, to imagine what drives him to such cruelty. Studying his tactical behavior, at least, may help us find weaknesses."

Amurel placed the fingertips of both hands upon the table to steady himself. "So, what do we know?" He didn't wait for an answer. "In order for him to rule such a vast territory, especially when he is leading the push into the north, he must have men who are loyal. What drives this loyalty, however, is not a sense of honor, or even the devotion he may feel towards The Dread Tyrant. As sure as I breathe, it is either fear or greed. Most of his commanders are opportunists, seeking to add to their own wealth or power by preying on those weaker. Other are simply afraid of the consequences of refusal."

"But what of it, Sir?" Orestes never had much use for speculative banter. "Ebon Khorel is not the first dictator to wield influence through fear, but he may be the strongest we've seen, given this god of his. We've got to find a way to combat his magic, or I'll be just as useful brandishing a wet fish as a sword, when it comes to it."

"Time is what we need, Orestes. Criesha will show us a way to stop him, I'm certain. My point about the King-priest, my good man, is that fear can be both a potent weapon, and an undoing. If you hold people in line through fear, they will despise you. Such hatred leads to betrayal, more often than not."

Saffron broke in, "You think we can find someone close to him to help us?"

"Perhaps in time, but I'm thinking on a larger scale at the moment – open revolt. Consider it. Just because the King-priest of Chelpa is evil doesn't mean his subjects are. Their conditions under his rule are part of the reason we're fighting him. There must be droves wishing they could throw off his yoke, but afraid to do so. Under such a crushing oppression, rebellions need only the spark of hope to ignite, and the Order of the Rising Moon can supply the tinder. What we need is a community with the courage to act on their discontent – and I think I've found one."

Amurel leaned in closer to the map, and the others mirrored him. "There is a village called Salmarsh near the Chelpian frontier. It supplied wood, peat, and other goods to the King-priest's army. Several weeks ago, they stopped. Word is, the locals are an independent crowd and never took well to being conquered. When the Blood Tear Brotherhood was sent to look into the matter, things got bloody and the people of Salmarsh rose up, killing the delegation."

"Sounds like my kind of town," Sir Kilborn added, his heavy tone dulling the intended humor.

"News has reached Lucnere," Amurel continued, "and you can bet they'll be sending more troops to force Salmarsh back in line. We'll use the Harpy Pass through the Wyvernwatch to approach undetected from the north, and give aid to the resistance. I'm told they're more organized than Ebon Khorel would suspect, but they could certainly use our help."

Sir Kilborn took over for Amurel, giving him a chance to wet his lips from a goblet of wine. "Our informants give the impression the King-priest is overconfident in his grip over his own lands, and has not taken the proper steps to secure them. There are reserve armies around the capital, but the majority of his troops are in far, forward positions. This mission will have two objectives: aiding Salmarsh in a successful uprising, thereby emboldening other towns to do the same, and halting the advance of Ebon Khorel's armies into the Free Provinces. If he suddenly has to consider the effects of fighting on two fronts, it may buy us time to forge alliances, raise more armies in the north, and find some way to counter his Channeling, as Orestes mentioned."

"We can't just let the enemy march unimpeded all the way to Selamus," Amurel reiterated. "We must sow doubt into the mind of the conqueror."

Saffron nodded, and her eyes considered the map, perhaps calculating the distance and travel time involved. "Any idea of the numbers?" She was perhaps the most eager for invasion, increasing her chances to discover the whereabouts of her sister, Dhania.

"We know soldiers have moved from the capital, but it's too soon to tell how many are designated for the rebellion. We won't know until they turn west, Lady Saffron." Saffron's eyes met Amurel's, but he couldn't read what was behind them.

"If they've already left the capital," her words followed a brief silence, "we'll need to move quickly, and leave soon."

"We break camp in the morning," Amurel confirmed. "Orestes, this will be cavalry only. You'll be taking the rest of the men to resupply in Greyhorne."

Orestes nodded.

Amurel and his council discussed their plans well into the dim evening, and the preparations to depart were underway by the time most of the Order of the Rising Moon had earned their beds for the night.

"I'm back," Jaiden observed as midnight-grey clouds raced by, around and beneath him. "Would that I had never left." He was standing on two, fully-healed legs, absent of pain.

Starlight momentarily poked through vacancies in the cumulous rush – there one second, gone the next. Though it remained breathtakingly wondrous, this realm had a movement and energy lacking the first time he visited.

A pale, green beam of light suddenly cut through the clouds, but by the time Jaiden followed its path to the ground it disappeared, leaving an unmatched beauty standing in its place. Criesha appeared even more tantalizing to him than before, enhanced by her absence.

"Self-pity does not become you, Jaiden Luminere." Her voice was soft and compassionate, despite the judgment of her words. "You are capable of so much more, but must learn to fight for what you desire."

"M'lady," Jaiden bowed his head reverently, but not so low that his eyes couldn't continue looking upon her illuminated countenance. "I was hoping for the chance to see you again."

"You will have the chance for a great many other things, if you submit your will to my service." As she spoke, Criesha trailed the fingers of her right hand slowly down her torso, between her breasts and down to her belly.

Jaiden's eyes went wide and his mouth dropped agape. "What must I do?"

"You must learn to serve others, first, before you'll be fit to serve me. I want you to join the Order of the Rising Moon."

Jaiden looked from side-to-side, wondering if this was some sort of trick. What if he was really still lying in his cot, ensorcelled as he slept? "I was thinking of doing just that," he mentioned warily, "but I'm afraid I'll never be of use in battle again."

"Because of your injuries?"

"Well, yes," he said, looking down at his leg. "Of course, when I'm here, everything seems to be right."

"Keep your courage up, Jaiden." Criesha stepped slowly closer. "Once you show you are ready to serve me, to give yourself completely to the way of life I demand, I will heal your body. Within my realm, however," she gestured with open palms to the starry night around them, "you will always be your better self."

Criesha was close enough now that Jaiden would only have to extend his arms to touch her, yet he dared not. At this proximity he could feel the unseen current between them, binding them, empowering his blood. He was scared to lose that feeling, and eager to do what he must to reclaim the health he'd always taken for granted.

"If you can do that – if you can fix me..." The words escaped quietly, for it was a hard thing to admit aloud he was broken, even though such knowledge had consumed him since his meeting with Ebon Khorel. Jaiden closed his eyes before finishing, "I would do anything." He collapsed to his knees, overcome.

"Devotion is a beautiful thing." Her voice was beside him now and he felt the silk of Criesha's hair against his cheek, the moisture of her breath on the skin of his ear. "All manner of rewards shall follow, should you prove yourself worthy to be my Champion."

Jaiden gasped as he felt the wetness of her soft tongue on his neck, followed by her hand on his chest. Once again he felt a surge of vitality, and his manhood immediately responded to her touch. Could this be happening? He dared not open his eyes, nor even move, lest it cause her to stop. Her mouth moved from his throat, until he could feel her breath against his. "Join the Order, obey Amurel, and walk the path."

Jaiden pursed his lips, anticipating the crush of the goddess's against them, but was denied. The energy, her touch, the pleasurable sensation boiling below his waist all disappeared. When he finally forced his eyes open, it was to the sight of other soldiers packing their bedrolls. The camp was coming alive, deconstructing itself around him.

What was going on, he thought? Clearly he'd been dreaming, yet both times he'd dreamt of Criesha felt unlike any other midnight reverie he'd experienced. He felt present, lucid, alive – even more vital than during wakeful hours. Could there really be something more to it than his own imagination? He decided if he could figure out a way, he'd try to test these dreams in the future.

For now, however, he needed to wash up and get breakfast in a hurry, or risk being left behind. Jaiden slid awkwardly from his cot and propped his crutch underneath his arm. Limping toward the exit, he heard one of the soldiers call after him, "Hey, cripple, you need to break down your hammock before you leave so we can fold up the tent."

Jaiden stopped and turned. "I was leaving it for your mother – she's probably still in there somewhere."

"Why you lazy sack of orc-dung!" the man yelled, scrambling to his feet.

"Ho, Geoffrey, calm down!" his neighbor called, racing to restrain him before he knocked the crutch out from under Jaiden, or worse. "It's not worth it; you don't want the lieutenant dogging you over this joke of a soldier. He's not even one of us, friend." The speaker stared over Geoffrey's shoulder at Jaiden, a look of disgust on his face.

"Well, if you do stick around, gimp, you'd better start watching your back. And don't expect us to pick up the slack for you!"

Jaiden had already cleared out of the tent before the final words were spoken, but he heard them, as did everyone nearby. His face was hot and his arms quivered as he steamed toward the breakfast table. People cleared a path in front of him, and no one else spoke a word in his direction.

Chomping on a sweet biscuit with ham shavings, he looked around the bustling camp, silently daring anyone to test his ire. He saw a boy, possibly ten years old, holding a water bucket and staring at him imploringly, half-a-dozen paces away.

"What are you looking at?" Jaiden barked. "Bring me that water."

The boy did as he was told, carrying the wobbling bucket with two hands, intent on not spilling. Jaiden stuffed the remainder of his biscuit into his mouth and bent over to cup water from the bucket to his face. It was cold and refreshing, instantly improving his sour mood.

"Do you have a towel?" he asked after washing. His tone was firm, but without anger. The boy nodded and presented the rag he'd kept slung over his shoulder. When Jaiden had sopped up all the dripping, he saw the boy still watching him. "What's your name?"

"Tikvi, sir."

"What kind of a name is that? Nevermind. Why are you watching me, Ticky?"

"It's Tikvi," he retorted before drawing in and shrugging.

"Well, speak up. I'm not going to bite." The boy just shrugged again, drawing a sigh from Jaiden. "Are you here with your father?"

"I'm an orphan, sir. And, I guess I was hungry."

"Hungry? There's food right here on the table, help yourself." Jaiden gestured to the dwindling spread of morning rations.

Tikvi raised his eyebrows, "We're not permitted to eat until the fighting men have finished, sir."

Jaiden recognized the look that came from not truly belonging anywhere. "That's foolish. You're going to be a fighting man one day, aren't you?"

Tikvi nodded eagerly.

"Well, then. Here you go." Jaiden grabbed another biscuit and half an apple from the ration table, and tossed them to the page. "All right, off with you now. I have to go find the lieutenant."

Tikvi stuffed the entire biscuit in his mouth, the apple in his pocket, and grinned, before taking up his water bucket and ambling off.

It took Jaiden ten minutes of inquiry before he finally located Lieutenant Orestes. "Jaiden Luminere, reporting, sir."

"Jaiden, yes. Sir Golddrake mentioned you. You're his personal project, it seems." Lt. Orestes appeared to be the epicenter of the bustling camp. He finished instructing one man on what supplies needed to be acquired at their new location, and another on the precise route they would be taking there, before returning his attention to the Order's newest recruit.

"Have you decided to join up, then?" Orestes's tone was serious, and the full mustache hiding his upper lip made him look even more severe.

Jaiden immediately rethought the decision, but answered, "I suppose so," nonetheless.

"There's a brief ceremony involved, but it will have to wait for Sir Golddrake's return." The lieutenant appraised Jaiden's crutch and unbalanced stance. "You're not going to march all the way to Greyhorne, are you? Very well, hitch a ride in one of the supply wagons, and report to Captain Millstone when we arrive. He'll get you sorted out with the infantry."

"Yes, sir."

Jaiden talked his way into the back of one of the wagons, but only after threatening the driver with the wrath of his superiors. From that bumpy vantage he watched the hundred cavalry of the Rising Moon depart southward, white tabards and shining armor glinting in the midmorning sun, longing to be one of them.

Chapter 8

Shared Enemies

"How much farther do you suppose it is?" Sir Kilborn asked Amurel as their horses trotted along the soft earth.

"Not more than a league or two. We should arrive before the Brotherhood, but make sure the troops are ready in case our intelligence is sour."

"Aye," Sir Kilborn answered and peeled off, riding back along the column of cavalry to assure their attention.

Amurel's eyes were active, taking in his surroundings while watching for movement. Even with the visor raised, his helmet muted most sounds, though the constant drumming of the horses' hooves still echoed in his ears, along with his heartbeat. It wouldn't be long now.

They had indeed crossed into a foreign country. The scenery had transformed from the rocky valleys and rising cliffs of southern Halidor to a living landscape of soggy greenland. Though the true swamps were farther west, closer to the River Chelhos, the ground here seemed near saturation. A variety of wild tree groves broke up the gentle sloping lines of rolling hillsides.

Low-lying, grey clouds blanketed the region from direct sunlight much of the time, working their way around the mountains to the north. Amurel regarded the environment, not as unfriendly, but as decidedly less crisp than his ancestral homelands in the Cradle. The air, the land, the horizon, all bled together as if created by a distracted painter.

Observing the landscape atop Bastion, Amurel sought to calm his nerves by imagining he was no longer headed to battle, but visiting a new locale on holiday instead. Perhaps meeting friends of the family for a retreat in the country, he mused – not that he'd kept many such friends since the dissolution of his estate. Still, as the cool wind tightly whipped the banner on his lance, he felt awed by the possibility that any of the groves they were passing might be a sacred conduit for the magic of his mistress.

A mountain pool, a hollow tree, a ring of stones – the beauty of the natural world held myriad repositories of her magical influence, and it remained incumbent upon the members of his Order to protect such places. Most people simply weren't aware how nature preserved the residual power from when the gods walked the world, even when they experienced that energy. The wonder inspired by these sites was rarely recognized for what it was – a seed of magic.

Lost momentarily in his appreciation, Amurel snapped to attention when he noticed the first wisps of dark smoke rising from the south. Upon clearing the nearest line of trees, the black columns that had birthed them came into full view. Half a league south, along a track of cleared timber, Amurel could make out the signs of conflict.

Thatched roofs blazed, and the delayed echoes of metal on metal clanged like tiny bells from afar. Sir Kilborn drew alongside him once more, and they shared a look before Amurel clipped his heels to increase their pace. The column followed suit behind him, their thundering hooves and brilliant white cloth casting a clear beacon of their approach.

As the cavalry of the Order drew nearer, Amurel counted a half-score of black-clad riders wheeling their horses to avoid a hastily constructed rampart. Some lofted torches over it as perhaps a hundred darkly dressed foot soldiers swarmed around them, clambering through breaches in the low wall.

The oncoming charge of knights diverted some of the infantry from storming Salmarsh, and the enemy horses also gathered quickly into formation.

Assessing his opponents on the gallop, Amurel decided it was worth the risk to use their speed against the Chelpians. With the rampart to one side and teeming wetland behind their targets, the Order of the Rising Moon would have to take care not to extend their charge too far. With no pikes to threaten them, though, the dark-armored enemy presented a tempting target.

A few of the Chelpian riders broke ranks and bolted eastward, rather than face the oncoming force. The rest advanced and the two sides met – a colliding mass of muscle and steel, leather and wood.

Amurel lowered his lance and pierced an unlucky soldier. The impact yanked his arm back as he held his shoulder tight, the thud joining dozens of others, adding to the cacophony of battle-cries, trampling hooves, shattered shields, and screams of the wounded. As his well-trained cavalry penetrated the enemy ranks, leveling them as a scythe through sawgrass, Amurel caught a glimpse of flashing white light to his right, beyond the rampart. It vanished before he could turn his head, but he had no time to wonder at the cause as more immediate concerns consumed him.

Dozens of Chelpian troops had managed to scale the town's improvised fortifications. No permanent wall surrounded Salmarsh, but from the look of things, a shallow pit had been dug recently, and the excavated earth packed behind it to discourage approach on horseback. However, it now also deterred the Order from aiding the town directly.

As Amurel wheeled Bastion around after their pass, he had to contend with the Order's horses cramped together in tight quarters. Thick woods lay behind, and their momentum was completely spent. Sir Kilborn joined him in discarding their lances and drawing swords, pushing their way back into the fray, side by side. Their charge greatly depleted the enemy, but the resulting engagement was sure to be more chaotic.

Unconcerned for his own safety, Amurel worried that every added moment securing the outer field would be hazardous for the townsfolk. For now, those who fought across the low wall remained beyond his aid.

Upon seeing the scores of horsemen approaching from the north, white coats and banners emblazoned with a crescent moon of brilliant violet, Baron Rogan's instinct was to shake off the mirage of wishful thinking. However, since meeting Palomar, the boundaries of his expectations were being reinvented. "Did you summon them?" he called to the Aasimar hovering two body-lengths above.

Palomar broke into a broad grin, his perfect teeth just as bright as his luminous, pearlescent skin. White-feathered wings tipped with gold, each as long as his body, flapped rhythmically from his shoulder blades, keeping him aloft.

"I told you, Baron, the cause of justice is contagious." He spoke telepathically, often leaving Rogan unsure who else could hear him. Even weeks after finding him, the effect remained uncanny.

"That you did, my friend. Perhaps we'll survive the day, after all." Rogan held a polished saber in his right, gloved hand. His armor was supple, reinforced black leather, permeated by holes designed to increase flexibility, leaving the scarlet tunic he wore beneath visible.

He stood his ground twenty paces from the rampart, within sight of the crossbowmen poised to cover him from their concealed positions down the adjacent alleys. Although eager to join the fray, Rogan had the patience to let the enemy come to him. Over the last four years of freedom-fighting, he learned the value of a well-prepared ambush. It became especially difficult to hold back, though, as he saw several of the men he'd personally convinced to stand and fight, cut down before him. The blades of the King-priest's soldiers did potent work against the crudely-armed citizens of Salmarsh.

"Palomar!" Rogan pleaded to the Aasimar, eyes not straying from the enemy.

"*I need them closer, Baron,*" he responded, his voice too calm for the situation, as usual.

"Fall back!" Rogan called to his allies fortifying the barrier, who eagerly obeyed. Several more perished during the maneuver, becoming easy targets during their withdrawal. In planning their defense, Rogan recognized the limited number of archers as a serious liability, and didn't want to risk trading volleys against a superior number of marksmen.

He'd positioned the majority of defenders behind cover, with only enough at the rampart to discourage an entrance by the cavalry. Most of the townsfolk had already been evacuated to a camp hidden within the nearby swamp. He knew casualties were unavoidable, but such knowledge never inoculated fully against the sting of loss.

Rogan tensed as the last of the wall-defenders hurried past him, a wave of black-clad soldiers close behind. Palomar's hovering presence seemed to dismay them, granting a gap between escape and pursuit. When the angelic figure made no move to attack, though, they closed on Rogan.

His saber was poised, and his left hand gripped the smooth, stone handle of his uril-chent dagger, ready to unsheath. He opened his mouth to remind the Aasimar, but as he did, the singing started.

Two notes of his haunting, celestial voice was all it took to call forth the magic. A blinding globe of white light formed around Palomar and accelerated outward in all directions. The Chelpians were caught off guard and staggered to a halt before the overwhelming radiance, their eyes singed by its brightness.

Rogan knew what was coming and had closed his eyes as soon as the first sound issued from Palomar's lips. Still, he perceived the white blast through shut lids, pausing four heartbeats for it to fade before drawing his dagger and opening them. His naked blade created a sphere of dimness, absorbing the natural light and painting everything inside with shadows.

Taking advantage of his enemies' disorientation, Rogan leapt forward and quickly dispatched two of them with his saber. He easily skirted their neighbor's awkward responses, then backtracked, hoping to lure his opponents after him. The Aasimar flew higher and started singing a new melody, bolstering Rogan and the woodsman of Salmarsh with a sense of bravery that defied the odds they faced.

As the Chelpian infantry staggered forward, blinking in hopes of returning their compromised sight, they wandered directly into the path of the waiting crossbowmen and hunters. The archers of Salmarsh let loose their arrows, swiftly felling half a dozen more surprised foes.

Rogan watched as the new frontline of Chelpian soldiers assessed first him, wreathed in unnatural dimness, then the winged Aasimar above, chanting mysterious words of power. Doused in bewilderment, they turned to retreat, only to find their comrades on the other side of the wall already slain, or surrendering to the invading cavalry. Unanimously, they gave themselves up as well, casting down their weapons.

Sheathing his dagger to return to light, Rogan mustered forth his remaining charges, waiting behind the shelter of buildings to strike from concealed positions. Palomar ceased his song and descended, folding his wings behind him, his golden hair wild from the wind.

"Round up the enemy and seize their weapons," Rogan called to the warriors of Salmarsh. Then, to Palomar, "Let's go meet our saviors, shall we?"

"*I must see to these fires before they spread, Baron.*"

"You've got a song for that?" Without giving an answer, Palomar took flight again, heading toward the roofs set ablaze by the Chelpian marauders.

Rogan sheathed his saber and bounded atop the earthen rampart. He saw scores of mounted knights in white tabards starting to separate into lines, as two stationary riders called out orders. A half-dozen prisoners in dark armor were being forced to their knees on one edge of the field.

One of the riders pointed Rogan out to the speaking commanders, who halted their instructions to gaze upon him. They spoke briefly to one another before one removed his helmet and steered his horse closer to the wall.

"Hail!" He raised his right hand in greeting. "I am Sir Amurel Golddrake, Master of the Order of the Rising Moon. Do you speak for this town, or are you one of our enemy, come to parley?"

Rogan bowed deeply before responding – no easy feat atop the narrow precipice. "Greetings, Sir Golddrake, to you and your men. My name is Emmert Rogan, former Baron of Thispany, and I am no enemy. I speak for the free people of Salmarsh."

"Then let us talk more, so we may give each other wise council, friend. But first, is there a place in your town we may keep the prisoners secure and our horses less visible?"

"Certainly. Send your delegate in on foot, and I will have a man assist him. More have surrendered inside. I will meet you, Sir Golddrake, on the north end of town, if you would be kind enough to lead your horses that direction?"

Rogan leapt back down the wall to give instructions to the townsfolk. He headed west toward the interior of the town, to the edge of where the fire had spread earlier. "Palomar, would you come with me?" he yelled to the rooftops, where steam rose instead of the black smoke of burning thatch. "I was thinking of using the Public House to host our formal introductions. I would prefer if you waited inside so we could reveal your presence to only a few, at first."

"*So be it.*" The answer entered his mind, though he had no visual contact with the Aasimar.

"My thanks." Rogan slipped between buildings and headed north toward a short bridge, which served as the only entrance to Salmarsh from that direction. He spread the "all clear" as he walked, making sure everyone knew the battle was over. The bridge was only three body-lengths and stretched over a gully nurturing a slow-moving brook.

An exuberant pair of axe-wielding brothers guarded it. They had instructions to take out the bridge's supports, should the enemy attempt to gain entry from the north. Luckily, they didn't start chopping when the Order of the Rising Moon arrived ahead of Rogan. The brothers stood abreast, blocking the way across, however, until he called to them.

"Morton! Genri! Thank you for your diligence. These men are guests, and you may let them pass." Rogan jogged the rest of the way to the bridge and clasped the still-suspicious brothers on their shoulders. "Please show their quartermaster to the Falkin pasture, where they may keep their horses."

Rogan nodded to the blonde-maned Master at the front of the procession. "Welcome again to Salmarsh, Sir Golddrake. You have a formidable retinue, and fortuitous timing. If you and your officers would join me, there is a table in the Public House reserved, and I'm sure we can find provisions for your men."

"You are most gracious, Baron Rogan."

"Just 'Rogan' will suffice. I am, after all, an outlaw now."

"History will be the arbiter. We aim, at least, to have a hand in writing a better one. By all means, lead the way."

Rogan took Sir Golddrake and a pair of his officers, one of which was a striking woman of Begnari descent, along the town's dirt paths to a two-story, wooden building. The distance was short, but weighed by an awkward silence. With his back to the riders, Rogan wasn't sure if they were communicating secretly behind him, or just taking note of their new surroundings. Rogan was still trying to decide how much information to share with these seemingly benevolent strangers, when they arrived at their destination.

When the riders dismounted, Rogan's attention was seized by two details. First, Sir Golddrake, the Order's Master, was lame. Second, the silk-veiled Begnari woman was not one of the Order. Once on solid ground she unclasped the oversized, white cloak that encircled her, revealing a closer-fitting ensemble of desert red. The upper garment left her sun-kissed shoulders and belly exposed, and her long skirt hugged the curves of her legs as she took sure strides toward the door. Her figure, her dark eyes, even her clear sense of confidence was striking. Rogan was intrigued.

He followed his visitors closely into the Public House, eager to witness their first reactions to the presence of Palomar. He was not disappointed.

"A visitor from the afterlife!" Sir Golddrake exclaimed, pointing.

"Legends of old!" the man beside him added, placing his right palm over his heart.

"I... I've dreamt of you," the woman gasped, seeming both surprised and pleased. Everyone turned in her direction. "Last night. You handed me a bloom I didn't recognize, strange and beautiful. When I took it you began singing a melody, and my own voice rose in harmony, though I'd never heard the tune. The petals in my hand burst into red flame, and the dream ended."

Palomar nodded deliberately, as if perhaps he shared knowledge of the woman's dream, or at least understood something about it. *"There is power in song, my lady."*

She gasped and Rogan smiled, remembering his initial response to telepathy. Momentarily mesmerized, Rogan recovered when he felt the Aasimar's gaze upon him.

"Pardon me, where are my manners?" Rogan stepped past his guests and took a spot to Palomar's left, facing them. "Once again, I am the former Baron Rogan, and this is Palomar. He is an Aasimar, a being not native to our world. I shall let him explain his origins further, but first, it would please me very much to receive your introductions." He held his hands outward to the visitors.

"Of, of course," Sir Golddrake stammered, overcoming his awe. "As I previously stated, I am Sir Amurel Golddrake. This is my second-in-command, Sir Geldrick Kilborn, and the talented Lady Saffron min Furasi. I am Master of the Order of the Rising Moon, chartered by the Prince of Dawn's Edge, dedicated to her Exalted Radiance, Criesha."

Rogan and Palomar shared a half-turn glance.

"It has begun, then," the Aasimar intoned. His face remained an emotionless mask, but energy hummed in his words.

"What has begun?" Saffron asked.

Palomar looked in her eyes and shrugged, as if she should know the answer, *"Your gods have clearly returned their interest to this mortal realm."*

Sir Kilborn's jaw dropped.

"How are you doing that?" Sir Golddrake questioned, raising his palm toward Palomar, as if it might contact something invisible between them.

The Aasimar cocked his head sideways with a quizzical look. *"It is how I communicate."*

"You are a marvel. I have felt the change you speak of coming," Sir Golddrake nodded. "Criesha's sacred revelations have given me a glimpse of what the future might be."

"I don't know how you came to be here at our moment of need, but it does feel like something larger at work," Rogan cut in. "I have lived in Chelpa my entire life, and though I have some grasp of the perception many outsiders hold, I can tell you it was not always as now. Before Ebon Khorel rose to power a decade ago, this land was not a harsh place to grow up. Certainly, there have always been opportunists making things difficult, but nothing compared to the crushing worship of The Dread Tyrant, Gholdur.

"I was arrested on suspicion of treason and served three years in Blackthorn Prison, without any opportunity to defend myself. Such a thing was unfortunately common, back when anyone dared to openly criticize the King-priest. So, the rebellion went underground.

"I escaped prison with the aid of another of Palomar's people, and though we failed then in our attempt to end the King-priest's reign, I've been striving against him ever since."

"There are more of you?" Saffron asked Palomar directly, though it was Rogan who answered.

"Many more – though they don't look like him. Palomar is the butterfly, if you will. Dampers are the caterpillars, and the

King-priest keeps dozens of them prisoner underneath Blackthorn.

"I went to see a historian, a scholar friend of mine in Crioc, after my encounter with Ebon Khorel some years ago. I saw firsthand the destructive magic he wields, and sought to gather more information on where that sort of power came from, and the origin of the Dampers as well."

"Was this scholar of yours a believer in the old gods?" Sir Golddrake took a step closer with his question, his own interest in the subject apparent.

"He seemed to think there is merit to the stories, yes. I don't know how much of them are true myself, but what I've seen certainly convinced me there is a basis for the tales."

"Gentlemen... Saffron. Might I suggest we take a drink and sit before delving further into story-telling? I, for one, am thirsty after the day's long ride and hard fighting." Sir Kilborn strolled behind the bar to search for mugs as he continued. "Not to mention, a little brew might help me start believing children's stories about gods and such."

"Geldrick!" Sir Golddrake admonished.

"Criesha's pardon, of course."

Palomar studied the older knight for a moment. *"You do not believe in beings from other realms? How would you explain my presence?"*

"That's exactly what I mean, begging your pardon, too. You look real enough... but either way, I'm in need of ale."

"I can get behind that," Rogan added. He helped distribute the full flagons as Sir Kilborn poured them, then gave everyone a chance to find a seat at one of the large tables. He pulled out a chair for Lady Saffron after she declined to partake in the ale, attempting to polish off his rusty manners. Palomar remained standing, his wings making it nigh impossible to fit comfortably in the high-backed chairs.

"Common legend has it," Rogan continued, "that the gods were banished centuries ago by a secret congregation of powerful, mortal Shapers, sometime after the Gift of Arkmus. My friend shared, however, that it was not the gods themselves who walked the world in the first place – only their Avatars."

"This is true," chimed in Palomar. *"The Veil of Nessus prevents physical beings crossing from one realm to another."*

"So it was only the Avatars," Rogan carried on, "the impure, physical manifestations of the gods' psyches, that were banished. The gods, according to my friend, simply chose to abandon us after this great insult. It appears, for whatever reason, at least some of them have returned their attention to us. Unfortunately, Gholdur the Tyrant seems to be the first."

"And now my mistress, Criesha," Sir Golddrake pondered.

"Your world is about to change, again," Palomar added.

"Ebon Khorel is Gholdur's most potent Channeler. I've seen him morph into insubstantial shadow, even call searing flames down from the heavens. His armor is forged of an uril-chent alloy that turns back steel as if it were wet grass. I don't know of any mortal means to defeat him." Rogan took a sip from his flagon before hitting them with the punch.

"That's why, if you're serious about defeating the King-priest, I'd like your help freeing the Dampers from Blackthorn Prison."

"And exactly where is Blackthorn?" Sir Golddrake inquired.

Sir Kilborn answered. "I know exactly where it is, unless my geography lessons were taught by an imbecile. It's two hundred miles deep into Chelpian territory, overlooking the River Chelhos, is it not?"

Rogan nodded, "You are correct, Sir."

"I'm sorry, friend," Sir Golddrake said, "but that is too far for my men to travel into hostile territory."

"We would have the element of surprise. Ebon Khorel would never suspect it."

"And we would never make it back alive. Even if Criesha herself anointed the path to the prison gates, and we were able to claim victory, the King-priest would cut us off with his northern army before we even got a sniff of the border." Sir Golddrake took a deep breath and composed himself. "Now, we've won a victory here. Salmarsh is on the frontier. We should look to fortify this position, to use it as an example for other towns within the Empire – that they too can revolt against oppression."

Rogan didn't want to sour this budding relationship, but couldn't help feeling a little desperate. "That is an important endeavor, yes. But with all due respect, it is not how we're going to topple the King-priest. We need the Aasimar for that, and with your help I know we can free them. You're the allies I've been waiting four years for." Couldn't these newcomers understand, no one knew as well as he what they were up against?

"No offense to you, sir," Sir Golddrake stood and addressed Palomar, then turned back to Rogan, "but, impressive wings aside, how exactly can these *Aasimar* turn the tide of battle in our favor when we are outnumbered five-to-one?"

Rogan looked to Palomar, who took a tentative, half-step forward.

"No future outcome can ever be guaranteed, but my kin have protected the slopes of Mount Celestia for eons."

Sir Golddrake let out a sigh, reeking of impatience. "I am very happy to meet you both, and am certain we will revisit this later, but for now I must look to my men and make sure they are up to task. Perhaps we should gather again for supper and discuss the immediate future of Salmarsh, once we've had a chance to assess things?"

Rogan pursed his lips. "Of course, Sir Golddrake. Take what time you need, and we shall dine together this evening."

While the knights made their way from the Public House, Saffron lingered behind. "Pardon me, Baron, might I have an extra moment of your time?" Palomar overheard the request and gave a polite nod before following the others outside.

Once she was no longer in the presence of the Order, Saffron's shoulders slackened and she removed a long pin from her hair, sending the confined, sable locks cascading over bare shoulders. "I hope you don't mind the informality," she said, unclasping her veil, "but it can be hard for me to relax around men of such discipline. I do not wish to forget who I am."

"I don't mind at all." Rogan's gaze was transfixed on her now-bare face, as if he had been granted a glimpse at a rare treasure.

Saffron smiled. "Good. I was hoping for an opportunity to ask you about something that may not affect the direction of nations, but is of no less importance to me."

"Go on." Rogan encouraged, leaning closer. He couldn't imagine what this beautiful stranger might possibly need from him, but his intrigue deepened.

"You have been working toward a rebellion for some time, no?"

"Since I escaped my imprisonment, yes. Which, of course, was baseless," he added, not wanting to give the impression he was a common criminal.

"I assume, then, you have informants in or around the government of the King-priest?"

Oh, here it comes, he thought. Rogan just knew she was about to ask him to do something he really didn't want to do. "It would be fair to say I sometimes hear things..."

Saffron brushed back a dark tendril of hair from in front of her ear. "I have a favor to ask, then." She smiled, not only with her lips, but her eyes.

This one knows what she's doing, he thought, and prepared himself as he returned her smile. "I am at your service, Lady Saffron."

"I am from the province of Sesfaran in the Emirate of Begnasharan. I was travelling to Selamus with my sister to play for the prince, when our caravan was attacked. We were both taken as slaves, but sent to different camps. Sir Golddrake and his men rescued me, but I am still searching for Dhania. Please, can you help me find her?"

Rogan was taken aback. There was no deception or pretense in her eyes, only true concern. "I'll do what I can," he found himself saying without considering the response.

"Thank you." Saffron rose on her toes and kissed Rogan on the cheek. "She is very beautiful, and probably being kept in one of the pleasure gardens, if that is helpful."

Suddenly, the door to the Public House swung open and Sir Kilborn thrust his way inside. "Scouts have returned and there's no time to lose!"

"What is it?" Rogan's heart fell to his stomach.

"The force that attacked earlier was just a first wave. More of the troops deployed from Lucnere came west than we thought; they just took a different route. A thousand men, including Blood Tear assassins and Gholdur war-priests are on the move. They'll be here by nightfall. Amurel's leading us out of here as soon as can be managed."

"We can't just forsake Salmarsh!" Rogan had only come to this town a few weeks ago, after finding Palomar, but he'd invested much in its rebellion and felt responsible for its defense.

"Baron, the decision is made. You and Palomar are welcome to ride with us. In fact, we hope you will. But we're moving quickly, and the townsfolk will have to fend for themselves." Sir Kilborn left without another word, while Rogan dangled between duty and desire.

"Come with us," Saffron spoke for his heart. "I will ready a horse for you and your winged friend – does he ride?"

"He does. Flight is tiresome." Rogan sighed. Leaving his brethren felt like a decision he would regret, but not following this woman was beyond his power at the moment. "All right, give me an hour to make arrangements with my people. I'll bring Palomar and meet you at the northern bridge."

Rogan had no doubt that, one way or another, this choice was going to define his future.

Chapter 9

After a Long Climb

The journey to Greyhorne was miserable. It rained most of the way, and Jaiden was stuck in the back of a covered stock wagon, surrounded by smells of dirt, grease, dried sweat, and wet horse. Although the destination was only about forty miles northwest of Halidor Keep, the ascension into the foothills of the Wyvernwatch Mountains was rough. The uneven terrain added to the unpleasantness of Jaiden's ride, and he was relieved to climb out of his shifting coffin on their arrival at the end of the second day.

He had plenty of free time during the excursion, leading his mind to wander to his latest rendezvous with Criesha. After thinking more on it, he had practically convinced himself she was just a pleasant delusion brought on by his injuries. Imagining she was real enticed him, though, even if he could only visit her in another realm.

For the first time he pondered what it meant that a goddess would choose him for a special purpose. Did she, with her unearthly insight, recognize something in him he failed to notice? He was good with a blade – maybe the best – but what else did an orphan from Selamus have to offer a supernatural entity? She said she desired obedience – maybe that's all there was to it. If he served her, perhaps they would both end up getting what they wanted.

He stretched his limbs after climbing down from the wagon. He winced against a surge of pain from his right leg as it adjusted to bearing his weight. The rain had ceased for the moment, but the ground was muddy from its afterbirth.

A long night of unpacking lay ahead for the Order of the Rising Moon, but Jaiden wanted no part of it. Given his limited mobility, he'd probably only end up getting in the way.

Instead, he decided to relax with some time away from the other soldiers. He would be seeing his fair share of their ugly faces in the coming weeks. Unsure exactly what he'd be asked to give up once officially signing on, Jaiden rationalized the best thing might be to find somewhere he could have a stiff drink. He could always report to Captain Millstone in the morning.

Still using the crutch Saffron made for him, Jaiden limped from the growing bustle of men unloading the wagons toward the darker portion of the town's center. He didn't want to be noticed or bothered, and figured to find an establishment in the shadow of the mountains serving something stronger than water.

Sure enough, a tavern called "The Ringing Hammer" awaited on a side street, several rows west of the town's central square. Almost all the other buildings along the row looked dark and deserted, though thick, beeswax candles in the windows advertised the tavern as open for business. The wet pine steps creaked under his weight, and he was spared the awkwardness of opening the heavy door when a patron made his exit just as Jaiden reached the porch.

"Good evening," Jaiden attempted as the unshaven man shouldered by. He and his ambulatory implement received silent judgment from the man's bleary eyes, but no words were given.

"I guess this isn't *that* kind of place," Jaiden muttered as he shuffled through the door. The kind of place it did appear to be was a working-man's watering hole. No fancy adornments on the walls and no polished candelabras, for sure. A stuffed elk's head hung over the bar, around which huddled rough-looking souls.

The patrons bore signs of tiring labor: dirt on the cheeks or salt streaks along the shirt from a day's worth of dried sweat. Jaiden guessed from the earthy smell that many of the regulars were miners. Nearly every table away from the bar sat empty, and not a single soft curve of woman brightened the dreary room.

With no serving wench apparent, Jaiden headed straight for the bar. He had no desire to engage the locals, but the only empty stools were already flanked by patrons. He kept his eyes down to avoid contact as he limped noisily across the sawdusted floor.

He kept his coin purse hidden underneath the top fold of his right boot, tied with a string, while on the move – he'd done so since his father first taught him the value of money. While thankful the Chelpians hadn't discovered it, the fact he'd never received payment for his service at Halidor Keep stung. Bemoaning its lightness, Jaiden tucked the purse into his belt and took a seat on the nearest stool, accidently bumping his crutch into the man on his right.

"Hey, watch it, would ya?" A man with salt-and-pepper stubble cradled his drink, which had lost a little off the top, defending against another possible assault.

"I, I'm sorry. Not really used to this thing, yet."

"Recently injured, huh?" The man to Jaiden's left imposed a bit further than necessary to get a clearer look at Jaiden's leg. "What's wrong with it?"

When he turned to face the inquisitor, Jaiden nearly kissed the man, his face was so close. Jaiden's wool leggings didn't divulge any obvious sign of his maligned condition, so it appeared an honest-enough question. The man was middle-aged, but had an older face, worn from years of toiling in the elements. He reeked of his labor, and Jaiden guessed he hadn't seen a washtub for at least a week. Still, the odor of his liquored breath was the stronger at this proximity.

Jaiden inched his face backward until his neck was straining and raised his eyebrows, unconvinced of the need for such intimacy. "I'm a soldier. I was injured at Halidor, less than a fortnight ago."

"You don't say?" The man returned to vertical and reached into his pocket for a coin. "A flagon of 'eel's breath' for the soldier!" he called out to the bartender, slapping his silver onto the bar.

"Eel's breath?"

"Yeah, haha, wonderful stuff. It'll get you where you want to go." The man took a swig of his own brew, then looked Jaiden over again after lowering his cup. "Name's Mosely. There's been talk around here of some fighting down south. This 'sorcerer-king' fella from Chelpa stirring up trouble. So, soldier, what are you doing up in Greyhorne? Not a deserter, are you?"

"What? No, of course not. I'm here with the Order of the Rising Moon. And it's the 'King-priest of Chelpa.' Thank you for the drink." Jaiden exhaled deeply then tilted his flagon, hoping the beverage would go down easier than its name suggested. It didn't, and Jaiden almost spit it back up.

"Whoa-ho, easy there, soldier! You've got to sort of, work your way into it. Slow sips at first, 'til you get your sea legs." The miner demonstrated with another practiced gulp. "Well, I just wanted you to know I appreciate all you fighting lads keeping us safe."

Jaiden was at a loss. He couldn't remember ever receiving blind appreciation, and didn't have it in him to tell his admirer they'd been slaughtered at Halidor. "And thanks to you too, Mosley, for... everything you do."

"Haha, you're all right, son," Mosely laughed, swatting Jaiden a little too roughly on the back.

Jaiden downed the remainder of his drink despite the burn, wishing he could be left alone like everyone else in the bar. He knew he probably should have offered to buy his new friend a round, but wasn't sure when more coppers would be coming his way.

"Well, thanks again. I need to *mosely* on back to camp now. My captain will be expecting me."

"Haha, Mosely on back! I see what you did there." He turned to the man seated to his left, looking to share his enjoyment of the pun. "My name's Mosely. Did you see what he did?" Mosely's neighbor did not appear amused in the slightest.

Jaiden forced a grin as he rose and positioned his crutch under his right arm. More quickly than when entering, Jaiden limped across the creaky floor and out the door of "The Ringing Hammer." He stumbled while maneuvering down the steps, prompting his left hand to pat where he'd stored his purse.

It was absent, no longer tucked in his belt. He hadn't heard the cling of coins hitting the ground, but searched the dark with his left foot anyway. Criesha was just a sliver tonight, her green light not much to see by. The blue tint of the trailing Hurn was even dimmer.

After a few rounds of frantic pawing with his boot, Jaiden gave up and cursed his luck. He had just started making his way back toward the wagons when he froze. He remembered Mosely slapping him on the back and it suddenly came together. That filthy drunkard had stolen his coin purse!

Jaiden stalked back up the stairs, ignoring the pain it caused. He burst into the bar, his eyes immediately locking on the stool Mosely had occupied: empty. The stool to the right of where Jaiden had been sitting was empty, too, though both of the men's drinking vessels remained on the bar.

"Barkeep!" Jaiden hobbled over to the melancholy chap who had served his beverage. "Where did these two go?"

The bartender shrugged as he wiped a tankard with a well-used rag, keeping the same, sour look on his face. "I dunno, maybe they left out the back?"

Jaiden bit his lip to resist saying more, but moved with heavy strokes of his crutch toward the rear of the dive. A short hallway split across his path. To the right, a set of steep stairs climbed to the top floor, while the left led to a latrine and another exit. The stairway was too daunting at the moment, and he didn't figure a thief to hide in the building with an easy retreat available.

He trudged into the foul-smelling alcove and out the door into fresh mountain air. He scanned the alley for movement. The dark was prohibitive, but he listened, steadying his breath in hopes of catching the sound of fleeing footfalls. Nothing.

"Of all the welcomes." Jaiden shook his head, resigning himself to his loss. In truth it wasn't much, but the idea of being robbed incensed him. It left him with no choice but to commit to the Order. With his injury, he knew it would be months before he could get hired on to another military unit. Sir Golddrake's outfit could at least be counted on to feed him in the meantime.

Feeling all too sober, he made his way back toward the wagons, both his leg and his pride hurting a little more than when he arrived. By the time Jaiden meandered into camp, most of the set-up work was complete. He marveled at how efficiently the Order of the Rising Moon operated. Everyone had an appointed task that benefitted the whole, and performed their service without complaint. Or, almost everyone.

Most of the camp was either bedding down or on watch. Greyhorne didn't have an obvious problem with the presence of the Rising Moon's company, allowing them to set up camp on the outskirts of town. Jaiden presumed some prior arrangement, since no one seemed to question his new comrades dropping by for an extended visit.

Jaiden didn't wish to draw attention, and was worn out after his ordeal at the tavern. He didn't relish going from tent to tent looking for a vacancy, announcing the fact he'd skipped out on erecting shelter in the first place. Instead, he followed another lesson he'd learned from his father: when in doubt, bed with the horses.

Sneaking to where the animals were tied, most of which were either nodding off or grazing absentmindedly on the sparse grass, he dropped onto a soft pile of dried hay, set out for the morning feeding. Covering up with a layer thick enough to keep warm overnight, it wasn't long before Jaiden began lightly snoring, dreaming of pickpockets and uncompleted chores.

Jaiden awoke to an itchy nose, and was surprised to find a stray cat curled in the hay next to his face. He pushed it away and battled with a sneeze, before it finally won out. His surroundings were a harsh reminder of how the previous night ended, and he figured he'd better hurry to breakfast, if this was anything like the last camp. No point starting out a new day broke *and* hungry.

Luckily, once he got enough distance from the horses, all he had to do was follow his nose to the breakfast table. The aroma of freshly-cooked sausages was a pleasant distraction from the fatigue lingering after his harried sleep. Adding some bread and butter, Jaiden felt capable of taking on the morning. He hoped to find Captain Millstone without appearing like a hapless initiate.

Across the stone-riddled field, Jaiden spotted a familiar boy lugging a bucket of water toward the wash basins. An idea struck him, and he grabbed another piece of buttered bread before limping after the lad.

"Tikvi!" he called, trying to catch the boy's attention before losing him. The lad turned at the sound of his name, and Jaiden was pleased he'd remembered. "I've got something for you." Jaiden ceased walking and simply held out the bread.

Tikvi looked both ways, making sure no one else was paying close attention, before setting down his bucket and claiming his early snack. He broke into a wide grin before chomping voraciously on the offering.

"Whoa there, slow down." Jaiden watched as the entire piece of bread disappeared in three bites. Tikvi seemed completely satisfied with his mouthful, though, so Jaiden shrugged and made his request. "I need you to tell me where Captain Millstone's tent is. He's in charge of the infantry."

"Mmmhmm," Tikvi nodded, his mouth still stuffed. He pointed a buttery finger at a gray, canvas pavilion flying a purple pennant. A dark-haired man with a thick moustache stood out front, holding a spear. He gave active instruction to two, youthful soldiers on how to wield the simple weapon.

"Thanks, Tikvi." Jaiden tousled the boy's hair, never removing his eyes from the Captain. He cut toward the pavilion, straightening his posture as much as possible while leaning on his crutch.

"Captain Millstone?"

"Yes? Who do we have here?"

"My name is Jaiden Luminere, sir. Lieutenant Orestes told me to find you once we arrived. Said I'd be joining the infantry under you."

"Is that so?" The captain looked Jaiden up and down, assessing his new recruit. "What's the story on your injury, Jaiden?"

"A hydra, sir. Bit me in the leg while I was defending Haldior Keep." Jaiden hoped to make it sound like no big concern.

"Fiends of the Fire Wall, is that so? Well, you've got guts – not a lot of brains, though, huh? We're used to that in the infantry, so you'll fit right in. Go inside," he pointed with his thumb to the tent behind him, "and grab yourself a tabard and a change of clothes out of the open chest. There are extra packs beside it, so get one of those to store your gear, too."

Jaiden nodded and turned to follow orders.

"Have you been sworn in yet?" Captain Millstone added.

Jaiden froze. He knew this was going too easily. "No, sir."

"Well, Sir Golddrake will take care of that when he returns. For now, hustle up and join me in Doring Meadow as soon as possible – sparring practice in a quarter-hour. We're bound to see action soon, and I don't want to find any of my men on the end of a pike because they were rusty."

"Yes, sir." Jaiden wasn't sure how that would go with his mangled leg, but after the long wagon ride he was thankful for the distraction and a chance to get some exercise. The supplies weren't difficult to find, and once the rest was tucked into his new pack, he donned the white tabard of the order. His fingers traced over the violet, crescent moon emblazoned on his chest, and his thoughts wandered to the full, quarter-moon lips he'd kissed during the best of his dreams.

Jaiden's life had been so strange the last fortnight, and he had no reasonable explanation why. What was he sure of? He knew his leg was ruined, but had he really done battle with a many-headed monster? He could feel his heart aching in his chest after heavy exertion, but had he really been scorched by the leader of their enemy? Were his dreams of Criesha just a fantasy, created by his mind to cope with the loss, or were the stories of the old gods true and one of them had actually decided to make him her champion?

He admitted it sounded crazy, yet here he was in the military camp of a religious order dedicated to the same goddess. Sir Golddrake believed he was special, too. Perhaps, that was enough. As long as he wasn't alone following some ridiculous road to nowhere, maybe he could stay the course and figure out the truth along the way. It wouldn't be easy on his own when he could do little for himself.

A horn sounded in the distance and Jaiden snapped back to the here-and-now: sparring practice. Captain Millstone would be waiting for him to show up, and he didn't want to make a poor impression on his new commander. He slung his pack over his shoulders and exited the tent. The heavy cracking of wood already echoed from the mock combat, guiding and enticing Jaiden. He knew how to wield a sword, and put on a show doing it.

When he reached Doring Meadow, the ongoing fight had devolved into a wrestling match, the circle of spectators closing in further as the participants took to the ground. Screams and cheers were offered, and it was clear what began as a simple sparring lesson was suddenly personal. Captain Millstone and another soldier waded through the ring of boisterous humanity to break up the rowdies.

"Enough of this! Order! Order in the goddess's name!" the captain called as he finally wrangled the fighter on top by his shoulders. The man on bottom had a bloody nose, while grass and dirt clung to both their tabards. The crowd quieted once the brawlers were separated. "This is not what we're here for. You act like that on the battlefield and you're good as dead." Both men lowered their heads as Captain Millstone berated them. "More than that, the man next to you is probably dead too, because you exposed his flank. Get back, the two of you!"

The captain stood in the center of the circle, fuming, as the crowd spread wider, wary of his ire. "Now, somebody show me they know how to treat their weapon with respect. Who's next?" The once-noisy congregation of soldiers evaporated into a collection of men, silent as the Monks of Narvelle.

"I'll give it a whirl," called Jaiden, calmly standing outside the round. Everyone turned his way, and the crowd parted to allow him entry.

"Ah, the new recruit." Captain Millstone paused, but didn't say anything about his leg. "So be it. Get on in here." He picked one of the wooden sparring swords up from the ground and handed it to Jaiden. "And who wants to challenge this brave champion?"

"I'll have some of that."

Jaiden recognized the voice. When the speaker came forward, he saw one of the men he shared a tent with at the last camp – one who had previously taunted him. He wore a smirk on his face and approached slack-shouldered and loose, as if expecting an easy victory.

The crowd spread outward, allowing about ten paces between sides. Though mostly flat and worn down, the meadow had uneven patches where the grass grew thick, and Jaiden knew he would have to be careful of his footing.

With lack of mobility his greatest weakness, Jaiden decided to start in the griffon's stance, and let the enemy come to him. He held the sword aloft, gripping with both hands, pommel even with his head. His opponent's smirk curled into a menacing smile, and his cold eyes betrayed thoughts of delivering his first strike at Jaiden's injured thigh.

"Begin!" the captain announced.

"I'm going to give you the beating you've been asking for, cripple." Seeing Jaiden's sword held high, the man faked a lunge to his right, and then charged from the left, sweeping his wooden blade inward toward the knee of Jaiden's compromised leg.

Jaiden was ready, swiveling his hips and swiftly bringing his own sword screaming downward, parrying the blow with a resonating *thwack*. The man's charge left him off-balance as he passed, and Jaiden used the momentum of his downswing to circle his weapon around and thump his opponent on the backside.

The onlookers erupted with laughter, and the soldier's face reddened at the indignity, once he stopped his forward stagger. Nearly snorting steam, he turned and took a two-handed grip on his blunted battle-implement. A rapid assault of blows ensued, coming from one side, then the next, three, four, five. Jaiden blocked them all, swirling his sword with practiced turns of his wrist, his body barely moving, save for short steps back with every parry. The fluid movement of his weapon spoke for him, while his opponent called out "Heeya!" with every new effort.

Lulling his attacker with continuous defensive strokes, Jaiden waited until he was sure the man had no thoughts toward protecting himself. He gave ground purposefully to continue the illusion he wasn't a threat, then, as the braggart was looping his sword arm from right to left, Jaiden pivoted to show him his profile. The switch in position was enough to make the man miss without deflecting the strike. Instead, Jaiden followed the movement of his opponent's blade with his own, filling the natural opening that appeared as he crossed his body and smacking him on the pate.

The resulting *crack* seemed to startle everyone present, as Jaiden also lulled them into assuming he was on the retreat, though his skill at manipulating his weapon was clearly beyond his foe's. His challenger winced at the blow and his knees buckled as legs gave way.

The next moment he was on the ground, dazed and defeated. A few heartbeats passed in silence until his movements suggested no lasting damage had been done. The circle broke into unsure applause, but Jaiden found satisfaction in his victory, regardless.

Captain Millstone stepped forward to check on the downed man, and after a quick assessment, gave Jaiden a nod of respect. Jaiden suppressed an outward grin, though he was inwardly beaming. He handed his wooden weapon to another soldier as he limped out of the circle's center to retrieve his crutch. He hung around long enough to watch the next pair of fighters, but then snuck off to find his tent for a nap. The late morning's exercise left him exhausted.

In the evening, Jaiden was surprised to receive an invitation from another soldier to join a private game of *Skirmish*. He had played the card game a few times before, and knew wagering was usually involved. He hadn't forgotten the theft of his coin purse, and considered it an opportunity to start replacing his losses, if he could find a way to cover his bets.

He didn't have many possessions beyond the clothes he just acquired from the Order, and all the soldiers had those. Perhaps he could parlay promised lessons of swordsmanship for coin, at least to start. He couldn't think of anything else, and hoped he'd impressed some of the camp with his earlier display of prowess.

He couldn't help noticing the splendid twilight hour as he made his way to the tent hosting the game. The horizon had eloped with a serene shade of purple, and the pursuing clouds were doused rose and gold. The air was comfortably dry, cozily warm, with only the intermittent punctuation of a cool breeze – just a reminder to appreciate it. He'd ignored for too long the sublime moments often recognized in the past. Jaiden realized then that more than just his body needed healing.

Tell-tale sounds of jest and friendly ribbing spilled out from a nearby tent into the eve, honing Jaiden to his destination. He exhaled deeply, preparing for possible disappointment, and ducked inside.

"Jaiden, pull up a stool!" Lothander, the soldier who had invited him, summoned between gasps of laughter. A round table, too big for the space, sat with an assortment of benches and stools surrounding it. A couple lanterns hung from the tent's support rods, and each of the half-dozen players at the table held identical grey mugs. There were cards, face up on the table in front of each player, as well as a pile of speckled kidney beans.

"It's five coppers a bean, Jaiden, how many do you want?" Lothander asked as he stepped from the table and opened a foot locker.

"Well..." Jaiden stalled, undecided between giving an explanation and lying.

"We'll settle up after the game, just let me know what you're in for," Lothander insisted, seemingly unconcerned about payment. Jaiden wondered if his host was merely good-natured, or if the Order conditioned its members to become overtly trusting.

He executed a quick count of one of the other player's beans to gauge how much they were playing for. "Give me twenty-four," he settled, not wanting to contemplate the ramifications of losing more than he won. Where would he get a dozen silver sovereigns?

Lothander counted out twenty-four beans from a cinched pouch in his locker and set them in front of Jaiden, who claimed an empty stool. The men on either side shifted to make room, and Lothander made introductions around the table.

"This is Dohrke, Emanti, Siler, Rafe, and Gayorg. Everyone, this is Jaiden, our champion from this morning." They all raised their mugs and bowed their heads in unison, playing to Lothander's mock flare.

Jaiden shrugged and laughter broke out again. "What are you drinking?" Jaiden was curious whether the choice of beverage was making them all so merry.

"A special spirit, in honor of our foreign mistress," Lothander offered as he handed Jaiden his mug and went to scrounge up another. "Rafe brews it, but don't let the rest of the squadron know. He calls it, 'Saffron's Dew.' I doubt the captain would approve." He shoved Rafe's shoulder as he raised his newly poured cup to his lips.

"Hey, I named it out of respect, all right?"

"Sure you did, Rafe," Dohrke added. "And I'm sure this mug is as close to sipping from her cup as you're going to get, my friend." Once again the table erupted in laughter.

Jaiden took a polite swig and watched as Dohrke gathered the cards on the table. They each had a different creature pictured on them, and he noticed the one showing a gorgon had a slight tear in the top of the card. Dohrke shuffled the gathered cards in with the remains of a deck, then dealt five apiece to each player as Lothander retook his seat.

"So, what are we playing?" Jaiden inquired, though he'd already been told during Lothander's invitation.

"*Skirmish*," responded Dohrke. "You know it?"

"Aye, I've played it a few times, but could I get a quick reminder?"

"Three rounds of cards, betting before each," Dohrke explained. "Everyone chooses which creature to play first, but keeps it face-down until we all reveal. The first card is your base creature for that round. Each one has both a value and a special attribute. The second and third cards modify the attributes of an opponent's base card and then your own, respectively, shifting their value. You can bow out at any time, but lose anything you've already wagered. Whichever remaining player ends with the best, modified base creature wins the skirmish, and the beans to go with it."

Jaiden nodded. "Understood, let's play."

The dealer changed with every hand, and after one trip around the table, Jaiden felt comfortable he'd remembered each of the card's values, while only down three beans for the experience. Furthermore, he was laughing, drinking, and actually enjoying himself for the second time that day, an uncommon feat given the past couple weeks. Another circuit around the table found Dohrke and Gayorg completely bereft of beans, with Jaiden's pile doubling. The evening was wearing on, and the responsibilities of the Rising Moon began early, so Lothander announced they would call it a night after each remaining player took one last turn as dealer.

Jaiden suffered harsh, consecutive hands, and fell to only twenty beans, fewer than he started with. Worry crept in as he remembered he didn't have the coin to settle any losses. Only two skirmishes remained before the game ended.

He looked at his cards carefully, deliberating the best course. He chose the *Troll* as his first card, and wagered four beans. It was a strong creature, starting him off in second position. He bet another four beans before the second cards were revealed, but unfortunately, Siler lay down the *Hell Hound*, whose fire breath nullified his *Troll's* regeneration. It was a devastating turn of events, and Jaiden had to bow out or risk giving away even more of his stash.

"Tough luck there," spouted Lothander, who consequently came out on top, taking down the pile and relieving Rafe of his last beans in the process. "All right, last one fellows."

Jaiden had only a dozen beans left, and he silently prayed to Criesha for some intervening magic as Emanti dealt the final round of cards. What could it hurt, he thought? He kept his eyes closed until all five of his cards were given, then opened his lids as he lifted them.

Had it worked? He was holding the *Shimmering Dragon*, the strongest starting card in the deck. He didn't want to scare anyone off so he only bet half of his remaining beans, though it took restraint not to shove them all to the middle of the table. After the initial cards were revealed, Lothander let out a groan and declared himself out of the bidding. Emanti and Siler kept their reactions to a minimum, still holding on to hope.

They had played the *Wyvern* and *Hill Giant*, respectively, both strong cards. Jaiden looked for a solid way to attack one of their creatures. Yes, the *Dryad* would counteract the *Wyvern's* poison, weakening Emanti's card significantly. Jaiden waited until they had all chosen their cards, and wagered his remaining six beans.

Emanti saw he was bested once they were revealed and bowed out, holding onto the rest of his healthy winnings. Siler's *Corrupted Spider's* web mitigated the *Shimmering Dragon's* flight, but Jaiden still held a slight edge going to the last card. With him out of beans the betting was over, and he concentrated on finding the best way to enhance his dragon. He finally decided on the *Behir*, who would double his limbs – a nice addition.

He waited on Siler to make his decision, and saw a smile creep to his face as he chose his card, which had a slight tear on the top. Jaiden suddenly remembered it was the *Gorgon* – his dragon would be petrified! He scanned his hand one last time, desperate.

"Let's see 'em, for all the beans!" cried Lothander, who seemed to be getting a vicarious thrill from the heavy betting.

"Wait!" Jaiden saw his chance. He felt guilty knowing what Siler's card was, but figured it was a grey area of cheating, since he wasn't the one who'd torn the card. He exchanged his *Behir* for a *Mirror Mephit*, who would reflect the *Gorgon's* gaze back upon it.

When they flipped the cards everyone let out a yell, either impressed or dubious at the perfect play on Jaiden's part.

"You had to have looked or you wouldn't have switched!" accused Siler.

Lothander intervened, however, making it unnecessary for Jaiden to concoct a lie for cover. "Don't be a sore loser, Siler. It was a tough play, but it could've gone either way. Great game – a fabulous way to end the evening."

Siler stared coldly at Jaiden as they waited to redeem their beans back to Lothander for coin, but didn't say another word.

Jaiden walked out with six silver sovereigns, a small fortune, considering he began the night with nothing.

Criesha had risen high, and her soft, green hue painted the encampment as Jaiden trekked back to his tent. He felt invigorated by his winnings, and decided the night was still young, after all. With the majority of the soldiers emitting a lamentable symphony of snores, he determined to head into town to celebrate.

Steering clear of "The Ringing Hammer," Jaiden went deeper into the alleyways of Greyhorne in search of other diversion. After a few, well-placed inquiries, he located the kind of establishment he was looking for. Growing up around brothels, Jaiden felt no shame upon entering "The Four Feathers." His father often found comfort in whorehouses during a long campaign, and would tip the parlor girls a little something to watch after his boy while he was indisposed. Jaiden had memories of women, reeking of perfume, fawning over him and telling his father how adorable he was as his dad retreated with his entertainer of the evening. He remembered a particular incident of his cheeks being pinched incessantly by a rotund prostitute named Big Gertha. He couldn't wait for his father to finish so they could leave.

Of course now, he was the paying customer. Jaiden passed a bulky man with an oaken rod tucked into his belt, just inside the door. The parlor was hazy with lingering smoke, and held a mixture of intoxicating smells he found common to such places: perfume, sweat, and the remnants of recent sex.

A slight-framed strumpet, her brown hair in tight curls, swooped from an unseen corner and laced her arm through his.

"Are you looking for some fun, soldier?" she asked in her best, practiced imitation of a sultry voice.

Jaiden looked over her face, which was pleasant enough, and decided, *why not?* He nodded, "Lead the way, madam."

She smiled in return and took him down a narrow hall, thankfully foregoing the stairs to the second-floor rooms. The chamber they entered was narrow, a slight bed and cheap end-table the only furniture. He had seen several portals lining the hallway, and the walls between rooms were thin – the groans of a vigorous customer on the other side an intruding indicator of why they were there.

Jaiden closed the door. His leg was bothering him from the long walk over, as well as the sparring earlier in the day. "May I sit?"

"As you like," his hostess responded with a wave of her hand toward the bed. As he passed her, she cleared her throat to draw attention to her open palm.

Jaiden placed the silver coins in her hand, which quickly closed around them. Then, he claimed the corner of the bed and unbuckled the thick, leather belt around his waist, so he could peel off his tabard and the cotton tunic underneath. Bare-chested, he rested back on his hands and nodded for her to do the rest. She tucked her payment into a pocket of her dress, gave a wicked smile, and dropped to her knees, grasping his left boot to pry it off.

"No-no-no," he halted her. "What's your name?"

"Annabell."

"Not the boots, Annabell." He didn't want to point out that's where he was hiding his coin purse.

"As you like," she repeated and reached higher to untangle the drawstring on his trousers.

Jaiden closed his eyes, leaned his head back, and imagined the hands touching him through his pants belonged to Saffron. He began to stiffen, and Annabell cooed appreciatively as she pulled his pants further down to expose him. Suddenly, her hands stopped moving.

"What happened to you?"

Jaiden's eyes shot open and he looked down at Annabell, who was staring at the bandage wrapped around what remained of his right thigh. It had started bleeding again from over-exertion, and a growing red spot soiled the white cloth.

"It's just a battle injury. Ignore it."

"Does it hurt? Should I get you something?"

"I said ignore it!"

Annabell looked up at Jaiden's face, jarred by the bite behind his command. "As you like," she said, her voice relinquishing the note of concern that had crept in. She continued her ministrations, but he had gone soft. She tried for another few moments, but it was no use. All Jaiden could do was look at the blood spot on his leg. He felt the wound throbbing, and he couldn't be sure, but it looked like the circumference of the crimson stain increased slightly with every heartbeat.

"Let me try something else." She stood and began loosening the cords of her corset. When she removed it to reveal her bare breasts, Jaiden could see her torso had its share of scars as well. He momentarily wondered how many times she'd been beaten during her line of work, or if that was what led her to it, but pushed such thoughts away. She gave a guarded smile and he smiled back, then lay flat on the mattress and looked up at the ceiling.

He closed his eyes again as he felt the warmth of her mouth cover him, and concentrated on conjuring images of Saffron walking in one of the long, tight skirts she preferred. He could feel himself starting to grow firm again, when suddenly the Saffron in his mind turned her chin over her shoulder to glare at him. "You wouldn't even know what to do with this," she said, and as soon as she did, he lost all the rigidity he'd gained.

Annabell felt it, too. "Is there some sort of problem?" she asked, removing her mouth and wiping a strand of saliva from her bottom lip.

Jaiden opened his eyes and sat up. "Yes, there's a problem. I didn't pay you good silver to talk." He pulled his trousers up, covering his half-vacant thigh as well as his limpness.

"Ahh," she gasped indignantly as she stood, "I'm sorry, I was just trying to help."

"How did you think you could help, with those sad tits? They look like they've been blistered by the red ache."

Annabell's arms crossed over her chest and her face tensed up. He wondered if she was about to cry, but instead she spit her own venom. "You're one to talk, you aberration. You're a useless cripple, and that black spot on your chest looks like your mother used your heart as a hot cloth!"

"What did you say about my mother, whore?"

The yelling drew plenty of attention, and the door swung open just as Jaiden grabbed his clothes in one hand and took a step toward Annabell. The barrel of a man he'd seen by the door in the parlor reached in and enveloped Jaiden in a crushing grip, hoisting him off the ground. Despite struggling, Jaiden was powerless to break loose.

"You can't treat me like this, I'm a paying customer!" His plea fell on unsympathetic ears, and the guard deposited him several steps outside the brothel. He pointed a stern finger in Jaiden's direction. "Don't think about coming back!" he warned in a deep, menacing tone.

Jaiden was running hot, but only managed one step back toward the door before wincing in pain. Both his leg and chest shot surges of agony through his body, and he collapsed on the porch of "The Four Feathers." He could barely breathe, let alone stand, and his anger faded as he focused on regulating his heartbeat, realizing the exertion had incapacitated him.

People stepped around him as they entered and exited the establishment, probably taking him for nothing more than a drunkard. After perhaps an hour he was helped up by a pair of men in white tabards, though he hadn't noticed if they were leaving "The Four Feathers" themselves, or had been dispatched specifically to clear him off its porch.

Either way, he ended his night staring at the shadows near the ceiling of his tent, wondering how his life had gotten to such a state.

Chapter 10

Finding the Lessons

When the uproar began, Jaiden was lying on his cot, recovering from the previous night's adventures. The horns and hollering incited confusion and a brief panic, until the likely reason occurred to him – the return of the cavalry. He sat up, eager to find his crutch to go hear the news.

Outside his tent, the entire camp buzzed with rumors of a strange newcomer, and it seemed the entire Order was making its way to Doring Meadow to hear the Master speak. Growing weary of his hampered mobility, Jaiden limped impatiently behind the crowd to the open meadow, which was packed with members of the Order by the time he arrived. He itched to hear the outcome of the mission and hopefully gain Sir Golddrake's ear as soon as possible about taking part in the next expedition, but found it difficult to make headway past the gathering throngs.

Sir Golddrake, another knight, and a pair of strangers not wearing the garb of the Rising Moon, sat atop horses at one end of the field. One was a pale, muscular specimen with golden hair and feathery wings folded behind him!

The Master was addressing his charges, "...and should be afforded every courtesy as our guests and allies. Furthermore, Palomar has declared his intention to join the Order with the next group of initiates. We have given the King-priest of Chelpa something to consider in his own territory, as he invades our free lands.

"We shall break camp tomorrow and head east to the Dawn Way, then north to Synirpa. The castle at Windhollow Rock is undermanned, and we will help fortify it until reinforcements arrive. Battle may find us, however, so steel yourselves, men. Honor to Criesha."

"Honor to Criesha!" the crowd repeated. Sir Golddrake and the other riders headed back toward the main camp, but the congregation was slow to disperse. Discussions continued, mostly about the winged stranger. Some speculated he was a visitor from the heavens of Mount Celestia, others an emissary from their goddess. Most agreed, however, his presence was a clear sign their cause was favored.

Was this the being Ebon Khorel was looking for? Jaiden tried to squeeze his way up to the departing horsemen, but realized the crowd and his leg conspired to make it hopeless. He decided to remain at the meadow, at least until the masses cleared out. He would speak to Sir Golddrake about the details of his interrogation later.

The gentle spring day called to him, and Jaiden slipped between idle soldiers until he came to a collection of boulders marking the level edge of the field. Beyond them, the ground sloped downward until eventually dropping off the hillside. The surrounding mountain range loomed purple in the distance, a reminder of how insignificantly a single moment stacked against the eternal patience of the earth. Still, men are not mountains, Jaiden thought, and he was content in that moment to reflect on the grandeur around him.

High grasses grew around the rocks where he sat and moss licked their faces, making them an ideal spot to enjoy the vista. He wasn't the only one who came to this conclusion. Saffron approached and settled on a waist-high, smooth-topped boulder. She was holding a flower up to her face by the stem; its purple petals, kissed with white, caressed her cheeks as she inhaled its fragrance. Her eyes acknowledged him, but she didn't speak.

Jaiden straightened his posture and cleared his throat. "That's a beautiful blossom."

"Jaiden," she nodded her greeting, the remnants of a smile on her lips. "I am pleased to see you are no longer confined to your tent. That is good. The fresh air will help you mend."

After she sat on the boulder next to his, he scooted closer. Nodding at her flower, he asked, "Did you pick it yourself? Where did you find it?"

"No, Baron Rogan gave it to me. It is a Bellflower, they typically grow in high places."

"Who is Baron Rogan?" Jaiden inquired, ignoring the extraneous floral information.

"He journeyed with us from Chelpa. He is involved with the resistance there, and came along to help Amurel with strategic planning."

"Hmm, I don't think you can really trust anyone from over the Chelpian border."

"And what about me, Jaiden?" Saffron lowered the bloom to her lap. "I am not from your kingdom. Can I be trusted?" Her voice carried a sharpness, warning of dangerous waters.

"Well, where I'm from isn't really a kingdom..."

"Pssh. You know that is not the point."

"Saffron, the point I'd like to make is that if you would let me, I could do a lot more to make you happy than simply pick you a purple flower." He leaned as he spoke, narrowing what distance remained between them.

"Is that so?" her tone deepened, matching his.

"I know you think I'm young, but I know a lot for my age. I could make you feel good."

"Jaiden?" Her voice was little more than a whisper, her lips only a foot-span from his.

"Yes?"

"You are not unpleasant to look at, but you have no idea how to talk to a woman." Saffron turned her head and slid off the rock. She started walking toward the camp, hips swaying enticingly in her blue skirt. Without looking back, she delivered a few final words. "Sir Golddrake kept speaking of you during our ride. You should pay him a visit."

Jaiden watched her leave, shaking his head in disbelief even as he enjoyed the view. What was it going to take to get through to her? He sighed and rested a while longer on the boulder before summoning the energy to make the trip back.

When he did reach the camp's center, he found a pair of guards posted in front of Sir Golddrake's tent. It seemed unusual, but when he gave them his name, he was directed to enter. The winged creature stood facing Sir Golddrake, who turned toward Jaiden as the tent flap closed behind him.

"Jaiden, I want you to meet Palomar. He is an Aasimar, come to us from another realm."

Palomar formed a fist with his right hand and placed it over his chest, bowing his head in greeting. His skin was alabaster-white and flawless, his hair and eyes the color of wrought gold.

"Palomar," Sir Golddrake continued, "this is Jaiden Luminere, the one Criesha guided me to find."

Jaiden was mesmerized by the otherworldly Aasimar. He managed to nod in attempted politeness, though his gaze never broke from the stranger. He had wings like an eagle, folded against his shoulders, and stood half-a-head taller than either man.

"*I have been told of you, and your pain.*" Jaiden heard his voice, but Palomar's lips didn't move. "*I am sorry for your injury.*"

"What the...?"

"Oh," Sir Golddrake chimed in, shaking his head. "I meant to warn you. Palomar is a telepath; he communicates with thoughts. I wanted you to meet, especially since you'll be entering the Order together. You might also have things to teach one another."

"I'm not sure what I could—"

"Captain Millstone told me about your display of swordsmanship yesterday," Sir Golddrake offered.

"*I have not lifted a weapon since coming to this world, some years ago,*" Palomar communicated. The voice in Jaiden's mind was sure and level, a relaxing combination. "*Now that I am joining the war, I would very much like to learn. In turn, I may know songs you could benefit from, and memories of my homeland you may find useful as well.*"

"Well, I'm not much of a singer, but I would be happy to share some of what I know," Jaiden answered.

Palomar smiled.

"Excellent," added Sir Golddrake. "I have arranged for you both to share a tent with the other initiates, so you can bond with those you will be learning alongside. Palomar, I look forward to continuing our discussion on the trail tomorrow. Jaiden, I have reserved a few hours this afternoon to work on your horsemanship. Please report to the quartermaster after the midday meal. We will have an opportunity to speak of other things then, as well. For now, I must take a short rest. The journey has exhausted me."

"As you wish." Jaiden bowed awkwardly, then followed Palomar, who must have intoned his farewell to Sir Golddrake's mind alone, out of the pavilion.

"I can give you a lesson now, if you wish." Jaiden didn't want to sit idly for the next hour, waiting for his chance to finally get on horseback.

"That would please me – like you, I find myself eager to learn." Palomar's astuteness caused Jaiden to wonder if he was able to read thoughts as well. He would have to keep on guard until the Aasimar proved himself trustworthy.

Jaiden led them to Captain Millstone's tent, where the officer graciously lent them a pair of sparring weapons. Soldiers turned to stare at Palomar whenever they walked by, finally compelling Jaiden to speak. "Doesn't that bother you?"

"Does what bother me?"

"Everyone gawking," Jaiden replied, as if it was obvious. "Minding you, instead of their own matters."

"I look different, and they've never seen my kind. It will pass as I become familiar." Palomar's tone was convincingly indifferent. *"From what Baron Rogan tells me, the looks would have been far worse before my transformation."*

"Transformation?"

"Yes." Palomar stopped, and Jaiden halted a few steps after. *"I suppose there are a few things I should tell you, since we are entering the Order together. Sir Golddrake believes you are special, and I would like the opportunity to discover what he feels, but doesn't yet know. I would like us to become* friends."

"Well, I've never heard it put so bluntly. Thank you for the offer. I cannot just declare us friends, but if we work closely and get along doing so, I don't see why we couldn't end up as such. Shall we?" Jaiden gestured back to the path they were walking. "We're not far from the stables and pasture, and there's an empty corral that suits our purpose."

"I shall follow your lead." Palomar took slow strides, since each of his easily matched three of Jaiden's shuffles. He waited until

the horses were within smelling distance before venturing back to Jaiden's previous question.

"*I am not the only one of my kind on your world, though I may be the only to reclaim the form you now see. I was one of a company of Aasimar punished for a choice we made. We were cursed by our Lord, given hideous, decrepit bodies, and stripped of all memories of our home on Mount Celestia. Our existence became suffering, made more unbearable by the singular knowledge that we used to be something better – we knew clearly that we had lost, though we could not remember what.*

"*We were banished and sent to this realm; all who beheld us despised our grotesqueness. Unable to defend ourselves, many were killed until the King-priest of Chelpa found a use for my kind, which he called 'Dampers.' One of the lucky ones, I was never discovered by such men, and made my way through the wild to the foot of the Nerram Orodruin – the Firewall Mountains.*"

They had reached the corral, but Jaiden didn't want to interrupt the Aasimar's tale. "*I was drawn to a specific crack in the earth, though I didn't know why. Within this fissure I made my home, kept warm by the magma that flowed from its depths. Over time, the strangest thing happened.*"

Palomar's pitch rose slightly. "*The longer I dwelled in this place, the more memories of my previous existence returned. It began with segments of a tune, then series of images, and finally entire songs. I rediscovered the magic I had known as an Aasimar, and eventually a new song formed in my mind – we call it the 'Song of Redemption.' After singing this complex and wonderful harmony, my body changed back to the one before you.*"

Palomar's story enthralled Jaiden, transporting him back in time to when his father told him snippets of old sagas at bedtime. "That's incredible," he said, returning to the present. "Do you think something in the cave affected you?"

"I do now, after meeting Baron Rogan. I wasn't careful when I first recovered my wings, and was spotted during flight. Rumors spread quickly, and luckily he found me before the agents of the King-Priest. He shared his experience in Blackthorn Prison, and how many Dampers were held there. He knew of one other who made the transformation, and said the energy from the ore they mined underneath the prison, and ultimately the channeling of the King-priest, triggered that Damper's memory as well."

Jaiden rolled his eyes. "Well, it seems like this 'Baron' fellow knows a little something about everything."

"I am sorry to have droned on. Please, I am eager to learn what you can show me." Palomar extended his arm toward the empty corral.

"Right." Jaiden flipped him a wooden sword. "First, I want to show you some of the various fighting stances you can use, and the advantages of each."

Jaiden spent the following hour teaching nuances of swordplay to the Aasimar, who seemed to have an insatiable thirst for learning. They were enjoying themselves immensely, having lost all sense of time, when eventually Sir Golddrake approached on horseback.

Amurel watched for a while before making his presence known, impressed by the imposing form of the Aasimar on the offensive, as well as the absolute fluidity with which Jaiden manipulated his sword, regardless of his hampering injury. Amurel's tutelage was aimed at mitigating Jaiden's weakness, and the work would not be easy, so he finally cut in.

"Ho!" he called from just beyond the pen's gate. "Are you ready for riding lessons?"

Jaiden was demonstrating a wrist rotation, but looked up when he heard Amurel's summons. He raised a hand in acknowledgement, then traded words with Palomar before they both made for the gate.

Once they were closer, the Aasimar addressed them. *"Sir Golddrake, Jaiden Luminere, I ask your leave to ruminate on all you have shared with me today."*

Both men nodded at the Aasimar, who trotted a few steps past Amurel's horse before flapping his wings and taking flight, quickly spanning the encampment. They watched for several seconds, Amurel envious of the being's freedom of movement.

"That whole 'talking in my head' business will take some getting used to," Jaiden said.

"Assuredly so," Amurel agreed. "The world is full of wonders, Jaiden. As for the matter at hand – you learning to ride – first tell me, do you have much experience?"

"I've been on horseback a few times, but cannot claim to truly know what I was doing."

Amurel nodded. "All things considered, the beginning is a fine place to start. Follow me to the stables, and I can show you how to saddle your mount." Watching Jaiden struggle to make up ground behind him, Amurel felt pity, even though he had been crippled from birth. He imagined it a greater frustration to fail at that which had once come easily than to simply aspire to the unreachable.

Once they arrived the stables, Amurel dismounted and looped his reins on a hook in one of the wooden posts. He patted his steed's neck reassuringly before turning his attention to finding a suitable mount for his protégé.

"Each horse is a valuable member of our family, Jaiden. Of course they are a financial investment as well, but should be appreciated for their courage and labor, and treated with respect. My stallion's name is Bastion, and we have been safely through many adventures over the years. Unfortunately, we had several animals return from the most recent mission without their riders." He stopped in front of the stall housing a white-and-grey-flecked specimen.

"Ah, Inferno. How are you this afternoon, boy?" Amurel stroked the slender bridge of the horse's nose, then motioned for Jaiden to come closer. "Here is a sturdy lad for you. Don't let his name scare you; he's even-tempered, but swift as a forest fire. Grab his bridle, there, and slide it over his head."

Amurel opened the hinged plank to the stall and patiently instructed his pupil on how to outfit and saddle his mount, adjust the stirrups, check his hooves, and other steps of general grooming. Jaiden indicated he had no idea taking care of a horse was so complicated, but held an immediate fondness for Inferno, who seemed to enjoy licking his hand.

Next came the basics of mounting, which Amurel knew from experience were not going to be simple for Jaiden. He had no problem reaching the saddle, but lifting his left leg into the stirrup when his right could not support him proved tricky.

"You're going to have to use your upper body strength to hold on until you can brace with your left heel."

Jaiden slipped on the first few attempts, before finally succeeding. Inferno whinnied at the shifting failures, but remained patient with his new rider. Getting his left foot firmly in the stirrup was only half the battle for Jaiden, though. Amurel noticed the wincing that every movement elicited, though his student didn't complain.

From his rigid, standing position in the stirrup, Jaiden still had to swing his right leg over the rump of his mount. He hesitated to follow instructions, as a failed try at this maneuver would no doubt be excruciating.

"Perhaps we should improvise," Amurel conceded. "Try sitting on the saddle first, then take your foot out of the stirrup and slide your right leg over in front of you."

Jaiden seemed much more willing to comply with this direction. Slowly, with his jaw tight and one hand poised for balance, he used the other to drag his injured leg over the horse's back. His forehead beaded with sweat from the effort, but finally Jaiden sat atop Inferno, ready for his next lesson.

"Grab the reins, give me a moment to mount Bastion, and I'll lead us back to the corral." Amurel took Jaiden through the proper riding postures, how to steer and give commands to his horse, and transition from walking to trotting. Despite the repetition and regular grimaces at the jostling of his injured leg, Jaiden took to it with admirable persistence.

Amurel discovered he took many things for granted having gained knowledge of horsemanship during his upbringing, yet found pleasure and pride as his protégé grasped a new concept or advanced a skill. He remembered what it was like to learn firsthand the animal's capacity for both strength and subtlety of movement, and to forge a bond of anticipation and empathy. He became so wrapped up in teaching that the hours dissolved, unnoticed. Not until daylight had severely faded did awareness of the afternoon's unmarked passage strike.

"I must apologize, Jaiden. I did not intend to push you so hard to start."

"I don't mind. I want to learn," he called out, bringing Inferno's trot to a halt beside Bastion.

"Good." A thought crept into Amurel's mind, and after a moment of consideration, he gave it voice. "I know you're not ready to join the cavalry, but you would learn more quickly riding with us than poking around with the infantry. I'm going to transfer you from Captain Millstone's command to mine, if you think your leg is up to it. Once we reach Windhollow Rock, you, Palomar, and the other initiates can finish your preparations to officially join the Order."

"Wonderful!" Jaiden smiled. Even now, he was still concentrating on his recent lessons, clicking and pulling Inferno's reins, trying to get his horse moving backward and sideways simultaneously.

"Very well. Let us retire the horses. They've worked long too, and need rest for tomorrow's journey. I am overdue for a planning session with my lieutenants, but I want to see you at the stables at sunrise."

"I'll be there, Sir."

Jaiden had not anticipated how sore he'd be after a full day of sparring and riding. The walk to his tent alone was twice as difficult as that morning. When he arrived, Palomar was seated on the ground, scanning a parchment scroll unrolled before him. Three sleeping pallets were arranged around two hammocks, which spread away from the central support pole.

A tin plate with bread and a pile of the unimaginative mush that often served as camp dinner rations was sitting on a low, wooden stool beside one of the hammocks, along with a cup of water.

"Greetings." Palomar's welcome sounded in Jaiden's head as he looked up from his reading. *"I saved you some dinner."*

"Thank you." Jaiden limped to the stool, and winced as he replaced the plate with his backside.

"Are you hurt?" Palomar sat up straighter, concern shaping his eyes.

"I suppose I should be more careful," Jaiden admitted. "There's always some pain, but now it's everywhere."

Palomar stood and took two steps closer. *"With your permission, I may be able to help."*

Jaiden was wary of anyone touching his leg and tightened in response, though he recognized Palomar was unlike any physician he'd ever met. It might be worth a try. "If you think it will work, then I guess so."

Palomar nodded, took a deep breath, and began to sing. Though Jaiden wasn't yet used to the intrusiveness of the Aasimar's telepathy, it also seemed odd to now hear an actual voice coming from his mouth. The two did not match.

The song began as a low humming before a higher set of notes joined in, as if the voice had split in twain. Jaiden felt compelled to close his lids as a wave of relaxation washed over him. It only took moments before Palomar quieted, leaving Jaiden astounded at the results. He felt remarkably better; his muscles forgot their fatigue and the throbbing in his thigh ceased.

He opened his eyes and regarded Palomar with a new sense of admiration. "How, how did you do that?" He lightly patted his upper leg, curious if he had been made whole again. Unfortunately, the muscle he'd lost was still missing, but he couldn't deny he felt less pain than he had since being wounded – while awake, anyhow. "Are you a Shaper?"

Palomar eased into a gentle smile. "*I suppose it is not too different. Sir Golddrake explained to me there are those who can manipulate the magic left behind by the Avatars of your gods, when they walked this world.*

"*My songs are similar, I suppose, though their source is different. Some of them use the power of the elements, from which all matter derives. Others merely play on the perceptions of the mind, using a being's own potential to make them feel or experience the world differently. The first kind needs no audience, but the song you just experienced, for instance, only has the ability to change things for those who hear it.*"

Jaiden bit his lower lip, not sure if he fully understood, yet certain he had just experienced magic firsthand. "Well, I'm glad you are with us and not against us."

"As am I, Jaiden. I have begun teaching your Lady Saffron some of my methods. She has a knack for composition, and is a rare specimen. Time will tell if she bridges understanding to utilize the potential I see in her."

Jaiden blushed at the thought of Saffron and wondered if perhaps he could use music to show he was worth her time. "She is special, isn't she?"

Palomar cocked his head to the side, as if unsure how to interpret the look upon Jaiden's countenance.

Chapter 11

Caught on the Road

Realizing it would take some time to tack up his steed, Jaiden rose early to feed, groom, and saddle Inferno. Others were packing supplies and moving them to the wagons before anyone else made an appearance at the stables. Palomar promised to bring him breakfast so he would not have to limp all the way to the mess table for sustenance.

Heeding his lessons from the previous day, Jaiden was mounted and ready by the time Palomar arrived with his morning biscuit. The Aasimar greeted him, handed over breakfast, and mounted the stocky mare Sir Golddrake lent him in Salmarsh. *"It might be a muddy track today from the look of things,"* he said.

The morning was gray and overcast, with a cool breeze carrying hints of a rainstorm from the south. "Indeed, the sun may not show its face at all. Thank you, again, for your song this morning. I'm sure it will help on the long ride."

"Think nothing of it, though the effects rarely last more than an hour or two. I can sing for you again if we break our march at midday. Ah, and there goes the Master now. We should meet him." Palomar gently tapped his heels to his horse's flank and Jaiden did the same, following to where a longer line of cavalry was making its way to the southern trailhead. At its fore was Sir Golddrake, shadowed closely by a cadre of other riders, including Saffron.

With her dark, braided hair and fiery-hued outfit, she was easy to spot amongst the masses of white-and-gray-clad soldiers. Palomar quickened his horse's pace to catch up with the assembling leadership. Jaiden attempted to follow suit, imploring his steed to trot, but Inferno failed to respond. By the time he made it to the growing column of riders, he'd arrived somewhere in the middle, and Inferno fell in line as he had countless times, ignoring the inexperienced rider urging him otherwise.

Amurel Golddrake led the march down the steep foothills of the Wyvernwatch Mountains, flanked by Sir Kilborn and Saffron. Immediately behind were Baron Rogan, Palomar, and Lieutenant Orestes, who proudly bore the billowing standard of the Order atop a sturdy lance.

The hundred horsemen of the Rising Moon were split, one group riding at the vanguard of the column, the other trailing it, protecting the middle of the train. Six supply wagons, each drawn by a team of draft horses, ferried the worldly belongings of the Order, and over two hundred souls marched alongside, comprising the infantry and non-military support staff.

Amurel thought it important to remain mobile, and he had a charter from the Prince of Dawn's Edge allowing passage between provinces. The authority of the Prince did not truly extend beyond his own province, but for political reasons, none of the Northern Dukes had yet contested the writ. Amurel made it a point to visit each of them and offer his services, so they left him to travel freely, allowing he might answer their call should they need his Order's protection in the future. These were, after all, uncertain times. He sent swift riders ahead to announce their intentions to the Duke of Rosegold, who he knew would be grateful for their arrival. Amurel also wanted intelligence on the position of Ebon Khorel's troops, whom he'd lost touch with during the recent excursion.

The air grew warmer as they descended from Greyhorne, and signs of spring's rebirth were evident along both sides of the road. The recently dormant grass had a fresh green luster, and wildflowers bloomed from every surface they could take hold, peppering the slopes with patches of gold and lilac.

By the second day they were heading southeast, and the land flattened out considerably. The ephemeral conversation followed suit, until after lunch Rogan once again launched his argument about the significance a successful assault on Blackthorn Prison would hold.

"I know you said you would give it more consideration, but I was wondering if you had come to a conclusion yet, Sir Golddrake?"

Amurel sighed, "I have, Baron."

"And?"

"Whereas we are in agreement to the benefits such a victory would bring, I have to consider the tactical facts, and I simply don't think our chances of success merit the attempt." He could read the disappointment in Rogan's tensed features. "To travel that far into the Empire of Chelpa, we would need to bring our supply wagons or the cavalry would never make it. Bringing the wagons would slow us considerably, and negate the primary advantage of a cavalry strike in the first place. Even if we took the fortress unawares, it would be a hard victory, and I have to assume enemy forces would cut us off before we could escape. I just fail to see how it could work."

"There are problems to overcome, certainly," Rogan countered, "but we have several advantages: Palomar, my knowledge of the prison, surprise, and from what I've seen, the most dedicated and best-trained army in the Cradle."

"I admire your passion, Rogan, and I certainly would like to help free the other Aasimar from bondage – but we are no army. Not yet, anyway. The discrimination that makes our Order effective will always limit its size, and unless we start getting more resources from the nobles we aid, I don't know how long I can keep us outfitted."

As Amurel finished his thought his attention shifted to the horizon. He raised his hand to signal a halt, and Sir Kilborn echoed his command to the troops.

"What is it?" Rogan asked.

"*A rider*," Palomar responded.

They all waited, straining to see signs of the allegiance of the horseman, who was driving his steed hard. A dust cloud spit out behind him, obscuring his identity from this distance.

"One of ours," Sir Kilborn finally determined.

"Orestes, hold them here. Geldrick, with me." Amurel urged Bastion forward, and he accelerated to meet the returned rider. Sir Kilborn trailed after, the crescent moon on his small banner shifting with the ripples of fabric as it unfurled in the wind. In short order they closed the gap and all three came to a violent, rearing halt.

The scout bowed his head, "Hail, Master Golddrake."

"What news has you returning so soon and with such haste?" Amurel questioned. "Surely you are not come from Windhollow?"

"No, m'lord. The host of Chelpa prohibited me. They are encamped along the road, not twenty miles from here, just north of the beaten Fortress Halidor."

"Indeed?" Amurel considered their options. "You did well to warn us. Were you spotted?"

"No, m'lord. Leastways, not by the host. It is impossible to tell if they had spies along the road."

"Understood. We shall have to cut cross-country, it seems." Amurel caught the attention of the scout's eyes focused beyond him, and his neck stretched to get a better vantage. "What is it?" he asked, wheeling Bastion around.

Sir Kilborn turned in his saddle as well. "There's something going on."

The three-wide column of their horses was spreading and turning, though they were too far to determine a reason. Amurel strained his eyes to no avail, but he could just hear Lieutenant Orestes' voice echoing sharp commands. "Marshall, let us make haste!" Without another word they put heels to their horses and urged them to speed, returning to their brethren.

What started as a rumbling of voices behind Jaiden quickly acquired jittery movements and calls of dismay. Soldiers ceased marching and turned to see if the alarm was justified, their speculation adding to the confusion. Too many bodies stood in the way for Jaiden to spot anything useful, but he heard rampant cries of "attack!" and "alert the Master!"

Seconds later, a rider galloped by the right flank of the column, headed to the front. Inferno sensed the growing anxiety around him and became restless, pawing the ground with his hooves. Jaiden was shushing and patting his steed, trying to calm him, when a clearer voice called out, "Arrow formation, cavalry. On me!"

Horses spread, wider than the road, while Jaiden impotently urged Inferno to join them, having no knowledge of the various formations and commands. The assembling line of horses edged westward, the way they had come. The infantry gathered along the road in the space vacated by the cavalry. Jaiden felt very much in the way, and finally convinced his mount to amble south of the wide, dirt track, out of the middle of things.

The first line of infantry hoisted their pentagonal shields in an almost interlocking pattern, the butts of their spears planted firmly at their instep. Behind them, another row of foot soldiers pulled drawstrings and set quarrels, readying their crossbows. The Order of the Rising Moon's discipline was on full display; within moments nearly everyone was in a position to defend or launch an assault.

From his new vantage point, Jaiden could make out the cause of the alarm. A host of horsemen, their steeds draped in black barding, closed in from the west. Their advance carried intent, and he guessed not a soul amongst the Order believed it benign. Yet, impassable mountains blocked the west, with the River Chelhos farther beyond. How could an army approach from this direction, unless they materialized from thin air onto the Harpy Pass?

The terrain further conspired to create difficulties if combat proved unavoidable. While the trail they followed was wide and flanked immediately by flat swaths of grass on either side, the land beyond to the north of the road inclined sharply. It would be treacherous to lead a horse over the hilly outcroppings. The south, while more hospitable, was deceptively uneven. The ground was green and soft, masking the extent of its many dips and rises. Jaiden had noticed a creek running alongside their road for much of the morning, though it receded and emerged at irregular intervals. If horses were coaxed in that direction, unwary riders would risk plummeting to disaster.

The acting cavalry commander held his men in check, though their horses snorted and pawed nervously at the ground, aware such maneuvers always ended in a charge. Sir

Golddrake was nowhere to be seen, and Jaiden craned back to the east, looking for the banner carried by his lieutenant. Though a number of horses made their way from the vanguard around the bloated midsection of the caravan, he did not notice the Order's standard-bearer among them.

As reinforcements from the front of the column rushed past, Jaiden made the rash decision to join them. His bravado with a sword and the lure of glory dwarfed the small part of him that recognized he was not prepared for mounted combat. Jaiden could hear battle cries in the distance – the other force had accelerated to a charge. Still without their Master, the ranking officer determined they could no longer afford to wait. The Order of the Rising Moon was going to meet them.

"Knights, advance!" With a sudden, unified surge the cavalry in front of Jaiden pushed forward, rapidly shifting from a trot to a full run. Inferno matched them, and while Jaiden held on as best he could, trying to balance in the saddle, he suddenly realized he wasn't even carrying a lance.

"Whoa, boy!" He pulled sharply on the reins and his horse reared back in protest. Time slowed as the rest of the cavalry line continued advancing down the road like a wave on the beach, pulled back into the sea. Frothing and foaming in brilliant white tabards and shining armor, their beauty was interrupted by violent collision with the enemy.

The most terrible sound Jaiden had ever heard followed: screams of beasts and men, lances splintering on shields, bodies thudding with impact. The white of the Order was replaced by the black of their foe, as if a conjurer had swapped them with some sleight of hand. As the enemy broke through the lines many continued toward Jaiden, who remained alone between cavalry and infantry. With no time to retreat from their path, he hastily drew his sword to defend himself.

Luck hovered on his side as the crossbowmen behind him took aim and released their shots. Several of the charging warriors closest to Jaiden rocked back in their saddles, pierced by bolts. They continued their approach unable to raise their lances against him, and Jaiden cleaved the nearest one as he passed, toppling the soldier from his saddle.

To the west, the road was a crowded mass of mounted soldiers engaged in a life-or-death dance of hacking and evasion. More ebony-clad riders pushed around the edges, though, making for the wagons, which were already defending against those who had streaked past Jaiden.

He decided that was where he could be most useful, and this time Inferno didn't fight him. He rushed into the fray, which swelled the middle of the caravan as more foot soldiers joined the fight. Unfortunately, this made it impossible for the forward half of the Order's cavalry to get around and help.

Once more stationary, Jaiden's innate understanding of balance and leverage took over – shortening strokes when exchanging swings with mounted foes, elongating them when sweeping down on unhorsed opponents. Immediately upon dispatching one darkly donned soldier he looked to engage another, finally spotting a cluster of four enemy riders. Numerous felled men in white lay at the feet of their steeds. The leader was wielding a heavy-bladed axe and wearing a chain hauberk. On his head rested a helm shaped like a spider, its spindly legs reaching around shadowed eyeholes.

Jaiden had a sudden flashback of being tortured by the King-priest, and his chest jerked in pain at the memory. That helmet belonged to one of the men who had stood over him, watching. His grip tightened around the hilt of his sword, and he yanked the reins with his free hand, urging Inferno to turn. He yelled, clenched his jaw, and kicked heels to his horse's flank.

As he pursued the group, they disappeared from view around the far side of one of the wagons. By the time Jaiden rounded the corner they had pinned in a pair of unarmored support troops, whose backs were pressed against the side of the supply wagon. The man dropped his sword and raised his hands in surrender. The other, a boy of about twelve, picked it up and held the weapon with both hands, pointing it shakily in defiance. It was Tikvi.

"No!" Jaiden roared as he snapped the reins, watching as the Spider-helmed soldier raised his blade. Inferno only managed two steps before the down-stroke of the axe knocked the boy's sword from his hands and continued on, cleaving his clavicle and slicing a wound halfway down his chest. The boy's severed ribs failed to contain his insides as he collapsed.

Before Inferno had taken two steps more an explosion of sound blasted Jaiden's left ear. A sonic eruption, delivered by the channeling of a Gholdur war-priest, splintered the wood of the wagon, panicking Jaiden's horse. Inferno swerved southward and bolted; Jaiden was pushed sideways out of his saddle, though his feet, tangled in the stirrups, kept him from falling to the ground. The violent, up-and-down motion, the ringing in his ears, and the agony of his injured leg twisted against his horse's flank, combined to completely disorient him.

He couldn't tell how long he was suspended upside-down, his head dangling over the swiftly passing ground, but thankfully his foot finally came free and he toppled onto the grassy earth. He landed facedown and remained motionless, wishing the ringing in his head and the throbbing of his leg would both quiet. The image of Tikvi being struck down caused him to weep, wetting the grass with stores of pent-up tears, until the overwhelming sensations closed off his consciousness.

It was a dreamless state, though, and he returned to the sound of steel against wood. While alarmingly close, it was better than not being able to hear at all. Jaiden used his arms to push his chest up and lift his face out of the grass, but his leg prevented him from moving further. Just lying still was agony.

Through tear-blurred eyes he spotted Saffron, a whirling red cyclone, her dark ponytail whipping behind her like a slaver's lash. The dark-armored soldier fighting her hesitated, then slashed, his blade striking shield where her body had been a flash before. Saffron, with the grace of the wind, brought her right foot down, pivoting on it to halt her spin, and redirected into a forward thrust of her spear. The attack caught her hapless opponent off balance, and the meticulously sharpened tip of her implement did its work, piercing the unprotected space between his ribs. He slumped to the ground as she withdrew her weapon.

Saffron looked over her shoulder uneasily before springing to where Jaiden was lying. "Good, you're alive. Amurel will be relieved." She dropped her spear and knelt on the thick, matted grass beside him. "Any new wounds?" she asked while looking him over. Though spatters of blood tainted his white tabard, it was free of any deep red stains indicating mortal injury.

"I don't know. My leg?" Jaiden was so consumed by it he wouldn't have been able to feel anything else, regardless. Unwilling to look himself, he watched for Saffron's reaction as she moved her gaze downward. With her veil covering the lower half of her face, only her eyes spoke – yet they were foreign, and he couldn't decipher their message.

"We've got to get out of here before we're noticed." She picked up her spear, stood, and added "wait here," before striding a dozen paces to where her horse chomped on the long grass. Jaiden could do nothing but wait, though he saw another horse, draped in black, standing with its head bowed beside Saffron's.

After securing her weapon and shield to her saddle, Saffron returned bearing a long, leather cord. "This will hurt, but likely no more than what you are already feeling. We need to turn you over." She crouched beside him once more, this time at his hip. She grasped his leg with both hands, one at his calf, the other mid-thigh. "Roll toward me, Jaiden. Push with your hands." Her voice was urgent and more firm than usual, and he did as told.

New jolts of agony surged as the pressure shifted on his leg, but within seconds he was settled on his back. Jaiden's face flushed with sweat, and he concentrated on breathing to try and block the pain and urge to vomit, while Saffron bound his leg with cord. Gathering his courage, he crept onto his elbows to watch her work and survey the damage. The lower two thirds of his leg bent at an impossible angle as Saffron lifted it to work the leather strap around.

"It broke again; my guess is all the way through. Not much is holding it together, Jaiden. I don't see how you can keep it, but this should hold your leg in place for now, if you stay completely off it. Perhaps a surgeon can do something."

Saffron tied off her knot and hastily wound the other end of the cord around Jaiden's upper leg. He had no words, his jaw clenched to help suffer her ministrations, but silently vowed not to relinquish his leg.

"You'll need to ride with me," Saffron said as she finished. Draping Jaiden's right arm over her shoulder, she struggled to raise him off the ground. He used his left leg as best he could to help, but still felt disoriented. She let out a shrill whistle once they were standing, to which her horse lifted its head. It looked at her, shook its mane, and slowly paced over. "Good girl. Now down, Sheen, down."

The animal whinnied but obeyed, kneeling first on its front legs, then lowering its hind ones as well.

"Good girl, are you up for two today?" She helped Jaiden straddle the saddle, though he felt like he could slip from consciousness at any moment. "Up, girl, up."

With some effort, the mare lifted itself onto its legs, Jaiden grasping its neck to keep balance. He happened to look north and saw the road, perhaps a half-mile away, crowded with black figures.

"It is as Palomar warned; their squadron of foot soldiers has caught up. We'll have to find a way around." Saffron stalked the horse in black, whispering reassuringly until close enough to grab its reins. She led it to her own mare, withdrew a length of rope from her saddlebags, and quickly tied a line between the enemy horse's reins and the horn of her saddle. "Hopefully they have no intention of following us, but I wouldn't be surprised otherwise."

Saffron put her foot in the stirrup and gracefully hoisted into the saddle behind Jaiden. Reaching around him, she took the reins and commanded, "Go, Sheen." The horse walked slowly, carefully at first, adjusting to the weight of a second rider. The ground was uneven and obscured by the thick, verdant grass, further justifying caution.

With the sun arcing downward they headed southwest, both to put distance between themselves and the Chelpian army, and to backtrack. After an hour of no visible pursuit they cut back north toward the road. Saffron spoke little – Jaiden, not at all. He was sweating profusely and tried to empty his mind, numbing the pain by distancing his consciousness.

"There is a collection of caves within the hills that abut the eastern face of that mountain range. Amurel has shown it to me, and he holds it a sacred place. That's where he aims to lead his men, if they are able to elude the enemy. Before I left to find you, he told me the road to Halidor Keep was blocked by the King-priest. We shall all have to travel more secretive paths to reach our destination. It will not be easy."

Jaiden heard, but gave no response. Those concerns were beyond him as he struggled just to keep from falling off horseback. He was dreadfully thirsty, but his mouth felt so dry he found it difficult to ask for water.

"Looks like we are being followed, after all." There was no concern in Saffron's voice, however, and she nudged Sheen into a quarter turn so Jaiden could see with his own eyes. Inferno stubbornly kept his distance, but trailed them nonetheless.

Jaiden gave a weak, snort of a laugh, though he wasn't sure why he found it funny. "How much further?" he was finally able to ask, after circling his tongue around his mouth to moisten it.

"We've got a few more hours until sundown. We're almost to the Harpy Pass. I'd like to cross it, find the back way to the Moonlight Stairway, and gain some elevation before bedding down. I'll have to lead on foot once we start climbing, so it will be slow-going."

She pressed on, and he resigned to enduring. The dirt of the wide trail they had ridden along that morning was churned loose by the passage of so many, and puffs of dust rose with the horses' steps, further drying Jaiden's nose and mouth. No longer able to swallow, he finally pleaded for water.

"Of course," Saffron sympathized as she dismounted, "my apologies." She dug a canteen from her saddlebags, took a short swig, and offered it to Jaiden. "Drink as you like; there are many streams in these mountains. Now, let's have a look at that leg." She walked to the right side of her steed, where Jaiden felt her hands lightly upon him. She was delicate, and caused no more pain. "Good, the cords are holding. I know it hurts, but I won't be able to do anything more until we stop for the night. You can hold on, yes?"

Jaiden wasn't sure he could, but nodded anyway.

"Sheen needs to rest as well, so I'm going to leave you two here and take the other horse to look for the path. It shouldn't be too far, if I remember correctly. See those blossoms on the ridge?"

He tilted his head upward and saw, forty paces east along the top of a gentle slope, a sprinkling of frosted violet.

"Periwinkle," she continued. "I noticed them as we passed, and moments later Amurel pointed out a goat path leading to the Moonlight Stairway. I shall return anon." Saffron took the canteen from Jaiden and replaced it in the pack. She patted her steed's nose. "Stay Sheen, I need you to take care of him." Without another word she slipped her spear from its harness, mounted the black-cloaked horse, and headed east down the trail.

Thankful for the momentary stillness and quiet, Jaiden leaned against the horse's neck and closed his eyes. With surprising quickness, he descended into an uneasy slumber.

Chapter 12

Giving In

When Jaiden awoke he was lying on a saddle blanket on the ground and the first stars were showing themselves. A small fire crackled nearby, centered within a cozy, wind-carved grotto on a rocky hillside. The smell of cooking meat had roused him, and craning his neck, he saw Saffron kneeling over the flame, adjusting the position of a spitted hare. Her hair was unwound and her veil nowhere to be seen. He shifted ever so slightly, wincing as pain shot up from his leg, earning Saffron's notice.

"It wasn't easy moving you around," she said, without looking up from her task. "But you never woke, so I deem your sleep was important. We crossed a stream a ways back, so I watered the animals and refilled our canteens – I found yours with your horse, who caught up while we stopped."

Jaiden looked around their campsite. All three horses, Inferno among them, had been unpacked and tethered with rope to her spear, which was wedged horizontally between uneven surfaces in the rock face. Saffron had snared a rabbit, built a fire, and set up a place for him to sleep – though he saw no other blankets laid out. "You did all this?" he asked, genuinely impressed.

"It is surprising what a woman can accomplish when men are not trying so hard to get in the way."

"I, I didn't mean...thank you for coming to find me. I didn't think I would make it through the day. I'm famished – is that hare almost cooked?"

Saffron laughed. She finally looked up at him, eyes smiling, face lit by the glow of the fire. She was certainly beautiful, but he couldn't even describe why. Something about her darker complexion, her smoky irises, and the roundness of her nose and cheeks enticed him. She looked so different from the girls he knew growing up.

"And there I thought we were about to share a sincere moment. Yes, Jaiden, the food should be ready." She used the hem of her long skirt, edged with golden cloth, to remove the hot spit from the fire. She winced as the heat became too much, and let it drop onto the tin plate she'd set out.

"You certainly do come prepared," he said, raising an eyebrow at the dishware.

"Unlike these Knights of the Order," she quipped, "I believe in complete self-reliance, and don't count on the serving cart being nearby when I need something. You, for one, should be thankful for it."

"Oh, I am – don't get me wrong. I am completely, without a doubt, thankful."

"Indeed," she responded, incredulously. She drew a dagger from the sheath at her waist and sliced bits of meat from the bones. When she finished, she brought the plate and a canteen closer, set them beside Jaiden, and sat cross-legged opposite him. "Eat." It sounded like an order.

Trying to be polite, Jaiden waited until she had selected a piece of meat for herself before taking any. Once in hand, however, he quickly tore into the cooked flesh, finding it tender, juicy, and flavorful. "This is terrific," he said, mouth still full. "What is it I'm tasting – other than the rabbit? I can't quite place it."

Saffron waited until she'd swallowed to answer. "It's lemongrass. It grows in the warmer parts of Chelpa. Baron Rogan picked some before we left, and told me how to prepare it for cooking."

"Ugh." Jaiden couldn't contain his disgust.

"What? I thought you said you liked it."

"I love the dinner, Saffron. It's just I have had enough of this *Baron Rogan*." He cut her off before she could say it first, "I know. I really ought to meet him."

Saffron didn't say a word, but a smile crept across her face. She tried to hide it by lifting another slice of the cooked rabbit to her lips, though she paused to savor and swallow before taking another bite.

Jaiden sighed. "So, what is it about this Baron fellow? Do you like him because he's wealthy?"

Saffron coughed, nearly choking on her food. "Who said I liked him?"

"Oh, you don't like him? Well, we have that in common, because I don't think I like him either. Who knows what other interests we might share?"

Saffron narrowed her eyes and shook her head. Jaiden groaned and finished his meal. Between their silences, the occasional crackle of the fire reminded them of its presence, though it did not bar the growing chill in the air as evening melted into night. When they both had their fill, Saffron tossed the remains into the fire. The last thing they needed was the smell of a carcass luring scavengers.

While she put away and rearranged her supplies, Jaiden took a long swig from his canteen and stared at his leg, still bound by the cord Saffron wrapped around it. Though the blood staining his pants had dried, the gnawing of the wound was constant. He knew it had broken again, and at best would be starting over in the healing process. Deep down a seed of fear had taken root, however. Unlike the first time, his defiance was being subdued by a new awareness – the realization that his leg was dying. He hoped it wasn't true, but believed it was.

"What do you think happens when you die?" Jaiden stared into the fire, relaxing his eyes until they lost focus, detaching from his pain, mesmerized by the dance of the flame. "My father told me men have an immortal soul, and that your actions while you live determine where it goes afterward. Brave men's souls go to the Warrior's Hall, the wicked to the Lake of Fire, the cruel to the Abyss."

Her cooking implements packed, Saffron took up a fleece mantle and her lyre before returning to sit by the fire. "And what if you are none of these things?" She draped the fleece over her shoulders and nestled the lyre in her lap while she listened.

"Then your soul goes to the Grey Wastes of Limbo, or so he said."

"Do you believe your father's words?"

"I don't know. It doesn't seem fair. What if you hadn't yet become what you were meant to be?"

"Ah," Saffron tilted her head downward and struck a series of notes on her lyre. "*Deshiri hujat ib Yunë castilah. Sun hallih shezat ya fhallan,*" she sang.

Jaiden's confusion drew his eyes from the fire. He'd never heard Saffron speak Begnari before.

"Destiny flows from the mouth of Yunë. We are all prisoners of her words," she translated. "It is from a song of my homeland."

"It's beautiful." It occurred to Jaiden for the first time Saffron may be homesick, but he didn't ask. "I saw a boy I knew, Tikvi, killed today during the fighting. He was brave; I saw him pick up a weapon while the man beside him cowered. But he was just a boy." Jaiden's eyes moved from Saffron back to the fire. "I don't want to end up in Limbo."

The crackle of the fire punctuated the heavy silence that followed, until finally Saffron responded. "The tradition of my people states we are all bound to the elements. They make up everything: the sand, the sky, our horses – every one of us. Our spirits return to the elements as jewels when we die. Diamonds from the earth, pearls from the sea, the stars from air and fire."

"Do you believe that is what happens?" Jaiden had never heard such a thing.

Saffron smiled. "I think they are stories, Jaiden. But every story holds at least a bit of truth."

He was not sure what to make of her answer. He knew he didn't understand this woman, yet wanted to bathe in her voice. "I hope Tikvi ends up on Mount Celestia. That's where Palomar said he was from." He shrugged. "It can't be too bad if it's full of Aasimar, I suppose. Will you play me something on your lyre?" It was time to change the subject. He could feel his throat tightening and his eyes begin to sting.

On the heels of his words an icy wind whipped through the hollow and nearly extinguished the fire before fleeing. "Perhaps something to warm our blood?" Unlike Saffron, he had no additional clothing for warmth. It was all packed away in one of the wagons, and he hadn't planned on cutting a path through these high hills.

"I will play something in remembrance of your young friend." Saffron lifted her lyre upright and plucked at its fine strings. The dexterity of her fingers amazed Jaiden, reminding him of the way she danced in battle. When her haunting voice joined the melody, he couldn't help shutting his eyes, awash in emotion.

She sang in Begnari, but the mood of the words translated well enough. The song was simultaneously sad and hopeful; slow, deep sounds from Saffron's voice, sparsely punctuated by higher tones of the lyre. Unbidden tears escaped down Jaiden's cheeks as he mourned all at once the loss of Tikvi, his father, and his future as a soldier.

His eyes opened to capture Saffron's for a moment, but hers lowered quickly. He knew she must have caught the wetness on his skin, glistening in the firelight, but she ignored it and kept singing. It was the first time in his life he could remember crying and not caring that someone saw. As he gave in, the tears came faster, overflowing as if a dam holding back his sorrow had finally collapsed. At last Saffron's voice hummed to a quiet stop, her last pluck of the strings lingering in the rock depression like a shadow refusing to leave when the candle is put to bed.

The sky had fallen dark and a multitude of stars sparkled overhead. Jaiden turned from the fire and lay on his back, searching the constellations for something familiar. From the corner of his eye, he saw Saffron stand and head toward the horses, no doubt to pack away her lyre. He took the opportunity to wipe the wetness from his face.

"That's a beautiful instrument." Jaiden coughed to clear his throat. "Did you bring it from home?"

"It was a gift from the Prince of Dawn's Edge, actually. Mine was lost when I was captured by the Chelpians." She placed two more broken branches on the fire and sat on the blanket beside Jaiden. "The only thing I recovered was a trunk of clothing. Amurel took me to see the Prince shortly after rescuing me – playing for him was the reason I left Begnasharan in the first place. I had intended to stay and study music in the capital, but first I must find my sister."

"Do you know if she's still alive?" Jaiden realized it was the wrong thing to say as soon as the words left his mouth.

"Of course she is!" Saffron turned her back to him and lay down, but surprisingly slid closer, until her back pressed against his left arm. He was unsure how to respond.

"It's cold, and it's only getting colder," she said, reading his mind. "The blanket beneath us is the only one we have."

Neither talked for some time and Jaiden was unwilling to move, afraid that in doing so he might lose contact with the woman beside him. He felt Saffron's back curve and press into him ever-so-slightly with every breath, and he timed his own breathing to match hers. Finally, tired but unable to fall asleep, he ventured to speak again.

"I can see my father's favorite stars." He took two breaths, trying unsuccessfully to determine if Saffron was still awake before continuing. "They make up the Swordsman, there, in the northeastern sky." He pointed with his right arm, but Saffron failed to move. "He really loved to fight, I think, but he always said it was up to each of us to find the things worth fighting for. I practiced every day, hoping for the chance to make him proud. And now, he's gone."

A twig snapped in the dying fire and a distant wind rustled the branches of far-off trees. "You can still make him proud," Jaiden thought he heard Saffron whisper, but when he turned his head she gave no indication she was awake. Perhaps he imagined her words? Either way, the chilled air and throbbing of his leg kept him up for what seemed like hours.

When Jaiden opened his eyes he was lying on a soft mattress. Draped in green satin, the bed was raised an arm's length above a floor of ghostly vapor. Stars still filled the night sky above him, but he felt neither cold nor pain. Propping on his elbows, he saw he was naked and his leg in perfect condition, as if never bitten. He lay back down and closed his eyes, realizing where he was, wanting to savor every blissful moment.

"Have you made your decision?"

Jaiden sat up with a start at Criesha's warm voice beside him. Out of nowhere she'd appeared on the bed, looking immaculate in her forest-green gown. With her presence came the distinctive surge of vitality that put all his sense on alert. He looked into her eyes, realizing for the first time the deepness of their blue, almost black irises. How had he not noticed before?

"You still have not pledged yourself to the Order, and are not walking the path of my Champion. Have you forsaken me?" The moonstones and silver in her hair caught the starlight and distracted Jaiden, interrupting the coherency of his thoughts. He dared not look lower yet, sure the view below Criesha's regal neck would unwind him completely.

"I, I have chosen to join the Rising Moon. Sir Golddrake has planned for the ceremony, I just haven't had time to study yet," he tried to recover. "There are a lot of rules, if you ask me."

"Easy to live by, once you embrace them. The key to overcoming these challenges, Jaiden, is to give up what you think you want for yourself, and imagine what others might need." Criesha pushed closer. "Believe me, once you start acting selflessly you will find it not only makes you happier, but you will tend to end up with everything you wanted in the first place."

She placed a soft hand on his solid, muscular thigh, the same spot mutilated in the waking world. Her luminescent skin cast a green hue upon his tanned flesh, and Jaiden watched her fingers glide toward his hip. Criesha's touch alone sent a surge of pleasing energy through his body. Within a breath his arousal showed, the anticipation exhilarating him. He watched her hand, willing it to move across his lap and take hold of him, though not daring to suggest such a thing.

Instead, Criesha continued to slide it up to his muscular chest, coming to rest over his heart. "You have been wounded physically, Jaiden, and I cannot know what that must be like, but I want you to believe I can make it better. Not only can I heal your hurts, I can share things beyond your current understanding. But you must prove yourself ready, and soon. Gholdur is a dreadful adversary, and be assured he is bestowing ever-greater gifts upon his chosen Champion. I need a representative as well, but it must be one who is worthy. Prove yourself to me."

"It's not that I don't want to, my lady. You must believe that."

Criesha withdrew her hand, the loss excruciating. "Then do it. The time for talking is past, Jaiden. Your actions will speak for you." She stood and withdrew two steps before turning back. "I hope they please me."

"Might I stay here a while longer?" He searched those bottomless blue eyes for pity.

"I will make you dream until sunrise," she said, before stealing silently across the floor of clouds.

"Thank you," he replied, falling back into a pleasant repose.

Jaiden awoke to Saffron stirring in her sleep, nuzzling closer for warmth. He was on his back with his arm around her. Her head rested in the hollow between his chest and shoulder, her arm flung across his torso. Her legs had entwined his uninjured one, which was buried in the folds of her skirt.

The grey of morning greeted him, while the cold of a long night had sunken into his bones. At least it numbed his leg, though not immediately feeling its throbbing worried him, too. He didn't rush to get up, letting Saffron sleep and inhaling the aroma of her plentiful, sable hair. Her woolen mantle was spread across their midsections, doing a poor job of covering their frigid extremities. Without it, though, they would have been even worse off.

Looking down, he suddenly realized something was left behind from his dream-world encounter with Criesha, besides a newfound sense of dedication – a clear rise in the fleece garment around his lap. With his left arm tucked around Saffron, only his right was available.

Moving slowly, careful not to disturb Saffron, he slid his hand underneath the mantle in an attempt to adjust himself. It was no use; he was stuck, pressed too firmly against the fabric of his trousers. It was going to take either both hands or removing his pants entirely. Jaiden struggled to think of things that would kill his arousal, but with Saffron's body on top of his, the heat of her loins radiating directly onto his leg, it was no use.

His failed attempts to dislodge himself ultimately woke her, and she inhaled deeply as she lifted her head from his shoulder, disoriented.

"Oh," she said when she saw Jaiden's face only inches from hers. "Oh!" she repeated as she looked down to find Jaiden's hand manipulating his erection. She pushed off of him quickly and was standing an instant later.

Seeing her reaction, he looked down and realized what it looked like. "No, no, I was just stuck," he said. Sitting up, he quickly used both hands to maneuver into a less-obtrusive position.

Saffron raised both palms and turned to the skeleton of the previous night's fire. "I don't want to know."

Jaiden sighed. "Can you hand me my crutch? I need to go relieve myself."

"I said I don't want to know." Nevertheless, she grabbed Jaiden's crutch from the pile of supplies removed from the horses and handed it to him. "I'm going to restart the fire for a quick breakfast, but we should be on our way soon. We've got a lot of ground to cover."

The last pair of days were the toughest Sir Amurel Golddrake had seen as a knight errant. Their battle on the road from Greyhorne was an eruption of utter chaos. Though a fair number of enemy cavalry had been slain, many managed to retreat in both directions. Amurel struggled to keep his knights from pursuing those who fled, for there was no time to explain that the bulk of the Kingpriest's army lay ahead to the east.

There had been no time to fully regroup either, as Palomar, aloft, spotted the squadron of trailing infantry closing in from the west. With the maintained trail cut off in both directions, the supply wagons had to be abandoned. Quickly weighing down men and horses with everything they could carry, the dead and grievously wounded were forsaken as well.

Criesha forgive him if he'd left other survivors behind. Palomar volunteered to stay back until the last possible moment to help as he could, but the sun had risen twice since then, and he'd seen no sign of the Aasimar, either.

The less-travelled paths over and around the foothills of the Wyvernwatch Mountains were narrow and slow to navigate. In order to increase their speed and chance at survival should the enemy pursue, he'd ordered what was left of their numbers to split up, giving Sir Kilborn command over the second group. After two days of leading without him, he realized what a blessing his old friend was.

Without intelligence on the exact positions of Ebon Khorel's armies, he couldn't risk heading directly for the castle at Windhollow, which would have been the easiest route. The only practical decision, given the uncertain circumstances, was for the Order of the Rising Moon to regroup at a place he'd anointed the 'Caves of Criesha.' An easily defensible location, the expansive cavern had only a single approach, and held a cache of supplies now essential with the wagons gone. In need, they could hold out in the Caves for some time, and though at risk of being cornered, it would be dangerous for an enemy to remain exposed on the steep approach for long.

Amurel prayed to Criesha that any of his men who became separated would remember the way. He chided himself for allowing Saffron to go after Jaiden, when he was likely already lost. His belief in the lad may have cost him double, for it would be a dire toll to continue without both.

Baron Rogan remained safe, thankfully, and his experience in organizing rebellions proved useful in keeping the men on task and their morale from collapsing. Amurel's brooding over his own burdens shouldn't be allowed to create a negative effect on the motivation of his troops.

At last, his group was nearing their destination. The entrance to the caves appeared as a black shadow on the hillside from afar, where it stayed shielded from the sun until the evening hours. On the eastern face of the cliff, it could only be reached after ascending a winding series of switchbacks, though the trail was wide enough for two horses to comfortably walk abreast.

Bastion was none too happy with the rocky terrain, picking his way carefully to avoid turning an ankle or worse. Amurel's truth was that, even with the undetermined number of other casualties, his horse was the one he could least afford to lose. Weariness made continual attempts to claim him, but he was too eager to reach the hidden sanctuary to give in.

With praise and the promise of a well-earned rest, he urged his horse up the last two switchbacks, where the stone had been cut by ancient hands into a line of smooth, broad stairs. Bastion whinnied in response, recognizing these steps signaled the end of the long, climbing road. Upon reaching the top, Amurel looked back at the train of soldiers following up the path. Only smatterings of horses mixed with the scores of men on foot. He hoped more of the cavalry survived and would catch up.

Everyone from crossbowman to cook must be fatigued, but he knew much needed doing before rest was earned. There were beds and fires to be made, saddlebags and packs to unload, and neglected wounds to be tended. Amurel would check the roster himself to account for every man present and missing. He wanted to know the exact state of the Order.

After a brief respite, he would have to send out scouts to gather reliable information on the whereabouts of their foe, and send a new emissary to the castle at Windhollow Rock as well. First, however, he was going to give Bastion a break from the saddle and groom him.

Understanding the beasts would be uncomfortable too deep into the caves, he claimed a shallow corner where the slanted sunlight still carried the reminder of open air, to serve as the temporary stables. After dismounting and untacking his horse, Amurel took a brush from his saddlebags and worked in long, thorough strokes to remove the dust from Bastion's coat. He whispered promises of water and nourishment soon to come, though he'd have to rely on someone else to move the water barrels closer.

"There you are, Sir." Rogan's horse clopped forward to join, its hooves striking echoes against the stone of the cavern floor. The former baron swung down and stretched his legs, sore from too long in the saddle. "Would you like me to finish up for you while you see to your men?"

Amurel saw Rogan watching for a reaction out of the corner of his eye, as the southerner unburdened his own steed. "No, thank you. I enjoy the work." His eyes kept to the lines of his animal. "It's an opportunity to keep our bond strong." Amurel patted Bastion on the neck, and his horse whinnied and dipped his neck.

"What about your bond with them?" Rogan tilted his head toward the soldiers still filing into the caves.

"You think I don't spend enough time with my men?"

"I think leading men is trickier than befriending them."

Amurel chuckled wryly and shook his head. "Baron, you do speak your mind." He brushed a few more strokes, then handed his brush to Rogan. "Are you implying my time grooming Bastion would be better spent giving orders to my worn-out soldiers? They've had a rough time and need to rest, not be pushed harder."

Rogan accepted the brush and went to work on his own mount. "Sir Golddrake, I would never presume to tell you how to handle your own Order, for I do not share all your convictions – though I believe our goals are the same." He sighed and averted his eyes.

"I was imprisoned with all manner of criminals for three years, and the similarities between them and typical soldiers might surprise you."

"Now you're comparing the Order of the Rising Moon to a band of thieves and murderers?" Amurel's voice rose enough that some of the men unloading supplies nearby stopped and took notice.

Rogan smiled at them, continued cleaning his horse's brown coat, and made sure to speak softly. "Of course not. What I am trying to say is that I had the opportunity to spend a lot of time observing men in situations where their spirits might be crushed at any moment.

"I know we were surprised on the road, and you did a noble job protecting the lives of your men, but after the way we left – the confusion, the haste, splitting up – uncertainty lies in the hearts of these men."

Rogan stepped closer to Amurel and placed a hand on his shoulder. "Show them *you* are certain. *You* are resolute. They need that more than they need rest." He paused for a moment before adding, "In my opinion," then resumed grooming his horse.

Amurel was considering the Baron's words when Sir Kilborn hailed him.

"You're always a step ahead, it seems," the knight said as he crested the last of the steps into the Caves of Criesha.

"Your age is slowing you down, old man." Amurel smiled. "I trust you found your way safely through the hills?"

"Aye, no sign of pursuit." Sir Kilborn eyed Rogan deliberately for a moment, but continued, "We lost a pair to their injuries along the way, and some time with it. We tried what we could to save them, but had no experienced surgeons around – messy business."

Amurel probed the inside of his cheek with his tongue and nodded as Sir Kilborn dismounted. "I don't suppose you found any sign of Lady Saffron or Jaiden?"

"None." Sir Kilborn withdrew a pair of hard biscuits from his saddlebags and handed one to Amurel before biting into the other. Rogan remained silent and continued grooming his horse. "I don't see how they could've made it past the Chelpians, even if she found him. She's a clever girl, I know, but I don't see the benefit of waiting around for her, either. She's not even one of us. And neither was he, yet, unless I missed the vows."

Amurel broke his biscuit in two and offered half to Rogan, who declined. "No, there had not yet been time for an initiation ceremony, but we care for the freedom of all, Geldrick. And I hold myself responsible for their safety."

"Well," Sir Kilborn posited between swallows, "all of our safety is in jeopardy until we find out more about the enemy's location. We don't want to be caught unaware here, or wander into a hornet's nest on the ride out."

"Agreed," Amurel replied. "We'll take the night at least to rest, and get a better sense of our losses. In the morning, I'll find scouts fit for deployment."

"I'll leave you two to talk," Rogan said, handing the brush back to Amurel. "I'm sure I can find something useful to do. Maybe I'll find a good spot outside to set a small signal fire for Palomar, something he could spot from the air; I wouldn't want him to miss us once it gets dark."

Amurel caught Rogan by the shoulder as he passed. "I'm sure he will show up soon. He's too remarkable to let himself get captured."

"Thank you. You are right, of course," Rogan added. Think about what I said earlier, Sir Golddrake."

Rogan took his leave to get the lay of the land and stretch his legs after uninterrupted hours of riding. The hilltop hideaway intrigued him. Though the rock walls and shadowy depths were reminiscent of the bowels of Blackthorn, where he spent years in hard labor, there were stark differences. The air was cool and circulated from the north end of the windblown peaks to the south – the prison had been oppressively warm and stagnant. Quartz and other crystals lay embedded in the cave's uneven surfaces, and the slanting radiance of the sun played off them to give the impression of a living space.

As Rogan circled the perimeter, he was surprised how far the cavern bit into the hillside. He borrowed a torch from some of the men opening barrels of foodstuffs preserved in the cool depths. The ceiling barely rose beyond arm's reach after descending further than fifteen paces, but there was room for three hundred men or more to bed down, if they kept close. The open maw of the cave led to smaller cracks and tunnels beyond the main chamber, and Rogan wondered if the Order had explored them all, or if unexpected encounters might still await an intrepid soul. He held no desire to find out.

Heading back to shallower depths, he decided to look for paths out of the cave other than the one they used for approach. He found no easy way, but a lip of rock at the southeastern edge of the cave continued out to a ledge, which wound around a boulder and onto a lessened slope on the lee side of the hill. Grasses and stubborn shrubs dotted the incline in a patchwork of dull green and brown. Even a few, mostly bare trees jutted out in defiance of the rocky terrain. Their trunks were twisted as if shaped by the wind, but their fallen branches supplied enough dry wood for Rogan to consider a signal fire.

He gathered what he could with one hand, still carrying his torch, whose flame whipped incessantly in the spiraling gusts. It took a while to find a usable spot shielded from the wind, but he stacked his wood and several handfuls of dry grass to serve as tinder. The sun had nearly fallen to the horizon and darkness would blanket the foothills soon enough, so he set his torch to the pile, lighting a signal fire he hoped Palomar might spot from the air.

It would have been easy to stay there, warming by the fire in solitude, resting from a weary day. Rogan, however, knew he had work to do. The soldiers could handle setting up the caves for their stay, but he had another agenda. He'd heard the rumors among the men during their retreat – many saw Palomar's arrival as a sign from their goddess. Using that, he'd been swaying them toward liberating Blackthorn Prison, telling of the other Aasimar imprisoned there. It was a half-truth, of course, but if the Master of the Order couldn't be convinced by Rogan's arguments, perhaps Sir Golddrake could be influenced by the desires of his own men. He wanted to reach as many as he could, and let the stew simmer before broaching the subject again with their leader.

When he returned to the cave, it was significantly more crowded than when he'd left. The south end had been designated as the kitchen, as the air current helped smoke escape from the cooking fires. Two huge cauldrons were nearing a boil, and he could smell the pleasant aroma of venison and potatoes being prepared.

Unexpectedly, he thought he caught a note of female speech from deeper in the cave. He wove around tired soldiers in the direction it seemed to come from, until he caught it again. Could it be? Hurrying toward the back of the cave, he broke through a line of men and there she was – Saffron, stooped over, inspecting a man's wounds with the aid of a lantern. Nearly a score of wounded men, actually, lay lined up in a carved depression of rock. Their backs propped against the smooth curve of the wall, Saffron appeared to be presiding over the impromptu infirmary.

She stood and addressed two eager-looking lads on the verge of manhood, designated as her helpers. "I need a kettle of hot water from each of you, needle and thread, and as many clean bandages as you can find."

"Yes, Lady," they intoned together, heading off to gather the requested supplies.

Saffron's eyes passed over Rogan's presence initially, then returned as recognition struck her. She smiled. "Baron Rogan, you are not easy to spot in this dimness."

Looking down, Rogan realized that next to the white tabards of the Order, his black and scarlet armor was especially unobtrusive in the frail light. "It is good to see you safe, Lady Saffron." He bowed his head. "Your long absence worried us all."

"It didn't worry me." The response came from the man Saffron had been inspecting.

"Pardon me?" Rogan cocked his head sideways in an attempt to see the speaker, seated behind her.

Saffron closed her eyes and blew a wayward strand of hair falling across her face. "Baron Rogan, meet Jaiden Luminere." She gestured to a dark-haired northerner with a brutal-looking injury to his right leg.

"Jaiden...ah yes, the one Sir Golddrake mentions often. I heard you were spectacular with a sword. A shame about the leg," Rogan gestured to his exposed, mangled thigh, where the blood-stained cloth had been cut away in preparation for treatment. "I've seen too many warriors fall before their prime."

"This one's going to get back up; I assure you that. Did you also hear how a goddess has chosen me as her Champion?"

Saffron shook her head and turned back to Rogan. "He has been through a lot. I am doing my best to help him mend."

"Of course." Rogan reached out and laid a hand on her shoulder, caressing it slowly. "I didn't mean to interrupt treatment. I would like to speak with you, when your obligations allow."

Jaiden pointed toward the subtle touching. "Hey, what was that?"

Rogan ignored him and smiled at Saffron, who huffed initially, before mirroring his smile.

A bustling amongst the soldiers caused Rogan to shift his attention, reluctantly, behind him. Before he could clearly see the cause, he heard it in his head.

"I knew I would catch up to you sooner or later, Baron."

Rogan perceived the accompanying toothy smile before the crowd broke wide enough to let the Aasimar into view.

"Palomar, you found us!" He stepped forward and embraced the angelic creature, much to their mutual surprise. "You managed to escape, unhurt?"

"*I did. Hopefully, I helped a few others do the same.*"

"Did you spot my signal fire?"

Palomar nodded, "*And put it out upon arrival. The last thing we need is an untended fire setting the entire hillside ablaze.*"

"What took you so long getting back? Your wings should've allowed you to bypass the difficult terrain."

Saffron stepped past Rogan to make herself seen, rubbing against his shoulder in the process. "Greetings, friend. I am pleased to see you safe."

"*Lady Saffron, I am delighted to be in your presence once more. Have you kept up your singing practice?*"

Saffron glanced toward her patient. "I found opportunities. Jaiden's leg was reinjured and needs attention, though. Would you like to assist in my operation?"

Palomar's eyebrows shot up. "*Of course, any way I can. How is Jaiden?*"

Rogan noticed Palomar's thoughts were in his head as well, though his friend was speaking to another. He briefly wondered whom else Palomar chose to include during their conversations. Could the whole cave perceive them now?

"Come see for yourself, he's right over here." Saffron led the Aasimar to the infirmary and Rogan followed, stinging she had not asked him to help, regardless that he lacked the desire to do so. The errand boys returned with their water kettles and clean bandages, as well as needle and thread to sew the wound shut.

Saffron confiscated a nearby lantern and lay out the supplies on an unrolled cloth beside Jaiden.

"My friend, it seems your valor has once again been costly." Palomar smiled broadly, a hard thing to do while looking at the remnants of the soldier's thigh.

"Palomar!" Jaiden and another, more distant caller, invoked the Aasimar's name simultaneously. Rogan and the others turned to find Sir Kilborn approaching, lifting his hand to draw attention.

The elder knight stopped short when he saw Saffron crouched beside Jaiden in the corner. "My goodness, you all showed up. Better late than never, I suppose."

"Greetings, Sir Kilborn. How are things with the Order?"

"They're downright sideways is how they are. Sir Golddrake would like to speak to you straight away to get your report. I imagine you as well, Lady, if you've anything to add. We're sending out riders at dawn." Sir Kilborn fidgeted, first with the fingers of each hand, and then with the end of his short beard.

Palomar extended his wings, spreading the feathers as if he were stretching, then folded them once more behind his shoulders. The movement caused Sir Kilborn to take a backward step. *"I do have news I think the Master should hear, but it will have to wait. I've promised to help Lady Saffron perform surgery, and it certainly looks like young Jaiden is in need."*

At the mention of his name, Jaiden raised the wineskin he'd been sipping, in preparation for the imminent incisions. "Just make sure the knife is clean, huh?"

"Be still, Jaiden," Saffron chastised, preparing to flush the wound with hot water.

Sir Kilborn's eyes moved from Jaiden to Saffron, Palomar, and finally Baron Rogan. "Very well, I suppose none of you actually *belong* to the Order, and are therefore not under my command. Whenever it pleases you," he snapped a stiff bow, "the Master would appreciate your input, so he might proceed determining the fate of all these men." He concluded by spreading his arms, palms raised, giving a deep grunt, and trudging off in the direction he had come.

Palomar's brows were arched over wide eyes. Saffron waved her hand dismissively, not even bothering to turn her attention from her task. "Palomar, can you grip tightly just above the knee?" The Aasimar knelt and did as asked.

Seeing he was no longer useful, Rogan went after Sir Kilborn. "I'll smooth things over," he called over his shoulder, certain no one was listening.

Jaiden took another long swallow of the wine as hot water washed over his wound. It scalded yet strangely soothed him, though he knew the worst was still to come. "I don't think I'm ready, Palomar," he said, staring straight into the golden pupils of the Aasimar. "I don't want to lose my leg."

"I am not going to take it off – not yet, anyway," Saffron scolded. "I am going to set it again, cauterize, and stitch it closed."

"*Perhaps this will help.*" Palomar sang.

The calming tune was similar to the one Jaiden had already heard on several occasions, but familiarity did nothing to wane its compulsion. Immediately the pain in his leg dissipated, and whether it was the wine or a new effect of the vocal variation, keeping his eyes open suddenly became a struggle. The last thing he saw before falling asleep was the white skin of Palomar's face, virtually glowing in the near dark. The image stayed with him as he began to dream.

Opening his eyes, Jaiden still saw Palomar in front of him, though all was quiet, save the distant movement of air. He noticed the accoutrements of his dream world – grey clouds constituting the floor and ceiling. Ample space surrounded him, though it was the lofty chasm of an immense palace, not the limitless night sky.

"This is odd." Looking down, he found his leg in perfect condition, though the goddess was absent.

Palomar shrugged. "You are dreaming."

"You, you spoke with your mouth."

"Indeed. Jaiden, you are at a crossroads." Palomar stood and walked toward a door at one side of the vast, open chamber.

Jaiden followed. "What do you mean?"

"You have spent most of your life trying to prove yourself. You are concerned with how others think of you, but mostly try to sway their view by seeking to impress them." Palomar stopped in front of the door and waited on Jaiden to catch up.

"How would you know, anyway?"

Palomar continued, resisting the bait. "You are eager to show people what they should think of you, while not allowing them to know you well enough to make up their own minds. This is a problem."

"Oh, is it?" Jaiden quipped, unsure he wasn't just arguing with himself. He had never dreamt of the Aasimar before. "I don't know, I think I have done pretty well so far, all things considered."

"You feel lost because you fear losing the very thing that made you stand out – your fighting prowess. I am here to console and also guide you, Jaiden. The key to life beyond fighting is to change your perspective on what brings you joy."

A lump grew in Jaiden's throat, and he had trouble swallowing. "What would you suggest?"

Palomar sighed. "I can tell you the turning point in my own existence – when I began to put the needs of others ahead of my own. When my efforts served another, I never partook in a useless endeavor. Every selfless action is filled with meaning." He nodded toward the door. "Go on, open it. There is nothing to fear on the other side."

Jaiden reached out and grasped the elegantly carved handle. "Where does it lead?"

"Open it and find out."

Releasing a controlled exhalation, Jaiden pushed on the door and as it opened, so did his eyelids.

Blackness surrounded him, but after a moment his eyes adjusted, and Jaiden noticed a scattering of dim lanterns around the cavern. He looked down at his leg, throbbing with every heartbeat, and saw it thickly wrapped.

I knew you would pull through, Jaiden," the Aasimar's warm voice glid into his mind.

Palomar was seated on the ground beside him, wide awake, while everyone else in the cavern seemed to at least be attempting to sleep. "How late is it?"

"*It is early, I think. Not yet dawn.*"

"Have you been here the whole time?" Jaiden carefully sat up and slid to prop his back against the cold, cave wall.

Palomar smiled, his bright teeth eerily visible in the dark. "*I do not need sleep as you. Meditation is enough to keep me refreshed.*"

"I had a dream. You were in it." Jaiden's eyes strained to catch any change in the Aasimar's countenance, but it was useless.

"*That is not surprising. My hands saw much of your blood.*"

"I was considering studying for the initiation, you know, to the Order. I know Sir Golddrake left us that scroll, but in truth, I cannot read." He was not embarrassed by this deficit, for he knew the majority of the infantry was also illiterate, but it was an obstacle to preparing on his own.

"*Nor can I – not your Ilanese, anyway. Luckily, Lady Saffron can, and she read it to me in return for the songs I have been teaching her. I would be pleased to assist you in your preparations. It would only strengthen my own resolve.*"

Jaiden swallowed hard past the same knot he'd encountered while sleeping. "I would appreciate that."

"*After breakfast, then? Baron Rogan convinced Sir Golddrake to wait until morning for council, but I don't think he'll put it off much past sunrise.*"

Jaiden could not hold back any longer. "How is my leg?" he blurted. "Is it ever going to get better?" Silence stretched out, intermingling with the dark. Finally, the deliberate, unsatisfying words filled his mind...

"Destiny will decide, my friend."

Chapter 13

Redirection

Rogan trailed Saffron into a deep recess within the Caves of Criesha. Her lamp provided just enough light to prevent running into a wall, though they had to step carefully on the uneven floor. Embedded crystals glistened like hidden fairies as the light struck them. Saffron's black hair was relaxed, unbraided, concealing her shoulders in dark waves. She looked only half-real in the dimness, an apparition perhaps, mysterious yet alluring. She could have been leading him down a tunnel to the Abyss itself – he would have still followed.

Finally, other lights shone ahead, and they passed through a narrow opening to a natural hollow forming a room at the end of the corridor. Far enough from the main cavern to provide privacy, the space was just large enough for the six participants to stand an arm's-length apart. Rogan kept closer than that to Saffron.

"I see we're the last to arrive," she said, holding up her lantern. Sir Golddrake and Sir Kilborn, as well as Lieutenant Orestes and Palomar, had already gathered. "I apologize if we've kept you – the night has been long on deed and short on sleep."

"I appreciate all you have done for the men, Lady Saffron," Sir Golddrake said. "These past days have been difficult, and that is why I have asked to speak with you all. We were not prepared for an ambush, having become used to choosing our battles."

"Do you think someone gave our position to the enemy?" Rogan saw that as a distinct possibility, but Sir Golddrake bristled.

"No, I do not. My soldiers are loyal to a man." He challenged Rogan with his eyes, but softened when no response came. "We must learn to be more vigilant, however, and take care, lest too much is said to outsiders."

Rogan opened his mouth, but Sir Golddrake stayed him with a raised palm. "Present company excluded, of course. I know you've fought long against the King-priest, Baron. I have seen your prison marking, and Palomar explained what it meant."

"What is your next move, if I may ask?"

"That depends on what the Aasimar has to tell us," Sir Kilborn answered. Five pairs of eyes fixed on the angel-winged council member.

"You are correct, Sir Golddrake – these have been difficult days. I do not wish to dictate the choices you make for your men, though I intend to become one, shortly. However, what I have learned may lead us to an agreement on proceeding."

"Well then, out with it."

Rogan raised an eyebrow at Sir Kilborn's eroding patience, but watched his unearthly friend simply glance at the aged knight with a calm smile. Did he speak directly to him, privately? Rogan wondered, but it was impossible to tell.

"As you know, once the retreat sounded I stayed behind, hoping to save as many of the wounded as I could from a likely cruel end. I carried several survivors, one at a time, and deposited them among the tall grasses south of the road. It was anguishing to choose, as many could have been saved.

"Yet, I knew time was against me. When I could risk it no longer, I claimed some rations and salves from a supply wagon, and flew to our hiding spot. There, masking my song with the wind, I commanded the growth to fold over and conceal us.

"We lay still for hours, listening to the cries of the remaining wounded as they were dispatched, until all grew silent and I dared forth to seek the enemy. The wagons were gone, though the bodies of the fallen remained, unburied – I fear that stretch of road shall remain haunted for an eternity."

Rogan shook his head at the recounting of wasted life, but Sir Golddrake's face remained a mask.

"I flew westward first, backtracking to see if any Chelpian forces lingered. With none to be found, I suggested the survivors take the supplies and make their way back to Greyhorne if they could, for there were bound to be foes along the east road, and cutting cross-country would prove hazardous in their condition.

"Once night fell, I flew high under the crescent moon, searching for the campfires of an army. It was only a few miles to their encampment. The cover of night could have concealed more, and I am unused to open war, but my guess puts their numbers at a thousand men.

"Resting my wings until dawn, I started north with the morning, to see if any of the enemy pursued you. When I found no signs, I made my way back to the road and continued north, remembering your scout's warning of another force lying ahead. It is true. A much larger force, three times the size by my count, travels north along the road. I stayed far off to avoid detection, but they were easy enough to see, clad in black and stretching for miles along the thoroughfare."

"How far away were they?" Sir Golddrake asked.

"If they kept moving, they would now be further north than we are. I followed for some distance, and detected no intention of leaving the road."

Orestes broke his silence. "They'll be on to Windhollow – get there before we can, even if we rode this morning."

"Aye," Sir Kilborn agreed.

"Damn." Sir Golddrake bit his lip and ran fingers through his golden mane. "The Duke of Rosegold won't be able to hold the castle against so many."

"Nor will we be able to help them, coming so late with so few," Rogan added.

"I'm afraid the Baron's right, Sir. We're short seventy-four men by my count. You know I'm no coward," Orestes continued, "but I've seen my share of battles and know the difference between brave and stupid. Marching on those hordes now would be a meaningless sacrifice."

Sir Golddrake nodded and sat on a stoop of rock jutting from the floor, resting his weakened leg. "What we need is time to replenish our numbers."

"Nay, we need to grow them," Sir Kilborn added. "We need all the provinces to band together and stand as one. We need a miracle."

Rogan knew the answer, of course, but he'd already shared it. Sir Golddrake had brushed his petition aside several times already, and bade him not speak of it again.

"I do not know if it would qualify as a miracle, but there is an obvious way to gain an advantage."

Sir Golddrake looked at Palomar expectantly. "By all means, speak. Or... share."

"Quite simply, Sir, my kin. Free them from their bonds and I will teach them the Song of Redemption. A flight of Aasimar would be a powerful weapon. Unexpected, to say the least."

"Oh, that again." Sir Golddrake shook his head and waved his hand. "I thought I was already clear that an assault on Blackthorn Fortress was a fool's errand."

"More foolish than your alternatives? You said yourself, what you need is time. This might draw the King-priest's attention."

"We tried that already with Salmarsh – it didn't make a difference," Sir Kilborn bit in.

"Salmarsh is not Blackthorn." Rogan could hold his tongue no longer. "I guarantee Ebon Khorel would notice an assault on a stronghold so close to his capital. Besides, it's looking more like you have nothing to lose. At this rate, how long do you have before your lands fall under his dominion?"

Sir Golddrake looked to Sir Kilborn. "When do you think he could reach Selamus?

"Pshh," Sir Kilborn pushed against the open air. "It hasn't come to that, yet."

"When?" he repeated, his tone demanding an answer.

Sir Kilborn shrugged. "Winter, maybe."

Rogan saw his chance. "I know it seems insane to you, but I spent three years in that prison, and believe we can take it. I believe we have to try. *I* have to try, and know it could make a difference toward your goals as well. You've seen how your own men respond to Palomar. They believe in him. Think what you could do with twenty Palomars as your allies. Recruits would flock to your banner." He shared a look with the Aasimar, and raised his brows.

Rogan read Sir Golddrake's hesitation as a sign to finish. "Let me plan it. I know my country well, and still have contacts who could help us. I could sneak back, alone, and make all the arrangements while you gather strength here and prepare to move."

Sir Golddrake looked at his longtime companions. "What do you think?"

Orestes answered first. "It is risky, but it may be our best chance to make a difference, considering our circumstances. I think the men would be behind it."

Sir Golddrake nodded and turned to his second-in-command. "Geldrick?"

"Aaah," Sir Kilborn looked away. "You know we're better defenders than instigators."

"Yes. But would we have a chance?"

"Only the Goddess knows, son. Only the Goddess knows."

Sir Golddrake turned to Saffron. "And you, m'lady. What do you think of such an endeavor?"

Saffron had remained virtually silent since they arrived. "I owe you for my freedom, Amurel, but my strongest obligation is to my blood. I believe I have a better chance to find her in a Chelpian prison than amongst the camps of their forward soldiers – though neither place would surprise me. If this is my best chance to find her then I will go, even if it means my death. I will do what I must to find Dhania; meager chances of success are an excuse for inaction, and hold no interest to me."

Sir Golddrake held her gaze for several seconds, but she did not blink. "Thank you all for coming," he said, finally. "I will pray on it."

When Jaiden woke again, Palomar was nowhere to be seen, and the distant light of day made a bright backdrop at the opposite end of the caves. He was hungry, but dared not stray from his straw pallet, lest the new stitches on his leg burst open. Furthermore, Palomar's song from the night before had worn off, leaving even the slightest twitch of his thigh agonizing.

Looking around the depression, he counted about a dozen other wounded men, all likewise stranded. He didn't recognize any of them, but thought about his dream the night before. Perhaps helping someone else might take his mind off his own troubles, but where to start? The soldier to his right was fully reclined and had bandages wrapped around his forehead. His hands were on his chest and his fingers were moving, so at least he was awake.

"Ho, there," he called. "My name's Jaiden. Jaiden Luminere. What's yours?"

No response came, save the continued tremor of his digits.

"I do not think he can hear you," blurted the man to Jaiden's left. "He hasn't moved for hours."

"What about his hands?"

"Yeah, odd isn't it? He took an axe to the head during the fighting. He seemed all right the next couple days, and then, well, you can see."

"Oh," Jaiden said, craning his neck for a better look at the reclining man's face. "That's horrible." He turned to assess the man who had spoken. He was sitting up, too, his tunic split down the middle. White cloth looped around his midsection, and his hands pressed on his stomach as if to keep his insides from spilling out. A crimson stain soiled the cloth behind them.

Following his eyes, the man offered with a strained voice, "Sword to the gullet. All things considered, I think I'd rather be him," he nodded back at their comatose companion. "Where's your friend with the wings? It would be nice if you could get him to sing one of them songs again."

Jaiden hadn't considered how much worse his situation could have been. "I, I don't know."

"Well, I hope he decides to come back. That song was relaxing."

"Excuse me!" Jaiden called to a lad passing by. He was about Tikvi's age. The boy stopped and looked at him, but did not speak. "Would you mind terribly bringing us some breakfast? Not feeling the most mobile at the moment."

The boy nodded.

"Oh, and could you fetch Palomar if you see him? He's the tall man with the gold eyes and white, feathery wings."

The boy looked at Jaiden as if his hair were on fire.

"It's fine, I'm a friend of his." The uneasy look persisted. Jaiden sighed, "Don't worry, he won't bite – just tell him Jaiden's looking for him."

The lad scurried off, leaving Jaiden unsure if either request would be met.

"I am Fhezwick, at your service," said the man with the punctured stomach.

"Fhezwick? That's awful, who named you?"

The soldier shrugged, shrinking back.

"So, Fhezzy, what shall we do so we don't die of boredom?" Fhezwick was low on ideas, so Jaiden sat with his stomach grumbling for the next quarter hour, watching the rest of the camp go about its business.

The intrepidness of young boys was riding high that morning, however, and Jaiden received favor on both counts. Palomar approached, savior-like, balancing a bowl of warm broth in each hand. *"A messenger told me of your hunger."*

"Palomar! Great to see you."

"Have I been absent so long?" He handed one bowl to Jaiden and the other to Fhezwick, who nodded his appreciation.

"You have no idea." Jaiden glanced at his neighbor, who was already slurping down his meal by the wooden spoonful. "I have to have something to do. I wondered if you might teach me some of what I'll need to know for initiation."

"Certainly."

"First, though," Jaiden averted his eyes from Palomar's, "do you think you might sing another song? My leg feels like it's burning, and it helps the other patients as well."

"Of course." His words seemed tinged with sadness, but once the Aasimar intoned his Song of Soothing, the pain in Jaiden's leg receded. When finished, he sat cross-legged in front of Jaiden, and opined about the strictures of the Order of the Rising Moon.

"First thing you need to know, and probably commit to memory, are the 'Five Corners' of the Order. They are the foundation principles that guide our behavior, and the symbolic reason the Order of the Rising Moon carries pentagonal shields, by the way. I've been told by Lieutenant Orestes that we shall receive our personal shields upon completion of the Swearing Ceremony."

"Well, that will be nice."

"Honor – it is imperative to remain honest and fair in all dealings, even with adversaries. Loyalty – all commitments, whether to others or the ideals espoused by the Order, must be faithfully maintained. Courage – even when facing grim odds, bravery and fortitude are essential. Obedience – dutiful compliance to recognized authority is demanded. Charity – generous actions to aid the less fortunate should be our daily bread."

Jaiden felt the weight of responsibility just listening to the words. "You already memorized all that?"

"*It is not so much.*"

"Perhaps not for you, but I am used to doing things my own way; never really had much use for rules." Jaiden thought of the nights he was recently robbed, accused of cheating at cards, and then kicked out of a brothel.

"*We have not even come to the rules yet, Jaiden.*" Palomar laughed, but it was with his true voice, not conveyed through telepathy, and it had a metallic aspect Jaiden found surprising. "*Think of these as the challenges we face in our everyday behavior. Some will come easily, but we all have our shortcomings. Mine, for instance, has always been obedience. No doubt there will be Corners to work on, but at least you have courage mastered already.*"

Jaiden reached down and smoothed his hand over the space where his thigh had once been whole. "Aye, or stupidity."

Palomar squeezed out a tight-lipped smile.

Jaiden swallowed hard. "I think 'Charity' might be my biggest challenge. That is where I will start."

"*Sounds like an excellent idea.*" Palomar stood. "*You should eat your broth before it cools further. We can continue the lessons later. Sir Golddrake has been meditating on whether to assault Blackthorn, and I am eager to hear his decision.*"

"You want us to go? It would be an excellent chance to test our mettle."

"*I admit I am being selfish. I do not think I can sit by much longer without trying to free my kin. Baron Rogan feels the same. I would be more hopeful if Sir Golddrake were with us.*"

"Will you let me know what he decides?"

"Certainly. Be well."

"Thank you for the song!" Jaiden called out as the Aasimar took leave.

"I didn't want to interrupt, but do you often have conversations with yourself?" Fhezwick asked.

Jaiden dismissed him with a roll of his eyes. "It's called 'telepathy'," he mumbled, no longer looking in Fhezwick's direction. "Boy!" he called to the same lad he had harried earlier. This time the page was passing by with a rag, whetstone, and tin canister. He stopped, looked over at Jaiden, and his shoulders sagged before changing course.

"What have you got there?" Jaiden asked as he looked over the boy's armful of contents.

"I am to sharpen and oil the swords, sir."

"You don't have to 'sir' me. Anyway, it is your lucky day. Give me what you have, and bring me a lantern and the blades. I will tend to them. It will at least give me something to occupy my time."

The boy hesitated. "I—"

"Hurry along now, before I change my mind." Jaiden accepted the load from the boy's arms, and without any questions, he scampered off to gather the inventory of weapons. He returned a few moments later, though he was unwilling to leave the task solely in Jaiden's care. The two of them spent hours honing and oiling the Order's steel, until it was sharp and well preserved.

Palomar did not return until the following midday, and by then, word of Sir Golddrake's decision had already spread through the camp. Jaiden heard the news from Lothander, who came to visit once he tracked down sightings of Jaiden to the infirmary.

"There has been a change of plan, my friend. Have you heard?" he said.

"Blackthorn?" Jaiden guessed.

"That's right." Lothander's face fell a little, as if he had missed an opportunity. "We are no longer marching to Windhollow Castle, but heading south into enemy lands. It will mean a few more days in the caves, unfortunately."

"We do not go immediately?"

"Nay, the Master is staggering our departure. We will travel in secret," Lothander's hands were demonstrative as he spoke, "in smaller groups to avoid detection, and not all of us are going. The Order is splitting to help maintain the ruse. The rest will stay up north and regroup at Selamus. Apparently that Baron fellow from Chelpa is heading down first to make some arrangements. I hope he does not betray us – but, the Master trusts him well enough. He has befriended the Aasimar as well, so that's good enough for me, I suppose."

"Hmm, I wonder," Jaiden said. That was *not* good enough for him, and he was eager to change the subject. "Have you still got those Skirmish cards?"

Lothander's eyes lit up at the prospect. "I have them in my pack."

"Perhaps we could play a few rounds with the men here?" Jaiden motioned to his fellow patients. "It's awfully boring sitting here all day."

"I know what you mean. We have only been allowed outside in shifts to avoid attracting attention. I shall return shortly."

The hours passed more quickly as they played, and Jaiden tried hard to learn the names of his remaining wounded compatriots. The patient to his right was gone when he woke that morning, and Fhezwick informed him he had not survived the night. It gave Jaiden a shiver to imagine it could have been him. Would anyone remember his name?

When Palomar returned, the game had already wound down, and he promptly apologized. *"I am sorry, my friend, but I could not come sooner."*

"Don't let it worry you, Palomar. I'm a grown man, and it's not your job to look after me."

"But I said I would return when I heard news, and I did not. Sir Golddrake had a mission that demanded my immediate attention."

"I understand, truly. Say, would you help me stand? If I don't get at least a little sunshine I think I might wither away." Jaiden reached out for Palomar's grasp. Just as the Aasimar bent to assist, however, he was chided into stopping.

"Oh, no you do not!" Saffron commanded. "He is not moving from that spot until I put this on him. I have worked too hard to see all my efforts undone by your infernal impatience, Jaiden."

She was nearly upon them by the time Jaiden spotted her out of the darkness, leaving him unsure precisely where she sprouted from. She carried what looked like a leather sleeve draped across one arm, and carried a brass vial in her opposite hand.

"Lady Saffron," Palomar arose.

"What are you putting on me?"

"Relax, Jaiden, this will help." She knelt directly between his legs. He could smell the perfume she wore, subtle as it was. He looked upward and tried to find some distraction in the shadows as she tore away the fabric from the already split right leg of his trousers.

A moment later he felt her rubbing a cool ointment onto his bare leg, and it was too much for him. Without looking, he felt his arousal taking hold, a tightness growing in his undergarments. Why did he keep ending up in these positions? Saffron was going to think him some sort of aberration. His face flushed, though it was probably too dark for her to notice... no way she would fail to notice what was happening below. Was Palomar watching, too? Jaiden shut his eyes, wishing he could just disappear entirely.

Saffron said nothing, however. She worked her way down his leg, until almost its entire surface was slick with the treatment. Then, she worked the sleeve over his foot and up his leg. "Pull it tight," she instructed, though the sharpness of her voice had been replaced by a tint of compassion.

Jaiden opened his eyes and looked at his leg, realizing the purpose of the endeavor. The leather sleeve fit snugly over his leg, with a hole cut out for his kneecap. He grasped the top and pulled until it was finally in place.

"There," Saffron said. She began working her way up the crisscrossed cord on the side of the sleeve, pulling it tight, then tying it off at the top. She rocked back on her heels when finished, admiring the result. "Not a bad piece of work, if I say so myself."

"Did you make this?" Jaiden asked, immediately aware how helpful its binding support would be for his leg. Overwhelmed, he fought back the sting of forming tears.

"That I did. I took measurements the other night while you were sleeping." She stood, her work done. "I am leaving in the morning with Baron Rogan, and wanted to be sure it was complete."

"You're leaving?" Jaiden felt a rush of concern he could not explain, overpowering his unexpressed gratitude.

"Aye." She looked at Palomar for some reason. "Sir Golddrake wanted someone to go with the Baron, and I want to look for my sister, so I volunteered. Besides, we can masquerade as a couple, which should lower suspicions."

Jaiden's concern exploded into full-fledged panic. "Is that a good idea? I mean, what if it is some sort of trap?"

"Trap?" Saffron's face was painted with confusion. "I know it may be perilous, but I shall manage."

Palomar bowed to her. "*Successful journey, Lady Saffron. Practice your songs when it is safe to.*"

"I will," she nodded in return. "I have made progress. Perhaps I can show you when we meet again?"

"*I look forward to it.*"

"Good evening, then. I have much to prepare for the morrow. Take care of that leg, Jaiden."

"Thank you," he finally managed to say as she smiled and walked away. Then, to Palomar, "What am I going to do? He's going to be alone with her for days, maybe weeks!"

"*You are going to learn the expectations of the Order, one of which is chastity, so you can put all those thoughts,*" he pointed at Jaiden's still-bulging erection, "*out of your mind.*"

"Oh, what do you know about it? Are there even female Aasimar?" Jaiden sighed and grasped the sides of his head.

After a moment of silence he looked back at Palomar, who stood with arms crossed in front of his body. "Go ahead, you might as well tell me the rest."

"Indeed. The Order of the Rising Moon prohibits the accumulation of personal wealth, demands obedience to Criesha and her anointed leadership, and obligates you to defend the weak. You must fight for the protection of relics and places sacred to the Goddess, freedom from oppression, and the destruction of the unnatural."

"Is that all?"

"All I can remember at the moment."

"Good. Palomar, could you do me a favor?"

The Aasimar uncrossed his arms. *"Has the pain returned?"*

"It has, but that can wait."

"What is it?"

"I need you to help me outside, locate Lothander, and tell him to bring me a lute. I've got some practicing to do."

Chapter 14

The Birth of Fire

Baron Rogan checked his pack one final time, though it seemed everything was accounted for. He could not shake the feeling, however, that he was forgetting something.

"Are you ready?" Saffron asked, hoisting her own pack onto her back. She was wearing heavier, less colorful clothes than usual, per his suggestion. He couldn't remember seeing her in anything other than a skirt, actually. Rogan knew these gray pants and tunic weren't her style, but they needed to blend in, and her typical choice of garb would instantly mark her as a foreigner.

"Aye, let's be on our way."

Sir Golddrake and Palomar were standing at the entrance of the Caves to see them off. Rogan and the Aasimar clasped wrists in farewell.

"May the sun shine ever at your back."

"I do not know what that means, but I'll take it," Rogan smiled. "All will be fine – I am going home, in a way." He turned to Sir Golddrake. "Give us a week, and then start sending your men. No more than twenty at a time. Hunting parties, remember?"

"Understood. May Criesha illuminate your path," he touched his fingertips to his forehead, then drew them away. "Be safe, Saffron...I hope you find your sister."

Saffron leaned forward and kissed Sir Golddrake on the cheek. She waved farewell to Palomar, but shared no words. Rogan thought he saw dampness in her eyes.

With the sun still concealed behind the western mountains, they began down the winding trail on foot. Horses would not be a boon on the sloping terrain, and once they made the River Chelhos they would have to abandon them anyway.

They traveled light on rations in favor of remaining armed. Stealthy as they hoped to be, neither was naïve enough to forfeit the reassurance of a weapon. Rogan brought his saber and uril-chent dagger, while Saffron kept a long-knife and bow for hunting. She preferred a spear but he forbade, knowing it would bring too much attention.

Saffron retraced the paths through the hills she had taken with Jaiden, heading for the Harpy Pass. They moved with greater speed, though, unburdened by injury or the care necessitated by laden animals. Rogan kept up, though his guide's spryness impressed him. They spent the first day on a pace that precluded much conversation.

They stopped only a few times to drink and share a biscuit, for Saffron drove them hard toward the dusk. She seemed to grow stronger and more alive the longer they went. Saffron remembered the several streams she crossed on her first trip, and waited until they reached one to allow them rest, though the sun was merely a glow beneath the horizon. By the time they made camp, Rogan was exhausted and famished.

"This country is beautiful, is it not?" she asked, as she struck up a campfire. Rogan paused from laying out his bedroll to take a look around. The hills were mostly silhouettes against the dim, pink sky, but the air was crisp and fresh, smelling of pleasant plants he could not identify.

"I suppose," he shrugged. "I spent half of my free life in cities, the other around my manor in Thispany, mostly."

"And what was it like there?" Two strokes of her steel and she'd caught a spark on her tinder.

Rogan drew nearer, ready to warm his hands by the growing fire. "More damp," he said, sitting cross-legged on the dirt. "Lush greens, though. The soil is rich in the midlands. Most of our land was farmed, but a bit of wild forest painted the northern edge. My father would take us hunting there, even as young boys; I fell in love with it. I continued even after my parents passed on, and looked forward to taking my son when he was old enough."

"You had a child?" Saffron asked, one eyebrow and the pitch of her voice raising simultaneously. "You have not spoken of him before."

Rogan forced a weak, toothless smile. "I lost him the night I was arrested by the King-priest's men, along with my wife."

Saffron studied his face. "I am saddened to hear so. I have never been married, but my brother died when he was very young, and I saw what it did to our mother. No parent should have to survive their offspring."

Rogan sighed, trying to keep his pain packed beneath the surface. "This world can be a harsh place. All we can do now is honor their memories with our actions."

Saffron reached over and grasped the edge of his hand, giving it a gentle squeeze.

"So, what about your homeland?" Rogan asked, anxious to change the subject. "I am sure these were not the circumstances you had in mind when you left to journey abroad, but I do not recall hearing any stories of Begnasharan. Is it much different than here?"

"Ha, nothing is the same, Baron." She let go of his hand and gestured upwards. "The sky has not so many clouds, the earth is dry, and there are many places where dunes have overrun to the horizon. But, we have cities, too. Life clings harder where I come from. Everything is precious, nothing wasted.

"I was lucky enough to be born into a family of privilege, but I take nothing for granted. The desert will polish the bones of a wealthy woman just as quickly as a peasant. When I was very young, I heard a woman playing the lyre as I wandered the bazaar with my ma-ma. That was when *I* fell in love, as you did hunting. I begged her to buy me one so I could play, and cried for three days when she refused. Finally, pa-pa said he did not want to see me dry up into a pillar of salt, and purchased one." Saffron smiled.

"I played every day. I played until my fingers bled. I got quite good, and in not so long a while, I was playing before the Caliph."

Rogan could not help but smile, seeing her so animated. "Wonderful. Is that what led you here?"

She cocked her head to the side, then down, her voice falling with it. "Music was supposed to be a way to see the world, and I begged my parents to let my sister come along." Saffron shook her head. "She is young, younger still than perhaps Jaiden." Mentioning his name, she laughed and rolled her eyes. It did not escape Rogan's notice.

He swallowed hard before speaking. "How long have you known him?"

"Whom?"

Did she really think her nonchalance would fool him? He cleared his still-pesky throat. "Your patient."

"Jaiden? Not long, I suppose we met a few weeks ago, if you could call it that. He was near-dead – nearer than now, anyway. I do not know why Sir Golddrake makes such a fuss over him; supposedly he has an important destiny."

"Is that so?" Rogan asked, incredulous.

Saffron shrugged.

"And what do you suppose my destiny is?" He leaned back on his hands, wondering if she would play along.

She reached into her pack, sitting on the ground beside her, and retrieved some travel rations. "Unfortunately, I am no fortune teller." Instead of a prognostication, he got another cold, hard biscuit. "Sorry, it is too dark for hunting now. Perhaps once we hit the lowlands."

As they ate their meager dinner, the wind made more noise than they did. Looking toward an early start the next day, Rogan suspended his attempts at wooing and curled up on his bedroll, close to the fire. "Good night, Lady Saffron."

"Good night, Baron Rogan." She was still up, gazing at the stars, when he drifted into a chilly, lonesome slumber.

Their second day in the hills saw a similar pace, and Rogan wondered if they were indeed feeding from the same store of rations. Saffron seemed to have boundless energy, far outstripping his. She gave no notice of his struggles, though she took pause from time to time to inspect one flower or another, and remarked on how various and beautiful the blooms in the high country were.

He took those opportunities to catch his breath, and it was always too soon before they were off again. She seemed to have a firm grasp of the topography, and showed no concern when their waterskins got low. Sure enough, before they were empty, a creek or reservoir would be right around the next hillside.

The afternoon was wearing on when Saffron finally stopped along a high ridge to take in the view. "Ah, there it is!" When Rogan caught up, he peered over the edge and saw the road.

"Well, that is a sight for sore eyes. I think I've got half the mountainside stuck in my boots."

"We should be able to make the Harpy Pass early tomorrow, if we keep on through moonrise. Our pace will be much quicker once on the road."

Rogan groaned inwardly. How could it be any quicker than it was? After they navigated down the final hillside, he stopped to remove his boots. Sure enough, a fine collection of rocks tumbled out when he shook them. "So, what do you think about hunting? Or have you not tired of those biscuits yet?"

"I think straying from the road will cost valuable time, as long as the surrounding territory still has elevation. Once we cross into Chelpa, there is a wood not too far south that should make a good hunting ground."

She was right, of course. Rogan remembered the location she spoke of from when they fled Salmarsh. He was good and ready for some meat, though, and started salivating at the thought of spit-roasted venison.

His thoughts were interrupted by a lonesome howl echoing through the hills. He shared a look with Saffron and they both held still, listening for a response. It came a moment later, though some distance off. "You are right, hunting can wait. We should get down to the road and put some miles on it before nightfall." With no argument, they did precisely that.

Walking was less taxing on the steadier grade of the trail, which cut between steep slopes. Rogan realized they were probably only a league or two west of where the Order of the Rising Moon was waylaid, and he wondered if the soldiers Palomar rescued had made it safely past this point on their return to Greyhorne.

The wind picked up considerably during the night, extinguishing the small fire they built for warmth. The slapping of tree branches against the stone cliffs woke Rogan, though the clouds were so heavy he could see little in the absence of their blaze. He barely made out the shifting of shapes in the dark, and was about to call out to Saffron when she surprisingly dropped her bedroll directly beside his.

A moment later she was lying next to him, pressing closer until he felt her back against his chest. He said nothing, but draped his blanket over them both, and put his arm around her, hugging tightly. Cold as it was, he eventually fell back asleep with her hair against his cheek, her unique scent filling his nostrils and infiltrating his dreams.

It was still dark when Rogan woke again, this time from something hitting his face. He stirred but brushed it off, not yet alert enough to realize what was happening. A deep breath later no doubt remained, as the heavy clouds that rolled in the night before dumped their load with sudden vengeance.

They both jumped to attention and rolled their bedding as quickly as they could. Rogan was thoroughly soaked by the time he slung on his pack. He looked to either side of the road, devoid of obvious shelter, the sky menacing as far as he could see. Though difficult to judge, he guessed it was near dawn.

Between bursts of lightning he could see the back of Saffron's hair woven into its customary braid, though the front clung to her face in wet tendrils. She pointed down the road in the direction they were heading, as the pounding rain nearly drowned out her speech. "We might as well keep moving – we can't get much wetter than we are."

Rogan nodded, agreeing, but unhappy with the circumstances. They jogged westward toward the Harpy Pass, as if speed could outrun the falling sky. After several minutes of splashing they gave up, succeeding only in tiring themselves and splattering mud on their clothes.

They resumed the previous day's pace, and even though the sky brightened minimally after dawn, the sun remained hidden behind perpetual clouds. The rain continued, unabated for what Rogan counted as the longest hours since escaping prison. They saw no other soul upon the trail, though that was not unusual in this part of the country, even when not in the midst of a deluge.

The elevation climbed again as the Pass cut through the true base of the Wyvernwatch Mountains. Sir Golddrake warned them to be vigilant for brigands. The Harpy Pass was a favorite detour of smugglers, and provided a multitude of outcroppings with access to the path.

Finally, with the danger of landslides and flooding growing into a serious concern, the downpour relented. Rogan was sure everything he wore or brought with him was hopelessly water-logged. With no sun showing to warm the air or their skin, the travelers started shivering in their wet clothes.

"What do you think, should we build a fire and dry out our belongings?" he asked.

"What are we going to burn? Everything is as soaked as we are."

"We need to get out of these wet clothes, Saffron, or we'll catch a fever long before we reach the river. Let us at least check and see if we have anything dry to wear."

"Certainly."

Setting their packs on a low ledge of the abutting cliff faces and opening them, they sifted through the contents, testing anything made of cloth for relative dampness.

"Nahh," Rogan groaned, finally giving up. "Nothing salvageable. I'll have to wait until we can make camp and get a fire going to hang it all."

"Perhaps you should learn to pack better," Saffron said, pulling out one of her traditional long skirts and waist-baring tops, which had been folded together inside the fleece mantle she brought. "Not the proper outfit for this weather, but it will be warmer than wearing these wet things. Look away, please." She turned her back to him, removed her jerkin, and peeled off her knitted shirt.

Mesmerized by the smooth, tan lines of her back as her arms stretched over her head, Rogan found it impossible to immediately do as asked. As her torso rotated slightly to pull her dry shirt over, he caught the swell of her right breast, and finally shut his eyes. His breath quickened with the image fresh in his mind. He had not been with a woman since his wife, and had not felt the urge until meeting Saffron.

Rogan listened as she pried off her boots and wriggled out of her wet breeches, his imagination supplying what his lack of sight denied. A long moment later she declared it safe to look, and he caught her tying the saturated clothes onto the back of her pack. She had donned the same desert-red outfit she'd worn the first day he saw her. It left a lot of skin exposed, though he knew it was more suited for the hot winds of her homeland than this chilly mountain pass.

Neither complained of the cold, however, as they moved on. Rogan did not see the sun directly until it had dipped below the clouds, though no more rain fell. By then he was looking for a place to camp, rarely holding such anticipation for a simple fire. A break in the ubiquitous vertical rock of the cliff offered a promising spot.

A flat shelf, wide enough to support a small copse of majestic pines, rose a body-length above the level of the pass. The back end ascended steeply up the mountain, but it was traversable on all fours if necessary. Rogan told Saffron to wait while he scrambled up the rocks to scrutinize the area more closely. He particularly wanted to inspect for footprints in the mud, lest any highwaymen used the spot recently for an ambush.

He had yet to turn up anything when another wolf's howl broke the easy silence, much closer than the ones they'd heard in the hills. It came from the east, behind them, but more startling was the response that sounded somewhere just beyond sight, on the other side of the northern cliff. This was answered by still another nearby canine – they were being hunted.

"Get up here!" he called to Saffron, racing to the edge of the shelf to give her a hand. A pair of wolves bounded down a tight alley of fissures in the northern rock face, sprinting straight for Saffron as she grasped Rogan's wrist.

One of the animals leapt on her back as he lifted her, causing her feet to slip and collapsing her onto the rock. The wolf snagged the stave of her bow in its maw instead of her neck, ripping it from her pack as it fell back to the ground. Her wet clothes came with it, temporarily draping the wolf while Rogan hoisted her the remainder of the incline.

"Are you hurt?" he asked, swinging her over and out of the way. The second wolf leapt and gained purchase on the slope, almost making it onto the shelf before Rogan kicked it down with the sole of his boot. The beast yelped, then joined its partner in snarling and pacing below.

Rogan drew his saber as two more wolves came running down the trail from the east. "What are our options?"

Saffron stood and looked over the edge. While the drop was not excessive, all it would take was a turned ankle to doom them. "Unless you hope to outrun wolves, the sword may be all that is left." One of the wolves made another lunge upward, but retreated when Rogan slashed in its direction. "I could shoot them if you want to retrieve my bow."

"I will have to pass. What we need is a wounded calf to wander by and distract them."

"Or fire," she said, trailing off, as if an idea had taken root.

Rogan could not afford sparing the attention to decipher her thoughts. The wolves tried fervently to ascend the shelf, one after another, and his hands were full keeping them at bay. They were learning, too. After swinging his saber at one, a second would leap during his backswing.

Out of the corner of his eye he saw Saffron bend over, busy with something – he hoped it was helpful. One of the wolves bit the bridge of his boot and he overreacted, trying to shake it off. His preoccupation left an opening, and another wolf took it. It brushed past him, and he lost his balance trying to swing at it. "Saffron!"

She turned and rolled right as the wolf lunged for her. It knocked over the pile of kindling she had assembled, and snarled as she gracefully pushed herself up and drew the knife from her boot in one, fluid motion.

Rogan knocked the wolf from his own boot with his other foot, and stole a quick glance toward Saffron – he could not let her come to harm. He struggled to push back from the ledge and stand, feeling suddenly clumsy. The wolf growled and circled Saffron, assessing, its mane bristled in threatening display.

She began to sing in Begnari. Rogan could not imagine a more odd time to break into song, but just as he made it to his feet, another wolf came scampering up the ledge. He had no choice but to focus on repelling it, or the shelf would soon be overrun. Three more wolves arrived and howled as if claiming victory.

Suddenly, a flash of red lit up the shelf, and the wolf opposite Saffron let out a horrid, whining yelp. It dashed past Rogan and down the ledge, its fur on fire! He looked at Saffron in wonderment. She was still singing with arms extended forward, the knife in one hand, the other, palm out. She was staring at her open hand as she took careful steps to the edge of the shelf. In it, a tiny blossom of pure flame grew, until its petals opened. Saffron pursed her lips and blew, sending the fire bloom shooting toward another of the circling wolves. It cried out as the flower struck it, immolating the fur of its hind quarters.

The two ignited animals ran off in panic, while the others circled and howled in confusion. Rogan wanted to do the same.

He had seen Palomar evoke spectacular effects from his singing, but he was a being from another realm. This was Saffron!

He waved his blade and yelled at the animals as menacingly as he could manage, and sure enough the wolves took off after their departed pack-mates. Saffron ceased her song as soon as the retreat was complete, then stood with a blank expression, as if also surprised by what had just happened. A moment later, though, it shifted into a pleased grin.

"How did you do that?" Rogan asked as he embraced her, relief that she was unharmed washing over him.

"Magic," she replied, almost laughing the word. She let their bodies remain close for a few seconds before stepping back. "Please, you are still soaking wet."

"Oh, my apologies. I'm glad you're safe, that's all... since when can you do magic?"

"Palomar says I was touched with the gift, and only need to learn how to use it. We've been practicing, but I've never been able to control it like that." She said no more, but her eyes were alight with a wonderful secret she appeared unready to share.

Saffron sheathed her knife as he put away his saber. "I am not sure I will be able to sleep tonight, but we should still set up camp if you think it safe. We need to get you out of those wet clothes and warmed."

"I feel plenty warm now," he laughed. His heartbeat was still at double speed. "We can keep watch, and get a fire going. I don't think those same wolves will trouble us again if there is any sign of a flame."

"I will get started on the fire," she winked. "Could you retrieve my bow?"

"Of course. I suppose hunting will have to wait another day. How are we doing on those delicious biscuits?" He climbed down the ledge to the road and found the bow, which had fallen into a ravine during the commotion. Luckily, it seemed to have escaped damage. He gathered her fallen clothes as well, and by the time he hoisted them up and climbed the shelf himself, Saffron had a small fire burning.

"I don't know how much tinder is available here. Most of the wood is wet, so we should take advantage of the flame while we have it. I'll look about for more dry branches."

While Saffron scouted the area, Rogan hung a length of his rope between two tree trunks near the fire. He unpacked the two changes of clothes he brought and strung them over the line to dry. Once they were up he stripped, so he could hang those garments as well.

When Saffron returned to the campfire's halo with an armful of wood, she nearly dropped it. "What are you doing?" Her eyes were closed by the time he turned to face her. She was standing in place, holding a pile of pine twigs and branches.

"I'm drying out my clothes. Don't worry, I left room for yours as well." He suddenly remembered how she had asked him to turn away while she disrobed, and her meaning dawned on him. "Oh, forgive me, I did not mean to offend." Surrounded by men for so long, in prison and during the rebellion, he had forgotten the modesty required by female companionship. He grabbed his still-damp blanket and wrapped it around his waist. "I'm covered now," he offered.

She opened her eyes slowly, dubious of the truth. "Baron Rogan, do I need to remind you we are not betrothed?"

"I am aware, m'lady."

"Hmmm." She stacked the wood next to the fire to dry, and stuck another branch into it. "Please act like it, then. I shall take first watch." Saffron spread the contents of her pack and hung the wettest garments on Rogan's line, while he ate his dinner rations in silence.

Worn out and unwilling to start an argument, he curled up as close to the fire as safety allowed, and tried to get some rest. As he drifted off to sleep, he heard Saffron humming a gentle tune, which put him at ease.

The night passed without a return of the wolves. Saffron woke Rogan for his shift, and he spent much of the time either tending the fire or watching as she slept. He had the sinking feeling that bringing her along was going to lead to trouble, but he also knew he was powerless to refuse when she volunteered to accompany him. Her presence was, quite simply, invigorating.

Morning came with their clothes less damp, if not their spirits. He hoped things would improve once they got out of the Pass and into more open country. He would have given half of Thispany for the flank of a wild boar. It would be a hard thing to go another full day with only those cold, hard biscuits to eat – and few of them remained.

The slope of the trail started declining around midday, proof they were almost through the mountains, and the adjacent cliffs gave way to less steep abutments shortly thereafter. By mid-afternoon they bid farewell to the Wyvernwatch, though they intended to follow its roots westward as far as the tongue of the River Chelhos. No established path existed to guide them once they left the Harpy Pass, but Rogan assured his companion he would not lead her astray.

"Just keep the mountains within sight to our right, and it's hard to go wrong. Now, are you going to put that bow of yours to use, or should I? There is a promising wood to the southwest, there."

Saffron, back in her traveling breeches and tunic, unfastened her bow and quiver and handed them over. "Since you enjoy it so much, why not go ahead. You certainly have more experience stalking the animals here. Besides, I want to investigate some plants. This region is mostly unknown to me, and awaits discovery."

Rogan was not about to argue, as his stomach eagerly anticipated a hearty meal. He gladly took the bow and made his way toward the young forest. "Meet me at the tree line in roughly an hour," he called back, already setting his mind to the hunt. He wanted to avoid distracting thoughts of Salmarsh, which lay only several leagues to the south. They did not have time to investigate, but he hoped the townsfolk had not fared too poorly in the wake of the Blood Tear's retribution.

It took him a shade longer than an hour, but he assumed Saffron would not begrudge him the time, given his success. He managed to bring down a second-year buck. When he emerged from the canopy of the woods, he whistled to alert Saffron, and began preparing his prey for cooking.

She emerged within minutes, carrying an assortment of leaves and stems, and congratulated him on his kill.

"I will get a fire going," she said, happily.

"I'll filet some thin strips we can salt and store for later." Rogan wanted to show Saffron she was not the only one who thought ahead. "I brought an empty sack for such a purpose. Anything there useful for cooking?"

"Perhaps you could tell me. A couple of them have pleasing scents."

They spent the next few hours preparing, cooking, and eating the venison, flavored with a bit of green onion. When they had eaten their fill and packed away as much as they could justify carrying, Rogan suggested they relax until their meal digested. He sat cross-legged and removed a piece of folded leather from his shirt pocket. Saffron, lying nearby, perked up when he removed delicate splinters of bone from inside the leather.

"What are those?"

"Lockpicks," he answered as he polished the tools with a soft, black cloth. "Xyanarind ivory," he explained before she could ask.

Saffron watched him at work for a short while before reclining once more. "Do you know how to use them?"

There was a challenge in her tone, but he could also hear the smile on her face without looking. "Of course. I am an outlaw, remember?" He did not mention he made them himself from a comb that used to be his wife's, or that polishing them was soothing, because it made him think of her. When he finished, he knew it was time to go.

The day turned quite warm and they shed their outer garments as they walked through green fields of high grass. A fine afternoon for a lazy stroll, Rogan allowed himself to pretend he was doing just that, and not heading toward enemy territory on a dangerous mission. The fantasy was all the more appealing with Saffron at his side. She showed such curiosity for the tiny marvels of spring he took for granted. Her presence was an almost cruel reminder of the possibilities life held before his path altered, but he made no effort to push such thoughts away.

Chapter 15

Talon Barge

Finally south of the road, they maintained a steady, but leisurely pace, managing good time across the gently rolling terrain. For four days they crossed open-skied pastures, meadows of wildflowers in bloom, and small wooded groves, until at last the firm ground gave way to spongy turf. They were nearing the snaked tongue of the River Chelhos, fed by Lake Pelmar high in the peaks of the Wyvernwatch Mountains.

"I know a small settlement on the river where we can acquire a rowboat for a few silvers," Rogan mentioned as they trudged through muddy swampland. "We will have to be careful once other people are around. You should speak as little as possible."

Saffron opened her mouth to respond, but he answered her unspoken objection first.

"You look unique enough as it is. If others hear you speak, there will be no doubt you are a foreigner, and that will just bring questions. Chelpians, especially since the King-priest took power, are a suspicious lot. We don't want more attention than we can help. In fact," he said, reaching around to grab her braid, "this will have to be undone. You should wear your hair over your shoulders. Better yet, let as much fall over your face as possible. It will help conceal your features."

"All right, stop pawing at it! I can fix my own hair." She ran her fingers through its strands to expand it, then tousled the edges until it became tangled. "There," she said, "does it look unsophisticated enough for you?"

Rogan sighed, unsure her fiery attitude was going to allow them to pull off the charade. He could not help admiring her wild, uncompromising spirit, regardless of whether it might get them thrown into prison. Deciding not to waste more effort attempting to subdue her expression, he accepted he would simply pay the consequences as they came.

Evening was thick upon them when they finally reached the settlement – more a homestead than true village. Lanterns were lit to help with finishing the day's chores.

"Wait here," Rogan instructed as they made their way up the line of a crooked fence. The cabin ahead had the look of a fisherman's place, with extra nets hanging on wooden frames in the yard and an upside-down, dug-out canoe resting against the side of the building.

A man with weathered skin, his back permanently bowed from patient hours waiting for a tug on his line, sat on a bench in front of a low table down by the water's edge. Several fish were spread across its surface, and the man proficiently worked his knife through them, one-by-one, gutting and scaling.

Rogan raised his hand in greeting as he approached the fisherman, trying to look as non-menacing as possible with a saber sheathed to his belt. The man raised his head to look at Rogan, but never stopped his knife's work. He peered past Rogan to account for Saffron, then once again bent to consider his task.

"Good evening, sir. Well met."

"Not many strangers come around these parts, and none that don't come from the river."

Rogan couldn't find a question in the man's observation, but decided that being direct would serve him best. A rowboat already floated in the water, tied to a mooring. "I understand. My wife and I don't mean to stay longer than we have to. We need passage down the river, and I was wondering if we might make a purchase from you, if you have a spare boat. That canoe against your house, for instance?"

The man stopped gutting and looked up. They locked eyes, and Rogan did his best to maintain the contact without challenging.

"I suppose you'll be needing a spot to spend the night and some fresh fish for dinner as well?"

"I would be obliged, sir."

"Mmhm." The man chopped off two of the smaller fishes' heads, then held their bodies up by the tails and handed them to Rogan. "You can take the canoe and use the shed in back for shelter, though it's shaping up to be a fine night out in the yard, too. If anyone asks, they're gifts. Of course, you can leave a donation on the porch – we don't get taxed on donations."

"I understand. Thank you for your kindness." Rogan carried the fish back to Saffron. "Don't ask," he said as he nodded toward the fisherman's back yard. "We should be safe to camp here tonight, and have some variety in our bellies."

"I was not complaining. Do we have transport for tomorrow? I look forward to resting my feet."

"Aye, that dugout against the wall. He offered it up rather easily; we shall have to inspect it for holes in the morning."

"Maybe it was the fact you are wearing a blade and he did not want any trouble?" she offered.

"Perhaps. I think I'll sleep lightly tonight." Rogan exhaled and adopted a happier tone, "For now, let us fry up these fish. You have some of that lemongrass left, do you not?"

Saffron bit her lower lip and nodded, then set to rummaging through her pack.

Reclining on their bedrolls by the crackling fire in the afterglow of their meal, which was so tasty Rogan relaxed his suspicion of the fisherman's motives, he noticed how noisy a spring evening in the wetlands truly was.

Croaks and calls from bullfrogs and insects created a discordant symphony all around them. It was strangely comforting, though; a lullaby sung by an anonymous thousand, who he preferred stay unseen. Yet, falling asleep proved difficult. Saffron had no such trouble, but Rogan's mind was busy worrying about all the ways things could go wrong once they reached Talon Barge. He would be exposing himself in one of the busier cities in the Empire – the King-priest would no doubt have eyes and ears everywhere.

Finally, he stared into the fire, hoping it would make him weary. He would gladly give his freedom, if it meant succeeding in his cause. He owed that to the Damper who offered him a second chance at life, though Rogan knew it was never as simple as trading one thing for another. He had to execute his plan precisely, for so much hung in the balance – the hopes of Saffron, Palomar, and the lives of all the soldiers he was bringing along on his quest. Rogan was getting the chance he wanted, though it came with so much responsibility.

Sleep eventually arrived, but between the frogs and his busy mind, it was far from restful.

By the time Rogan arose in the morning, the fisherman had already departed. At least, his rowboat was gone. Saffron was down by the river, lurching over their new canoe, its front half bobbing with the current.

"No holes," she informed him.

He nodded and shook the sleepiness from his head. "I was only joking about that." Still, her mouth was tight with concern. "Are you truly worried?" He approached the riverbank, his boots squishing into the soft ground with every step. "I am sure it is a perfectly reliable vessel. What, have you never been on a boat before?"

Saffron rose to look directly in his eyes. "Once," her voice was distant with memory, and barely loud enough for him to hear, "on a slave barge, across this very river."

Rogan did not know how to respond. Finally, he simply nodded. "This trip will be much different."

After returning to the shed and packing his bedroll with haste, he withdrew his coin purse and sifted through for what he thought would be a generous, but fair donation. The fisherman made things easier than they could have been, and Sir Golddrake gave him plenty of funds to secure arrangements prior to the Order's arrival.

Rogan left his coins on the porch as instructed, setting a stone beside them to mark their presence. His debt paid, he pushed the remainder of the canoe into the river, jumping inside as it broke free of the muddy bank.

Saffron in front and Rogan behind, they each took up a paddle and maneuvered toward the faster current in the middle of the tongue. She fumbled a bit at first with the unfamiliar motion, but Rogan was patient, and with regular communication they achieved a fine rhythm. Ultimately, it mattered little, for the journey was completely downstream and the flow of the current accomplished most of the work on its own.

Once safely in its grasp, they pulled their oars in, and Rogan relaxed. "Just sit back and enjoy it, Saffron. Not much in this world is more peaceful than drifting down a river with the sun shining overhead. I will steer us if necessary."

"Indeed, I have missed the sun." She bent forward and flipped her hair in front of her, clearing it from her neck. Loosening the front of her shirt just enough to pull it past her shoulders yet remain modest, she let the rays warm her sandalwood skin. "How long until we reach the city?" she asked, her voice barely reaching him from her lap.

"The way we're moving, a few hours at the most."

They spent those hours mostly in silence, alone in their thoughts. It was barely past midday when the port of Talon Barge came into view. The River Chelhos widened at the joining of the tongues, and still the city bulged well onto its waters. Watercraft aplenty navigated into port, bringing cargo of goods and visitors alike.

The wharfs bustled with fisherman, merchants, dock workers, and customers. A well-known destination for all sorts of contraband, it was the most popular place in the Empire for acquiring unusual items.

Seabirds circled in hopes of stealing untended fish or bread, as Rogan guided their boat toward the area designated for fishermen. He paid some coppers to a local for letting them dock alongside his rig, and watching over their boat for at least a few hours.

"We should start by finding my contact, Cyril." Rogan had to yell to be heard over the multitudes bargaining on the wharf. "He will get us situated in town, and hopefully be able to make all the arrangements we need."

Saffron nodded, doing her part by staying silent as much as possible. She kept her head rigid as she followed Rogan, though her eyes were busy taking in all there was to see. They both kept on the lookout for anyone wearing the insignia of the office of the King-priest, or the telltale black of the Blood Tear Brotherhood.

Rogan wove through the crowd with a deftness indicative of his experience navigating the largest population centers of the realm. Once they made it past the warehouses of the docks, the streets became more orderly and less like a mash of hermit crabs all scrambling for the same shell.

In the merchant district, cobblestone streets replaced the boardwalks of the adjacent docks. Rogan searched the signs of shops as they passed, looking for the *Silver Trumpet*. Passersby occasionally leered at him or Saffron, but nothing indicating intent beyond sizing up his potential as a mark, or admiring the beauty of his partner.

At last he spotted the store, and in the doorway beneath the sign, stood Cyril. Rogan reached back and took Saffron's hand, pulling her with him across the alleyway.

"I hear you've got a giant tortoise you're looking to get rid of," Rogan jibed as he strode up to the blind side of his old acquaintance.

Cyril turned, surprised, but laughed when he saw who was speaking. "Rogan, you old dog! How in the Nine Hells are you? I would have wagered ten-to-one I'd never see you again, once I heard you ended up in Blackthorn."

"Shhh, do not say that so loudly out of doors." Rogan was only half-jesting. He was well aware this was not the safest place for him. Still, he thought it proper to make introductions before going inside. "Cyril, may I present Lady Saffron. Saffron, this is Cladius Cyril. Are you still a viscount, or have your titles all been stripped as well?"

"Oh," Cyril groaned in an exaggeratedly gruff voice. "You don't know the half of it, Rogan. Very pleased to meet you, Lady

Saffron. You are clearly too good for the company you keep, but I shall not hold it against you." He winked.

Rogan tugged lightly on the man's full, dark beard. "What is this on your face, huh? Been attacked by some sort of river rat, have you? What do you say we talk more indoors?"

"Certainly," Cyril responded, swinging open the door to the *Silver Trumpet*. "Come in, come in, and welcome to my showcase of exotic wares."

All three stepped inside the shop, and Cyril closed and locked the door behind them. No one else was inside at the moment, through wondrous trinkets and baubles were displayed throughout the space.

"I was just waiting on a delivery when you walked up. My man should be here any moment – do not mind the intrusion. He doesn't speak much Ilanese, but it's an important shipment. I am keeping the store closed until he gets here."

"May I look around?" Saffron asked. "The brasswork reminds me of home."

"And where is that, exactly?" Cyril cocked one eyebrow as he assessed her. "Wait, let me guess...Begnasharan?"

Saffron looked over at Rogan, then lowered her eyes, shameful for keeping up her disguise so poorly.

Rogan pursed his lips and changed the subject. "Have you been back to Lucnere recently, my friend?"

"Ahh," Cyril pushed the air with his hand, "why would I want to do something like that? With this 'northern conquest' in full bloom, you're likely to walk in a free man, and walk out conscripted to the army. I tell you, Ebon Khorel has just about pinched the last drop of decency out of the capital. It's getting bad here as well. He's got a secondary palace built just downstream, probably to keep a closer watch on what comes in and out of the docks. 'Hope's End' it's called, and that's the gods' truth.

"So, I am guessing they did not let you just walk out of Blackthorn, no?" Cyril continued. "What does an outlaw baron need so badly he would risk coming within the shadow of his enemies?"

Rogan's smile faded and his eyes set firmly on Cyril. "It may take a while to explain, and I do not wish to interrupt your business. Perhaps we could come back after you close tonight, and discuss it over a few bottles of wine?"

"Ooh," Cyril groaned as before, taking a seat on a high, wooden stool. "Why does this sound like it ends with me doing you a dangerously big favor?"

"Nothing I wouldn't be willing to pay you handsomely for." Rogan took a step toward the door and Saffron ceased her browsing to join him. "Tonight?"

Cyril nodded. "Aye, an hour after sunset. I'll bring the wine."

Rogan turned the bolt on the door and reached for the handle, when Saffron conspicuously cleared her throat. He looked back at her and raised his eyebrows.

"Dhania?" she hissed a whisper.

"Tonight, Saffron. Trust me," he whispered back. "There is someone else I need to see first." He raised his voice to give a final "so long" to Cyril, then led them back onto the streets of Talon Barge.

"What is it?" Saffron questioned.

"Cyril can do a lot of things for us – he knows a lot of people. But, he knows a lot of people, if you catch my meaning."

"I do not." Saffron crossed her arms and stopped following, waiting for Rogan to explain himself.

He sighed and took her by the shoulder, guiding her along to keep moving while he talked. "Asking after the whereabouts of a particular Bengnari slave girl is most likely going to require Cyril talking to a few a sources himself. I certainly did not want to have that discussion in front of his deliveryman, had he shown up. The sort of people who can provide answers about slaves are either slavers themselves, or people who work for slave owners. In your sister's case, that owner is likely to be the King-priest."

They rounded a corner and took a side street leading toward a district where the buildings were more crowded, allowing less light. "We don't want to attract that sort of attention before we even find out if Cyril can help us with smuggling Sir Golddrake's men down the river. I need to make sure he's still a viable option, and setting up a meeting was the start. There will be no point in stirring up a fuss and drawing scrutiny to our intended operation until I speak to my other contact, anyway. That's where we are headed now."

"I am glad you know what you are doing," Saffron admitted, "because I would have handled this entire situation another way. So, who is this other contact?"

"He, uh, is a little less savory than the viscount." Rogan stopped in front of an unmarked door. They were no longer in the merchant district, and the smells of piss and vomit wafted in from the nearby alley. "Maybe you want to stay out here?"

Saffron shook her head. "I do not think so."

"Very well." Rogan knocked on the door five times, three quick ones followed by two spaced out. He heard a bar sliding out of position, followed by a hollow thud. The door budged inward a few inches, and a pair of eyes stared from the darkness beyond. They looked from Rogan to Saffron, silently deciding, before the door opened wide enough to step inside.

The antechamber was pitch-black, but a rectangle of light opened as their host whisked back a curtain, leading to a larger room. Rogan held his tongue as he followed their silent guide, hoping Saffron would know enough to do the same. The room beyond the curtain was hazy with heavy smoke, and the person who let them in joined a dozen others who were puffing out of long, curved pipes.

A similar number of bodies were strewn about the room in varying states of consciousness, lying on mats or cushioned benches. Some stared at their own fingers as if they didn't belong to them, while others entwined with one another, leisurely touching the exposed flesh prevalent among both the men and women.

A few individuals in the room remained astute, and Rogan strode purposefully toward one of them. He was a thin-framed, middle-aged man, sitting in an armless chair, wrapped from ankle to neck in what appeared to be a burlap suit. The soles of his feet were pressed together, jutting his knees outward. His hands remained motionless in his lap, but his eyes followed Rogan's progress as he crossed the room.

Kneeling on the floor in front of the man, Rogan spoke softly to him. "Kasim, it's me, the Baron."

The man cracked a smile, revealing a mouth with very few remaining teeth. He nodded, slowly.

"Kasim, the time has come. We're going to liberate Blackthorn, but I need to know if you can get a message to the Dampers. Do you still help with the deliveries into the mines?"

Kasim turned his right arm over and lifted up his sleeve, revealing a skull-shaped burn scar, but still said nothing.

"All right. When you pick up the next shipment, I need you to find Corbin. He's been a prisoner there forever, everyone will know him. Tell him – now this is very important," Rogan clasped the side of Kasim's face and stared straight into his eyes, making sure he appeared lucid. "Tell him, 'The Mating Day Ceremony will be bittersweet this year.' Can you do that? Will you remember?"

Saffron tapped Rogan on the shoulder, "Do you have any confidence in this man?"

Kasim saw her face and once again gave a tooth-challenged grin.

"I do. Kasim is a good man; he will not let us down." He patted Kasim gently on the side of the face and stood. "Well, that just about does it here. Time for us to leave. Let's find a place to eat dinner, then we can head back to the *Silver Trumpet*."

Saffron shrugged. These were, after all, not her people.

After finding their way outside, Rogan once again took the lead, taking them back toward the wharf. He had a surprise for Saffron to help with the homesickness he imagined she must feel. During his last visit to Talon Barge, during the winter freeze, he had come upon a small eatery among the docks, serving Begnari cuisine. He had not sampled the food himself, but he wagered it must have been months since Saffron had eaten any native fare.

Before long and without too much trouble, he was able to find the spot, and luckily, it was still in business. Saffron's eyes lit up and her hands clasped over an open mouth when the cook rattled off the available dishes. She gave Rogan a heartfelt hug, and her eyes teared up.

He mentioned he was paying, and she proceeded to order three meals so they could share and sample some of her favorites. All of them were spicy and flavorful, and though Rogan had trouble pronouncing the names of the dishes, he was content to eat sparingly and simply bask in the abundant happiness Saffron exuded. He knew then that he wanted to go on making her happy, a feeling previously reserved for Riah. The thought excited and frightened him.

"So, how exactly did you conjure that fire, back with the wolves?" He hoped she would've spoken of it on her own before now, but decided it was as good a time as any to ask, in part to distract from his upwelling of emotion.

She squinted at him for a moment, looking intense, before slackening and shrugging casually. "It was my song. Palomar has been teaching me, but that was the first time I succeeded. My guess is, it was the danger."

Rogan wanted more. "How does one simply sing fire into existence? I cannot."

"Nor could I, before then." She took another bite of the pastry she'd chosen to cool her palate. "According to Aasimar lore, there are seven, key note combinations tuned to either the deep consciousness or the elemental planes." Witnessing the incredulous look across Rogan's face she added, dubiously, "I know."

"Each of these note combinations is a trigger for turning what comes next in the composition from possibility to reality. Every singer, therefore, has seven possible manifestations of magic. The key is not only pairing the correct combination, but constructing a song that will not only tap into the power of one's will, but describe, in a very specific way, what the manifestation will be.

"I have been working on several compositions, but nothing quite came together until the wolves. I suppose I hadn't been feeding it enough of my will – that is what Palomar said was always the trickiest part for new singers. Now that I know what it feels like, I should be able to put my other songs to the test."

Rogan leaned back in his chair, marveling. How could he not believe it? He had seen it happen, and grown used to Palomar's power. "Well, let me know when you figure out what else you can do."

Before long their stomachs were full, though it was still a chore to pull Saffron away from the table with remnants of her native dishes dotting the plates. The sun had set, however, and it was time to visit Cyril once again. "Let me get through the negotiations for Sir Golddrake before you mention your sister," he warned. "I know how important she is to you, but this is going to be expensive as it is, and we do not need to give him any more leverage."

"I thought Cyril was your friend?"

"As close to one as I have in the business world, but trust me, this is still about business to him." Rogan took them back to the *Silver Trumpet*. The crowded streets were already thinning as citizens headed home in advance of the government-imposed curfew. From an hour after dark until an hour before dawn, only agents of the King-priest were allowed to roam the major cities of Chelpa.

The viscount was waiting just outside his doorway, and ushered them in with due speed. He glanced both ways down the thoroughfare before closing the door behind them, which he immediately bolted shut.

"How were sales today? Did your new shipment arrive as scheduled?" Rogan could not have been less interested in the mundane transactions of the shop; he knew it was just a front for Cyril's real business, the sale of information and movement of black market merchandise. He thought it wise not to let Saffron onto how personally involved his contact was in such matters, lest her emotions become their undoing.

"Oh yes, things progressed smoothly today," Cyril answered. "But of course, curiosity about my old friend's visit preoccupied my thoughts most of the afternoon."

The shop was in near darkness – only a single brass lamp, resting on the counter, illuminated the space. Cyril took it and continued toward the back of the shop, where a flight of stairs rose to the second floor. The light, pale though it was, reflected off dozens of shiny objects lining the shelves. Saffron leaned to get a better look, even as they left the baubles behind.

At the top of the stairs, Cyril unlocked a sturdy, wooden door, reinforced with iron edges. He replaced the key in a pocket inside his vest and swung the door open. "Welcome to my War Room." Rogan glanced about as their host busied himself lighting a candelabra and more lamps. Like a large attic, the room was packed tightly with the viscount's exotic spoils.

In the center was a round, wooden table, so well-polished its surface shone like glass. Six high-backed chairs, carved with intricate tribal designs, were arranged around it. Several large, stuffed creatures were mounted on stands, fierce and strange combinations of tusks, fur, and scales, unknown to Rogan. Two open coffers boasted piles of gold coins and jewels, and three similar chests sat with lids closed.

Suits of armor, painted shields, and exotic weapons encircled the table at a respectful distance, and numerous crates and boxes lined the walls, too far beyond the light's reach to share the secret of their contents.

"Please, take a chair." Cyril waited until his guests were seated before joining them. He picked a chair beside Saffron and leaned closer to her, feigning the need to hear Rogan better.

"You have an impressive collection." Rogan nodded as his head continued to swivel around the room. "I presume this is all contraband?"

Cyril shrugged. "They are items of interest to me. But enough of that, what is it you came to see me for?"

"I was hoping you could get us the use of a ship."

"That is easy enough," Cyril said, tucking his upper lip beneath his lower. "Where is it you wish to go?"

"Not far at all, just down the River Chelhos." Rogan decided to play coy as long as he could.

"Well, then I do not think you need me, my friend. There are a number of downstream ships taking on passengers every day."

Rogan leaned closer himself, mimicking Cyril. "Ah, but we need a ship for a hundred men," he whispered, then sank back in his chair. "And their horses," he added. "And the whole process needs to be handled beyond sight of the authorities."

Cyril sank back as well. "I see. Yes, that is more of a problem."

Rogan shrugged. "That is why I came to you." He gestured to the contents of the room. "I know you have a way of... getting around problems."

"Mmmm," Cyril hummed as he thought. "That would take a galleon – too big. I would have to split you into two ships. When would you need them?"

"We would depart at midnight, a full day before Mating Day," Rogan answered.

"That would at least give me a few weeks..." the viscount seemed to be speaking to himself. His attention suddenly snapped back to his guests. "Where are you going with an army, Rogan?" He looked at Saffron, "Who are you really, Lady?"

"This has naught to do with her," Rogan cut in. "She has other motives, which we will get to shortly. Let us talk price." He drew a small sack from his belt and dropped it on the table. The sound of the gold coins clanking within drew Cyril's focus back to the negotiations.

"Assuming I can return the ships to their owners in good order, I could do it for a thousand."

"A thousand gold crowns! You have lost your wits, my friend."

"How badly do you need these ships?" Cyril crossed his arms over his chest.

"Whether I need them badly or not, I cannot afford a thousand crowns. Are you looking to retire? Five hundred is all I can manage, and for that pretty sum, I will also need you to find housing for the men and horses as they arrive in Talon Barge."

Cyril roared with laughter. "Oh, I see perfectly. Taking advantage of an old friend, is it?"

"You know very well it could have just as easily been you in that prison, Cladius." Rogan's tongue was suddenly sharp. "I, who lost everything, never said a word."

Cyril clenched his jaw as he considered Baron Rogan's plight. "You are going to Blackthorn, aren't you? That is what this army is for – your revenge."

Rogan kept his mouth shut and Saffron looked from one man's face to the other, perhaps waiting to see who would burst open from the tension first. Finally, Cyril relieved the pressure with a long, heartful sigh.

"I wish taking a hundred men to battle would bring them back to you, I really do. All right, I will take your five hundred, but I also want whatever uril-chent is available, should you succeed in taking Blackthorn. Are we agreed?" Cyril stood and held out his hand.

After a second's pause, Rogan clasped it and they shook. "Agreed."

Not another second passed before Saffron spoke up. "There is a favor I would ask of you as well, Viscount Cyril." Both men turned their heads and looked down, having forgotten for a moment Saffron was still present.

"What would that be, my Lady?" Cyril sat back down and took the opportunity to place his hand on Saffron's knee.

She looked down at the unwelcome intruder, but restrained from forcibly removing it, forcing a smile instead. "I was hoping you could assist me by locating my sister. She and I were both taken as slaves when our caravan was attacked by the King-priest's men several months ago. We were separated, and while I was later liberated, I have not seen her since."

"An all-too-common tragedy under the current regime, I am afraid." Cyril's hand tightened on her knee. "How would one pick her out among all the other slaves, if they were to go looking?"

Saffron straightened her posture. "Her name is Dhania min-Furasi. Our features are similar, though she is three years younger. Her hair was a hand-length shorter than mine, and I have not cut it since we were separated. She is a shade shorter than I, unless she's grown."

Rogan took over, "She is a young, Begnari woman. Beautiful, from an educated family. I am sure she stood out to more than one lecherous eye. She would have commanded a heavy price, so you can start with wealthy slave-owners. She would have been taken in winter, during the slow season, so the records should be lighter."

Cyril removed his hand and stood. "I would be honored to look into the matter for you." He winked at Saffron. "Now, it is after curfew, so you shall stay here for the night. There are living quarters downstairs, beneath the shop, and I keep several spare rooms. Please, accept my hospitality."

Rogan stood as well, putting his hand on Saffron's back to guide her toward the stairs. "That is very kind of you, and we are more than happy to take advantage."

"I will get started right away trying to find your sister, Lady Saffron min-Furasi." Cyril gave what Rogan interpreted as a reassuring smile.

"What about the curfew?" Saffron asked as she reached the door.

Rogan answered for him. "Our friend Cyril is the sort of man for whom the curfew does not present a problem."

Cyril laughed as he closed and locked the door behind them. "Well put, Baron, well put."

Chapter 16

Only as Good
as the Armor

Rogan stayed in bed for a solid hour after waking, luxuriating in the feel of a proper bed. He could not remember the last night he had slept on anything so soft. Moments like this, he dearly missed his life as the Baron of Thispany. He was waiting to hear back from Cyril, and would likely spend the next few days bored, until the Order of the Rising Moon began arriving at the *Silver Trumpet*.

Staring at the ceiling, brushing his hands over the cool sheets, he could envision the other alternative quite clearly—the King-priest's soldiers bursting in to arrest him. It would only take one question asked to the wrong individual, one secret action witnessed, or one unaccounted-for motive for the entire mission to go horribly wrong. Between his old acquaintances, Saffron's zealotry toward rescuing her sister, and the Order's penchant for honesty, enough variables existed beyond his control to keep him nervous. Rogan felt the pressure bearing down on him like the walls of his old cell in Blackthorn.

Yet, for the moment he had a soft bed, a roof over his head, and access to good food. He would try to enjoy the illusion of peace while he could. Eventually, he heard footsteps pass his room and start up the stairs, and decided it was time to rise. It would be unwise to let Saffron stumble into trouble on her own.

After dressing, he found her perusing the shop on the main floor. Other customers browsed as well, but Cyril was nowhere to be seen. A woman he did not recognize was minding the store, so Rogan lured Saffron back downstairs to join him for a late breakfast in the kitchen. He was hungry, but his primary concern was reiterating the importance of limiting their exposure to the untrustworthy inhabitants of Talon Barge.

"I was not going to leave the *Trumpet*," Saffron reassured him. "Not until you woke up, at least."

Rogan shut his eyes and sighed, before gazing directly at her. "I know we walked about freely yesterday, but now others are acting on our behalf, possibly stirring up unwanted interest. We simply cannot risk drawing attention and having someone follow us back here. Not until we know more from Cyril, at least. There is too much at stake now."

"Fine! But you do not have to explain it like I am a child." Saffron snapped off a bite of her toast, staring Rogan down.

She chewed thoroughly before swallowing. "Cyril had better show up soon."

Rogan endured uneasy silence for the better part of an hour before their host finally materialized, and was mildly surprised to find him vibrant and wearing different clothes than the previous evening. He had assumed his contact spent the entire night out, gathering information and making arrangements. "Welcome home," Rogan said, stifling his incredulity. "You certainly have some skip in your step."

"I always possess verve on such spectacular mornings. The sun is shining, the birds are singing, and I stand to make an absolute fortune once I get a hold of that uril-chent ore." Cyril embraced Rogan, "The King-priest has held a monopoly on the stuff since it was discovered. You cannot imagine what one crate would sell for at auction."

He kissed Saffron's cheek, drawing a flinch, and handed her a wildflower with yellow petals. "I have good news for you as well, Lady." Cyril cocked his head sideways and corrected himself. "That is, of course, depending on how you weigh the first part against the second."

Saffron grabbed ahold of his vest with both hands, appearing ready to shake the information out of him, "What is it?"

"The first part is — it seems terribly likely your sister is nearby. My man remembers a Begnari girl being brought in to the slave markets around the time you described. Ebon Khorel apparently thought highly of her appearance, and decided to keep her in his own harem. Perusal of the records indeed fails to show a sale was ever made." Cyril swallowed hard and Saffron released his vest.

"What does that mean?" She looked from Cyril to Rogan, waiting for an answer. "Where is she?"

The viscount took a step backward before explaining further. "It means your sister is probably still a part of the King-priest's personal stable of slaves. It is doubtful she was sent all the way to Lucnere, so she most likely resides at his palace of Hope's End. It is on an island, merely half a mile south of Talon Barge, in the middle of the River Chelhos."

Rogan's chin sank to his chest. He knew Saffron's mind.

"I am going after her. Rogan, we have to go after her."

He could not look her in the eye, though he felt hers on him. He shook his head, still not meeting her gaze, knowing how tenuously balanced their efforts toward the liberation of Blackthorn were – and how hard it would be to tell her "no." Breaking into the King-priest's palace was an invitation to disaster. "Saffron, I know how much she means to you."

"Do you?"

His head snapped up.

Saffron's voice quivered as she spoke. "I am the reason Dhania was even on that caravan. I told our parents I would look after her. Can you imagine what she has been going through, every day, since she was taken?"

Rogan's mind flashed back to the night he was arrested. Once again he was in his manor house, being forced to watch as his wife was bent over the table. He shook away the memory, and could barely find his voice. "I know."

Tears streaked down Saffron's face as the guilt surfaced. Rogan also knew what that felt like. She wiped her cheek and took a moment to compose herself. Rogan could see her deciding what to say next, and realized that even if it meant burning the world down, he could not stand in her way. He had mused in prior weeks that Sir Golddrake's code was his weakness – now he realized Saffron was his.

"Rogan, I am rescuing my sister, no matter what. I know it would be easier if you were with me, but I will not ask that of you. I do not wish to jeopardize your mission to help the Aasimar, but Dhania needs me, so I am going."

He could not stop her, so how could he refuse to help her, since abandoning Saffron would certainly lead to her capture? The three of them stood silently in the kitchen for what seemed like a hundred heartbeats. Saffron was waiting for Rogan to say something, and Cyril apparently dared not move a muscle until he did.

"Viscount, I am going to need to borrow those fifty crowns I gave you last night."

"Of course, Baron. I know you are good for it." Cyril forced a smile.

"Lady Saffron, there will undoubtedly be fighting to do, so we are going to need armor, and I know just the man for the job. My friend," he turned to Cyril, "I will need to know as much as possible about the palace's protection before we leave."

"Of course, I will have my man do some reconnaissance."

Rogan and Saffron borrowed a pair of chestnut-brown cloaks from Cyril, donning them before departing. With hoods up, they took to the streets of Talon Barge once again, heading to the Arms Quarter. Rogan knew the area would be swarming with Chelpian forces, and more than one agent of the Blood Tear Brotherhood.

Control was the King-priest's obsession. Nowhere was this more evident than the industries that fed his war efforts. Smithies, craftsmen, and engineers had been forced to work for Ebon Khorel; those who resisted were either shut down or arrested for treason. Of course this coercion bred resentment, and Rogan had found that wherever strong wills toiled, submission was never complete.

Early in his days as a resistance fighter, he had forged an alliance with a particular armorsmith. The only thing Natrone loved more than his work was the chance to see it used against the King-priest. He filled his orders as necessary to avoid the wrath of the Dread Tyrant's mouthpiece, but he kept his best work for the rebellion. Natrone had a particular affinity for working with leather, and he had designed the armor Rogan normally wore. Unfortunately, he had not brought the suit on this trip, unable to justify the extra weight in his pack, or the chance of being recognized.

The Arms Quarter of the merchant district was heavily populated by soldiers, and more rigorously guarded than the rest of the district and the docks combined. Rogan knew they risked being stopped simply because they were not soldiers. He made sure, before they left, to put a few coins in a smaller pouch in case they were searched, or he needed to negotiate a quick bribe. He would have left Saffron behind, had the task not required her presence for measurement.

"It is absolutely imperative, Lady Saffron," Rogan mentioned on the walk there, "for you to remain silent and take my lead during this outing, no matter how much discomfort it brings you. Are we agreed?" He received no response beyond a searing stare. "Excellent."

A short iron gate marked the entrance to the Arms Quarter, and a guard stood at attention beside it. His spear looked sharp and his shield polished, but Rogan approached with confident strides.

"State your business, civilians." The guard's dour expression carried over to his intonation.

Rogan tried to match it. "We are inspectors for the Crown. His Majesty has demanded we look over a recently arrived batch of uril-chent to make sure of its quality." Cyril had told him the King-priest sometimes used non-military alchemists for such things.

"I have not been made aware of any such business today."

"That does not surprise me," Rogan said. "We were only just told ourselves."

"Why is she along?" The guard pointed at Saffron with his spear.

"Because she is the damned expert. Now, can we get to work?" Rogan hoped appearing to lose patience would assert his legitimacy, but his hand migrated toward the hilt of his dagger, just in case.

The guard snorted, "You can get to work when I say so," but did not seem interested in raising further trouble. He returned his spear to its resting position. "Do not dally."

Rogan nodded, but did not thank the man. He knew of guards who disappeared from one shift to the next at Blackthorn, the rumors suggesting they asked too many questions about the wrong person. One of the problems of being a tyrant, of course, is that fear cuts as a double-edged sword.

He held open the gate and waited for Saffron to pass through before slipping behind her. They took cobbled paths straight to Natrone's workshop, keeping heads bowed to avoid inadvertent eye contact. The other soldiers left them alone, no doubt assuming they had been vetted. Rogan let out a grateful sigh once they stepped into Natrone's place and shut the door.

"The pieces will be ready when I said so, and not a day earlier," a voice called from the other side of the room. The stone floor and walls gave the proper impression that this was a venue for warriors, owned by a hard man.

Shields made in a variety of shapes, sizes, and materials were mounted along the walls in display. Wooden stands on thumb-sized wheels littered the space, each bearing a frame-mounted suit of armor. The inventory created a maze of sorts, blocking the view from one end of the shop to the other. Rogan took Saffron's hand and wove through the impressive collection of protective wear, much of which he could identify as masterpieces. When they had nearly reached the back, Rogan spotted Natrone – he sat before a piece in progress, patiently stitching a stretch of boiled leather onto a more supple backing. He looked sideways at them, but could not recognize a face behind the hoods, and returned his eyes to his work.

"I am not sure what you are here for, but I am working as fast as I reasonably can."

Rogan pulled back his hood. "Might I convince you to work on two things at once, then?"

Natrone looked up at the sound of his voice. "Well, I'll be a thrice-skinned cat." He glanced about his shop as if expecting rauggin to be eavesdropping from the shadows. "What in the Nine Hells are you doing here, Baron?"

"It's probably better if you don't know, but I am in a bind and we need some armor."

"We? You mean this wispy lad needs some, too?"

Saffron drew back her hood and crossed her arms over her chest.

"I loved the last set you made for me." Rogan wanted to butter his bread without overdoing it. "Might you have more of that design? I have gold."

"Well, why didn't you say so first?" Natrone stood, causing Saffron to take a step back. He was a giant of a man, barrel-chested and a full head taller than Rogan. "There is a line of suits I have been working on off the ledger. Unique stuff, like what I made you – only better. I've made some modifications to increase their strength and flexibility, but would never see it on the Brotherhood. Come, take a look for yourself."

Rogan felt rewarded to find his faith in his friend was not misplaced. Natrone was a true innovator, driven by his own desire to create perfection. He led them to a nook along the northern wall concealed by drawn, black curtains. Natrone whisked them aside to reveal a secondary workshop, full of tools and scraps of assorted materials. More shields lined the wall panel, which slid to the side to reveal a secret alcove. Within stood another four armor stands, bearing specimens unlike anything worn by the combined armies of the region.

Two were dyed midnight black, the others rust, tinged by blood – full-bodied suits of leather armor. Created with an extra layer of cured hide, they had holes seemingly everywhere, as if some brilliant, giant moth had gotten into the wardrobe and feasted on them. "The cut-outs allow the skin to breathe and stay cool, and the joints to move without constriction," Natrone commented while gazing admiringly at his handiwork. They were, quite honestly, the most striking pieces of armor craftsmanship Rogan had ever seen.

"Are they effective protection with all those holes?" Saffron asked.

"Aye, that's what the extra layer is for." Natrone's pride showed through the matter-of-fact tone of his voice. "You might take a scratch, but the spaces actually slow the motion of a blade, distributing force. Plain and simple, you are not cutting through this with a weapon – it's kank hide."

Rogan felt the sleeve of one the black pieces. It was soft, supple – moreso than typical leather. "This one looks about my size," he smiled.

Natrone nodded. "I actually had you in mind – used your measurements from the one I made you months ago. I guessed you might be landing in more trouble." He looked over Saffron with a critical eye. "I'll have to make some adjustments on this other one for sure – take out the chest, tighten up the limbs. All right, Wispy, take off that cloak; I need to get the lay of the land." He reached into a pocket and pulled out a coil of black string with evenly-spaced white marks across it.

Saffron shot a look at Rogan, protesting the proposal of the burly man's fingers circumventing her, but he shrugged and she acquiesced.

"How soon can you have it ready, my friend?"

"Haha, friend is it? How soon do you need it?" Natrone looped the string around Saffron's chest, waist, and hips, measuring her body and calling numbers aloud to help memorize them.

Rogan waited until Natrone finished with her arms and legs. "Tonight?"

"Ha," Natrone bellowed in response. "Now I know you're mad. Tomorrow. Late. And that is only if the blasted, Blood Tear Ambassador of Impatience doesn't show up to keep pressuring me to complete his order first."

"Fair enough," said Rogan, retrieving his pouch of gold crowns. "We will be back tomorrow, before sunset. Come, Saffron," he beckoned, "let us leave the man to his work."

She gave him a sideways glance and opened her mouth briefly, but ultimately held her tongue.

Rogan and Saffron made it back to the *Silver Trumpet* unmolested. He could tell the next day was torture for her. Rogan still had some errands to run about town, preparations for the arrival of Sir Golddrake and his men, but he would not allow Saffron to leave Cyril's shop. She simply brought too much attention, and her ever-more-agitated behavior only convinced him of it.

Before leaving to return to Natrone's workshop, Rogan practically had to force her to eat something. She was too nervous for an appetite, but he knew they would both need their strength. It got worse when Cyril announced his informant was nowhere to be found. He did not report back to the viscount, and was absent from his usual haunts. Rogan took it as more than a bad omen, but Saffron refused to be dissuaded.

"Do you think the armor will be ready?" she asked, pulling at the end of her sleeves as they walked.

"If he's still the man I knew, it will be. Cyril did not want to tell you himself, but he regrets that you and your sister cannot return to the *Silver Trumpet*, once we break into Hope's End. There will be a search for Begnari women, I assume, and people know he was trying to track one down the other night. It is too much of a risk for the viscount and our other plans to hide you there."

She kept silent upon hearing the news, but after a few, long breaths simply said, "I understand."

Rogan patted her back, wishing he could be of more comfort. "Clear your mind, Saffron. We will need your wits tonight."

They reached the Arms Quarter just before sunset, and neither one particularly wanted to try talking their way in again. Though still wrapped in their brown cloaks, they brought their full packs along as well, since they were heading straight from the armorsmith's to the docks. Armed and burdened for travel, Rogan knew it would be a difficult sell to convince the King-priest's guards they were merely innocent citizens out for a stroll. Tonight, they would have to embrace the shadows.

Rogan led them around the perimeter of the Quarter, staying well beyond the fence until they got close to Natrone's shop. They abandoned the paved pathways and cut across the grass, staying behind structures and trees to keep out of sight. The fence was only chest high, not tall enough to present much of a problem, but they absolutely had to avoid detection by the soldiers frequenting the district.

Already using the dusk to their advantage, Rogan aided their cause by unsheathing his dagger, placing them in a globe of dimness as the uril-chent alloy sapped ambient light from the air around it. He watched as a pair of armored men walked the path inside the fence, patrolling the border of the Quarter to dissuade any mischief.

After waiting for them to pass, Rogan counted down from twenty before covering the final fifteen strides of open ground to the metal barrier. Saffron kept close, behaving as though she were his living shadow. He boosted her over before grabbing the top and thrusting upward, taking care not to catch the hem of his cloak on one of the iron prongs atop the fence. Their luck held the short remainder to the workshop, and they slipped in without attracting attention.

"Great hammers of Grothgar, if you were two minutes earlier we would be a sorry lot!" Natrone bellowed when he realized who had just entered his shop. "This imperial peacock kept going on and on about his new position at the river-palace, and how with Ebon Khorel so long-absent on his campaign, his harem girls were just ripe for the plucking. Indolent bastard, does he think I want to hear about how easy his duty is, surrounded by beautiful women, while I slave through the day working for these pushy half-wits? Still, it is lucky he left before you arrived. Let me close up shop."

Rogan chose not to say anything, but he paid heed to the armorsmith's comment. If the King-priest had not shown himself for some time, it could work to their advantage. The guards at Blackthorn prison were always more attentive when their superiors were in the vicinity. It was a shame Cyril's contact never reported back, but he could use this information in his infiltration plan.

For all his previous complaining, Natrone came through; the alterations were already complete. The men gave Saffron the privacy of the curtained alcove to undress, while Rogan donned his armor in the main room.

He was pleased with the fit and feel of the new suit — unrestrictive, light, tough. Wearing it was empowering. He would be protected, yet still able to act decisively – a major boon in hand-to-hand combat. He still wore his scarlet tunic underneath the black, and fancied himself a poisonous spider, ready to strike with quick, deadly fangs.

When Saffron emerged from behind the curtain, however, Rogan's jaw dropped. She looked svelte in the red leather suit. The supple armor fit exquisitely, hugging her curves and leaving her femininity no place to hide. The cut-outs provided alluring glimpses of Saffron's tanned physique. Unlike Rogan, she did not wear a tunic underneath.

"I feel naked," Saffron said, standing with hands on her hips.

Despite her words, Rogan noted she did nothing to cover herself. "Well, you did not have to take everything off."

"I did not remove *everything*, but it wouldn't fit right with my tunic. It was too snug." She shot a glance at Natrone, remembering how he'd called out her measurements at the fitting.

He, in turn, gave a silent look to Rogan and shrugged, though a slight curl shaped his lips.

"You look fine," Rogan covered. "Besides, I recall an outfit or two of yours baring some skin. More importantly, how does it feel? Can you move well enough?"

Saffron jumped in the air and took a full spin before she landed, spreading her arms for balance. She alighted with the grace of a jungle cat. "I suppose."

"Here," said Natrone, as he walked to the wall and dislodged one of the hanging shields. It was a disk, less than two feet in diameter, made of hickory cast in bronze. The motif engraved upon it included three, stylized sand dunes and a scimitar. "I know the Baron never properly learned how to use one, but if you are going into battle, you shouldn't want for a good shield. The design reminds me of your people." He handed it to Saffron, who immediately tried it on for size.

"Thank you; it is exquisite. *Imshihi ezmaran kubahi uhm*: may your generosity return to you many-fold." She bowed and took the shield to the rest of her belongings, investigating a way to strap it to the back of her pack.

Rogan clasped his friend on the shoulder, though he had to reach up to do so. "You have come through for me once again, and I am in your debt."

"Ah, forget all that." Natrone brushed away the thought with his hand. "You pay in advance, which is more than I can say for the King-priest – I'll be lucky to see my rightful wages by autumn. Just send him to the Burning Wastes if you see him, huh? That's all I ask."

"I will try, my friend."

"May your swords strike true," Natrone called as the pair left his shop, hooded cloaks concealing their identities once more.

With Saffron's shield on her back they looked dangerously like mercenaries, so Rogan did the best he could to take an unpopular route toward the docks. The sun was all but down, and the shadows long as they crept one alley at a time toward the water, trying to stay out of view. The few citizens afoot were hurrying home ahead of the oncoming curfew, and none showed concern for a couple of cloaked figures slipping past them in the twilight.

Night was fully upon them when they reached the wharf, where scores of workers still labored in the moonlight to unload the moored ships. The curfew was abrogated for those properly employed, and lines of torches provided additional illumination to the docks.

"I dropped some supplies off at our canoe earlier – things we may need – so we should be ready to go, assuming no banditry has taken place." Rogan's pace quickened once they were on the boardwalk, belying his outward calmness as they approached their transport to Hope's End. "Cyril presented me with a gift for you from his War Room as well, to soften the blow of your exile, I believe. He wanted you to know it was not because he didn't enjoy having you around."

"I understand," Saffron acknowledged, "there are no grudges. I am grateful for the help he has already given me.

Something about him gave me the shivers, anyway. All I care about is rescuing Dhania."

The canoe remained where Rogan left it that afternoon, and the canvas tarp he placed over it was still drawn tight. A row of nearby torches cast barely enough light to mark the edge of the dock. Saffron misjudged the shadows and nearly plummeted into the river as she bent to peel back the cover.

"Whoa!" Rogan reached out just in time to steady her. "Let's not get wetter than we have to tonight." He helped her clear the way into the canoe, folding up the tarp to take with them. In the belly of their boat lay a spear with a haft of black ash. Its total length was almost equivalent to Saffron's height, leaving it short enough to be wielded with one hand. The head was serrated steel, elongated and embedded to reinforce the shaft. Flexible and strong, it was the perfect weapon to match Saffon's experience.

She smiled from ear to ear and immediately reached out, eager to lift the spear and feel its weight. She drew back her hand, instead carefully moving it aside with her foot as she climbed into the canoe. "Is it Begnari?" she asked as Rogan followed her in and untied the line. "The spear looks like what our armies use."

Rogan shook his head. "Actually, it's from the jungles of Chelpa. The primitive tribes there favor spears, not having much access to metals, but this one belonged to a war-chieftain. I thought you would like it, though. I saw you fighting during the ambush, and we may have some to do tonight."

Saffron took up her paddle and noticed two sacks, in addition to the packs they had carried, already stowed. "What else did you bring?"

"A few things we may need, and a few others I hope we don't," he responded. "Let us cast off and get moving, shall we? This night is likely to be long enough as it is."

Without another word, they paddled away from the docks into the dark embrace of the River Chelhos. The vastness of the swift waters was amplified by night, nearly swallowing them in blackness. Its current seemed more powerful with no clear view of the banks to provide perspective, and louder with their sight abated by the heavy clouds moving in to shroud the moons.

Chapter 17

Hope's End

What started as a distant collection of candle flames grew into an impression of the palace as they drew nearer. Hope's End stood as Cyril described, on an island in the midst of the river. Its eastern side faced the Chelpian shore, where a small harbor built on an abutting island received traffic from the mainland. Rogan, however, steered them toward the western face, where a shallow shoreline led abruptly to the towering, stone walls of the palace.

Originally designed as a fortress, the structure had more than adequate defenses. The crenellated outer wall stood three stories high with bastions at the corners, where men could rain arrows or stones on their enemies from cover. A drawbridge protected the only true gate into the palace from the east – Rogan and Saffron hoped to scale the wall furthest from it.

They dipped their paddles into the water as quietly as they could during their approach, though Rogan could not spot any movement atop the walls. He hoped the darkness would serve them just as well. His heartbeat accelerated as the canoe washed to a stop against the wet sand of the shore. Unlike the thrill that accompanied battle, this feeling was danger of the unknown – true fear. He would have to control and use it if they were going to succeed. He offered a silent plea that Saffron mastered hers as well.

Rogan jumped onto the bank and pulled their boat further in until satisfied it was secure. The hull was a mere arm's length from the palace foundation. He offered his hand to Saffron, who took it and stepped onto land. They removed their cloaks and threw them back into the canoe. Saffron grabbed her spear and shield, while Rogan untied and rifled through one of the sacks.

He withdrew two pairs of metal claws. One set was attached to bands that fit around his palms, while the other slipped over the toes of his boots. "This brings back memories," he said to himself as he slung a coiled rope over his shoulder and across his torso. The lapping of the river against the shore created enough noise that he felt safe for the moment, as long as they did not do something foolish. Rogan's mind had been spinning through scenarios during most of the approach, preoccupying him too much to speak, but he needed to ensure they agreed on strategy.

"We have no idea how many guards the palace has, or who of consequence might be present, so we want to draw as little attention as possible." He hoped the tightness of the King-priest's grip all these years had lulled their enemy into a false sense of security, but did not dare express this out loud for fear it would sabotage their luck. "I imagine the majority of look-outs will be positioned near the gate, where any ship of consequential size would have to dock. Less time inside means less chance for detection, so be decisive without being rash. Still, we should watch out for one another, especially if one of us has to focus on another task."

Saffron nodded her compliance. "Of course. I have never heard you speak so quickly, Baron. Are you anxious?"

Rogan's brow furrowed. "Since you have your spear and shield to manage, I'm going to scale the wall first and throw our rope down to you. I think we will have to risk leaving it tied for our escape." Rogan paused, trying to read the dark pools of her eyes, but the night and shadow of the walls were too deep. "You should be prepared for anything when it comes to your sister. She might be a changed woman – different than you remember her. Who knows what she has been through? She might be drunk or drugged when we find her, assuming she's here at all. You need to be ready to accept it if she isn't, and concentrate on us getting out alive." He exhaled stiffly. "Are you ready?"

Her response was calm, but determined. "I will not fail Dhania. I cannot."

It was enough for Rogan. He reached up and slapped the wall with his right hand, forcing the claws into its surface. He prayed they would hold, and that the noise of the river was enough to drown out their sharp *clink*. Repeating the process with all four limbs, embedding one hand then the next, raising one foot at a time, he chipped into the palace stone. Much as a lizard made slothful by the cold, Rogan crawled up the hard surface until within a couple body lengths of the top.

From there, he paused to survey the battlements, but still saw no guards from his limited vantage. He made sure not to look down, fully aware how precarious his hold on the wall was. The air was humid, but at least at this height a breeze cooled the sweat from his face. His arms and shoulders burned from the continued exertion, but soon Rogan was hoisting his leg over the top of the wall.

He immediately ducked to eliminate his profile from any observers on the eastern side of the palace. Once more he checked for nearby guards, but the only discernable movement was the whipping of banners mounted atop the bastions. Was something occupying everyone's attention, or were they being insidiously invited in?

Rogan looped his rope around the nearest crenellation, tying it off before casting the other end down to Saffron. It was his turn to be patient. Wearing her shield on her back and her spear tucked into her belt, she scaled the wall with steady movements. By the time she rejoined Rogan, he had already stowed his climbing claws in his pack.

"I'll lead the way – you watch our back," he said, leaving his saber sheathed and drawing his dagger. Up on the wall there was little light for his uril-chent blade to steal, but over the years its stone grip came to comfort him. Saffron donned her armaments as well, nodding her readiness.

Rogan had no knowledge of the palace's floor plans, and it would be a waste of time looking for someone who did. On a whim, he chose to head toward the northern bastion, hoping he would find stairs leading to the lower levels. Suspicious they had not yet seen a sentry, his eyes strained in the dark, searching for the slightest hint of danger.

When he drew within a few steps of the arch that opened to the interior of the parapet, he spotted their first foe. A guard slumped in his chair, lightly snoring. A nearby trap door no doubt provided a path downward, and the corner chamber held nothing else of note. Rogan hesitated, considering if he might simply sneak past the guard. They might have to come back this way, though, and could not risk him waking up and finding their rope. They had too much to lose.

Regretfully, Rogan crept into position behind the man, and with decisive movements used one hand to smother the guard's mouth while plunging his dagger into his chest. His victim's arms flailed to the side before his entire body slumped once more into a permanent sleep. Rogan looked up at Saffron, who witnessed his execution, half-expecting to find judgment in her expression. None was present, and she helped him dispose of the body over the western wall.

Kneeling to the floor, he cracked the hatch to peek below. A short shaft led downward, iron rungs protruding from its westward wall. The light of torches glowed beyond, and Rogan nodded at Saffron as he swung the trap door fully open.

He went first, descending the one-and-a-half body lengths to the floor. A long corridor stretched southward, and he could see at least one other hallway breaking off in the direction of the palace center. Sconces on the wall bore torches every half-dozen paces, though only every-other-one was lit, providing shadowy illumination. He had not taken two steps toward the first of these when footfalls echoed on the stone from an adjoining passage.

Rogan motioned for Saffron, who was already all but down the ladder to go back up, while he pressed firmly to the wall, trying to flatten himself. In her haste, Saffron's shield clanked against one of the metal rungs, though she managed to disappear above the square hole.

The approaching footsteps stopped. "Did you hear something?" a man beyond sight asked.

"No, but if you did it was probably my stomach. I have not eaten since noon-hour."

"I could make do with some supper myself. We should drop by the kitchens after you return those tomes. I swear, why anyone would want to learn to read in the first place is beyond my reckoning."

Two men, dressed in long tunics cinched at the waist with silken sashes, turned the corner heading away from Rogan's position, without so much as a glance in his direction. They turned again down another corridor shortly after, and Rogan could hear the hollow sound of their boots trailing off, as if they were descending stairs. He snuck over to the ladder and motioned for Saffron to come down.

"That was close," he whispered once she joined him.

"What was close?" she answered.

"A couple of men, but I think they were unarmed. We should follow them."

"What? Why? I thought we wanted to draw as little attention as possible?" Her objection had merit.

"I did say that, didn't I?" Rogan winked. "I was just thinking if I had a harem, I would want vaulted ceilings, so it's unlikely we'll find her on the top floor."

Saffron rolled her eyes. "That is your reasoning?"

Rogan shrugged and turned down the corridor, heading the same direction the men had walked. He stole a peek down the hallway the unarmed men had come from, but there was no door for some distance. Sure enough, the second option yielded a brief landing, which led to wide, stone steps. With Saffron close behind, he crept down to the next landing, preparing to pounce should anyone be present on the floor below.

No one was in sight. Rogan knew he should not question good fortune, but it disturbed his senses that resistance was so slight. This palace belonged to the King-priest, after all. Perhaps the enemy *had* become lazy over time – reliant on the cumulative effects of oppression. Rogan returned to the moment, as choices needed to be made. Double wooden doors stood straight ahead, and hallways broke off north and south, perpendicular to the stairs. Also, off to the left, the stairs continued down another level.

"This must be a jest," Saffron said, interrupting his thoughts.

"What's that?" he questioned, trying to keep his eyes on both hallways at once.

"I was here in my dreams last night. I was standing on these very stairs."

Rogan turned to look at her, trying to ascertain whether she was serious. Though her eyes were cast in his direction, she was clearly struggling to access her memory. "Well, what did you do in your dream? I suppose it's as good a way as any to navigate these halls."

Saffron's focus turned to Rogan in earnest, and she nodded. "Down. We should go down another flight." She stepped past him and took the lead, continuing confidently down the next set of stairs. They bottomed out on the floor below, but Saffron closed her eyes briefly, and when she opened them, strode down the southern corridor with new assurance.

The torches on the ground floor were spaced further apart in their sconces, the dimness amplified by Rogan's dagger. They were moving quickly, hardly sneaking anymore, and he followed her around a pair of corners before coming to a stop. An open door lay ahead, and the sound of many voices escaped through it; laughter, discussion, and boasting intermingled.

"Must be the mess hall," he whispered. "We should find a way around."

Saffron shook her head, and he saw her shoulders relax with a deep exhalation. She continued down the hallway with a purposeful stride, parading right past the open doors, keeping her eyes straight ahead. Rogan stayed put and watched, waiting to see if anyone came to investigate her passage.

His rapid heartbeat kept him company for what seemed an eternity, but no guards issued forth. Saffron stood at the far end of the hall, gesturing with her spear for him to join her. He put his fist to his forehead, but could not think of anyone to pray to for such a situation. Rogan sheathed his dagger, lest the change in light catch someone's attention as he passed. Then, with even strides, he walked in front of the door and down the corridor until he caught up with his companion. He dared not turn around, relying on Saffron's reaction to inform him they were still unnoticed.

"That was not smart, Saffron," he finally whispered as they turned the next corner.

"This is the only way I know. If we deviate, my dream won't do us any good."

"Is your dream doing us any good? How could we tell?"

"Shh," she silenced him. "This is it." They stood before a short passage shooting off from the main hall. At the end of it loomed a closed, iron door.

Rogan's eyebrows rose. "Are you sure?"

Saffron walked up to the door and pulled its handle, but it did not budge. "Ugh," she grunted, a little too loudly. "It's locked."

"Let me see what I can do." Rogan brushed her out of his way and got on his knees to examine the keyhole. "Cross your fingers it's not barred from the other side," he said as he slung the pack from his back and fished through it for a scrap of folded leather. He withdrew his delicate, ivory picks and went to work on the door.

"I was not sure you knew how to use them." Saffron extended her shield-arm downward, resting it while she waited.

"You learn all kinds of things when you are stuck in prison," he retorted, squinting as he felt for just the right positioning and pressure. A satisfying *click* told him his job was done. "And there we go." He put away his tools and stood, trying the handle again. The door swung open, and inside was pitch black.

"This does not have the looks of a harem to me," Rogan observed as he entered the dark room beyond. "Grab a torch, would you?"

Saffron grasped her spear with her shield-hand and picked a torch off the wall from the hallway. She joined Rogan in the small room, but it seemed as if they had come to a dead end. It appeared merely a storage room of some sort. Shelves sat on opposite ends of the rectangular space, and sealed barrels crowded the floor.

"Why would my dream lead me here?" Saffron wondered aloud as she held the torch closer to the shelves, examining their contents.

"I do not know. Perhaps it was just a dream?" Rogan tapped his foot impatiently, and was surprised when it returned a hollow sound. The entire first floor of the palace had been stone, but this was something different. "Down here," he said, taking the torch from Saffron and dropping to one knee. A wooden trap door was hidden in the floor, much like the one leading down from the bastion.

A latch locked it in place from the top, but it was no matter to swing it aside. Rogan and Saffron shared a glance before he hoisted the hatch open. Unlike before, there was no ladder to be seen, only a sheer drop into complete darkness. Rogan dropped the torch, and it landed with a thud on another stone floor, two body lengths below.

He ducked his head beneath the surface of the floor, but the torch did not illuminate much from the ground. He did not imagine Dhania was being kept here, but something was, locked out of the way for a reason. Rogan's curiosity won out over his initial trepidation. "Shut that door," he nodded to Saffron, and then lowered himself as far as he could for a drop into the dark.

The landing stung his feet, but he was otherwise unhurt. He picked up the torch and quickly surveyed the room. A cellar of some sort, it definitely was not used to store wine. All manner of strange implements populated the room, metal and wood, worth investigating. He found a wooden step ladder against the nearby wall, and positioned it underneath the trap door. "Lower yourself on this," he called up to Saffron. "There does not appear to be anyone else down here."

"Take my shield." She passed along both it and her spear before slipping gracefully down to the ladder. "What is this place?" She squinted in the frail light to make out the contents of the cellar.

"I cannot say." Rogan set her battle regalia on the floor and offered his hand to assist her down the ladder. She took it, and together they walked around to get a better look. Strange-looking tables and upright frames, outfitted with chains and manacles, created most of the clutter. Racks lined one of the walls, on which unusual blades, hooks, and clamps hung.

Buckets of dark liquid rested on the floor beside some of the tables, and on closer inspection, Rogan could discern stains on the furniture, which could have only come from... blood. Saffron realized the implications at almost the same moment.

"This is a torture chamber," she said, solemnly.

"Well hidden, too. I wonder how many prisoners have disappeared here?"

As Rogan drew closer to the far end of the room, the light from his torch began to dim. He checked to see if it was burning low, but that didn't seem the case. "What is this?" he wondered aloud as he came within view of the wall.

Standing against it were humanoid figures, motionless. They were identical, black, metallic. Saffron walked right up behind him and peered over his shoulder to get a good view in the low light.

"Are they suits of armor?" she asked.

Rogan reached out and touched one – it was cold, colder than the normal chill of metal in a dark place. "They do not appear to be hollow," he remarked, leaning in closer. There was a slit for the eyes, but when he reached inside, it only receded to his second knuckle. He tried to move the body with his free hand, but it was too heavy and did not budge. "Definitely solid," he followed up. "And uril-chent, judging by the torchlight."

"Uril-what?"

"It is the ore we mined at Blackthorn Prison. My dagger is made of it."

"Ah, your dimming dagger. So, what do you think they are if not armor?" Saffron asked the question he was already thinking.

"I wish I knew. This alloy is valuable, though. I do not imagine the King-priest would waste it on mere statues."

"Well, there is little we can do now." Saffron sighed. "Dhania is clearly not down here. Shouldn't we get moving? Who knows how long before the guard you have slain is discovered?"

Rogan turned from the motionless, uril-chent figures and stared at the woman before him, remembering why he was here. Even in near darkness, he could see her beauty. "You are right, of course. Let us be on our way."

After a single step Rogan froze, senses on alert. "Wait, I heard something." They both stood motionless, ears straining; their single torch, dimmed by the proximity of the uril-chent, cast only a weak glow. "There it is again!" Rogan whispered.

It was barely audible, but had the faintest echo, like the flick of a fingernail against a bare blade. Rogan crept in the direction of the sound, listening for it again. It took another dozen, rapid heartbeats, but he finally heard it a third time, and realized the source. "The bucket."

Rogan lifted his torch, which brightened slightly as they gained distance from the statues at the far end of the room. Suddenly Saffron gasped and nearly jumped out of her skin, causing him to flinch as she grabbed him.

The ceiling was overlaid with a metal grid, from which spikes protruded downward. Impaled upon them was a man's body, further suspended by chains around his wrists and ankles.

"Great ghosts of Balazar," Rogan squeezed out, still only a whisper. Blood dripped slowly into the buckets below, indicating he was nearly dry.

Saffron finally released Rogan and drew her hands back. "Who do you think he was?"

"Some poor soul..." even as he spoke the words, his memory conjured a reminder of Cyril telling them his spy had failed to report. He wondered if this could be him, but shook off the speculation. Nothing could done about it now, and he felt the urge to clear out of this room as fast as possible. "We should find your sister."

Saffron nodded and went first, climbing the short steps and surprising Rogan by leaping the rest of the way without assistance. She caught the lip of the opening and pulled her lithe body up with minimal effort. He handed her spear and shield over, one at a time, followed by the torch, and waited for her to move aside before jumping and hoisting himself up as well.

Swinging and latching the trap door shut, they tried to leave the storage room just as they found it. Once again careful not to make unnecessary noise, they snuck back to the main hallway and replaced the torch. Rogan took the lead once more, since Saffron's dream had led them astray.

He did not want to risk crossing the mess hall again, so they continued down the hall eastward, determined by his best guess. Another short corridor broke off to the north, but instead of a door at the end, a spiral staircase awaited. Following the main hall a little further led to the mumbled sounds of conversation ahead. Rogan gestured for Saffron to hold, and peeked around the next corner.

Twenty-or-so armed guards milled about a large chamber, waiting before a huge set of double doors, which he assumed led to the main gate. So that's where they all are, he thought. Could they be setting an ambush? If the man in the underground chamber was Cyril's infiltrator, had they learned something from him?

Rogan inched back to Saffron and quietly informed her, "We are taking the stairs."

The whole structure creaked and groaned as they ascended, and Rogan silently cursed every step. No sooner had he reached the next floor than a woman appeared, carrying a pile of folded clothes, headed for the stairway herself. They both froze upon spotting one another. The middle-aged woman, apparently unsure what to make of him at first, looked down at the climbing Saffron and immediately determining something was amiss.

She opened her mouth to call out, and Rogan knew he had to act quickly. He pounced forward just as she began to scream, knocking the clothes she carried to the floor and cupping his hand over her mouth. Only a fraction of a second's terror escaped her lips before being muzzled.

Two blinks later Saffron was beside him, singing softly in her native song. The tune seemed to soothe the woman, who relaxed in Rogan's arms. He quickly looked to see if they had drawn the attention of any armed fellows; none entered view.

"We are not here to harm you, my lady," he said in a firm, calm tone. "I am going to remove my hand now, so you can speak. Please do not cry out. We only want to know where the girls are kept – the pleasure slaves. Can you tell us?"

Rogan slowly removed his hand, while Saffron kept singing. He was starting to relax too, and felt oddly at ease, given the situation.

"They are another floor up," she stated, her voice trembling slightly.

"Please, take us there?" Rogan asked.

She looked directly into his eyes and he recognized the worry in hers. She nodded, however, and he released her. The woman walked tentatively to the staircase, looking back at her captors every few steps. Saffron kept humming until Rogan was on the stairs behind their guide.

Up they went to the third floor, and despite his assurance, Rogan finally drew his saber and dagger, keeping a few steps behind the laundry woman. She led him down a pair of twisting hallways to an open antechamber, where she shrieked and lunged forward, seeking the protection of a pair of guards.

Dressed in chainmail and holding glaives, they stood before a pair of wide, ornate doors with brass handles. They leveled their weapons upon spotting Rogan, maintaining positions in front of the door. The woman cowered on the floor between them, curled into a tight, protective posture.

Rogan was still assessing the tactical situation, realizing the considerable reach advantage of his opponents, when Saffron joined him in the antechamber. Her arrival threw the guards, who apparently did not know what to think about seeing a woman armed for battle. She took advantage and charged straight for the one on the right, easily deflecting his thrust with her shield and closing enough to render his glaive useless.

The second guard tried to help his companion, swinging his weapon sideways in an attempt to behead the brash attacker. Saffron answered by sliding to her knees and raising her shield to stave off the blow. As her momentum carried her closer to the guards she twisted her body to the left, bringing her spear up with a thrust of her right arm.

It caught the guard to her left between the ribs and he cried out in pain, dropping his glaive to clutch the wound. Not wasting a second, Saffron released her grip on the spear and jumped to her feet. She torqued her leveled-off shield behind her with incredible force, smashing the other guard's face and slamming his head into the door behind him. It bounced off with a thud, and he immediately sank to the floor, unconscious. The guard with the spear in his chest sank to his knees, his punctured organs no longer able to sustain him.

Rogan was in awe of how quickly Saffron dispatched their enemies. He had barely moved. "Remind me never to make you angry," he said, stepping forward. He gestured to the laundry woman. "What about her?"

Saffron placed a boot on the body of the dead guard and pried her spear loose. "Open the door!" she commanded. The woman was sniveling, but managed to climb to her feet and pull one of the wooden doors ajar with both hands.

The spacious, decadently furnished Pleasure Garden of the King-priest lay beyond. Curtains, pillows, and all manner of cushioned surfaces imbued the chamber with a sense of comfort and luxury. It contained a fountain, planted trees, and a ceiling that opened to the sky above, letting in the soft light of celestial bodies. Two dozen women or more, clothed in fanciful outfits of silk or even precious metal, lounged about the premises. The nearest had backed away from the door, alerted by the sounds of fighting.

Others were oblivious, sleeping or simply lost in a haze of distraction. Fragrances smothered the air, fighting for dominance as they mingled together: incense, perfume, pipe smoke, even the heady musk of sex.

Saffron stormed into the room, scanning the faces for her sister, but Rogan's focus was on the guards slowly stepping forward to stake their territory. Clearly among the most rewarded soldiers to have landed this duty, Rogan assumed they were either extremely loyal or extremely deadly – possibly both.

He counted six who were clearly visible, though places to hide in this den of pleasures were ample. This time Rogan was the first to charge, seeing the guards taking up positions to encircle them.

The harem protectors wore black cloaks over their armor and iron helms concealing their faces. Wielding swords and teardrop shields, Rogan surmised they possessed more battle-training than the pair Saffron had so easily dispatched. Perhaps the earlier absence of guards was only meant to lure them inside, after all.

The enemy sprung into action as Rogan entered their midst, and hearing his battle cry brought Saffron's attention back to their danger. Rogan traded parried blows with one of the guards and then sank back toward Saffron, allowing her to focus on the right side of the room, while he took the left. She lunged forward with her spear only to have it blocked, while a second guard seized the opportunity to swing his sword at her flank. She moved her shield just in time, but it was clear with their numbers her opponents could just keep snapping; eventually, their teeth would hit.

Many of the slave girls screamed as the fighting broke out, but at least they had the sense to get up and push back to the far end of the room, out of danger. Rogan hoped, for Saffron's sake, her sister was among them.

He did not have the advantage of a shield, but had never seen the need for one. Rogan preferred to remain nimble, though he also strongly preferred not to be outnumbered three-to-one. It certainly divided his attention, and he had the sinking feeling that he was going to once again have to rely on the special qualities of the uril-chent to get out of this alive. As he lunged forward again to engage the middle guard with his saber, he heard Saffron starting to sing behind him.

This song seemed somehow different from the others. Though still in Begnari, it was full and clear, and tinged by fury. He didn't know if she was employing magic again, but he let the sound infuse him, feeding an anger he sought to harness. His arms moved faster and his blows beat back his opponent, who tripped over a padded bench while giving ground.

The two flanking Rogan were surprised by his advance, and slow to make up the distance. The moment the guard fell to the ground Rogan was on him, pouncing like a predator to finish his kill. The guard relinquished his sword to grapple with Rogan, trying to keep his dagger from thrusting into his exposed neck.

The delay was long enough for one of the other guards to slash the back of Rogan's right arm, cutting deep into his triceps where one of the holes in his armor left him vulnerable. With a cry of pain accompanying a surge of strength, Rogan drove his dagger into the throat of the man beneath him, then quickly rolled away to seek cover nearer the wall.

A pulse of heat swam through Rogan's body, coming to rest in his injured arm. A dozen tiny needles seemed to prick from the inside, but seconds later left no sign of a cut arm, no weakness of a severed muscle.

Momentarily out of danger, his attention shifted to Saffron, who was a hurricane of fire doing battle on the other side of the room. She spun with the speed of a cyclone, still singing, and embers trailed in the wake of her spearhead, glowing red with heat. Saffron thrust her weapon into a hanging tapestry, piercing and setting it ablaze. She yanked it away from the wall and onto one of her mesmerized opponents, cloaking him in a garment of fire.

He screamed and backed away, unsuccessfully trying to remove the artwork without actually touching it. She focused on the next guard, spinning and pivoting, bounding off obstacles in the room as if she had placed them on purpose. Her opponent was overwhelmed, unable to discern from what angle the next blow was going to come.

The third guard on her side clearly wanted no part of this elemental warrior princess, and whether a coward or simply smart enough to recognize the situation, he bolted for the door, either intent on escaping with his life or gathering reinforcements.

As Saffron finished off her foe with a spear to the stomach, Rogan noticed the other two guards near him had also become distracted by the incendiary display. One ran to push his ignited ally into the fountain to extinguish him, while the other stood in place, contemplating his next move.

In the confusion Rogan charged, sweeping his saber's blade across the back of the stunned guard's leg, crippling him.

"I surrender!" he called out, dropping his sword, acknowledging defeat. "Mercy!"

The two near the fountain had abandoned their weapons and shields as well, and steam rose from the torn tapestry, doused in the cool water. Occasional gasps and squeals still erupted from the congregation of concubines huddled together at the back of the room, the braver ones peeking around plants or sculptures to get a view of the action.

A woman's voice rose from the crowd, "Saffron! Im shulak hadeem!"

Saffron's head snapped in the direction of the voice, her eyes frantically searching for its source. "Dhania? Dhania!"

A young Begnari woman, bearing a striking resemblance to Saffron, peeled out of the group of harem slaves and ran forward, smothering her mouth with her hands and sobbing into them. She collapsed to her knees before covering the distance between them, but Saffron was to her an instant later, enveloping her in an embrace and weeping as well.

Rogan prodded the remaining guards toward the wall, away from their weapons. With Saffron distracted, he didn't want them regaining their courage and taking up arms again.

"If you want the girl, take her and go," one of them said. "We will not miss one slave."

Rogan could not decide if it was a trick, or simply the man's sense of self-preservation speaking.

"You wait much longer," another chimed in, "this place will be swarming with more guards than even that one can handle." He nodded in Saffron's direction.

Perhaps they only wanted a chance to control the scene before others arrived, but it certainly was a risk to linger now that they had found Dhania. "Saffron, we need to leave," Rogan called as he backed toward her, still pointing his saber at the guards.

Saffron wiped her eyes, kissed her sister's forehead and stood, bringing Dhania to her feet as well. She did not, however, lighten her embrace. "Which way out?"

"There is a door this way," Dhania grabbed her sister's hand and pulled her toward the back of the chamber. She pointed at the guards across the room, "Only they have the key." She spoke Ilanese, but her accent was even thicker than Saffron's.

Rogan faced his prisoners, "Hand it over."

Looking as though his secret had just been exposed, one of the guards pulled a chain, looped through a small, silver key, from underneath the neckline of his tunic. Rogan ripped it off him, then ran to the far end of the room to unlock the door.

"Dhania, take us with you!" one of the other girls begged, her hands extended toward her fellow slave, daring to take a step closer.

"I am sorry," interjected Rogan. "We have no room, nor any time." He wanted to promise he would return to set them all free, but too much danger lay ahead, and he did not want to lie. As he held the door open for Saffron and Dhania, more women pleaded to come with them, but as soon as he was through the door, Rogan shut and locked it again.

He looked at Dhania; her fresh face held the same beauty as her sister, only more innocent. "I truly regret it, but if we freed your friends now, none of us would get out alive." Dhania nodded, her eyes wide as she considered him.

Rogan placed them not far from the bastion they originally descended, if his bearings were correct. He led them with haste down the hallway to their right, and when it ended, took a left. In the distance they heard cries of men being called to arms. Spurred on even further, Rogan was relieved when the passage ended with only one more hallway.

Turning right, he saw the iron rungs in the wall leading up to the battlements. Rogan went first, and as he helped Dhania out into the cool night air, he realized her outfit left much to be desired in terms of providing warmth. Her torso was wrapped in layers of silk that only extended to her ribcage. Her skirt was the same material, and only reached mid-thigh. A matching silk veil completed the ensemble. No shoes to speak of. He would be glad to at least offer his cloak once they reached the canoe.

"Look out!" she called and pointed behind him. Rogan turned to see a guard rushing across the wall in their direction, spear in hand. He stopped where the rope was looped around the crenellated stone, and started to lift it over.

"Don't!" Rogan cried, running forward to save their escape route. He was too late. The rope went over the edge and Rogan almost went with it, lunging to grab hold as it skipped down the side of the stone to the beach.

The guard grabbed him by the waist to hoist him over as well. Rogan scrambled to catch the side of the wall as he felt himself lifted, but suddenly the guard released him and he dropped to the ground, relieved.

Saffron was pulling her spear from the guard's body by the time Rogan realized what happened. "You almost went over," she said, stating the obvious. The concern in her voice, however, was real.

"We lost the rope," were the only words he could find.

They peered over the edge together – their canoe looked tiny, so far below. Bells rang as the general alarm was raised, and Rogan could see more guards on their way across the wall from the far side of the palace. An arrow clanked off the stone nearby, causing all three of them to flinch.

"We have to jump," Saffron said, ducking from any unseen arrows.

"Is it deep enough?" Dhania questioned. "You know I am afraid of heights."

"I'll go first," volunteered Rogan. "If I make it, don't wait too long." He leaned over and kissed Saffron full on the lips, leaving her stunned. Then, climbing onto the edge of the wall, he jumped as far as he could out toward the water.

The impact felt like being slapped hard on the bottoms of his feet, but the channel cut deep and he didn't hit the riverbed. Water rushed up his nose, but after a few seconds of disorientation he pierced the surface of the water. It took him a moment to locate the shore, but by the time he was pulling himself onto it he heard another splash.

Saffron's shield dropped first, wedging into the sand, followed by her spear. Rogan looked up just in time to see her sailing through the air, and followed the course of her silhouette down to its inevitable splash as she collided with the river.

He saw Dhania swimming to shore and waded back out knee-deep to help her in. She took his arms, and when he lifted her body out of the water, he couldn't help but gasp. Wet, the silk she wore was completely sheer and clung to her body, revealing every inch of it. Even though it was night, the moonlight shared enough.

Rogan looked away, but not before the image had burned into his memory. He walked her onto the shore and immediately to the canoe, where he offered one of the cloaks they borrowed from Cyril. Saffron crawled out of the water on hands and knees, having trouble finding her breath.

She waved Rogan off as he tried to help her to her feet, so he grabbed the spear, shield, and rope dropped from the wall. Someone hurled a spear from above, but it missed and plunked harmlessly into the water.

"We had better leave before their archers show up." Rogan dumped his armful into the boat and waited for Saffron, still out of breath, to climb in. He pushed the canoe into the river and leapt into the final seat. Dhania had already taken up one of the paddles, and he grabbed the other. With swift strokes they took off downstream, eager to put distance between them and Hope's End.

Only when the lights of the palace had shrunk once again to candles, did Rogan allow himself a break from paddling. "We made it," he said, looking back at the daughters Furasi. "We actually made it."

They were looking at one another, and though they did not respond with words, he saw Saffron's cheeks wet with tears. She would tell him it was only the river, dripping across her face, but he knew better. He looked ahead, not wanting to intrude, and concentrated on steering their boat toward the western shore, beyond the realm of the Empire.

Chapter 18

Calling Up the Storm

The day Saffron went south with the Baron, Jaiden began making an effort to live the tenets of the Order of the Rising Moon. According to Palomar, it was the best way to learn them. Jaiden wanted to change, wanted Saffron to notice his transformation; if that did not work, he would woo her with song.

Lothander did not disappoint him, finding a lute so Jaiden could practice during his free time in the caves. He had not touched one in years, but the fingering came back quickly, and he was soon composing a song dedicated to the absent object of his affection.

Getting used to the structure the Order provided, and the discipline it demanded, did not come easily. Jaiden made an effort every morning to take up a helpful task with no personal gain. Spending a few hours every day polishing boots or weapons, peeling potatoes – nearly any mundane chore that did not require standing – only left him hungrier for excitement. With none to be found, he was still waiting to reach the point where he felt gratified by his service, as Palomar promised.

He spent his afternoons alone, working on the song. Not a natural talent, he made slow progress, memorizing the music and lyrics little by little as he wove them into a story of his longing.

During these hours of seclusion, in the shadowed depths of the Caves of Criesha, Jaiden first noticed the smell. Unsure at first what it was, he came to realize his leg had acquired an unwholesome scent – like a sack of rotting potatoes. He regained some mobility after Saffron bound his leg in its sheath, and paired with Palomar's morning songs to soothe his pain, he had convinced himself his leg was improving. In truth, there were worrisome signs – he could prod parts of his lower leg without feeling, and now the unmistakable stench.

He did not tell anyone, carrying on as if nothing was wrong, but he spent almost all his time alone to avoid betrayal by his pungent aroma or the pit of dread taking hold inside. Jaiden tried not to pay it heed, but an inner voice grew, whispering the end had come.

Palomar spent the first days after their arrival tutoring Jaiden on the particulars of the Order's minutia, but had rarely been around since. Sir Golddrake kept him busy scouting and carrying messages in preparation for their next move.

Five days after Saffron left, Sir Golddrake announced his decision that fewer than a hundred men would be selected to liberate Blackthorn Prison. The rest would be heading to Selamus, to bolster the capital against possible invasion and await the return of their brethren. Jaiden knew he would have to do whatever it took to be one of the chosen.

The Master asked for volunteers, since the journey into Chelpa was by far the more dangerous mission, but no shortage of willing participants came forth. When Jaiden petitioned for inclusion, Sir Golddrake told him he would only consider it if he were fully committed to the Order.

"I am ready," Jaiden responded without hesitation.

"So be it," answered Sir Golddrake. "Tomorrow, then, you and the rest of the would-be initiates will be tested, declare your intentions, and swear loyalty to the Rising Moon before your new brothers."

That night Jaiden had trouble sleeping. He was cold and could not seem to get comfortable on his mat. His leg itched in its sleeve, but he did not want to risk loosening it, afraid of what he might find.

The following day began much the same as the one before, but around noon Lieutenant Orestes dropped by to gather the initiates for their test. Jaiden, along with five other men and Palomar, walked out of the caves and into the sunlight of the stone steps. They sat in a crescent formation and were asked to talk about what they had learned while traveling in the presence of the Order.

"Humility."

"Bravery."

"Honor."

None of the responses were revealing, but as the others took turns sharing their observations, Jaiden thought hard about how his life had changed since Saffron and Sir Golddrake found him nearly dead, in the aftermath of the Halidor decimation.

"I have learned that, no matter how independent we think we are or strive to be, we can all benefit from someone watching over us." Jaiden's answer silenced the others for a moment, but drew nods from the Lieutenant and Palomar, seated beside him.

"I have learned," Palomar contributed, "that choices are sometimes hard. There is not always an easy answer or obvious solution. I do not envy Sir Golddrake those difficult choices, but when good intentions are there we must strive not to hold a bad outcome against him."

"Hey, his lips weren't moving when he spoke!" one of the recruits said.

Palomar smiled at the lad, and perhaps directed a few words toward him alone, for his mouth dropped open like a baby bird's.

"That is all for now," Orestes declared. "The point was simply to spend some time reflecting. Tonight, by the light of Criesha, Sir Golddrake will complete the ceremony. He will swear you in and present you with your shields. Make sure you wear your tabards, and by the sacred starlight make sure they are clean." He sniffed the air noisily. "Someone around here needs to take a bath," he said, standing and dismissing them. Jaiden's eyes darted from side to side, searching for recognition by the others of what the lieutenant smelled, but none presented.

The afternoon sped into evening, where time reverted to a crawl as the ceremony drew near. Jaiden felt nervous, though he had come to fully embrace his decision to join the Order. Perhaps the impending weight of responsibility, an unaccustomed burden, bothered him. What he only half-realized was the sentiment he shared that afternoon cut both ways. He would now share the task of looking after hundreds of other men, just as they would watch out for him.

The standard tabard did not work with Palomar's wings, so they fashioned a leather harness to fit around his torso, bearing a small replica of the Order's shield at the center of his chest.

The other initiates were dressed in the bright white tabards of the Order, and gathered near the entrance of the cavern, where the slanted moonlight fell freely upon them. Everyone was summoned for the event, to bear witness to the oath and officially welcome the new members into the fold.

Sir Golddrake grasped the hilt of his sword with both hands, blade down, and extended his arms. "Initiates, repeat after me: I swear to dedicate myself to the Order of the Rising Moon, in both thought and deed, until death or my Master releases me. I will honor the goddess, Criesha, with every action, and revere all she holds sacred. I will protect the magic in nature. I will defend the helpless from harm. I will give my life if it will save my brother. Honor, loyalty, courage, obedience, and charity – these are the five corners I will build my life upon – let all else fall to the wayside."

After the initiates spoke the words, Sir Golddrake sheathed his sword. One at a time, he received the pentagonal shields of the Order from Sir Kilborn, and bestowed them on their new owners.

Jaiden cradled his like it was an infant. The moment struck him harder than expected. That shield was the first object of worth he felt belonged to him. Painted white, with the crescent moon in violet at its center, it was beautiful, solid, his.

When the last initiate received his shield, the assembly roared with applause and cheers. Had it been winter, the celebration might have caused an avalanche. The passing days of isolation with no sign of Chelpian agents put the Order's caution on reserve. People he had not yet met congratulated Jaiden on his acceptance into their band, though more expressed their sentiments to Palomar.

Mead flowed freely, and the drinking continued far into the night. The mood of the camp was at its peak since they had taken to the hills. It seemed so long since the men had any excuse to release joy. Beautiful as it was, the Caves of Criesha were a constant reminder of their retreat.

Jaiden tried his hardest to drown concerns about his leg, relinquishing his freedom, and the possibility he may never wield a sword in meaningful combat again. After several hours of revelry, though, he found himself sitting alone in the moonlight on the same steps he occupied that morning. His dizzy mind drifted idly to images of his green-skinned goddess, before settling on Saffron. By the gods he missed her, and it made him feel foolish. Not in the mood for introspection, he stumbled off to his sleeping mat, sure his dreams would be visited by the raven-haired woman who seemed to be getting the better of him.

Two days later, the Order began splitting up. Most headed north toward Selamus, though they had to be careful to bypass the castle at Windhollow Rock, which Palomar reported was under siege. That meant staying off the road, and the journey would be a long one, especially for those on foot.

The first group of southbound troops left around the same time, a dozen or so, making their way through the hills to the Harpy Pass. Jaiden, excited and relieved Sir Golddrake had granted his request, was to be among the last to leave. His wounded leg continued to deteriorate, but he had to hold on and make this mission count. He had not dreamt of Criesha since reaching the caves, and no longer held out hope for the promises she had made him. Freeing the prisoners from Blackthorn might be the last useful thing he did before winding up an amputated invalid, begging for alms on the side of the road – the last thing worth remembering.

It was still the middle of the night when the canoe carrying the former Baron Rogan, Saffron min-Furasi, and her younger sister Dhania, came ashore on the western bank of the River Chelhos. The air was not overly cool, but their plunge from atop the wall of Hope's End left them wet, and Dhania was shivering.

Saffron helped Rogan pull their boat onto the beach. "We need a fire," she said, looking to her sister.

"I do not disagree," Rogan answered, leaving the oars while grabbing the rest of their supplies from the dug-out hull. "Yet, we cannot be sure if we are pursued. It would be too clear a signal to anyone following on the river."

"I can carry something," Dhania offered in her thick Begnari accent, seeing his hands were full. When Rogan hesitated she added, "I am not a child," and took one of the wet sacks directly from him.

"Baron Rogan, meet Dhania min-Furasi." Saffron's introduction implied her sister's identity was enough to explain her attitude. "Dhania, this is my friend, Rogan, former Baron of Thispany."

Rogan bowed his head, but the only response he received was a head-to-toe sizing by the younger sister. "Let us move inland past the tree line, and we can start a fire there." Neither woman proffered an argument, so they trudged over the wet sand, only to find the ground beyond the beach just as soggy. Insects began to harass them, and reaching the trees they discovered a frond-inhabited swamp, instead of a hardwood forest.

"Just lovely; where are we going to find dry wood in this bog?"

"Lady Saffron, you need only know where to look." Rogan moved from tree to tree, trying to find the right specimen with only the pale green moonlight to aid him. "Ah, there we are." He set down his burden and drew his dagger, using it to peel the bark off a nearby tree in long strips. "The inside of this is very flammable. I will gather enough for our fire, if you can find us a dry enough spot to make camp."

Within minutes Saffron located a workable patch of high ground, just spacious enough to accommodate the three of them and a campfire. She organized their packs, resting them against tree trunks, and was drawing out a change of dry clothes for her and her sister when Rogan joined them with arms full of stripped bark. He used his flint to get a flame going, then sat back to rest his weary body. His belly growled, but he was so tired he barely had the motivation to change out of his armor into something dry, let alone bother eating. Food could wait until morning.

With the fire providing warmth and a pleasant glow, Saffron handed a spare outfit to Dhania and stepped behind a tree, just beyond the radius of the light, to change. Her sister sought no such refuge. Standing in full view of the fire, she cast off the cloak Rogan lent her and started to raise her wet, silk top over her head.

Saffron was already halfway out of her armor when she realized her sister had not followed her example. "Dhania! There is a man present," she chided.

Dhania paused, but did not lower her shirt. "So? Do you not think men have been present these past months when I have changed clothes? And not so attractive as him, I can assure you."

She looked straight at Rogan, their eyes locking on one another. He knew he should resist, but found it beyond his power to look away. She resumed disrobing, watching him watch her as she exposed her body.

"Besides, I am pretty sure he enjoys it," she smiled. "Don't you?"

Rogan realized he was as good as trapped. Any response would lead to trouble, so he simply remained silent and closed his eyes.

"Dhania, it is not proper!" called Saffron from behind her tree, struggling to change as quickly as she could.

"Proper?" countered her younger sister. "Since I left Begnasharan with you, what part of my life has been proper? Was it proper I am still unmarried, but taught by other slaves how to service their King?"

Rogan opened his eyes, but Dhania had stopped dressing to argue with her sister. Utterly helpless, unable to move or say anything, he felt pity for Dhania and guilt for his earlier arousal. He was certain, however, he should not be present to witness this.

"Was I being proper when forced to service those slaves as well, or when the guards took turns with me when sure the King was away?" Dhania's voice cracked and tears of rage streamed down her cheeks.

Saffron reappeared wearing dry breeches and a soft, grey tunic. She encircled her sister in her arms, and Dhania's head dropped to her shoulder as she wept a season's worth of tears.

Rogan finally found his legs and grabbed some dry clothes from his pack in silence. The women did not seem to notice him, and with Saffron still whispering words of comfort to her sister, he stole out of camp into the swamp.

He changed out of his armor in seclusion, and though weary, he waited nearly an hour before returning. He had no idea what he would say to either of them. He did not truly know Dhania, though felt he already might, given she and Saffron were clearly close. His feelings for Saffron were alarming after being alone so long, and holding so tightly to the memories of his wife, but he recognized them all the same. Rogan hoped he had not damaged what they had, but her sister's presence certainly complicated matters.

He decided to gather more bark for the fire, and when he returned to camp, both Saffron and Dhania were sleeping soundly beside one another, covered by the same blanket. He slid his bedroll a little further from them and added the extra fuel to the fire. After laying out his armor to dry, he finally gave in to his weariness, too exhausted to keep watch. They would have to trust the darkness thwarted any pursuit.

The women were up first, and had already packed by the time Saffron shook Rogan awake. The smoldering remains of the fire expelled a thick, grey smoke, which had trouble clearing the canopy of wet leaves overhead. Saffron handed him a quarter loaf of bread after he sat up and rubbed his eyes.

"So, what is the plan from here?" she asked as if nothing had changed from the night before.

He took a sizable bite off the loaf and thought as he chewed. "Well, I suppose that depends on the two of you. You found your sister, and are on the right side of the river if you wanted to head home. Given the circumstances, I don't think anyone would blame you."

He spoke as if her leaving would be inconsequential, but his heart felt like it stopped beating, waiting for her to tell him she had decided to stay.

"I owe a debt to Sir Golddrake. Besides that, I want to see the King-priest pay for what he has done to Dhania, and countless like her. Not to mention, I am not sure your plan would succeed without me." She patted him on the shoulder and dropped to one knee to whisper in his ear, "Though, you should ask permission, before stealing another kiss." She followed with a peck on his cheek, then stood. "So," she declared in her full voice, "it is back to Talon Barge, then?"

Rogan looked at her with wonderment and envy. She made decisions so easily, with such clarity and confidence. He packed up his bedroll after stuffing the remainder of the bread into his mouth. Once he had chewed and cleared his throat with a swig from his waterskin, he addressed her declaration.

"If I may speak on behalf of Sir Golddrake, I would say that while we are both pleased by your decision to remain committed to our quest, we cannot all show ourselves back in Talon Barge, given recent developments. You and your sister would likely be spotted and recognized within three steps, and our entire enterprise would be forfeit." Rogan sighed, trying to devise a safe way to keep the ladies close to him.

"First, I suppose we should cast the canoe back into the river and let the current take it downstream. I should have done it last night, but thought you might want to use it to clear out. If anyone from Chelpa is after us, we do not want a clear indication of our landing point. Secondly, we should follow the river, though not too closely, north. This is the realm of Crioc – they have no king, they're more a collection of independent settlements who feel a commonality, uniting them against outsiders. It should be safe, more or less, to keep you on this side of the River Chelhos."

"I take it you are returning to see the viscount? If we cannot come with you, how will Dhania and I join you at the prison, still stuck on the western shore?"

"A ferry runs between Talon Barge and Lirole Run, the town on this side of the river. We will travel that far together, and I will continue on to Cyril's. I shall send for you by ferry when the ships are nearly ready to depart. Is that acceptable?"

After receiving Saffron's silent nod, Rogan led them back to the beach to take care of the canoe. From there they began the trek upstream toward civilization. The wetland terrain proved an annoyance, slowing their progress significantly, and they took most of the day covering the two leagues to the crossing.

The evening ferry was almost ready to depart by the time they arrived at Lirole Run. Rogan paid up front for the sisters' room and board, then caught the barge across the river, back into Chelpa. With so many considerations regarding the arrival of the Order and keeping them from detection, he could not afford to entertain distraction. He had to trust the sisters could fend for themselves for a fortnight.

After an hour, the ferry arrived in Talon Barge. "What is your business in Chelpa?" the harbor guard asked when Rogan's turn came to depart the ferry.

"I am an import acquisition agent for the *Silver Trumpet*. Just returning from trade negotiations in Moeria." Rogan forced himself to make eye contact, though his first inclination was to avoid it. He certainly looked the part – he was filthy, bedraggled, looking as if he had spent time in the wilderness – and yet retained an air of refinement.

"Where is your merchant seal?" the guard followed-up, his tone bland from asking the same questions dozens of times over.

"Ah, that's the thing." Rogan shrugged, leaning in closer to whisper. "It was a very difficult trip, and one of the carriers I hired disappeared in the jungle one night with some of my luggage. My seal was in that pack." He was determined not to let the increase in his pulse show on his features.

The guard's eyes darted up, scrutinizing Rogan more closely. The rouse must have been convincing enough. "Get a replacement before your next trip."

Following the tilt of man's head, Rogan nodded swiftly and stepped forward, exhaling only after his back was to the guard. By the time he approached Cyril's shop he was already thinking about a hot bath and the soft bed he had left behind. Lost in thoughts of these pleasantries, he did not notice the black-clad soldier standing watch until he was almost at the door.

Panic seized him, but he was too close to veer away without being obvious. The soldier did not move to arrest him, so it seemed he was unrecognized. The *Silver Trumpet* was a place of business, after all, though he realized it might seem odd for him to enter, laden with a pack of his own. He had no idea what he would say about the contents if searched.

Rogan was too tired to think of an alternative, and he had to get in touch with Cyril eventually to find out how the plan to smuggle in the Order was progressing, so he bolstered his nerves, continued to the door, and confidently swung it open. The soldier standing by eyed him as he passed, but made no move.

"Ingersol, a timely return!" called Cyril, approaching from behind the counter.

Rogan looked at him, confused, but as Cladius stepped forward to welcome him, he shifted his eyes meaningfully at a dark-haired man wearing a black tunic and boots, standing in the corner.

"How did the scouting trip to Moeria fare? Is everything in order for us to begin operations there?" Cyril clasped him in an uncomfortably long embrace, whispering, "Blood Tear Brotherhood," before separating.

"Everything is as it should be, Master Cyril." Rogan played along as he stepped further into the store, shifting his belongings to shut the door behind him.

"Well, you must be weary from your long trip. Go ahead and take your things below, and we can talk all about it after this gentleman has concluded his business." Cyril looked directly at the man in the corner this time. Curfew was moments away, and it was obvious no regular customers would be casually shopping so close to the deadline.

Rogan nodded and went downstairs, stowing his gear in the spare room he previously occupied. He returned to the foot of the stairs, remaining quiet as he listened for signs of trouble above. The warm bath would have to wait. He heard speaking, but no raised voices, and within a quarter-hour the front door was locked.

"Whew, that could have been a disaster," Cyril said as he appeared at the head of the stairs. "I think the agent bought it, but we shall have to be careful. He arrived first-thing this morning and stayed all damn day, scaring away most of the customers. I took it as a sign of your success, but one never knows."

Rogan relaxed and moved aside as Cyril passed him and headed for the kitchen. A pot of soup already warmed over the hearth fire, and he ladled a bowl for each of them.

"How would a spot of wine suit you?"

"Wonderfully," Rogan answered as he took a seat at the table.

"So you managed to actually pull it off? I cannot say I wouldn't have wagered against you. Is the Lady Saffron well?" Cyril's attempt to keep his concern subtle failed, though Rogan played along, letting him pour the wine and delaying an answer until he had his cup in hand.

"Well-enough, I suppose. I left her and her sister in Crioc." Rogan raised his cup as Cyril held his own out to propose a toast.

"Here is to sticking it to Ebon Khorel, one victory at a time."

"I will drink to that."

"So," Cyril's voice carried an edge of excitement as he also sat, "you must tell me all about it. I have wondered what the inside of the King-priest's island palace looks like. Are the walls encrusted with jewels?"

"Haha, whatever gave you that idea?"

Cyril shrugged, a slight look of embarrassment crossing his face.

"Well, the pleasure garden was a little extravagant," Rogan conceded, playing to the interest of his host. "It had a huge fountain, trees, and women – scores and scores of the most beautiful women."

"Ahh," Cyril sighed, looking out into space as his imagination wandered.

"But tell me about things on this end." Rogan hoped he had done enough to placate Cyril's particular fondness. He felt unsure about sharing the details of the previous night's endeavors just yet. "Did the Blood Tear Brotherhood give you much trouble? Are we still on schedule for our ships?"

"As I expected, after your little raid last evening, questions were certainly asked. You can bet the Brotherhood will want to find some answers before word of the incident reaches the King-priest. Of course I am not the only one my informants will talk to, and apparently they sang pretty quickly about my inquiries, when pressured by Blood Tear agents.

"What they found out I do not know for certain, but they arrived this morning demanding to search the premises. I even had to let them into the War Room, though of course I had already moved some of the more sensitive contraband to another location last night.

"They had the place staked out all day, and you can bet they will be watching for a few more, even if more subtly. We need to be careful about where we go when we leave here, Rogan, at least for a while."

Rogan nodded his understanding. "I suppose it is to be expected. I am sorry we put you in such a predicament. I know how frustrating the lack of freedom in the Empire can already be, without additional scrutiny."

"Ahhh," Cyril dismissed the notion with a wave of his hand as he took another sip of wine. "Think nothing of it. It is the price to pay for fighting back, no? I suppose you have been enduring it for years?"

"Well, things are a little different when you're trying to remain hidden. You have a business to run."

"Businesses, actually," Cyril countered, "which is lucky for you. I have already contracted the two ships for transport. Your friends will be riding upon the *Riverdog* and *Cutthroat*. The names should give you an indication of the kinds of people I am forced to work with, given the circumstances. We will be travelling under the guise of a major logging expedition to Moeria, for which I have already submitted the request for a charter. I had to spend a little extra coin making sure it is expedited and ready for our departure."

Rogan nodded as they both took a break from talking to spoon soup into their mouths. His belly grumbled greedily in anticipation. It seemed Cyril was coming through after all, though he wondered how much of that had to do with helping a friend, and how much was the lure of the fortune to be made off an illicit shipment of uril-chent.

"However," Cyril finally continued after emptying half his bowl, "given the watchful eyes of the Blood Tear Brotherhood, we cannot have your army showing up at the *Silver Trumpet*, even if only a few at a time. It will look too suspicious."

Rogan had not thought of that, but had to agree. "Where, then?"

"Someone, meaning you, since they won't recognize anyone else, will have to wait along the road and catch them before they reach Talon Barge." Cyril gave a moment to let the notion set in before continuing. "I will take you to my warehouse tomorrow, and you can lead them directly there. I have arranged to store some logging equipment there to appear legitimate, should the authorities decide to stop in."

Rogan sighed. It would be hard to give up his comfortable bed for indeterminate nights on the roadside, but he knew Cyril was right. They did not want to invite further intrusion by the Brotherhood, and the Order wouldn't trust a stranger to deliver such a change in plans. He figured he could spare another three days of indoor luxury before starting his watch.

"Alright." Rogan tipped his bowl and drank the last of his meal. "I am going to take a long-overdue bath, and will see you in the morning."

Rogan spent the next few days helping mind the store, freeing Cyril to continue making arrangements for the journey to Blackthorn. The morning of the fourth day, Rogan borrowed a horse and rode east out of the city, taking a few days' worth of rations and his bedroll. He found an amiable farmer, with property adjacent to the road, who let him board his horse and sleep in his barn in exchange for a few hours of labor a day.

The rest of the time, Rogan kept an eye out for travelers. After two days with no sign of the Order, he began to worry they had run afoul of Chelpian soldiers, and pondered riding on to find them.

The next day, though, while shoveling a mixture of manure and hay at the top of a hill, overlooking the trail to Talon Barge, he spotted a contingent of three riders and a dozen footmen, donned in drab travel-cloaks, approaching from the east. Rogan dropped his pitchfork and bounded down the far side of the hill, keeping out of sight until he traversed most of distance between them. He considered calling out before showing himself, but did not want to startle them, or worse, give himself away if these were not his men.

The group halted as Rogan finally wound into view, staying elevated from the road in case he was mistaken. Despite his care, his haste left him too winded to speak, though he raised his palm to request a moment's recovery. One of the riders drew back the hood from his head and spoke in surprise.

"Baron Rogan?" It was Sir Kilborn.

Upon recognition, Rogan felt at ease. He explained the change in their situation, asking them to wait while he retrieved his steed from the farmer's stable. He led them into Talon Barge and took them directly to the warehouse, which had been outfitted with basic living amenities and room for their horses.

Sir Kilborn, gruff as he came across, was obviously more at ease after having a chance to share the story of their journey with Rogan, and seeing firsthand the plan was advancing without too much interruption. For his part, Rogan felt more comfortable leaving Sir Kilborn in charge, knowing he would keep his men disciplined and not let them wander off to cause trouble in the wide city.

The concern was real. Imparting upon a group of young men just how different a Chelpian city was from the Northern Provinces remained a difficult task. As brash as fresh soldiers tended to be, it was recipe for trouble.

For the next week, a routine developed. Not wanting to risk the attention of sending messengers back and forth too far along the road, Rogan would ride to the farm to await the next group, then lead them into Talon Barge. Some had stories of passing enemy troops, but kept their composure, their foes too intent on reaching their destination to harass them much. The cover of hunting was reasonable enough to dissuade action, even if suspicion was present.

Sir Golddrake's contingent was the last to arrive, and they held a quiet celebration in the warehouse once all the members of the Order were safely accounted for. Sir Golddrake led a prayer, thanking Creisha for her protection over their journey, and Rogan found himself joining in. Surely it could not hurt.

He asked after Palomar, noting the Aasimar was not present. Sir Golddrake told him he waited some ways off, and would fly directly onto the ship under cover of night, once they put out to water.

Mating Day was fast approaching, and the *Riverdog* and *Cutthroat* both put into port at the docks, awaiting their cargo. After his counter-surveillance left Cyril confident the Blood Tear Brotherhood no longer kept constant watch on him and his shop, he showed up at the warehouse to inform them it was finally time to board.

The horses were led on first, and as expected, they were a bit uneasy stepping onto the ships. Rogan climbed the scaffolding of a building under renovation, some distance away, and took up position on the roof. From that vantage he continued to watch the Order of the Rising Moon as they boarded and carried on supplies, looking to see if he could spot anyone else who appeared interested in their activities.

He did not detect any unwanted attention after an hour of surveillance, so he climbed down and let Cyril know he was leaving to gather Saffron and Dhania. Catching the midday ferry across the river, he planned to return that evening in time for them to cast off. Rogan was astounded everything was turning out. In his experience that almost never happened, especially with stakes so high. The thought put him on edge, as he expected each passing moment to be the one something went unexpectedly wrong.

Neither of the ferry rides provided such an occasion, however, and by sunset he had reunited Saffron with Sir Golddrake and the rest of the Order. To a man they received her enthusiastically, and her sister garnered plenty of attention herself:

"I simply must plan a trip to Begnasharan when this campaign is over – seems like the perfect place to find a wife."

"Lady Saffron, you did not warn us how beautiful your sister was. Your father must be a proud and weary man, watching over the two of you."

"I'll give you one warning," Rogan broke in as a circle of admirers closed around the Furasi sisters. "Remember your oaths, lads."

He made sure to smile as he spoke, fighting his jealousy as the soldiers embraced the women in greeting. He knew they had not been in the presence of the fairer sex for some time, and these women in particular were intoxicating, but the lustful stares Saffron and Dhania evoked pricked his self-control.

For her part, Dhania played right back at them, and it took both Rogan and Saffron's full vigilance to ensure the flirting and innuendo did not escalate. He took comfort in Saffron's like-mindedness, and working with her to contain her sister kept the mood frivolous.

Stars poked through the evening canopy as the *Cutthroat* and *Riverdog* eased away from the merchants' wharf of Talon Barge. Rogan paced the deck of the *Cutthroat*, unable to breathe easily as they approached Hope's End. He was grateful Dhania was below getting some rest, and not present to see its imposing shadow looming on the horizon.

A stretch of over eighty leagues remained before the landing at Blackthorn Prison, and the ship's captain promised they would make the trip within two days, "less the world flipped upside-down." That was not a lot of time to plan, but plenty of time to think. Rogan had now been freed from Blackthorn longer than he spent there, but his incarceration still held power over him. Some nights he would wake and forget where he was, convinced the last few years were a dream and he remained locked inside his tiny room, the heat and stench of the mines clinging to him.

He feared after showing up and fighting his way in, he'd find the Dampers already dead. Cyril assured him there were monthly uril-chent shipments coming upstream, but that was far from a guarantee the Dampers were alive. Not only did Rogan owe his freedom to a Damper, he was determined to help them because no one else would.

A sudden flapping noise startled Rogan, and he turned to see the ghostly pearl skin of Palomar flash past him as the Aasimar alighted on the ship's deck.

Members of the crew Cyril hired on to do the sailing gasped and cried in alarm at the arrival of the strange, winged creature.

"Do not be panicked," Rogan yelled, raising his hands. "He is a friend, and of no danger to us."

"I am sorry if I alarmed you, Baron. I have been hiding my presence for days."

"Palomar! It is most excellent to see you again."

The gawking and murmurs continued unabated, though once it seemed unlikely Palomar was going to be harpooned, Rogan ignored their astonishment. Only a few lanterns were lit on the forecastle, but Rogan caught the glint of metal upon Palomar's chest.

"I see you have made an addition to your wardrobe."

The Aasimar looked down and realized Rogan was speaking of his shield-harness. *"Yes, it suits me, I think. I do not understand the will of Criesha as some of my new brothers seem to, but for now I trust in the virtues of the Order to guide my path."*

Rogan could only shake his head at the oddity of such an outsider following a goddess of men. But then he felt it altogether odd that beings no one could see appeared to have such profound influence on the world these days.

"My harness is not the only thing new," Palomar admitted. *"See what else Sir Golddrake has given me!"* Palomar reached behind his head and drew forth the largest greatsword Rogan had ever seen. *"A shield made flying too awkward, and this seems to be more my style, anyway."* The blade looked to be nearly as tall as Rogan, and its hilt long enough to accommodate both of Palomar's ample hands.

"Well, I'll be an executioner's bucket... that is a huge weapon. Are you able to wield it?"

"*I am getting the knack. Jaiden Luminere has kept me practicing during our journey south. He is an expert swordsman, and a fine teacher.*" Palomar waved the blade in a circular motion above his head, then brought it down in a chopping motion to demonstrate. Seeing the uneasy look on Rogan's face at having such a large piece of sharpened steel swinging before him, Palomar stowed the weapon once more in its harness.

"*Not to change the subject, but how many ships are in your armada?*"

"What do you mean?" Rogan asked reflexively, not ready for the question. "We have two caravels. You are on board the *Cutthroat*, and the *Riverdog* behind us carries the rest of the soldiers."

"*And the smaller ship behind her?*"

"What smaller ship?"

"*Granted, there was more distance between them, and it was difficult to spot with its black sails, but I certainly passed a third ship.*"

Rogan scrambled to the aft of his boat and peered upstream, but he could not see past the *Riverdog*. "You are certain?"

Palomar nodded.

"Perhaps it is a part of the King-priest's fleet, heading toward Hope's End." Rogan looked east at the silhouette of the island structure. Their ship steered close to the western shore to give the palace a wide berth, and they were just passing it. His theory made sense given the recent infiltration, but Rogan felt a return of the uneasiness he experienced prior to Palomar's arrival.

"Once we're a little further downstream, would you check to see if it is still following us?"

Palomar bowed his head, *"Of course."*

Rogan could not help peering back into the darkness every minute or so, until finally his obsession was too much for even Palomar to bear.

"Alright, I shall see if the boat is still behind us." The Aasimar stretched his feathery wings and leapt into the air, flapping them downward until he gained enough height to clear the sails. The moonlight painted his feathers a greenish blue, not unlike the sea on a summer day. Rogan followed the arc of Palomar's flight until the dark and distance consumed him. Then, he could only wait.

The seconds passed achingly slowly. Was it a minute without word? Two? Rogan stared into the sky to catch the first sign of the Aasimar's return, but Palomar's telepathy reached him first.

"Sound the alarm, Baron! They are here and they mean us harm."

Rogan waved his arms frantically and shouted to catch the attention of anyone on the deck of the *Riverdog*, but the wind swallowed his voice, and the heavy darkness rendered his gestures useless.

He ran to the helmsman. "We need to warn the *Riverdog* they are in danger from another craft. Can you slow the ship and bring us alongside? I am sure the captain would approve."

The sailor shot him a smug look before calling out, "Aye-aye." He turned the wheel starboard and yelled, "Drop the foresails! Coming about! Act lively on the aft look-out! Signal the distress, rouse the captain!"

Aboard the *Cutthroat*, Jaiden was disappointed to find Saffron had been taken to the other boat, but he eventually realized it might be for the best. His song, while close, was unfinished, and the most challenging battle of his life drew near. The mission came first, and such a distraction might rob his focus. Brave deeds would speak better than any words he could muster, and the time for wooing was after such a display. Should he fall, he might also be spared making a fool of himself his memorial. Yet he still wondered if Saffron wanted to check on him and was unable before boarding, or if she had forgotten and no longer cared.

The ride south from the Caves of Criesha to Talon Barge shaped a change in his perspective. Impossible to hide the deteriorating condition of his wounded appendage from Palomar, he confided the truth to both the Aasimar and Sir Golddrake. He was unsure he wanted to go on living without his leg, but realized keeping it would likely mean his death. It might already be too late. He implored them with how badly he wanted to do something meaningful, and how this mission was his last chance to achieve such a goal. He was half-expecting to die, and fully prepared for their pity when he told them so.

Pity, however, was not what he received. Sir Golddrake stated that, while death was a possible outcome for all on this mission, he firmly believed it was not Jaiden's time. He believed Criesha had a special plan for him, and that he should have faith in the course of the goddess. Jaiden did not mention he had visited with Criesha several times in his dreams, but that lately she had abandoned him.

To hear another person, someone he respected, assert that he was meant for more than a slow death from disease, or even a quick death so early in battle, gave him chills. He wanted to believe as well, but such faith seemed the shortest path to disappointment. Whatever his fate, his choices brought him here, sailing down the River Chelhos with a future undetermined.

Though dubious at first, never seeing a ship so large, Jaiden was coming around to the merits of water travel. One could move great distances with little effort, and his cabin was eminently more comfortable than the saddle. He was contemplating his possible future as a sailor and beginning to drift off to sleep, soothed by the steady movement of the boat, when raised voices and a loud thump from above stirred him abruptly.

"What is going on?" another soldier asked, his feet dangling from the bunk above. Another yell, accompanied by the sound of splintering wood, and suddenly the entire cabin was scrambling to put on boots and find a weapon. Jaiden found his crutch and was rising from his bunk as the first of his neighbors ascended the steps and unlatched the door to the ship's deck.

Beyond the door was chaos. The first man who stepped beyond it was pierced by the point of rapier and spilled back down the steps. Yelling, cursing, orders being shouted, and the clamor of steel against steel exploded before the door was kicked closed. Several cabin mates picked up their fallen comrade and lay him on an empty bunk. One tore the sleeve from his tunic and pressed it against the wound to stanch the bleeding.

No one seemed eager to try the door again. Jaiden picked up the injured soldier's discarded sword and steeled his nerve, then limped up the three steps to the cabin entrance. After a deep breath he shouldered the door open and stepped out onto the deck. It was worse than he imagined.

One of the sails was on fire, and the ship swarmed with what he presumed to be river pirates. Another, smaller boat bobbed alongside the *Riverdog*, latched with thick ropes and grappling hooks. Bodies from each side littered the slippery deck, which pitched wildly back and forth as the two hulls bumped one another.

Jaiden saw the *Cutthroat* attempting to move into position beside them, but it was having trouble battling the current, outpacing the stagnant pair threaded together. Their help might come too late – the *Riverdog* may have to fight its way through this alone, he realized.

The two hulls smacked again, and the deck lurched beneath his feet. His crutch slipped, losing contact with the floor, and he tumbled into the back of one of the attacking pirates. The pirate turned and pushed him off to create separation, then hacked at Jaiden with his cutlass. Stumbling backward, Jaiden was barely able to raise his sword high enough to deflect the blow.

A stray rope hanging from the damaged rigging swung to his left. Jaiden took hold of it and wound once around his wrist, stabilizing his shaky stance. He parried high then low, following the second with his own cut to the midsection, too fast for the unsuspecting pirate. His longsword cut easily through the unarmored belly of the outlaw, whose surprised look quickly drained with the loss of his intestines.

In the midst of the fighting, Jaiden heard singing from above. Stealing a glance upward he saw a white form that must have been Palomar, hovering, enveloped in a mist that saturated the flaming sail. Instantly reassured, he called on his cabin mates, who were waiting on the steps for an opportunity to join the fight.

More soldiers spilled out of the forecastle as well, and the pirates suddenly had the collective look of a scared dog who picked the wrong fight. Although more used to fighting on vessels such as the *Riverdog*, they were no match for a larger, trained fighting force, not to mention a roused Aasimar.

The Order cut down another ten of their enemy before the objective obviously shifted from looting to retreat. Some tried to dislodge the grappling hooks, while others jumped directly overboard, opting for the quickest route of escape. Within minutes, the deck of the *Riverdog* had been cleared of still-breathing assailants and separated from the parasitic, pirate vessel. Palomar had completely doused the fire from the sails, and a victorious cheer went up from the remnants of the crew.

Sir Golddrake did not cheer, however. All told, they were now sailing south with a dozen fewer men. When Rogan got word of their losses on the *Cutthroat*, he cursed himself for his earlier prayer. He was a fool for ever asking – bad luck had struck anyway, and now he would have to reconsider his plan.

Chapter 19

Assault on Blackthorn

From Sir Amurel Golddrake's perspective, the Order of the Rising Moon was already heading into the endeavor light on numbers. The attack of the river pirates, and subsequent loss of soldiers, only exacerbated the problem. He was uneasy relying so heavily on subterfuge for martial success, but the losses gave him little choice other than to trust Baron Rogan's plan.

Rogan's contacts were in play, and his knowledge of prison operations made them dependent. Amurel could only pray to Criesha he was not sending his men to a meaningless slaughter.

A wide mudflat, several leagues north of Blackthorn, provided an opportunity for them to anchor the ships close to land. In the shallows, the twenty-five horses they brought were unloaded. After the animals were led ashore, Amurel, Sir Kilborn, Jaiden, and the other designated riders made their way to the road. It saw few visitors, and was the only path from which Blackthorn was accessible. The knights headed south until they were within sprinting distance of the fortress. There, at the edge of the jungle, all they could do was stay hidden and wait for the gates to open from the inside. That was Rogan's job.

After depositing the cavalry, Baron Rogan and the others took the ships to dock at Blackthorn Prison. The day was pleasant enough, as mid-spring days in Chelpa often were, and Rogan took a moment on the deck of the *Cutthroat* to close his eyes and bask in the warmth of the sun on his upturned face. The cool wind blowing through his short, thick hair, allowed the brief illusion this was just an innocent, spring day.

But it was not – this was Mating Day. The prison guards at the docks would not be expecting a shipment of goods, so suspicion at the arrival of his ship – the *Riverdog* trailed behind and would join them later – was to be expected. Mating Day would serve as his excuse, his way in. An old observance, its customs were renewed and perverted when the King-priest came to power.

Originally meant to celebrate the natural fertility of the season, Mating Day occurred on the middle day of spring, included feasting to honor the earth's bounty, and private acts of coupling, behind closed doors, to honor the gift of children. Rogan remembered such a celebration with his wife years ago – the day they conceived their son.

Under the current regime, however, it had essentially devolved into a public display of sanctioned rape. In many communities, young women were selected and forced to publicly mate with a chosen male, which sometimes became several men.

The military population at Blackthorn was denied such a celebration, due to the astute concern that if the inmates caught wind of it, a riot might ensue. If the temperament of the guards was anything like it used to be, however, Rogan saw little chance of them turning down a special gift from the King-priest.

The danger to Saffron would be severe, but she insisted on volunteering once he shared the plan, recognizing it was the best way to gain the tactical advantage they desperately needed. At least a hundred, seasoned guards with military experience resided on site, and though it was now a prison, Blackthorn still possessed all the strategic defenses of the fortress it was designed to be. Strong walls, a moat, anti-siege engines, and skilled archers combined to make a forced infiltration beyond foolish.

The prison sat high on the cliff ahead – a daunting vision. A lump stuck in Rogan's throat. How did he ever imagine he could pull this off? He was wearing the new armor Natrone had made him. Saffron donned hers that morning. Dhania would remain in the deepest hold of the ship until one of them retrieved her after the fighting was over.

His saber and dagger already sheathed at his hips, Rogan swept and fastened a crimson cloak, bearing the Royal insignia of the Inquisitor's Office, around his shoulders. He would carry Lady Saffron's spear and shield, as well. Playing the role of the Mating Offering, she would have to enter unarmed.

The ship was about to anchor, and Rogan went below to find Saffron. She was standing beside Palomar, his hands clasped over hers. Their heads were tilted forward, his chin buried in her hair. Though their eyes were closed and neither made a sound, Rogan had no doubt Palomar was speaking to her, perhaps sharing some final words of encouragement. He felt he could use some, too.

Finally, the Aasimar lifted his head and looked at Rogan. *"She is ready. I cannot thank you both enough for this – I understand the danger you face. My people shall never forget your compassion and bravery."*

Rogan stepped forward and clasped Palomar's shoulder. He was so nervous, he felt even trying to speak might cause him to lose his breakfast, so he trusted in Palomar's perceptiveness, leaving his thoughts unsaid. He offered his hand to Saffon, who clasped it with her own trembling hand and followed as he led her back up to the deck to disembark. Selling their story from the outset would be important.

Wrapped in a brown travelling cloak, she drew the hood to conceal her sex from the general prison population. The River Chelhos flowed well beneath the fortress proper, so anything unloaded from the docks had to be brought through the mines. Neither Rogan nor the prison guards wanted to deal with the frenzy that would break out if the prisoners knew a woman walked amongst them.

"I will be ready for your signal, and to unleash the wrath of Mount Celestia. Good luck, and may Criesha's light shine upon us." Palomar stayed below as Rogan and Saffron broke into the sunlight.

The *Cutthroat* came to a halt, and no fewer than five guards awaited an explanation on the docks. A pair of archers covered them from the small, defensive post near the mine entrance. As the boarding plank was put in place by the sailors, Rogan could already hear the demanding questions of the commanding officer.

"What is this ship, and what is the purpose of its landing at my dock?"

"No need to yell, captain." Rogan tried to use his most entitled tone of voice. "His Imperial Highness, Ebon Khorel, has sent me to extend his gratitude for the faithful service of all of your men. In other words – I have a gift for you." Rogan grabbed the edge of his cloak and whisked it around, making sure its insignia became visible.

"Inquisitor," the captain's insistent inflection tapered considerably, "how unexpected. What kind of a gift?"

"A Mating Day gift." Rogan extended his hand sideways and Saffron stepped forward to take it, simultaneously pulling back her hood. She kept her eyes low in appropriate deference to the men, and Rogan winked at them for good measure.

Gasps and murmurs of instant appreciation followed, culminating in the captain's stammering response, "What, here?"

"Oh, certainly not," Rogan responded, trying to sound insulted. "A specimen this exquisite must be used for the viewing enjoyment of all. The ceremony will commence in the main yard, as soon as everyone can be gathered, of course. Now, if you would be so kind as to provide an escort, I am sure we would all like the festivities to begin as soon as possible."

His idea seemed to be working even better than Rogan had expected. No one asked questions about who the ship's other passengers might be, or any business other than the one he proposed. He found it easy to play along, making up simple answers while stringing along the guards' hopes they might be picked as volunteers for the demonstration.

Stepping back into the mines, though, was accompanied by a rush of memories – the work, the pain, the lost years of his imprisonment, all packed into unwanted flashes. Rogan pushed aside the distraction the moment he saw the first Damper. He had forgotten how repellant their forms truly were, and how it tainted the way everyone treated them.

He alone knew their complexity, how twisted their story. No one else wanted to think of them as anything other than a tool. Rogan didn't blame the other prisoners for feeling that way, for he had done the same. He tried to hide his interest in the Dampers, stealing glances to get a count of how many might still be around.

By the time he and Saffron were climbing the long, winding Tower of a Thousand Stairs, word had gone out to the staff, and all the prisoners were being rounded up for an early return to their cells. None of the guards wanted to miss the upcoming show, and did their best to clear the mines as soon as possible.

Rogan was impressed by Saffron's restraint as well, silently enduring the soldiers' crude comments about what they would like to see done to her, and the creative ways they would use her if given the chance. Once they transitioned to the halls of the prison, Rogan could appreciate just how hot and stuffy the mines were. Sweat dripped from their climb, and the fresher air was a welcome guest.

"This way," said the guard captain, taking a left turn down a short hall, while the rest of his men continued forward. Preparations to lock down the prison for the afternoon were no doubt numerous. The captain led them to a courtyard, where the return to daylight temporarily blinded them after the dark of the underground tunnels.

"Inquisitor..."

"Captain," Rogan responded with flare.

The guard gave an uneasy laugh, before stammering, "Might I, well, that is, I was wondering..."

"Out with it, man. No one here but the two of us." Of course, Saffron didn't count.

"Well, if you do need a volunteer to start things off, I was wondering if I might have the honor. The men, well, they look up to me, and I think it would help morale. Also, the rotations are going longer with the war, and I have not seen my wife in two moons."

"Ah, I get your meaning," answered Rogan. "Sir, I cannot think of anyone who deserves it more." *And may you be the first to die*, he thought silently.

The captain broke into a wide grin. "Thank you. Thank you, Inquisitor."

A platform near the center of the yard was set up with a chopping block for executions. Rogan led Saffron to it, explaining to the captain, "I suppose we will set things up over here." Once he'd put some distance between them and the guard, Rogan whispered to Saffron, "How are you holding up so far?"

"I can think of an honor or two I would like to bestow upon the captain," she hissed from under her hood.

"All in due time; it will not be much longer now." Rogan, still holding her shield and spear in his left hand, used his right to shade his eyes as he looked around the top line of the outer wall. None of the posted guards seemed to have any cause to be alarmed yet. Rogan worried some ally would get over-anxious and act too soon. He hoped for enough of a distraction inward to keep the sentries from noticing Palomar, or the delayed approach of the *Riverdog*.

"We should sit," Rogan determined. Once they were both settled on the platform, Rogan set the spear down as nonchalantly as possible so it would not roll, and lay the shield flat as well. "Your arms, should you need them, my lady."

"My thanks, sir," she mimicked his tone. Rogan smiled, glad Saffron's sense of humor was intact. "Am I ready for this?" Saffron spoke the question aloud, but Rogan got the impression she asked it of herself. Her heels tapped repeatedly against the base of the platform.

After a sigh, she drew down her hood, then apparently thought better of it and removed her cloak altogether, deciding it was time to draw more eyes to her. Her hair was braided into its long ponytail, and although she wore armor, it was unlike anything the men of the prison had ever seen – supple and crimson, with flashes of skin beneath piquing their interest.

Almost immediately, men began to spill from various inner doorways of the fortress, gathering into the courtyard, ready for the Mating Day ceremony to begin.

"Do you think our soldiers will be in position?" Saffron asked quietly. "The moments between us starting and them showing up are likely to be the longest, most intense of our lives."

"Saffron, I am shocked to hear a lady speak so bluntly." Rogan tried to jest, though his heart pounded the truth of her words. "They will be in position," he added soberly, "or this will be over extremely quick. Either way, there is naught we can do about it now."

The crowd had swelled, but it parted as two armored figures, trailing black capes and wearing frightening, beast-like helmets, made their way from the fortress to the execution platform. Rogan and Saffron stood at their approach.

"What is the meaning of this?" the metallic voice behind one of the helms asked. "On whose authority have you ordered this spectacle? All ceremonies must be approved and overseen by the proper servants of the Dread Tyrant."

"I would not have dreamed of starting until you arrived to preside, good sir. The event, however," the glee in Rogan's voice quickly departed, "is sanctioned by the King-priest himself, and as his appointed officer, I am only seeing through his wishes."

A stare-down ensued, though Rogan felt certain he could not win, since the eyes of his opponent were hidden. Nevertheless, it was the Gholdur war-priest who flinched first and backed off his initially harsh approach.

"*We* are here now, Inquisitor, and shall take over enactment of the ceremony."

Boos rained down from the crowd, who were obviously aware that wherever the Dread Tyrant got involved, enjoyment seemed to evaporate. The priests must have been used to it, for they walked to the platform without a reaction or hesitation.

"You will want to be off the platform when I get started," Saffron whispered as Rogan passed. They shared a look, but he knew better than to doubt her.

The war-priests took over his place on the platform, and as Rogan stepped away, the impression he was seeing Saffron alive for the last time seized him. The captain edged hopefully closer, but seemed less confident now that the priests had taken over. Rogan distanced himself from the crowd, backing toward the main gate, though he was at least twenty long strides from it. His hands migrated to the hilts of his weapons, and the sweat that started on his climb up the Tower of a Thousand Stairs returned, beading his face.

He couldn't be certain the entire Imperial presence of the prison had gathered, but the assembly had swelled to at least a hundred. A few silhouettes still dotted the wall, and no doubt a handful of uninterested stragglers remained inside the fortress, but the audience was surely near capacity.

Given their helmets, it was difficult to tell where the priests were looking, but they flanked Saffron, and the silence of anticipation spread through the crowd. The priests, however, were not the next to raise their voices.

Saffron raised her arms and sang out in a powerful, moving voice, shocking the entire Blackthorn contingent. Her lyrics flowed forth, indecipherable yet assertive, pouring over her in visible form. Bright orange and red streaks of light danced from her mouth over her body, wrapping her in a cocoon of energy. Not even Rogan knew what to think, but he alone had the sense to distance himself even further. The streaks grew thicker into tongues of flame, licking the surface of Saffron's body without consuming her. Her voice grew bolder.

The crowd was mesmerized, captivated by the beauty of the magic before them, unsure of its purpose, unable to look away. Rogan realized they too must be haunted by the experience – he could still see the fire when he closed his eyes, and it continued to grow.

When Saffron was barely visible through the dancing flame she hit her crescendo, sending a nova of red-orange heat exploding across the platform. It scorched the war-priests as well as the first row of spectators, knocking them prone with its shock-wave. A few of the onlookers' clothes, as well as the executioner's block, caught fire.

Before the dumbstruck look melted off most of their faces, Palomar swooped down and landed between the platform and the guards, also singing. His angelic presence drew most of their attention – quite the feat, given what they just witnessed.

Saffron picked up her spear and shield and yelled at Rogan, "Go!"

Snapping to action, Rogan bolted for the gate. Even looking the opposite direction, he could sense the bright flash of Palomar's blinding aura from the corner of his eye. He ran straight to the winch controlling the drawbridge. Drawing his saber, he pounded the lever stabilizing the counterweight with his spare hand. It shifted position and one stone fell, raising another on a pulley. He could hear the rapid descent of the heavy bridge beyond the gate, crashing to its final position within seconds.

The gate itself posed a more difficult obstacle. He had to pry the heavy support beam out of its brackets, a job meant for a man on each side. Sticking his saber into the ground, he laid his back against the gate and pushed his shoulders just under the beam.

Across the yard the guards had armed themselves and were pressing on Saffron and Palomar, who backed slowly toward him, trying to keep from being surrounded. No sign of the Order's soldiers. He hoped they were able to maneuver through the mine without meeting resistance or becoming lost. His directions had been simple, but it could be difficult for the uninitiated to navigate the tunnels. He needed to get this infernal gate open so he could rejoin them.

As soon as he placed his hands wide and started pushing up on the beam, a black-feathered arrow pierced the gate with a chipping sound, mere inches below his left arm. It startled him and he dropped the beam back into place. The angle of the arrow indicated a shot from above, but he could not immediately find the location of the archer. Summoning all his strength, he roared and once again pushed upward. The beam budged, but started to tilt as he lifted higher, threatening to slip back on his right side. With a final effort he gripped the bottom of the beam and slid it away from the gate, then let go.

The wooden support fell to the ground, jostling from the impact in a series of vibrating thumps. The gate was unbarred. Rogan grasped a bracket on one side of the seam with both hands, leaning back to pull the gate open. The *swoosh* of another arrow brought a jolt of pain through his entire arm as it pierced beneath his left shoulder.

Through the crack between the separating gate doors he could see the mounted knights of the Order fast approaching. Palomar and Saffron were in dire need of reinforcements. Pushing on, Rogan concentrated on one side at a time, leaning his right shoulder to the outside of the door and groaning until it swung to an inward angle.

He moved to the other side and did the same, clearing the way just as the hooves of the horses struck the drawbridge. A thunder of hollow-ringing stamps echoed as the cavalry passed. Rogan fell to his knees, weary from the effort. He winced as he reached back to grasp the arrow, testing to see how deep it had gone. Not likely a fatal wound, he stood and unsheathed his dagger, knowing he would feel better once he removed the arrow and found an enemy to stab.

The entire ride from the beach to the grove where they hid, Jaiden felt like he was going to vomit from the excitement. Then came the waiting, which was excruciating. Once Palomar flew over the wall, however, signaling the start of the final charge, the uneasiness had all been worth it. At last, Jaiden felt the exhilaration of charging into battle on horseback.

With his shield upon his left arm and the reins is his hands, he placed his trust in Inferno, letting his steed's training take over. A moment of worry snuck up when it looked like the gates might not open before they arrived, but once he saw them swinging inward the adrenaline took over and he drew his sword, ready to face whatever foes awaited inside that fortress.

Unlike the fight on the deck of the *Riverdog* two nights ago, there was plenty of space to maneuver, though his side was now the one outnumbered. The courtyard of the prison was a vast square of grainy earth, with sparse patches of grass struggling here and there. The enemy was concentrated ahead, hemming in the Order's foot soldiers toward the far end of the yard. Sir Golddrake led their charge in that direction, but Jaiden peeled to the left when he spotted Saffron and Palomar facing grim odds in the northeast corner of the square.

They were surrounded by ten men, clad in mail and black cloaks. Even amid the cacophony of alarm bells, war-howls, hoof beats, and clanging weapons, Jaiden could make out Palomar's singing. As Inferno brought him closer, he could see the blade of the Aasimar's greatsword, crackling with white energy.

When Palomar swung and contacted an enemy's sword, a peel of thunder rang as if lightning had struck, and the weapon flew from his opponent's shocked hand.

Saffron followed with a cobra-quick thrust of her spear, impaling the suddenly defenseless man. Yet a pair of warriors circled behind her, and one swept the haft of his spear at her ankles, tripping her. As she fell to her knees, Jaiden pressed the flanks of his horse to hasten to her aid.

The second soldier behind Saffron brought his blade downward, though she managed to raise her shield and meet his blow. Jaiden let out a battle-cry and swung his sword. The man attacking Saffron heard and turned in time to see Jaiden bearing down on him, but not quickly enough to prevent being nearly cloven in two.

His fellow with the spear was likewise surprised and trampled by Inferno, who danced and leapt sideways to clear his feet from the entanglement of the man's body, smashing him further in the process. The other nearby warriors backed slightly, possibly reassessing their tactics with the addition of a mounted opponent.

Jaiden was not waiting for them to figure out a new plan. He urged his steed into their midst and Palomar followed his lead, pushing them back with huge sweeps of his thundering sword. Saffron regained her feet, only to turn when the sound of chanting rose behind her, where the enemy had already been cleared.

One of the war-priests, a cudgel in one hand while the other clenched near his chest, was standing fifteen paces away, channeling the dark power of his god. The midsection of his armor was charred black by Saffron's fire-burst, and she strode forward to finish the job. She had only covered half the distance, however, when the priest kneeled and struck his hand against the ground.

A line of black, as if the earth was rapidly changing to ash, raced from his fist along a path toward Saffron. When it reached her legs they turned black as well, up past her knees, and Jaiden watched as she struggled to take another step. The war-priest finished chanting and stood, repeatedly slapping the head of his cudgel against his open palm as he stalked forward.

"Jaiden!" Saffron called, panic in her voice. "My legs – I cannot move my legs!"

Jaiden swiveled to strike once more at his opponent, but his blow was parried. He glanced over his shoulder again toward Saffron, who collapsed to her knees, nearly keeling over completely.

Palomar turned as well to see what was happening. *"Go to her, I will hold them off."*

Jaiden nodded and yanked on the reins, causing Inferno to whinny and circle in Saffron's direction. He galloped forward, but to make matters worse, an arrow arced from above, right on target with Saffron. She deflected it with her shield, but was still rooted in place by the war-preist's spell.

Inferno interposed between Saffron and the war-priest, who halted his approach when Jaiden extended his sword. Looking back, Jaiden saw some of the enemy working beyond Palomar's reach toward them. The Aasimar could not hold six men at bay simultaneously.

"Son of the Abyss," Jaiden cursed and sheathed his sword. Inferno reared and struck out with his hooves when the priest took a step forward, causing him to rethink his advance. When his horse came down, Jaiden leaned over and stretched out his free arm to Saffron. She moved her spear to her shield hand and gripped his offered wrist as tightly as she could.

With all his strength, Jaiden yanked Saffron up onto Inferno's back, directly behind him. He spurred his mount forward just as enemy reinforcements arrived, leaving them in a wake of dust and up-churned grass. With his friends safe, Palomar leapt into the air and flew to find where he was most needed.

"Thank you for saving me," Saffron managed to say between deep breaths. "He used some dark magic."

"I am only returning the favor," Jaiden replied, happy for the opportunity. "Hold on!" he yelled as he turned his mount suddenly to avoid a pair of allies knocked into his horse's path by a sonic blast, similar to the one that victimized him on the road from Greyhorne. "We have to do something about those war-priests!"

"The Dampers!" Saffron clutched him tightly around the waist to keep from falling, bringing her lips directly behind his left ear.

"What?" Jaiden heard her, but had no idea what she meant.

"Rogan said the Dampers absorbed the King-priest's divine energy. There!" she pointed toward a doorway leading into the prison. The Order's foot soldiers had spilled forth from it and were still nearby, shielding it from enemy troops. "See if you can get us to that entrance."

Jaiden did not understand what Saffron had in mind, but he needed to reach a safer place to deposit her before rejoining the fight. He urged Inferno forward, weaving around the skirmishes taking place over most of the courtyard.

"The feeling is returning to my legs!" Saffron's excitement nearly cost her place on the back of Jaiden's horse as she released her grip to pinch her thigh, testing whether her impression was true. To prove it was, she sprung down from Inferno as they neared the open doorway, and quickly disappeared inside.

Jaiden trusted she knew what she was doing, and moved to rejoin Sir Golddrake. The cavalry was proving effective, and it seemed to Jaiden that the numbers on both sides were now almost even, granting the Order an overall advantage with their superior troops. Between their knights and Palomar, he assumed they should carry the day if they could only subdue the war-priests.

But Jaiden had not counted on the archers, either. It took time for them to coordinate and get into position, but nearly a dozen of them now moved along the outer wall, picking off the Order's men wherever they found clear targets.

Palomar was hovering near the Master of the Order when Jaiden caught up. Two of the war-priests had taken up position on the execution platform, surrounded by guards to protect them as they invoked the power of the Dread Tyrant, Gholdur.

"We need to clear that platform," Sir Golddrake yelled from behind his visored helm, struggling to be heard over the cries of several nearby allies suddenly doused with hot tar from above. "Are you with me?"

"We are," Palomar responded for the group, quicker than any of the men could speak the words. With the completion of his thought an arrow, launched from an archer on the wall, struck Palomar in the abdomen. His flight faltered briefly, but it was enough for Jaiden to see the Aasimar was hurt. He had silently wondered whether his winged friend was actually invulnerable. An uncomfortable expression marred Palomar's countenance, but vanished an instant later. *"Perhaps I should deal with our enemies on the walls?"*

"Of course, Palomar," Sir Golddrake said. "Jaiden, come. You and Sir Kilborn with me. Hee-ya!" he spurred Bastion forward, and the nearby group of cavalry charged to the middle of the courtyard to take on the war-priests.

Some of the foot soldiers had gotten the same idea, tired of taking repeated losses to the corrupting power of Gholdur's servants. Half-a-dozen of them moved purposefully in formation toward the platform, and closed before Jaiden and his contingent. They paid for their bravery.

Working in conjunction, the war-priests called down a column of bluish energy from the very air above their enemies. It smote all five of the soldiers, and as the column collapsed on itself a moment later, the bodies of those consumed lay motionless and smoldering in a smoking heap.

The sight was enough to halt Sir Golddrake's charge. The riders all pulled back on their reins, horrified by what they had just witnessed, and afraid to suffer the same fate.

Jaiden Luminere defied their collective hesitation. "They still have to be stopped."

Urging Inferno forward he drew his sword, intent on making the war-priests pay for their deeds. Two seconds later the others followed, muttering prayers to Criesha to spare them from a similar fate.

The priests turned their attention to the oncoming riders, and their protectors directed their shields toward the charge. Ominous chanting began anew, and the war-priests clasped one another's hands to strengthen the focus of their channeling.

A sound like rushing air filled Jaiden's ears as he closed on the platform. He glanced upward and saw a swirling vortex of blue energy about five body lengths above. He lifted his sword to strike the guard standing nearest the edge of the platform as he passed, hoping to at least take one out before turning into a pile of molten flesh.

The column of divine power rushed downward as before, but never reached Jaiden or his companions. Instead, it redirected sideways, like a cyclone leaping from one point to another. The blast of energy was pulled harmlessly to the Dampers, who Saffron had brought out to the courtyard from their cells. It enveloped them momentarily in a bright glow, before all trace of the column vanished.

Jaiden's sword ripped through the legs of two guards, clanging off the shield of a third. He circled around to see Saffron charging an enemy soldier, leaping into the air and striking from an unexpected angle, as was common to her fighting style. The war-priests howled with rage, yelling orders for the Dampers to be dealt with.

It didn't appear Saffron had considered their physical defenselessness. Jaiden watched as a band of black-clad soldiers broke off their attack on the Order's infantry and hustled toward the spindly, mucus-covered creatures. Saffron would not be able to handle them all herself.

He looked back at the platform, where Sirs Golddrake and Kilborn, along with their vanguard, seemed to be giving the war-priests' contingent all they could handle. Jaiden knew what he had to do. He urged Inferno to a gallop, trying to intercept those bound for the Dampers. He was nearly there when a black-feathered arrow lodged into his horse's rump.

Inferno stumbled severely and the shift was enough to send Jaiden, already leaning forward, tumbling over the saddle and skidding violently to the sandy turf below. His body twisted as he fell, and his injured leg struck hard, re-breaking upon impact. A flash of white-hot pain erupted behind his eyes, and he shut them instinctively.

When he opened them again his pain was gone and he was among the clouds, staring into the face of the Goddess. He did not dare blink, lest she disappear and he lose these last, unspoiled moments before death.

"I have missed you." Jaiden spoke plainly, honestly. He had no more interest in games.

Criesha did not blink either, and her deep, blue eyes bathed him in a look that brought comfort and arousal. He was filled with a longing to be consumed by her, until nothing of himself remained.

"You have grown, Jaiden Luminere. You finally fight for something besides your own glory, and have learned what it means to serve."

"I want my life to mean something," Jaiden admitted. "I want to be a part of something worth remembering, even if it is not remembered."

Criesha smiled, and it filled him with joy. "So you shall, Jaiden Luminere, Champion of Criesha. You will be my vessel on your mortal world, and my companion in this one."

The Goddess leaned closer, the green glow of her perfect skin washing over his face as her lips touched his. Jaiden closed his eyes and they kissed. As it deepened, he felt a surge of vigor beyond anything he could remember or even describe. He felt as if his muscles grew to twice their size, as if his lungs would swell out of his chest as he took in a new breath. Their kiss became even more passionate; tongues breached lips and swirled together, and he was sure he had gained the power to move mountains, were they to dare stand in his way.

The air around him quickened, until the breeze was so strong it enticed him to open his eyes to discover the cause. When he did the wind stopped, the clouds were gone, and so was Criesha. He was lying on the ground in the courtyard of Blackthorn Prison, and only a few heartbeats seemed to have passed while he was gone.

A black-cloaked guard in ring mail armor stood above him, swinging his spear back with two hands in prelude to skewering a defenseless Damper. Jaiden, left for dead, surprised both himself and the guard when he was able to push onto his knees and use his shield to bash the spear out of the man's hands.

Unlike previous forays into the dream-like world of Criesha's realm, the vigor he felt while there carried over to his waking world. He jumped from his knees to his feet and felt no pain doing so. Looking to his right hand, he saw the sword it gripped radiating an aura of greenish light the same hue as the dominant moon on a cloudless night. With a confidence absent since the siege of Halidor, Jaiden attacked with the controlled fury of an animal trained to kill and kept too long in its cage.

The first guard fell to his sword before reaching the spear he dropped. Jaiden was too quick for his enemy's reactions. He could generate enough power from one stroke to the next, without need to wind up or recoil, that he simply abused their defenses. Jaiden could evade the swing of a sword and redirect his momentum while his opponents were still in their follow-through.

Guards two, three, and four fell in rapid succession, hardly even threatening this new terror on the battlefield. Saffron almost attacked Jaiden as he moved past, clearly not expecting help from her backside. "You are using both legs!" She glanced at his glowing sword. "Has Palomar unleashed your inner magic, too?"

"Explanations later," he replied, keeping his eyes fixed on the Chelpian forces. Side-by-side they advanced, and Jaiden made sure none of the enemy could get close enough to harm the Dampers. He waded into the midst of a melee, sundered a soldier's shield with a powerful down-stroke, and eviscerated his esophagus as he brought his blade upward again.

When the rest of the nearby fighting men saw this display, combined with the unearthly luminosity of his weapon, they ceased hostility and willingly gave up arms in surrender. Even the last war-priest on the execution platform, deprived by Sir Golddrake and company of his remaining protectors, relented and sued for mercy.

Though the toll on the Order of the Rising Moon had been heavy, Blackthorn Prison was won.

Chapter 20

Spoils of Victory

Though the battle was hard-fought, Jaiden had enough experience to realize winning the fortress of Blackthorn was only the first challenge. The Order of the Rising Moon lacked the numbers to hold the prison against an inevitable assault by the Empire of Chelpa, and they held no real interest in doing so – but the Chelpians hardly knew that. The true obstacle before them was extricating their troops safely back across the northern border.

The ships were of no help to them now. As per their bargain, Cladius Cyril was using them to haul away as much raw uril-chent as could be pulled from the mines beneath Blackthorn.

He offered a free ride to any prisoners who willingly helped load the material into his cargo holds.

Once word of the attack reached the ears of the King-priest, and the Order had every intention of spreading it, the Chelpian authorities would have an easy enough time deciphering how the invaders arrived. Returning to Talon Barge would be inviting an ambush.

Cyril was aware of this and stated he had no intention of returning to the riverside city with these same boats, nor in the near future under any circumstances. He was not above laying low, and informed the Rising Moon's leadership he would continue downstream with his bounty until reaching the sea, and then cross the Cauldron of Xyanarind before unloading it.

The remainder of the Order was going to have to find another way. They agreed a controlled release of the news of their victory would best serve their purposes, for though they wanted to draw the King-priest back from his northern conquest, they also needed ample time to escape enemy lands.

Jaiden was invited to attend council with Sir Golddrake, Baron Rogan, Sir Kilborn, and Lady Saffron. Palomar declined, citing his zeal to teach the Song of Redemption to his kindred as soon as possible.

"I think we should keep at least some of the prisoners until a few more Dampers have made the transition to Aasimar," Rogan suggested. "Let them see the number of angelic creatures growing, before we release them."

Jaiden nodded and turned to Sir Golddrake. "Such a story would no doubt cause great alarm amongst Ebon Khorel's elite. When the King-priest captured me at Halidor, he was desperate for news of Palomar. To hear he now faces a host of Aasimar might give him second thoughts about opposing us at all." He felt Rogan's eyes on him and glanced to see both the Baron and Saffron staring. Uncomfortable under their gaze, he returned focus to his Master.

"Agreed." Sir Golddrake shifted his weight on his crutch and sat down on the closed lid of a nearby footlocker. "Uncertainty about the force they must conquer might slow a violent response against the fortress, and buy us more time to escape.

"Leaving Palomar and his fellow Aasimar to guard Blackthorn should not carry much risk. Once imperial reinforcements arrive they can simply abandon the prison and fly to safety. How long, Sir Kilborn, until our wounded are ready to travel?"

Sir Kilborn stroked his beard while considering, and Jaiden noticed it was longer than he remembered. He must not have trimmed it since leaving the caves.

"Not as long as it will take to bury our dead – more have crossed over than are left standing." He dropped the hand from his face and shrugged, "We should be able to depart by third dawn."

The Order arrived with twenty-five cavalry and twice as many footmen, though they were down to a mere thirty souls. Jaiden counted. Saffron found enough horses in the prison's stables for every remaining man to have a mount, which would boost their speed across the dangerous country.

Over the next couple days, Jaiden's popularity among his brethren vaulted tremendously. They already knew how capable Jaiden was with a sword in his hand, and upon revealing how

Criesha miraculously healed him during battle, he achieved legendary status.

Sir Golddrake positively beamed with pride when they spoke. "I told you your destiny awaited you." He declared before his men that Jaiden Luminere was their goddess's Champion, and more victories would follow in their wake.

For his part, Jaiden felt reborn. The tremendous joy at being whole once more was something he never anticipated, even while wishing for it with all his heart. He planned not to take a single breath of his regained freedom for granted, and rededicated himself to his training. Realizing their return to the Northern Provinces might not be an easy trip, he nevertheless found it difficult to refrain from making plans for the future, now that it was once again something worth looking forward to.

In his effort to start anew, Jaiden even spent time with Baron Rogan, wandering the corridors of the uril-chent mines. The man deserved thanks for planning the assault and for helping Saffron rescue her sister, from what he was told. In the dark, cramped confines of the mine, Jaiden's growing appreciation for what Rogan had gone through softened his lingering dislike. Although there was room for him to stand erect, Jaiden crouched slightly as they walked. He felt mildly claustrophobic, and could not imagine working in such a place every day for over three years.

Rogan reached up and ran his hand along a vein of obsidian ore in the ceiling, only a narrow span above his head. Smoother than the surrounding black rock, it glinted when the light of his torch touched it at the proper angle. "There it is – the uril-chent in its natural form. Before I got here, the men would all get sick after a month or two of mining. Something about the raw metal brings on illness. Until it is refined and mixed into an alloy, the ore is exceedingly dangerous. Prisoners kept dying off until the Dampers were brought in; the gods only know how they figured out that connection."

"What put you in here, if I may ask?" Jaiden heard that Rogan had been imprisoned, but no one seemed able to share why.

Rogan seemed to consider carefully before speaking. "When the King-priest was first establishing his power over Chelpa, he sought to neutralize any of the nobility who might speak or act against him. As you can guess, his regime was not popular, yet many of us still underestimated the deeds he was capable of seeing through. I was put in this place, I suppose, because I was seen as a threat to the control he craved."

Although not a very specific answer, Jaiden gleaned enough to suit his curiosity. He imagined they were both men shaped by the events they had endured. "I am sorry for you; it must have been very unpleasant here."

Rogan smiled at the understatement. "Jaiden Luminere, you have no idea." He took a quick look down the passage they were following, then turned around. "You have probably seen enough. Let us return topside, shall we?"

Jaiden agreed, choosing not to add he felt physically uncomfortable in the warm confines of the tunnels. When they had climbed the Tower of a Thousand Stairs, Rogan went his own way, making an excuse about preparing for their departure the following morning. Jaiden suspected he really wanted to sneak off and visit Saffron, but did not push the issue. He desired to speak with Palomar once more before they parted ways.

In two days since the battle, Palomar had spent almost every moment of his time with the rescued Dampers in a suite of rooms, separated from the mortals. Sir Golddrake decreed that their privacy be respected, and Palomar rarely came forth on his own.

Jaiden knew he was trying to teach the Song of Redemption to his kin, but the task was apparently more difficult than it sounded. A short visit would not be too much of a bother, he decided, and he had a question he thought his winged friend might be best suited to answer.

Approaching the wing where the Dampers had retreated for their metamorphosis, Jaiden could hear singing from well down the hall. The voices themselves were strong and in tune, but it sounded as if the music was discordant. When he peeked into the room where the song originated, he saw Palomar was not the only Aasimar present.

Three others had joined him, and they were all sitting cross-legged on the flagstone floor, singing a tune that a dozen Dampers tried to faithfully emulate. They all stopped suddenly when several spotted Jaiden.

"Sorry to interrupt," he said, biting his lower lip. "It really was lovely."

Palomar rushed to stand upon seeing him in the doorway. *"Kindred, this is Jaiden Luminere. He is the one who has been instructing me on swordplay."*

"Yes, the one with the glowing sword. We remember." A second voice intruded upon Jaiden's mind, startling him, though he should have guessed the others would communicate the same as Palomar.

"Jaiden," Palomar gestured toward the Aasimar standing nearest to him, *"this is Illicurus. He was a Marshall among the Aasimar before our... change."*

Illicurus stared at Jaiden, unmoving, and did nothing to give away whether it had been he who spoke. His skin was alabaster just as Palomar's, but instead of spun gold, the hair on his head was an icy blue, as if made of frozen water. The tips of his wing feathers were likewise colored, and he wore a commandeered tunic, tied around his waist to cover him.

"Greetings." Jaiden lifted his palm. Looking at them together, he could hardly imagine two creatures less alike than the Dampers and Aasimar. "What caused your change, anyway? Didn't you say it was some sort of curse, Palomar?" He blurted the question before thinking, only realizing it might be a sensitive subject when he saw the look that passed between Palomar and Illicurus.

"I suppose it would be all right to share our story with a mortal," Illicurus projected tentatively, his mindspeech more deliberate than Palomar's. *"We have already paid the price for our choice, after all. Our shame should not be any greater for having the truth known."*

Palomar nodded at his superior and kept his head low, deferring to Illicurus to recite the tale of their fall.

"It is difficult to describe to one of your realm what it is like on Mount Celestia. Your world, Jaiden, is essentially flat. Oh, there are instances of different elevation, hills and valleys, but this is not what I

mean. Here, the earth is but one layer, which can be folded and bent to different heights, but remains a continuous plane on the whole.

"Our home is different. You can ascend Mount Celestia and find numerous layers along the way that extend beyond the horizon. It is like a series of interconnected realms, at the same time separate and yet one. The higher up the Mountain, the more – what is the right word, Palomar? The more glorious the inhabitants, one might say. And you cannot even compare the splendor of our two worlds. Your greatest garden, your most beautiful waterfall, your most breathtaking sunrise, they would all be common fare on Mount Celestia."

Illicurus did not seem hesitant as he described his home world, and Jaiden wondered what the earlier exchange between he and Palomar was truly about. His friend continued to keep his head low, and the other Aasimar and Dampers remained sitting, their heads lowered as well.

"We Aasimar naturally reside fairly high along the slope, though all creatures may move freely to layers lower than those of their birth. Near the roots of Mount Celestia there are also doorways into other realms, if you know where to find them – some that lead to unsavory places.

"A tribe of lesser beings, Ulimar, had built a settlement unfortunately close to one of these doorways. Constantly harassed by creatures from the darker realms, they had a hard time protecting themselves as the attacks became more persistent. The Lord of the Second Layer, Hiruth Jeshu, may his light shine forever, bade a company of Aasimar go stay with the embattled Ulimar and protect them from encroaching predators of the dark.

"We could not simply take the Ulimar to a higher layer for safety, for their birth prevented it. We defended strike after strike from the denizens of the Darker Planes, who simply would not leave our charges alone. Enemies were drawn to them, it seemed. What was more, so ferocious became the attacks that we began to lose Aasimar to these incursions as well. As their Marshall, I found that unacceptable, but our Lord insisted the lessers be protected.

"One day, after losing another several Aasimar to a raid, we decided it was enough. Each Aasimar was worth ten of the Ulimar, perhaps a hundred, we reasoned. Why should we continue to die to save these creatures too weak to defend themselves? So, the next time the beasts came from the dark, we did not repel them. We flew off a distance and watched as the Ulimar were eradicated, weary of wasting our lives for theirs. This decision did not sit well with Hiruth Jeshu, may his light shine forever, and we were punished severely."

Jaiden filled in the rest of the story for himself. The Aasimar's curse had been to become weak themselves, banished to this less-spectacular world to pay their penance. He empathized that Palomar had to endure pain and sadness, but he could not say he thought the punishment completely undeserved.

"So what will you do now, once you all have been restored to your old bodies?" Jaiden thought it a fair question. After hearing the Aasimars' tale, he assumed they would want to return to Mount Celestia as soon as they were able.

"I, for one, would seek not to repeat the mistake that brought us here," Palomar answered, finally raising his head. "I will not abandon our Order, Jaiden, even though we are not from the same realm. I will stay as long as the evil of the King-priest endures, or until it is clear I am no longer needed to defeat it."

Palomar looked at Illicurus as he shared his next words, *"I hope to convince the others to stay and fight as well, given our collective debt to the Order for our freedom."*

The Aasimar Marshall stared at Palomar, but shared no words with Jaiden.

"I should let you get back to your task, but I wanted to seek your advice before we leave, Palomar."

"What would you like to know?"

In the midst of such powerful creatures, Jaiden suddenly felt too humble to ask. He found himself looking at the floor, avoiding his friend's golden pupils as he searched for the right words. "I have always known how to fight, so that is not the part I am worried about... it's just that, well, none of these people knew me before my injury."

"And?"

"I mean, none of them have really expected anything from me before. Now, all of a sudden, I am 'Criesha's Champion,' and I'm not sure how to handle people depending on me." It sounded so awkward, once spoken out loud.

Palomar's lips tightened, but Jaiden could not tell if he meant to smile or frown. *"Merely recovering from your injury has already changed the Jaiden I knew. It will not be the last time such a thing happens."* Palomar placed his hand on Jaiden's shoulder, and he looked up to meet the Aasimar's gaze. *"Though others may lift you up, seek not the heights for yourself, and you should do well. If you become great, as I believe you will, let those you serve be the beneficiaries of that greatness, and it will never be a burden."*

Jaiden nodded. "Thank you, Palomar. I trust you know we depart in the morning? I wanted to bid you farewell in person, and tell you I look forward to the next time we meet."

"*As do I, Champion of Criesha.*" Palomar clearly smiled, and Jaiden could not help but do the same.

He wished luck to all the present and soon-to-be Aasimar, then took his leave and sought out his final dinner in Blackthorn. They would be covering as much ground as they could, hoping to avoid confrontation, and restful mealtimes might be in short supply. It was also the last night he anticipated not sleeping on the ground, for a while anyway. Even if his bed was only a prison bunk, he had his own room, and wanted to get one last night of rest without the usual symphony of snoring to contend with.

Jaiden had avoided Saffron since the battle, too nervous to make the move he had looked forward to for weeks. Strangely, anticipation of a longer life had made him a coward in some ways. He retreated to bed early, bowing out once again, though he fell asleep thinking of her beautiful face, and wishing her warm body was beside his.

Air moved gently past Jaiden's face, caressing it with warmth and lifting him gently from the depths of sleep. Upon opening his eyes, they confirmed what his body already knew – he was high upon a world of clouds, resting among the stars. Soft, green moonlight, tinged blue by Hurn, the smaller moon that ceaselessly chased Criesha across the night sky, bathed the mist supporting him.

Within a few paces, a raised bed rested on a pillow of billowing clouds. A focused beam of moonlight shown upon the center of midnight blue sheets – an invitation to Jaiden's attention. He sat on the edge of the bed and ran his hand through the beam, letting its light dance across his fingers. Though they appeared to pass through air, his sense of touch informed him he was caressing the soft skin of a woman.

Amazed, he withdrew his hand and examined it, but it appeared unchanged. Jaiden closed his eyes and ran his hand through the beam once more. This time, he clearly felt his fingers running along a surface like silk, with something more solid underneath. Trailing upward, he would have sworn he traced the swell of a woman's hip, and was about to open his eyes again when he felt fingers running through the waves of his hair, convincing him to keep them shut.

"I have been waiting for you to reach this moment." Criesha's voice melted over him like butter on a hot roll.

Jaiden raised his left hand opposite his right, grasping a slim waist that twitched at his touch. He could not stand it any longer and opened his eyes. There, straddling his waist and grasping his hair with both hands was his Goddess, her luminescent skin showing through the diaphanous gown that only played at covering her.

Contrary to her usual appearance, her sable locks were set free. They meandered across thin shoulders and down between her shoulder blades. Criesha leaned lower and Jaiden lifted his chin, anticipating another kiss like the one that miraculously healed him. Before their lips met, however, she gripped his head tighter and held him still, only an inch away from her alluring mouth, where bliss awaited.

"I am going to show you the life that awaits my faithful Champion." She made sure his eyes met hers, to leave no chance of misunderstanding. "It remains up to you to choose this existence for yourself, but you cannot go back and forth – should you forsake me, my favor will be lost to you forever."

Jaiden nodded, ready to give in, ready to devote every remaining breath he would ever take, if she would only kiss him. Criesha's hold relented and her mouth collapsed onto his. They kissed deeply and his hands roamed up her back, drawing her body closer. Once he tasted her lips, her tongue, he wanted more. He wanted to explore her entire being with his mouth, and started with her neck.

It seemed so fragile, so vulnerable, making it all the more lovely. He pressed his tongue against the soft skin just above where her neck curved into her shoulder, and nibbled lightly with his teeth. She quivered at the touch, and Jaiden wondered amusingly if another man existed who could claim to have made a goddess moan.

His hands grasped the sleeves of her gown, and as he peeled them down her arms, their clothes suddenly disappeared. With no more impediments, his hands moved forward and cupped her breasts – they were full, round, and hung slightly from her lithe frame. His mouth lowered to join his hands, and as he squeezed her soft mounds, his lips closed around one nipple, then the other.

As with her neck, he sucked first and then gently used his teeth, pulling lightly on their tips. Her hands continued to hold his face, and her hips were rotating, moving her wet sex back and forth over his hardness, coating it with her juices. Criesha reached behind her with one hand and guided Jaiden inside her. She sank down and took him almost completely into her slippery warmth.

Jaiden's eyes opened wider and he released her nipple to groan. A surge like a hundred orgasms fired through him, making every inch of his body pulse with pleasurable electricity. The feeling was worlds beyond anything he had ever experienced with another woman.

She pushed his muscular chest back until he was lying flat on the bed, and slid her hands lower, gripping either side of his rippling abdomen. She applied just enough pressure to lift her hips, and began riding him up and down. He grabbed hold of her rounded buttocks and assisted in moving her faster, nearly releasing and then swallowing him, over and over.

Criesha's face and sex tightened simultaneously while her wetness increased, and she let out a prolonged moan. When he looked down, he saw his shaft coated in luminescent liquid. His own pressure built rapidly, and when she clenched him once more, he climaxed deep inside her. It felt like his spirit left his body with his seed, joining with the goddess in a state of pure bliss, before sinking back and reclaiming his body once more.

When he was finally spent, she collapsed forward onto his chest and listened to his racing heartbeat until it calmed.

"If you continue to be my Champion – to do my bidding on your world, to devote yourself to me and forsake all others – you will be rewarded beyond what your mortal realm can provide. This was only a taste, to show you a glimpse of what might be yours. Serve me well, and you will manifest new power whenever my favored moon is full in the sky."

Jaiden tucked his chin to kiss the top of her head as he placed an arm around her. "Exactly what power do I have now? Obviously you healed my body, and I am forever grateful, but what about the glowing sword?"

"As long as you remain a pure vessel serving my will, any weapon you wield shall be imbued with sacred moonlight. No armor made by man will resist such a blade."

Jaiden rested his head back. The possibilities swam through his mind. With Criesha as his patroness, he could become the greatest warrior alive. The thought was intoxicating. He had visions of leading his own army, battling demons at the foot of Mount Celestia – only to wake and find he had been dreaming.

Still in the commandeered cell in Blackthorn, it was impossible to tell what time it was with the door shut. He reached down and felt his lap – it was wet. Sitting up, he crept to the door and cracked it open. Faint sunlight filtered into the hallway. Dawn had arrived, and they would be leaving soon, assuming Palomar made progress teaching the other Dampers during the night. Jaiden figured he had just enough time to change pants before anyone noticed.

When he emerged into the courtyard to greet the others and ready the horses, nearly a dozen Aasimar were gathered, carrying on a silent conversation with Sir Golddrake, by the looks of it.

Palomar saw Jaiden as he walked closer, and included him into his telepathic discussion. *"You look infinitely more comfortable moving without that crutch. Sir Golddrake was telling us your expected* route, and where we should be able to meet up with the Order once serving our purpose here. Do you feel fit for your long ride?"

"Aye. I've so missed taking regular strides, I wager I could march all the way back to Halidor if need be."

"Then I wish you all good speed until we meet again."

Palomar, Jaiden, and Sir Golddrake bowed their heads in farewell. Their gesture was lost on the other Aasimar, who stood waiting for a verbal cue the conversation had ended, and seemed confused when the humans departed without one.

Jaiden found Saffron in the stables with her sister, talking to Baron Rogan as they saddled their horses for the ride out. "Fair morning," he said to the group, not minding his interruption.

"Fair morning to you," Saffron answered, stepping past Rogan to approach Jaiden. "I have not seen much of you since the caves – it is wonderful you are walking again."

Jaiden tucked his lower lip and nodded at Saffron as he swung his saddle atop Inferno. His horse shifted in his stall under the additional load.

"And how is your horse recovering?" She cupped a hand over her throat and shifted her weight so her hip flared out.

"I was worried the first night we may have to put him down, but Palomar calmed him and it has been a boon. Luckily, the arrow was not too deep, and he seems to be healing. Aren't you, Inferno?" He patted the horse's rump, opposite where it had been penetrated. The horse whinnied and nodded his head, coaxing a laugh from Saffron.

"It looks as if he is," she said. "By the way, have you met my sister yet?" Saffron turned and grabbed her sibling by the hand, breaking her away from a conversation with Rogan to introduce her. "Jaiden Luminere, this is my younger sister, Dhania min-Furasi. I suppose you two are about the same age."

Jaiden dusted his hands off and extended one to Dhania, who glanced at Saffron before offering hers back to him. He clasped it lightly, and lowered his head to kiss the back of her hand. "I am honored to meet you, Dhania, and pleased you have been brought out of bondage."

"Pleased to meet you as well, Master Luminere."

Jaiden could tell she was uneasy with the formal custom, and sought to make her comfortable. "No need to be proper with me... I am no Baron, after all," he smiled, tilting his head at Rogan.

Dhania smiled as well and exhaled through her nose, before retracting her hand.

"I, for one, cannot wait until we've left Chelpa far behind," Jaiden remarked, turning to finish preparing his steed.

Sir Golddrake was already mounted and trotted to the edge of the stables before calling to the lot of them. "Let's finish up in there. The ships have departed and the prisoners released – it is time for us to make for Selamus."

"Yes, Sir," Jaiden was the first to call out. Shortly after, they led their horses into formation in front of the gates. Sir Golddrake and Sir Kilborn led the way, and Jaiden felt compelled to stay near the front of the column, close by. Rogan kept to the rear and Dhania pleaded to stay back as well, so Saffron capitulated. Palomar lowered the drawbridge, and to his final salute, the remaining cavalry exited the prison fortress.

The immediate descent from the cliff on which Blackthorn was built was a barren slope of sharp, jutting rock, with only one safe path down. When the ground leveled off it was immediately engulfed by Skulwood Jungle, which persisted for several leagues northward before giving way to more tamed, cultivated lands.

The trail out of Blackthorn was the only one maintained through this part of the jungle, making it unlikely for anyone to be travelling along it not on official, prison business. Jaiden found the encroaching flora and thick canopy of the rainforest slightly sinister, as little sunlight penetrated to illuminate their path. The Order was forced to ride in a column two-abreast, and even so, the way became crowded at spots.

Unlike their journey through Chelpa before the assault, Sir Golddrake insisted they proudly display their white tabards on the ride back. He reasoned they were moving too quickly for any force strong enough to threaten them to assemble and intercept, even if they were reported. The sight of mounted knights not fighting for the King-priest might dismay their enemies, and establish doubt in those who assumed Ebon Khorel's grip on the country was unassailable.

Jaiden supported this decree and took it further by asking to bear the Order's banner as they rode, letting their foes know exactly who they were up against. They rode due north, as much as the terrain would allow them, straight for Halidor Keep. The quickest route to reach Selamus from there was along the Dawn Way, though unspoken trepidation permeated the riders as to what they might encounter on such a path. The latest information they received suggested the King-priest had already won the lands as far north as Synirpa, and the castle at Windhollow Rock. Yet, their ride through the enemy's own country provided nothing in the way of resistance.

While trudging through a muddy hamlet the day after a rain, they stopped to draw water from its well. Sir Golddrake asked several of the villagers for permission, but no one claimed to be in charge. With no objections, they filled their waterskins as quickly as they could.

Jaiden scanned the dreary collection of huts and sagging fences – even the livestock appeared depressed. He was still holding the banner, propped up by a loop and knot at the base of his saddle, when a boy of seven or eight summers approached and tapped him on the boot.

"Are you here to fix papa?" he asked.

Jaiden looked down, and leaned closer to the soft-spoken boy. "What is wrong with your papa?"

"The bad men whipped him, and now he cannot work. They will whip him again if he cannot work."

"Well, we are here to stop the bad men from coming. When we are through with them, the bad men will not lay a hand on your papa again."

The boy smiled at Jaiden and ran off toward a dilapidated dwelling. Sir Golddrake, who overheard the exchange, nudged his horse closer once the boy disappeared into his home.

"We are here to bring hope, Jaiden, not to make promises we may not be able to keep. Be aware of the difference." With that, he led his horse over to the well to check on the progress of the refilling process. Jaiden remained silent, but watched his Master from behind, questioning him for perhaps the first time. He had every intention of fulfilling his promise, and it had not occurred to him to doubt they would be successful.

Chapter 21

Touch of the Moon

T he Order rode for four full days, making good time, before finally leaving the boundaries of Chelpa behind. Just across the border, Sir Golddrake decided to spend the evening within the ruins of the abandoned fortress where he first encountered Jaiden. Using the crumbled walls as shelter, the camp split around half-a-dozen scattered fires. The soldiers were more at ease than previous nights during their ride, as if safer on home turf – no matter the place they were bedding down had been destroyed by Ebon Khorel only half a season ago.

"The ghosts of Halidor shall haunt this place for many years, I fear. So many died." Saffron slid her hand along one of the broken stone walls of the keep, just at the edge of the nearest campfire's halo.

"And I would have been one of them, if not for you." Jaiden reached to put another log on the fire, and then leaned back against the remnants of a former battlement. The night was clear, and the stars lit the canopy of the sky like a thousand candles. With so many visible, each one could have burned in remembrance of a soul taken by the King-priest.

"You give me too much credit, Jaiden. You would not have survived unless your own desire to live was strong." Saffron remained at the boundary of the fire's glow, where shadows danced heavily upon her as the flame licked back and forth across its pile of fuel.

"I think we have all survived much since winter," added Dhania. Jaiden could not remember hearing her say more than a few words during their journey, and only when he spoke to her first.

"Here-here!" Rogan raised his flask of wine and folded his feet in front of the fire. "A toast to our collective will to survive."

Jaiden raised his flagon, chiming in with Rogan and Dhania as they repeated, "to our wills!" He stared straight over the fire into Saffron's eyes as he spoke, and she, without a drink, stared back at him. He would have given a handful of silver to know the thoughts dancing behind her eyes.

"So, Jaiden," Rogan's speech was tainted by the slightest slurring, "you seem to have Sir Golddrake's ear. What's the head man got planned for us? Are we really going to ride straight up the Dawn Way to Selamus? Last I heard, Ebon Khorel's northern army was in charge at least as far as the next castle. I mean, look at this place – it's not as if the locals have returned to rebuild. We might want to take a hint from that."

Jaiden was unsure what spurred Rogan's questioning, or if he meant there to be a challenge behind it, but he seemed to be indulging in more wine than usual. Jaiden proceeded with caution. "Truth is, Baron, the last intelligence we got on the King-priest's whereabouts was almost two moon-cycles ago. He could be almost anywhere by now. I trust Sir Golddrake. He means to get an audience with the Prince, and reunite with the rest of his men as speedily as possible. If we took a less direct route, we'd only be guessing on how to avoid the Chelpians anyway."

Saffron stepped out of the shadows and sat next to her sister. The orange petals of the exotic jungle flower she had pinned in her hair matched the blazing heart of the campfire almost perfectly. "I think I know Amurel better than most, though we have not been acquainted overlong." Was she attempting to keep things peaceful? "Having taken so many casualties, he will look to replenish the Order's numbers before engaging the enemy openly again. I believe he intends to petition the Prince in Selamus for more men."

"Better him than me," quipped Jaiden. "The politics of court would drive me insane. Give me a sword over a crown any day."

"I do not think anyone wants to see you in a crown." Rogan laughed, as if his statement was hilariously funny. Jaiden assumed it was the alcohol, until Dhania joined in the laughter. Perhaps he simply missed the joke.

Saffron looked at the two of them laughing and smiled, shaking her head at their lack of restraint. She turned back to

Jaiden, and from across the fire he saw her smile break into a tooth-baring grin when their eyes met again. Finally, she laughed as well, and he could not help joining her, the contagious release of weeks of mounting stress overtaking him.

"What is so funny over there?" asked a soldier from a nearby campfire. They continued laughing for another minute, though more subdued, preferring to keep amusement amongst themselves. Not long after, everyone migrated to their bedrolls, thankful for even the imperfect shelter of the dilapidated keep to welcome them home.

In the morning, they packed and started north again along the road. The conversation was light, and despite the drinking of the previous night, the column seemed alert, watching for signs the army of the King-priest might lie ahead.

As usual, Jaiden rode immediately behind Sir Golddrake, bearing the standard of the Rising Moon. Unimpeded, it would still take them nearly a week to reach the province of Dawn's Edge. Jaiden left the shining capital of Selamus years ago, having seen plenty of its bustling streets while growing up. He first learned to fend for himself among its hills, before his father decided he was old enough to tag along to the mercenary camps.

The Dawn Way was the longest paved road in the Cradle, its stone connecting the seats of four provinces, running from Halidor all the way to the Northern Reaches. The two largest cities of the region, Synirpa and Selamus, were built in its path, though numerous towns had sprung up adjacent to its length. It provided the easiest route for trade, and was usually kept well patrolled by the nobility of each province.

As one such town came into view, Jaiden was apprehensive about the welcome they might receive. On the one hand, the populace might see their arrival as a sign order was being restored, but on the other, perhaps they would be blamed for not defending them when the King-priest's army came through.

He almost asked Sir Golddrake if they would be stopping, but held his tongue. His eyes stayed busy, however, surveying the wake of Ebon Khorel's passing. The buildings nearest the road had been torched, though the damage seemed localized. More disturbing was that not a single soul appeared to watch or greet them.

Sir Golddrake must have been unnerved by it as well, and raised his hand to call a halt. He said something to Sir Kilborn, who broke off to his right, followed by the knight beside Jaiden. Sir Kilborn and his escort rode to an elongated building Jaiden guessed might serve as the town hall. They dismounted and drew their swords – Jaiden's right hand released the banner staff and went to his own hilt.

Sir Kilborn tentatively climbed the front steps to the building's wide, double doors and opened one. As he peered in, Jaiden craned his neck to see, though the distance and angle made it hopeless. After only a few seconds, Sir Kilborn shut the door and returned to his horse. With no sign of danger, Jaiden released both his breath and the grip on his weapon.

When Sir Kilborn reached the column once more, he was shaking his head. "It might as well be a charnel house." He spit, as if his mouth needed to be cleansed of what his eyes saw. "There were flies – the smell was awful. They've been dead for some time, and clearly no one around to bury them. My guess is some sort of a plague."

"The whole town?" Sir Golddrake questioned aloud to no one in particular, looking to either side of the road once more to perhaps catch sight of even a single survivor able to tell the tale of what brought such a deadly sickness.

"Not knowing what it is, I do not think we should stop here," Sir Kilborn added.

Sir Golddrake nodded and gestured to the others they were to keep moving. "We will assure they are buried once we have answers."

The next village they came to was smaller, yet hit by the same, mysterious illness. This time bodies lay outside in their yards, or on the pathways from one house to another. The skins of the dead stretched tightly over their corpses, blemished by pervasive patches of blackened spots. If any were spared, they had abandoned their homes trying to escape the ravages of the contagion. None remained to explain the cause.

A growing sense of dread rose in Jaiden – what if those they were fighting to keep free in the first place had all been stricken by this foul disease? What would keep him and the rest of the Order from catching it as well?

That night they made sure to camp beyond the reach of civilization, heading a fair distance west of the road just to be sure they did not come into contact with any carrier of the plague. They boiled the water from a nearby stream before using it to fill their drinking bladders.

Sir Golddrake tried to reassure them with a hopeful message. "We will reach Synirpa tomorrow – surely there will be answers there. The city is too large to have succumbed to a plague this quickly."

Jaiden was not so sure, but kept his concerns private as he slipped into an uneasy sleep.

Clouds swirled nosily in a vortex around him, stretching upward to the sky, leaving Jaiden unsure whether or not he was in danger. Suddenly, they billowed upward and spread harmlessly above, revealing the boundless night sky. He was sitting on the bed with sheets of midnight blue, wearing a long, loose-fitting tunic of silver, tied at the waist by a purple cord. The material was soft and light, barely leaving an impression on his skin.

"Tomorrow, the moon that bears my name will be full, and you shall receive your next gift."

Jaiden turned his head to find Criesha kneeling behind him. She wrapped her arms around his chest and leaned to nibble gently on his ear, her moonstone earrings dangling smooth against his neck.

"What gift might that be?" he asked, not really caring as he closed his eyes and enjoyed the warmth of her tongue on the ridge of his ear.

The goddess slid around his body into his lap, keeping one hand tangled in his dark, wild hair.

"One I think you might find a need for...henceforth, while the full moon still rides in the night sky, the touch of both your hands together will cure a body of any pestilence." She stretched her neck to meet Jaiden's mouth in a deep, hungry kiss. "So long as you remain faithful to me, of course," she added as she pulled away.

"Of course," he nearly moaned the words. He wrapped his arms around her body – touching her made his flush with an ecstatic current. How could he ever do anything but what his mistress required?

She slipped off his lap, lowering her head to kiss his inner thigh. Criesha's short, sheer gown rode up to her waist as she moved, and Jaiden stared at her round, exposed buttocks. She pushed up the hem of his own tunic and took the tip of his member past her soft, wet lips.

With expert efficiency she took him toward another unearthly climax, making him feel as if his body had dissolved into pure energy and become one with the stars. For a long while he could not even remember a word she had told him, only that feeling of transcendental bliss. Its afterglow stayed with him as he rose in the morning and prepared for a long day of riding.

They came within view of the Castle at Windhollow Rock around dusk. Unsure of what they might find, Sir Golddrake resisted putting the entire group at risk. For recently being under siege, the castle appeared in excellent shape – nothing like the ruins of Halidor Keep.

Jaiden volunteered to investigate, and once he did, Saffron declared she would go as well. Sir Golddrake rejected the idea at first, but withdrew argument when Jaiden insisted Criesha would be with him. Saffron nimbly convinced him her passing knowledge of medicine and plants would allow her to find clues others might miss.

Together, they navigated the treacherous, twisting trail to the front gate – the sheer drop to the rock canyon below was one of the castle's best defenses. Drawing near, Jaiden announced their approach to anyone who might be inside. No one presented on the wall to greet them, and by the looks of it, the entire fortress was abandoned. Once they reached the final, straightened stretch to the gate, Jaiden spotted a flash of color behind one of the arrow slits in the turret to his right. Something inside was still alive.

A small, square cut-out in the gate swung inward a few moments later, and a shadowy face appeared, declaring in a throaty voice, "Seek your rest elsewhere, travelers. Only the plague visits Windhollow Rock, until it has run its course."

"We would enter, regardless," Jaiden said. "You may tell the Duke of Rosegold, or whoever is now Lord of this castle, that the Order of the Rising Moon seeks an immediate audience."

"Hmmmm," the throat answered. "The Duke does live, for now, and I will deliver your message, but do not presume that will gain you entrance. Wait for my return." The wooden square closed, leaving Jaiden and Saffron with little to do but be patient.

"At least not everyone is dead, yet," Saffron mentioned. "There may be something helpful to gain if I can examine a living specimen."

The sun was nearing the horizon, and had partially dipped behind the hill housing the foundations of the castle. Windhollow Rock resided on the very site from which its stone was quarried. Laborers had scooped out half of the hillside to use as materials for construction. Even the ground surrounding the foundation of the castle was excavated. The result created a fortress unique for its vertical rise; the main gate stood nearly halfway up the structure instead of at the base, and was accessible only by a narrow, precipitous trail. To scale the walls from the bottom would require a significant feat of climbing, making Windhollow Rock difficult to assail by numbers alone. Apparently even the King-priest never gained entrance, for as the emissary indicated, the Duke was still inside.

Finally, the gate swung inward. Jaiden shrugged at Saffron as they awaited formal acceptance into the stronghold.

A short, stocky man with thinning hair peeked out from behind the gate. The knuckles of his left hand were blackened, their skin cracked and blistered. "His Grace will see you if you choose to enter," the raspiness of the man's voice seemed more pronounced, now that his face was visible. "But he bids you consider such action carefully, as all who reside here are doomed by this hellish curse."

"At the very least we should cover our mouths and hands, and be careful not to touch anyone who might be infected," Saffron said. "We don't yet know how the sickness spreads."

Jaiden was already wearing gauntlets, but he took a rag from his saddlebags to cover his nose and mouth, tucking it into his coif. Saffron once again wore the veil she'd removed during her stay in Chelpa to disguise her origin, but donned a pair of leather gloves before they proceeded into the castle on foot, leading their horses.

Their guide sighed. "You may leave your steeds here," he said as he shut the reinforced gate and took up a nearby torch. "No sense taking them to the stables where they could be infected – it's overrun with vermin."

The courtyard was a tighter fit than Blackthorn or even Halidor, as the architecture was mostly concerned with upward expansion. Jaiden looped his reins around an empty iron sconce along the inner wall as the raspy-voiced man passed, and Saffron followed his lead. Soon enough they were indoors, ducking under a stone archway into the shadows of a dimly lit hall.

"His Grace and most of the others have taken up the Great Hall as their final refuge. It is not far."

Jaiden's glances down several corridors yielded similar glimpses of death. Bodies, blackened and besmirched with bloated pustules lingered in the otherwise abandoned spaces, illuminated by scarce torchlight – burying the dead had apparently become too burdensome. At least their guide spoke truly enough and it was not far to the Great Hall, though the scene awaiting them was even more depressing.

A nearly wasted Duke of Rosegold slumped in a high-backed chair at the noble's feast table, his face marred like the others who had contracted this disease. Scattered about the room, another two dozen at most of the infected still clung limply to the world of the living. None responded visibly to the newcomers' arrival. Only half the candles overhead in a large, iron chandelier were lit.

"Your Grace, visitors from the Order of the Rising Moon," the guide announced, his throaty speech making Jaiden wish someone would offer him a cup of water.

The Duke raised his chin and then, slowly, his hand, showing his faculties survived. "So, you did not heed my warning to leave us be?" His voice, though not loud, was remarkably clear, given his condition. "Is that because you are stubborn, or do you carry tidings of such monumental importance you would forfeit your lives to deliver them?"

"Perhaps a little of the first, Your Grace," Jaiden responded. "Though in truth, we are compelled to this audience by our own search for news. We have encountered towns along the Dawn Way stricken by the same affliction as Windhollow Rock, but with no survivors left to tell the tale. We hoped someone here could explain the nature of this contagion, and how it has spread so quickly."

"Your timing is poor, Knight of the Rising Moon. I recall, some weeks ago, expecting the arrival of your reinforcements, only to be left fighting off the King-priest on our own. Now, your belated presence serves only to doom you to the same fate we thought had been avoided by the enemy's retreat. We do not have any answers here, I am afraid. Only death."

Saffron challenged his decree with more questions. "Do you remember when exactly, your Grace, the sickness began? How long does it take to run its course?"

The Duke stared at Saffron, and Jaiden imagined him working out whether he should respond to a common woman – a foreigner at that – who had the audacity to speak in his Court. Only, the Duke was not really *at* Court; he was slowly and painfully dying in the Great Hall amidst the remains of his Court, who were likewise suffering.

"It was some weeks ago," he finally started in his surprisingly clear voice. "Difficult to remember now, as the passage of time has not played the same since the sickness began. I do know it was mere days after the Chelpians broke their siege. We fought them back from the walls for three long days and nights.

"The King-priest tried as he might, calling down fire and hurling burning pitch against our firmament, to little avail. As you can attest, the approach to our gate is narrow, and their soldiers learned quickly the fall from those heights is final.

"After a lull in the fighting that very first night, I took a risk to sneak out three riders who might speed word to our yet unresponsive allies. I sent one south to find Sir Golddrake, one north to the Prince in Selamus, and perhaps foolishly, a third east toward Naresgreen." The Duke deteriorated suddenly into a fit of coughing, but regained his composure to continue.

"To our surprise, as morning broke on the fourth day, the host of Chelpa was nowhere to be seen. They had packed up during the night and marched east, or so it seemed from the tracks leading away. I was sure it must be some kind of trick, and we remained watchful for the enemy's return, but they have not shown themselves since."

Jaiden found it difficult to believe Ebon Khorel had simply retreated. He had never heard a single story of such an occurrence. "Your Grace, did your messengers ever return with tidings?" He knew the Order would have been difficult to locate, but Jaiden wondered how the other rulers would respond to such a plea for help. He had his suspicions – the Northern Provinces' lack of unity stood as a tragic shortcoming for years, now blooming its significance.

The Duke's head bent at the question and his voice softened, leaving his guests straining to hear. "Not a one, though I have no reason to believe they ever made it past the King-priest's lines."

"What makes you say that?" Saffron chimed in.

This time, however, the Duke seemed not to heed the source of the question, his vacant stare heralding his regression into the land of memory. "As night fell on the enemy's departure, a pair of scouts I'd sent to track the Chelpians returned, sooner than expected. They found Hesrick, the emissary I sent east, barely alive along the road. He was delirious with fever, and when asked how he came to be there, only repeated nonsense about meeting a 'man of bone, with a thorny crown.' He clearly never made it through to Naresgreen, whether cowardice or contrivance blocked him, and he died in the infirmary without ever recovering his senses."

"And the others?" Jaiden asked.

"Neither was heard from, nor did we receive aid – though it may be for the best, given how our fortunes turned. I cannot assume any of the messengers reached their destinations."

"I take it the sickness began after this Hesrick was brought into the castle?" Saffron inquired. She did not seem interested in receiving an answer, but Jaiden inferred from her furrowed brow that she was working through a line of thought to its unhappy conclusion. "Was he injured in any visible way when found, or simply ill?"

"Hesrick was delirious with fever, but had not been assaulted," the Duke lashed out. "This 'man of bone' he spoke of was just a hallucination. He lasted a week, but was never able to communicate with reasonable intelligence, and neither are you as far as I am concerned, madam."

Jaiden's eyes got big and he touched Saffron's arm lightly when he saw her about to speak again. The Duke of Rosegold coughed and struggled to catch his breath, visibly drained by his outburst. After a moment of calm he continued, his tone more subdued.

"Simply look around you," he gestured to the gaunt remainder of his court, "this is our reality, and the folly of you coming here. Yes, it occurred to us eventually that Hesrick's illness was not a coincidence, but what does it matter? It was already too late. Others were stricken before he passed, and there is no cure we have found." The Duke's chin sank to his chest and he mumbled, "We are all doomed."

Jaiden's hope sagged, for he had seen the evidence of the contagion's finality with his own eyes in the villages to the south. "And what of the city, Your Grace? What of Synirpa?"

The Duke shook his head. "I locked the doors to Windhollow and forbade any to leave once seeing how completely the disease was spreading, but not in time. Only days after others here fell ill, a delegation from the town arrived to beseech my aid against a sickness rising in the merchant quarter. 'A curse,' they called it. What succor could I give? I turned them away."

Saffron spoke softly, only to Jaiden, lest her words invite harshness from the lord of the castle. "A curse may be exactly right. A natural disease may pass through contact, sure, but from one village to another, so quickly?"

Jaiden whispered back, "Could it not have been spread by travelers along the Dawn Way, by those who did not even know they were sick?"

"Given enough time, I would agree. Only, with the King-priest coming north from Halidor, who would be bold enough to travel to all those places directly in his wake?"

Jaiden glanced back at the Duke, slumping in his chair. He didn't seem aware of his visitors carrying on a conversation in his presence – they may as well have been ghosts, or the other way around, he acknowledged. "Are you saying you think Ebon Khorel himself is responsible for the plague?"

Saffron's eyes widened and she shrugged. "It fits, does it not? If he could do something like that – if Gholdur the Tyrant could grant him that sort of power," she shivered upon invoking the dark god's name, "why not let it do the work for you? Why bother storming a castle when you can safely wait for its inhabitants to rot?"

"Khorel is an affront to nature!" Jaiden called out, his rising voice causing the Duke to stir in his chair. Looking from the pestilence-riddled noble back to Saffron, Jaiden felt an uneasiness rising from the pit of his stomach. Of course she was right. He knew from his own experience that the King-priest was more than capable of ruining innocent lives in the pursuit of his goals – that he might even relish it.

But something else bothered Jaiden, something besides the idea of a divinely-induced sickness called down to ravage the enemies of Chelpa. It gnawed at him like a memory, lingering beneath the surface, one he couldn't quite gather to consciousness. It was an answer to their problem, given before he knew the problem existed, and he could not remember what. Something said to him in a dream... that was it!

Jaiden looked directly into Saffron's eyes. She raised her eyebrows, unable to decipher his gaze, waiting for him to verbalize the thought working its way through his mind. Instead of speaking, he shifted his gaze to the Duke, and then to several others in the room. Their skin, now illuminated by a mixture of torch and moonlight, showed the blackened decay and open sores of their affliction. Jaiden raised his head to the ceiling and swiveled to take in the high walls, looking for the narrow windows from which the slanting light of the moon, Criesha, pierced the room.

Daylight had completely passed away, and Jaiden pushed a long, wooden table across the stone floor until it met the western wall, where the radiant beams were strongest.

"Jaiden?" Saffron asked as he jumped to a bench and then atop the table. He peered outside, tracking the sky until he found the namesake of his goddess, still low in its nightly arc. The moon was full.

Upon this confirmation, he stepped down from the table, still not answering Saffron. He did not want to speak his thought aloud, risk sounding like a fool, until he put his faith to the test; the idea stopped him mid-stride. That is what it was, after all – faith. If he was only dreaming during his visits to that other world among the stars, he would pay the price now. But how could that be? His leg was whole again – that much was real.

Jaiden covered the ground to the Duke's throne in quick steps. Such an approach would have earned an intercession of the noble guard in times past, but no one was left with the strength to defend Rosegold's lord. The Duke looked up, merely watching as Jaiden stood over him and removed his gauntlets.

Saffron, who followed his movements more slowly, called from behind, "Jaiden, do not touch him, you'll become infected!"

She was too late. He placed both palms upon the crown of the Duke's head and closed his eyes. He did not know exactly how to do what he was attempting, so he let his emotions guide him. "May the pure light of Criesha cleanse your body," he said, envisioning the soft cheeks and boundless blue depths of his Goddess's eyes. He felt a surge of comforting warmth, then opened his lids and parted his hands.

The face looking up at him was not the same one from a moment ago. The Duke, though middle-aged, looked years younger with his skin cleared. Only a few wrinkles around his eyes hinted he was not a man in his prime. He raised his own hands, lips quivering as he marveled at the difference – once again strong and useful, unmarred by sores and decay.

"What is this?" he bellowed, looking up at Jaiden with searching eyes.

Jaiden did not know what to say. His throat caught as he opened his mouth, and he was forced to swallow hard without providing an explanation. He looked over his shoulder at Saffron, but with her veil on he could not read her reaction.

As the Duke of Rosegold stood, Jaiden moved aside and kneeled next to an almost completely wasted man, sitting in a heap against one of the long, wooden feast tables. He repeated his actions, clearing his mind as he laid his hands on the man's head, and spoke the same words. This time, however, he kept his eyes open, and could feel Saffron and the Duke watching.

The change began immediately. No bright flash, no crackle of energy, no outward sign at all betrayed that something was happening – only it was. This man's skin cleared as well, and he lifted his head as if coming out of a stupor.

"It's a miracle." The Duke's observation sounded more like acceptance of what his eyes saw than exultation at the fact. His gaze moved from his revived courtier to Jaiden. "Are you some sort of Shaper?"

Jaiden shook his head. "If this is magic, it is the Goddess's and not mine."

"Criesha?" the Duke asked. "You are telling me the legendary Goddess of the Moons and Magic, a myth not worshipped in the Cradle for ages, is performing some sort of healing through you?" Coming from one who had just returned from the brink of death, it sounded to Jaiden like a challenge.

"It would appear so." Jaiden looked over his shoulder again, as Saffron stepped closer. He was as stunned as any of them, perhaps more so, being the newly discovered conduit of his deity's power. He offered a hand to the man he had cured and helped raise him to his feet.

"This was hinted to me in a dream," he offered, finally finding his voice. He looked straight at Saffron as he spoke. "I only remembered it now." He blushed, thinking about what happened in the dream world to distract him. "We must hurry, though. If all I was told holds true, I only have until the full moon sets to channel her power."

Jaiden looked around the hall at the gathered survivors of Windhollow Castle. "There are enough to start here. Saffron, you must return swiftly to Sir Golddrake. Beseech him to have the Order ride to Synirpa and spread the word. Gather anyone who has the sickness and bid them travel to the castle."

She nodded and turned her body to leave, but held her head a moment longer to cast a final look at Jaiden – a look he could not, with her face still covered, read. Their eyes met, then she strode in the direction of the courtyard.

"Whatever you need, Sir Knight, you shall have it." The Duke clasped his shoulder.

"Pardon, Your Grace, but I am no knight."

"Truly?"

"Truly, Your Grace, but I thank you for your offer. We should prepare this room to receive the sick. Who knows how many may come?"

"Too many," the Duke replied, a far-off look in his eyes. "And it is already too late for many more."

Jaiden knew the truth behind that a statement, but chose to stay mindful of those he could help, starting with the Duke's own court. One by one, he lay his hands upon the wasting bodies of the ill, and cured them of the Dread Tyrant's plague. As he did, the Duke led the newly cured in moving tables and benches, creating a path along which the expected sick could make their way to Jaiden.

Saffron emerged from the gate of Windhollow Rock at a speed entirely unsafe for navigating the precarious, winding trail, especially at night.

The cavalry was mostly unhorsed, preparing to camp in a glade along the Dawn Way, within view of the castle. Rogan had even picked out a nice spot underneath an aspen tree. Yet Sir Golddrake was atop Bastion by the time Saffron cleared the snakelike approach, hurrying to meet her.

Rogan noticed she had ridden out alone, and feared what it meant. He strapped on his saber and hustled forward to hear the news. He had time to imagine an ambush, perhaps an accident of some sort, or an emergency related to the disease requiring young Jaiden to remain behind.

To hear instead that the impetuous warrior had miraculously healed the Duke, strained his trust in Saffron's reliability.

"He has asked that we ride to Synirpa, and quickly lead as many of the sick as will come to the castle to be healed," Saffron continued.

"Why the immediacy?" Sir Golddrake questioned, obviously less incredulous than Rogan.

"Jaiden claims he will only be able to cure the illness while the full green moon rides in the sky."

"We must act swiftly, then." Sir Golddrake turned in the saddle to face the rest of his men. "We have not earned our rest yet, it seems," he called in a resonant voice. "Prepare yourselves and your mounts, for we ride to Synirpa with haste. We must gather all the infected who still live and escort them to Windhollow Rock."

Sir Golddrake left Sir Kilborn to see his orders through. Without hesitation, he urged Bastion northwest along the road toward the second largest city in the provinces. Saffron followed his lead, leaving Rogan and the rest of them scurrying to pack their gear and catch up.

"It sounds like a long night ahead," he mentioned to the soldier beside him as they saddled their horses once more. The animals whinnied and snorted their displeasure at being burdened again without a full night to recuperate.

"I know, girl," Rogan commiserated with his mare. "It is a sour course to swallow, but we must all dance to the Master's tune."

He swung onto his steed and put his heels to her flank, joining the line of the Order already riding north into the young night, underneath the green glow of the complete and watchful moon.

The ride stirred something within him, a feeling like surging memory springing forth from forgotten depths. This sweeping mood raised goosebumps, though the air had not yet lost its accumulated warmth of the day. This same night air, however, was undoubtedly causing a transformation – along with the moonlight, and the trees passing by east of the road like ancient sentinels, and the road moving swiftly like a river beneath the hooves of his steed, burrowing inward.

Rogan became aware of the world around him as if his senses were heightened, and in this state a thought from years ago – something guarded, kept buried by a desire stronger than his consciousness – swam to the surface of his recollection. He could not explain what moved him, but he suddenly wept, the wind streaking tears from his eyes as soon as they formed.

It had been a night just like this – still warm but with cold to come, Criesha full overhead, bathing his manor in ghostly green light. The smell of smoke was heavy in the air, and the light changing to red as his house erupted in a conflagration. His wife and son were still inside. He had struggled to break away, but the Blood Tear Brotherhood pulled a sack over his face and struck him on the back of the head.

What was happening to him? He remembered it all: the almost-deafening anger, the physical exhaustion, the untapped sorrow threatening to flood him like the melting mountain snow, the heat of the flames, even from far away, the ubiquitous burning smell... the crying. Why had he forgotten the crying?

It was brief, but as he was thrown in the back of a cart he had regained consciousness for a moment, and in that blur of confusion and darkness was the sound of a child – his child, his Dominic – wailing for the loss he could not possibly comprehend. Why had he not remembered his son was still alive?

Synirpa lay no more than a league from Windhollow Rock, and Rogan saw his companions slowing to a halt with the looming skyline outlined in green to the west. His head still reeled from the memory as he pulled back on his reins, joining the crowd where a path diverged from the main road toward the gate of the moonlit city.

"The eastern bridge is out," Saffron declared as the last of the horses came within earshot.

"Where is Master Golddrake?" The irritation in Sir Kilborn's question was not masked, though no one present could claim fault. Rogan had come to realize this was not a man who liked surprises, but if Sir Golddrake had ridden on alone, it would have been his choice to do so.

"He commanded that you and most of the rest should follow him north and west around the hill," Saffron gestured to a tree-spotted mound a stone's throw beyond. "A second gate sits on the far side of the city, and he wants to spare no time. Once you gain entrance, he bids you rouse and lead as many of the sick as you can find back to this eastern gate."

The Orders' horses stamped and shook their manes, used to battle following such brief, hard rides. Sir Kilborn's mount strode along the road once more and had to be forcefully steered back to circle around Saffron. "And the others?" he prodded tersely after a delay.

Saffron paused two more breaths before answering. She lowered her chin, choosing not to face the older knight. "I need a half-dozen to remain with me here to build a new bridge."

Rogan had not been included, but he already knew he was staying to help Saffron. He imagined Dhania would as well. Still, he watched for Sir Kilborn's reaction with interest. He knew it bothered Sir Golddrake's lieutenant when those outside the Order were entrusted with too much responsibility.

"Pick your men," Sir Kilborn responded flatly, then turned his eager steed loose to gallop in pursuit of their leader.

Saffron watched him go before moving her gaze to the heavens, checking the height of Criesha in the sky. "Any volunteers? Who are carrying the axes?" It only took a matter of seconds for six men to claim their chance to assist the Lady Saffron, and she dismissed the rest to ride to the far gate of Synirpa.

Rogan joined her in dismounting, and they led the remainder of their company to the bank of the encircling stream that formed the natural perimeter of the city. The old bridge had been disabled, though its foundations were still intact. He needed a distraction, to put his hands and mind to work, lest he torment himself with the new memory that sprung forth under this haunting moon. Now was not the time to dwell on its implications.

"We should get to it," he said to Saffron, taking charge without asking. "I'll swim to the other side to assess the far bank. We're going to need more light to work by, and new timber for the span."

Saffron opened her mouth, but shut it without speaking. She placed her hand on Rogan's arm and squeezed briefly. Perhaps she heard something shaken in his voice. "Alright. Dhania and I will take measurements. I fear it is going to be a night without rest."

Chapter 22

The Miracle at Windhollow Rock

The majority of the bridge's components remained just inside the Eastern Gate of Synirpa, a pleasant surprise. Convincing the guards to let him use them for reconstruction, however, proved a task beyond Rogan's abilities of persuasion.

"The bridge was disassembled for the protection of the city," one of them said, "and nothing, short of a declaration from the steward or the Duke of Rosegold himself, will satisfy a reversal."

When Rogan, still dripping from his swim, pushed his argument that the King-priest's army was nowhere to be found, and repairing the bridge was the only way to save their sick, the guard pegged him as a native of Chelpa and accused him as a likely spy. Rogan was ready to strike the man for his insult, but the hot look that washed over his features forewarned the guard, who drew his sword in deterrence.

Across the stream a fire was burning, and the sound of axes biting trees echoed over the space between its glow and the woods beyond. Rogan could hear Saffron's voice, and saw the feminine silhouettes of her and Dhania standing not far from the flames. He cupped his hands on either side of his mouth and called to her, deciding a fresh approach might be more fruitful. "Saffron, I could use your help over here. I am having difficulty... relating to the locals." She turned her head and tilted it toward her sister's outline before approaching the far side of the stream.

"What seems to be the trouble, Baron? Are you ready to lay the ropes?"

"Yes, but then I think you should cross over. They've got most of the bridge piled up just inside the wall, but the guards won't let me near it."

"I see." Saffron tossed the coil of a thick, wound rope in a near-perfect arc across the stream. Tinged green, it looked like the tongue of an exotic frog unfurling to catch an insect.

Rogan caught the descending rope awkwardly in the dark, its impact stinging his bare hands. They each wrapped their end around the remaining stone foundations until the length between was taut, then tied knots to hold it secure. Repeating the process on the other side, they soon constructed a sturdy base on which to lay the planks.

"One moment," Saffron called across the stream before returning to where her horse was grazing. Rogan watched as she unpacked her lyre and slung it across her back by its leather strap. Next, she removed her riding boots and left them as she crossed back over the cool grass in her bare feet.

"What are you doing?"

"Silence," she admonished, though without bite. "Let me concentrate, or I shall end up as wet and sour as you, Baron." Arms out wide for balance, Saffron stepped onto the thick rope they had just strung over the running water. She did not look down, but Rogan did, and while the current was not swift, the channel's dark waters were cold, and deeper than their width suggested.

Saffron's sure feet folded around the curve of the woven hemp, and Rogan found himself holding his breath as she placed one in front of the other, steadily covering the span of the stream. When she was within arm's length he reached out, and she took his offering, gracefully leaping the rest of the way.

She smiled easily at him, and Rogan could not help grinning also. "Well done. I could not be blamed if I mistook you for a cat." He bowed in jest before remembering their plight and recovering a more serious manner.

"These fools have all the supplies we need, but will not yield them to me."

Saffron adjusted her weight and pulled the strap until her lyre swung around her hip. "I understand. Let me see what I can do." She walked toward the open gate, leaving delicate footprints in the dirt of the path.

Braziers burned fiercely on either side of the entrance, illuminating the quartet of armed guards who curiously watched her approach. Rogan followed, but made sure to stay several, long strides behind to prevent his presence from disturbing the natural aura of enchantment Lady Saffron exuded.

Instead of attempting to reason with them, however, she cleared her throat and plucked a few strings on her instrument to assure it was in tune. Then, she played. The men drew closer, no doubt wondering why a beautiful, bare-footed foreigner was serenading them at the gates of Synirpa.

"Weary now, the night has come, let it bring my body peace,
Tired from travel, tired from grief, let the dark bring some release,
I buried her two moons ago, and still my naked tears,
Fall unchecked, they keep me blind to all but the vanished years..."

As Saffron sang the "Dirge of Ladeon," Rogan watched the faces of the guards change; eyes softened, mouths slackened, and he felt the tension in his own muscles melting away. No one spoke while Saffron's lyre and voice held sway. When the last note from her strings drifted too far on the night breeze for them to hear, she let the stillness fill the distance between them before making her plea.

"I am in desperate need of your help. There is but one chance to save the afflicted of your city. We need to rebuild this bridge as quickly as possible, so they may make a swift journey to Windhollow Rock before the setting of the moon."

The foremost soldier nodded and broke his silence. "Of course, my lady. It shall be done." He turned and instructed his comrades, "Alright, lads, let's get to it." Without complaint, the four of them worked in pairs to haul the long planks of the dismantled bridge from the stockpile to the stream.

Rogan knew he could not have denied her anything at that moment, but was fascinated that the same seemed to be true of Synirpa's night-guard as well. He had seen her conjure fire through song, but this was something different.

When Saffron turned to face him, Rogan was still marveling at her. "Was that—" he started, before she cut him off.

"It would go faster with six; should we help them?"

Rogan stared a moment longer, but did not push. He could not be certain if magic was at work, but he understood Saffron's desire to keep her newfound abilities secret. "Of course," he said, finally. "We should have Dhania gather the others so they do not waste effort felling new trees."

He looked up as a chill breeze stirred distant branches and then blew past him. Night-grey clouds had moved in, masking some of the stars with a threatening presence. The full moon continued to rise, as did progress on the bridge, and Rogan decided to put off attempting to decipher all the strangeness happening beneath it.

While he circumvented north and west around the city, Amurel could see plenty of lights shining beyond the wall, even at this late hour. The citizens of Synirpa were still on alert after the approach of the King-priest's army, though it never reached them. Bastion snorted beneath him, testing the night air for hints of upcoming battle, and signaling his appreciation for the chance to stretch his legs in a gallop.

"No, boy, no enemies tonight – we are only fighting time." Soon they arrived at the city's northern gate, having crossed the water by a small bridge to the east, where the stream continued its northward course, parallel to the Dawn Way. Though the wide doors were swung open, a quartet of armed vigilants stood ready to greet him.

What sort of greeting he could not be sure, as two of them braced polearms against the instep of their boots, set to receive a charge. Another bore a shield and drew his longsword, flanked by a final man wearing the uniform of Rosegold. He held an outstretched palm toward Amurel, indicating he should cease his advance toward the gateway.

Reining Bastion in, his steed continued to stomp the packed earth of the trail leading into the city. Even with this noise, Amurel could hear the growing clamor of hooves in the darkness behind him as his men drew nearer.

The guard lowered his barring arm and spoke, "Who is it that rides in haste to the gates of Synirpa, armored but bearing no standard?"

Amurel bent to whisper in his horse's ear, trying to sooth Bastion's restlessness, so his coming answer could be heard more easily. He did not miss the silhouettes of a half-dozen archers coming into view along the ridge of the wall above. "I did not wish to raise alarm, good man, but I rode ahead of my standard-bearer. I am Sir Amurel Golddrake, Master of the Order of the Rising Moon. You are correct that I come with haste, for the night is short and there is no time to lose. I bring tidings out of the castle at Windhollow – all those with the plague should be ushered to the Duke's hall before the setting of the moon. There, the divine power of my goddess shall restore them."

The guards looked at one another as if verifying they had all heard the same declaration. "Forgive me if you are who you say, but to me you sound like the one who has been stricken with an illness of the mind. And now this host approaches in your wake; is this some trick?" The speaker turned and gestured anxiously to someone behind the wall beyond Amurel's sight, and the gates swung a quarter of the way closed.

"Please, no! They are friends," Amurel countered, realizing he may have gone too far mentioning an otherworldly power. Most men still viewed the gods as merely the characters of ancient tales.

"Archers, make ready!"

Amurel hissed and turned Bastion away from Synirpa. He rode toward his followers to slow their advance before they were fired upon as enemies. The last thing he needed was to lose more soldiers to a misunderstanding in the dark.

How could he make these men believe him? "Criesha, show me the path to further your will," he whispered, just before reaching Sir Kilborn and the others.

"What news, Sir?" his commander asked as soon as they halted their mounts.

"It appears they mean not to allow us entry to the city. Unsure of our allegiances, by my measure."

"Utter ridiculousness," Sir Kilborn countered. "They should recognize our banner, once we advance."

"*If* we advance," Amurel said, "I am afraid we'll have a hail of arrows to contend with."

"Hrmmm. Is this what our land has come to – friends cannot even assist one another without a threat attached?" Sir Kilborn looked back at the train of soldiers, waiting for a command. "Let me talk to them, Sir, with just a banner man. We'll leave the rest of the men out of range for the moment."

"I leave it to you." Amurel waived his hand toward the city gate.

"Logan, with me," Sir Kilborn ordered. He urged his steed toward the lights of Synripa, the sigil of the Order of the Rising Moon unfurling from the lance of the rider behind him.

Amurel watched them shrinking in the dark. When their forms became illuminated once more by the torches near the wall, he thought about what Rogan had said to him about leadership. He realized he should be there, with them, demonstrating his will.

Instructing his followers to wait for his return, Amurel urged Bastion once more toward the gates of Synirpa. When he reached them, his second-in-command was leaning forward in his saddle, hands folded over one another on the pommel, and the city guards were laughing.

Sir Kilborn swiveled his head at his Master's approach, then turned back to the gate. "Sir Golddrake, may I introduce Lineus Redfeather of Crimsonmoon." The apparent leader of the night's watch raised his palm in greeting. "I have no doubt your fathers knew one another. Lineus remembers me from my jousting days, if you can believe it."

"I loved watching the Prince's tournaments as a lad."

"Then we will have no more trouble entering the city?" Amurel wanted to get straight to the point. Lives were at stake tonight.

"Of course not, milord. Pardon me for my duty." Lineus bowed.

"Excellent. Then, I shall summon the men. If you wish to help," he raised his voice to include anyone posted on the wall as well, "we need to gather all the infected citizens of the city, and lead them to Windhollow Rock. There is one at the castle who can heal them, but we only have until the moon sets."

Without waiting for a response, Amurel made haste drawing forth the riders of his Order and dispersing them into the streets. Further delays could not be tolerated. He ordered them to fan out, sending a small contingent to start in each quarter of the city, and authorizing them to do whatever necessary to complete their task. He began with a small group in the southwest quadrant, which consisted of buildings constructed on wide, gradually elevating terraces. They went from door to door, seeking out those who were ill, and beseeching neighbors to spread the word as well.

Most of the stricken were bed-ridden, the plague robbing them of nearly all vitality, but some were in the streets, unable to move. Those had been left to die, as no healthy soul dared to risk contracting the disease in order to aid them. Amurel realized they would need to gather wagons in order to save all the people who were alive, yet too far descended into their illness to walk.

Some of the city guard joined in the evacuating effort, but only with those tasks not requiring physical contact with the sick. Amurel couldn't blame them, and directed a volunteer passing by to secure as many carts for transport as possible. Amurel had an eye on a neighborhood further south, far enough up a sloping embankment that none of his men had yet approached. He wondered how many might be tucked away, unnoticed in such a place. Coaxing Bastion forward to investigate, the heavens broke, loosing a cold rain thick enough to obscure his vision.

Bastion whinnied his disapproval, but trudged forth until they reached the base of the rise. The dirt path that cut its way between the stone-lined terraces had already been transformed into a channel of mud, with overflow coursing down to form a widening pool at the feet of Amurel's horse.

"There-there, boy." Amurel absently patted Bastion's neck as he strained to scan the top of the incline for movement. He found the torrent no more inviting than his steed, but wanted to assure no one was left behind. Just as he was ready to move on, he spotted what looked like a child hobbling across the courtyard, heading for shelter. His perspective only put the upper half of the girl in view, but suddenly the child dropped below the ridgeline, as if she collapsed from her effort.

How could he move on knowing even one remained who could be saved? Amurel looked around and did not see anyone who could help. *I am that girl's only chance at survival.*

He considered the slick pathway upward with apprehension, but prodded his steed onto the rise. Bastion's hooves splashed in the basin of rainwater at the foot of the hill, and he stepped up one leg at a time. When his second foreleg planted, the weight of Bastion's body and Amurel atop him sank his hooves several inches into the mucky path. He skipped forward in an attempt to compensate, but that only set him scurrying for secure footing as he slid back down.

"Whoa!" Amurel spoke to the mud as much as to his steed. He shared Bastion's trepidation – his horse's feet were his feet – and an injured leg would be catastrophic for them both. Amurel pulled the reins and circled back behind the pool, where he could be sure of level footing. The rain continued to plummet, and he knew the conditions would only deteriorate.

It was too much weight, he and Bastion together, to scale the terraces. His horse alone probably could not make it either, and little good it would do the plague victims above. Amurel already knew the answer to the problem, and that more than the cold was the cause of his shivering. Racing clouds obscured the moons, and he desperately desired a sign from Criesha. Without her presence, or the help of his horse, he may as well be on an island.

Amurel sighed and patted Bastion's neck once more. "You are not to tell anyone about this." He gazed to the top of the path and judged the distance. "Perhaps seven body-lengths," he said to himself. "You can do this." He swung down from his saddle and momentarily held onto his horse to keep steady. Then, leaning forward, he hobbled a few awkward steps to the embankment, splashing through the ankle-deep, rising water, until his hands planted into the mud of the ascending path.

The mail gloves gave him a better grip in the slick torrent, and he dug one hand, then the other, into the slope as he hauled his body upward. Rain poured into his eyes when he lifted his head to check his progress, so he tucked his chin and concentrated on making sure his hands gained sufficient purchase before hoisting his body further.

Amurel's chest and biceps were on fire by the time he reached level ground. Looking back down, the distance seemed further, though Bastion kept a patient watch, putting Amurel slightly more at ease.

The courtyard looked more like a killing field than a neighborhood plaza. Bodies lay strewn across the grounds, their blackened, pocked bodies ravaged by the plague. The number of deaths overwhelmed him, and Amurel wondered if perhaps this area was known to have been hit hard. That might explain why no one from the town militia headed this direction in the first place.

Focus on finding the girl, he thought. Surely she, at least, was not yet dead. Propping up his torso on his hands, Amurel slid his strong leg underneath him to rise. Once standing, he could differentiate more clearly among the bodies. A slight twitching brought his attention to the form of a young girl, not yet ten summers, face down on a cobbled pathway. She appeared on her way toward shelter when she'd collapsed.

Amurel limped more slowly than usual, taking care on footing the downpour had turned treacherous. When he reached the lass, she was in poor condition, though still alive. Her skin had not deteriorated as much as the corpses around him, but painful-looking blotches of sores marred her exposed arms, and though her eyes were open, Amurel would not vouch for her consciousness.

"It will be all right, child." He thought it important to talk, to offer hope, even if the girl could not hear him. "I am going to take you to get better," Amurel said, though still unsure how. First, he gave the courtyard a final scour to make sure no one else showed signs of life. "Can anyone hear me?" he called. Unclear they could, above the rain, duty demanded he make the attempt. "If you can," he shouted at the houses with closed doors and shutters, "take your sick to the castle before dawn, and they shall be cured." He had to believe that Criesha, through Jaiden, would not betray him on this.

No response arose. "Come, lass, let's get you out of here," he said more softly, though not looking at the girl as he spoke. Instead, he was checking over the rest of the courtyard, searching for anything to help him actually fulfill his promise. He could not drag another body with him – he would need both hands – and he could not carry the girl and still walk.

An untethered hand-cart, lying just off the walkway near a house, offered possibilities. Amurel approached to investigate, finding a case of garden tools and a short length of wire abandoned underneath. They would have to do.

Using the head of a spade, he quickly dug notches into the wet, wooden handles of the cart. He wound the ends of the gardening wire around them, leaving a loop of slack between, hoping it would serve. He pushed the cart across the wet, stone path, which was level and fairly smooth. Leaning forward, Amurel used the cart to maintain balance, though its unencumbered weight was slight enough for his one good foot to push along. Carrying the child would prove another matter.

When he reached the girl, thunder roiled from above. The stars were completely blotted out. Unable to bend far enough while standing, he knelt in order to cradle the child, then awkwardly lifted her over the lip of the cart to deposit her. The girl's limbs folded at Amurel's manipulation, but their owner never escaped her haze of debilitation. "You are going to hold on for me, yes?" With no response, he decided his own determination would have to suffice.

Amurel tried, but as he feared, the added drag of the girl lying in the cart proved too much for his lameness to overcome. He simply could not stand and push off hard enough to budge the cart through the mud between them and the path leading down from the terraces. Subjugating his dignity, he spun the cart so its handles faced the slope, and got on all fours between them.

He strung the wire across the top of his chest and shoulders, his mail protecting him from its bite, and crawled forward on his hands and knees like an ox. For a moment, he feared it would not be enough, but then the wheels came loose from their rut and the cart followed behind Amurel, sharing his progress.

The mud was slick and he knew, as he clawed his fingers into the ground, there was no way he could have kept his feet while attempting to carry the girl. Exhausted, he reached the edge of the top terrace and saw Bastion below, worrying at the absence of his master, but waiting all the same. With a last effort he drug the child from the cart, hugged her to his chest, and slid feet-first, on his back, down the slope. Water sprayed to either side as he cut down the channel, until he landed with a splash in the shallow pool at the bottom.

The sudden stop after the rush of the drop surprised him, and his bottom stung briefly from the impact, but neither he nor his unconscious charge seemed significantly worse for the wear. Bastion lowered his head to nuzzle Amurel's face.

"Kneel, Bastion," he commanded. His horse complied, though settling down onto the wet ground disturbed him, and he shook his mane in complaint.

"I am sorry, my friend, I promise to make it up to you." Amurel worked the limp body of the girl onto the saddle first, before straddling behind her. "Up, now, up," he called, and Bastion struggled to rise to his feet with the extra burden. After a shaky misstep, he succeeded. "Good boy, there you go," Amurel praised before turning them eastward, off to find how the rest of the evacuation was progressing.

Thankfully, none of the other neighborhoods proved so difficult to access, and word spread quickly through Synirpa, though the rising storm made some residents reluctant to come forth. The presence of so many already in the street, however, proved too much of a lure for most. Their curiosity, coupled with the fear of being left behind, seemed to triumph over the deterring elements.

Amurel was pleased to find Saffron and Baron Rogan had not let him down. It took several hours, according to their report, but by the time the masses accumulated at the city's eastern gate, his uninitiated comrades had repaired the bridge to at least the point of functionality. The rain started to abate, and as Amurel led Bastion beyond the outer wall, a sliver of green moonlight slipped forth from the veil of black clouds.

His heart lightened, and he felt confident enough to whisper to the girl propped in his lap, "You are going to be just fine."

The storm worried Jaiden. The rain announced itself in force, pounding upon the roof of the castle. Not one for omens, he still realized the downpour would make travel from Synirpa to Windhollow Rock more difficult. He considered going out to meet the sick, but determined his initial decision was more prudent. Though impossible to know how many might need his help, he guessed the number would be great. If so, it would be dangerous tending them in the open. Not only would they be easy targets, should agents of the King-priest be lurking, but the risk of masses closing in at once would be real. Innocents might be trampled or suffocated by the eagerness of their neighbors. Furthermore, the wind, rain, and thunder would all make communicating instructions more difficult, and it was important to minister efficiently. Unnecessary time in the rain was also an invitation to further sickness, even if of a mundane sort. No, the sour weather only increased the importance of having a dry, orderly place to share his gift.

This gift that he could scarcely believe was real, confirmed that Criesha was worthy of his trust. Whatever doubt lingered before was erased by both his own benevolent healing, and the power she channeled through him on this night of the full moon. After tonight, he would be the goddess's, completely.

In the hours since Saffron left to rally the Order, Jaiden and those he healed within the castle started preparing the fortress to receive the potential oncoming throngs of infected citizens. They arranged furniture to create a natural path for the sick to approach and then move away, so an orderly line could be maintained. Debris, deposited and ignored since the sickness began taking its toll in earnest, was cleared away. With no shortage of work, Jaiden made a search of the castle to ensure no still-living person was forgotten.

When he found a western-facing window, he looked for any sign of the approaching sick, but the shroud of the collapsing night sky was too thick to penetrate.

Patience, he thought to himself, returning to the great hall – not one of the five corners of the Order. A good thing, too, since he was unsure he could ever learn to master it.

A couple of hours after it had begun, the rain began to subside. It lightened until he could no longer hear it striking the roof. A hand upon Jaiden's shoulder caused him to look up from his seat. The Duke of Rosegold stood beside him.

"Perhaps it is a good sign no one has arrived. If the city was able to quarantine its sick before the disease spread too widely, maybe the illness was quelled."

Jaiden knew the Duke was only trying to reassure him, but didn't think such a macabre thought constituted a 'good sign.'

He had already seen how rapidly the pestilence spread through the villages consumed along the Dawn Way. With no messenger, Jaiden feared the Order of the Rising Moon had been ambushed by forces of the King-priest between Windhollow and Synirpa. He would not voice that worry, however, lest such words manifest into truth.

"You have already secured our gratitude," the Duke gestured to those occupying the hall whom Jaiden had saved, "and have done a great thing, even if no more can be accomplished tonight. Still, I will keep vigil with you until the moon sets." He sat beside Jaiden, who nodded at the older man's gesture.

"Your Grace, a rider approaches," the seneschal announced as he burst into the room. He immediately bolted back the way he came, no doubt to gather more substantial news. Both Jaiden and the Duke arose and followed, eager to see the visitor with their own eyes.

Jaiden recognized Saffron even from afar, and though she rode swiftly, no sense of panic influenced her movements. She dismounted before the final, treacherous approach and lit a torch, leading her mare on foot to the portcullis, which rose with the Duke's command. Only the slightest drizzle fell from the open sky.

"Is everything well?" Jaiden asked as he took the torch from Saffron and handed it to one of the onlookers. The quartermaster, whom Jaiden healed only hours ago, took the reins from Saffron and led Sheen away to be cared for.

"It is." Spoken by any woman other than Saffron, Jaiden would not have believed those words, judging by her appearance. Her dark hair was wet and matted against her forehead, her outer cloak likewise soaked and flecked with mud thrown by her horse's hooves. "But for all the labor this night has already seen, you have at least as much remaining."

"You succeeded, then?" Jaiden looked over her shoulder, expecting a line of the sick nearing the gate. "The ill are coming?"

"They are," Saffron answered, heading toward the inner keep. She saw the Duke and asked, "Might I trouble your kitchens for a hot beverage, your Grace? The rain has left me with a bit of a chill."

"Of course." The Duke directed the few servants still around to start a fire in the kitchen-hearth, bring hot water, and prepare for more visitors.

Saffron shed her riding cloak as they walked. "The diseased number in the many hundreds, and at least that number again alongside – not only their caretakers, but those who come solely to bear witness to the miracle. Sir Golddrake's knights are providing escort."

Jaiden ceased moving at her words. He had not considered that Criesha's gift might make him such a spectacle. "The night is no longer young," he said, walking again. "How long before they start arriving?"

Saffron shrugged. "Most of the distance was covered before I rode ahead to prepare you. The first should be here within the hour."

"Then I should make ready. It might be wise to break bread now, for there may be little time to rest ere morning." Jaiden stopped again and took her hands in his. "Thank you, Saffron, for aiding me in this. I know these are not your people, but every one of them leaving cured tonight does so in part, due to your actions, and I wish I could make some proper payment."

Saffron cocked her head sideways and squinted, as if not recognizing the man speaking to her. "You are welcome, Jaiden Luminere, as are they. I do not need payment – no people should see such misery."

While Saffron sought out the warmth of the hearth and sipped her tea, Jaiden nearly inhaled half a loaf of freshly baked bread he'd found cooling in the kitchen. He then retreated to a secluded corner of the great hall, knelt, and bowed his head, gathering his thoughts. Was it a joke of the cosmos that he, who had only trained to kill, would likely now be known as a healer? "Criesha," he started with uncertainty, having never prayed before, "I trust you will not abandon me. Please continue to share your grace, so that tonight I may pass it along to those in need."

Jaiden endured the remaining minutes in quiet solitude, until the seneschal announced the arrival of the sick. The Duke of Rosegold bade the remainder of his servants and household to admit the droves and treat them well, mindful they had been in like condition recently. The knights of the Rising Moon were received as honored guests as they arrived, though Jaiden noticed only a few actually entered the grounds.

"Where are the rest of our men?" Jaiden asked as Saffron patiently led the first of the infected over to him. More trailed as far back as he could see.

"Sir Golddrake has them patrolling alongside the column, no doubt. They have guarded the citizens since we left Synirpa."

"Is there danger?"

"None found yet," Saffron responded as she presented the hand of the first arrival, an elderly woman who could barely be recognized as such, after the ravages of the disease. "But Sir Kilborn especially is wary of an ambush, I think."

Jaiden nodded and placed his hand on the head of the afflicted woman. He cleared his mind of other concerns to focus on channeling the Goddess's grace. "May the pure light of Criesha heal your body."

As wondrously as before, all signs of the pestilence vanished. She looked at her hands, wrinkled but free of sores and dead flesh, and Jaiden watched a smile stretch across her face. Her eyes wet with joyous tears, the woman embraced him tightly.

"Blessings to you, sir," she cried against the side of his face, her voice choking like the squawk of a waterfowl.

Jaiden returned her hug awkwardly, eager to escape the situation. He was uncomfortable accepting thanks. "You are welcome, madam, but many more await."

She withdrew and looked at the line behind her, nodding in understanding. "I am healed!" she announced to the room, rousing murmurs even as Jaiden tended the next in line.

He carried on, placing his hands on foreheads and reciting the words. Staring at each face, marred by the disease, then watching it transform back to something recognizably human, took his breath away on more than one occasion. So many had come. Jaiden healed for what seemed like hours, only to glance up and see the line still extending out the door of the Great Hall.

His throat dried out and his voice started cracking. Before he bothered tracking down one of the Duke's servants to ask them for water, Saffron appeared with a jug and cup. "I thought you might need this," she said, pouring the clear liquid from one vessel to the other.

"My thanks," he replied, taking a moment to swallow several gulps of the cool water. The next man in line eyed the cup and licked his lips, but waited without a word for Jaiden to finish. "It must be late," Jaiden observed as he handed the drained chalice back to Saffron.

"Early, I think," she replied. "Dawn is not far off. Moonset will come soon after."

At mention of the time, Jaiden could not help but yawn. "You should get some rest, my lady."

Saffron shrugged, "I will wait up with you." She refilled the cup and took a drink for herself. "If you only have until the moon sets, you will not have time for them all." She walked away toward the kitchens, leaving him with that unpleasant thought.

Jaiden's stare lingered on her dark hair for several seconds, until the man in line issued a purposeful cough to reclaim his attention. He returned to his healing efforts, but stole a glance at the windows, unsure in his weariness if the meager light shining through them was cast by the sun or moon.

After what seemed another hour or two at the least, with his right elbow throbbing and stiff, Jaiden saw the line displace, making way for someone. As the cause drew nearer, he recognized Sir Golddrake by his limp. Sir Kilborn trailed the Master, carrying an unconscious child in his arms.

"Jaiden," Sir Golddrake nodded in greeting, his blonde locks falling across his eyes. He leaned on a polished, wooden cane Jaiden did not remember seeing before.

"Sir Golddrake," he nodded in return, too weary to bother standing.

"I have seen many leaving the courtyard, already cured – absolutely wondrous. Is it true what Lady Saffron told us; you only possess this healing power while the full moon hangs in the sky?"

Jaiden nodded. "That is my understanding of Criesha's gift."

"Then there is no time to lose, Jaiden."

Sir Kilborn set the child on the floor at his feet before speaking. "Dawn has broken, and the setting of the moons is nigh upon us."

Sir Golddrake grasped Jaiden's forearm. "The Order has been exposed to the disease while gathering the townsfolk. We need to make sure none of us develop the sickness or carry it further."

"But what about the rest already in line?" Jaiden spewed before he could help himself.

Sir Golddrake looked back at the afflicted and sighed. "It is regrettable, but our duty is to the Order first."

"But is not the purpose of the Order to protect people just like these?" Jaiden's fatigue betrayed his exasperation.

"Save all you can," Sir Golddrake answered, "though I do not suppose time remains to save them all. We must hurry. You may begin with Sir Kilborn and myself, then this child." He looked down on the young girl Sir Kilborn had been carrying, before continuing. "We will summon the rest of your brethren with haste."

"I do not—"

"Every wasted word is a death sentence." Sir Kilborn spoke firmly, cutting off any debate.

Sir Golddrake patted Jaiden's shoulder. "There is a good lad." He bowed his head to receive Criesha's blessing, just as the rest.

Jaiden felt conflicted, but realized the truth of Sir Kilborn's words. Taking the time to argue did no one any good. What would he say, besides? He did not want any of the Order to die of a disease they would have only contracted in service of the sick. Still, he could barely stomach choosing who among the innocent perished, and felt nauseous as he spoke the words, "May the pure light of Criesha heal your body."

They could only assume it worked, with no symptoms to judge. No warmth coursed through Jaiden, though, making him dubious that preventative blessings were beneficial. If only Criesha would tell him for certain, he thought. He decided to lean on obedience, as the Order mandated, and offered no further argument. Still, he could not shake the impression he was only using a new kind of crutch.

As Jaiden laid hands upon each member of the Order, some of the healthy citizens of Synirpa spoke up for their own who had not yet received healing. A vocal minority claimed the remaining population had been waiting fairly, and should not be abused. They demanded the knights wait their turn, but the Duke appeared and gave permission for the Order to remove them from the castle if they did not settle. They quieted at the sight of armed, disciplined men staring them down. Jaiden was thankful the agitators apparently had no idea of his time constraints, or they may have resisted more vehemently.

He continued chanting through the disturbance, and tended each member of the Rising Moon, in addition to Baron Rogan and Lady Saffron. A short while afterward, perhaps a dozen plague victims in, the charm ceased working.

A man bowed patiently in front of Jaiden as he rested a palm on his head and spoke the words, but nothing happened. Glancing at the narrow windows, he noticed the full morning light breaking through them. He coughed to clear his dry throat and spoke again, making sure the failure was not due to lazy inflection. Still, nothing. The blackened face rose to meet his gaze, and Jaiden saw sad eyes reading his own. He was too tired to keep from weeping. The euphoria of working miracles, sustaining him for the last dozen hours, had vanished, leaving him drained. His shoulders shook as a single sob crested his weary soul, too sudden to catch. Though he had saved so many, this man would not be one of them, and he could not help feeling guilty for that.

A whisper cracked from his dry throat, "I am sorry." Jaiden wiped his eyes and looked across the great hall at the remaining line, trying to gauge how many suffered beyond help. Still backing out of the room, he thought he could make out the end a few dozen deep. He had no words big enough for the moment. The next person in line pushed forward, eager to receive his blessing, but Jaiden drew his hands back, suddenly aware it may be unsafe to touch the infected.

"What are you doing?" the man scolded, not far enough gone to be severely weakened. "It's my turn, why won't you heal me?"

A murmur spread through the room. Jaiden stood, hands still drawn back. The man's hands were suddenly on his shoulders, shaking him, moving inward toward his neck. "My turn," he croaked. Jaiden stumbled backward, his knees buckling as they hit the bench behind him.

"That is quite enough!" Saffron appeared beside him, startling the aggressor with her sudden assertion.

Jaiden heard swords being drawn, followed by Sir Kilborn's voice. "Clear the room!"

Shrieks of alarm spoiled the air, and eruptions of protest followed as chaos spilled forth. Saffron grabbed Jaiden by the arm and yanked him toward the kitchens, out of harm's way. He followed, peering over his shoulder to see the rest of the sick being herded from the room at the tips of weapons.

Saffron led him through the kitchen and out another door, up some stairs, then down a hallway. Fatigue prevented him from keeping track of their route. His life seemed surreal. He no longer felt his feet as they took steps, and all he wanted was to sleep. At last, she opened a door and took him through.

The room beyond was small, but comfortable, with a soft-looking bed and other, well-made furniture. He sat on the mattress, only resisting several seconds before lying back. Jaiden's lids closed, though he was vaguely aware of Saffron prying off his boots.

"You rest," he heard her say, though he was already burrowing deeper into the blankets. "I will make sure we are safe."

That sounded like a good idea. Behind closed lids, Jaiden's mind continued to spin. Too tired to think clearly, visions and broken bits of conversation continued to harry him. *Dream*, he willed himself. *Dream of her.* A moment later he was fast asleep, on his way to the realm of the night sky.

Chapter 23

Growing the Banner

Jaiden was allowed a few hours rest, but all too soon a page showed up to rouse him. He woke to a new identity. Everyone knew his name, and every stranger he passed while navigating toward the great hall greeted him with a smile and a kind word. The castle at Windhollow Rock buzzed with energy. The population had swelled since the previous day, and bent its efforts toward restoring the citadel to its proper state, after the Chelpian siege and plague-induced disrepair.

"There you are," Sir Kilborn blared as Jaiden stepped into the late-morning sunlight, much too loudly for only being a few steps across the courtyard. "Sir Golddrake sent me to find you.

Grab something to eat quickly; we ride as soon as the horses are tacked."

"Where are we going?" A rising suspicion he'd missed out on some crucial information while sleeping overtook Jaiden.

"Synirpa. You are a popular man after last night's performance. We are taking advantage. New recruits are being mustered at the city gates, and the Master requires your presence."

Jaiden looked around the courtyard, his lack of sleep leaving lingering confusion. He had no recollection of where his belongings were stored, nor where his horse was stabled.

"A good knight does not spend his days in idleness," Sir Kilborn said as he returned to his duties.

"Am I a knight now?" he called after, but his superior failed to acknowledge. Jaiden's stomach grumbled and he decided to heed Sir Kilborn's suggestion to find food. What he wanted even more was a few additional hours in that comfortable bed – a few more hours with *her*.

Shoveling a few spoonfuls of porridge down his gullet from a cauldron in the kitchen was as close as Jaiden came to a meal before another soldier dropped in and yanked him away by the arm. Sir Kilborn's sense of punctuality was beyond questioning. Inferno was saddled and waiting in the courtyard; he stomped and snorted as Jaiden took hold of the reins.

"What are you complaining about? I'm sure you got more sleep than I did." Jaiden patted the stallion's neck before swinging atop and hurrying after the rest of the squadron, who were already on their way beyond the front gate.

The winding path down from the castle was still precarious enough in daylight to warrant caution, but once they reached the wider ground their horses picked up speed. The cool wind against Jaiden's face and the warmth of the still-rising sun combined to melt away some of his weariness. Inferno seemed to welcome the chance to stretch his legs as well.

The countryside glistened with remnants of the previous night's deluge, and Jaiden found it difficult to reconcile its rippling, green beauty with the decay he had been attending to. By the bottom of the hour they approached the final rise prior to the terrain leveling off to reveal the city of Synirpa. Beyond its apex, however, a column of black smoke billowed upward, tainting the otherwise azure sky.

Alarm seized Jaiden, and he cursed himself for being in too much of a hurry to don his chainmail. If the city was already being razed, he imagined Sir Golddrake and most of the Order were already in a hard fight, if not worse. Sir Kilborn seemed to have the same thought ahead of him, digging his heels into his steed's flank. Their small group charged up the hill, Jaiden expecting to confirm the worst once he crested it.

What awaited them was not at all what he expected. Still a way off, the city of Synirpa rose above the height of its outer wall, which looked completely intact. No army or cries of battle broke the horizon. The smoke billowed from a fallow field somewhat nearer. A huge pile of *something* was burning in the heart of it. Jaiden relaxed in his saddle, and Sir Kilborn slowed their pace, with no sign of strife to rush toward.

Jaiden assumed it was only rotten crops set to the torch, perhaps, though the thick smoke made it difficult to tell from a distance. As he drew nearer, the reality struck him harder than the blow of a greatsword. They were bodies, burning in the field. How many was hard to discern; two hundred, five hundred? Stacked in a broad pyramid, the work was likely done in haste as part of the cleansing process.

He cured so many the previous night, it had not occurred to him how many might have already perished. The castle had faced a similar decimation, though their smaller population diluted the impact. Rage against the enemy and regret at his own helplessness battled in Jaiden's blood, leaving him suddenly hot.

None of his companions said a word, though he saw them all staring at the burning corpses. The remainder of the ride, which carried them to an assembly at the open, eastern gates of the city, was filled with grim silence. A crude bridge spanned the creek running parallel to the road. On the near side, members of the Order idly watched over the horses, while the majority had crossed the bridge on foot.

Sir Golddrake stood behind a sturdy table, while other knights mimicked his posture behind several more. A crowd had gathered, though most appeared to hover without a definitive purpose. For those who possessed one, that purpose was clear to Jaiden even before he carefully crossed the makeshift trestle to join his Master.

The beginning of a line, composed of mostly young men not unlike him, pushed out from the tables opposite Sir Golddrake. The recruiting had begun. As Jaiden approached the crowd, he turned to look once more at the smoke billowing up near the horizon and thought it an odd backdrop for the endeavor – a reminder of his failure.

"Ah, and here he is." Sir Golddrake beamed when he saw his protégé, and moved quickly to capitalize on his arrival. He addressed the crowd, whose attention was dangerously close to dissipating. "May I present Jaiden Luminere, Champion of Criesha, and the healing hand behind the Miracle at Windhollow Rock!"

A murmur rose among the gathered, dying seconds later. Jaiden felt dozens of eyes suddenly upon him. Many people pointed as well, singling him out from the other soldiers donned in the white and purple. An unnatural hush descended, raising the expectation for him to speak. He looked to Sir Golddrake for guidance, but received only an encouraging nod.

Jaiden swallowed hard, nervous. "Greetings, townsfolk of proud Synirpa," he said, raising his arms and projecting his voice to reach over the crowd. "I am no different than many of you. I was born in the Cradle between the mountains, and have lived a simple life. I could have been a farmer, or a tanner, but for the happenstance my father was a soldier. I learned my trade from him, like perhaps you learned from your own fathers.

"The day I stopped being ordinary, though, was the day I fully committed to the Order of the Rising Moon." Jaiden stole a glance at Sir Golddrake, wondering if this was the sort of thing he expected. "Because on that day I became something more than a lone man trying to make his way in the world." His voice grew louder and surer as the words seemed to spill out on their own. "On that day, I embraced the realization that everything you do means more, when it is done in the service of something greater than a lone man can ever be on his own. Now I serve the goddess, Criesha, I serve the Master of the Order, Sir Golddrake, and I serve all of you in the defense of our lands from the Dread Tyrant and his King-priest."

"Huzzah!" The cry went up sharp and clear from his brethren within the Order, followed by an elevation in the murmurs of the crowd at large.

Sir Golddrake lifted his arms to gain their collective attention, seizing the momentum of Jaiden's speech, and channeling it toward his purpose. "All of you have the opportunity to follow the same path that led Jaiden to the great deeds he has already achieved. You need only pledge yourself to the Order of the Rising Moon, and I will take on the mantle of guiding you, by Criesha's light, toward your own meeting with glory!"

When Sir Goldrake lowered his arms, young men swarmed to the tables, eagerly signing the Order's enlistment scrolls. Jaiden raised on his toes to better his vantage, curious how large the growing crowd had swelled. A hand clasping his shoulder interrupted his observation.

Sir Golddrake was grinning, and had clearly bathed since the previous evening. Aided by his bright, golden locks and pristine, white tabard, the Master looked younger than Jaiden remembered. "Your words and presence here mean a lot to our efforts, Jaiden. Thank you for both. I am still overwhelmed by what you were able to accomplish last night. I told you from the start Criesha had plans for you, did I not?"

Jaiden smiled and nodded in return, "You did, Sir."

Sir Golddrake's gaze meandered over the plethora of potential recruits. "This is just the sort of boon we needed. Hopefully our numbers will continue to swell all the way to Selamus." He turned back to Jaiden. "We have done good, here."

Jaiden looked at Sir Golddrake's hand, which never released the hold on his shoulder, and then instinctively down, realizing he was being used for balance. He remembered also being crippled when Saffron and Sir Golddrake found him among the ruins of Halidor, and felt a rush of embarrassment. He craned his neck back, avoiding eye contact, and caught the rise of black smoke from the far field. "I suppose we have," he answered vacantly.

Eight years had passed since Rogan last attended a banquet hosted by nobility. Even though the occasion honored someone he would rather not pander to personally, and he had been stripped of his own title, his anticipation rose as the hour of the event approached. The lighting of candles, the preparation of the feast, the arrival of guests wearing their finery – it was all so familiar, yet from another lifetime.

After speaking to him privately, the Duke of Rosegold generously accommodated the former baron with clothing from his own wardrobe. Rogan imagined Sir Golddrake must have initiated a similar conversation, as it appeared most of his entourage were adorned in vestments not previously in their possession. Perhaps the closets of the dead had been put to use.

Rogan stood in a corner of the great hall simply observing, as he was fond of doing in the olden days. Four rows of long tables were already set with plates and goblets, and servants finished the preparations as guests killed time bantering. Of course Sir Golddrake and his inner circle were present and huddled near the Duke, including Sir Kilborn, and now Jaiden Luminere. No longer hindered by injury, the young warrior was steadily gaining influence – he was the Guest of Honor, after all.

A few men and women of middle-age or older, likely minor lords and ladies of the province, lingered near the epicenter of power like flies drawn to cow dung, though they remained quiet themselves. Just as Rogan wondered whether entertainment had been arranged, the first, tame notes of a tune were plucked from the strings of a lute in the corner, opposite Rogan. A pair of other musicians soon joined to liven the atmosphere.

Rogan scanned the crowd made up of important plague survivors, residents of the castle, and wealthy landowners. The faces may have been different from those he knew in Chelpa, but the room felt the same. A particular face eluded him, however, the one belonging to the only person he was eager to see.

"There you are!" The exclamation startled Rogan and his heart jumped. Dhania stood to his left, with her sister behind.

Saffron was smiling. "I thought you were never caught by surprise, Baron." Her voice was languid, dripping like tickled honey, and he swore her eyes flashed in the candlelight.

He cleared his suddenly tight throat. "Lady Saffron, Dhania." Rogan bowed as he spoke their names. "You both look lovely this evening. I swear you two could be twins." He was not lying. There must have been a Duchess Rosegold at some juncture, though Rogan could not imagine she made such an impression in her own dresses. Saffron's gown was the color of emeralds, deep and dignified. Her dark hair was pulled up and woven in delicate plaits, spiraling around her head in an intricate pattern.

Dhania, not to be outdone, cut a striking figure in a pearl dress, whose alluring neckline blatantly decreed she was no longer a child. The cloth's color contrasted so starkly with her sun-kissed complexion, it was as if she was daring the room to ignore her. Rogan felt certain that would not be the case. Three milky, teardrop stones, ensconced in silver, dangled from each ear like wind catchers. Her hair, not as long as Saffron's, remained down to play about her shoulders. The sisters shared the same eyes and mouth, though Rogan had noticed Saffron's nose was rounder, and she still held a height advantage of half a little finger.

Realizing his eyes had lingered too long on the plunge of Dhania's dress, Rogan raised his head and grinned, "Shall we find a seat at the table?" He extended both arms, crooked at the elbow, which the ladies accepted after sharing a glance.

Rogan perused the banquet hall for seating accommodations, settling on a spot far from the Order's delegation. He had spent too much time with them lately, and hoped to paint a different portrait for this evening than the one that dominated the previous fortnight. He politely scooted the short bench back from the table, allowing Saffron and Dhania to slide in on either side, then stepped over to maintain his spot between them.

The majority of the hall found their seats over the next few minutes, and servants began to pour the wine. The Duke sat at the head table with an elderly couple who might have been his parents, though the three chairs to his left were notably vacant. Rogan understood the need to celebrate, yet could not escape thoughts of the grim backdrop over which the banquet took place.

When everyone's flagon was full, and the carved boar brought to the serving table, the Duke of Rosegold stood and raised his cup, prompting his guests to do likewise.

Dhania covered her mouth to stifle a giggle next to him. "I've already run out of wine," she whispered, leaning in and giving a brief tug on the arm of his fine, scarlet tunic.

"Fear not, there is more," he conspired back before raising his own cup and turning attention to the Duke.

"I am a proud man," Rosegold began. "For those who have dined in my hall before, you may have noticed." He gestured to the walls where, vacant the night before, trophies of bestial heads were mounted. "Some – behind my back," he gave a wink, "may have even accused me of being stubborn. That stubbornness is part of the reason Windhollow Rock has never fallen to an enemy."

A boisterous "Hurrah!" went up from a number of veterans in the room.

"But I am not too proud," the Duke continued, "to stand before you this night and offer my most humble thanks to a man who has not only saved my life, but hundreds of others since yester sunrise. That man is with us tonight, so let us drink to him now." The Duke raised his cup slightly higher. "To Sir Jaiden Luminere!"

"Hurrah!" the cry went up again, this time echoed by nearly the entire crowd. It stung Rogan to see Saffron cheering along, laughing as the neighbor on her other side clinked cups with her. He joined the rest in taking a sip of wine, and sat with them after the Duke did so also.

"I am sorry, your Grace, but I am no knight." Rogan heard Jaiden's still-boyish voice acknowledge. "Though I am proud of my father's name, I remain Jaiden Luminere, servant of Criesha and the Order of the Rising Moon."

Rogan looked at Dhania, raised an eyebrow and shook his head, eliciting another giggle. He drained the remainder of his goblet, then caught the eye of a servant and gestured to his and Dhania's cups. "More wine," he mouthed silently.

After procuring additional beverage and sharing a silent toast with Dhania, Rogan turned to say something clever to Saffron. She was still staring at the head table, and he followed her gaze just in time to see the Duke of Rosegold laying sword-to-shoulder, bestowing a knighthood upon Jaiden.

Saffron turned to Rogan, beaming. "This must be very exciting for him," she said, without a hint of sarcasm.

Rogan searched her face for something he did not find. "Perfect, I would imagine." Saffron squinted, as if not catching his meaning. "You know," he swiveled from Saffron to Dhania to include them both in the conversation, "after the last couple of days, I have been considering a homeward journey."

Saffron's smile vanished, replaced by concern. "Why would you think of such a thing? I have not judged you as a man who gives up."

"I am not talking about giving up," Rogan answered swiftly, before sighing. "Lately, I have felt more like a minnow in a foreign stream. I only came north the first time because we had to flee Salmarsh, and had little time to decide otherwise. Then I stuck around to procure help freeing the Dampers from Blackthorn." *And because of you*, he thought while looking directly into Saffron's eyes, in case they could pierce his consciousness.

"But now all that is done," he continued aloud, "and the Order seems to have matters well in hand in these lands. What more use can I be here?" Rogan paused, giving Saffron an opportunity to ask him to stay – to tell him she wanted him near.

Dhania, however, spoke first. "But if you went home, you would be in danger. Are you not an outlaw, there?"

Rogan shrugged. "The danger is no different than I have faced since escaping imprisonment. In Chelpa I have contacts, I know my way around – I could be *useful*."

Saffron nodded quietly, as if she understood. A small victory. After a brief silence, she seemed to have gathered her thoughts. "You cannot leave yet, Baron. Wait at least until Palomar returns with news from the south. You need knowledge of the developments there before choosing how best to proceed. No place may be truly safe, but it would be foolish to cross enemy lines again without at least the intelligence the Aasimar will have gathered."

Regretfully, she made sense. To walk blindly into the hornet's nest of Chelpa in the wake of their success at Blackthorn would be folly. "I suppose I could wait a little longer, until Palomar finds us. Keep this to yourselves, but I think I am starting to miss him." A rueful smile curled his lips. "And I have long desired to see the shining citadels of Selamus. I have heard stories of the silver towers since I was a youth."

Dhania gave Rogan's right arm a squeeze. "Then it is settled? You will stay with us at least a little longer?" Her face was full of expectation.

Rogan sighed and nodded, just as a platter of carved boar was set nearby on the table. He politely served the ladies before taking meat for himself, and as the meal began he decided to keep conversation as light as possible. This was a night to take advantage of the finer things and ignore, if only for a while, the distractions of adversaries, whether political or personal.

He made sure to compliment their host, the beauty of his companions, and surrender his mind to the wine, music, and feasting. Inevitably, his thoughts turned to his past – sneaking around the banquets at the manor in Thispany, meeting his Riah, and falling in love. When he could no longer concentrate on the conversation at hand, he excused himself and sought out the fresh, late-spring air.

The last, rosy haze of evening clung to the horizon as a deeper purple descended to usurp it, and Rogan found himself climbing long, spiral steps to the upper levels of the outer keep. From there he found access to walk the top of the wall, seeking out a view to make his own concerns seem small.

The stars crept out one by one as Rogan wandered the high perches of Windhollow, measuring the turns of his life that had led him there. Until a few months ago, his direction seemed clear. Once the King-priest of Chelpa took everything from him, his thoughts drove only toward survival and vengeance. Then, the sacrifice of a Damper had complicated life. He still yearned to end Ebon Khorel, but not only for his own satisfaction.

Rogan realized now, his was but one of thousands of lives turned upside-down, and he was fighting to create a better reality for his homeland. Ironically, only after his title of authority had been stripped did he feel responsible for his people. So what was he doing in the Cradle, these northern provinces between the mountains, far from home? He could have found an excuse to remain in Blackthorn with Palomar, or ridden back to Thispany, where he still knew loyal men.

His reasons came back to the Lady Saffon. She reminded him of everything he had before his arrest, that there is more to live for than revenge. Was her influence responsible for the memory of his crying son, the son he abandoned with the rest of his lost life? What else could Saffron return to him, he wondered?

"Don't be foolish," he chided himself, listening to the echoes of his own boot heels as he followed the battlements back toward the keep. After all, Saffron was from another land and she had her own agendas, which he did not fully understand. Yet, were he forced to swear, he could not deny feeling something between them. He saw firsthand in Blackthorn what regret could do to a man. Would the rest of his life be tortured if he failed to at least ask her how she felt?

His thoughts heavy about him, Rogan did not notice the woman leaning forward, forearms against the parapet, until he was a mere ten paces from her. He inhaled sharply when he saw her, thinking his mind had somehow conjured Saffron to him, but breathed out when he realized it was Dhania. Her pale dress still stood out, despite the muted shades of nightfall. She did not seem to notice his approach, either.

"I see I am not the only one who needed to consult the stars tonight," he said before taking a spot next to her. She glanced at him and forced a smile, before looking back over the eastern countryside, haunted by the shadows of a distant forest. "Anything particular on your mind?" Rogan offered.

She shrugged. "Just thinking about how far away home is. As much as I wanted to get away and see something of the world, my adventure has not turned out like I envisioned."

Rogan peeked at her face, which seemed more stern than usual in the dark, then back toward the horizon – easier to talk of loss when you didn't have to see one another's eyes. "No, I suppose it didn't. But you have your sister here; I know she cherishes you deeply."

Dhania sighed. "Yes, but she is not home. Saffron is dear to me, but I miss my mother brushing my hair. I miss my father's tiny presents when he returns from the bazaar."

Rogan heard the smile in her voice without looking. Pearl flashed in the corner of his eye as Dhania whipped her neck to face him.

"Do not tell her I said this."

"I won't," he promised. "Have you talked to Saffron about returning to Begnasharan?" he probed.

"No," Dhania confided. "It is not time yet. I can tell she cares for these people, and wants to see this through. I would not ask her to leave until she is ready."

Her answer surprised Rogan, and he decided to search her eyes to help understand it. Alas, the night was too full for his attempt to read her face. "Even after all you have been through, you don't feel like you deserve to speak for what *you* want? I cannot imagine Saffron would place the plight of these Easterners, even if they are friends, above her own flesh and blood."

Dhania's eyes narrowed and she cocked her head slightly. "I know this. I love her, and that is why I would not ask. Saffron does not need Begnasharan like I do. Of course I wanted to see new places, but I always planned to go back. I am not so sure about her. Saffron has always had a hunger for learning. It is no secret she was gifted with much talent: her music, discovering the name of every plant she sees, mastering the wind-dance when she was younger than I am now. But there will always be more for her, and she must be free to find it."

Rogan was impressed. "How old are you again? I certainly did not understand things so well at your age." He tilted his head back and made a vain attempt to start counting the stars. "I was already married by my eighteenth summer. She was the love of my life, and all I knew." He heard Dhania exhale and swallow, but she did not speak, so he continued. "She died...she was killed by servants of the same king who captured you." Eight years later, it was still a difficult thing to say. "We had a son together, and I thought he was lost as well, but now I'm not so sure." Rogan found his lips suddenly trembling, and felt the pinch of tears starting to form. "That is also why I feel I should leave. I need to find out for sure whether he is still alive."

As Rogan blinked the welling tears from his eyes, he suddenly felt Dhania's soft hand on the side of his face. She turned it toward hers, and a second later rose on her toes to press her lips against his in a gentle kiss. He was shocked, felt a rush of panic, but did not pull away. He watched her face as best he could in the dark, her eyes closed, yet for some reason could not produce a thought other than it felt nice. As he felt her tongue applying pressure against his lips, he gave in for a second before regaining his faculties. He recovered enough to place his hands on her shoulders and gently return Dhania's heels to the ground, separating their lips.

Rogan cleared his throat, trying to buy time as he thought of what to say. Whatever it was, it had to be put delicately. "I, uh, I think I'm going to find some more wine." He walked back toward the keep, closing his eyes and shaking his head as soon as he was past Dhania. *That* is all you could come up with, he thought. He didn't turn back, unsure if he could handle whatever look Dhania might be giving him. At least he spoke the truth – he did need more wine.

Chapter 24

Gods and Men

Jaiden awoke to the rumble of thunder outside. A third consecutive day of rain loomed, though today he had to ride in it. Sir Golddrake gave them a short reprieve from travel after the banquet, deciding it prudent to wait a few days to assure the illness did not resurface among the Order, lest they spread it further. Thankfully, none of the men became sick.

Nearly half of them would remain garrisoned at Windhollow Rock, under the gracious hospitality of the Duke of Rosegold, to train the new recruits. With his own forces depleted by the plague, his Grace had the room, and would benefit from having armed soldiers nearby. The whereabouts of the King-priest's northern army was still unknown to them.

Jaiden, however, was tapped to accompany Sir Golddrake to Selamus, the shining capital of the province of Dawn's Edge. He was returning home. Reluctantly, he threw back his blanket and set his feet to the cold, stone floor without thinking. He lifted them quickly, wincing at the unpleasant intrusion to his half-sleep, and repositioned on his stomach, clinging to the residual warmth of the bed. Head upside-down, he peered over the side of the mattress to locate his chamber pot.

The pressure in his bladder bestowed the bravery necessary to cross to the corner of the room. Rain sounded on the roof as he relieved himself, and his eyes began to shut as the steady sound and dissipating pressure lulled him back to a reduced consciousness. Surely the Master would not have us head out until the weather breaks, he thought. Jaiden was about to crawl back under his blanket when a knock rattled his door.

"Sir, the morning meal has been served," a voice spoke through the wooden barrier. "Sir Kilborn asked me to inform you that the Order departs at the bottom of the hour."

So much for warm, dry thoughts.

Only a dozen of the Order took the winding path down from the castle at Windhollow Rock that morning, but Baron Rogan, Lady Saffron, and her younger sister accompanied them. Jaiden could not fathom what effectual difference it made, but now that he was a knight, he rode a little straighter in his saddle. He was sure Inferno could tell, as his horse's steps seemed crisper, more precise.

They rode north along the road in a column, two abreast, with Sir Golddrake at the fore. Saffron ended up at Jaiden's left, and he noticed her glancing his direction on more than one occasion, though she said nothing. The rain washed the green countryside in grey, and heavy clouds hung low, muting the sun, as an ineffectual lantern in a fog.

After an hour the rainfall lightened to a misting, and Saffron drew back the hood of her riding cloak. "I have noticed you sleeping later these past few days; are you feeling well?"

Jaiden thought it odd for her to be paying such attention to his routine. "I feel wet, but otherwise cannot complain." He was not about to admit he had been sleeping longer to spend more time in his Goddess's embrace. "I suppose I was drained after the long night of healing, and just taking advantage of the comfort of a warm bed."

"I am glad that is all. I was concerned you might have acquired the sickness." Saffron followed with a weak smile.

"Oh, no, nothing like that. I am healthy as a horse." Jaiden patted the neck of his stallion for emphasis. "Right, Inferno?"

Saffron's smile brightened, and they fell back into silence. The column rode into late afternoon before breaking. The worst of the weather seemed left behind, though, the clouds parting enough to show traces of an azure background.

While the horses were being watered, Jaiden stretched his legs and took a swig from his own drinking bladder. When he lowered it, it nearly dropped from his hands. Saffron had somehow crept beside him without making a sound. "You startled me." He wiped the spilled liquid from his lips.

"This is fertile country," she said, looking west. "You must have excellent farms around here. The practice fascinates me.

In the Emirate where I grew up, only land near the rivers was good for growing, and it was protected as sacred ground."

Jaiden shrugged. "Farming always seemed boring to me. Waking up early, doing the same thing every day, tied to the same plot of earth. A couple more days along the Dawn Way we'll enter the hills. Now that's beautiful country – rolling green as far as you can see. Excellent ambushing opportunities." Jaiden put away his waterskin and sighed. "You never really know what lies beyond the next rise. Well, until you see the eight hills of Selamus. There's nothing quite like it."

"I have to agree," Saffron replied. "I was very much impressed by your city. I was to play there for Prince Falcionus... before our caravan was ambushed. Sir Golddrake took me there shortly after rescuing me. I did not go to the palace personally, but when the Prince heard my story, he gifted me a new lyre."

Jaiden nodded solemnly, a touch jealous not to be the first to show her the area where he grew up.

"How long, do you think, before we reach the capital?"

"It shouldn't take more than five or six days, depending on how we push the horses. Assuming the road is clear," he added.

"That should leave plenty of time, I would think." Saffron took steps toward the reservoir to claim Sheen by the reins.

"Time for what?" Jaiden asked.

"Time to practice," she called back. "In case the Prince still desires me to play."

Remaining vigilant, the Order could not find any signs that Chelpian forces came before them. Farmsteads were intact, and no indications remained of any large encampments along the Dawn Way. Jaiden's thoughts turned toward seeing familiar places, though he had no proper home to return to. His father had neither plot nor cottage to pass to his son, though comfort could still to be found in the haunts of his youth.

On the evening of the third day out from Windhollow, as twilight settled lazily upon the land, Jaiden spotted the hills of his home province creeping closer from the horizon. "Dawn's Edge," he said, absently. "A village sits at the base of the headlands, just across the border." He intended his statement for Saffron, but didn't look to see if she was listening. "I hope we stay there tonight. There is a tavern called 'Pork & Porridge,' and they have the best spiced cider. My father and I would always stop for some when we passed by."

"That seems a sound plan to me," she responded. "Perhaps Sir Golddrake is familiar with it as well?"

"It would not surprise me," Jaiden finally turned to look at her. The dying light was soft against her features, and he could not ignore Saffron's beauty – though he had been trying. He had not dreamt of Criesha since leaving the castle. He cleared his throat and looked away.

Sir Golddrake apparently did share his plan, announcing shortly after that they would be stopping in the border village of Fallow for the night. In the dimming light, eager to exchange the saddle for a soft bed, neither Jaiden nor any of the riders noticed the sixteen pairs of wings gliding toward them from the southern sky. Silent as death, the Aasimar descended to alight in a semi-circle, cutting off progress along the Dawn Way.

"Palomar, is that you?" Sir Golddrake shouted as he came to a halt.

But who else could it be? Jaiden broke ranks and rode forward to meet his friend, recognizing the glint of gold at the tips of one set of wings, even in the failing light. "Greetings, Palomar! A relief to see you and your kin safe."

"*Joyous greetings to you as well, Jaiden Luminere.*" Palomar lifted his palm in salutation. "*It is lucky our paths have crossed. We did not think to see you until reaching Selamus, though my brethren and I are weary from many days of flight.*

"*Master Golddrake,*" he set his countenance upon his commander, "*there are few of you left. I hope you did not find more trouble in your own lands than we in Chelpa.*"

Sir Golddrake clicked and his steed trotted forward, closing the distance. "Trouble of sorts – though our numbers are not lessened by attrition. There is much to tell."

"*No doubt from both our parties.*" It was not Palomar's voice in Jaiden's head, but another, emanating an icy calmness. One of the other Aasimar stepped forward, and Jaiden recognized Illicurus by his frost-blue hair. "*Perhaps we should make camp, and Palomar can apprise you of our stratagem's success. As he said, we are weary.*"

Jaiden looked to Sir Golddrake, who seemed to weigh his words before speaking. "If your Aasimar can manage, we were set to halt today's march at a village less than a league to the north. Will this suffice? It will provide more comfort than camping alongside the road."

Illicurus had already turned to scan the northern horizon. *"That is acceptable."* He strode up the road, the other Aasimar following in silence.

Palomar had always been so warm with Jaiden that he never considered how eerie or quietly menacing a group of them could appear. They each had swords sheathed at their waists, and it occurred to him there were more Aasimar than humans present. He felt ashamed the realization made him uneasy.

"It is probably better we travel on foot from here, so we can arrive with an escort. Our sudden appearance could be unnerving for your kind," Palomar iterated as he also turned to walk the Dawn Way.

Jaiden wondered, not for the first time, if the beings' telepathy was something more than pure communication. He made a clicking sound with his tongue and nudged Inferno forward to keep pace, Saffron and Rogan advancing alongside him.

"Palomar, I am pleased you found your way back," Rogan's voice carried an undeniable note of fondness. "Though truthfully, if I had wings I might be elsewhere."

The Aasimar smiled and shrugged. *"Nevertheless, I see you have found reasons to stay. Lady Saffron,"* Palomar bowed his head, *"your inner fire burns bright as always."*

"I am thankful for your safe return, my friend," she smiled.

Jaiden felt a sense of awkwardness growing, and decided to extricate himself from the situation. "I should probably get back in line, now, but I cannot wait to hear your story."

"And I to share it. Some insights beyond the machinations of war have been brought to my attention, which I believe you and Sir Golddrake, in particular, may be interested to hear."

Jaiden nodded and peeled his horse off to circle back into his proper place. He saluted the Master as he passed, hoping his breech of protocol would not earn sanction. Sir Golddrake did not betray his thoughts by returning the gesture.

Less than an hour later, with the sun vanquished behind the mountains, the odd troupe arrived at the wooden gates of Fallow. The Aasimar held back, allowing Sir Golddrake to enter the village first. As they approached the Pork & Porridge tavern, located prominently on the major avenue of the hamlet, men came out to greet them and take their horses.

Sir Golddrake raised his hand in salutation to a man just outside the door of the establishment, and Jaiden could tell from the welcoming grin on the weathered face of the portly gentleman that the two had done business before.

"I thought I might be seeing you soon, Amurel!" His voice was a bellow that cut through the night air more efficiently than the lanterns in the windows. "News has already reached us of Synirpa."

"Has it, indeed?" Sir Golddrake answered as he swung down from his steed.

The tavern owner grunted disapprovingly as he watched the knight limp forward to clasp hands. "I was told you were performing miracles, but I see that's not the case, or you would be skipping into my establishment." The man bypassed Sir Golddrake's offered palm and enveloped him in a crushing embrace.

"You know you cannot believe everything you hear, Verino." Despite his paralytic position, Sir Golddrake was smiling.

Jaiden dismounted and handed the reins over to a chest-high lad, who dutifully led his horse around the building to the stables. Jaden bent to touch his toes, stretching out the tightness from his legs, but looked back toward the gate when he heard gasps from bystanders. The Aasimar had been spotted.

"No need for alarm," Sir Golddrake announced, attempting to head off the ascending unrest. "They are fighting with us against the King-priest."

The Aasimar stalked closer, and as the light of the Pork & Porridge cascaded upon their forms, a brilliant kaleidoscope of colorful feathers and hair differentiated the otherwise similarly perfected bodies of the creatures. Staring at them along with everyone else, Jaiden was shocked he hadn't noticed during their approach that several of the Aasimar were female. He counted four of them now, with frames slightly smaller than their male counterparts. Three of them bore long locks, with the fourth capped by short, mussed, magenta hair.

Jaiden had overheard Sir Golddrake ask the Aasimar, before their arrival at Fallow, not to communicate with the villagers using telepathy. Palomar was the only one who had learned any Illanese, so he volunteered to be their spokesperson. Illicurus initially objected, but apparently relented after a conversation Jaiden was not privy to.

"What in the Nine Hells are they?" Verino asked, barely above a whisper.

"They are called Aasimar, and they come from another world. We are lucky to have them on our side," Sir Golddrake explained.

"I am certain we are..."

"Come, let us go inside, Verino. I have waited long enough for my mug of spiced cider."

Taking Sir Golddrake's lead, people began filing into the tavern. Once the entire Order, all the Aasimar, and a smattering of curious onlookers had packed in, there was barely room to stand.

"Here, Jaiden, I saved you a seat," Saffron said as she grabbed his hand.

He took it thankfully, then set about gaining the attention of a barmaid to order a round of drinks. Service was understandably slow, but once the drinks were flowing and the initial awe of the Aasimars' presence wore off, the atmosphere became surprisingly jovial. Most of the men were happy to be back in their own province, and the Pork & Porridge felt like home.

After enjoying a couple hours of lightheartedness, Jaiden and Saffron were tapped by Sir Golddrake to follow him from the common area into a back room.

Baron Rogan, Sir Kilborn, and Palomar sat close around a sturdy table, with the aloof Illicurus alone on the other side, wings spread more than Jaiden thought necessary. After allowing Sir Golddrake and Saffron to take their seats, he chose a spot between Saffron and the blue-tipped feathers of Illicurus.

"I am sorry to pull you away from some well-earned relaxation," Sir Golddrake began, looking around the table at each of their faces, "but plans must be made for how we proceed, and for that I need to know where things stand in the south. Palomar has told me a little already, though I wanted to eliminate the need for re-telling. Since I value all of your perspectives, I wanted you to share in the tale."

"*Thank you, Sir Golddrake. After battling Gholdur War-priests, and now seeing Ebon Khorel use his powers in person, I have a better idea of what we're up against.*"

"You saw the King-priest?" Jaiden could not keep from asking.

"*We did. And it was Ellingle who identified the handiwork of the Juda-cai,*" Illicurus added.

Palomar lowered his head in the Aasmiar Marshall's direction. "*Of course. Her experience provided much illumination.*" Palomar sighed audibly. "*Let me begin with what we saw. Reaction to our seizing Blackthorn Prison came swiftly. Within two days of the Order's departure, we spotted troops moving toward us out of Lucnere. We were ready for them, naturally.*

"*As per our agreement, the available uril-chent ore had been loaded on Cyril's ships. With some ingenuity and the cooperative shaping of my brethren's songs, we then temporarily rerouted the river and flooded the mines. It will take some work to make them operational again.*"

"It's only too bad you couldn't tear the whole place down," Rogan interjected.

"*I understand your sentiment, Baron, but of course we needed the walls to make our stand and draw out the King-priest. Though swift, the initial response from the Chelpians was inadequate. They were mostly ordinary soldiers, unprepared for our wings, let alone magic. They lay an ineffectual siege, but took casualties from us.*"

"It was comical," Illicurus added, "to watch them trying to batter the gate, and then scale the walls with little more than a few archers to cover them."

"They had to withdraw after a couple of days," Palomar continued. "They realized it was foolish to remain in the open against us, given our resources. Then, we waited. I was sure an answer would come – we just did not know when.

"We took turns flying out north, east, and south every day, watching for enemy movements. Four days later a storm rolled in from the south. From atop the prison I could see the massive, dark clouds advancing from above the horizon. The same day the storm manifested, however, a heavy fog, dark as shadow, rose out of nowhere to obscure the land north of the jungle for untold leagues."

A dull ache informed Jaiden he had pressed his elbows too hard into the table, leaning forward to follow Palomar's story. Looking around, he saw he was not the only one on edge but forced himself to relax in his chair, realizing the words were not even issuing from the Aasimar's mouth.

"We could all sense something beyond nature at work, and prepared to be besieged once more. The enemy did not disappoint us. The fog met the jungle, curiously following the same road you took north out of Blackthorn. The sky was dark as twilight with the advancing clouds, and the wind strengthened. I could taste the impending rain on it.

"A rustling came from the jungle as the fog advanced, as if it were a solid force disturbing the trees. Lightning illuminated the sky, and thunder cracked close behind. It seemed we were about to be caught between two colliding maelstroms. I flew to the outmost position on the northern wall; my eyes were trained on the mist as it finally broke free from the rainforest.

"As another bolt of lightning struck overhead, it briefly illuminated numerous shadowy shapes within the dark fog. Our archers made ready, though we knew not what we were facing."

Illicurus suddenly unfolded his wings, startling the rapt table. Saffron grabbed Jaiden's arm in response, then followed with nervous laughter and downturned eyes as she released it. The Aasimar's dry, unapologetic tone suggested he was unaware of the tension. *"This King-priest obviously was not taking any chances in dealing with us."*

Palomar ignored the interruption and continued. *"Once it rolled right up to the front gate, the fog evaporated, replaced by a horde that would be any general's nightmare. These were not the troops we faced at Salmarsh, nor even like the smattering of War-priests garrisoned at the prison. The forces Ebon Khorel brought to bear were not unlike the Abyssal fiends we would fight on Mount Celestia.*

"Front-and-center was a huge, ebony battering ram, covered by a slanted, reinforced roof. A number of hooded men, moving like acrobats, used wooden poles to vault straight onto the outer wall, where they stuck and began to climb like tree frogs.

"But my attention was grabbed by a large, lizard-like abomination. Tall as a house, it had five, ferocious heads, each with an iron collar around its neck. Chains spiraled outward from those, held by hairless men with markings and metal piercings upon their faces."

Jaiden rubbed his once-injured thigh at the description of the hydra. "I know that beast," he said, the memory thick upon him.

"And still, that was not all. Creatures like large, tusked dogs sprang forward and snarled in anticipation of an extra meal. Their eyes shone red in the dimness. Plenty of soldiers came too, wearing heavy shirts of

steel and black shields – much better armed than the force we faced earlier.

"The floor beneath my feet shook as the battering ram pounded the gate. My brethren acted quickly, firing arrows and then consolidating along the battlement. We decided breaching the gate didn't matter as long as we kept the high ground.

"It did not take long for them to break through, and once they did, the beasts charged into the fortress with abandon. Metherin sang a song to influence the scent of some of the nearby soldiers – they became like wounded prey, very appealing to the beasts. That bought some time, but we soon became busy with those who had scaled the walls.

"We blinded them with our aurora and the fight was going well, but it kept me from noticing the arrival of the King-priest himself. In fact, I think he meant to remain unobtrusive, but right as the rain started to fall we felt it – all of the Aasimar – a strong pull of power at the edge of the jungle. I had felt it before. It was the same pull that called me to the caves where I hid and recovered my memories as a Damper. For a moment I despaired as I realized our enemy had found some of the Living Fire."

"I knew we should have gone back to recover it," Rogan hissed. "There was just not any easy way with the Blood Tear Brotherhood on our trail."

"No, there was no easy way." Palomar shook his head sympathetically. "And we cannot be sure that is where the King-priest found his. Either way, he has some now, and Gholdur has taught him how to use it. That, added to the stories your historian friend told you, and my companion Ellingle's own interactions with them, is why we are now fairly certain Gholdur the Tyrant is one of the Juda-cai."

"Can we go backward for a momemt?" Sir Golddrake put his hands in the air to stop the deluge of new information. "In order to make sense of all this, I am going to need you to finish the tale first. Then, we can discuss strategies. Please, Palomar, continue with the siege."

Palomar nodded his apology. *"Of course, Master Golddrake. The storm had arrived, and when I felt the presence of the King-priest, I found he was away from the rest of the Chelpian forces among a cluster of bodyguards. They were all donned in black armor, astride black horses, but the rain obscured further details.*

"I rallied a handful of my brethren to fly down and engage him, hoping we might end this war quickly. Just as we leapt from the battlement, however, I saw that Ebon Khorel had stretched out a hand in our direction.

"There was a buzzing in my ears, I was surrounded by light, and the next thing I knew I was on the ground, getting drenched in the downpour. Dazed, I was lucky one of my fellows reached me first. He helped me to my feet, but no sooner had I stood than he pushed me hard to the side. This time I saw the burst of light where I had just been. It accompanied a snap, a smell like burning hair, and a metallic taste on my tongue. A painful surge coursed up my legs, followed by the deafening crash of thunder. Thankfully, my wits stayed with me, and I realized the King-priest was actually commanding the lightning upon us.

"Needless to say, it was time to leave." Palomar leaned back and sighed, as if re-telling the story had released some of the tension from the experience.

Illicurus took up where he left off. *"I ordered our withdrawal and we ascended in a spiral pattern to deter our enemies from focusing on any individuals who may be wounded. We headed west across the great river, then began our long journey to Selamus, where Palomar promised we would meet the rest of his human allies."*

Jaiden looked around the table at each person present, though none of their faces gave away anything other than an appearance of consideration. He understood, with so many things to think about, but after a few more seconds he couldn't wait for someone else to ask the questions he knew they all must have.

"So, were any of you wounded? How are you feeling, Palomar?"

"The lightning was not a direct hit, thankfully. My legs felt numb and weak for a few days, but I have since recovered. I appreciate your concern. All told, we suffered nothing worse than cuts and bruises, fortunately."

"The King-priest was at Blackthorn in person... how long ago was that?" Sir Golddrake pressed.

"A week," came Illicurus's cool response.

"Baron, you probably know the King-priest's behavior better than anyone here. Do you think he would seek to pursue the Aasimar?"

Jaiden watched Rogan press his palms together. Perhaps feeling eyes upon him, Rogan turned and stared at Jaiden, but his expression didn't change. After a moment, he looked back at Sir Golddrake. "Ebon Khorel has an obsession with the urilchent we extracted at Blackthorn. If the mines were flooded as Palomar says, I think his first priority would be to return them to order. That would take time and more slaves."

"Not to mention more Dampers, of which there are none, as far as we know."

"Let us hope so, Palomar."

"Good," added Sir Golddrake. "Then we should have some time. Please, share my thanks with all of the Aasimar. I know the danger you faced was real, but it may make all the difference." He turned to Sir Kilborn next. "Pick a man to carry the news back to Windhollow. We need eyes at Halidor to give warning when the King-priest marches north again."

Sir Kilborn nodded his understanding.

"I am not sure how much difference it will make, unfortunately, now that he has Living Fire."

"What exactly is the 'Living Fire,' Palomar?" Among a room of soldiers, Saffron's voice sounded sweet and slow, like molasses. Jaiden's eyes were drawn to her full lips, and his mind began to wander, before he forced his attention to Palomar.

"As I have explained before, the Veil of Nessus prevents physical bodies from travelling between worlds, or planes or existence, if you would. Some planes may touch or merge, and special doorways can sometimes be created, but there are rules governing such magic as well. It is complicated.

"I believe those you call the 'old gods,' are beings known on other planes as the Juda-cai. They could not travel here themselves, but were able to send Avatars. Ellingle, our companion, has met one such Avatar on her travels. The Juda-cai are immensely powerful, and struggle for dominance against one another on their home plane, as well as across other worlds. Yours is but one such battlefield. While their Avatars were present they exuded power, especially when invoking magic. This power permeated the air around them – even the earth and living *things would have absorbed some of it. Like light, however, it could not be captured, and continues to surround us.*" Palomar turned his head back-and-forth, as if looking for the mysterious power of the Juda-cai at their very table.

"*An exception, however, are some gemstones that formed when the Avatars were still present. Rubies especially, perhaps because of the heat and pressure present during their formation, have been known to trap some of that direct, magical essence exuded by the Avatars of the Juda-cai. Such stones are known as the Living Fire and can be used by those who practice the Art to unleash extraordinary power, comparable to that wielded by the Avatars of the Juda-cai.*"

"And now the King-priest has one of these rubies?" Jaiden asked, clasping his head in both hands. "Wonderful!"

"*I do not think it is wonderful at all, Jaiden.*"

Jaiden raised an eyebrow at Palomar and shook his head.

"Certainly, we shall have to be on guard when we face him," said Sir Golddrake. "But we should not forget; we have not only a flight of Aasimar, but the Champion of Criesha on our side. We will not hand victory to the Empire of Chelpa without a fight."

Jaiden saw Palomar look at Illicurus, and saw Sir Golddrake notice as well.

"You are all with us, Palomar, aren't you?"

Illicurus responded. "*Your Order liberated us from captivity, and even though my greatest desire is to return to Mount Celestia, we shall honor your bravery with our allegiance... at least until the King-priest is brought to justice.*"

Palomar nodded as if he had been unsure what answer Illicurus might give.

"Excellent!" Sir Golddrake pounded the table with his fist. "Now, if you will consent, I would like to slow our approach to the capital. I know many of the towns between here and the Eight Hills, as well as estates of wealthy men. Between Jaiden's growing reputation and an appearance from the Aasimar, we can drum up healthy support for the Order before reaching Selamus. With any luck, that will put enough pressure on Prince Falcionus to publicly throw his support behind us as well. If I know the Prince, he is too concerned with popular opinion to be found on the wrong side of a movement such as ours."

"Oh, we're a movement now?" Sir Kilborn laughed incredulously. "Here I thought we were a military outfit."

Jaiden shrugged as they all stood from their chairs. He certainly felt a part of something more than that.

"Jaiden, would you accompany me to the stables? I should like to see how the horses are doing."

Jaiden nodded. "I suppose so."

Palomar smiled and held out an arm for Jaiden to lead the way, *"Very well."*

When they had passed beyond the Pork & Porridge's common room, still noisy with revelry, and into the fresh night air, Palomar confided. *"I wanted to talk to you privately."*

"You don't say?" Jaiden smirked.

"Well, I heard stories from the other men about how you performed a miracle while at Castle Windhollow?"

"There is truth to that, but only insofar as I delivered the blessings of Criesha."

"So you channeled Criesha's power to heal the sick?"

They reached the stables behind the tavern, where the boy Jaiden handed Inferno over to was putting away the last of the feedbags. He stared at Palomar with an open mouth as they approached, but said nothing.

"You could phrase it so if you like." Jaiden picked up a brush, resting on a rail, and went over Inferno's coat in long strokes. The stallion groaned his appreciation.

"Do not misunderstand; I am not implying anything is amiss. Only, it is likely Criesha is also one of the Juda-cai."

Jaiden lifted his palms up, "Is that bad? I do not really know what it means."

"Not bad, my friend. It is simply best to remember that the Juda-cai have their own agendas, and lesser beings such as we, are ultimately but pawns in their game."

"I think I am a little more than that to Criesha."

Palomar tilted his head to the side, and Jaiden was glad the stable was too dim for the Aasimar to see him blushing. *"Now it is I who do not know what you mean."*

Jaiden peeked around the horses, but could no longer see the stable boy present. "Criesha and I have a... special sort of relationship. I have promised myself to her."

Palomar's eyebrows furrowed. *"How can this be? She does not reside on your world."*

Jaiden shrugged. "We meet in another place, when I am dreaming."

"You are wed to a Juda-cai in your dreams?"

"No, it's real. It's just, well, we can only be together when I'm asleep. It is real." He nodded.

"I see. I apologize for my reaction, Jaiden. The idea is strange to me. I would still caution you to be wary, however. The Juda-cai gain power in their own world through the spread of their influence on others. Take care you are not manipulated from any course you feel to be right."

"She's not manipulating me." His voice reached a higher pitch. "We want the same things."

Palomar smiled and placed a gentle hand on Jaiden's shoulder. "Very well, my friend. I hope for your sake that remains the truth. Now, I sense we are both weary. I will go meditate, and leave you to your dreams." He patted Inferno's flank before taking a few steps from the stable. He stopped for a moment, but didn't turn. "It is good to see you well, Jaiden." Without another word, Palomar returned to the tavern, leaving Jaiden to indulge his horse.

Chapter 25

Decisions of the Heart

Rogan was thankful for the Aasimars' return, not only to catch up with his friend, Palomar, but because doing so afforded him an excuse to put distance between himself and Dhania. He knew Saffron noticed her sister snuggling up beside him the last couple nights on the road. For warmth, Dhania had said, but the nights were not overly cold.

As per Sir Golddrake's strategy for support, the Order did not head straight to the capital city, but created a visitation circuit including a number of smaller towns and outposts in the province of Dawn's Edge. Rogan paid only marginal attention while meeting minor nobility of the region. He had no reason to believe such relationships would be lasting, as this was not his home.

The Order split to cover more ground, and as part of Sir Golddrake's unit, Rogan at least got to sleep in the houses of wealthy men. He also got to watch Saffron min Furasi ply her significant charms, only to later skillfully deflect the dozen or so would-be suitors vying for her attention. He wondered if tempting such men was Sir Golddrake's intention for keeping her close.

Whatever his plan, it seemed to Rogan to be working. Rogan witnessed Sir Golddrake secure impressive contributions of funding, supplies, and recruits eager to make a name for themselves. Had his life not been altered by the Blood Tear Brotherhood years ago, Rogan no doubt would have engaged in similar pandering, for one reason or another.

Three days after the Aasimar had rejoined them, Rogan was watching Sir Golddrake give a riding demonstration to a potential patron, when a courier arrived at the estate. The letter was not for the estate's owner, but rather the Master of the Order of the Rising Moon. When Rogan approached out of curiosity, Sir Golddrake showed him the invitation to dine with Prince Falcionus in two days.

"Just what we have been waiting for!" Sir Golddrake grinned as he patted Rogan on the chest and finished his demonstration.

Rogan handed the letter to Saffron. "Were you not on your way to play for the Prince when your caravan was attacked? I suppose you have come full-circle."

"That is one perspective." Saffron scanned the page, but Rogan was unsure she would be able to read much of it. "The circumstances are much different now, of course."

Rogan caught the sadness in her remark and felt shame dragging down the inside of his chest. After what she had been through this year, how could he resent the attention other men were giving her? She had done nothing wrong. He dared to put his arm around her shoulder and kiss the hair on the side of her head. "What say we corral Sir Golddrake and prepare ourselves for the palace?"

Saffron nudged him and shimmied from under his arm, but the smile had returned to her voice. "I think Amurel is enjoying himself far too much."

Looking into the yard, Rogan saw the Master of the Order executing a jump over a fallen log. "Yes," he echoed. "I think these past few days have been all he could ask for."

It took another day for all the Order's soldiers and Aasimar to be rounded up, but at last Rogan was on the final approach to the Shining City of Selamus. He had heard occasional tales of its immensity back in his homeland, but figured them the exaggerated stories of those with a need to impress.

Within sight of the capital, however, he marveled at the truth of those boasts. The city ascended from the crests of several broad hills of varying heights, the outer slopes of which were cultivated for green vineyards and clinging orchards. Walls and towers of white stone gave the impression of a spiral, working its way toward the centermost, zenithal hilltop where the palace stood. The protected inner slopes of the Eight Hills bore wide terraces filled with grand houses, which he imagined trickled into the valleys.

When they reached earshot of the front gate, Rogan heard murmurs like waves descending from the onlookers assembled atop the fortified walls. His curiosity got the better of him as occasional gasps and shrieks punctuated the droning hum; surely a small retinue of soldiers on horseback would not elicit such gawking.

He peered over his shoulder to see what was garnering so much attention – of course, the Aasimar. His awe diminished with familiarity, almost forgetting they looked spectacularly unlike normal men. He decided he should probably get used to the reaction.

The Order rode in first; he and Dhania brought up the rear of the column. The Aasimar followed on foot, their broad strides covering significant ground with each step. The Dawn Way continued northward, with the capital set just off to the west. A wide branch of the road carried them into and through the city, winding around the smaller hills until it climbed straight to the doors of the palace.

Selamus was throbbing. Every avenue and open space seemed filled with activity, whether women cleaning rugs, men carving stone or crafting ironwork, or even children harvesting the bounty of the vineyards. Instead of an opulent wasteland of excess, it appeared a diligent landscape of production, and the people seemed to be enjoying it, which struck Rogan. He wondered if the greatness of the city had been built on the backs of such workers, or if they only inherited the fruits of slavery, like Lucnere.

Throughout Chelpa, at least since Ebon Khorel came to power, not many seemed to relish the work of the day, even if not formally servants. Rogan innately understood this was a place worth protecting. Even as an outsider, it would be a shame to watch it burn.

The architecture was magnificent, too. Whether a collection of common houses or a grand mansion on the road to the palace, there was a continuity of style. Arches, spirals, and curves abounded, as if the buildings mimicked the slopes of the hills they were built upon.

Their pace slowed and the horses struggled as they finally began climbing the centermost promontory. Rogan assumed they were heading for the palace, but a sudden detour took them down an abutting path. The beasts were clearly relieved for the change to level ground, and he did not have to wait long to find the cause of the turn.

Calls of greeting carried back from the front of the column, and word spread quickly among the men until it reached Rogan in the rear – Lieutenant Orestes had come to greet them. As discussion commenced at the fore of the formation, Rogan took the opportunity to rise up in the saddle and stretch his legs.

He looked back over the edge of the slope, marveling at the view. He had not realized how far they ascended. From this vantage, the layout of the city carried an artistic sort of order only a genius could plan. Buildings fell into rows of alternating grey and brown, with swaths of green swirled in a display at once chaotic, yet not without its own rhythm. The blue sky reigned over all, and Rogan was just picking out birds against billows of white when Sir Kilborn disturbed his reverie.

"The Master has requested you accompany him to the palace."

"Of course." Rogan's response comingled with a wistful sigh as he turned away from his indulgent view.

Sir Kilborn nodded and led his horse back to the front. Rogan followed, cutting around the paths of companions as the majority followed the Lieutenant to a less prominent destination. Once they cleared some distance, he saw those who comprised the chosen contingent were the same he expected: Sirs Golddrake, Kilborn, and Luminere, Saffron, himself, and two of the Aasimar – Palomar and Illicurus.

Because of its position on the hill, the palace stayed hidden for most of their climb, until the final bend of the road. Rogan was no stranger to royal seats, having visited the palaces in Lucnere and Crioc, but this one stood alone. It wasn't clearly more opulent than those other residences of power – just strikingly unique.

Unlike the King-priest's abode, the palace at Selamus was no fortress, and held no air of intimidation. Instead, it seemed designed as an invitation to appreciate and experience the greatness of what could be accomplished by human hands. Pedestals flanking the steps to the entrance displayed a gold sun and silver moon, as if decrying the site an equal to those celestial bodies.

Rose-colored glass was prominently inlaid among the white, stone façade, creating a warm dance of reflected sunlight. This aura made Rogan feel as though he was about to step into the halls of a dream. The outer walls were not completely vertical, but slanted inward for several stories until they met with expertly carved, polished wood, which flared outward again.

Like the curved horns of a ram or the winding tendrils of a grapevine, these spirals added to the impression that this was more than a building, perhaps a living entity all its own. Three towers of gradual ascendancy jutted toward the sky. They each bore a tall steeple, upon which flags seized the wind, displaying different emblems unfamiliar to Rogan. As much as he admired the view, he realized the rest of his companions had already started up the steps of the palace, so he hurriedly dismounted and rushed to join them.

Attendants took their horses and guards flanked the ornate doors, though those opened from the inside upon their approach. Rogan noted Sir Golddrake utilized a gold-headed cane he had never seen before. Perhaps Orestes passed it along earlier when they met, he thought. A seneschal appeared clasping a sleek, wooden rod that bore what Rogan assumed was the royal standard, and greeted the Master of the Order with a slight bow.

Sir Golddrake hunched his shoulders forward in return, and quiet words were exchanged before they were led into a wide foyer. The sound of falling water tickled Rogan's ears as they passed a pair of flanking pools, fed by streams pouring forth from the walls above them. Lily pads bearing white flowers floated in the reservoirs, and he heard Saffron gasp as a hand played up to her lips. She looked back and smiled, the wonder in her expression warming him. Then Jaiden spoke, and it quickly chilled.

"I stared up at the palace on the hill all my life, but never thought I would see it from the inside."

Saffron turned to him, "Is it not breathtaking?"

Rogan noticed Palomar staring up at the ceiling. "How does this compare to your home on Mount Celestia?"

"It is breathtaking, as the Lady Saffron suggests. I think it compares favorably to some of the temples in my native realm."

Illicurus snickered suddenly and his lip curled upward as he gave his fellow Aasimar a look, but he articulated no thoughts to Rogan.

The seneschal took them through more open rooms with cathedral ceilings, all basked in early-afternoon rose and gold radiance, before stopping in front of a closed door. "Court has not yet come into session, but His Excellence wanted to greet you in person before your official announcement this evening."

The seven visitors were admitted into what looked to Rogan like a mixture between a library and sitting room. Three walls held shelving full of books, while the fourth was an array of tall windows providing ample illumination. A pair of sturdy tables and numerous comfortable chairs and lounges filled out the space.

"His Excellence, Prince Falcionus of Dawn's Edge greets Sir Amurel Golddrake of Dawn's Edge," the seneschal announced with vigor. The prince stood near a door, which was nearly concealed within one of the walls of literature, an open book in hand. He wore a white, floor-length coat, pale vestments underneath, with a gaudy blue gem centered in a thick chain of silver around his neck. Two guards in ceremonial, gold-filigreed armor, holding spears, stood at attention on either side of the door.

"Yes, Umberto, that will quite do," said Prince Falcionus as he took a step closer and shut the book.

"Your Excellence," Sir Golddrake straightened his posture before bowing, going deeper than he had in his exchange with the seneschal.

"How are you, Amurel?" Prince Falcionus had a tidy, graying beard that came to a point beneath his chin, but there were few lines on his face, and Rogan guessed him to still be late in his prime, not more than ten years older than himself. As soon as he said the words, the prince's grey eyes cast themselves upon the two, tall, angelic creatures behind Rogan.

Ignoring his own question, Prince Falcionus muttered something unintelligible, before speaking clearly. "Gods be with us, I had heard the stories in recent days, but did not believe them until my own eyes have born witness."

"Uh," Sir Golddrake attempted to maneuver along with the prince's attention, "may I present two of the Aasmiar who have been fighting with us? To your right is Marshall Illicurus, and this is Palomar to your left. He has already sworn allegiance to the Rising Moon."

"Has he?" the prince mouthed absently. Palomar dipped his head in deference, though Illicurus made no such gesture.

"*You have much to be proud of, Prince Falcionus,*" Illicurus's voice filled Rogan's head with its steady, disinterested tone. "*This is as fine a human city as I have seen during my brief travels in your lands. But might I ask, why merely a Prince and not a King?*"

Umberto the Seneschal gasped and Sir Golddrake immediately opened his mouth to speak, but the prince raised his hand to halt him.

"*Marshall*, was it?" Falcionus began by looking Illicurus in the eye, then paced about the room as he spoke. "To answer your question: the Cradle of the World has a history like a winding road. The Seven Provinces were long united under a single king, but that did not work out well for its people. In the end, it did not work out well for that final king, but since then each province has ruled itself. The Dukes each come from families with deep roots in their region, and their own prosperity is tied to it as a result. Selamus," he gestured to the walls around them, "as the historic capital of the old kingdom, still holds a prominent place in the collective minds of the Cradle. As a sign of respect and a deference to our *very real influence*," he turned back to stare straight at the Aasimar at this last phrase, "the head of my family has been allowed to carry on a royal title, though it is understood there shall be no king."

Illicurus's answer was quick. "*Unless one forces you all to submit, I imagine?*"

Prince Falcionus's lips quivered briefly, before he forced them into a smile. "Ah, but that is exactly what our good Amurel is here to prevent, or I've misheard?" He turned back to Sir Golddrake, who nodded in response.

"Your Excellence, that is indeed why I have returned to Selamus."

Falcionus raised his hand again, "And we shall address all those matters at Court, have no fear. For now, introduce me to the rest of your retainers."

Rogan saw the prince's eyes trained directly on Saffron, and he extended his hand to her as he drew nearer. Looking unsure, she tentatively took it in a light grasp, and bent at the waist to kiss the back of his royal hand.

"This is the Lady Saffron min Furasi from Begnasharan," Sir Golddrake tried to keep up.

"My, you are far from home, are you not?"

"Yes, Your Excellence." She kept her eyes lowered and released his hand.

"I did not know such flowers bloomed in the western deserts." The prince's eyes lingered on Saffron, assessing her bare shoulders and continuing downward.

Rogan could not remain silent and watch. "Lady Saffron is a talented musician, Your Excellence."

"Is she, indeed?" The prince responded without moving his eyes.

"She is, and was actually on route to play at the invitation of your Court, some months ago." Rogan was unsure she would want him to share this information, but he would have declared a third arm was growing out of his backside to interrupt the man's hungry stare.

Prince Falcionus turned to consider Rogan, raising his eyebrows in question as to who was addressing him. Rogan cleared his throat, spurring Sir Golddrake to make the introduction.

"Yes, Your Excellence. This is Emmert Rogan, former Baron of Thispany."

"Another foreigner?" the prince uttered with slight distaste.

"Baron Rogan is one of the few men known to have had a direct confrontation with the King-priest of Chelpa, and live to tell." Sir Golddrake's justification was unexpected, but Rogan approved.

"Is he now?" The prince seemed to reconsider his standing. "Impressive."

"And here," Sir Golddrake continued, seizing momentum, "is my Marshall, Sir Geldrick Kilborn. He is the head of a proud family."

"I know it," replied the prince.

Sir Kilborn bowed his head, "Your Excellence."

"And finally, on the end, is Sir Jaiden Luminere."

Rogan rolled his eyes at how proud Sir Golddrake sounded.

Prince Falcionus clasped his hands together. "Ah, the Miracle at Windhollow Rock! Another story I was unsure whether to believe."

"I assure Your Excellence that it is all true." Sir Golddrake beamed.

"Well, Willem is crafting an extravagant gift of our appreciation for you, Sir Luminere."

Jaiden looked from side to side, seemingly unclear if the prince was indeed talking to him. "Thank you, Your Excellence," he finally managed to sputter.

Falcionus puckered his lips and looked over the entirety of the group, before nodding. "You are all welcome to Selamus, and will of course be my guests at the palace while in our fair city. Unfortunately, I have much to do before holding Court, so I must take leave of you now..." he stopped just before reaching the door, spun, and added, "though it would be my pleasure if you would play something for us tonight, Lady Saffron."

Not waiting for a response, he turned on his heel again and raised a hand, prompting one of the guards to silently open the door. When the prince disappeared, the seneschal briefly took back control of the room.

"If you will follow me back to the main hall, there are porters who will show you to your accommodations. Sir Golddrake, we still have some arrangements regarding your petition, and the Shaper of Selamus has requested a brief visit with Sir Luminere and one of the Aasimar before tonight's festivities."

Palomar shared a look with Illicurus and volunteered. With most of the others occupied, Rogan thought it might be the perfect chance to reconnect with Saffron, absent the constant interference manifest since Talon Barge.

Initially, becoming knighted seemed such an abstract honor. Jaiden thought it a suave nuance, being addressed as "Sir," but that was about the only benefit he saw in the whole ordeal. He had since walked through the halls of the palace on the hill, held meetings with nobility, and wherever he went, people seemed to have heard of his deeds. Now, he'd received a summons to the chamber of the famous Shaper of Selamus, a man professed to be capable of making your spine shrivel with a mere incantation.

As the porter led him and Palomar up yet another flight of stairs, Jaiden wondered when the fantasy would come crashing down upon him. Looking over the railing, near the top of one of the towers, Jaiden induced a moment of vertigo.

"Are you unwell, Jaiden?"

"I would feel a lot better if I also had wings." He leaned away from the edge of the stairs and blinked a few times to readjust his equilibrium, before soldiering on. At last they reached their destination, and the porter knocked on a heavy-looking door at the end of the stairway.

"Come in," came the muted response.

The porter turned an iron ring to unlatch the unlocked portal and swung it open, leaving Jaiden and Palomar to enter of their own accord. Jaiden looked back at the Aasimar, who seemed content to wait his turn. With slow steps he crossed the threshold, imagining the room beyond to be dank and full of unrecognizable skulls.

In fact, a suite of rooms awaited, all perfectly comfortable from Jaiden's vantage. An enormous window, slanting with the tapered roof near the apex of the tower, let in a flood of sunlight. With a welcoming balcony and sturdy furniture throughout, including a hanging, wire bird cage housing a green feathered avian, Jaiden was forced to relinquish his anxiety. The bird twittered and flapped its wings briefly when Palomar entered the space.

"Ah, so it is true!" The voice came from a man sitting behind a desk on the far side of the room. "What a wonderful day it is!" He finished scrawling something with a quill and then stood to approach. As he entered the rectangle of sunlight upon the floor, Jaiden could see the outline of his thin body through his robes, though his wrinkled face otherwise showed good health. "Come in, come in, please," he waved them over.

As Jaiden crossed the room, he saw a second man reclining on a shaded couch, opposite the window. He stood as Jaiden entered his view, and though he was also thin, he wore more closely-fitted clothes, and bore a stick of charcoal and a spool in his hands.

The man who spoke clasped Jaiden's hands in his own. They were cold, and the iris of one of his eyes was clouded over. "I am Willem, though some know me as the *Shaper of Selamus*." He laughed as if the title itself was a joke.

"And I am Jaiden Luminere."

"Welcome, welcome both. And who is your feathered friend, Jaiden?" Willem laughed again, thoroughly amusing himself.

"You may call me Palomar."

"Extraordinary!" Willem turned to Jaiden, "He uses telepathy, my boy." He then spoke louder to Palomar, as if the Aasimar's choice of communication rendered him hard of hearing. "I say, Palomar, you are not from this plane, are you?"

"That is correct. I am native to Mount Celestia."

"And did you get here through a Planar Gate? Where is it, might I ask?"

"No, Willem. I was sent here directly by my lord, Hiruth Jeshu, may his light shine forever."

"Fascinating. And I presume you have the gift; you are a Shaper, as well?"

"I am, after a fashion. But my shaping is harmonic; yours is somatic, if what I have heard of this world is correct?"

"Somatic and verbal, but you are mostly right." Willem clasped his hands together and shook with excitement. "We shall have to talk further, Palomar, but I hate to waste any more of Dorric's time." He gestured to the other man. "Dorric, here, is the royal tailor, you see, and I am in need of some measurements, my boy."

Without further invitation, Dorric whipped the end of his wire around Jaiden's chest and unspooled enough to encircle him. Jaiden raised his arms out of the way and let the man work.

"Very well," Jaiden stated, struggling to find a connection between being measured for clothes and a conversation with the Shaper of Selamus. Still, he obliged as the dexterous Dorric maneuvered his arms and legs to get what he needed.

"Is it true you have both survived battle with the King-priest of Chelpa?" Willem asked, drastically changing the subject.

"We have, though just barely, I would say."

Jaiden nodded his agreement.

"And though he employs magic, he is most definitely not a Shaper. I believe him to be a servant of the Juda-cai. Does that mean anything to you, Willem?"

"I have heard that name before... in a text expounding on the old gods, if I am not mistaken." The Shaper of Selamus walked back behind his desk and started searching one of his many shelves.

"The city will need you, Shaper, should Ebon Khorel reach its gates."

"Ha! Then I would say younger men and feathered men had better do all they can to make sure that doesn't happen. This city hasn't the vaguest idea what I am truly capable of, or the King-priest, I'd imagine. And I don't mean that in the same way!" Willem abandoned looking for the book. "Oh, I have some enchantments left in me, for sure. And I can make anyone sorry who might try to pilfer my Lydia." The bird chirped at its name and Willem sighed, calm descending once more upon the room. "But I am old, and beyond fighting back armies, I can assure you."

Willem suddenly shook his head, as if clearing an unwanted idea from his mind, "But none of this is why I asked you here. I wanted to thank you in person, Jaiden Luminere. I heard about the sickness in the southern provinces. I... I have a granddaughter in Synirpa – my only grandchild. A letter arrived from her mother yesterday, and if not penned by my own offspring I would have thought the author mad. She relayed the story of what happened at Windhollow, and how you healed our precious Kylie. I don't think I could take losing her so young." The last few words were difficult to make out, as Willem choked on the tears welling in his eyes.

Jaiden was moved. He looked down at Dorric, who seemed to understand and pulled back from his work. Jaiden covered the few paces between them and embraced Willem. "She is going to be fine," he said, patting the old man's shoulder. Jaiden never met his own grandparents, but always imagined them similar to Willem.

"I have what I need," announced Dorric, though no one responded.

By the time Jaiden relinquished the Shaper, the tailor had already taken leave. "What was that all about, might I ask?"

Willem wiped his cheeks and smiled, "The prince has commissioned a gift for you, Sir Luminere, and I am going to make it unique."

Rogan spent much of the afternoon exploring the royal gardens with Saffron, but failed to seize the opportunity. Every time his courage rose enough to put his feelings into words, she became distracted by another flower or plant she'd never seen before, and the moment passed. Finally, they parted to prepare for Court, where he toiled for an hour dressing in the outfit the Duke of Rosegold bestowed him. This time he was the one distracted, refining and reciting a declaration fit to woo Saffron the next time he managed to get her alone. The words just never sounded quite right.

He was likely missing the petitioning as a result, but held it of little consequence. Rogan hoped Sir Golddrake would receive what he needed to strengthen his Order, but it hardly mattered if he was present to witness the outcome. He found it critically important, however, not to make a fool of himself while confessing his emotions to the woman he hoped might one day become his wife.

He wanted to find a creative flower analogy, both for its poetic effect and to show her he understood her interests. Everything he thought of sounded too contrived, or simply imbecilic. Deciding it would be a mistake to miss the event entirely, he pressed a damp cloth over his face and tried to convince himself he was ready. "Just speak what you feel, Emmert, from your heart."

Rogan left his room and did his best to remember the path to the Gallery, assuming they had already moved on to the banquet. Before long, he heard music lingering in the halls, and he followed his ear until he saw servants bustling to and from the celebration. Another party in Jaiden's honor, he thought, shaking his head; no, he needed to focus. Tonight was not about Jaiden Luminere, but opening up to the woman he had fallen in love with.

The music grew louder, and movement in the room caught his eye before anything else – people were dancing. Perhaps just the opportunity he needed to get Saffron to himself. An excuse to draw her close could not hurt, either. He stood at the edge of the room and scanned its expanse for signs of her signature color. Saffron told him she would be wearing a red dress.

He first looked along the edges of the room, where tables still held a sprinkling of those too shy or otherwise ill-conditioned to populate the dance floor. Not finding her, he shifted his search to those dancing, and a moment later his heart dropped. He spotted Saffron, and that she looked stunning came as no surprise, but she was dancing with *him*: Jaiden. As he twirled her around awkwardly – obviously a novice – Rogan could see they were both laughing.

A wave of nausea rose from his stomach to wash over him, and a droplet of sweat was suddenly running down his temple. Rogan instinctively turned to spare himself the sight, but then froze. He was done running from this. However difficult, he was going to find a way to tell Saffron what he needed to, tonight.

Making his way along the edge of the dance floor, he deftly avoided joined pairs until he saw Dhania sitting at a table along the wall. She gazed longingly over the crowd, her eyes following the languid movement of well-dressed dancers as they glided before her. Rogan sighed. There was only one thing to do.

"M'lady, would you care to dance?" he asked, offering an outstretched hand. Dhania looked up, just noticing him, and smiled.

"Of course, Baron." She stood and took his hand, navigating around the table until she was beside him. As a new song started to play, some couples left the floor, while others changed partners. "I do not know the steps to these dances," she confessed, though already placing a hand on his shoulder.

Rogan met her eyes. "I will lead you through it. I have been to my fair share of such events, and presume many of the dances are the same here as in Chelpa." He listened to the tempo of the music, stole a quick glance at the next couple over, and nodded. It was a *swego*, which he knew. He grasped Dhania's waist and began stepping: toward her, then away, then to the side as they turned. She followed his lead flawlessly; she was clearly either a natural or had some training.

For several, blissful minutes he was completely wrapped up in the dance. The choreography and dashing woman across from him held his attention completely. Dhania looked so happy, and he could not deny it felt good to share that and lose himself in the moment. Her hand was soft in his, and Rogan realized how much he missed this. Of course, the last time he danced, Riah was in his arms.

He caught Sir Golddrake's eye as he circled around, and the knight raised his glass toward Rogan from his seat, pairing it with an insinuating tilt of his head. A flash of panic speared Rogan. Did it look like something was going on between him and Dhania? Were others getting that impression? As the song ended, he hurriedly looked for Saffron, wondering if she had spotted him. He could not find her immediately, but quickly put a step between himself and Dhania.

He bowed to her, "Thank you for the dance. You are light on your feet."

"I could go for another, if you like…"

"I would not deprive the entire room of your company," he said. "I am sure other gentlemen are waiting for their chance." His eyes continued darting, searching for Saffron.

Dhania's fell. "I see."

Rogan quickly bowed again and turned away. He finally spotted the red of Saffron's dress across the floor, and made haste to reach her before the musicians cued up their next piece. She appeared to be returning to her table when Rogan pulled even and grasped her hand. Saffron gasped but relaxed when she saw who it was.

"Baron, I had begun to worry. You missed both the petitions and dinner – are you well?"

"I will be just fine if you dance with me." The music started again and he whisked her into his arms, not waiting for an answer.

She squealed, momentarily losing her balance, regaining it only after reaching out and taking hold of his body. "Ooh, my apologies." Saffron followed her stumble with a hearty laugh.

Rogan studied her closely as they fell into the rhythm of the dance. Something was off. "Have you had much wine?" he asked.

Saffron's lips curled upward and she placed a finger up to them. "That is between me and the sommelier," she answered, her eyes still smiling.

He let out a sudden cough. "Is that so?" He pulled her waist toward him, closing the space between them. She leaned her cheek on his shoulder.

"No more questions, Baron. Just dance."

Rogan held her close and swayed for what seemed an eternity, until it ended too soon. He did not even hear the music stop, but eventually one of the prince's servants interrupted by tapping on Saffron's shoulder. The man swallowed deeply and kept his eyes trained somewhere above their heads.

"Your pardons, milord and lady, but His Excellence requested Lady Saffron play for his pleasure now."

Rogan looked over her shoulder at Prince Falcionus, who sat on a throne overseeing the room, a chalice raised to his lips.

Saffron cleared her throat and straightened her dress, then flipped the hair that had fallen about her shoulders behind them. "Of course," she eventually answered. "I shall retrieve my lyre with haste. My sister is watching over it." She took two steps toward her table then turned and briefly curtsied. "Baron," she saluted before continuing on her way.

The dance floor was clearing as the musicians temporarily abandoned their instruments in favor of the wine servants had begun circulating. Rogan momentarily considered his next move before settling on finding a seat at a table where he knew no one. His head was too full at the moment for conversation.

He watched closely as Saffron crossed the floor with her lyre, bowed to the prince, and took over one of the chairs emptied by the hired players. She spoke loudly enough for most of the room to hear, her accent drawing thicker than in quiet conversation, marking her as a foreigner.

"This is a song I love that reminds me of my homeland. You will not know the words, but it does not matter. Hopefully, you will love it too." She plucked a few strings absently, the lonesome notes floating out in search of companions. They had almost completely drifted away when she began playing earnestly; a harmonic avalanche ensued, chasing all the silent spirits from the room.

Her honeyed voice followed closely, dripping thick Begnari that stuck to the memory and would not let go. Rogan could not look away. The movement of her hands, so precise, mesmerized him. He already knew the wine had gone to her head, but its influence was hidden during her performance, playing a tune she must have passionately practiced hundreds of times. He closed his eyes and could still see her, and in his mind she was playing just for him.

When her song ended, Rogan opened his lids, and for a short moment thought his desires had manifested – the rest of the Gallery was completely silent. The entire audience seemed unsure of the appropriate reaction. Saffron's eyes were shut as well, and he imagined her waiting for a response before opening them.

Rogan lifted his hands to clap, hoping to breach the awkward silence, to let Saffron know how talented she was and how she had moved him, how he wanted her head upon his shoulder once more.

But Prince Falcionus beat him to it. He began clapping and the room quickly followed his example, as if waiting for it. Maybe they were? Regardless, Rogan added to the cacophony of appreciation that soon became deafening. Saffron looked out at the crowd, her eyes fixing on something, and stood to curtsey, only to lose her balance and stumble. She avoided falling, but Rogan decided he needed to talk to her before she got her hands on another glass, or she would be incapable of understanding him.

He stood, intent on being the first to congratulate Saffron, but once again the prince, who was nearby, foiled him. His Excellence seemed determined to monopolize her for a while, bringing a circle of his pompous followers into the conversation. Rogan resigned to biding his time, seeking out a beverage of his own to negotiate with.

The wine amplified his courage, and by the time he finished his glass, he was not only ready to confront Saffron, but decided he was no longer going to wait.

"Baron, I missed you at the petitioning, I figured—"

Rogan heard Palomar's thought but did not see him, and was not getting sidetracked. He raised his head and kept walking, weaving through the crowd, which had devolved into a mass of imbibing gossipers. When he reached Saffron, she was engaged in a one-sided conversation with a man twice her age, who seemed tickled by the sound of his own voice. The weight of the unseen world distilled itself, in that moment, upon this singular decision – whether Rogan dared speak his heart to her, and begin the frightful unravelling of reason. Another breath gone, he stepped forward, though toward his doom or salvation, he couldn't be sure.

"Lady Saffron, may I speak to you alone for a moment? The matter is urgent."

Saffron looked from the graying man to Rogan and then back again. "Please excuse me, Sir, I think I am needed elsewhere." Rogan extended his hand and she took it, breaking into laughter as soon as her back was turned, too abruptly to go unnoticed. "Thank you for rescuing me. I was so bored I was about to immolate myself. Where are we going?" she asked.

Rogan did not say a word, but tightened his grip around her hand to make sure he did not lose contact in the maze of bodies. He led her out of the Gallery, and down one of the hallways he had taken on the way from his room. Only when he was confident they were alone, and had some distance from the rest of the party, did he stop and turn.

"Where are we?" Saffron asked, looking around at the walls as if they might give her an answer.

Rogan had been concentrating for the last few hours on what he planned to say in this moment, but now that it had arrived he wanted to do something else even more. Reaching up, he cradled her face in both hands. His thumb briefly played with a loose tendril of dark hair before he closed the distance between their bodies. He felt her inhale deeply, and then crushed his lips against hers. His kiss took away all sense of himself for a moment – only his longing need remained.

For the duration of two shallow breaths Saffron submitted, accepting Rogan's advance; then, her hands pressed against his belly, pushing him away. He reluctantly withdrew his lips, though his thoughts were still clouded by desire.

"What's wrong?" he asked, the urgency shaping his voice.

"What are you doing, Rogan?" she countered, wiping his saliva from her lips.

"What? I'm...Saffron, it's me." He realized he was not making any sense and peered down at the floor, forcing himself to take slow breaths.

"I know who you are, Baron," she said, seeming to regain control. "Why are you kissing me?"

At that moment, two men walked around the corner from the direction of the Gallery, in the midst of a conversation. "I know they have wings, but that doesn't mean the histories all have to be re-written. Sure, I can believe the part about other realms, but gods and goddesses?"

"I don't know, it must be possible..." The second man, spotting Rogan and Saffron, clearly got the impression he'd intruded upon a private moment. "All right, well, I think I'll take the long way to the gardens." The men both retreated the way they came.

The interruption gave Rogan time to pull his thoughts together. "Saffron, I didn't bring you here to kiss you, I just couldn't help myself. The truth is, I have wanted to kiss you for some time because I've fallen in love with you."

Saffron's brow pinched and she crossed her arms. "Baron, I enjoy your company and you are a fine man, but you have already been married. You have a life waiting for you in Chelpa once you chase down justice. I cannot pull you away from it, but it is not the life I want. I'm sorry; I just do not envision a future where we can be romantically involved."

Rogan shook his head, unwilling to hear her words. "Saffron, please do not dismiss us so easily. Forget the way you think events might unfold – what do you feel? Yes, I have been married, and the loss of my wife stunted the realization of my feelings for you. I did not want to feel that sort of love again, because of the cost I paid for it. But being around you, getting to know you... I know now I cannot let the ghosts of my past prevent me from pursuing the happiness we could share together." He reached out his hand and took a step closer, but she shook her head and quickly backed away.

She seemed to have difficulty speaking, and when she did, immense sadness carried her voice. "I am sorry," she gasped, bringing her hand to her face and turning away. Saffron fled toward the Gallery without turning back.

Even if he thought it wise to go after her, Rogan found his legs suddenly unwilling to move.

Jaiden could not remember having had so much fun without a sword in his hand, with the notable exceptions of his liaisons with Criesha. Lords of Selamus, including the Prince himself, had praised him for his service to the Northern Provinces. He ate the best food, drank the best wine, and had to admit that Saffron had even made learning to dance enjoyable. His childhood dreams of visiting the palace on the hill had never been so vivid.

The day had drained him of vigor, yet left him satisfied. He met so many interesting people, like the Shaper of Selamus, his mind was still preoccupied playing over those interactions as he ambled down the final hallway to his appointed apartments. He was counting the doors, trying to remember which was his, when he noticed another presence from the corner of his eye.

Looking up, it took him a moment to recognize the lithe silhouette leaning with the back of her shoulders against the wall. Saffron's red dress clung alluringly to the front of her arched form, its excess fabric draping from her thighs toward the floor. She stood erect as he drew nearer, and smiled coyly as he reached for the handle of his door.

"I have been waiting for you," she said with a tone that was still seductive, despite slightly slurring the words.

Jaiden nodded as he opened his door and gestured for her to enter. "It certainly seems that way." He immediately walked to the wrought-iron stand beside his bed and poured water from a jug into two cups, offering one to Saffron. "Can I do something for you, my lady?"

"I've watched you for a while, now, Jaiden Luminere. When we met you were brash, melancholy, self-absorbed." She sipped from her cup, but made an unpleasant face when it dawned on her it wasn't more wine.

"Thank you for your flattery," Jaiden said, raising his cup in a mock toast and taking a drink.

Saffron shook her head, "But you were also undeniably talented – and stupidly brave."

"Well, then, I suppose that all balances out." He studied her face, trying to discern if she intended on paying him compliments or giving him a lecture. The fact she was drunk and he had never seen her this way, also unnerved him.

"The last several months, however, you have changed. I've seen you act kindly, even when you don't know others are watching. You have sacrificed, placing the needs of others ahead of your own." As Saffron spoke, she closed the distance between them, and soon her hand was on his head, fingers running through his dark, untamed hair.

"I'm sorry, am I still awake?" He reached up and gently took hold of her hand, then lowered their entwined fists between their chests. "Because this is starting to remind me of how my dreams have gone lately."

Saffron's eyes squinted slightly, as if she were trying to decipher his meaning. "Jaiden, I am trying to tell you that I have taken notice, and am finally ready to share myself with you in the way you wanted." She leaned forward, shutting her eyes as her full lips puckered.

Jaiden acted quickly, releasing her hand and stepping to the side. "Well, I cannot say I saw this coming." She opened her eyes when he moved.

"I know I said before nothing would happen between us, but I changed my mind. You have become just the sort of man I always saw myself falling for." Saffron blushed as she absently ran a hand down her torso, between her breasts, tracing the soft fabric with her fingertips. "More than once I have noticed your reaction to me." She broke into a grin and looked up at the ceiling, "Suffering scimitars, I hate that you know just how attractive you are!"

When she looked back at him her face turned serious, mirroring his. "Saffron," he spoke quietly, as if saying her name pained him. "Three weeks ago, all I could think about was how badly I wanted you, and that I wasn't worthy. I even wrote a terrible song, hoping to impress you. But I belong to the Order of the Rising Moon now, and have taken a vow to be faithful to my Goddess, to the exclusion of all others. I take my oath seriously, and cannot give you what you seek, though I am beyond flattered."

Saffron's laughter echoed through the room. "Are you jesting? Jaiden, do you remember telling me how good you could make me feel, and then waking up outside a brothel in Greyhorne? You probably did not know I heard about that, but I did. And you expect me to believe you have taken some vow of celibacy, and furthermore intend to honor it, even when I am standing here offering myself to you?"

Jaiden did not know how to respond, but was fairly sure anything he said would be insufficient, so he merely tightened his lips and searched her eyes for empathy.

"You are insufferable!" She cast her half-full cup of water to the floor, smashing it into dozens of clay shards. She stalked to the door, put her hand on the latch, and froze. Regaining some control, she kept her back to him as she spoke. "Do not expect me to wait for you." She gave Jaiden a moment to answer, and when he did not, opened the door and left.

After Saffron rejected him, Rogan did not want to be around anyone. He felt like a fool, humiliated and self-delusional, and wished for the world he had wings like Palomar so he could fly back to Thispany that very night. Since no feathers began sprouting from his back, the next-best move was to pilfer a jug of wine from the kitchens and head for the exit.

He passed a few people on the way to the front doors, some coming in, some leaving, but thankfully, no one he recognized. The night air, at least, was pleasant. A few clouds obscured the stars, but it was warm enough not to regret the decision, which could not be said for his other recent choice. Why had he thought Saffron would feel the same way? He saw her dancing with Jaiden earlier. In fact, she had been introduced to at least a dozen other men in the past week who would be able to offer her more than him.

Rogan sat on the front steps of the palace and took a deep drink from his jug. The vintage was sweet, but he downed enough to feel its heat warm his throat. He shook his head and took another sip, trying to figure out how swiftly he could find his horse in the morning and start the journey home. Prince Falcionus would have to forgive his departing without a formal good-bye.

Leaves rustled suddenly off to his left, and he heard laughter in the dark from beyond the steps. A young couple stumbled onto the moonlit path, their arms encircling one another. Oblivious to his presence, they held each other tight; their laughter silenced as mouths met.

"Unbelievable," he said, shaking his head and standing as he tipped back his jug yet again. He was not going to endure watching other people blissfully kiss after his own attempt was so brutally rebuked. *At least I can be alone in my own room.*

The problem with that line of thinking was he could not remember precisely how to get back to his room, and ended up wandering the palace halls for another half-hour before finding it. The wine did not help, and by the time he shut his door, all he wanted was to get into bed. He half-heartedly washed his face, then took off his boots and tunic. Rogan had not intended to lie down immediately after, but a few moments later he was horizontal, drifting toward a wine-induced coma.

He still wasn't even aware his head had hit the pillow when a noise disturbed him. Rogan opened his eyes but did not move. The sound repeated. Was someone knocking at his door? He grunted as he sat up. The lone candle he had forgotten to put out still cast a dim halo, but was not much to see by. Not yet fully lucid, he stood and shuffled to the door, failing to consider who might be behind it. Upon opening it, Rogan thought he might possibly be stuck in a nightmare. Saffron had returned to twist the knife in his heart. Only, that's not what she did at all.

Without a word, she pounced. Her arms flew around his neck, her legs wrapped around his waist, and her mouth attacked his with surprising ferocity. His hands moved to her thighs to support her as he stumbled back, absorbing the momentum of her leap.

He attempted to mumble a question, but Saffron's lips made articulation impossible.

"Shhh," she said as she pulled her mouth away, "don't say anything."

Odd as it seemed, her voice put him at ease. It grounded him in reality, and for the moment, it was enough to know she had changed her mind – for that much was clear. He slid one of his arms around her back and held her firmly to him until he could feel the heat through her dress against his skin. He wheeled around, returning her kisses with vigor, and moved the hand on her thigh under the hem of her dress.

She gasped as he moved it higher, prodding along her soft flesh until he found his mark. Rogan lay her on his bed, and together they managed to scramble her dress completely off. For a brief moment, he paused and looked down at her, drinking in her beauty. Then, with the hunger of a man deprived for nearly a decade, he did all he could to make sure they both remembered that night. The solitary candle on his shelf expired well before Rogan had spent all his passion.

Chapter 26

Nothing Can Last

Another knock at the door kicked Rogan out of his dream. Lying face down, a string of drool linked his chin to the mattress when he lifted his head. He reached to his left and felt Saffron's bare, slightly damp skin. "Mmm," she responded, still mostly asleep. *So, last night* did *happen.*

Although he gave no bidding to enter, the latch on his door jiggled as if someone were trying, unsuccessfully, to turn it.

"Baron Rogan, can you please open your door? I brought you breakfast, but can't hold the tray and turn the latch." The thick accent gave the voice away, and instantly Saffron shot to alertness, pulling up the blanket to cover her nakedness.

"Dhania!" she hissed at Rogan.

"Bloodhounds of Beyond!" he exclaimed as he reached over the side of the bed, frantically grasping for his trousers.

"What is my sister doing at your door?" Saffron whispered harshly.

"How would I know?" he retorted, pulling one leg into his pants only to find it was the wrong one.

Saffron had recovered her gown and was gathering the material as quickly as she could to slide it over her head.

"I cannot hold this forever!" Dhania complained, the latch once again shaking up and down. At last she negotiated it and the door swung inward, just as Saffron's garment slid down her torso to her hips.

Dhania stood in the doorway with a wooden tray stocked with several dishes, holding bread, fruit, and warm tea. They all came crashing to the floor when she saw her sister in Rogan's bed. "What is going on in here?!"

Rogan had never seen an expression quite like the one displayed on Dhania's face. He placed it an equal mixture of surprise and rage. His immediate instinct was to tell her that the situation was not what it looked like, but he kept his mouth shut, realizing it probably was.

Dhania pointed at Rogan while looking at her sister. "Did you?"

Saffron stood and leaned to search the floor as she spoke. "Dhania, I was not myself last night." She slipped one of her wayward sandals on her feet and continued to look for the other. "It was a mistake – I was weak."

"A mistake?" Rogan was incredulous. "Saffron, last night was a lot of things, but I don't think you can say a mistake was one of them. Did you not once tell me events occur for a reason?"

"And you!" Dhania turned her ire toward him. "First you kiss me, then you lay with my sister? I cannot believe I brought you breakfast." Dhania threw her hands over her eyes, "Such a bastard!" She spun and accelerated down the hall, leaving the doorway full of broken pottery.

"You kissed Dhania?" Saffron shook her head as she placed the other sandal on her foot. "Then you have the nerve to tell me you love me, and do... what we did last night?"

Rogan shrugged and held his palms up. He opened his mouth to explain himself, but was suddenly tongue-tied. As Saffron left his room, he finally found his voice, *"She* kissed *me!"* She did not stop or respond, and he did not really want her to. He flopped back onto the bed, put a pillow over his face, and growled.

"This is not what I rode all the way to the capital for!" How could one of the most amazing nights of his life turn on its head so quickly? He did not know whether to try and find Dhania first to smooth things over, or chase after Saffron to get an explanation of why she described the bliss they so recently shared a mistake. Nine Hells, she was probably doing that with Dhania right now.

Perhaps the setback was a sign – like the ones Sir Golddrake supposedly received from his goddess. Maybe the cosmos was pushing him toward returning to Chelpa and looking for any signs his son was still alive. Nothing was more important, right? The North seemed to be doing fine without him, and he knew he could at least be useful to the oppressed towns in his native country.

It was settled – enough of this distracting confusion plaguing him of late. He would wish Sir Golddrake the best of luck and be on a south-bound horse that afternoon.

Amurel faced a difficult decision; the Order of the Rising Moon was at a crossroads. In his petition for provisions and monetary allowances, Amurel promised the Order of the Rising Moon would do all it reasonably could to protect the interests of Selamus and Dawn's Edge from outside threats. Prince Falcionus offered even more than he had asked for, though Amurel had not anticipated him placing such shrewd stipulations on his otherwise-generous gift.

Food, clothing, medicines, weapons, horses, and even more wagons to help transport the abundant supplies would all be made available to the Master, on the condition that Prince Falcionus gain the title of secular Commander of the Order, and a share of leadership – including tactical and dispensary input – equal to Amurel.

Essentially the Order, which Amurel sacrificed his familial lands to establish, would no longer belong to him. His ego told him to seek other terms, other nobles to invest in him, and maintain control of the Order at all costs. None of them would be as wealthy or influential as the prince, however, and if he spurned Falcionus after seeking his aid, the man may use that influence to further impede Amurel.

He sat on his bed, sword across his lap, polishing the steel as he worked over the problem. His ultimate goal had to be not only preserving the existence of the Order, for which he needed the prince's supplies, but its purpose as well. If they were not serving Criesha's agenda, the goddess would no doubt abandon him, or worse.

The morning sun painted his quarters a bright rose as it filtered through the colored windows. "Goddess, please lead me in the direction you desire. It is difficult to know what is best."

He spent much of the previous evening mulling over all the possible scenarios he could conceive, and watching as the extended nobility of Dawn's Edge paid homage and vied for Jaiden's attention. *Sir* Jaiden Luminere, since the Duke of Rosegold had knighted him. *The Savior of Synirpa.*

As Amurel reflected, an idea crept to him, whether from the depths of his own mind or the fruit of a divine seed – something to counter the prince's play. Jaiden was the key, but Amurel was not convinced everything could develop as he hoped. Much would be left to faith.

Jaiden was beloved by the nobility, and Amurel suspected much of that adoration was possible because the young knight posed no political threat. He owned nothing beyond the sword at his side, after all. Yet, they innately knew common folk would see him as one of their own, and therefore he had value as a potential pawn.

Prince Falcionus was not immune, of course. Why else was Jaiden last night's guest of honor? This was not Rosegold, after all, and Jaiden had yet to serve anyone in Dawn's Edge, though he hailed from the province. After making such a show of praising the young swordsman, it would be difficult for the prince to turn around and denounce him, even if only in a symbolic way.

Amurel held his sword up to the light and twisted his wrist, bouncing rays off its gleaming surface. He took pride in properly maintaining his arms. Yes, Jaiden was the answer. It may be too much to ask of one so inexperienced, but Criesha had chosen him as her Champion. The youth had developed under not only his own tutelage, but the influence of both Palomar and the goddess. She had undeniably entered his heart, just as she had Amurel's. He could be trusted to at least strive toward Criesha's example.

Amurel felt content, doing what he must for the benefit of the Order. He would rely on Criesha for the rest. He sheathed his sword, picked up his ornamental cane, and gathered the contracts he received at the petitioning. On his way to Jaiden's apartments, a voice from the hallway behind called to him.

"Sir Golddrake, do you have a moment?" It was Baron Rogan.

"I have a few to spare, Baron," he said, over his shoulder. "Though in truth, I am in route to negotiate an important contract."

"I shall not hold you long, Sir," Rogan said as he caught up. "I merely wanted to extend the courtesy of informing you in person that I am returning to Chelpa today."

"So soon? I thought you might wish to stay in the palace a while, after how far we have come."

Rogan wrung his hands while explaining. "The hospitality has been more than adequate, but I have personal matters that need attending. Not to mention, I will likely be of more use in my homeland than I could possibly be in your Company."

Amurel regarded Rogan and thought back to the battle at Salmarsh, when he first encountered him. "Fair enough," he nodded, and extended his hand. "I wish you a swift and safe journey."

Rogan clasped his wrist. "I shall be ever thankful for your assistance freeing the Dampers...uh, Aasimar. Perhaps we will meet when Ebon Khorel is brought to justice?"

"I will count on it, Baron." Amurel watched Rogan retreat down the hallway a few paces before continuing his own trek to find Jaiden.

He knocked on the door when he reached his room, but heard no response. After a moment's pause, he tried the latch and found the door unlocked. "Jaiden?" Amurel opened the door halfway and peered inside. Jaiden was sitting cross-legged on the bed, bare-chested, eyes closed, as if in some sort of trance.

Amurel knocked loudly on the door once more, but still no movement from the bed. He widened the portal enough to enter and limped closer to the non-respondent Jaiden, who finally opened his eyes as Amurel came close enough to touch him.

"Sir Golddrake?" Jaiden looked around the room as if these were not the surroundings he expected.

"Are you feeling all right, Sir Luminere? It is nearly noon, and does not appear as if you have completely risen from last night's slumber."

Jaiden stepped onto the floor and set about making the bed. "I awoke hours ago. I was just communing with Criesha," he said, matter-of-factly. After tucking in the edges of his blankets, he worked on getting dressed.

"As in, speaking with her?" Amurel asked, amazed.

Jaiden nodded as he fastened his belt. "There was talking, yes."

Amurel put even more of his weight upon his walking stick. "And, how often do you commune with the Goddess, thus?"

Jaiden's eyes lifted as he calculated. "Recently... nearly every day."

Weeks had passed since Criesha last contacted Amurel, and her guidance usually came in the form of enigmatic portents left for him to decipher. Only rarely had she spoken directly. Had he fallen out of favor? "Well, I am glad you have become close, and trust her direction will lead you to righteousness." Even as he said the words, they felt empty as a lie.

"As it happens, I need to talk to you about a decision I have made." Amurel sat on the bed Jaiden had vacated. "Prince Falcionus has granted us his favor in acquiring the supplies we need to continue our campaign against the King-priest."

"That is excellent," Jaiden replied, folding a spare tunic left on the dresser.

"It does not come without cost, however, and I am bound to take the Order in a new direction. New recruits have been flocking to us since Windhollow, and such growth is more than one man can manage." Amurel had to swallow hard before getting out the words that followed. "For this and other reasons, I am splitting the authority of the Order into three parts, and I would like you to have a share in the leadership."

"Me? I have only belonged to the Order for two moons—"

"But you embody what I want our members to emulate: you trust the Goddess, you are brave and battle-ready. Other traits, such as wisdom, will come in time."

Jaiden's mouth was agape, but it took several seconds before words formed. "I am flattered, I think. And, I would be honored to hold such a position. May I ask who the third commander is to be?"

Amurel didn't want to give the impression he had been strong-armed into his choice, and maintained a relaxed tone. "Prince Falcionus shall govern alongside us as the secular Commander of the Order."

"The Prince?"

Amurel could not place the emotion accompanying Jaiden's response. "The Prince is not as familiar with our edicts, so I am requesting that for the time being, you stay here and help direct our efforts in Selamus, where you can instruct him as needed and oversee the training of the recruits. I will take a shipment of supplies south, restock the Caves of Criesha, and gather our forces drilling at Synirpa."

"Master Golddrake, I would much prefer to ride south as well – I am eager to settle things with the King-priest in person."

"All in due time, Jaiden." He sighed. "I understand your enthusiasm, but we still need to grow our numbers, and you are in the best position to do that here, in the capital. Let the people see you, let them rally to our cause, and soon enough you will be back on the front, I promise."

Amurel tapped the end of his cane against the stone floor and stood. "Now, we must close negotiations with the Prince, and it would be a boon to have you present. We will work out the specifics of our respective responsibilities afterward. What say you?"

"I am at your service, Sir Golddrake."

"Good, then let us track down the seneschal." Amurel left the room with Jaiden in tow. He hoped when he broke the news of his decision, the prince would be sufficiently boxed into a corner – unwilling to either slander the promotion of Sir Luminere, or reverse his terms.

In less than an hour, the prince granted an audience, no doubt eager to bolster his martial influence among the provinces. Amurel kept his head high as he entered the throne room, however, giving no indication of supplication, and Jaiden trailed him by several paces. A number of other courtiers were present, mostly disinterested looks upon their faces.

"Ah, Sir Golddrake and Sir Luminere, I trust you both enjoyed yourself at the banquet last night?" Prince Falcionus led, his voice confident with a hint of expectation.

"A splendid event, Your Excellence." Amurel bowed his head briefly, but snapped it aloft before continuing. "If I may proceed directly to the point, Sire, I have an answer for the generous offer you made yesterday."

"Of course – I have always known you as a deliberate man and appreciate your candor, Sir Golddrake." Prince Falcionus raised one eyebrow. "Shall I have my administrator draw up the supply transfer, then?"

"As you like, Your Excellence." Amurel paused. "I am prepared to cede you a share of authority equal to mine, over the Order of the Rising Moon, in return for the goods and funds discussed during our negotiation."

"Very good, I am glad to hear it." The prince's quivering voice betrayed his attempt at calm.

"I am also proud to announce that I have bequeathed an equal share upon Sir Luminere, giving us each authority over a third of the troops, and responsibilities commensurate with our particular strengths." Amurel watched closely as the Prince's mouth immediately shut and his face tightened.

Falcionus's gaze fell beyond Amurel and then settled back upon him; his voice lost all of its previous luster. "Our agreement was that I would control half of the Order."

"Our agreement," Amurel countered, "was that you and I would share equal authority over the Order, and I have honored that condition. Sir Luminere is now an equal partner as well. Do you disapprove of my choice?"

The prince silently took measure of the room, more of which seemed to be paying attention given the interesting turn of events. Amurel waited for a response, deliberately keeping his eyes trained on the prince's face. He had him right where he wanted him.

Finally, Falcionus spoke, his tone shifting to an altogether different inflection. Amurel placed it as grim resolution. "It would be an honor to join a brotherhood that included the esteemed Sir Luminere. I will consider our bargain struck, and look forward to ushering in a new era of security in the Cradle."

In a private meeting that evening, the three partners negotiated how responsibilities were to be divided, and Amurel felt satisfied that Jaiden's ascension would keep the Order of the Rising Moon on its intended path. It took another two days to make all the preparations, but now he was to ride south again, escorting a train of fresh supplies closer to the front.

How long the King-priest would be delayed at Blackthorn remained unknown, but Amurel hoped if he moved quickly enough he could establish an outpost at the ruins of Halidor, to provide warning of the enemy's advance.

Sir Kilborn was coming with him, but Amurel left Lieutenant Orestes behind to assist Jaiden, who had yet to learn the intricacies of running a militarized organization. Palomar decided to stay with the young knight as well, though Illicurus and the majority of the Aasimar were accompanying the southbound troops. Amurel was surprised, but pleased, that Saffron insisted on coming with him. She cited her need to reckon justice with the King-priest, and that a southern victory would leave her closer to home.

When all was made ready, Amurel mounted Bastion and rode with the vanguard, leading a long column of over two hundred infantry, support personnel, laden wagons, and a small contingent of mounted warriors, each pared with a spare horse as well.

Prince Falcionus seemed pleased to finally see him off, and the streets were lined with well-wishers who mistook their procession as some sort of celebratory parade. Amurel wondered if many of them even knew the Empire of Chelpa had recently entered the neighboring provinces to the south.

It took them a week, at a modest pace, to reach the Castle at Windhollow. The weather remained fair, though the afternoons grew hotter, and the Duke of Rosegold openly welcomed their arrival. The state of the castle was much improved from when they arrived going the other direction, appearing to function at full capacity. The common spaces were tidier, and men drilled with bows and swords in the outer courtyards.

"It looks as if you have returned full order to your house, Your Grace," Amurel said to the Duke as he dismounted.

"Thanks in part to your men, Sir Golddrake. How was your journey, and what are these magnificent creatures you have brought with you?" The Duke of Rosegold gestured to Illicurus and his fellows, who trailed the horses by several body lengths.

"Ah, I forgot they were not with us on our previous visit. Your Grace, may I introduce Illicurus, Marshall of the Aasimar. They are our secret weapon, you might say, against the dark magic of the King-priest."

"No longer secret, and not really yours, but a weapon, no doubt." Illicurus stepped forward upon his introduction, considered the Duke, and then took measure of the citadel from the inside. *"An impressive fortress you have here – much more defensible than the palace at Selamus. We should be able to hold it indefinitely."*

The Duke looked at Amurel in seeming disbelief, no doubt reacting to the Aasimar's telepathy. "I certainly would like to think we could, though we are glad to have any assistance in defending her." He put his arm around Amurel's shoulder as they made their way in to the quieter halls of the castle.

"And although definite strides toward preparation have been made, it would be a lie to say that everything has gone smoothly since you left. There have been minor uprisings in Synirpa – backlash from those whose kin were not saved from the plague and have somehow found fault for that in your men. No bloodshed yet, but some vandalism and quite a bit of tongue-lashing."

"I see," Amurel responded, his brow creasing. "I shall address that early on the morrow. Most of our men and supplies stayed behind at the city while I shore up affairs here – we will be moving on shortly."

They came to the Great Hall, where the men feasted together a fortnight prior. "Have you news of the enemy?" the Duke questioned. "We have not seen nor received word of their presence since they abandoned their siege. I trust it is too much to hope the Chelpians have given up ideas of conquest."

Illicurus joined the conversation, though he had been lurking several long strides behind Amurel and the Duke. "*We encountered the core of their forces deep within their own country weeks ago. They could be between the mountains shortly, if they deployed soon after.*"

Amurel stopped and sighed. "Indeed, Your Grace, we believe they are only gathering their strength. Nothing, short of defeat, will halt their advance. We've ridden for days now. If I might rely on your hospitality for one night, we can discuss these matters more at dinner this evening, and my company shall depart in the morning."

"Of course, Sir Golddrake." A few weeks of recovery made the Duke noticeably healthier, and though he was the older man, Amurel envied his vitality. "Your Order is welcome here, and you must be weary from travel. Take your rest, and we shall speak at supper."

"My thanks." Amurel nodded and the Duke of Rosegold gave a polite smile before heading back the way they came.

"*There is little pretense about that man,*" Illicurus observed. "*Not like the Prince.*"

"His Grace is a straightforward man, yes. He can be severe, but one knows where he stands with Rosegold."

"*This is a very defensible position, as I mentioned.*" Illicurus looked at the high ceilings and solid stone walls of the Great Hall, the blue tips of his wings shifting as they unfurled behind him. "*Hopefully, it does not fall from the inside.*"

Amurel turned to ask what he meant, but the Aasimar was already heading toward a side passage housing a stairwell ascending to the next level. He had no energy to pursue or decipher the aloof outsider's innuendo. Amurel gladly shifted thoughts toward a soft bed and a few hours of rest before dinner.

A unit of the Order's fighting men, well-supplied and trained, remained garrisoned at Windhollow Rock in case the castle came under siege once more. Amurel also made sure the Aasimar under Illicurus's command were familiar with the surrounding terrain, should they have need to locate and enter the fortress from the air.

Amurel met the rest of his troops outside of Synirpa. Given their swelling numbers and the fact the Order of the Rising Moon was not directly affiliated with the province, they set up camp a safe distance from the city walls so as not to induce suspicion or spark an unnecessary conflict. Amurel had left Sir Kilborn in charge of the encampment while he pushed ahead to visit the Duke at Windhollow, and he was waiting to brief Amurel when he returned in the morning.

"Well, things are a right mess, but I am getting it sorted out. You have between four and five hundred souls waiting to take their oaths, some of whom were only weaned a month ago by the look of it." Sir Kilborn ran a gloved hand over Bastion's nose as he walked beside him. "Then someone on the far side of camp tapped into the ale stores, when I strictly limited rationing to water. Numerous trainees are hungover, and one of the smaller canopies even caught fire." Sir Kilborn snorted, as if he could barely believe what he was working with.

"From the reports I've received thus far, however, the exercises have progressed well, and nearly a hundred of the recruits are passably battle-ready. Any news from the Duke?"

Amurel did not bother dismounting. He wanted a quick ride around to assess the camp on his own. "The castle is in good hands. It should continue to serve well as a fall-back position, if needs be.

"I was given a word of caution about dealing with the general population. A bit of trouble regarding hard feelings over the healing, it seems. If our men have cause to enter the city, make sure it is in groups no smaller than four, and no larger than eight. We don't want to incite violence, but I don't want us easy targets, either."

Sir Kilborn shook his head. "Some people have a strange way of showing thanks."

"It's hard to imagine all the loss they have experienced. I am more interested in keeping our men safe than passing judgment on the grieving."

"Aye," Sr Kilborn agreed.

"I am going to stretch Bastion's legs on a hasty inspection. Have you set up a command tent?" Amurel asked.

"Bearing the standard," Sir Kilborn nodded toward a large pavilion near the center of the encampment.

"Good. I shall return anon and we can sift through the roll together, divvy up assignments, and plan the first initiation." Amurel nudged his horse to the right and then picked up speed, riding in a wide circle around the Order's temporary home. He looked for situations requiring corrective intervention, but also wanted to get a collective sense of the new recruits' disposition.

The land was green. Soft, pillowy grasses made an ideal blanket for the labors of battle preparation; it did not hurt as much when you were knocked to the ground, and was comfortable enough to sleep on without a pallet. Amurel saw men diligently working, and by the time he finished his inspection, was satisfied that whatever foolishness had occurred in his absence was duly corrected by his arrival. Sir Kilborn's value, evident once more.

When he entered the command tent, Amurel found more than just his second officer waiting. Saffron, her younger sister, and a man around his own age had gathered as well.

"Lady Saffron, how are things with you?" Amurel removed the mail gloves from his hands. As usual, a table centered his tent and he limped over to take a seat on the bench behind it, beside Sir Kilborn. "I planned on wading through some bureaucratic necessities," he gestured to the unrolled scrolls on the table, "but if there is a matter you need to bring to my attention first, I am more than happy to assist."

"My thanks, Sir Golddrake. I do not wish to waste your time, but Dhania pleaded to me on behalf of this man."

"His name is Bremmil," Dhania insisted, "and he has something very important to tell the Master."

Amurel considered the younger sister for a moment, and then turned his attention to the man. "Is this true?"

Bremmil flashed a smile at Dhania before adopting a more serious appearance. His olive complexion and thick, dark hair reminded Amurel of Baron Rogan. "Yes, your lordship, I believe it is." His accent was thicker than Rogan's, and clearly cemented his origin as Chelpian.

"Sir Golddrake will do. Are you from the Empire?" Amurel had to address his identity before moving further.

"I was born and raised a few leagues from Lucnere, yes."

"And you have come all this way to join the Order of the Rising Moon? You know we intend to defeat your native King?"

All remaining pleasantness drained from Bremmil's features. "I cannot serve such a tyrant. I know what my land was like before him, and even though life was sometimes hard, it was never so bleak. This King is not good for the country."

"And how did you hear of our Order, specifically?" Sir Kilborn followed, picking up on Amurel's suspicion.

"I did not know of it until I came north. I was conscripted into service in Lucnere. I trained in the army with no choice, but knew I could not serve and fight for that ruler. When I saw the chance, I deserted. I could not go home, so I came north to these lands and this great city. Now, as a man free to choose, I wish to fight against the King who gives so many others no choice."

"He is very brave," Dhania broke in. "He told me last night all about the incredible odds he faced to make it this far."

Saffron shot her sister a look. "Let the man speak for himself, Dhania."

Amurel drummed his fingers on the table before speaking. "I am impressed with your resourcefulness, Chelpian. It could not have been easy to escape your unit, and then travel so far without being caught. I am sure the Blood Tear Brotherhood loves to make examples of deserters."

Bremmil showed his teeth again and shrugged. "Luck has been on my side."

"Indeed. And so, what is it you wish so desperately to bring to my attention?"

"My Lor—Sir Golddrake, everyone knows the common way north into the Cradle, the valley your men call the Gap of Halidor. It is by far the easiest way to bring an army from the Empire. But the King of Chelpa now knows another – and I overheard his commanders planning to use it."

"Have they found the Harpy Pass?" Sir Kilborn directed his question at Amurel, ignoring the southern informant.

"It would not surprise me," he responded. "We were ambushed not far from it after leaving Greyhorne."

"Yes," Sir Kilborn agreed. "A difficult place to keep troops supplied, but we should dispatch scouts to watch over it and give us warning."

The tall form of Illicurus ducked beneath the canvas and entered the command tent, unannounced. *"Pardon, Sir Golddrake, but Ellingle just arrived from Selamus at the behest of Sir Luminere."* Illicurus stopped moving and speaking and stared straight at Bremmil, who was likewise openly assessing the Aasimar. The feathers of his wings bristled, their icy blue tips twitching, as if in warning. His voice began before his gaze shifted back to Amurel.

"One of the nobles from the northeast province has petitioned the prince for aid, claiming orcs from the Black Hills have been massing on his border. He fears invasion."

"Grace of Criesha, is it not enough we have the King-priest to contend with?" Amurel stood from his seat, placed his hands on the table, but did not move his feet.

"The young knight you left in charge might be unsure of what is needed, but I have experience in strategies of war. I could move quickly to assess the situation, and give my recommendation to the Order in Selamus. I could be back to this camp in under a fortnight."

Amurel was surprised to hear Illicurus volunteering for such a task, but he remained still, not showing any emotion.

"Ellingle could coordinate the Aasimar in my absence..."

Finally, Amurel nodded.

"I am sorry to hear of even more troubles, Sir Golddrake, but I was not finished with my own news." Bremmil boldly stepped to the other side of the table and mirrored Amurel's stance, placing his outstretched fingers upon the flat surface. "I fear the secret path through the Wyvernwatch Mountains is farther north than you suspect. They said it followed a finger of the

River Chelhos, winding around the peaks into the hills west of here."

Sir Kilborn failed to hold in a gruff snicker. "That's absurd! I think the people of Rosegold would be aware of any track that led through the mountains into their territory."

Amurel nodded but held the gaze of the foreigner, who annoyingly seemed to be amused.

"Disregard the intelligence if you like; you know your business. I thought it my duty to inform my superiors, as I will be taking my oath shortly." Bremmil brought his hand up in salute, and then turned to leave. He side-stepped Illicurus, then held his hand out to Saffron's sister as he was about to exit.

Dhania looked from Saffron to Amurel before taking the new-comer's hand, and leaving the command tent.

"Smug one, isn't he?" Sir Kilborn fingered his beard and snickered again. "I wonder if he knows joining up means holding hands is about as far as he will get with the ladies."

Amurel saw Saffron shoot his second-in-command a rebuking look before she stepped toward him. "Nevertheless, you should send a scout west as well," she said, coolly.

"I intend to. The way news is going today, nothing would surprise me. We will hope it is just smoke, but I want to be ready to ride as soon as possible if the worst is confirmed. Saffron, will you make sure a hundred horses are prepared for tomorrow? I will send a rider today, and we will expedite the first initiation ceremony to this evening."

"What are you planning to do, Amurel?" Sir Kilborn asked.

"I am going to make sure we are not taken by surprise and flanked."

Amurel could sense it was going to be a restless night. He swore in the first hundred new members of the Order, and while such an auspicious occasion was traditionally followed by revelry, he had forbidden drink for the second straight night. He knew they might be leaving for war in the morning, and wanted their minds sharp.

The sun had gone down, but most of the camp had yet to retire. Soldiers were too wound up with the promise of potential glory rising with the morning sun, and seemed intent to greet it. Amurel leisurely patrolled the camp from horseback, along with Sir Kilborn. He wanted to be seen and project a countenance of resolve to his followers. He hoped they saw him as neither frivolous nor grim – merely one whose mind was firmly set upon future action.

Campfires spotted the field, but were kept low. Further warmth was no longer a concern, as the nights had lost their bite, growing comfortably cool near the onset of summer. As Bastion bowed his head to nibble the leaves of a low shrub, Amurel let his gaze wander to the southwest, where the blue-green glow of Hurn and Criesha, the dual moons, highlighted the rooftops and tower walls of Synirpa.

Though the King-priest had not lain siege, the city's populace had been indirectly decimated by the evil power of his god. Amurel made a silent vow to spare them from a second scourge, be it sickness or the sword.

"Look at that," Sir Kilborn interrupted his thought.

Following the direction of his comrade's gaze, Amurel spotted the bright feathers of an Aasimar's wings, nearly a hundred paces off. They belonged to Illicurus, who curiously seemed to be conversing with the Chelpian who brought the tale of the hidden path through the mountains.

"Our Marshall did not seem so warm with the foreigner this afternoon."

Amurel tried to get an idea of the nature of their current exchange, but it was difficult at such distance. "Who does Illicurus seem welcoming to?"

"There is the bare truth," Sir Kilborn conceded. "Perhaps he's trying to gather everything useful he can out of the lad, or using a mind trick to determine whether or not the newcomer is feeding us a load of horse manure."

"Stranger or not, he is one of our brethren now," Amurel said, soberly. He turned to look off to the west. "If our rider made good speed, we will learn for sure in the next day or two whether he can be trusted."

Just as Bastion lifted his head, content with his late snack, Amurel watched Bremmil turn his back on Illicurus and head for the nearest campfire. He noticed Saffron's younger sister stand and greet the man with an embrace, though Saffron herself was nowhere to be seen.

"Remind me in the morning, Geldrick, to ensure our captains emphasize the importance of maintaining all our vows to their subordinates."

"Aye," answered Sir Kilborn, and with a flick of his reins, the two continued their patrol of the camp.

Illicurus left sometime before sunrise, and was already on his way north by the time Amurel had dressed and emerged from his tent. By midday, Saffron reported the horses and supplies were ready should they need them, leaving only the uncomfortable waiting Amurel loathed to endure.

He oiled both his sword and armor, and went through the roster of recruits once again, preparing lists of training regimens and prospective future assignments of command – anything he could think of to kill time. At last, a soldier notified him that not one, but two riders approached rapidly from the west.

Sir Kilborn was beside him by the time he grabbed his crutch and made for the wide field that rested beyond their camp. Amurel saw his scout, dressed in his white tabard adorned with the crescent moon, pushing his brown steed straight for them. A second man, wearing brown leather and keeping to the scout's flank, rode just as hard. They only slowed when necessary to avoid crashing into Amurel and the entourage surrounding him, all eager to hear the fate lying before them.

"It's true, Master Golddrake!" the scout shouted, his breath short as if he and not the horse had been pushed. "I got as far as the village of Holjek, and they were already preparing for the worst. A line of dark-clad men bearing black standards were spotted coming down from the hills."

"I hail from Lodale at the base of the Wyvernwatch," the man in brown followed. "We have already been overrun, and I was dispatched by our town warden to beseech aid from the Duke."

Amurel felt something in the pit of his stomach tighten. "How many?"

"Four or five score, I was told," answered the scout.

"That again or more assaulted Lodale," said the second.

"I suppose the waiting is over," Amurel shared with Sir Kilborn. "Pick a man you trust familiar to Sir Luminere. Have him escort Bremmil north to Selamus so he can brief Jaiden on everything he knows about the Chelpian army. I want him to ride for Windhollow as soon as he is able. The Prince will have to deal with the Black Hill orcs, should they pose a threat."

"Aye."

"I will prepare the troops. We'll take two companies west, and leave the rest encamped here. I will ask Lady Saffron to join us, and request Ellingle send what Aasimar she can spare."

Sir Kilborn nodded. "So it begins."

Amurel returned the gesture and looked west, over the vast pasture of green spreading to the horizon. "So it begins," he repeated, barely more than a whisper.

Chapter 27

Matters of Trust

Amurel and his unit arrived too late to save the structures of Lodale, though not to exact revenge for its people. Black smoke still rose from the burned-out houses as his cavalry came within view of the town, built at the eastern base of the Wyvernwatch Mountains. The terrain was steep in some places and uneven in most – unsuitable for a charge from horseback.

"We will ride closer, then engage them on foot," he commanded, regretting it meant he would have to stay back from the fighting. Given the circumstances, he had little choice, though Amurel loathed being unable to partake in the danger he ordered others into. Sharing risk was a defining feature of true leadership.

He trusted they would be victorious, all the same. His men were well-trained and better equipped than what he had seen of Chelpian soldiers so far. It did not hurt that a pair of Aasimar came with him, as well.

They passed the citizens of Lodale in the high pastureland half a league east of the town. Fleeing first, they stopped when not pursued to watch helplessly as their homes were put to the torch. The enemy seemed more intent on looting and destroying than hunting down the evicted townsfolk. When Amurel got closer, it appeared the Chelpians lacked any organization at all.

Some clearly noticed the final approach of his men, but they failed to rally into any defensive formation. Amurel, astride Bastion, watched from a hilltop as his dismounted troops entered the town, systematically breaking any pockets of dark-cloaked resistance they encountered. The Aasimar descended upon the few looters keen to flee. The fighting was over in an hour. It was all too easy.

This cannot be the regular army, Amurel thought. So what exactly was going on? The question occupied him as he rode down to join his men.

"Skirmishers, and not very good ones," Sir Kilborn confirmed as soon as Amurel found him. "Very little in the way of armor, and no discernable training in tactics. This was not an invasion bent on occupation."

"Then what?" Amurel asked aloud, though the answer already crept to the surface of his thoughts. "You think we were lured here?" The possibility alarmed him, and Sir Kilborn's dour expression suggested his second-in-command felt the same.

"Leave a single patrol to gather and guard the townsfolk. The rest of us ride immediately. We will regroup with Saffron's unit and see if they encountered the same at Holjek. If so, we need to continue through to Synirpa as swiftly as the horses can manage."

Within a quarter of an hour the bulk of Amurel's unit was riding eastward, trying to cover as much ground as possible before sundown. The high country was beautiful, though tiring for the horses. To Amurel's right, the horizon was a jagged line separating afternoon blue sky from pale purple peaks. To his left, seemingly endless hills folded upon one another, carpeted in long grass that swayed in the steady breeze, born of the altitude. This was the edge of the Cradle, and no doubt held many secret places, untouched by men, that still exuded the magic sacred to his goddess. The virgin wild, he knew, needed to be defended as much as the cities and towns of the Northern Provinces.

The uneven footing made it too treacherous to ride after dark, and unfortunately the sun set before his unit came within sight of Holjek. Amurel spent an uneasy night wondering if a deception more devious than what they encountered at Lodale had awaited Saffron's squadron.

As the first rays of sunlight touched the rolling grasses of the highlands, Amurel had his men in the saddle and on their way to rendezvous with Saffron. In less than an hour they arrived at Holjek, which was still under the control of its citizens, defended by the Order of the Rising Moon.

Lady Saffron seemed to have things well-in-hand, and Amurel found her instructing a small crowd on the basics of spear-fighting. He noticed women were among them, as well as a few he would still consider children. She looked his way as the sound of Bastion's hooves upon the pebble-strewn earth announced his presence.

"I did not expect you from Lodale so soon, Sir Golddrake. Do you doubt my abilities so much you had to check on me after one night?"

Due to her accent, Amurel was sometimes unsure when she was speaking in jest.

"Never have I doubted you, Lady Saffron. The force we encountered further west was no more than a collection of raiding skirmishers, and I feared that meant your opposition might be the stronger."

"It appears not. We arrived before the brigands attacked, mostly because the people here had the wits to prepare their own defense, which held them at bay. I thought it prudent to shore up a few weaknesses before venturing to strike, should another threat arise after we depart. I presumed we would have more time before your return, Sir."

"You have done well, my lady. Now that we are here, what did you have in mind for your next move?" Even though he was formally in command, Amurel thought it would be informative to observe his various delegates in action. The need to share even more responsibility may lie just beyond the horizon, he guessed.

Saffron pressed the butt of her spear into the earth and lifted her chin higher. "The enemy backed off when they saw reinforcements arrive. They probably realize they cannot win, but have not abandoned their objective yet. I want to catch them before they do, and hopefully we can capture someone who will talk.

"I will send the Aasimar to fly behind their position and cut off escape. At the head of twenty cavalry I shall ride at them hard. If they surrender, so be it. If they break ranks, the archers creeping up from either side shall pin them with arrows. If they retreat whence they came, the Aasimar will cut them off with sword and song."

Amurel had to admit, this was a woman who seemed sure of herself. "Very well," he nodded. "Make it happen."

Saffron took her leave to deliver the commands and make preparations for the ride. Amurel decided to observe from atop a platform behind the villager's palisade. Though the enemy kept a fair distance, he could make out their location by the slow movement of black lumps against the greenery of the hillsides. He was eager to see how Saffron's plan unfolded, and also wanted extra time to think.

As eager as he was to return to Synirpa, a thought had rooted in Amurel's mind that he could not shake. He knew sowing doubt was the King-priest's objective, but it did not change the fact enemy troops, feeble or not, were able to sneak behind his lines. The Order couldn't cover that much land, yet he was sworn to protect the weak.

How could he ensure the entire countryside remained safe, yet not dilute his forces to be useless against a major assault? The question demanded further attention; he would pray on it later. For now, he turned to the south, where he could see

Saffron's riders bearing down on the skirmishers. The enemy, unprepared for a fight against trained soldiers, spread in disarray to escape the wrath of the cavalry. Much as Amurel expected, the archers felled a third of their number before they surrendered. The fight was over before it had truly begun.

He congratulated Saffron on her victory before turning his attention to those she captured. No useful intelligence was extracted from the prisoners, though Amurel did not judge them liars. They simply did not know much in the way of plans or purpose, and no definitive leader stood among them. Those facts, however, still served to paint a picture.

Clearer than ever he saw these incursions as a distraction, either to lure his forces from Synirpa, waste his time pursuing trivial combats, or at the least, undermine the north's sense of security. Perhaps all three were the goal, which he couldn't argue had been accomplished. That knowledge started a sinking feeling in his gut, which he tried to subdue as he ordered his troops' return to their main camp.

They had a fifty-mile ride northeast back to the seat of the province, and a long, two days for Amurel to speculate on possible disasters that may have befallen in his absence. His worries failed to manifest, however. Tents still filled the fields outside Synirpa, and the wagons of supplies were loaded and waiting for the journey south. Almost like a sickness of his mind, though, Amurel could not find a reprieve from his suspicion that something was amiss.

Saffron did her best to put him at ease and even played a soothing melody to calm him, but sleep did not come easily. With no recent reports, Amurel hungered for news as well as action. He decided to leave immediately, the morning after his return, to escort the supply train bound for the Caves of Criesha. He desired not only to replenish the stores they had consumed when last taking refuge, but to feel the presence of his Goddess, which came more often in her sacred space.

Sir Kilborn and Lady Saffron both insisted on coming with him, but before leaving, he dispatched two scouts to the ruined keep at Halidor. "We will come there next," he told them, "so be alert. I want to know of any signs of the enemy between here and the border over the last fortnight."

His men nodded their understanding before riding south, into the misty morning.

A week had passed since his anointing, and Jaiden was already weary of his new responsibilities. Then, an emissary from the province of Crimsonmoon brought an appeal for the Prince to send troops, which seemed like a second chance for Jaiden to see action. An alarming number of orcs had amassed near the northern border, and the Duke wanted to deter an invasion.

Yet Prince Falcionus downplayed the danger and refused to send his men afield, speaking of his responsibility to defend Dawn's Edge. A few savages on the outskirts of the provinces, he claimed, were no equal to the threat of the King-priest invading from the south.

While Jaiden did not disagree with the assessment, he saw no reason why both threats couldn't be addressed. After all, was that not precisely why Sir Golddrake split the responsibilities of the Order? As long as he was guarding the south, what prevented Jaiden from slipping to the northeast and crushing a disruptive gathering of orcs? They weren't even human, for Criesha's sake.

The argument played out again as Jaiden stood at attention in the throne room. The Prince and his advisors were awaiting the entry of Sir Golddrake's envoy, who arrived much sooner than expected at the gates of Selamus.

"I have been Prince of Dawn's Edge since before you could lift a sword, Sir Luminere."

"I appreciate your experience, Your Excellence, I do. But one thing I know about enemies, especially those with the reputation of the Black Hills Orcs, is that it is much better to strike before they have time to organize. Perhaps they are only gathering for some savage celebration and intend to disperse. But if not, what might be a small problem today could swell into a major liability." Jaiden knew he would not win this argument – not with the Prince of Dawn's Edge – but lessons learned from his father were difficult to silence.

The seneschal stepped into the gilded, cavernous room followed by two men, robed in white tabards of the Order. "Your Excellence, may I present Lothander Highgarden and Bremmil Barigor of the Order of the Rising Moon."

The olive-skinned man with thick, dark hair stepped forward and bowed. "Your Excellence, I bear news and council from Sir Golddrake, Master of the Order. But first, let me say what an honor it is to stand in your presence, here in the finest city on Elisahd."

Jaiden rolled his eyes, not feeling guilty in the slightest for interrupting. "Lothander! Greetings, friend. I am glad to see you've made your way to the capital."

Lothander raised his palm and smiled widely. "Jaiden, er, Sir Luminere. How is all with you?" He put a hand to his face to shield his mouth from the others, though the distance between them was too far for a whisper. "I brought my Skirmish cards, if you fancy a game later."

Bremmil looked from Lothander to Jaiden and forced an insincere smile, before returning his attention to the Prince. "Your Excellence, I am a native of Chelpa who has recently earned the trust of Sir Golddrake and joined his Order. I previously served in the army of the Empire, and have knowledge of their movements and tactics that his lordship thought might benefit you in your planning."

Jaiden straightened his posture at the announcement. "And what news from Synirpa? Is Sir Golddrake continuing to the Caves as he intended?"

The recent initiate cast a glance over his shoulder at Lothander before continuing. "There has been a minor detour, my lord. Your enemy has infiltrated the Cradle further to the west, as I warned they would. Sir Golddrake took some fighting men to halt their advance."

"My goodness," Prince Falcionus stated calmly from his throne. "I hope it is nothing too threatening."

"No, Your Excellence, I do not think so. The pass through the mountains is too narrow for a very large force to navigate."

"Did Sir Golddrake ask that I bring reinforcements down the Dawn Way?" Jaiden interjected.

"In fact, no, my lord." Bremmil's words were short and his pitch heightened. "If I may continue with my report?" After a shared moment of silence he did just that. "Sir Golddrake said he has the matter well in hand, but given the slippery nature of the enemy, you should be on alert for attacks against the capital. I know from personal experience, the armies of Chelpa are adept at subterfuge and have ways of surfacing where you least expect. Upon my recommendation, Sir Golddrake suggested you vigilantly patrol the areas around the City of the Eight Hills, so as not to be caught by surprise."

Prince Falcionus smiled. "Now, that seems like sound advice. Keeping Selamus from harm should be our priority – for as long as the capital stands, the Northern Provinces will have a stalwart bastion to look to."

Jaiden frowned. "I still think it would be wiser to meet our enemies and deal with them on our own terms, not wait for them to strengthen their positions. Sir, are you sure Master Golddrake is in no need of reinforcements?"

The pitch of the Prince's voice heightened as well. "Sir Luminere, we all heard what the messenger said. You are outnumbered in this – you should learn to trust the judgment of those more experienced. Start sending out staggered patrols to ensure the highlands are secure. My men will continue drilling on city defense procedures. Now, if that is all?" Prince Falcionus stood from his throne, and the room bowed.

"Actually, Your Excellence – if I may have a word in private?" Bremmil asked, lifting his head quickly to catch the Prince before he got too far.

"No, messenger, you may not. You are from the South and I do not know you. But I will give you two minutes in the western antechamber to speak – guards present, of course."

"Thank you, Your Excellence."

Jaiden waited patiently until the Prince and Chelpian messenger left the room before moving. He joined Lothander and put an arm around his shoulder as they departed through the main exit. "Ah, my friend, I feel as if I am going to miss the entire war stuck in this palace."

"There are worse places to be, Sir." Lothander lifted his head, taking in the vaulted ceilings.

"Just Jaiden, please. You knew me before I was knighted. I'm not one for all this ass-kissing, anyway. What do you know about the conflict this Bremmil spoke of? Is it really of no concern?" He dipped his neck and squinted slightly to better assess his friend's face.

Lothander shrugged and Jaiden let his arm fall away. "Sir Golddrake did not inform me of his plans. He rode west from Synirpa with a hundred men, and the rest were preparing a journey to re-stock the Caves of Criesha with supplies. They won't leave until he returns, though. Sir Kilborn did instruct me to tell you, when we were alone, that the Master sent the Aasimar Marshall to assess the threat in the Black Hills. He is supposed to bring you a report on his return."

"Illicurus running errands? Curious," Jaiden mumbled in reflection.

"What's that, Sir?" Lothander asked.

"Nothing important." Jaiden snapped back to the moment. "I will be glad to get more intelligence on the orcs. The timing worries me – seems like more than coincidence."

"There is one more thing I wanted to talk to you about, Sir, though I feel a little strange doing so."

"It's alright, Lothander," Jaiden reassured him. "I am not Master Golddrake – you can tell me anything."

Lothander pressed the fingertips of both hands together as he walked, presenting a toothless smile along with a creased brow.

Jaiden came to a stop and turned square to Lothander. "Come now; out with it."

"Well, Sir, after the Southerner and I left Synirpa and rode for a mile or so on the Dawn Way, we came across Dhania – Lady Saffron's sister."

"Came across? I thought she went south with the Order."

"She did – I mean, I saw her in camp, but she must have left ahead of us. When I suggested we escort her back, neither she nor Bremmil would hear a word of it. She said she was a free woman and could make her own decisions where to ride; I suppose I couldn't really argue with that. To be honest, I thought it might make the trip more enjoyable, having a pretty girl for company instead of just the Southerner."

Jaiden nodded silently. He imagined he might have thought the same in Lothander's boots.

"It's just, uh, when we would camp for the night," Lothander continued, "it was Bremmil that was enjoying her company – if you get my meaning. He just took his vows before we left, is all."

"I see." Jaiden was vexed. Though he felt some responsibility for the welfare of Dhania, given she was a foreigner in a far-away country, the last thing he needed was another soul to look after. Bremmil, on the other hand, clearly required a closer watch as well as discipline. "And is mistress Dhania in the city now?"

"She came with us to the palace," Lothander answered. "Bremmil told her to wait for him while he reported to the Prince."

"Did he?" Jaiden couldn't have this newcomer smuggling a woman into the barracks. "I will have the seneschal make sure quarters are provided in the palace for Dhania, and that Bremmil is suitably occupied over the coming days.

"It is good to see you, Lothander." Jaiden clasped his friend's shoulders with both hands. "Thank you for bringing the matter to my attention. We shall have to rustle up some players and get a game going after supper. If you will excuse me, I need to commune with the Goddess. I shall find you this evening." Jaiden nodded and turned down the corridor toward the new apartments gained with his promotion. He was sure Lothander could find his own way to the barracks.

Back in his room, Jaiden stripped down to his breeches and lit a crucible of the incense given to him by Willem the Shaper to facilitate concentration. His skin tingled in anticipation as he sat cross-legged on his mattress and closed his eyes. His favorite part of the day, he started the ritual the first afternoon after being tapped by Sir Golddrake for ascension in the Order.

He did not always reach her, but knowing he might kept him excited from the moment he ignited the incense until his communion began. Jaiden focused on the regularity of his breath, his chest rising and falling while his hands lay limply in his lap. He thought of the pale green light that accompanied her, the night sky full of stars, and felt a soft breeze stirring his hair.

When he opened his eyes he was still seated on a bed, though surrounded by the soft, silken veils of his mistress. The stars looked down on him, returning his attention. He was in *her* realm.

"My Champion," Criesha's soft voice teased his ear.

He turned to find his chin against her cheek, her luminescent skin bathing his in its glow. He leaned to kiss her but she drew away, pressing her hands against the bare muscles of his back. A low growl of dissatisfaction vibrated his throat. "Am I out of favor so quickly?"

"Patience, my Chosen. I do not visit you solely to accommodate your base urges. I am molding you into the person you need to be."

Jaiden swiveled his lower half to match his head, which had already moved to follow Criesha's alluring form. "To what end? I thought you chose me precisely because of the person I *am*."

"Potential, only." Criesha crossed her arms. "Is it not fitting I should instruct you? You are the mortal and I the goddess, after all."

Jaiden moved his eyes away, taking in the shifting shape of a small cloud as it sped by overhead. "I heard you called by another name."

Criesha's left eyebrow arched as she awaited explanation.

"I heard you were one of the Juda-cai: beings from another realm." Only after the words were spoken did Jaiden's gaze return to his hostess.

Her eyebrow lowered as her lips turned upward, and Criesha slowly sank to a horizontal position on the bed, her head cradled in one hand, propped up by her elbow. "Juda-cai, Goddess, Scepterina of the Midnight Heavens... does it really matter what others call me?"

Jaiden lowered himself to match her posture and adopted a more relaxed tone. "I have sworn to obey and dedicate my service to you – I think I deserve to know your true nature."

"One's true nature cannot be explained, it must be discovered." Criesha's eyes narrowed as she reached between his legs, taking him in her hand and stroking, "I discovered yours easily enough, Jaiden Luminere."

His lids began to close involuntarily as her electric touch stimulated his arousal. After a few seconds of indulgence, he forced them back open, unwilling to relent until receiving a clearer answer. "Who is the one lacking patience, now?"

Her arm ceased moving and she searched his eyes, testing his resolve. "Good," she said, releasing his manhood when he did not blink. "I am the keeper of magic, a boon to those who practice it. I am the watcher-in-the-night, bringing light to those who would otherwise dwell in darkness. Is this what you want to hear?"

Jaiden sighed. "Is it true you and your kind walked the world more than a thousand years ago?"

"There are many worlds, and time is measured differently in each." Criesha sat up and lifted her arms above her head. The sky around them lightened as if the sun had risen, then quickly dimmed again to the dark of night. She raised her eyebrows, "Did a day just pass? Here, I could teach you all you would ever care to know about my world, and when you went back to yours it would be the very next instant. Your body is somewhere else while your mind is with me. My body and mind are both elsewhere simultaneously. It does little good to explain what you cannot experience on your own."

"You did not really answer my question," Jaiden persisted as he, too, sat erect.

Criesha's laugh rang of honest delight. "Yes, Sir Luminere, a drop of my essence traversed the Veil of Nessus and walked the paths of your world in physical form a score of centuries ago, as you judge waking time."

Jaiden did not understand the implications of her words, but nodded and moved on. "A messenger arrived today saying that Sir Golddrake wished me to patrol the hills near Selamus. But why go looking for imaginary danger when I know where some lies?" Jaiden leaned back until he splashed onto the silk-soft sheets of the bed. "My heart tells me I should ride to Crimsonmoon and confront the orcs amassing there."

"Your talent is wasted on orcs. They thirst for war but cannot grasp the tactics necessary to win one. What of your duty to the Order? Does Sir Golddrake not command your allegiance?"

"Sir Golddrake passed leadership to me when he conceded the same to the Prince. I am responsible for my own men now, though I value his instincts."

Criesha lay beside him, tracing her hand across his bare chest. "As you should. He is a trusting man, and has experience and advisors to draw upon. It may be your place now, Jaiden, to learn from those around you, but do not be mistaken. I am preparing you for something greater."

A thought that had been nagging Jaiden for some time surfaced again, though selfishness had prevented him from voicing it before now. "Sir Golddrake is loyal to you – he founded the Order in your honor, after all."

Criesha arched an eyebrow. "This is true."

"Well..." Jaiden's nervousness almost prevented him from continuing, but the words finally came in a rush, "why haven't you healed his lameness as you did mine? It seems rather unfair."

The goddess's face showed something like pity, though her verbal response didn't match. "Do you think so little of our bond, Jaiden? I only have one Champion, and my greatest gifts are reserved for him. Just as I have you, Gholdur the Tyrant has his in Ebon Khorel, though the King-priest and the Dread Lord have a head start. You, and none other, hold the key to defeating them. Whoever wins will have the upper hand in transforming your world, for better or worse.

"So do not go seeking conflict until you must. Even if it results in loss now, the greater good is served by you being ready when the enemy can no longer be ignored."

Criesha slid atop Jaiden's body, placing her knees on either side of his waist. With a slow hand, she pushed the straps of her dress over each shoulder until it glided down her torso. "The next full moon is not far off, and there is some preparation to mastering your next gift. Are you ready to learn?"

Jaiden reached forward with both hands, placing them on the fabric bunched at Criesha's hips. He pushed his chin to his chest to both nod and watch as his palms moved up Criesha's waist to claim her breasts.

"The magic of your enemies relies heavily on deception," she continued, offering explanation as she reached down to guide him inside her.

All the breath left him at once, and he struggled to listen to her words as she began rotating her hips ever-so-slightly.

"Therefore, I will give you the ability to bathe yourself in an Aura of Truth. When you choose to do so, your position as my Champion will be unmistakable to your enemies, and they shall know you wield my power." Criesha leaned forward and placed her hands on Jaiden's chest, then raised her hips with a torturing lack of urgency. "But you shall see all within this Aura as it truly is, and no lie may be uttered from inside its glow. It requires a special sort of concentration to maintain, however, which is what we shall work on today..."

Three days outside the city left Jaiden mildly surprised at his eagerness to return. He had not been able to commune while out on patrol, and was feeling the effects of separation from his Goddess. He chose six men to act as lieutenants, including Lothander, and brought them with him on the first patrol, so they might learn the terrain and routes they would use when taking out their own units. True to his word, he made sure Bremmil accompanied them as an initiate, forcing him to do grunt work.

They found nothing noteworthy or suggestive of danger out among the hills, and Jaiden remained dubious about prioritizing such patrols. He wanted to head straight to his apartments in the palace when they reached the city, but knew an audience with Prince Falcionus would be prudent and proper.

Upon reaching the throne room, he found a bevy of Aasimar crowded into an inward-facing circle. A great rustling of feathers and perturbed movements pervaded, but no voices, and whatever lay in the center of the ring was concealed by the stretching rainbow of color-tipped wings.

Palomar must have spotted him, however, because his calming voice reached out to touch his mind, though Jaiden knew not where his companion stood. *"I am pleased to see you have returned, Sir Luminere. Illicurus has as well, and has instructed all the Aasimar to join him in flying south."*

"He what?" Frustrated at his exclusion, Jaiden waved his arms and waded through the feathery circle, determined to get to the bottom of the Aasimars' agitation. "Pardon me, my friends," he said as he squeezed between them, finally gaining their attention as he came face-to-face with Illicurus in the middle.

"Marshall, I was told to expect you with news from the Black Hills. Do you have a report?"

Illicurus continued to look another Aasimar in the eye as he responded. *"As I already told Prince Falcionus, the orcs were merely gathering for some sort of celebration – a coronation of their new chieftain, it seems. They pose no real threat, and after a little breast-beating they will no doubt disperse, once the majority regain sobriety."*

"And what is this business about flying the Aasimar south? I thought it was agreed that each Master would keep a third under his command, and Sir Golddrake has already led his allotment to Synirpa."

"Firstly, we Aasimar are not subject to the commands of the Order." Jaiden could hear the venom in Illicurus's telepathy. *"We have our own hierarchy, and presently, I am at the top of it. Secondly, I have decided to meet the King-priest on our own terms, and fully intend to do so."*

"I did not mean to offend, Marshall. Only, wars require all allies to operate under a unified strategy, if they are to be most effective. Surely, if we coordinate our—"

"I have coordinated with the Prince." Illicurus peered over his shoulder at the throne, where Falcionus sat holding his scepter, a nervous look on his face. *"It is decided."*

"But we do not all agree," responded Palomar.

Another voice, one Jaiden was unfamiliar with, jumped into his mind. *"We decided together to give our service to those who rescued us, Illicurus. We followed your deviation from authority before, and no one needs a reminder of where that left us!"*

"I am your Marshall, Ymrilad, and I based my decision on what is best for the Aasimar. We are away from home, as I am painfully aware every time I set eyes upon this crude wasteland, and have to look out for ourselves. Besides, as I already told you, the human prince agrees with me." Illicurus shot another glance at the silent ruler of Dawn's Edge.

"Pardon me, my friends." Jaiden looked from one perfect face to another in the crowd of angelic outsiders. "I do not mean to overstep my position, but if I remember the telling of your own story correctly, isn't 'looking after yourselves' precisely what left you cursed in the first place?"

Illicurus stared at him with an intensity Jaiden had never known, and for a full three seconds, all voices in the room fell silent.

"Our punishment, Sir Luminere," Illicurus began, his words pulsing with the strain of imposed calm, *"was for not properly obeying the directives of Hiruth Jeshu, may his light shine forever. In the absence of our Celestial Lord, the next highest-ranking Celestial is empowered to give such directives – and that would be me."*

Palomar interceded, deflecting the poison currently aimed at Jaiden. *"But Marshall, we are no longer on Mount Celestia. While I do not believe this dissolves us from authority, I would suggest the virtues we aspire to emulate should dictate our behavior. I swore loyalty to the Order of the Rising Moon, and honoring that means obeying its hierarchy, even though its leaders are not Celestials."*

"But you do not simply get to lay aside your original oaths because you have taken on others, Palomar." The fire in Illicurus's voice burned clearly. *"Have you forgotten your allegiance to Hiruth?"*

Palomar's tone remained steady as he pushed himself forward to stand beside Jaiden in the circle. *"We all did for a time, Marshall. Thus, we are here."*

"Bah!" Illicurus waved his hands dismissively. *"My command is going to help the humans who freed us defeat their enemy. It is clear we are their best chance for doing so, and will not show our strength by splitting up and hiding in the north."*

The second dissenting voice, belonging to Ymrilad, answered. *"This is not about doing what we think is best for these humans, or for ourselves. Do you not all see? We were stripped of our memory, of who we were, for taking matters into our own hands. How can you ignore the cruelty we endured in our cursed forms and not weigh it heavily? We owe these people for bringing us out of that torment, and should honor their wishes until the debt is repaid, however we measure that. I am not ready to say the scales have been balanced."*

Palomar nodded. *"I will stay with Sir Luminere and serve the Order of the Rising Moon until my death, or the King-priest of Chelpa is defeated."*

Jaiden felt a swell of pride and took in a deep breath, letting his chest expand to match. Illicurus gave him a measuring stare, before glancing briefly once more at the Prince. Jaiden's eyes followed, and he thought it strange Falcionus had not spoken during the entire debate. In fact he looked shaken, as if he'd recently seen the spirits of his ancestors. Were the Aasimar not projecting their argument to the Prince?

"So be it." Illicurus resumed his normal tone, as if disinterested with the entire proceeding. *"Those Aasimar still recognizing my rightful authority shall fly toward the Castle at Windhollow Rock on the morn. The more glory for us."*

Chapter 28

Haunt of the Bone Man

The day he left Selamus, Rogan thought only of putting as much distance between himself and Lady Saffron as possible. So why could he not get the images of that morning out of his head? Saffron's body glistening in the candlelight, Dhania appearing at the door to bring him breakfast, the smiles on each of their faces before they turned into... something else. He was done with them now, though, and would be happy to never meet another person from Begnasharan – doubly so a woman.

Travelling the Dawn Way south with as much speed as he could manage, Rogan came to Synirpa within a week. As he passed the familiar tract, he fought the urge to stop in and see some lads of the Order he'd spent long weeks with on the road. They had other things to worry about now, like staying alive for the next month, or whenever Ebon Khorel decided to finally stretch his arm north again. He knew it was only a matter of time.

As Rogan traversed the length of road between the seat of Rosegold and the castle at Windhollow Rock, his mind wandered to the memory the moonlight brought to him the last time he covered that stretch. It still amazed him he had blocked out the sound of Dominic crying, but he heard it clearly enough in his head now, echoing down the halls of the years between them – and he knew in his bones his son was somehow alive.

That was his goal, finding his son. The woman he loved, or the woman who loved him... it was unnecessary confusion that would dilute his purpose. Happiness would have to wait, and he was patient. He had already delayed such thoughts for over ten years; surely, he was better off doing so again.

Realizing the need for care, he slowed his pace once past the lands he assumed the Duke's forces patrolled. The country between Synirpa and the ruined fortress of Halidor had already paid a heavy toll in lives, a recipe for creating desperate men. Desperate men needed less of a reason to cut your throat for the promise of a full purse, or even a free horse.

Well into the evening, he reached the town they first found wiped out by the plague. Light was fading, but he wanted to push on. The memory of all those bodies packed into the great hall was enough to unnerve him. Even as the sun failed, more than enough of the moons remained to see by, though the shadows would not stop playing their tricks.

With Rogan's senses on alert, even the sudden movement of the wind in the trees or a creaking sign triggered suspicion. He could not shake the feeling something was watching him from behind the shutters of a gutted house, or imagining the almost-dead had risen to hunt down those who abandoned them to their fate.

As he stopped his horse to better listen, the sounds receded along with the wind, keeping their clues from him. The tiny hairs on the back of his neck stood outright, and a shiver made its way down his spine as he prodded his steed to a trot.

Sometime between midnight and the predawn hours, he decided he finally had to get some rest if he was to make any progress the following day. He tied his weary animal to a tree some fifty paces off the road, and lay beneath its boughs. The ground was cold and uneven, and Rogan promised himself the following night would be spent at an inn, if he could find one.

In another couple days, he made it all the way to the ruins of Halidor, where he decided to stop before crossing into his own country – the *Empire* of Chelpa, as it was now known. He remembered a time before it was so, before the kings of Chelpa looked outward with lust upon the territory of others. Rogan climbed a still-standing section of shattered stone wall and surveyed the southlands, his home, where he was officially unwelcome.

Though a thorn in the side of this monarchy, he strove for what most in the realm wanted, or so he believed – the opportunity to live without the constant storm cloud of fear casting its shadow overhead. There would always be poverty and undesirable tasks to perform, but the worry of unexpected punishment, of being conscripted into an aggressive army and sent to war, of being forced to dedicate your labor to a cause not your own, he could bring a resolution to those.

The land, however, still looked the same – at least from a wall across the border. He did not know whether that seemed an encouraging sign or deception. Could the land and sky be expected to warn you of the dangerous transformation taking place under its witness? Whatever the state of the current environment, he was entering it tomorrow and needed to decide what course he would take.

He required information, and that suggested regaining touch with his allies, of whom there were many. Rogan had resistance contacts in villages and cities across Chelpa, but needed to be smart about who he chose to see. As a wanted criminal, the Blood Tear Brotherhood would no doubt be on alert after his infiltration of Hope's End and the assault on Blackthorn Prison. It would be wise to involve as few sources as possible, which meant identifying the right ones ahead of time.

If his son was alive, who would know? Where would Dominic be now? Rogan could not lie to himself – he knew the Blood Tear Brotherhood would not have spared his child because they suddenly grew a conscience. If they did so, they had a reason, which necessitated taking the long view. His son would only be alive now if the regime thought he would be useful when he grew older. They would put him somewhere they could control, or at least keep eyes on him. Though he wished it were not so, the logical spot to start his search was Lucnere, the capital itself. Whether they placed Dominic in an orphanage or kept him locked in the palace dungeon, someone in Lucnere would have made that decision.

Rogan sighed, accepting the new direction of his fate. At least a large portion of the Imperial army, if not the King-priest himself, would be away from the capital, heading north. He swiveled on the crest of the wall, looking toward Selamus as the fading glow of the sun settled behind the mountains, toward Sir Golddrake and Saffron and... no, that was not his place. They would stand or fall regardless of his presence, and he knew he could do more good in his own county. His son needed him; he had already made the decision. So why was he looking back?

He descended the wall and sought out a soft patch of dirt to bed down on. His horse, tied to a nearby tree, nibbled on sprigs that pierced the earth around the ruins. Rogan could already sense the night would be restless, but he had to try. In the morning he would head due south, making his way to the town of Twin Pikes, where at last count he still had a few friends. The Dawn Way ended at Halidor, however, and he would have to watch for signs of the army as he cut cross-country.

Rogan's eyes were only shut a matter of minutes, it seemed, before an out-of-place sound grabbed his attention. A metallic clinking, like the rattling of chains against rock, reached his ears from nearby. He snapped to a seated position and listened intently, the dark of night fully drowning his vision, but the rattling faded.

His hand encircled the hilt of his dagger and he strained to hear, but the wind circling in the stones and his own heartbeat in his ears masked all other noises. Then he heard it again briefly, definitely metal, coming from somewhere among the ruins. Rogan rose to his feet and pressed his back to the block of stone he'd used for shelter, regretting his choice not to light a fire as his eyes strained against the dark. The sound drew closer. An unnatural chill fell upon him, piercing his skin and sinking all the way to his bones.

He carefully drew his dagger from its sheath, trying not to give any indication of his position to whatever was out there. Behind him and to the left, the shuffling clank came to an abrupt stop. Rogan noticed his breath was coming out in white puffs of vapor, the air was so cold. Time measured out in the rapid beats of his heart, and a brief eternity passed with no resolution to his anxiousness. Something had to be done.

Convincing his muscles to obey him proved no simple task, but Rogan counted down from "three" in his head and then leapt out from behind his stone shelter. Only four, long strides in front of him stood a young boy, staring up at Rogan's face. His skin and ragged clothes held a blue-green hue like they had absorbed all the light cast by the two moons, leaving the space around him an even darker version of night.

Manacles clasped around the boy's ankles, connected by a thick chain short enough to restrict a normal gait. More troubling was that the child's face seemed to have borrowed some of Rogan's features: his deep-set eyes, the angle of his nose – his mind immediately seized the possibility that this was his son. *How could this be?*

The apparition did not speak. They stood staring at one another for a couple dozen heartbeats before the boy suddenly turned his back on Rogan and started walking away, chains clanking with every step. Rogan reached out an ineffectual hand as his legs would not move. He was paralyzed from the waist down, and the words he longed to speak caught in his throat. He struggled to move, to urge the boy to stop, but all he could summon was a building tension in his chest that failed to dissipate, despite his efforts.

Not knowing what else to do and growing desperate, he looked to the uril-chent dagger in his left hand... if only he could release the pressure. He pointed the tip of the blade toward himself and with a decisive motion, plunged the dagger into his chest.

Rogan's eyes opened and he let out a primal scream as he bolted to an upright position. His face beaded with sweat, and his legs tingled. He had fallen asleep with them curled underneath him, and the restricted circulation numbed them. He stretched his legs and wiped his forehead with his sleeve before lying down again. With eyes open, he listened for the sound of metal on stone, but only the dry symphony of chirping crickets sang back to him.

He thought about the boy who looked like him, bound and speechless, and his chest tightened up again. Was it his son's ghost, come to haunt him to repay his abandonment? Did the apparition appear that way because Dominic was now one of the King-priest's slaves? Guilt washed over Rogan like a flood. He closed his eyes and wept until tears would no longer come, thankful his horse was the only witness. At last, exhausted by his release, Rogan fell asleep.

In the morning he made a quick meal of water and dried biscuits and was on his way. Passing into Chelpa, he wanted to reach Twin Pikes as fast as possible. He figured if he rode well into the dark, he could make it there by night's end. He swore he could feel the humidity build as he headed south. The clouds grew thicker and darker as well.

With no roads to follow in this part of the country, Rogan picked his way around the foothills as best he could, hoping no other obstacles presented themselves. The day passed quickly, his mind flitting between his vision of the previous night and the task of navigating. Did it mean anything? Was he supposed to interpret the purpose behind what he saw, as Sir Golddrake so often claimed to do? Soon enough, night approached again, and he found himself both longing for and dreading whatever might await him in the land of dreams.

Rogan rode through twilight, until only the stars and moon were left to guide him. He still had not spotted the town and while he felt he was close, the risk of getting lost while winding around the hills, or his horse turning an ankle in the dark, was too great. Twin Pikes would have to wait until morning. Rogan dismounted and led his weary steed by the reins up the side of the nearest hill. He wanted to make camp near a high perch, to see as much of the land as possible.

As he reached the crest, a flicker of light from the next hillside caught his attention. Someone had a campfire burning, though from this distance he could not tell if it belonged to shepherd or bandit. Desiring a fire of his own, Rogan had to investigate before settling in for the night. He led his horse back down to the valley and tied its reins to a thick copse of alders. Then, he crept slowly up the adjoining hill, opposite the fire, staying low and moving from one patch of sparse vegetation to the next.

When he got close enough to hear voices he lay on his belly, inching forward on his forearms and knees until he could catch what was being said. His sense was there were three men, though they spoke quietly so their words would not carry on the wind.

"No, we wait until midnight," a calm, deep voice said. "That is when the Bone Man was spotted in Yegetes and Salmarsh."

"Well," spoke another, high-pitched and anxious, "who is going to play the bait?"

"That is between you and me, Kerwin," the first man answered. "Lokitor's got the hawk-eye, so he will be doing the shooting. Is this moonlight enough for you, Loki?"

"Aye, it'll do. Just lure him out until he is clear of the trees," the man called Lokitor offered.

"But we cannot let him enter the town," reiterated the deep voice, "or Twin Pike will face the same fate as the others."

Something about that voice was familiar to Rogan... he searched his memory for a connection. Merrick of High Dell – that was it! The man helped Rogan more than once, including slipping him out of Lucnere when the royal guards caught his trail after an armory raid. He had not seen the man in several years, and Rogan hoped not too much had changed during the interim.

"Fortune favors the bold," he whispered to himself before rising and striding directly into the encampment. "I was wondering if I might warm myself by your fire," he said, loud enough so the others could hear him clearly. He kept his palms up so they could see he was empty-handed, and failed to flinch when the hooded Lokitor raised and pulled back on his bow. Luckily, he restrained from firing.

"Suffering snakes!" Kerwin called as he jerked back, losing his balance and nearly falling from the log stool he was sitting on. He was thin, with stringy, shoulder-length hair. "Where did he come from?"

Merrick stood and reached for the short sword at his side, but did not draw it. "What business do you have in these hills so late?" His tone was even as ever.

"What business do we ever have, suffering under the crown of the Dread Tyrant?" Rogan spoke casually, hoping his words and face would soon ring the bell of Merrick's memory. He watched as the man's lightly-bearded face twitched, obviously trying to place whether he had met this interloping stranger before, and where. Finally, the connection was made.

"Rogan of Thispany! By the churning river, what are you doing out here? I thought you'd be in hiding for a year after that ordeal at Blackthorn." Merrick released the grip on his sword and stepped forward to embrace Rogan.

In response, Lokitor relaxed and lowered his bow. "I take it this fellow is part of the cause?"

"My good Loki," Merrick answered as he clasped his arms around Rogan's shoulders, "this fellow *started* the cause, or may as well have."

"So what in the blue heavens are the three of you conspiring about all the way out here? You should be lying comfortably back in Twin Pikes. I know the place must be within a league or two." Rogan swiveled his head as though he might spot the town just over his shoulder. He noticed Lokitor lowering his head, while Kerwin glanced from one companion to the other. Neither of them seemed keen to speak. Rogan was even more intrigued. "What is it?" he asked, this time looking squarely at Merrick.

His old compatriot moistened his lips before speaking. "We're trying to save Twin Pikes from the same scourge that has ravaged sites of resistance outposts along the Verdant Passage."

Rogan's eyes narrowed. "What sort of scourge?"

"The curse of the Bone Man," Lokitor answered.

Rogan shifted his gaze to the hooded bowman for an instant, but when he was not more forthcoming it fell back on Merrick, who finally succumbed to its intensity.

"For the past few weeks, a savage disease has been cropping up in certain towns between here and Blackthorn. But not just any towns, Rogan..." Merrick paused while his hand absently stroked the graying whiskers of his chin, "only places that have harbored pockets of active resistance to the crown over the last several years. At each location, someone has reported an appearance of the Bone Man a couple days before the sickness takes hold. We think they are connected."

"A strange plague broke in the north several weeks ago as well, when the King-priest was laying siege to one of their castles." Rogan shook his head – it couldn't be a coincidence. "So who is this 'Bone Man' supposed to be?"

"Nobody knows," said Lokitor.

Kerwin, his voice slightly trembling, chimed in as he stoked the fire. "He walks the dead of night, they say. His visage is inhuman, fearsome like a beast's or dragon's. He is always bathed in a pale white glow, and insubstantial like a walking skeleton."

"If you believe what they say," chided Merrick. "I do not doubt imaginations are at work. Those telling the tales are always witless with fear, or feverish from the disease. Still, we have decided to do something about it."

"What exactly is that?" asked Rogan.

"We're going to hunt him," answered Lokitor, raising his bow for emphasis.

"I have studied the pattern," Merrick explained. "The victims form a line north along the Verdant Passage from Blackthorn Prison, and then east from Salmarsh. Twin Pikes is the next logical place for him to show up. You and I both know, Rogan, more than a few reside there who have acted against the regime."

"Aye," Rogan nodded. "I'd hoped to stay with some tonight if I'd better kept my bearings." He did not know these men's abilities, and perhaps they were more than competent, yet his gut told him theirs was a fools' errand, admirable though it was. "Where is Ebon Khorel, if you know? The last word I had, he had retaken Blackthorn. Do you know if he still occupies it?"

"The King-priest?" Merrick questioned rhetorically. "He could be anywhere, I suppose. Probably in Lucnere; unless he's not."

Rogan found the man's ambivalence puzzling. "And what about the army that marched on Blackthorn to seize it? Surely the whereabouts of his massive forces are not a mystery..."

"My efforts of late have not involved tracking troop movements, Baron," Merrick snapped. "My concern is for the hundreds of my countrymen currently wasting away from this godforsaken pestilence."

Rogan lowered his head and spoke softly. "I am sorry, my friend. Our thoughts lie in the same place. I just don't want the three of you biting off more than you anticipate. I do not think it coincidence that the King-priest abandoned his siege of Windhollow Rock immediately after this 'Bone Man' was spotted nearby. The disease followed in his wake through the province of Halidor and beyond. I fear the apparition may be an avatar of the Dread Tyrant himself – something you could not hope to kill with a longbow." The entire camp fell silent, leaving only the crackle of the fire to speak of any fear or doubt.

Lokitor sat back down on the flat rock he was using for a chair. Finally, he picked up a branch from their pile of gathered wood and placed it across the flames. "There is only one way to find out."

Kerwin nodded, followed by Merrick, and Rogan allowed himself a sigh. He certainly knew what desperation felt like. "Alright," he said, stepping closer to the fire to warm his hands. "What can I do to help?"

"Well," Merrick began, mimicking Rogan's stance above the small blaze, "we do not want the Bone Man entering Twin Pikes itself, so one of us will serve as a lure, out in the open on the approach to the town. Given the reports we have, he does something to disorient his victims, but we still do not know how they become infected. He may touch them directly, or bring a profane object in contact with their skin." Merrick gestured while he spoke, his hands circling like an unraveling spool. "Loki, with the bow, is going to be positioned on a hilltop with a clean line of shot."

Rogan turned slightly to regard the archer.

"He's one of the best," Merrick mentioned, as if reading Rogan's thoughts. "The other two should keep watch, but out of sight; we'll use hand signals to alert Loki to the Bone Man's approach, or make adjustments if something unaccounted for happens."

"What if you're wrong and he does not even make an appearance? How long are we willing to wait?" Rogan was still uneasy with the entire endeavor, but was not going to spend until sunrise trying to talk them out of it. He would need friends in the days to come, especially in his search, and a chance to do a favor could not be ignored.

Merrick crossed his arms and tilted his head to the sky. "As far as we can tell, he has always appeared when the moons were still high, usually just after midnight – we should be getting into position soon. Shall we draw lots to determine who shall be bait?"

The idea made Rogan very uncomfortable. He wanted to be helpful, and it would be a lie to say he was incurious to get a glimpse of this mythical Bone Man, but placing himself in harm's way against an unknown adversary, his only support an unfamiliar archer, would be unnerving. With only a one-in-three chance, however, he decided to check his objections until after the results.

Merrick quickly picked three strands of smooth cordgrass from the hillside and tore off pieces so that one straw was noticeably shorter than the others. "Short stem plays the lure?" He turned his back to the fire, and when he swiveled, the three pieces of grass protruded equally from his fist.

Rogan held his breath and drew first, letting the air out when he saw his strand was not the short one. Merrick turned to Kerwin, whose eyes darted back and forth between the remaining options, as if the lots might give away their length under scrutiny.

"They're not going to pick themselves, Kerwin."

The thin-framed man locked eyes with Merrick, swallowed hard, and chose. "Steaming dung piles!"

Merrick opened his palm to confirm that Kerwin had indeed drawn the short straw. "Don't worry, son, Loki won't let anything happen to you."

"That's right," said the still-seated Lokitor. "I made these arrows myself: steel from Lucnere's own foundries, serrated edges, and the best quail feathers for balance. I won't miss."

Kerwin nodded, resigning himself to his role. "You're right. I can do this. Should we take our positions, then? I want to make sure Loki has time to find the best spot."

Merrick nodded. "Let's douse this fire, but grab a brand first, Kerwin."

"I left my horse tied on the next hill," Rogan interjected.

"Leave it," Lokitor said as he poured water on the flames, eliciting a sharp hiss. "Animals might spook and give away your position."

Rogan turned to Merrick, who nodded his confirmation before kicking sand on the glowing embers. He hoped it would not be too difficult to trace back to where his mount rested;

otherwise, it would be a long walk to the capital. As gray smoke wound its way into the black air, he followed the triumvirate to the location they had staged for the bait.

A small, wooden cart, the spokes of one of its two wheels shattered, tilted sadly in the dirt on the side of a wide path. The trail wound through the valley of several hills, providing ample spots to watch from cover, relatively near-by.

"Is Twin Pikes close?" asked Rogan, breaking the silence they had shared during the short hike.

"Quarter-league to the west." Merrick tilted his head in that direction as he unpacked a pile of kindling from the cart and laid it on the ground.

Rogan strained his eyes and thought he could spot a shadow down the path, near the horizon. "Why are there no lights?"

"Strict curfew these days," responded Lokitor. "Not that his aggression is curbed under other circumstances, but the King-priest has declared Chelpa officially at war since you took the prison."

Kerwin set his flaming brand on the pile of wood and it caught quickly. Feeling the heat, Rogan realized he had missed it, even during their brief walk.

"Alright, this is where we leave you," Merrick said, placing a steadying hand on Kerwin's shoulder. "Loki, do you have your spot?"

The hooded man nodded, "Top of that hill." He pointed north, then turned and took one long stride before peeking over his shoulder. "Courage, Kerwin." After that, he bounded silently up the slope to his hiding place.

"We should take spots opposite one another," Merrick directed to Rogan. "Do you have a preference?"

"I will take the south side," he answered, desiring a vantage where he could keep eyes on both their target and archer.

Merrick nodded his ascent. "Here, take this." He dipped his hand into a pouch of white dust, and then passed the sack to Rogan. "Now if you spot the Bone Man, signal by shading your eyes like this." He stretched his open palm across his brow. "If anyone else is with him, raise the number of fingers indicating how many. If you hear something suspicious, but do not have visual confirmation, cup your ear." He continued making the appropriate gestures as he described them. "If someone other than the Bone Man arrives, for whatever reason, ball your fist over your mouth. If you see something that indicates Loki should wait to take a shot – both palms to your ears."

Rogan nodded, "Understood."

Merrick showed a brief, polished smile. "Don't worry, Baron, nothing will go wrong. Everyone knows you are surrounded by good fortune."

Rogan couldn't help but laugh and shake his head. He walked south off the path, heading toward the twisted trunk of a juniper just up from the base of a hill, and by the time he thought of a response, Merrick was only a shadow darting through brush on the other side of the trail.

Once he felt adequately concealed from any wanderers on the road, Rogan made an effort to identify the locations of his comrades. Kerwin was easy enough to see, sitting haplessly beside the broken cart with his campfire. The hillsides north of him, however, were shaded heavily from the moonlight. Rogan watched for any movement that would give Merrick away. He saw none at first, but finally a spot of white, reflecting in the starlight, waved from side-to-side. Dipping his right hand into the chalk pouch, he waved similarly, verifying his location to the others.

Lokitor's presence, however, was completely indecipherable from his position. He decided to simply trust the archer was hidden, ready to play his role. He hoped the man's night vision was keener than his as well.

Then came the waiting. The night air was cool for the season, but not unbearable; at least it helped keep Rogan awake. After half an hour of standing still, he heard a noise nearby, and his attention snapped to the source. It turned out to be a lone fox, bounding into the brush after a mouse or some other small prey. How much time passed after that, he was unsure, but his legs grew weary, and Rogan looked for a place to sit where he could maintain his view. He noticed the fire was diminished, even though Kerwin must have added more fuel by then.

Rogan inwardly chided himself for being caught up in fireside stories of walking ghosts, no doubt aided by the contents of his own dream the night before. And then, he heard the hum. Like a soft, resonant vibration, it roused him from complacency and drew his attention eastward. He saw a quick flash of white as Merrick raised his hand to his brow, indicating he spotted something.

Closer than he imagined, a figure broke free from a small copse of trees into the wide, dirt path. Shaped like a man, it was bathed in a pale, sickly glow and moved forward with deliberate steps. Trying to keep his wits while panic struggled to take hold, Rogan gave the signal that he, too, saw the Bone Man, though it was moving slowly enough he was sure Lokitor would spot it with plenty of time to act.

Using his tree for leverage, Rogan swung around the trunk to get a better vantage as the Bone Man drew closer. He could see why the spirit had garnered such a name. White, ivory plates, resembling bones, gave the creature its anthropomorphic shape, though empty spaces gaped where many of the muscles and sinews should have been, and its head was anything but human.

Like a beast with eternally opened jaws, the face was threatening and somehow familiar. Curved horns jutted from the sides of the head, above absent ears. The entire entity was bathed in a pale glow – ivory outlined in black – except for what looked like a crimson jewel at the base of its neck...

The Bone Man approached Kerwin, who stood to face it, appearing confused as to whether to hold his ground or flee. Rogan was unsure what Lokitor was waiting for, but was thankful for whatever stayed his hand. They had misjudged what they were facing, and Rogan raised his hands to his ears, desperate to keep the archer from giving away their ambush. He knew no steel-tipped arrow could pierce the Bone Man's protection.

Rogan recognized the menacing visage of the King-priest's helm, even though it had turned from dark to light, and remembered Palomar's suspicion their nemesis had acquired some of the Living Fire – rubies bearing the essence of the gods.

This had to be Ebon Khorel in disguise, and his uril-chent armor was nigh impenetrable.

The Bone Man, surrounded by a persistent hum, halted twenty-or-so strides from Kerwin and the cart. Rogan muttered under his breath for Kerwin to run, willing him to escape while he could. He hated not being able to help, but the four of them together were no match for the armored King-priest. Giving away their positions would not only put them all in danger, it would erase any advantage in gathering further intelligence. If Kerwin did not decide to run, however, Rogan knew the others would eventually rush to his aid.

Kerwin faced the Bone Man, but started to slowly back away, fear getting the better of him. The Bone Man raised a hand, fingers outstretched, and put an end to that. Kerwin's chest jerked outward as if drawn to the beckoning hand, and his head snapped back until his neck was stretched to capacity. Wicked-sounding words overlapped with the humming emanating from the Bone Man, to be subsequently joined by an outpouring fog. The mist coursed around the Bone Man in every direction, and Rogan instinctively backed up the hill a few steps at its approach.

Within seconds it enveloped Kerwin, and Rogan heard a hollow *clank* shortly after. The Bone Man lowered his hand and turned his head toward Lokitor's hill, even as Kerwin's body slumped to the ground. The fog began to dissipate, and Rogan held his breath to see what the King-priest did next.

Apparently Lokitor had enough discipline not to fire another arrow and keep himself hidden. After staring up the night-shaded hillside for a few moments, the Bone Man relented and retreated down the path the same direction he had come. An excruciatingly long wait ensued until the sickly glow had disappeared into the trees once more, and Merrick's chalked hand flashed as he ran to check on Kerwin, who had not yet stood.

Rogan joined him, and he heard the snap of branches as Lokitor hustled down from his hiding spot as well. Merrick held Kerwin's head in his hands, and though his eyes were half open, he was unresponsive to their commands to speak.

"Why did you wait to shoot?" Merrick nearly howled at Lokitor.

"Your friend here gave me the signal to hold!" he snapped back.

Merrick turned to Rogan. "Why did you do that?"

"You saw what happened when he did loose!" Rogan took a deliberate breath and cooled his tone. "I realized we were dealing with the King-priest."

"What?" Merrick and Lokitor asked in unison.

"The Bone Man and the King-priest are one. He's been infecting his enemies with this accursed plague." Realizing what he just said, Rogan stood and backed away from Kerwin. "You shouldn't touch him."

"What are you talking about?" Merrick retorted. "He needs help."

"He could infect all of us."

Lokitor looked from Rogan to Merrick, and took a step back as well. "He is right."

"I am *not* going to abandon Kerwin." Merrick stayed where he was, his friend's head balanced in his careful hands.

"Well, none of us should go to Twin Pikes now. That much is sure. And we should stay away from anyone else for a few days at least, until it is clear whether we are infected." Rogan looked back down the trail the King-priest had taken. "I am sorry to leave under these circumstances, but we might have an opportunity here, and I want to seize it. If I am right, the King-priest of Chelpa was just in our midst, alone and unguarded. He must have some place close to take refuge. I am going to try and track him."

Rogan paused for a second to let his words sink in, but could not afford to waste any more time. Both men remained still and speechless. At last he just nodded, adding, "I hope he is all right." He rubbed his palms together to wipe the dust off as he jogged east, looking for the spot where the King-priest broke off the path.

"Good fortune, Baron," came from behind, though he did not spare the time to acknowledge it. He spotted a promising gap in the trees lying at the base of two hills and followed it north, keeping his eyes peeled for any footprints in the moonlight. If he correctly guessed the Bone Man's identity, his uril-chent armor should have left some sign of passage in the softer earth. He made good time following the path of least resistance, and was rewarded several minutes later by catching a glimpse of the pale, white glow vanishing behind a rise ahead of him.

Rogan slowed his pace, desiring both stealth and perception once he spotted his mark. Just because the King-priest had approached the town alone did not mean reinforcements were not close by. He stayed close enough to keep the glow in sight, and followed for half an hour more before the ghostly light suddenly vanished.

He froze, frantic that he might have lost Ebon Khorel, and worried that the King-priest may have become aware of being followed. His mind was screaming the danger, but he knew his only choices were to run ahead in hopes of recovering visual contact, or abandoning the hunt altogether. *For Riah*, he thought, and broke into a sprint.

Ten seconds later he reached the spot he had last seen the light and stopped, his head swiveling to find any sign of the King-priest. He was in the last valley before the hills rose even higher to the edge of the Firewall Mountains. Yet, something was odd. To the north and south sparse trees and other vegetation continued to pepper the landscape, their leaves and branches highlighted by the green and blue tints of Criesha and Hurn, the companion moons. Yet to the east, between him and the mountains, nothing at all caught the moonlight, as if a great pocket of shadow hung over the land.

Rogan had no idea what to make of it, but then he got the break he needed. Something that had just been out of view did reflect the moonlight, and it was moving. Rogan dropped to one knee, reducing his own silhouette in case anyone was watching. Sure enough, as the clouds broke away from the green moon, enough light shone down that he could clearly denote a metal object passing through the valley, heading directly for the void of shadow. When it reached the edge and passed beyond, the reflection disappeared completely.

Dark, powerful magic was at work, and Rogan's doubt swelled again, shouting from within to turn back or rue the consequences. His thoughts shifted instead to the image of what he believed to be his son, straight from his dream the night before. What was it trying to tell him? Perhaps the truth he already knew – that finding his son would mean little if the King-priest continued to rule. He could not raise Dominic as he should, so long as they were living under the oppression of the Dread Tyrant. Rogan buried his fear and continued toward the cloud of shadow.

When he drew close he could hear muffled sounds from within, but they were irregular and distant, and he could not identify them. He examined the shadow in either direction for clues, though no obvious reason existed to favor one spot over another for entry. In fact, the entire surface of the mass seemed to be swimming this way and that, devoid of any pattern. With a final exhalation, he drew his saber and dagger and stepped into the veil of swirling darkness.

Rogan passed through instantly, and the other side revealed a sprawling encampment. Hidden from the outside world, he guessed the inhabitants numbered in the thousands. No moon or starlight penetrated the shadow, but plenty enough torches burned to see by. Rogan's first thought was to hide and hope he had not been spotted entering the camp.

Ducking behind a siege engine, with wooden wheels nearly as tall as him, Rogan peeked around its frame to get an idea of the camp's layout. Though the hour was late, plenty of soldiers still walked about: tending fires, feeding animals, and delivering messages. A deep, sustained moan caught his attention, and he followed the sound to a huge enclosure, where a many-headed reptilian creature was penned. The hydra that attacked Jaiden, he presumed. Taking stock of its numerous, tooth-filled maws, Rogan gained more respect for the young knight's bravery.

Other ferocious creatures populated nearby pens, though none as massive as the hydra. The tents seemed to stretch on endlessly, and it occurred to him that, this close to the border, the army could only be headed in one direction – back to the Northern Provinces. The King-priest obviously meant to finish the conquest they interrupted by releasing the Dampers from Blackthorn.

With no one aware of his presence or close to his position, Rogan sheathed his saber and began climbing the pitch-thrower to get a better view. From astride the engine, he searched the select tents flying banners for the royal emblem. He finally found it – a large crimson pavilion, curiously far from the center of the camp. Two guards were posted at its mouth, dressed in sleek, black armor, unlike any he had ever seen – except once.

He would have to move closer to be sure, but they looked very much like the uril-chent statues he found in the secret torture chamber at Hope's End. Rogan watched for a few moments to see if either guard moved, but not so much as a twitch was noticeable. Perhaps they were statues, after all. Still, he decided it safer to approach from behind and try to worm his way under the tent.

As stealthily as he could manage, Rogan climbed down from the siege engine and tracked his way around the edge of the camp. He remained within the dome of shadow to maintain his bearings, but kept his dagger drawn to benefit from the deeper darkness it created. Sneaking from cover to cover, it appeared the army was mostly bedded within its shelters, and those still awake did not perceive any threat. No doubt they trusted in the protection of their King-priest, and the cruel god he bade them worship.

He hoped Ebon Khorel retired as soon as possible after a late night – his attempt would be much easier if the King-priest was sleeping. After checking once more to make sure no one was approaching, Rogan set to work severing a few of the cords keeping the tent staked to the ground. With a satisfying snap they gave way to his dagger, allowing enough give in the thick canvas for him to pull up a section and wiggle underneath on his back. Although he moved as quietly and quickly as possible, his passage still disturbed the structure he infiltrated. He thought he heard the scrape of metal when he was through to his waist, and instinctively froze to listen closer.

The inside of the tent was almost completely dark, though a faint red glow above and behind him gave his eyes some light to work with. A faint, strange *hiss*, followed by muted footsteps, was all Rogan needed to hear to abandon stealth for quickness.

He pulled his legs through the loosened tent wall and hastily rolled over, tucking his knees underneath him in preparation to leap. A wide, raised bed stood an arm's length to his right, and around its edge one of the uril-chent statues, its eye-slit animated by hateful red flame, stepped to engage him. It held the metal shaft of a cruel-looking spear, with serrated blades, capable of slicing through leather and flesh, dipping below the pointed head.

The King-priest lay face-up on the bed, still sleeping, the Living Fire jewel embedded on a pendant around his bare neck, bathing his chest in a warm glow. Rogan decided to strike quickly and end the war with one plunge of his dagger, even if it meant paying the ultimate price. He twisted slightly on his feet and his calves tightened as he started to pounce onto the bed.

The statue was deceptively quick, however, and thrust his weapon forward to skewer Rogan mid-jump. He slammed his left foot down in a struggling effort to reverse his momentum. The exertion elicited a groan, and his forearm still caught one of the serrated blades, drawing blood from a gash just below his elbow. He also lost his balance and tumbled downward, crashing into the side of the wooden bed frame.

The living statue spared him no time to recover. The blade whistled in a downward arc to finish him, and Rogan had to roll away from the bed to evade it. He pushed himself to his feet, adrenaline fueling his muscles and sharpening his already acute reflexes. He caught the King-priest moving from the corner of his eye, and the statue coiled back with his spear, looking for his next opportunity to strike.

Rogan knew his own opportunity had slipped. He had no idea how to overcome an enemy made of metal with only his dagger, and the chanting to his right signaled the oncoming threat of magic. He feinted forward, causing his opponent to rock back on its heels, then swiftly turned and charged the side of the tent, plunging his dagger into the canvas and yanking down with all his might. He created just enough of a hole to grab the edges and dive through.

His spill to the ground outside knocked the breath from him, but he had no choice other than to climb to his feet, still gasping for air. Without looking back, he ran toward the edge of the shadow veil, trying to escape from sight before anyone emerged from the tent or brought other soldiers to attention. He passed through the smoky barrier and broke west, struggling to breathe as he ran, but not allowing himself to stop.

Rogan sprinted until his legs burned and he thought he would pass out from lack of air, and then pushed a while longer. He hoped the night would hide him, or that their desire to stay hidden would keep his foes from pursuing overlong. He thought of his failure as he ran, how close he came to achieving his goal only to fall short at the moment of truth. His anger fueled him, but finally, back in the hills, he nearly collapsed from exhaustion. Then another thought consumed him – he had to warn Sir Golddrake and the others.

They likely had no idea how close to the border this massive army was, nor the additional threats mounted against them. Facing such enemies would be difficult enough – to be taken by surprise would be catastrophic. Saffron and Dhania would be at risk. So would Palomar and the rest of the Order. The quest to locate his son would have to wait a little longer. Rogan needed to find his horse.

Chapter 29

Call to Arms

Amurel could always count on the solemnity of the Goddess's sacred Caves to reveal her voice. She filled his dreams the very first night they arrived.

In his vision he lay in a bed of thick, soft grass atop a hill. The night sky stretched above him, but a clear shaft of green moonlight illuminated his body. A black serpent wound around his feet and slowly slid up his legs, but Amurel was not afraid. The snake was shedding its skin, and as it travelled along his limbs, he felt them grow strong and healthy. Criesha's voice drifted down, filling him with a sense of peace. "You have served me well, Amurel," she said. "You will usher the Order toward a new beginning, and your service will not be forgotten."

He awoke with his faith and confidence replenished. Amurel was used to deciphering the sometimes-cryptic purposes behind Criesha's visits, but this time her message seemed clear – he would accomplish great things and be remembered for his deeds. He assumed that meant he would be victorious in the inevitable conflict to come. What's more, her return to his dreams assured him he was still in her good graces, even if her last appearance seemed a distant memory.

The journey up the narrow, steep path to the Caves had been taxing, especially with all the supplies. But after the painstaking climb, the Order's armories and larders were full once again, with more stores in reserve than before. Amurel's vigor was restored with sleep and the breath of his Goddess, and he knew the trek was the right decision.

When they had cut west from the Dawn Way to make for the Caves, Amurel sent a scout and engineer ahead to the ruins of Halidor to assess what steps could be taken to return the fortress into service, if only as a defensible outpost. He felt sure the King-priest would return to finish what he started in the Northern Provinces – it was simply a matter of time – and he would prefer to face the enemy at a natural chokepoint, such as the convergence of the Wyvernwatch and Firewall Mountains.

Amurel planned to meet his delegates on the road further south, allowing time for full consideration of the project. He was surprised to see three riders ascending toward the Caves on merely the second day of unloading and organizing their stock. A look-out notified him of the approach, and as he peered down from the edge of the stone steps, Sir Kilborn beside him, they tried to ascertain the identity of the third man.

It would have taken the scouts at least this long just to reach the fortress of Halidor, so they could not have made it there and back already. Yet, these were his men. As the riders drew closer, Amurel identified the black and scarlet armored leather at almost the exact moment Sir Kilborn confirmed, "It's the Baron."

Recalling their parting at Selamus, Amurel took it as a bad omen that Rogan had so quickly abandoned his plans. "No doubt they rode hard; let us make sure to have a hot supper ready when they arrive."

"Aye," responded Sir Kilborn. "Should I alert Lady Saffron?"

"Not directly," he decided. Though self-indulgent, he heard rumors about why Rogan actually left the capital, and wanted to make an assessment on his own by bearing witness to the reunion. He worried whether his friends would be able to work together effectively going forward.

"I have preparations to make. Please ask Saffron to join me in the deep meeting chamber. It is probably time we all sat down to discuss our upcoming deployments." Amurel took a couple, uneven steps in that direction, the click of his cane striking the rock giving a false sense of his determination. He stopped and added, "Greet the returning party personally, my friend, and bring them as soon as they are able."

"It shall be done." Sir Kilborn nodded and passed from sunlight into the shadow of the cave.

The new enrollment scroll stretched from the flat surface of Amurel's tiny wooden desk, all the way to the stone floor of the meeting cave. With their numbers swelling so rapidly, he knew the Order could not survive forever on the mere generosity of empowered nobility. They would have to start generating their own revenue – though those were considerations for after the war. At present, the task was simple to state and complex to achieve: defending the Northern Provinces of the Cradle from the encroaching Empire of Chelpa.

Amurel thought it clear enough that the best way to do so was by repelling the enemy at their border, and the old Halidor Keep was in the perfect geographic position to do so. Damage to the structure from its most recent conflict was severe, however, and the Duke of Halidor presumed dead. Lacking the certainty of a body, and with the obvious responsibility facing the lord of the southernmost free province, no one had yet asserted a claim to leadership.

This served as both a blessing and a curse. Amurel did not need to seek permission for his decisions in the realm, but had no effective way to petition individual settlements to combine efforts, either. The Duke's forces had been annihilated or scattered as well, and other than his own volunteers from the area, Halidor currently lacked any organized military.

"You sent for me, Sir Golddrake?" Saffron's voice pierced his preoccupied thoughts; he had not noticed the light of her torch approaching from the tunnel.

"Ah, yes, my Lady. The men I sent ahead to the ruins of Halidor Keep have returned, and I would like you to be present for their report." Amurel could not keep his eyes on hers as he omitted Rogan's presence. "I know your people have a different approach to warfare, and I welcome any insights regarding our strategy for repelling the King-priest. I also wondered if the rumors were true about what you did at Blackthorn, and if you might help us in combating his dark sorcery."

Saffron shrugged and allowed a soft smile. "It is still so new to me. Palomar taught me that song-shaping is tied to the elements, as well as matters of the mind. We are all attuned to a single element more closely than the others – he to the Air and me to Fire, I suppose." She stared at the burning end of her torch as she spoke, eyes losing focus as she invited in the flames. "Our magic tends to express itself with our attuned, elemental voice. The more I practice harnessing the essence, he says, the greater my control of its outcomes."

As if waking from a dream, she turned her attention from the fire to Amurel. "Different songs produce different results, but there is no map for me to follow. I am still experimenting with the connection between my will, the music I feel, and the expression of their union."

Amurel shook his head in awe. "I marvel at your gift, and your patience for discovery. It must not be an easy thing to control."

Saffron leaned forward and lowered her voice, though they were the only ones present. "Restraint is never-ending battle, fought on many fronts."

Amurel took his turn cracking a thin smile. Discipline was a trait he long felt the two of them shared – one of the reasons he admired Saffron so much. "Indeed." This time, with his head up, he did notice the aura of light approaching from the winding, black corridor. "Ah, that should be Sir Kilborn and the engineer."

Amurel kept his eyes squarely on Saffron's face, however, as the new arrivals filtered into the chamber. Sir Kilborn led a thin-faced man, who was in turn followed by Baron Rogan. Saffron's eyes grew large, and Amurel thought he detected a sharp intake of breath.

"Master Golddrake," Sir Kilborn tended toward formality in front of the uninitiated, "I've brought Tyregon of Doshale and Baron Rogan of Thispany – who bring dire tidings."

Rogan stared at Saffron before switching to meet Amurel's gaze. "Sir Golddrake," he nodded.

"Rogan," Amurel replied with a nod of his own. "I did not expect to see you again so soon, but I am glad for it."

Rogan emitted a doubtful snicker. "You won't be after you hear what I have to say."

Saffron's mouth opened to release an indecipherable sound, but she choked back whatever words might have followed and moved to Amurel's side of the desk.

He felt surprisingly bolstered with her behind him, like the oncoming news would not sting as much. "I suppose we should hear your tale straightaway, then."

"Very well." Rogan folded his arms across his chest. "I came across Ebon Khorel in the hills a day's ride south of Halidor Keep. In the dead of night I followed him into his army's encampment, which was concealed by dark sorcery. They have been moving in stealth, and have likely already crossed the border."

Sir Kilborn could not hold his tongue. "That means there is no point trying to fortify the Keep now."

Amurel closed his eyes and let his chin fall to his chest. He felt a headache rushing on as if launched from a catapult.

"And there's more, I'm afraid," continued Rogan. "Palomar was correct about the Living Fire. I saw a jeweled pendant around the King-priest's neck, and I fear his magic is stronger than ever before. Besides the many feral creatures kept by his beast-trainers, he has animated warriors forged of the uril-chent alloy he hoards. I suspect they are near-impervious to normal weapons, for the metal is hard and they possess no blood to spill."

"The statues we saw in Hope's End?" Saffron spoke as the connection seemed to dawn on her.

Rogan's eyes shifted to her momentarily and he nodded. "Even with the Aasimar at our side, it's going to be a tough fight, and we need to brace for it now. I think Windhollow is our best chance. The castle has already thwarted the King-priest once."

This was hard news. "You're sure Halidor Keep is out of the question?" Amurel asked.

Rogan nodded. "Absolutely. My guess is, the shadow has passed it already. We will be hard pressed to even get to the castle in time to make preparations."

"*We*, is it?" asked Sir Kilborn. "Did you not just leave us to look after private matters?"

Amurel was caught off guard to hear his right hand speak so. He shot Sir Kilborn a stare, but not harder than Rogan's.

"I have been striving to depose Ebon Khorel longer than anyone else alive—"

"Of course you have, Baron," Amurel jumped in. "My commander forgets himself, and we are happy to have you with us." He looked down again at the roster spilling off the desk – hundreds of names, but they were mostly untrained, and their enemy likely numbered in the thousands. "We need the rest of the Order, as soon as possible."

Sir Kilborn snorted, "Good luck getting the Prince to abandon his precious Selamus."

Amurel remained stern. "We need to convince him. It will be much easier to hold up the King-priest at Windhollow Rock than the Eight Hills. Falcionus has his own army beyond the Knights of Criesha."

"And I dare say he should send them too, Sir, but I can't imagine him doing so, can you?"

Sir Kilborn was right, of course. Amurel softened. "Maybe he will listen to Jaiden."

"Let me go," Saffron offered. "I may be able to assist in persuading the Prince."

"What does *that* mean?" Rogan asked.

Saffron narrowed her eyes at him, but turned back to Amurel before continuing. "I must confess I am worried for Dhania as well. If she returned to the capital, I would like a chance to see her and make amends."

"Your sister is not with you?" Rogan's insistence still failed to produce dividends.

Amurel bit the inside of his cheek. He preferred Saffron remain beside him, both for her influence and unquestioned usefulness on the battlefield. Yet, he remembered how the Prince of Dawn's Edge had warmed to her, and found it impossible to deny her, especially when the matter concerned her family. "Of course, Lady, I cannot think of a more adept emissary."

"Then I should be her escort," interjected Rogan. "It would be a shame to spare any soldiers – I suspect you will need them all."

For a moment, Amurel expected to see smoke rise from Rogan's armor, so hot was Saffron's stare. Her arms were crossed but the Baron matched her gaze, unwavering and patient.

"Fine," she said at last, in a way suggesting he might live to regret volunteering.

"Very well," Amurel concluded, certain now that something sour had passed between the two. He hoped they would find a way to reconcile, if only for the sake of their collective cause. "Sir Kilborn, ready the men to move out at first light. Send a rider ahead to Synirpa, and another to apprise the Duke personally. Lady Saffron, speak to Sir Luminere first. With any luck, the two of you can find a way to convince Prince Falcionus to succor us. I will lead our army to defend the castle at Windhollow Rock. Look for us there, and may Criesha deliver you with haste!"

Rogan had spent the better part of the day trailing Saffron's horse. She set a brisk pace, and although he understood her eagerness to make sure Dhania was safe, her impatience obviously doubled as an avoidance tactic.

He rose in his saddle to canter beside her, his horse's hooves clicking pleasantly against the stone-paved marvel of the Dawn Way. "Are we going to talk about this, or just ride all the way to Selamus in silence?"

Saffron brought Sheen to a sudden stop and glared at Rogan. "Oh, you want to talk about it?" He instantly regretted his approach. "What exactly do you want to talk about? How you professed your love for me after kissing my sister? Or maybe how you left the capital the morning after bedding me without even saying goodbye?" Her face flushed as she threw up her hands.

Rogan found his own sense of calm quickly boiling away under her accusations. "What did you expect me to do? I bore my soul to you, which wasn't easy, and you told me you weren't interested. Then you show up at my room an hour later and share my bed. Then the next morning, you say it was all a mistake. How is that supposed to make me feel? I'm not a handkerchief you can just use and toss away!"

Saffron's mouth dropped open for a moment, but she recovered quickly. "You don't love me, Rogan. You were drunk and just lonely since your wife died!"

Rogan was unsure what his face portrayed at the mention of Riah, but it garnered Saffron's attention. She took a deep breath and when she continued, seemed more in control. "We both had too much wine that night, and behaved unlike ourselves."

He wanted to respond, but the sting of her earlier words constricted his throat.

"I respect you tremendously, Baron. You have struggled through so much, and given years of your life to fighting for the betterment of your country. You have shown me kindness, and already risked your own life to help rescue my sister."

Rogan finally found his voice, though drained of its aggression. "Dhania did not deserve her lot, and I am sorry my actions upset her. I hope I have not damaged your relationship."

Saffron shook her head. "You are not to blame. I saw how she's looked at you since Hope's End, and discounted it because I assumed you would not be interested – and she will always be my little sister. But I was wrong to do so, and should have considered her feelings."

His unexpressed emotions had been building since leaving Selamus, and now that they found release, weariness replaced their domain. "I know it is not yet evening, but perhaps we can find a place to camp?"

She nodded and they rode in silence for another mile before locating a friendly spot. Once they settled in, Saffron played her lyre, and Rogan found his thoughts unexpectedly drifting to memories of Dhania over the last few weeks. They were all pleasant: the two of them smiling at one another or laughing over a shared joke at Jaiden's expense, the way she looked along the wall of Windhollow Castle before kissing him, or at the Prince's banquet as they shared a dance. How had he been so wrapped up in his own feelings that he missed hers?

Jaiden was slowly coming to embrace his new role of leadership in the Order. Thanks to Criesha's guidance, he realized some serenity could be found in sharing the burdens of responsibility with others. Always on the receiving end of orders in the past, it did not come naturally to him, telling others what to do.

Now, however, Palomar tutored the initiates on the doctrines of the Rising Moon, and Lothander proudly accepted a position as his squire, taking care of most of his daily needs. Lieutenant Orestes was exceedingly competent in managing the men's assignments. He somehow kept everyone busy doing something useful, while also tracking the disbursement of supplies and serving as the hub of communication for the three factions.

The men under Jaiden's command tended to be the most fervent in their loyalty and belief. Every day he was surprised by how reverently they spoke of the goddess they had never met, and their desire to please him when he gave lessons of the blade. That, at least, he enjoyed.

Though not as exhilarating as facing a true enemy, he pushed his body every day running sparring sessions and contriving battle scenarios for his men. Criesha planted the seed that, instead of requiring a nemesis to strive against, he could retain permanent motivation by focusing on becoming his perfect self. "Strive against complacency," she'd said.

So he toiled with sword and shield, both alone and with his men. He labored daily in the field with Inferno, working on balance and posture, reading his horse while learning to speak to him as well. He met with Palomar each evening to work on his letters; they were starting with Ilanese, Jaiden's native tongue. The Aasimar proved even more brilliant than he imagined and an excellent teacher, owning the knowledge of many lifetimes and a talent for assimilating new information quickly.

Still, Jaiden continued to make time for his meditations. He knew the people of Selamus rampantly speculated about his unique relationship to the goddess, often hearing them reference the miracle at Windhollow Rock while he conducted business throughout the city. He wore a plain cloak over his tabard to remain anonymous when leaving the palace, or risked being held up by admirers. Quite a following of Criesha worshippers had sprung up since his arrival, without any attention on his part. Supporters had already sought him out about the erection of a chapel dedicated to the goddess, and he spoke to them some of his devotion, but only Palomar possessed a true inkling of the depth of Jaiden's communion.

The inspection of a possible construction site drew him down from the Eighth Hill one morning, and when he ascended to the palace once more, a surprise awaited him.

"Lady Saffron has returned, Sir Luminere," Lothander informed him as they walked briskly down the hallway to his apartments. "And that Baron fellow, I think. I asked them to wait in the council chamber, but Palomar was with them and brought them directly to your quarters to catch you before daily meditation."

"It's fine, Lothander." Jaiden sighed, trying to convince himself he didn't feel the butterflies churning in his stomach. Not only did Saffron's appearance mean important news from Sir Golddrake was likely, but the last time Jaiden saw her, she was a bit put out. At least Palomar's presence would mitigate any residual malice. He hoped.

Stopping at the door, Jaiden remembered he still wore the disguising cloak and took a moment to shuffle out of it. He deposited the bundle of cloth in his squire's arms, patted down his hair and straightened his tunic, trying to remove any signs of dishevelment. After exhaling deeply, he dismissed Lothander with a nod and joined the reunion.

"I apologize if you have been waiting long," he said as his three guests turned from their conversation at his entrance. "I confess – I was not expecting a visit after so few weeks. Can I offer you something to drink?" No sooner had he spoken than Jaiden noticed Saffron and Rogan already held cups in their hands. He blinked and shook his head at the delay of his observation. "There is news from the South, I presume?"

"Nice rooms you have found for yourself." Rogan stood from leaning on the back of a finely upholstered lounge. He swirled the liquid in his goblet as his eyes paraded around the apartment, nodding at examples of the expensive décor.

Jaiden was thrown by the shift in subject. "Oh, thank you."

Saffron came next. "I spoke with Lieutenant Orestes on the way in. He said you put Dhania up in the palace, but no one seems to recall seeing her the last few days."

Jaiden's lower lip jutted out. "Really? That... seems odd."

Saffron's tongue pressed against the inside of her cheek. "Where is my sister?"

"The Lady Dhania's location does need to be ascertained, my friends," Palomar's wings stretched and folded back behind him, their golden tips shining in the late morning sunlight, catching everyone's attention, *"but perhaps we can conduct a search after delivering Sir Golddrake's urgent request to Sir Luminere?"*

"What request?" Jaiden looked from face to face, settling on Saffron's.

From the corner of her mouth she blew a strand of hair that had fallen across her forehead onto an eyebrow. "Of course." Her eyes darted to Palomar in recognition, but raced back to engage Jaiden's challenging stare. "The King-priest's army advanced in secret and was probably across the border of Halidor before we rode to Selamus."

"What?" Jaiden asked softly, his mind already calculating distances and time. He kept his eyes trained on Saffron, but stepped forward slowly until he too could lean on the lounge.

"We were at the Caves of Criesha," she continued, "when Rogan delivered the news. Sir Golddrake headed for Synirpa behind us and intends to defend the Castle at Windhollow Rock, though he implored you bring whatever forces you could muster to bolster him there."

"Orestes has already delivered directives to assemble, Sir Luminere, while you were out. I am afraid, however, that the Prince has travelled with a large portion of his command to establish the safety of the western boundary."

"When did this happen? There is nothing to the west but the Wyvernwatch," Jaiden spat. "I thought Falcionus was intent on defending the capital?"

"Apparently after news of mountain breaches in Rosegold, he wanted to be certain no such passes existed in his own province. Should I have Orestes send word to them as well?"

"Bah," Jaiden waved his hand dismissively. "Yes, but we cannot wait for them. Even if we left this afternoon, it will take us a fortnight along the Dawn Way to arrive at Windhollow altogether. Does Golddrake have that much time?" He thrust himself from the couch and walked toward one of the large windows, until he was bathed in sunlight. Jaiden stared at the heavy boughs of a mighty tree, blaming himself. "I should have ridden south with him."

"No disrespect to the Order," Rogan chimed in, "but I saw the size of this army firsthand. The North is going to need more than your collection of knights to face it. All the provinces need to band together, and quickly."

"I agree, Baron, but can only control so much. Joining Sir Golddrake and defending Windhollow is my priority now. Hopefully the nobility will follow the Order's lead and rally with us." Jaiden looked purposefully at Palomar. "Tell Orestes I have given the order to march on the morrow."

"And what about Dhania?" Saffron interjected.

It took a moment for Jaiden to register the switch in topics, but the concern in Saffron's voice compelled him. He could hear the usual sense of control slip, and understood she loved her sister, probably more than he had loved anyone. Then Jaiden slipped as well, wondering for a moment if he made the right choice, limiting himself to an otherworldly being. In many ways, Saffron embodied the vision of who he hoped to become. He realized, however, from the depths of his mind, that he would never get there without his goddess.

A soft smile concealed his flash of regret. "Give me a chance to speak with my squire. Dhania arrived to the city with him and another man. I suspect Bremmil may know where your sister is hiding." He wanted to add that he may be the one hiding her, but thought better of it. "I will question him by the end of the afternoon."

"I want to be there when you do," insisted Saffron.

"Of course. For now, though, I must ask your leave. I have a ritual to perform before I get overwhelmed with other matters."

Palomar understood what that meant, apparently, and moved to usher the others from Jaiden's chambers. "*I shall attend, too, if it pleases you. We may have more to discuss.*"

Jaiden nodded and waited patiently until he was alone. He realized the upcoming journey may make his sacred encounters harder to come by, and he intended to savor each one.

It took a few hours for Lothander to track Bremmil down, but eventually all the concerned parties gathered in the Prince's throne room, along with several guards and a scattering of curious courtiers. Notably absent was the Prince himself, though Jaiden secretly preferred it so. He wanted to utilize the Truth Aura he had gained during the recent full moon, without the scrutiny of the province's highest nobility, should he have use for it later.

Jaiden did not want to give Bremmil the impression he was under suspicion, yet wanted to be prepared if he had anything to hide. He nodded to Saffron, who was waiting beside the central approach to the throne, dressed in her red leather armor, a fierce look upon her face. Rogan stood behind her, with Palomar on the other side of the aisle, arms folded across his chest. Lothander led Bremmil just short of the throne's dais, then took a place behind him.

Jaiden stood before the throne and offered a quiet prayer to his mistress, invoking her gift. Gasps of surprise punctuated the room, confusing Jaiden, until he noticed the globe of golden-green light surrounding him. He ignored the aura and tried to act as if nothing was amiss. "Thank you for answering my summons, initiate."

Bremmil also tried to mask his amazement, though his eyes narrowed slightly before he answered. "Of course, Master Luminere, I am at your service." He bowed more deeply than necessary.

"I hoped you could assist me in determining the whereabouts of Dhania min Furasi. I am aware she travelled with Lothander and yourself from Synirpa to Selamus, several weeks ago."

Bremmil looked over his shoulder at Lothandar, before turning back to Jaiden. "Yes, I remember; a lovely young woman. I enjoyed her company immensely on the otherwise lonely road."

Jaiden heard a cursing exclamation and saw Saffron take a step forward from the corner of his eye, though Rogan reached around to hold her in check. Jaiden's tone became firmer, knowing Saffron's wrath may well fall on him if he did not yield results. "Dhania's sister is concerned that no one seems to have seen her over the last few days. Do you know where she is, Bremmil?"

The Southerner opened his mouth to speak, but seemed to have difficulty doing so. His mouth contorted, and panic flamed in his eyes before he finally found words. "I took her to the Chieftain of the Black Hill orcs as tribute."

Murmurs of shock permeated the throne room but were overpowered by Saffon's demanding voice. "You did *what?!*" This time Rogan could not hold her back and she strode directly for Bremmil, fists clenched.

"Lady Saffron!" Jaiden called out, extending his palm in her direction. "Please, restrain yourself." The sharpness of his own voice seemed to catch her, and he saw a look he guessed to be trust, flash across her face. She held her ground for the moment.

Jaiden turned back to Bremmil to follow-up on his revelation. "Where exactly did you take her, and when?" Once again, Bremmil seemed to struggle, perhaps seeking a way to mitigate the incrimination already provided. Jaiden brimmed briefly with satisfaction as his Aura compelled a truer response.

"I met Nejuk the Gouger and his entourage by night in a fallow field, just across the border into Crimsonmoon. There's an old, abandoned farmhouse north of the road. I left the Begnari girl with the orcs two nights past."

A quiet dread sank into Jaiden's stomach and he spoke more softly, unsure if he was prepared to hear the answer to his next questions. "For what purpose would you do such a thing – and on whose command?"

Disturbingly, Bremmil no longer seemed to struggle before speaking, and a wide grin ushered in his answer. "The orc king desired a noble hostage of his enemy as an assurance, and I convinced him she was a wealthy princess. All your lands are doomed, Sir Luminere. My Lord, Ebon Khorel, has a reach longer than you suspect. The orcs of the Black Hills are now his allies, and even your *friends* are susceptible to his influence." Bremmil's eyes darted almost imperceptibly behind Jaiden, toward the throne.

Jaiden caught the glance, however, and took a step of his own toward the smug Southerner. "Palomar, when is Prince Falcionus due to return?" He inwardly cursed himself for his lack of vigilance.

"Hard to say for sure, Sir Luminere, but I would not expect him back in the capital for at least another week."

"This realm will fall, Master Luminere." Bremmil spoke confidently. "You would be well served to seek terms with your new emperor before you can no longer make a show of strength. Ebon Khorel rewards his willing servants..."

Jaiden was no longer listening, his mind already preoccupied developing solutions to the growing manifest of problems he faced.

"Jaiden!" Lothander cried.

He did not notice from where Bremmil drew the dagger he suddenly thrust toward his chest, but recovered just in time to swipe the stab to the side with his forearm. Lothander dove forward and clasped his arms around Bremmil's ankles from behind, felling him to his knees. Jaiden kicked the weapon from his assailant's hand, and before the man could stand, two of the throne-room guards rushed forth and seized his arms. Palomar and Saffron were not far behind, and quickly flanked Jaiden.

"I'm all right," he said, anticipating their questions. "Take him to the dungeons," he ordered the guards. "I may have further need to interrogate him."

"Long live the Blood Tear Brotherhood!" Bremmil shrieked as they dragged him away.

"How could this happen?!" Saffron wailed as soon as Bremmil was clear of the room. "What do we know of these orcs, and why would they want my sister as a captive? She doesn't even look Ilanese."

Though she said "we," Jaiden knew the question, and her ire, were directed at him. "I doubt they would recognize the difference in human cultures," he said. "Orcs are brute creatures with minds wholly consumed by warfare. Luckily, they usually struggle against one another."

"They are not all brutes," Rogan interjected. "I knew an orc once – well, a half-breed – and his nature held an underlying gentleness."

"Half-human?" Saffron asked. "They can breed with us?"

Jaiden nodded. "I've heard of this, too. Abominations..." he stopped when he saw the implications playing out across Saffron's features. "Don't worry, we'll get your sister back unharmed."

"How can you promise that, Jaiden?" Saffron's chin quivered and her face was flushed, as if on the brink of tears. "How can you know she's *unharmed* now?"

"I do not wish to further upset Lady Saffron, but Sir Luminere, have you forgotten we leave for Windhollow on the morrow?"

"I will find Dhania," Rogan said, from behind Saffron. Jaiden, along with the rest of the room, turned to the source of the unexpected offer.

"Not without me," Saffron insisted.

"It will take more than the two of you. No doubt hundreds of savage orcs stand between Dhania and freedom." Jaiden knew his duty to Sir Golddrake, but felt the pull of personal guilt for not better protecting Saffron's sister.

"Perhaps sending Ymrilad would help – he is a capable defender."

Jaiden weighed Palomar's suggestion as his brain filtered the myriad responsibilities required to get the Order marching to war. He simply could not do both. He bowed his head, reluctantly giving in to reality. "Yes, send him with my blessing, if he is willing."

Saffron spoke more calmly than before, a hint of regret tinging her speech. "Thank you, Jaiden. I will leave as soon as possible. Tell Amurel I am sorry not to join him at the castle, but I hope to see you both as soon as destiny allows."

Jaiden nodded and she left the room with Rogan in tow. He waited a few more seconds before confiding in Palomar, his voice low so the other courtiers could not eavesdrop. "Did it seem to you that Bremmil suggested the Prince had struck some sort of alliance with the King-priest?"

"I would not invest too much into the words of a Blood Tear agent; deception is their daily fare."

"Normally I would agree with you, but he was incapable of lying within my aura."

"Is that what this is?" Palomar asked, gesturing to the iridescent globe surrounding Jaiden. "Still, *planting a seed of doubt is not the same as lying.*"

"I suppose. But if I leave Selamus now, are we going to return to find ourselves facing more enemies? Although Falcionus is the Prince, I fight to protect the people."

"*I believe there is enough to worry over without inviting dissention. Perhaps such questions can wait until a problem manifests. Speculation is moot if we fail to prove victorious over Ebon Khorel. Besides, how would it change your course? We cannot abandon Sir Golddrake in his need.*"

"True enough, my friend." Being on the verge of facing the King-priest's army was plenty to worry over. He bowed his head and muttered a short prayer of thanks to Criesha for her gifts, and the circle of light surrounding him melted away. Given time, however, he would try and extract more from the turncoat, though compelling a Blood-tear agent to give up secrets might prove a fruitless task. Bremmil would not be caught unaware twice. "I should continue preparing for the march."

"*Before you do, Willem the Shaper asked that I bring you to his chambers to receive a boon. He said it would aid you in the upcoming struggle.*"

A snorting laugh unintentionally escaped Jaiden as he stepped down from the dais. "I am not going to turn down any help at this late hour. Let us see what the Shaper of Selamus has to offer. Perhaps he holds a secret bit of wisdom we can use, or knows a trick to somehow double our numbers."

The pair saved their breath as they climbed the numerous steps to the Shaper's quarters at the top of the tower. Jaiden occasionally saw Willem around the halls of the palace, but had failed to take initiative uncovering the resource he suspected the old man could be. Timing had always been poor, and he had foolishly assumed there would be more chances to feed his curiosity.

Jaiden knocked twice when they reached the door at the top of the stairs, which was left open a crack. "Willem, are you in here?" he asked as he pushed the portal wider and took a step into the Shaper's apartments.

"Ah, Sir Luminere and my favorite Celestial! I was hoping you would have time to visit." Willem was on his tiptoes placing his pet bird, Lydia, back into her cage. "Come in, no need to be shy."

Palomar placed a hand on Jaiden's back and nudged him forward. *"You will need to go further inside to see."* An unusual excitement tinted the Aasimar's words, as if he was in on a secret about to be revealed.

"Ah, yes, sir," Jaiden stammered after a quick look over his shoulder at Palomar. "I am told you wished to see me before the Order begins our march tomorrow."

"Indeed, I do." Willem pushed the sleeves of his sky-blue robes back to his elbows. His cloudy eye still unnerved Jaiden when staring straight at it. Lydia let out a whistle as the pair drew closer, and Willem stepped away from her cage, drawing Jaiden's attention to the other side of the room.

Draped over what appeared to be an armor-stand was a thick, wine-colored cloth. "Now, we had intended to bestow this gift upon you in a more formal ceremony," Willem said, resting his arm atop the cloaked object, "but there is no time for that now, and it is something you should definitely have before riding off to battle. For saving my granddaughter, you have earned my gratitude."

Willem whisked the cloth aside to reveal a shining set of full plate armor. The mail glistened silver in the sunlight, offset with violet trim and intricate embellishments. The visored helm had a singular spiral horn thrusting outward like a unicorn, and the crescent moon of Criesha was emblazoned on the center of the breastplate.

Jaiden was stupefied and speechless, and peeked over his shoulder to see Palomar grinning in return.

"*A fair improvement from the old chain hauberk you've been donning, no?*"

"I... don't know what to say," Jaiden posited, still searching for the words. The armor was worth more than he and his father had made in their entire lifetimes, together. "It's magnificent," he finally managed, only after reaching a hand out to trace the metal and confirm it was no illusion.

"And it is more than just a pretty coat," Willem added, his voice brimming with excitement. "You will find when worn, the suit feels like it weighs almost nothing. But the second enchantment – well, I'll let you see that for yourself." The Shaper craned his neck from one side to the other, sizing up his guests. "Neither of you are armed?"

Jaiden patted his hips, confirming he had not brought his sword.

"No matter, I have something that will do." Willem retreated to his desk in the far corner of the room and came back holding a thin, iron rod, which he handed to Jaiden. "Any metal will suffice," he added, though Jaiden had no idea what he was hinting at.

Jaiden clasped the rod with both hands away from his body, waiting to hear why it was given to him. The iron was cold but not too heavy, about two feet long and thin as a riding crop.

Willem shrugged and gestured toward the armor. "Go ahead, have a swing."

Jaiden laughed briefly, expecting to be the butt of a joke, but Willem merely stood silently, waiting for his participation. "Alright," he declared, releasing his left-handed grip on the rod. He stepped forward and thrust as if the thin bar were a rapier. Though he had sized up the dead center of the breastplate, his strike went askew, missing the armor entirely.

Willem clapped and let out a gleeful squeal. "Oh come now, Sir Luminere, your target is not even moving!"

Bewildered by his embarrassing failure, Jaiden reset his base and hacked downward, this time simulating a sweep from his broadsword. He put his body into the blow, aiming for the middle of the right shoulder guard. As the rod came closer to the armor, he felt it forcefully deflected from its path, until it did no more than glance off the flank of the breastplate. The redirection caused Jaiden to stumble and nearly fall over.

"*Watch yourself!*" Palomar stepped forward to steady him.

Jaiden looked up at Willem, who had an unshakable grin on his face. "How is this happening?"

"Your armor *repels* metal. Is it not brilliant?" he squeezed out, shaking his fists in front of him. "The more force behind the blow, the greater the resistance. It would take a giant's war hammer to overcome the effect."

"It really is a fine suit, Willem. We will have need of protection in the coming days."

The Shaper's tone sobered almost instantly at Palomar's reminder of the trials ahead. "Aye, my friends. I wish I could give you more. There are worse things than weapons awaiting you at the hands of the King-priest, I'm afraid."

"You have done more than enough, Lord Willem." Jaiden handed the iron rod back to his host. "I appreciate your gift more than I can express, and will wear it proudly into battle."

"Well," Willem shrugged, "the Prince paid for it."

Chapter 30

The Defense of Windhollow

"We need to be quick, but careful," Amurel noted, and Sir Kilborn nodded in response, neither of them moving their eyes from the map spread before them. Two torches provided the only light in the deep meeting-chamber of the Caves of Criesha. Baron Rogan and Saffron had left the day before, while the Order of the Rising Moon worked to store supplies before a hasty return to Windhollow Rock.

"I want as much time as possible to prepare our defenses, though it won't do to rush into an unfavorable scenario. We need to ascertain the King-priest's whereabouts and what we're facing, as best we can."

"Might I suggest three pairs of scouts for reconnaissance, Sir?" Kilborn weighed in. "One north, to make sure the enemy is not already ahead of us, and two south." He traced a gauntleted finger across the map. "If they come upon Chelpian forces, they can return and let us know how far off. If they make it all the way to Halidor Keep, they can remain as lookouts at the crossroads."

"And the third pair?" Amurel's brow creased. He did not relish subtracting more men from the coming fighting effort.

"If they make it to Halidor," Sir Kilborn repeated, "the third pair can ride on to Greyhorne and raise the alarm there. The Order has connections – perhaps the town can send us aid. If not, they deserve to know the danger."

"Aye," Amurel agreed. They had encamped beside the mountain town on several occasions, but its location was easily cut off from the rest of the province. He looked at the minimal space between where the Caves and Synirpa were marked on the map. Then his eyes travelled the relative expanse between there and Selamus. He hoped Saffron and Jaiden were both able to make quick journeys, but his practical mind was already preparing for the likelihood their help would not come in time. "Time to get our horses ready, Geldrick," he said as he rolled up the map. "Let our troops know we leave in an hour, regardless of where the preparations stand."

The narrow switchbacks descending the hill always required concentration, though Amurel had little to spare. Fortunately,

Bastion had made the trek before and stepped carefully down the slopes without much need for guidance. Amurel's attention kept swimming back to his recent dream of Criesha. Her first visit in some time left him unsure as to its meaning. Sometimes it took days to come to terms with an interpretation, though he prided himself on extracting the intended meaning from her interludes. In this way, she had guided him for several years.

Considering what his goddess had done for Jaiden, he could not shake the idea Criesha meant to extend a healing blessing to him as well, perhaps after fighting bravely in the upcoming battle. The thought made him hopeful and nervous at once. What would it be like to run on his own? To jump and even sit without discomfort? He tried pushing down such ideas as they surfaced. This fight would be the hardest his men had ever faced. They would not have the advantage, even with the strong castle protecting them.

Though the foothills kept the going slow, at last the land leveled and the Dawn Way stretched before them. Its paved surface would convey them quickly the rest of the way, but Amurel paused nonetheless. They would be vulnerable in the open if another ambush awaited. The scouts had about an hour head-start and would be riding faster, which should give them ample warning if enemies lay in wait. Of course, not if the scouts themselves were ambushed; he had not forgotten their decimation a few short months ago.

He scanned the horizon both north and south, but no omens presented for interpretation. "Criesha protect us," he uttered, then urged Bastion onto the northbound road. By lessening their burden at the Caves, the Order made much better time on their return trip. The journey to Windhollow Rock was not exceedingly far, though the threat of ambush made the leagues stretch longer. An hour before sunset the northbound scouts returned, proclaiming the road ahead free of enemies. More at ease, Amurel set an ambitious pace. Riding well past nightfall brought them within sight of the castle's stone-gray walls, painted turquoise by the moonlight.

The Duke of Rosegold, flanked by two men-at-arms, greeted Amurel in the courtyard outside the stables, though most of the castle slept. "How now, Sir Golddrake? I expected you well on your way to Halidor."

Amurel handed Bastion's reins to another soldier. "I beg your pardon for the late hour, Your Grace."

The Duke waved off his apology. "Oh, I don't sleep all that well these days, anyway. So what news predicates your return?"

"The dire sort, I'm afraid." Amurel noticed that the Duke indeed seemed wide awake and focused, almost vibrant. Perhaps he expected to hear of war upon being roused. "Baron Rogan came across the Chelpian army not far across the border some nights back. We expect they are marching for us, and could arrive any day now."

"Well then," the Duke responded coolly, utterly unsurprised, "I suppose it is fortuitous the Aasimar arrived shortly ago."

"The Aasimar? Was Sir Luminere with them?" Amurel dared to hope that somehow Jaiden had started marching south on his own, knowing there had not yet been time for Saffron to reach him.

"Nay, no men came with them. That Illicurus fellow had a feeling we would be seeing the King-priest again sooner rather than later." The Duke looked around the courtyard, where men and horses still flowed through the gates. "Come, Sir, you and your folk must be weary from riding. Take your rest and we can talk strategy in the morning. I will set my men to preparing the castle."

Amurel assented, though he suspected that much like the Duke, he would not find sleep easily.

In the light of morning, the Castle at Windhollow Rock resembled a beehive bustling with activity. With the addition of Amurel and his troops, the place had become crowded, and it dawned on the Master that it would be impossible for the entire Order to simply dig-in behind the fortress walls. Their numbers had swelled too much, and most of his faction remained camped outside Synirpa.

The Duke had apparently risen early, and was overseeing defense preparations from the battlements when Amurel found him. "Your men seem to be handling this well," Amurel offered.

"Few of us remain from the last time the King-priest laid siege, but we have a fair idea what we're up against. They have the numbers, for sure, but will have a hard time spanning the gulf."

Amurel joined him in looking down the outside of the wall, which presented a drop of over a hundred feet to the cauldron of the quarry below. A crushing death against jagged stone awaited any who fell from such heights. The narrow, winding approach was the only easy way to reach the castle, a precarious journey for more than two riders abreast. Its slope and shape prevented a charge, and archers manning the wall could easily concentrate fire upon intruders. Even more daunting, Amurel noticed sturdy ballistae positioned at regular stations along the battlements.

Men passed back and forth along the wall, asking for pardon as they squeezed past Amurel and their lord. All around the grounds, soldiers and common laborers kept busy sharpening weapons, stocking arrows, preparing buckets of pitch to douse their enemies, and water to put out fires started by incendiary projectiles.

"The King-priest may not have shown his entire hand the last time," Amurel cautioned, though he was just as unsure of what to expect. Who knew what powers his dark pact with Gholdur yielded?

"Good thing we didn't, either," the Duke of Rosegold replied, nodding at the Aasimar flying javelins up to a high-mounted ballista. "This castle has never fallen, and we have Celestials now." He patted Amurel's shoulder reassuringly.

In turn, Amurel cast his gaze toward the eastern horizon, where the boundary of a thick wood could be distinguished. "What is that forest, there?"

The Duke craned his neck to look out over his lands. "That is the Balewood; marks the boundary of Naresgreen. Good timber there, and the best source for thirty leagues not controlled by the Eladrin." He studied Amurel's face and his eyes narrowed. "What of it?"

"I was just contemplating what to do with the rest of my men. We cannot all hole up in your castle, Your Grace. I want them closer than Synirpa, but not out in the open. I was thinking we might use the trees for cover."

The Duke's lower lip jutted out and he tilted his head. "That may work. You wouldn't be the first to hide in those woods, and they would at least break a charge if you were discovered early."

The sky grayed with seeded clouds from the south as Amurel weighed his options. The Duke's confidence was well-founded; Windhollow was an extraordinary citadel, which had already withstood one attack from the King-priest. And yet, doubt held firmly in Amurel's gut. If it was planned all along to weaken the north through plague and spread its armies by waging false attacks, then what other subterfuge might await? It simply did not feel like enough to trust in the hard stone and stalwart defense of the castle. Taking Windhollow Rock would open the doorway to the rest of the provinces, but could they even be confident in knowledge of the King-priest's goals?

Amurel made his decision – it would not do to have the majority of their forces locked behind high walls on an island. He had faith the vision his Goddess granted bound him for glory. "Your Grace, it is clear you know how to defend your own castle. The horses will do scant good behind your walls, so if you consent, I would take all you can spare and mount more of my Order. We'll set up a position in the Balewood." He grasped the outer rim of the palisade and leaned over the edge, peering across the tree-dotted fields toward the shadow of the looming forest. "It seems better than being caught in the open, and may allow us to flank the Chelpians once they arrive."

"I don't wager there will be need, Master Golddrake, but you have my consent," the Duke answered. "Your reputation for horsemanship is not unknown to me."

"My thanks," Amurel nodded. His affinity for riding was part of his decision. He strongly preferred meeting an enemy in open combat to waiting ineffectually within a confined space. "I will leave immediately, then. Without knowing the King-priest's whereabouts, every moment could be precious." He bowed and limped to the stairway, leaning on his favorite cane.

Once at the stables, he saddled Bastion, who whinnied at his preparations. "Yes boy, time for another ride. I hope you enjoyed your oats."

A voice from behind caught him unaware. "Surely you just overlooked telling me where you were off to?" Sir Kilborn's heavy shadow fell across the floor of the stables.

"Geldrick," Amurel paused, "I did not tell you because I want you to stay here."

"I will ride at your side as always, Sir." Sir Kilborn's arms were crossed; he was not submitting easily.

"This is the most dangerous foe we have faced, my friend. Ever." Amurel finished securing Bastion's bridle and turned to face his longtime companion. "You saw what the King-priest did to Halidor Keep. Even the Aasimar, together, fled before him. There is a better chance one of us survives if we fight apart. Besides, I will need you to direct our forces inside the citadel."

"*You* have a better chance of surviving if I'm watching your back, and that is all that matters," Sir Kilborn countered.

Amurel let out a sigh. "Not this time, Geldrick. What matters most is that we stop Ebon Khorel here. If we do not, he will scourge the north with wan resistance." Even Sir Kilborn's thick mustache could not hide his scowl. "Do not fret, my friend; Criesha has blessed me on this endeavor."

"All the more reason for me to stay close, then." Though his words did not relent, Sir Kilborn slowly unfolded his arms, showing resignation.

Amurel pushed out a weak smile. "We're going to camp near the edge of the Balewood forest. I will see you in a few days, when this is all over." Amurel tucked his cane through a loop and into a pocket on his saddlebags, then mounted his horse in a fluid motion. "Or, who knows? Perhaps the King-priest will not have the stomach for another siege and bugger on home."

"Ha, we can only hope."

Amurel looked straight into his friend's eyes, allowing a moment of solemnity. "May Criesha be with you, Sir Geldrick Kilborn."

A brief rumbling vibrated Sir Kilborn's throat, but then he placed a hand softly on Bastion's neck. "Criesha be with you."

Amurel led Bastion out of the stables and into the courtyard, where a company of mounted soldiers drew into ranks behind him and followed in a slow progression from the castle gates. The short trip to Synirpa gave him barely enough time to formulate a strategy.

The way he saw it, the enemy's strengths were superior numbers and the magic they channeled from Gholdur the Tyrant. He had to find a way to neutralize those advantages. The assets of he and his allies included the cavalry's speed, the flight and shaping prowess of the Aasimar, and the heretofore impenetrable fortress of Windhollow Rock.

One sticking point in his plan was his ignorance of the Gholdur priests' capabilities. He saw some of their work during the attack on Blackthorn prison, but Palomar alluded to the King-priest's more significant mastery. According to his story, Ebon Khorel might have conjured and controlled the power of a thunderstorm. Clearly, he was a threat they had to neutralize as quickly as possible.

If Amurel could keep a mobile force concealed in the woods, they might be able to flank the Chelpian army once it settled in. Using maneuverability to their advantage, they could cull the weaker ranks from the rear formations while simultaneously providing a moving target against the enemy's magic. Amurel hoped the strength of the castle's defenses, coupled with whatever surprises the Aasimar had in store, would be enough to frustrate their opponent into committing tactical mistakes. He also knew, though, the unexpected could force his own designs into disarray.

He was pleased to see deconstruction of the camp outside Synirpa already underway upon his force's arrival. His scouts apparently met no resistance while delivering his orders to the largely unseasoned troops. When the Order of the Rising Moon was smaller, training and quality of equipment were always strengths. Now, however, the majority of recruits were still raw, though his captains tenaciously drilled discipline and fighting techniques over the last few weeks.

Amurel spent the rest of his day receiving reports, issuing orders, and preparing the mobilization of supplies. He sent men to watch the Dawn Way in both directions; south for the approach of the oncoming hordes, and north with the hope of spotting reinforcements. Sunrise heralded deployment down the Tor March, the eastbound path leading through the Balewood toward the Fire-wall Mountains. Amurel's stomach churned all through the morning, anxious that the fight would be underway before he got his men into position.

The rain they seemed to dodge the previous day finally unleashed upon them, slowing his troop's progress. The days had already grown hot with summer just around the corner, so the downpour was not wholly unwelcome, but Amurel challenged his troops to pick up their pace.

His concerns turned out baseless, however, for they reached the edge of the Balewood in late afternoon, with no evidence of an invading army. The rain dissipated and he let his men settle in, reminding them to remain alert and prepared to mobilize at a moment's notice. The horses were to remain saddled. As darkness fell, Amurel only allowed the lighting of fires well beyond the tree line, where their radiance was shrouded behind the massive trunks of ancient elms.

He could not shake his own sense of anticipation, and stayed on his steed at the edge of the forest, staring back toward Windhollow Rock as twilight yielded to a canopy of stars. Had Rogan been mistaken? With Sir Kilborn not present to allay his doubts, he turned to Bastion instead.

"What do you think, boy? Did we come all this way for nothing?"

Bastion emitted a short, noncommittal grunt, then dipped his head to snap off a few leaves from the undergrowth just within reach. Amurel watched the open field for change until the last of the sky's purple was replaced by indigo. He could still hear his horse chewing, and it elicited a growl from his own stomach. "How are you so much wiser than me, boy? Time to get some supper, I suppose."

Amurel turned Bastion and made a clicking noise, which was enough to initiate their return to camp. He chose a fire that already had a pot of stew steaming above it and dismounted, handing the reins to a diligent page. "What are we cooking tonight?" he asked the group circled around the flames.

"Rabbit, Sir," the man stirring the pot responded.

"More or less," another added, drawing laughter from his peers.

"Pay them no mind, Master," the cook retorted, already ladling a healthy portion of broth into an extra bowl. "They just don't appreciate the nuances of a fine stew."

Amurel received the bowl with a hint of suspicion, but tried not to let it show. "I am certain it is delicious." He inhaled inconspicuously; it smelled good enough. He could feel the collective eyes of the group watching as he tentatively scooped a mouthful of the brown liquid and swallowed. It tasted good to him, but no sooner had he nodded his approval than one of his captains hailed from behind.

"Sir Golddrake, pardon the intrusion, but one of the Aasimar has just arrived."

Amurel shoved the bowl back into the hands of the cook and called in the direction of the page, "Bring me my horse!" He turned to the captain who brought the news. "Take me to him."

The man nodded and waited for Amurel to mount, then walked him to a more secluded clearing where an Aasimar with liquid bronze hair was waiting – Thuriken. Several other soldiers stood within earshot, hoping to get first-hand intelligence from the angelic ambassador.

"*Sir Amurel Golddrake,*" he bowed, "*Marshall Illicurus commanded I inform you the Chelpian army has been spotted on approach to the castle.*"

"Where and how far?"

"*To the south, but not along the road. They travel cross-country to no doubt limit detection, but will arrive tonight, lest they halt their march. We are content to wait for them at Windhollow, but the Marshall wanted you to know in order to prepare.*"

"You can give your Marshall my thanks, Thuriken."

The Aasimar bowed again, his message delivered, and walked westward toward the edge to the wood.

The time had come. That sobering thought occupied Amurel's head for a few moments before he could move on to issuing commands. "Captain, spread the word, but keep the men calm. We have no need for haste yet, and I don't want excitement leading to ill preparation."

"Yes, Sir. What should we have them preparing for, exactly?" he asked with eager eyes.

"We want the enemy entrenched," Amurel explained. "We'll creep south a bit through the forest, hopefully unnoticed, and circle around to their supply lines and reinforcements. I wouldn't be surprised if the fiends fought better by night, so we'll likely wait until dawn."

"Yes, Sir." With that, the man directed the onlookers who had overheard to go spread the word, and started toward the next clearing to do the same.

Amurel sighed. He already knew he was not getting any sleep tonight, though he prayed his men could. They would need all their strength for the morning's charge. He nudged Bastion back toward the border of the Balewood, prepared to stare into the darkness until fatigue took him. Once the open field lay before him, he climbed from his horse, so Bastion could rest his legs. Amurel sat on a patch of uncut grass and looked for his moon.

Criesha was falling away from full but still bright, and the steady blue of the smaller Hurn mixed with her light to paint nighted silhouettes a tranquil aquamarine. They chased across the northern sky, reminding Amurel that Jaiden was likely still far off in Selamus. "Help me fulfill the destiny you've planned for me," he murmured, then closed his eyes to continue praying in silence.

He must have found sleep after all, if only for a couple hours, as the moons had moved considerably when he caught himself tipping from his seated position. For a moment he thought he was dreaming, spotting an arc of red-orange light shooting across the sky, low to the horizon. At the end of its journey, it flashed brightly for an instant, accompanied by a distant, popping rumble. Another soon followed, and the truth dawned on him – the battle had already begun!

Amurel scrambled to his feet, nearly falling in the process. He placed his foot in the stirrup and grabbed hold of the pommel, then stopped, staring back toward the castle. He realized the start of the assault changed nothing. Sticking to the plan, they would still have to wait until morning to move. The forces at Windhollow Rock needed to survive the night.

Even though Amurel's muscles twitched with longing to join the fray, he swung into the saddle under controlled deliberation. He could at least confer with his captains and gather information. Simply sitting idle for hours might be too hard to bear. No sooner had he pulled the reins left directing Bastion toward camp, then Thuriken's voice in his head halted him.

"Sir Golddrake, I bring urgent tidings!"

Seconds later, Amurel caught the tint of the Aasimar's metallic hair and wing-tips in the moonlight as he silently descended to the ground. "What is it, Thuriken? I already noticed that the King-priest has arrived."

"Not at the castle, Sir. We are besieged, yes, but only with the purpose of pinning us in, I fear. The King-priest broke off and is moving west with the majority of his troops." Thuriken gestured emphatically across the open field. *"The Duke of Rosegold fears he intends to sack the under-guarded Synirpa. He beseeches you to intervene."*

"They have too much of a head start for the footmen to be of use," Amurel thought aloud. Then, to Thuriken, "Will the castle hold?"

"It is still early, but the Duke is confident. The walls are bombarded, but once the King-priest has moved far enough that his magic is no longer a threat, Illicurus intends to harry their siege engines."

Amurel nodded. The situation was far from ideal, but little was in war. "I will lead the cavalry back along the Tor March and try to cut them off. My ground troops will flank those who attack the castle at sunrise. Illicurus and the Duke can take advantage of that to initiate sorties if they choose."

Thuriken nodded his understanding. *"Good speed to you, Sir Golddrake. May the righteous ever triumph."* Without another word, the Aasimar leapt into the air and thrust his powerful wings downward, feathers glinting like dancing stars as he receded into the distant night.

The hour was late, but no rest dwelled in sight. Amurel quickly returned to camp, summoning his knights with all the immediacy he could muster. They could reach Synirpa in an hour if they pushed – under two if he let the horses conserve strength. Either way lacked assurance of arriving before the King-priest.

They rode hard to start, surging down the Tor March north of the embattled castle. Thundering hooves bore nearly three hundred warriors of the finest mounted force in the Cradle. Amurel tried to keep faith it would be enough to save the people of Synirpa. Once the distance was halved he slowed their pace, lest exhaustion dampen their prowess. The midnight journey seemed surreal with blue and green moonlight tinting the Order's white tabards the shade of dreams. The warm night wind licked the sweat from Amurel's neck as he passed orchard and field, still no destination in sight.

A fine night for a ride, he noted, under different circumstances. The land they passed was soft and tranquil, bearing no hint of the violence awaiting them. Eventually, however, the fires came into view. The eastern edge of the city was ablaze, and as Amurel drew closer he could see a steady line of dark shapes flowing north along the Dawn Way, parallel to the stream that abutted it. They were heading for the wide bridge that crossed it at the intersection of the Tor March, though their predecessors had already spilled out in force onto the field where the Order had recently resided.

Taking the bridge would be Amurel's first tactical goal. His men would ride down those pinned between them and the water, and prevent any more of the Chelpian invaders from crossing in peace. Even with the hindrance of night and the clamor of their own armies, some of the enemy horde had already spotted them – three hundred sets of hooves pounding the earth was far from subtle. But their tight ranks allowed little response.

When Amurel was close enough to pick out individual limbs he drew his sword and initiated the charge. He gave a fearful cry, picked up by his followers, which turned into a roar that seemed to panic the section of soldiers unfortunate enough to stand in their direct path. The enemy attempted to scatter in either direction along the Dawn Way, pushing futilely against the continuing march of their unaware brethren to the south. The resulting stalemate doomed them.

The column of Amurel's knights flared out as they drove into the wall of black-clad foes, cleaving some with fast-arcing steel as their horses trampled and crushed the bones of others. They secured the bridge within moments, some spilling across into the field beyond while others pushed their way south, pressing the advantages of horseback and surprise. The Chelpians along the Dawn Way continued to fall back. With only around ten paces of room to maneuver on either side of the road – water flanked one side and thick trees the other – their superior numbers were rendered meaningless.

Amurel had crossed the bridge with the first wave and led a frighteningly efficient attack on the far bank. The foot soldiers on the perimeter quickly fled toward the city, where the bulk of their allies congregated. Amurel followed their flight with his eyes, taking in for the first time the sheer volume of the Chelpian army.

The exhilaration of the initial charge faded as the enormity of the task at hand sank in. At least a thousand black forms had already crossed ahead of him. His resolve returned, however, as he noticed an enemy unit on horseback breaking free of the masses, riding in his direction.

"With me!" he called to nearby horsemen, rallying a contingent of his vanguard to follow against the approaching threat. Nearly a dozen knights gathered in formation and separated from the bulk of the slaughter, joining Amurel as he bolted toward the enemy cavalry. The two groups headed for a collision, led by Amurel in violet and white, and the Chelpian commander in chain armor and black furs, his face masked by a spider-like helm.

The distance between them evaporated with every thunderous heartbeat. With the aid of Criesha's light, Amurel noticed the opposing leader wielded a double-bladed axe and no shield, so at the last second he yanked Bastion to the right of the oncoming horse. The spider-helmed warrior had no time to shift his weapon to his left side, and Amurel extended his own shield-arm, slicing a gash into his enemy's left bicep as they passed.

Then he ducked, avoiding a blow from the rider passing to his right, and whipped his own sword in a wide arc, catching the back of his attacker as he whisked by. The rest of the mounted warriors engaged a moment later, a cacophony of metal striking metal ringing up to the night sky as their weapons clashed.

Bastion and Amurel were of one mind and the horse pivoted and leapt to the side, reversing direction quicker than any of the others could manage. Amurel was able to fell two of the Chelpians before they could even turn to face him. The enemy commander was soon upon him again, though, his heavy axe surging downward in a bid to separate Amurel from his arm. He parried the blow with his sword, but the force of it pushed the flat of his blade into the forehead of his own helmet.

Another horse beside him fell with a vibrating scream, and Amurel barely had time to push away his opponent's axe before Bastion leapt into the body of the attacker's horse to avoid the crashing beast beside him. The impact knocked the spider-helmed Chelpian askew in his saddle, one foot slipping free from its stirrup. Amurel's countless hours on horseback allowed him to recover a second sooner, which was all he needed.

His enemy's arms raised automatically to regain his equilibrium, and Amurel struck, extending his sword tip-first into the man's ribs. Once he broke past the chainmail, flesh offered little resistance. Bastion lunged forward to break clear of the clutter, and Amurel's weapon slid free of the warrior's body, opening a wound that surely included a punctured lung.

The man slumped over at first, clutching the gash with his left hand before simply sliding off his saddle to the ground. Amurel caught the last of their mounted foes being cleaved from either side by two of his men, of which he had only lost three. They were given no time to rejoice or recover the bodies, however, as a volley of arrows suddenly rained down.

The darkness made it difficult for the archers to assess distance, which may have been all that saved them. Even so, Bastion caught an arrow in his front shoulder, while another deflected harmlessly off the greave covering Amurel's right shin. He raised his shield and frantically searched for cover, but found none. Their best defense would be to keep moving and engage more of the enemy as soon as possible. Such worries soon passed, for once again the enemy found him.

In the distance, warning bells assured the entire populace of Synirpa was roused, and for a moment, everything else seemed frozen by their somber cadence. The Order had mowed down scores of enemy soldiers, and all near the bridge who had not fled perished. Half of Amurel's cavalry gathered behind him, forming a line that awaited the signal to charge. The other half battled steadfastly on the other side of the fast-flowing stream, stemming the advancing tide of soldiers.

Though he expected more arrows, another cluster of riders galloped forth from the midst of the dark mass laying between Amurel and the walls of the city, coming to a halt a hundred paces short of his position. Their bodies were blacker than the night around them, though the glint of moonlight betrayed metallic forms atop the horses – if that's what they were. The distance was too great to be certain, but both the steeds and their riders seemed to exhibit flashes of red flame where otherwise eyes would have been.

The figure in their center raised an arm, palm to the sky, and the gesture was answered seconds later by a thick column of red-gold fire surging down to Amurel's right, directly into his line of knights. Those struck directly were incinerated by the blast, while the horses nearby broke into a panic, screaming and bolting from the heat as best they could.

"Merciful Criesha!" Amurel cried, then responded with action. He gave no order but dug his heels into his horse's flank, spurring him forward. Bastion obeyed, bravely ignoring the arrow embedded in his shoulder. Amurel's men who still controlled their horses followed suit, forming a wave of thunder set to crash upon their enemies, outnumbered though they were.

The group of outlying black riders was not large, numbering only seven, though they made no move to retreat. Amurel considered whether they foolishly thought magic would protect them from the charging hooves and steel, but as he drew closer, his bravado quickly shifted to doubt.

The central figure was none other than the King-priest of Chelpa. He wore uril-chent armor and bore a chain around his neck, holding a glowing red pendant at his breast. The six knights surrounding him were not men at all, but rather the living statues of uril-chent Rogan had warned them of! Their chiseled black forms held barbed spears, and a slit across their faces burned with malevolent red light.

What's more, each of their horses appeared not made of flesh, but ethereal shadow and smoke. Fear of that beyond his understanding seized Amurel, but he remained resolute, asking his Goddess's protection from the Dread Tyrant's devilry. He drove directly for Ebon Khorel, ringed by his unnatural servants, and holding a wicked morning star in his right hand.

One of the uril-chent golems urged his steed forward to block Amurel's charge, thrusting his spear forward as he drew within range. Amurel deflected the attack with his shield, and as Bastion drew up on his hind legs to avoid crashing into his shadowy counterpart, Amurel brought his sword down heavily upon the golem.

The vibration of the handle jarred his hand as the blade shattered against the body of dark metal. All around him, the shouts of his men and the sounds of horses and steel rose as his knights joined the attack. As his sword broke, Amurel realized he had made a mistake, that this was exactly what the King-priest wanted.

The Order of the Rising Moon had Ebon Khorel surrounded by a collection of its most competent mounted warriors, but victory was not nearly as close. As Amurel discarded the broken hilt and drew the dagger at his side, he caught his brethren encountering his same futility. Blow after blow struck their foes, but neither metal nor smoke suffered injury.

The uril-chent golem before him callously drove his spear into Bastion's chest, eliciting a sound of desperate pain Amurel had never heard from his faithful steed. All too quickly, his horse's head collapsed, inevitably followed by his entire body. Amurel lost the grip on his dagger as his horse plummeted to the earth, and felt his own surge of agony as Bastion's considerable weight crushed his most useful leg beneath him. His shield impacted the turf instantly after, and his head whipped sideways into the ground, jarring his senses.

Through his daze, Amurel let out a moaning cry, summoned from his broken heart. In that moment he lost all concern for victory, danger, or the future. Bastion had been taken from him, and that was all he knew. A wayward hoof clanked against his helmet an instant later, sparing him from the decimation of his loss.

Something cold and wet suddenly soaked Amurel's face, and his tongue protruded from a parched mouth to taste it. His eyes opened slowly, squinting, though the room around him was dim. Everything ached, though the pain of his broken leg was most acute. Metal pinched his wrists, and his head throbbed as if he had been hung upside-down for a week.

He was bound, he realized, strung vertically by iron manacles upon crossed, wooden beams. A rectangle of light marked an open doorway, but the walls were hewn from stone. If he had to, he would guess he was somewhere in Windhollow Rock. Whoever splashed him must not have been satisfied, for another bucketful smacked him square in the face. This time his senses responded more quickly, and through the dripping water he saw a bald man dressed in a plain, gray shirt.

"Leave him alone!"

The familiar voice came from across the room to his right. Scratchier than normal, he had no doubt it belonged to Sir Kilborn. Amurel tried to lift and turn his head to see his friend, but the motion redoubled the pain, and he let his chin fall back to his chest. The man in front of him grunted then backed out of sight, and a second voice spoke from directly across the room.

"It is quite remarkable we were able to find you." An accent tortured the vowels, similar to the way Baron Rogan spoke, but more exaggerated. He surmised the speaker was Chelpian as well. "I was told the Master of the Order was a cripple, but did not believe it so until they brought you before me. Why would anyone follow a man with such a... deformity as yours? You must make up for it somehow, no?"

The man remained far enough away that Amurel finally forced himself to raise his head in order to see him. When he did, he immediately recognized the ornate black armor and ruby pendant around the man's neck – none other than the King-priest, himself. His olive-skinned face bore a black goatee, flecked with gray, and a small, curved scar marred the check below his left eye.

"You are Sir Golddrake, yes?"

Amurel did not bother to answer, but wondered who besides Sir Kilborn might be present.

"Don't feel like speaking, eh? Perhaps I can change your mind." The King-priest finally stepped forward, and once he closed within a body-length, Amurel was seized by a new pain. The skin over his entire body seemed to tighten and itch, and when he looked up at his right hand, he saw it shriveling before his eyes, his flesh withering on his bones. After a few seconds, Ebon Khorel stepped back and the sensation ceased, though the effects remained.

"What have you done, monster?!" Sir Kilborn shouted, though Amurel could not break his gaze from his emaciated limb.

Ebon Khorel ignored the outburst and spoke calmly. "I will be honest with you, and perhaps you can be the same. Your end will not be pleasant, Sir Golddrake of the North. There is nothing you can do to escape your fate, but perhaps, after today, we might understand one another better. Let me take this off – I do not wish our time to end too quickly."

Amurel lifted his eyes enough to watch the King-priest removing the pendant from his neck. Ensconced in a setting of gold and steel, the crimson jewel at its center burned with a light of its own. Everything beyond it seemed shrouded in a gray, color-dimmed haze. The King-priest turned and placed the Living Fire somewhere beyond his field of vision, then returned with what looked like a long band of leather in his hands.

"When I was a boy, my father's first love was ale," Ebon Khorel began as he knelt to encircle Amurel's shattered legs with the band. "His second was proving what a powerful man he was by thrashing me with a whip like I was livestock. If not that, there were always plenty of knives or heavy objects around. See this?" the King-priest pointed to the scar below his eye, after cinching the leather tightly above Amurel's knees and fastening it with a buckle.

The sudden compression made him wince, the subdued pain of his injuries jumping back to the fore of his consciousness. He still said nothing, unsure whether enough moisture remained in his mouth for his tongue to form words, should he deem speaking wise. Instead, he focused on steeling himself for what he expected to follow.

"The butt of a candlestick," the King-priest continued as he stood, his thick voice surging with repressed anger. "I used to wonder why my own father would treat me so, for I did nothing to provoke him. Then, as I got older and became stronger, I realized the joy of hurting things myself."

So quickly it surprised Amurel, Ebon Khorel punctuated his last statement by producing a thick, wooden rod from seemingly nowhere and powerfully striking the knee crushed by Bastion's fall.

A cry of agony escaped Amurel – he was too surprised to stop it. A second thud of wood and bone left him breathless as unbidden tears overflowed from his eyes. He reflexively sought out his punisher's eyes with his own, pleading for an answer that would not come.

"May the Nine Hells burn forever, I will find a way to kill you for this!" Sir Kilborn challenged from his side of the chamber.

"Why did your angels abandon the castle when I returned?" The King-priest asked calmly, once again ignoring the outburst.

Amurel's brow rose at the question, but his jaw remained slack. His leg pulsed with pain as if possessing its own, cruel heartbeat. He tried to derive meaning from this new information, but concentration was impossible.

Ebon Khorel sighed. "You're useless, aren't you?" He moved again, almost beyond Amurel's limited field of vision, then returned brandishing an implement that looked like a wicked, leather version of a serpent's forked tongue. "Well, almost useless."

He snapped the flail across Amurel's abdomen, ripping the soiled cotton tunic covering it and leaving blazing red streaks in the material's place. Amurel hissed and cursed as blow after blow rained upon his stomach and chest, stripping his skin until the raw flesh beneath was almost as prevalent.

"You don't expect sympathy, do you, Sir Golddrake?" The King-priest's tone grew in excitement as he inflicted more pain. "After all, you chose this for yourself the day you decided to stand against Gholdur's anointed vessel." Excitement then shifted to anger, though Amurel had not said a word. "How dare you attack *my* fortress, in the heart of *my* realm!" A final, vicious thrash drew a pent-up scream that had been fighting to force its way past Amurel's lips.

For a moment the torture stopped, though the air continued to burn the dozens of exposed wounds across his body. Once more, the King-priest seemed in control, but all Amurel could think to do during his respite was pray. He prayed Criesha would deliver him – heal him as she had Jaiden, or at least remove his suffering. Why didn't she? Had he not served her well? He prayed for Jaiden to stomp through the door and exact swift vengeance on this lunatic monster. Such an abomination could not be allowed to rule.

He heard muffled sobbing and guessed it came from Geldrick. He abhorred his old friend having to witness this treatment, and hoped he would not meet the same end. Amurel's lids sank and his head drooped on his neck, the will to live gone. Perhaps if he resigned to die, the pain would carry him the rest of the way.

A firm hand grabbed his chin, however, and its squeezing caused his eyes to open. "Not yet," the King-priest ordered softly, nearly whispering. "You do not get out so easily. Are you familiar with the emblem of the true god, Gholdur?" The King-priest forced his face to the left, where a round shield was propped against a table. It bore the image of a human skull, adorned in a crown of thorny roses. Tracks of blood seeped from the ghastly eye sockets.

"You will be my example, northman. Your countrymen will see you and know what it means to oppose me. You must look the part, however. I will find you a wreath of roses later, but for now, there is one more thing we can do." The King-priest grabbed either side of Amurel's head tightly, covering his ears. Then, with agonizing deliberateness, he placed thumbs over his eyeballs and pushed.

Amurel struggled to shake his head free, but the grip was too strong. He cried out, no longer ashamed to do so, and his scream echoed the protest from his friend as Amurel's eyeballs were pulverized into their sockets.

Chapter 31

A Deeper Darkness

The seasonal, late-spring downpour seemed appropriate, heaping a somber mood upon an already dismal setting. The hood of Rogan's travelling cloak was heavy with rain, and drops from its saturated cloth streaked past his face onto his saddle with every lumbering step.

Saffron rode quietly a length behind, but he knew she was worrying about Dhania and avoided speaking her fears, lest they become actual. Clearing the air during their ride to Selamus allowed them to reach a truce, each admitting they cared for one another, but that anything beyond friendship was doomed for failure.

Rogan felt strangely closer to her afterward, as if yelling at one another freed them to be honest, removing the need to filter their thoughts toward one another. He understood her better, and was learning to anticipate her moods. He didn't mind her silence now, knowing what was behind it. In truth, he felt similarly, concerned that Dhania's second capture would irrevocably damage her spirit, even if she remained physically unharmed.

Ymrilad set the pace, tirelessly striding east ahead of the horses. They travelled along the Solepass Road, out from the hills of Dawn's Edge. His long, emerald-green hair was tied back in a ponytail that dangled between his shoulder blades, almost to the spot where the powerful, feathered wings sprouted from his back. He kept those folded when he walked, their bright tips – the same vibrant color as his hair – standing out amidst the gray of the rainy afternoon.

Rogan didn't know much about the Aasimar in front of him, other than he often seemed to be of like-mind to Palomar, who vouched for his honor. He had proven more reserved in his communication, though perhaps due to the solemnity of his companions. Whatever the reasons, Rogan had plenty of time to think about what might happen when they reached their destination.

The farmhouse Bremmil mentioned during his interrogation should be coming up on the north side of the road within a league, and he wanted to retain the element of surprise when they arrived. Although the sounds of the rain might mask their final approach, Rogan also doubted Saffron's fire talents would be as potent under such wet conditions. They would stick to stealth as long as they could.

At last, the raised outline of a dwelling came into view. Back a hundred paces or so from the road, the rain-fuzzed structure appeared to be mostly wood, with a crumbled stone chimney and a thatched roof that sagged as if caught in a permanent exhale. Ymrilad stopped moving and broke the shared silence.

"My lord and lady, I believe this may be the place." The Aasimar shared his thoughts without looking back at his recipients.

Rogan narrowed his eyes and evaluated the surrounding terrain as best he could through the rain. Open pasture dominated the space between them and the building, though behind the structure loomed a thin stretch of elm trees, bordered by a thicket.

He turned his head and nodded to Saffron, which was enough to prompt her dismount. Rogan did the same, and they walked their horses north to the wood-line. Ymrilad followed tentatively, looking back at the house several times before reaching the modest cover of the elms.

"I know she's your sister, Saffron, but I have probably had more experience sneaking around over the last decade than either of you," Rogan said as they hung their reins over some low-reaching branches.

Saffron assented, "So what is your plan?"

Rogan checked the sky to gauge the hour, but the sun was completely shrouded by clouds. "Well, I am fairly certain it will be getting dark before too long. First, we need to know if the place is still occupied. I don't see signs of other horses, but we need to be sure." He took stock of their winged companion – his towering, muscular frame and green-tipped, bright white feathers screamed to be noticed. "Unfortunately, Ymrilad, you stick out like a fox in a hen house. If they have a look-out, you will be spotted for sure if we haven't been marked already." The Aasimar managed to look unhappy and confused at the same time.

"Saffron and I will stay low and try to get a look inside from opposite sides," Rogan continued. "We will signal to you if it is safe to approach, but try to be silent as possible. If Dhania is in there, and not in immediate danger, I want you two to cause a distraction. Lure them outside; I'll slip in and help her escape."

Saffron nodded her agreement, then asked, "And if the house is empty?"

"Then we look for signs of use, stay there tonight, and remain vigilant in case our prey returns." Rogan rested a hand on Saffron's shoulder and held her gaze. "If she is not here, we'll still find her." He nodded slightly, and she took a long blink before mirroring the gesture. "Let's go."

He crouched but still managed bounding strides through the wet grass, its slick surface sinking beneath his boots. Rogan swiveled his head while progressing across the yard, checking the road, the farmhouse, and the woods for any movement or signs of presence. Though no horses were tied up nearby, as they drew within an easy stone's throw of the dilapidated structure's rear, he noticed a hatchet lodged into the highest log of a woodpile. He pointed it out for Saffron's benefit, and headed around to take a closer look. Indeed, splinters of recently-split wood littered the nearby ground.

The roll of the land put the window on the back side of the house lower than the front, so Rogan left it to Saffron and continued circling the abode to make sure no one else was around. On the far end of the house was a worn, wooden door, attached only by the top hinge. A design had been scratched into its surface – a clawed hand with unrecognizable runes on either side. Numerous boot prints marked the dirt before it, heading both in and out. He checked the horizon to the east and south but no creature, orc or otherwise, stirred. Still, he drew his uril-chent dagger and found comfort in its sphere of dimness.

He listened at the door but all he could hear was the rain, and the portal was in such poor shape he couldn't move it unobtrusively. So, Rogan continued warily to the front of the house, past another door showing no signs of traffic, and backed against the stone wall beneath a window. Ever-so-slowly, he rose until he could peek over the protruding sill.

The panes were filthy, but he immediately caught the flicker of candlelight inside. Four or five shapes, concealed under dark cloaks, stood around a large, single room in an uneven, inward-facing circle. The light was too dim and the window too grimy to tell the number for certain.

He also found it impossible to tell if Dhania was among them, but he doubted she would be standing in any case. More likely, she would be bound somewhere out of sight, and it looked as if the figures were conspiring. He doubted any of them actually lived here – the congregation seemed too secretive.

Rogan quickly evaluated they could take five men if necessary, knowing just the sight of an Aasimar might make them reasonable. He crept back from the window and signaled for Ymrilad to approach. Even if they had someone watching, Rogan would still be able to get inside before warning could reach them. He peeked through the window once more, making sure the figures were still in place, before sneaking to the back of the house to join his companions.

"I did not see my sister," Saffron's hissing whisper accused as he approached.

"Nor did I," added Rogan, "but we cannot lose the opportunity to question those inside. Whoever they are, they seem to be meeting in secret, which likely makes discovering them dangerous." He noted Saffron was unarmed, and looked back toward the horses. "You should have your spear—"

"I do not need my spear. If these men have hurt Dhania they will burn in the flames of my wrath."

Rogan closed his mouth and drew back slightly. He had never seen Saffron's eyes so resolute. He unsheathed his sabre and handed it to her. "Still, it may make them think twice about not cooperating if we're armed. Ymrilad, there is a weak door on the side of the building. You should be able to kick it in. Lady Saffron and I will file in behind you. Be ready, but don't attack them unless they initiate, alright? I want to talk to them first."

"Of course, Baron."

Rogan looked at Saffron, raising his eyebrows when she didn't respond. She finally shrugged, "Agreed."

They moved to the far end of the building, where Ymrilad drew his sword and counted to three before smashing the door to splinters with the sole of his foot. If those gathered inside were surprised by the intrusion, they recovered quickly. By the time Rogan squeezed past the Aasimar they had spread out, the larger two drawing weapons.

Coming into the sheltered darkness, even from the suppressed daylight of the rain-soaked evening, made it seem deeper. Rogan had difficulty discerning more than the outlines of black cloaks and curved steel. There were five, after-all, though the armed pair stood a head taller than the others and possessed bulk to rival Ymrilad.

"Wait, there is no need for bloodshed!" Rogan shouted, hoping they hadn't already made up their minds. He held out an empty palm, but did not loosen the grip on his dagger.

"Who are you?" The question came from a deep, stilted voice belonging to the foremost silhouette. Though the words made sense, the effort with which they were spoken suggested casual familiarity with the language. A pair of short, arced swords stood ready in the creature's hands. Rogan's instincts told him those hands were orcish.

"We are only looking for a friend of ours, and were told she was last seen here." Rogan tried to sound as non-confrontational as possible. As his eyes adjusted, he thought he could make out tusk-like incisors within the hoods of the armed creatures.

A second voice, more natural and calm, answered from behind. "There are no women here now, save the one you brought; and you have trespassed where you are unwelcome. Why should we not slay you where you stand?"

No sooner had the man finished his sentence than Saffon replaced it with a low chant. Four candles and a dull, gray rectangle from the doorway provided the only light in the farmhouse, but it suddenly doubled as those flames pulsed on their wicks, growing in intensity.

"Do you think it would be easy to do so?" Rogan countered. "Violence is not what I want, but if she keeps singing you are going to have worse to deal with than my blade. So I suggest you tell us what you know, and we can be on our way..."

"Lady Saffron!" one of the men in the rear exclaimed, as if suddenly placing her face and unable to stifle the thought. The other cloaked heads turned in the man's direction, and he bowed his hood in apparent shame.

Saffron ceased her singing and the candles dimmed. "Do I know you?"

The man owning the once-confident voice stepped forward, between the drawn blades of either side, reconsidering his stance after the outburst. "Of course, there is no need for bloodshed, for we are not enemies." He walked to a table against the wall, lifted the candle resting on it, and took a seat in its place. "That is quite a trick you did with the candles, my Lady. You might find you share much in common with our master."

"And who might that be?" Rogan inquired, unnerved by the change in the man's demeanor. He almost preferred open antagonism.

"He shall make himself known to all, in time. As for the Lady's sister—"

"What do you know?" Saffron stepped forward, the naked blade of her borrowed saber a threatening reminder of the action she barely held in check.

The man seated on the table lifted the candle closer to his face, until its soft glow turned it into a mask of light and shadow. "We had nothing to do with it, but heard she was given to Nejuk the Gouger as tribute. She is probably in his camp by now, south of the Black Hills."

"Given by whom?" Rogan hoped the question would shed light on the identity or affiliation of this gathering. The mixture of men and orcs spoke of something bigger, something more threatening than suggested on the surface.

"The men of bleeding skulls give gifts to unite against the pale-skins," answered the dual-bladed orc.

"I am afraid if you want to get your sister back, Lady Saffron," the seated man continued, unflustered, "then you are going to have to offer the orc chieftain something more valuable – and I couldn't guess what that might be."

The previously silent orc gave an amused grunt. "Hmph, or challenge Nejuk for leadership, and take her back yourself." Both orcs followed with an eruption of gargling laughter that Rogan found horribly unpleasant. Despite the sudden levity of the orcs, he kept his eyes active and his dagger ready.

"Where can we find Nejuk?" Saffron demanded.

The man on the table shrugged. "Keep following the road east. Before you hit the mountains you will either find the Gouger or, more likely, his orcs will find you."

"*I do not trust these men in black.*"

Ymrilad's sudden contribution startled Rogan, though he imagined the words were not shared with the cloaked strangers. In all honesty, however, he had to admit the three of them probably appeared just as untrustworthy. "Is that the only help you can give? How do you know Lady Saffron?"

The man shrugged again, pulling the candle away from his face. "Tales of her singular nature have spread to far corners... as have those of the silent angels." His eyes coolly poured over the Aasimar. "I sincerely wish you success in finding the one you seek." He considered the saber Saffron still held in his direction. "For as I said, we had nothing to do with her abduction."

"What *do* you have to do with?" she almost spit her response. "Why are you gathered in secret?"

"You have your mission, my Lady, and we have ours. The master wouldn't like us spilling secrets – though I can't imagine you'd object to our goal."

Rogan had the feeling they weren't going to get anything further from these men, though his gut told him at least most of what they said was honest. His gut also told him if they lingered too long he might not be able to hold Saffron back from releasing her frustrations in a torrent of flame.

"Then we will leave you to your business," he said, taking a step back toward the doorway. "Saffron," he called when she failed to budge, "let's go." He nodded toward the door. She frowned but obeyed, as Ymrilad stood guard, joining them once they were both outside.

"*Do you mean to continue east, then?*" he asked.

"I mean to find Dhania, no matter what," Saffron answered before stalking purposefully through the rain toward the horses.

Five days later they came to the end of the Solepass Road at the thriving town of Battock. It was the last outpost of civilization in the Cradle. Further east rose the foothills of the Fire-Wall Mountains – to the north, the untamed frontier of the Northern Reaches. The Black Hills lay just beyond the border of Horizon Province. Not expecting such a lengthy journey, their supply of rations was nearly gone when they reached the town, and Rogan was happy for the opportunity to replenish it. He did not fancy the idea of battling a tribe of hostile orcs on an empty stomach.

Battock had a certain charm to it – a sense of adventure in the air that no doubt came from its position on the frontier. Under different circumstances, Rogan would have liked to stay a while and mingle amongst the locals and many travelers, escaping his own concerns in shared stories from other realms. On this occasion, however, he and his companions were the ones off to daring deeds, though it seemed to him more akin to knowingly entering an ambush.

He could not let Saffron down. Nor Dhania, for that matter. She had clearly seen something in him and given him her trust, when he knew such a thing to be difficult. He thought back to the kiss they shared on the battlements, and how he had attributed it to the wine and juvenile infatuation, when he had no right to do so. He dismissed her because of his own fruitless pursuit of Saffron, and he could not allow more harm to befall her – not after all she had been through.

A few, careful inquiries in town yielded several unconfirmed tales of orc raids on trading caravans and frontier villages, but none of the story-tellers had seen a single orc themselves. They marveled at Ymrilad, however. Some went as far as bowing before the Aasimar as they would a deity. Perhaps he was, after a fashion, Rogan thought.

They departed Battock by the eastern gate the morning after they arrived, though the paved, Solepass Road had ended. A wide trail, still regularly used, stretched before them, winding into the hills of their fate.

Saffron took charge, continuing toward the mountains along the trail, intentionally remaining conspicuous as possible. Ymrilad's appearance may be a deterrent, she explained, but hoped three lightly-armed wanderers would be too tempting for orc brigands to resist. They did not have to wait long to find out.

Barely an hour after losing sight of Battock on the western horizon, a trembling of hooves drew nearer. Once they realized what it was, Rogan and Saffron readied their weapons while Ymrilad took flight, whipping a dust cloud beneath him as he ascended. The source of the rumble was hidden from Rogan's view by the hillsides, but it grew louder and was moving quickly. At last, a line of horses broke free from behind a rise, two dozen or more, ridden by gray-skinned, muscular orcs.

The leader was especially massive, and directly following him were a pair of standard-bearers. Both of the banners were black, though one bore the simple white outline of three peaks, and the other the same claw and runes Rogan had noticed on the door of the farmhouse, days ago. As the train of orcs encircled them, Rogan struggled to settle his horse from near-panic while Saffron and her mount, Sheen, somehow appeared calm as statues.

"You have entered the territory of the Black Hills orcs," the leader shouted in passable Illanese, once his followers had fallen into position. Now they were still, Rogan could see the leader's features varied somewhat from those behind him. Though the tops of his ears were peaked and tusks bulged his lower lip, the eyes and nose seemed less bestial – more human. "Your horses and possessions are now ours. If you fail to give them up... so are your lives," he continued.

Saffron's expression was stoic, but she responded in a clear voice, "Are you the one they call Nejuk the Gouger?"

"I am Nejuk's legion commander, Taurn." The orc leader was looking at Rogan, not Saffron. "How dare you allow your woman to address me! Tell your angel friend to come down or we will shoot him from the sky." Taurn extended his right arm and gave an order that sounded like a bear clearing its throat. A half-dozen orcs further down the train produced black, curved bows, which they aimed at Ymrilad.

Undaunted, Saffron continued, "We have been told your chieftain holds my sister hostage. He must release her to me immediately, or your entire tribe will burn."

Taurn lowered his hand to the pommel of his saddle before seizing with laughter. "You are a bold one, Black-Hair. Are you certain you are not part orc?" All the levity then drained from his deep voice. "I was going to share you with my legion, but now I keep you to myself."

Rogan turned his head, trying to both count the orcs and look for a gap in their circle he might exploit as a possible way out. He wanted to trust Saffron, but realized her zeal for rescuing Dhania may push her farther than their ability to manage. The orcs were no doubt stronger and more savage than the men they'd vanquished in the past.

"Are you a creature of honor, Taurn?" Saffron asked.

"Creature? You can trust you and your friends will feel pain before you die!" Taurn grasped the hilt of the greatsword slung across his back, drawing the weapon with a snarl.

Saffron reacted quickly, dismounting Sheen and side-stepping to create space between herself and the others. She began singing, raised her shield, and set her spear across it, point-forward. Rogan watched the orc commander pause, a look of uncertainty molding his bestial features. Then the tip of Saffron's spear began glowing a dangerous red, and she twirled it quickly in a show of proficiency, a blaze of fire trailing the heated steel.

"I challenge you, then, Honorable Taurn, to single combat," she shouted so all could hear. "I am told your people often solve disputes in such ways."

"For what stakes?" Taurn turned to his companions and laughed, though it sounded uneasy. "We already outnumber and surround you."

"And I command magic that will turn you all to cinders. The choice is yours."

If she was bluffing, Rogan could not tell, though he noticed that in ceasing her singing to speak, the glow of her spearhead already waned. Taurn, however, seemed to consider the threat of sorcery seriously.

"You not use magic if we fight?" he asked.

Saffron shook her head. "Just warrior against warrior, 'til one of us yields. If you win, we will all submit to you with no further resistance. But if I win, you must take us to Nejuk, and leave us unharmed."

"I hope you know what you're doing, Lady," Rogan muttered through the side of his mouth. The plan seemed to be working, if only for the moment – Taurn dismounted and took a few steps forward.

"Your friends are fortunate I love to make battle, woman. You will not be." Taurn exercised a wide, looping swing of his sword, demonstrating its impressive reach while stretching his muscles.

Saffron quickly unclasped her riding cloak and cast it off her shoulders, revealing the supple leather armor Natrone made for her in Talon Barge. She would need unhindered quickness to overcome the orc's obvious strength, and Rogan could do little but watch and hope she was up to the task.

"*There is no help within sight, Baron. We are on our own. Should I join you?*"

Rogan had momentarily forgotten Ymrilad. He looked up and waved for him to land. No sooner had the Aasimar done so than Taurn charged Saffron, bringing his sword down hard with both hands.

So mighty was the blow, she did not even bother trying to deflect it with her shield. Instead, she crouched and lunged forward, sliding into the angle created by the length of his reach, and smashed the edge of her bronzed shield into the orc's chest. He stumbled back as the air left his lungs, nearly losing hold of his weapon – but not quite.

Taurn's left hand released his sword and grabbed at Saffron, coming up with her braided ponytail in his fist. He tossed her aside like a doll before she could follow with a thrust of her spear. The force of his shove took her feet from under her, but she didn't fight the momentum, instead using it to roll across her shoulders and back into her stance. She adjusted her grip on the ash shaft and readied for another attack.

This time the orc slashed horizontally in a wide arc, striking Saffron's shield with a ringing *clang*. Rogan winced, watching the impact nearly jar the shield from her forearm. She had to get in close again or Taurn would simply wear her down.

Saffron lunged like a viper, feigning a thrust toward his left shoulder. Unprepared for her quickness, he shifted back while raising his heavy sword to deflect the blow. Faster than seemed possible to him, Rogan watched Saffron push back off her extended right leg, lift the heel a finger's length off the ground, and spin. Like a dog chasing its tail, she crouched and whipped around, pivoting on her left foot until her extended right leg swept the off-balance Taurn's legs from under him.

The orc commander fell backward, flailing helplessly before landing with a satisfying thud. Saffron's boot snapped down on his right wrist a heartbeat later, and her spear's tip pressed just close enough to his throat to dissuade sudden movements.

"Do you yield, Taurn of the Black Hills?" Saffron asked between panting breaths.

Rogan leaned forward to better hear his reply, and his horse assisted by taking a couple steps closer. He could see frustration at being bested in the orc's eyes, but something else as well – respect.

"Why you want to find Nejuk? He will only make you a slave, like your sister."

"Do you yield?"

Taurn seemed to taste the words in his mouth first and find them unpalatable, before spitting them out. "I yield!" he shouted. "Do not harm the intruders."

Saffron nodded and stepped back from Taurn. "I will challenge your chieftain to a duel as well, and when I beat him, I will have rulership of the tribes."

The orc commander laughed as he rose to his feet and dusted himself off. "Outsiders cannot challenge for tribal leadership, and Nejuk is too strong."

"I'd wager you thought the same of yourself," Rogan added as his horse stepped him into the conversation.

Taurn shook his head, "You not understand; Nejuk has help from the Cursed One. He gives Nejuk magic and poisoned counsel. He is why we have left the Black Hills for this place. I would challenge myself, but his gifts make Nejuk too strong."

"Who is the Cursed One?" Saffron asked. "A shaman of some sort?"

Taurn shook his head and stabbed the tip of his sword into the ground before leaning on it. "Not an orc. Says he is part demon. Wields dark magic. Nejuk thinks he makes us stronger, but the Cursed One cares not for our tribe, and will make us fight too far from home."

"Part demon?" Rogan wondered aloud, looking to Ymrilad and Saffron. "Perhaps Ebon Khorel sent a Gholdur War-priest?"

Saffron shrugged.

"Most likely." Ymrilad offered.

An idea shot into Rogan's head. "Taurn, if we were able to bolster you with magic as strong as Nejuk's, would you challenge him then?"

Taurn raised his shaggy eyebrows, "What magic?"

"The Aasimar and I are both Shapers," Saffron concurred, seeming to catch on to Rogan's suggestion. "We could give you advantages, or perhaps even cancel Nejuk's."

The orc's gaze moved to each of them in turn as he considered. "For the good of the Black Hills tribe, I would do this."

"And if you won, you would let us and my sister go in peace?"

Taurn paused and then nodded, "If I have your word to help, Honorable Woman."

Another two days of riding brought Rogan and his companions, with a full orcish escort, to the cave-infested territory the Black Hill's army had claimed as its base. Along the way, sleep proved a fleeting endeavor, as it seemed every single orc snored like a snarling cougar.

"You know if this doesn't go well, we will likely have to fight our way through the entire tribe?" Rogan pointed out to Saffron as they made their way into the fortified camp.

Ramparts and palisades created a maze-like tangle of partitioned spaces. The late-afternoon sun was still too bright for torches to be lit, but Rogan could imagine how the place would look at night; formidable walls of sharpened timber decorated by macabre trophies of war, designs in red paint, and the iridescent eyes of battle-hungry orcs patrolling the grounds.

They entered a channel flanked by rows of wooden spikes protruding from the ground, in through one gate, and stopped before another. Taurn and his riders dismounted, so reluctantly Rogan and Saffron followed suit. The first gate closed behind them, and then the second swung open. More orcs poured through and began leading the horses into a corral. One of them spoke directly to Taurn in their native tongue, which sounded as harsh as Rogan imagined.

After a brief conversation, Taurn turned and explained in Illanese that he told the newcomer they were his prisoners. "It is easier this way," he explained, "but I will need your weapons to convince them." Saffron quickly handed over her spear, but Rogan and Ymrilad hesitated. "I give them back later." The Aasimar complied and Rogan handed over his saber, but left his dagger sheathed.

"I give Nejuk my report now," Taurn continued. "I will challenge for leadership. If he does not kill me outright, we fight at sunset." Taurn gave what Rogan presumed passed for a wink among orcs.

He and Saffron exchanged a look. They had not been told that was a possibility. They followed Taurn down a side path created by more spikes, where two armed orcs stepped out and snarled at them. Taurn quickly shouted orders in orcish and the guards backed down, their eyes blazing open suspicion.

At its end, the path opened into a wide, fortified circle where a bonfire blazed and a half-dozen orcs mingled. They all wore necklaces of bone. One, a foot taller than the rest and clad in black animal hides, approached. The gray skin of his face was scarred and gold capped his tusks. Heavily muscled, with the notched head of a harnessed axe peeking over his shoulders, he assessed each newcomer with clouded eyes. As the smoke-infused irises passed over him, Rogan had the feeling he was quickly dismissed as a non-threat.

The large orc spoke directly with Taurn. The language itself was sharp and angry, but the exchange boiled with an added tension. Interspersed with accusatory curses were fists banging on chests, and the gripping of weapons. Rogan thought they would come to blows in front of him. At last, Taurn spit on the ground and stalked out of the circle the way they had come. The display turned out to be ritualized.

"Do not linger," he said in Illanese as the orcs began closing in. Rogan and the others followed the orc commander back through the maze of palisades, until they arrived at an open space filled with hut-sized, conical tents. Taurn held the flap to one of these open and gestured for his "prisoners" to enter, scanning the yard for trouble as they did.

Once inside, he explained, "The challenge has been given. We fight at sunset, unless assassinated first." He looked directly at Saffron. "You are certain your magic will help?"

"Are you certain you can beat him if it does?" Saffron sounded as if she had doubts, and after seeing Nejuk in person, Rogan could not blame her.

"He is too sure of himself," Taurn assessed. "He will try to prove strength by finishing me quickly. I use that against him."

"Much as I did to you?"

Taurn's eyes narrowed, but he did not disagree.

"*You said the Cursed One has tainted his axe, such that wounds bleed more heavily?*" Ymrilad asked.

"Aye. Just one cut may kill me, even if the wound not deep."

"*And against his rage, even the bravest warrior trembles?*"

"It is unnatural."

"*And finally, his skin becomes hard, like stone?*"

"It is devilry." Taurn shook his head in disgust. "I have seen this trick in battle before. He will use it tonight. The Cursed One requires orcs to sacrifice, but Nejuk allows for his own benefit. It will take all my strength to cut him."

Ymrilad nodded. "*I should be able to take care of the fear. I can sing a tune to grant you almost boundless courage.*"

"I can make your blade so hot it will cut right through Nejuk's flesh, hardened or not," Saffron added.

"And his axe?" Taurn asked.

Rogan smiled uneasily, realizing he had no part to play in this battle. He patted Taurn's shoulder. "Try not to get hit."

"Huh, easy for you to say. That's what I get for taking up with humans." Taurn reclined on a pile of furs toward the back of the tent. Not much else adorned the space save a worn, wooden chest and a circle of stones that had seen fire. "My mother was human," he confessed after the silence wore on too long.

Rogan cast a glance in the half-orc's direction, but he was staring up at the tent's apex. Rogan waited for more, but nothing was offered. Finally, he spoke to his comrades, softly enough to avoid interrupting Taurn's reflection. "Saffron, you and Ymrilad will both be busy during the challenge, but I will not. It seems foolish to place all our hopes on Taurn's victory, when the outcome is uncertain at best."

"I agree, Rogan, but what other options do we have?"

"Well, I assume most of the orcs will be occupied watching the battle for leadership; Taurn said Dhania is most likely kept in the caves where this *Cursed One* lurks. From the sounds of it, he too may be busy with Nejuk's enchantments. I want to try sneaking in and seeing if I can find your sister. If things go poorly with the fight, maybe Ymrilad can at least fly her to safety."

"*And what about you, Baron?*" Ymrilad asked, noting the obvious flaw in his plan.

Rogan locked eyes with Saffron, and they spent a moment divining one another's intentions while hardening their own resolve. At last Saffron nodded, and Rogan spoke. "Lady Saffron and I have been in messes before; we will find a way out. Dhania's safety is more important. Would you help us, Ymrilad, if it comes to that?"

The Aasimar let out a physical sigh, before replying. "*If it is what you both want...*" He looked to Saffron.

She nodded without hesitation. "It is."

"*Then so be it.*"

The next hour passed tortuously slow. Taurn had loyal orcs posted around his tent to defend against premature attempts on his life, but finally demanded some time alone to prepare for the oncoming battle. The sun was barely above the eastern peaks of the Fire-Wall Mountains, its light soft and golden.

Opting for stealth, Rogan decided to leave his returned saber behind, trusting in his uril-chent dagger. He picked out a cave entrance he could reach without much danger of being noticed, and hoped the tunnel system Taurn had spoken of adjoined it to wherever Dhania was held.

"I have a song for you, my friend," Ymrilad offered as they walked to the edge of the tent clearing. "It will only last an hour or so after I stop, but will help attune your mind to the ways of the Panther – to be quiet and light on your feet."

"I would be thankful for any help. Thank you for standing by us on this mission, Ymrilad."

The Aasimar smiled. "I owe you and the Order a debt I can never repay. Life as a Damper was agony, and for me, without hope. To be restored to my former self," Ymrilad bent his arms at the elbows and flexed his muscles, "is a second chance to be who I was meant to be."

He placed a hand atop Rogan's head, closed his eyes, and began humming. Soon his lips parted and words joined the humming, which somehow continued. The song did not last long, and when it finished, Ymrilad's lids raised. "Remember, only an hour."

Rogan nodded. "Wish Taurn fair fortune for me." Then, he took position behind the largest survivor of a former rockslide to hide. Orcs soon sprouted from their tents, and many even left posts to make their way to the inner circle of the camp, vying for the best spots to watch the anticipated carnage.

Ymrilad returned to Taurn's tent, and Rogan waited a little longer before drawing his dagger. Once enveloped in its comforting shadow, he moved with astonishing fleetness from cover to cover, making his way to the chosen cave.

After scaling the rock face he crawled into the opening, plunging into almost complete darkness. He held still as his eyes adjusted, but worried about navigating in the blackness. He assumed the orcs would have lit the passages with torches, but could not see even a distant source of illumination at the moment.

One short step at a time, he pushed deeper into the cave, keeping his left hand pressed to the surface of the wall, while his right held his dagger. The tunnel opened up and turned sharply to the left. Relief washed over Rogan as the welcome glow of fire beckoned from further along the tunnel. He moved nimbly toward it and found a metal bucket full of torches resting beneath a hanging, burning brand. He selected one and lit the end, only to be presented with a new choice.

Another cave entrance sat opposite the ensconced torch, and the tunnel he approached from continued, gaining elevation, but a wider corridor also headed deeper into the mountain. He stilled his breathing and listened for a clue. A sound, akin to an orc groaning, echoed off the stone from far away, but he could not be certain from which tunnel it originated.

He looked either direction a second time. The thought of following the passage deeper into the dark of the earth raised the hair on his arms – so that is where he decided to go. Swallowing the lump in his throat, he extended his torch as far as possible and marched forward.

Distance underground was difficult to guess, for the tunnel wound like a snake further into the world until he truly had no idea which direction he faced. The groaning sound came and went, and the air grew warmer, though he expected the opposite. Rogan began to wonder if he could somehow use the beads of sweat dripping from his forehead to count time. Finally, but without warning, the passage spilled into an open cavern.

He stood on a natural balcony overlooking a narrow, underground lake. He saw fires reflecting off the water on the far side, so he dropped his torch and crouched to stay out of sight. He rolled his torch as best he could to conceal its light behind a stalagmite. Peeking from behind a second, he saw two forms carrying torches along the bank. They came to a bridge only a few planks wide, with no rails or ropes for balance, and began crossing.

Rogan tried to make himself as small as possible as they drew closer. He could hear the footsteps squeaking against the wet boards of the bridge, and the light grew brighter until it suddenly stopped moving.

"Get the supplies I asked for while I deal with this upstart. This foolish tradition is a waste of time."

The voice was in Rogan's head, but it wasn't Ymrilad's or Palomar's, and he got the feeling it wasn't speaking for his benefit. He wondered if another Aasimar had snuck in. Unable to suppress his curiosity, Rogan inched his head around, hoping to get a look at the owner of the telepathic voice.

Whoever held the torches were standing beneath his rock balcony, identities obscured from his current angle. He would have to move closer to the edge. He heard the harsh cadence of an orc voice.

"No. Do not touch her unless you want to be the next to volunteer," came the answer.

The telepath's projection was smooth, but firm – definitely something other than an orc. With utmost care, Rogan sheathed his dagger and crawled toward the edge of the overhang on all fours, eager to see who else was down in these caves. He was taking too long, though – the light began to move again, dimming underneath the balcony. With a final lunge, Rogan grasped the edge of the rock and stretched his neck as far as he could in one motion.

Viewing from upside-down, he identified two orcs, each holding a torch. A third figure walked ahead of them, but it bore no feathered wings. Slender, humanoid, and draped in a black cape, Rogan caught the definite outline of curved horns protruding from the side of its head.

The triumvirate walked into an arched opening beneath where Rogan entered the cavern, and soon disappeared as they turned a corner down the passageway. His gooseflesh returned as Rogan realized the horned figure must be the *Cursed One* Taurn had spoken of. And who was the *her* the Cursed One referred to, if not Dhania?

A sense of urgency seized Rogan. He could absolutely not let Dhania remain at the mercy of such a creature. He sprang to his feet, retrieved his sputtering torch, and looked for an easy way down from his perch. With no nearby handholds visible to help climb, Rogan decided to drop from the edge of the balcony.

He threw his torch first, using its light to identify what looked like the flattest spot to land.

The drop was almost two body lengths, but he had no choice. Time was running out. After hanging as low as possible from the edge of the balcony, Rogan simply let go. He landed on his feet, surprisingly, and maintained balance. The impact barely even registered on his joints, and he quickly scooped up his torch to continue across the bridge.

He kept a look-out for other lights, but none showed on the far shore. The reflection of his torch on the water showed the lake was undisturbed by current, though he tried not to think what denizens might lay beneath its dark, mirrored surface. Once he spanned the entire reservoir, a fresh call of discomfort echoed from his left.

Continuing to follow his gut, Rogan headed that direction. A narrow path ran along the shore for perhaps thirty-five paces, before the wall rising to his right gave way to an open chamber. Lying on the cave floor were two orcs. Rogan leapt back and drew his dagger, dimming the light of his torch. The orcs did not move, however, and as he stepped closer, he saw their hands clasped in irons. A chain connected them to the wall, though he could not be sure they were even alive.

The orcs' arms and legs were spread and their heads tilted back, eyes and mouths open. Just as Rogan stepped closer to get a better look, one of the orcs let out a sorrowful groan. Its mouth didn't move, but the sound rose from a sudden vibration of its throat. Rogan extended his torch toward the orc's face, then yanked it back when something moved inside its mouth.

A black tentacle, slick and slender like an oversized tongue, protruded from the open lips for a split second before retreating inside. Rogan was about to take a second look when the rattling of chains caught his attention. He looked at the hands of the orcs on the floor, but neither had moved. He heard it again, though the metallic sound came from somewhere deeper. Rogan stepped toward the far wall to find enough space existed to turn the corner into another alcove.

Torch in one hand, his dagger in the other, Rogan tiptoed into the chamber beyond, though even the dimmed light of his torch betrayed any stealth. Someone was huddled against the wall of the cave, trying to escape notice, but Rogan immediately recognized the glow of bronzed skin.

"Dhania!"

Saffron's sister shielded her face with her arms, but lowered them at the sound of her name. "Rogan?"

He sheathed his dagger just in time to catch her embrace. She held him so tight he thought he might suffocate, and began sobbing as she buried her face into his neck. He kept his right arm as straight as possible to put the torch a safe distance from her hair, while his left hand gently stroked her back. He wanted to hold her for as long as it took, but knew they did not have such luxury.

Forcing himself to step back, he took a better look to make sure she was unharmed. Her feet were bare, her ankles clasped in chains secured to the rock wall. She had been dressed in a black, fur loincloth, with a leather harness around her torso, leaving most of her flesh exposed. A design was painted between her breasts in black – the same clawed hand and indeciperable runes from the farmhouse door and orc banner. Around her head rested an ebony circlet, supporting horns that were a miniature mirror to those of the Cursed One.

"What were they planning for you? Are you hurt?" Rogan asked.

Dhania wiped at the tear tracks running down both cheeks. "No, not really. Just get me out of here, Rogan."

"I will," he replied. "I will never let anything hurt you again." Rogan had never meant anything more sincerely. "Here, hold this." He handed Dhania the torch, then fished in his belt pouch for his ivory lock picks. "We don't have much time," he said, working on her irons. "Your sister is near, but we may have to fight our way out if things go poorly." With a satisfying *click*, the manacles swung open. "There we go," Rogan said before standing and reclaiming the torch.

"I cannot believe you came for me after how I left things."

Rogan shook his head. Looking at her, barely able to comprehend what she had been through, all he wanted was to protect and take away her fears. "Water under the bridge, Dhania." He barely pushed it out past the lump in his throat.

Her obsidian eyes were about to spill over again and her lips were quivering, though she fought hard to keep control. Rogan could not take any more. Overwhelmed by relief and the need to suppress the pain he saw rising in her, he clasped her cheeks, wiping her tears with his thumbs as they fell. And then, he was kissing her. Unlike the first time, this felt right, and Rogan did not want to stop, though knew he must.

At last he relented, gave an encouraging smile and said, "Let's get out of here." He took her hand and led the way back, along the lakeshore and across the bridge. Unable to climb to the balcony, he had to choose another tunnel out. His heart worked at an unsustainable pace as he expected to find more orcs at every wrong turn, but they must have all been watching the battle for tribe supremacy. Eventually, he found a tunnel offering the promising smell of outside air and followed it to an opening.

Rogan tentatively stuck his head out into the hillside breeze, unsure of the danger they might be returning to. Only the last, orange glow of the dying sun peeked from beyond the horizon, and bats burst forth from several nearby caves, heading out on their nightly hunt.

"Baron, we were victorious!" Ymrilad's voice greeted him before any awareness of the Aasimar's presence. *"Taurn is the new chief, and has kept to his word."* The flapping of wings finally caught Rogan's attention and he looked up. Ymrilad's white feathers stood out in the twilight, and Rogan could not have been happier to see them.

Chapter 32

The Battle of Naresgreen

Jaiden made it as far as the Ducal Palace at Naresgreen before requests for help started pouring in. Crowesdale and Meadowhold, towns north of Synirpa, had both suffered attacks by the Chelpian army. No word of Sir Golddrake or his faction had yet surfaced, leaving Jaiden to fear the worst.

Having already mobilized with the intention of marching for Windhollow, Jaiden decided not to wait until the King-priest advanced upon Selamus. He redirected the messengers with dictates that any who wished to stand together, rally at Naresgreen. After years of self-reliance, it felt strange to suddenly have others looking to him. The province's Duke was still relatively young and eager to earn prestige, so he readily pledged his own troops to the effort. Given it was a defense of his own lands, the generosity doubled as self-preservation, but Jaiden appreciated the contribution nonetheless.

Within days, both new volunteers and the splintered remains of the other Provincial armies started straggling in – all except those of Dawn's Edge. Prince Falcionus probably still patrolled the far hills of his province with his faction of the Order, while the bulk of his regular army dug in for a stand at Selamus. If Jaiden's brethren did not materialize soon, he would have to plan his strategy without them.

Naresgreen's eastern border was marked by the great forest of Luin Menel, which superstition held was the realm of the fey Eladrin. Whether they existed or not, the woods were rooted in mystery, and men who valued their lives dared not enter. When he was a lad and heard stories of the Sky Kingdom, as it was commonly translated, Jaiden boasted he would brave its alpine peaks one day. From atop them, it was said one could see to the edge of the world.

As he surveyed the mustering soldiers amidst the brewing mists of war, he wondered if the Eladrin were real. He had believed when he was younger, then grew to doubt by the time he first left the streets of Selamus. After living amongst the Aasimar, however, visiting the dreamlike world of Criesha and witnessing the birth of Saffron's fire-shaping, he knew what sounded fanciful was sometimes true.

Jaiden shook his musings aside when he spotted Palomar approaching. His friend had been diligently gathering intelligence from their allies trickling in from the South, with the special intention of discovering any news regarding the other Aasimar. No sightings were reported yet, and Jaiden knew Illicurus's failure to surface drew Palomar's deep concern.

"What news, friend?"

Palomar grasped Jaiden's wrist in greeting. *"The King-priest's propaganda machine is hard at work; I cannot yet separate all the truth from the lies. Refugees share tales of a hundred thousand men, all in black with glowing red eyes, wiping out their villages. From more seasoned soldiers, the estimate is closer to a tenth of that number, though the enemy appears to be attacking on multiple fronts."*

"Any word on the fate of Sir Golddrake or the Aasimar?" Jaiden asked. His stomach churned slightly at the prospect of what he might learn.

Palomar clasped his hands together and raised them to his lips. *"I heard something about the Master, yes."*

"Did he fall at Windhollow?" Jaiden barely got the words out.

Palomar shook his head slowly, his golden hair catching the sun. *"I am afraid it's worse."* He paused, and Jaiden could feel the blood draining from his face in dreadful anticipation. *"I spoke with a captain assigned to the vanguard at the failed defense of Crowesdale. He seemed an honorable man. He had met Sir Golddrake when the Order visited his garrison in Rosegold once to barter for surplus, so he knew his face.*

"He says the enemy had him on display in a stockade upon a cart, surrounded by Blood Tear assassins. He was dressed in a tabard of the Order, but had been maimed to resemble the Dread Tyrant – eyes gouged and a circle of thorny roses pressed upon his head."

Jaiden raised a hand. "Stop." He could hear no more. A torrent of anger and guilt rose in his chest, but it erupted from his mouth as vomit. He turned to the side and folded in two as the shame purged from his body. If he had stayed by Sir Golddrake's side, his fate would have been different. Jaiden spit to remove the bitter taste and wiped his mouth with the back of his hand. "We cannot leave him like that, Palomar – suffering. We have to do something."

"*Are you unwell, Master Luminere?*" Palomar dipped his head, assessing Jaiden from a lower angle.

"I'm fine. How far is the King-priest's encampment?"

"*Surely not far. They could have been here already if pushing hard. Or, they may bypass us altogether in a bid for Selamus.*"

"Ebon Khorel won't risk it. His spies certainly know we're here, and he is not foolish enough to let us close in behind when the capital lies ahead." Jaiden stared westward, though the Dawn Way was beyond sight. "No, he will come for us – but not before you and I visit him..." he looked over his shoulder at the stalwart Aasimar, "if you're with me on this."

"*Of course,*" Palomar answered. "*What did you have in mind?*"

"We are going to find Sir Golddrake," he said, plainly. With Palomar in tow, Jaiden hiked to the stables and saddled Inferno. He found Lieutenant Orestes at the freestanding guard tower they requisitioned from the Duke for the Order's on-site headquarters.

"Orestes, Palomar and I are doing some quick reconnaissance. We need all these newcomers assigned to units by midday. Anyone with experience needs to be identified for leadership. I don't want our formations falling apart at the first charge because a commander freezes."

"Yes, Sir," the lieutenant replied, then returned to tallying troops and marking up orders.

Jaiden appreciated he was a man of few words. "Good, I'll be back by morning." He stepped outside and mounted his horse, heading for the practice archery range, where he grabbed an extra bow and a quivers of arrows.

"I always preferred the sword," he explained, though Palomar had not asked, "but my father insisted I train for ranged combat as well, in case necessity demanded."

"What exactly do you intend to do when we find Master Golddrake?"

Jaiden had an idea, but found it too difficult to speak aloud. "Can you lead us toward Crowesdale?" he asked instead.

Palomar let it be, nodding and launching into the blue afternoon, bearing south. Jaiden allowed Inferno the freedom to stretch his legs and give chase, relegating his concentration to maintaining balance in the saddle. It only took an hour or so of hard riding before Palomar descended and waited for Jaiden to catch up.

"I did not want to be seen," he explained as Jaiden slowed his horse to a trot and approached. *"The makings of an army lie another half-league in this direction."*

Jaiden looked back the way they had come. "Not far at all, but it is late enough they should be bedding down before going much further."

"Sir Luminere, before you do whatever it is you are intending, I should tell you what else I heard from my inquiries."

"Palomar, please, it's just 'Jaiden.'" He dismounted to stretch his cramped legs as much as to grant Inferno a reprieve from his burden.

"Jaiden, you should know what we might be heading into. I have no doubt now that the ruby pendant the King-priest wears is crafted of the Living Fire. Such a weapon not only enhances his channeling, but it appears to have granted him invulnerability."

Jaiden clenched his jaw then crossed his arms, resting them against his chest. "Of course he's not invulnerable. Everyone has a weakness."

"I do not fully understand the power of the Juda-cai, but I talked to several men who saw Ebon Khorel personally in battle, and they gave the same story. He rides surrounded by a cadre of armored devils, which no weapon can harm. The few who have been able to engage him in close combat have withered within seconds, as if they aged a hundred years at once."

Jaiden squinted and shook his head. Tall tales like that were how legends were born. "Palomar, such stories are natural to a side that loses a battle. My father warned me of it many times. He heard campfire retellings of warlords who stood ten feet high during his campaigns, only to find the next dawn they were no larger than he. All men bleed, Palomar. The King-priest and his goons are no different."

"I would agree with you, normally. But remember, the Juda-cai were a myth in your world not long ago. Last year, had you even dreamt of your Goddess? Had you dreamt of someone like me? There is magic in this world again, Jaiden, though it has slept a deep sleep."

Jaiden had no retort; the Aasimar was right, but he would not allow himself to be talked out of hoping.

"I say this not to dissuade you from your course, only so you can make an honest assessment of the risks you take."

"I appreciate it, friend." He relaxed his jaw and loosened his stance. "I am still going to try, though."

"And I will stand by you."

"Let's take some cover under those trees," Jaiden suggested. The western portion of Neresgreen was filled with wide-open fields, punctuated by un-cleared pockets of woodland. He guessed the approaching army would bed down before reaching this far, but he didn't want to be spotted in the open by a scout.

While they waited for evening to descend, Jaiden practiced lacing one arrow after another into the hollow of a large elm. Palomar provided helpful distraction by sharing stories of his life before the curse, though he would not speak of the days leading up to it. Mount Celestia sounded like a fascinating place, though he couldn't quite picture how its slope could climb upwards, and yet expand horizontally for vast distances as well. Palomar told him it was a different sort of mountain than the ones he could see from here, and that the spaces of each Plane obeyed their own set of rules.

The concepts preoccupied Jaiden until at last, as twilight fell, the story-telling was interrupted by the vibration of a thousand footsteps approaching. Jaiden stood and took hold of Inferno's bridle, lest his horse get overly excited at the prospect of battle.

"Should we fall back?"

"Not until we can see them."

"Won't that mean they can also see us?"

In truth, Jaiden fought back his urge to charge forward and engage. He longed for another crack at the army that had first gotten the better of him. An uneven line of gray broke slowly but steadily across the horizon, slowly morphing into shapes he imagined to be units of soldiers. Before taking discernable form, however, they stopped, and the earth became still. Jaiden leaned forward, the lower half of his face concealed by foliage, and strained his eyes. From this distance it was hard to tell much, other than the gray was no longer advancing. "They've stopped to set up camp." He looked at Palomar. "We'll wait here for it to get darker."

Though confident the army was through marching for the day, Jaiden knew he couldn't account for sentries or spies, so he set an arrow lightly to the string of his bow. When he saw the bright flecks of torches and campfires in the distance, he knew it wouldn't be long.

Jaiden was thankful the moons were almost new as true darkness replaced the dying half-light. He did not want the reminder of Criesha looking down on him tonight. He drew his white tabard over his head and left it draped across Inferno's saddle. Underneath, his tunic and breeches were a deep brown, much less conspicuous. He patted his horse's nose, checking to make sure he was secured, yet with enough slack to graze on the tall grass covering the countryside.

Jaiden replaced the arrow into his quiver and looked to Palomar. "I'm getting closer. Do you think you can remain unseen?"

"Like the wind," he said, as if his bright gold hair, pearlescent skin, and snow-white feathers were not hindrances to stealth. *"You lead the way, and I will join you."*

Jaiden decided to trust his companion. He ducked until the arch of his back was barely above the grass line, and cut a path through the overgrown turf, bow extended. Now and again he rose to peek, noting the distance of the fires and maintaining his bearings.

He spied a patrol of four sentries walking the perimeter, establishing a border he knew would be foolish to cross. As they turned to head in his general direction, he stopped advancing and sank as low as possible into the grass, wishing it grew a little thicker, even as it enveloped him. He waited, still as a statue, until the patrol had ample time to pass. Pushing up slowly on his arms, he surveyed what he could of the camp.

Tents and wagons, troops and cooking fires – Jaiden knew enough of the soldiering landscape to assess it quickly. His search stopped, however, when he noticed a man stooping atop a cart to offer water to another bound there. He heard a rustle of grass behind him and turned as a stiff wind blew aside a wide swath of the dry, non-pastured blades.

"Did you find him yet?"

Jaiden swiveled his head to locate Palomar, only to nearly fall to his belly when he found the Aasimar pressed down into the grass immediately to his right. "How did..." he started, then thought better of it. "I think so. Look there." He let his eyes direct Palomar's vision toward the man on the cart. His hands protruded from a wooden stockade and his head drooped as if he were dead, keeping his face from view. He wore a wreath of dead flowers around his head, however, and his hair, though filthy, was undeniably blonde.

Jaiden felt Palomar's hand squeeze his shoulder, and he slid his knees beneath him to take the strain off his shoulders. The man who attempted to slake the prisoner's thirst stepped down and walked away.

"The Rising Moon adorns his tabard – it must be Master Golddrake."

"I believe so," Jaiden agreed after swallowing the lump in his throat. His eyes weren't as keen as his friend's, but he felt the truth regardless.

"And you mean to shoot him?" The questioning in Palomar's voice told Jaiden it was the first time he deduced what the bow was really for.

"He is suffering." Jaiden did not take his eyes from the limp form of his mentor. "I aim to bring him peace." As he reached for an arrow, his companion began to sing, though so quietly they were in no danger of being discovered. Jaiden recognized enough of the short verse to place the melody. It was the song Palomar used to sing to ease the pain of his wounds. Remembering it, and imagining what Sir Golddrake went through at the hands of their enemies, brought sudden tears to his eyes.

"I don't think he can hear you, my friend," he whispered when Palomar finished. And yet, as he watched, Sir Golddrake slowly raised his head to face their direction – only his eyes were replaced by vacant sockets. "Merciful spirits," Jaiden mumbled.

"He heard me. I sent the song to him on the wind, and his pain is eased. He knows we're near."

Jaiden wiped the tears from his eyes and rose to his knees, mindful the patrol would come around again soon. He drew his bow and narrowed his gaze. They were perhaps fifty paces away, but the breeze had stilled and he knew he could make the shot if he concentrated. He aimed for the purple of the moon on Sir Golddrake's chest, barely recognizable from distance as more than a dark crescent. Had it really come to this? How could he take the life of the man who had brought him back from the edge of death? Who had believed in him when he doubted himself? Who had seen potential beyond any hopes of his own? And yet, given the state Sir Golddrake was in, how could he not?

As he let go of the taut, braided twine, he prayed the moment would not haunt him the rest of his days. The arrow sped through the night air, striking the center of Sir Golddrake's breast. A tremor of surprise shook his head for an instant before it once again slumped to his chest.

No one in the camp seemed to notice, or at least no cry of alarm rose as Jaiden and Palomar skirted through the grass in the opposite direction. By the time they heard noises suggesting discovery of their deed, Jaiden was only several strides from the tree where Inferno remained tethered.

"Time to fly, Palomar!" he said as he hastily untied and mounted his horse.

"I will make sure you are not pursued." The Aasimar took a running start to unfurl his wings, and then lunged upward. Great, sweeping thrusts of gold-tipped feathers pushed him

airborne, and within a few blinks, Palomar was high enough to be out of earshot. Jaiden focused on his own escape, urging Inferno to a speed that nudged the threshold of safety.

They reached the Naresgreen Palace grounds before midnight, with no disturbances from Chelpian forces. Jaiden checked in with Orestes, who had managed well in his absence. Jaiden shared the location of the troops he saw, declaring that battle would find them on the morrow if the enemy advanced. He did not, however, share what he had done, nor tell anyone of Sir Golddrake's fate. He was prepared to bear that weight alone.

Orestes, in turn, gave updates on their incoming allies, including a full two hundred of the renowned archers of Crimsonmoon. Their arrival was a welcome surprise, given how the Duke of that province had clamored for aid from the Prince against orc incursions.

At last, Jaiden retired at Lt. Orestes's insistence, realizing he needed sleep, but secretly afraid of what his dreams might hold. Visions of Sir Golddrake's eyeless face rising to stare at him with blank, blood-crusted sockets already tormented him during his return ride. Even after closing his own lids, Jaiden prayed for forgiveness to both Criesha and whatever spirit of the dead might be lingering after his deed.

Mercifully, though his mind churned with countless concerns and unanswered questions, it did not take long for him to fall asleep. There, he found peace among the clouds of the night sky, opening his eyes to the starry realm of his cherished Goddess.

"Put to rest your guilt, my Champion. No doom awaits for what you did out of compassion."

Jaiden heard Criesha's voice first, then caught the beam of green moonlight as it approached and transformed into the comely form of his deity. He sat up on the comfortable bed and regarded her with unsure eyes. "But it *is* my fault he was captured by the King-priest in the first place. I should have taken my men south weeks ago, not remained in Selamus to keep eyes on the Prince."

Criesha sat beside him and took his hand in hers. "But Prince Falcionus needed watching. I recently learned he negotiated with agents of the King-priest and planned to empty the capital of defenders, in exchange for a peaceful transition and place in the new order."

Jaiden's posture snapped rigid. "How do you know this?"

Criesha's unearthly eyes softened and she tilted her head a fraction. "The land of dreams is my domain – you may be my Champion, but you are not the only one I visit."

Jaiden cast his eyes downward, a surge of jealousy driving heat to his face.

"The Prince has paid for his betrayal, though," she continued. "He fell to an orc assassin, and his faction of the Order is moving to join with yours."

Jaiden lifted his head at the shocking news, his mind swarming with questions his mouth failed to translate.

"You are the only leader they have left, Jaiden. You must remain strong and true, or the influence of Gholdur will spread unchecked. You are the only one with a chance to kill his King-priest."

Just as he started to speak Criesha hushed him, guiding him to lay back down as she slid to receive his head in her lap. "What you need now is sleep, my Champion. Wake up strong. Act boldly. Never give up." With her last word he shut his eyes, content to feel her delicate hands through his hair, all questions forgotten.

He awoke invigorated after the best sleep he could ever remember. No longer protected by sleep, however, his mind turned back to the dark deeds of the day before. He thought of Sir Golddrake through breakfast and as he sharpened his sword, imagining each stroke of the whetstone represented another enemy he would fell. Once satisfied with its edge, he sheathed his weapon and made his way around the estate's fields, visiting the captain of every legion. He let them know the Goddess was with them and to have their men ready, as the day was finally upon them.

By the time he ended at Lt. Orestes's guard tower, the sun had passed its peak. Palomar waited as well, wearing the chest-shield given to him upon induction to the Order. His great, two-handed sword was slung upon his back, which Jaiden had not seen since Blackthorn.

"The Chelpians have drawn nearer, but halted their advance half a league to the southwest."

Jaiden nodded. "They are waiting for nightfall. Their beasts see better in the dark than we do, and they believe they're attacking a stationary target in the palace." He paused, looking from Palomar to Orestes, remembering what Criesha told him the night before. "They are wrong." He took a step closer to the table the Lieutenant was using for a desk and pointed to the map of the ducal lands. Orestes already had wooden markers for both their own, as well as enemy troops, placed upon it.

"I will lead the cavalry on a swift approach up the middle, here, hopefully catching them unprepared. We will wedge into their ranks, then use an Operian Crest maneuver to curl back around. If they pursue us, they will feel the sting of the Crimsonmoon archers, who will be stationed behind these lines, beyond range of their missiles." Jaiden moved the appropriate markers to illustrate his plan.

"And if they don't?" Orestes asked.

"Then we send in our heavy infantry to demoralize them with our discipline. The cavalry will split and flank their position and the archers will push to here, close enough to pepper their reserves who fail to engage. Our lighter infantry will guard the archers and act as support for the armored units. We don't give them a chance to use their siege engines or archers, and thin their numbers as quickly as possible."

Orestes nodded. "I'm sure the Duke will be glad to keep his palace out of it, if possible."

"If it doesn't go well," Jaiden concluded, "we fall back here and dig in. I know we have limited defenses, but the trenches we've dug and the walls around us will help. I've been told the Prince's faction is on their way."

"*I had not heard any reports from Selamus... but they will be welcome.*" Palomar looked at him wide-eyed, as if determining whether to openly question the source.

"Welcome, indeed," Orestes echoed. "About time Falcionus changed his tune."

"Give the orders to mobilize, Lieutenant, then get into your armor. I want you leading the infantry."

Orestes stared at Jaiden with a look of simultaneous surprise and appreciation. "Yes, Sir Luminere!" Jaiden knew Sir Golddrake valued his former man-at-arms too much to risk him in the field, but the man was a proud and capable fighter, and under the circumstances, Jaiden knew his presence could well save numerous lives.

Jaiden needed Lothander's help to put on his own armor, and Palomar followed him out.

"*Was it Criesha who told you?*"

"Told me what?" he asked as they crossed the open space toward his tent.

"*About the Prince's troops.*"

"Yes," he answered, not bothering to stop. He left Falcionus's death out of it. "They should be here within days, but not a help to us this evening."

Palomar nodded and stopped walking. "*I have my own preparations to make. I will see you on the field, Sir Luminere.*"

Jaiden raised his hand in acknowledgement, but spared looking into the Aasimar's eyes so soon after what felt like a lie.

Jaiden's full plate armor felt light as cloth upon him. The Shaper's gift truly was a marvel. The shining silver and purple steel, let alone the unicorn's horn protruding from his helmet, left Jaiden a visible and inspiring figure upon his steed. Inferno stood calmly at the head of the formation, ready for the pressure on his flanks that would urge him forward.

Jaiden looked down the line in either direction – two hundred of the finest mounted warriors ever assembled held for his signal. Hiding behind a short break of trees marking the border of the Duke's fields, he knew the Chelpian forces trying to take their freedom waited not far beyond those trunks and leaves.

The King-priest was used to being the aggressor, and would not be expecting his opponents to strike first. At least, Jaiden hoped so. Having given the Order's other battalions time to get into position, he drew his father's sword and held it high, signaling the cavalry to the edge of the tree line. They would need all the speed they could muster to reach their foes, taking advantage of surprise and lessening the impact of any attentive archers.

Inferno ducked to avoid the lowest branches, and Jaiden felt him quivering beneath, anticipating the coming charge. As the line of knights poked just beyond the cover of the trees, Jaiden got his first glimpse of what they were heading into. Someone had spotted them, and men scurried to file into formations. He decided it didn't matter – with no pikemen or horses at the head of the lines, they still had the advantage. An image of Sir Golddrake's first lessons on horsemanship teased his mind, bringing an added desire to make his mentor proud. A quick sweep of his arm brought his sword downward, and the thunder of eight hundred hooves soon drowned out all else.

Two hundred paces swept by in an instant, and Jaiden whipped his sword left and right as easily as a lash. Matching his previous experience against the Chelpians, he found most of their warriors wearing nothing heavier than reinforced leather. The Gift of Criesha imbued his weapon with a greenish glow as if touched by her moonlight, and men scattered in awe before him as he cut their fellows down.

The Chelpian troops were certainly not ready for their assault, but as the momentum of the Order's charge was spent, Jaiden got a glimpse of the sheer numbers they faced. As easily as they penetrated the first lines of ill-prepared soldiers, he needed to get the cavalry out to preserve them, lest the masses fill in the space vacated by the fallen and cut them off.

"Back!" he called, pulling Inferno's reins to bring him around. The weight of his horse rebuked a few footmen who had gotten too close, and the cavalry around him started turning as well. With enviable precision they made for the tree line, leaving confused soldiers scrambling in their wake. Jaiden looked back to see a few units being pushed forward by their captains, but none seemed eager to give pursuit.

Just before the horses reached the trees they peeled off in either direction to run parallel to the pines. As they parted, a squadron of longbowmen in bright red tunics stepped forward from under the trees, angling their bows upward in unison. Volley after volley, two hundred arrows at a time soared through the air then rained down as the Chelpian encampment scrambled for cover.

Jaiden stayed at the corner of the field, just beside the archers, to watch the battle unfold. The rest of the cavalry had their orders, circling around at a distance, hoping to be forgotten amidst new troubles.

At last, the Chelpians responded. Their own archers managed to assemble, greatly outnumbering the unit from Crimsonmoon, and returned fire. That was the cue for the next wave. Before the incoming missiles even landed, the Crimsonmoon archers took cover back under the trees. A brief silence hovered while the Chelpian captains tried to determine whether the assault was over. It was not.

The clink of chainmail reached Jaiden's ears a moment before he saw Lieutenant Orestes. He led the heavy infantry out from the trees, as if they were but living curtains on a stage, and this the next act. The enemy archers started up again, firing arrows at the oncoming soldiers, but these men all had shields. They raised them in tight formation, forming an effective roof over their heads. It only took a few volleys to realize they were wasting arrows.

Events had gone uncharacteristically to plan up to this point. Jaiden's extreme angle did not allow him to see far into the enemy camp, but the Chelpian infantry he expected to respond to the new threat was not forthcoming. Instead, a series of familiar bestial roars erupted in the distance.

Nearly to the edge of the enemy lines, Jaiden saw Orestes bring his men to a halt. Rising above them, the many monstrous heads of the hydra reared back and snarled threats. Despite the outcome of his previous encounter, anger boiled Jaiden's blood at the sight of the beast. He furrowed his brow and urged Inferno forward to intercept the hydra before it reached his men. His horse was not fast enough.

As he neared the tight formation, one of the serpentine necks lunged forward and rose up, a soldier of the Order dangling from the gigantic maw. Several of the other heads also struck with coordinated attacks, but came up empty.

When Inferno got close, Jaiden pulled him to a stop and quickly swung to the ground. He needed to move freely, and would not risk the life of his horse in such a battle. He charged to the fore of the fray, joining Orestes and a few others stepping forward to challenge the beast.

"Everyone else get back!" Jaiden shouted at the formation as he ran straight for the scaled body of the hydra. Before he closed, the beast shifted its position and one of its heads circled around to cut him off with a snap of its jaws. Jaiden raised his shield and lashed out with his sword, but not before the mouth hissed and retreated beyond reach.

"We have to coordinate attacks, just like its heads," he called to Orestes and the two other soldiers who remained in combat. The man who had been plucked up by the hydra fell to the ground with a thud upon release. Out of the corner of his eye, Jaiden could see he wasn't moving.

"Everyone strike on three. Ready?" Jaiden had to jump back and lower his shield to deflect another incoming snap from the hydra. The strength of the beast was still almost enough to make him lose balance. "One, two, three!" Jaiden showed the tip of his sword to the nearest head, and as it curled to bypass the weapon he spun completely around, using his momentum to slice a powerful arc up into the creature's exposed neck.

Though the hide looked tough, Jaiden's radiant sword cut through the flesh easily. The tactic of simultaneous attacks seemed to work; to his right, Orestes landed a stab into the nostril of another head. Jaiden was premature, however, in his satisfaction. All at once the heads retracted and the grayish-green body spun with surprising speed. The beast's massive tail followed, too thick for him to evade.

Jaiden raised his shield to absorb the impact, but the sweep collected both him and Orestes as victims, sending them sprawling to the ground. Dizzy and breathless, Jaiden had only managed to stagger to his knees when the shadow of a looming hydra head darkened the ground around him. He was vaguely aware he should be impaled on a hundred teeth any moment, but before that happened, the shadows beneath him vanished in a flash of white.

He closed his eyes and shook his head, hoping to regain his vision, but kept seeing repeated bursts of light. In between the pulses his sight worked fine, and when he looked up to face the hydra, he saw the cause of the display. Palomar hovered just out of the creature's reach, emitting explosions of golden-white energy from his body.

The effect blinded the hydra, whose heads first sought out the cause of its debilitation, and then retracted one-by-one as they succumbed to it. Unsure how long this opportunity would last, Jaiden eschewed his shield and grasped his hilt with both hands. He barreled toward the monster's base with as much force as he could muster, aiming for a spot below where the necks came together.

A war-cry forced itself from his throat in direct proportion to the strength summoned behind his blow. The tip of his blade sunk into the hydra's chest as easily as a dagger into a melon. He pushed it forward, watching the body of the beast swallow its green glow, until the crosspiece atop the hilt kept it from going further.

All five heads roared in unison, making Jaiden's feel like it would split, and the sinewy necks thrashed in a pattern-less chaos before crashing to the earth in the most final moment Jaiden had ever witnessed. He barely sidestepped the nearest neck as it plummeted, and his ears were still ringing when the triumphant cries of his infantrymen washed over him.

He retrieved his sword, and a pungent ichor leaked from its chasm. He looked for Orestes, and found the gentle Palomar lifting him to his feet. Palomar, who had saved them both.

Before he could share his thanks another roar went up – the cry of the Order's cavalry as they once again pierced the ranks of the Chelpians, this time from either side, further along their flanks. Jaiden delayed the exchange of congratulations, running to reclaim his shield and reunite with his horse. The enemy was in disarray, and he wanted to seize the moment.

The arrival of the war-priests changed his mind. As he drove Inferno closer to the center of action, bat-like wisps of animated shadow began to flutter by with a hiss. Jaiden did not know what purpose they served, but his father's lesson about the dangers of pushing ahead too quickly on the heels of victory registered in the back of his mind. Yes, they had executed his plans better than he could have hoped, but the war was not ending in a day. Better to leave the enemy questioning its resolve after a resounding defeat than let them salvage a sense of victory by rushing for a quick end.

He called his cavalry to fall back, and although he sensed some resistance, they ultimately followed his lead once he turned Inferno around. The sky itself seemed to dim as they hurried from the field of battle, and Jaiden waited at the tree line until all his men passed beyond its protection. His heart continued beating quickly for most of the ride to the Naresgreen estate, and they arrived just before sunset. When the count was completed, they had only lost three men in the afternoon of fighting, with another dozen injured. Though they would be missed, the spirits of his army were as high as the slivered moons that reflected down on their victory, and they celebrated further into the night than was probably wise.

Jaiden did not stop them, but retired early after breaking bread with Palomar and Orestes and thanking them both for their bravery. Oddly, the only thing that bothered him was the absence of the King-priest. He had not made an appearance, and Jaiden's gut told him Ebon Khorel was not present within the enemy's camp. So, where was he?

Back in his tent, Jaiden removed his armor and kneeled at the foot of his pallet. He offered thanks to his Goddess and prayed for continued success, though he unabashedly hoped to do so in person once he slept.

The next voice he heard, however, was not the honey-dripping intonation of Criesha, but that of Lothander, shaking him awake in his bed. "Sir Luminere, a messenger just arrived from the Prince's faction. They have been cut-off by the King-priest east of the Dawn Way!"

In the tired gloom proceeding the first direct rays of the morning sun, Jaiden rallied the cavalry to action. Within the hour, the men and their horses were fed, armored, and ready to depart. Half of the mounted troops and infantry, and all the archers would stay with Orestes to defend their current position. The remnants of yesterday's engagement still posed a threat, and could have been simply waiting for the second force to arrive.

Jaiden knew their ultimate success or failure lay with defeating Ebon Khorel, however, and such was his task. He rode west with a hundred horses as soon as they were ready, with the infantry hustling to catch up when able. Palomar flew ahead of the formation in short spurts, then landed to conserve energy. The Aasimar did not speak much that morning, but Jaiden was happy to have him along.

The fighting had started in the late hours of night, and it would be almost noon before their reinforcements reached the battle site, according to the position passed along by the messenger. Jaiden resisted the urge to spur Inferno into a full-fledged gallop; as much as he hated the thought of his brethren facing the King-priest without support, he realized they had to conserve energy for the up-coming fight.

Oddly, as the anticipated hour approached, the sky grew darker, though the sun should have been nearing its peak. A blanket of clouds stretched ahead of them, and a fell wind, hot and stale, visited in rolling waves, whipping at their banners.

"We are close, now."

Jaiden looked up to see Palomar hovering overhead.

"Jaiden, as formidable as it may seem, you have to engage the King-priest early, lest some other ill befall you."

"I am not afraid," he answered, though probably not loud enough for the flying Aasimar to hear through his helmet.

"You are the only one who can pierce his armor, so you must not fail. I will do all I can to ensure you have the chance – do not hesitate when it comes, no matter what chaos surrounds you."

"What are you getting at, Palomar?"

"Criesha visited me last night, and has shown me what must be done."

With that he flew ahead, picking up speed, leaving Jaiden to wonder at the weight of his words, and push past the twinge of jealousy he felt at being overlooked. Adjusting his line of sight, Jaiden realized why Palomar accelerated – they had been slowly climbing a shallow incline for some time and finally reached the apex – below, the sights and sounds of furious battle called up to him.

The landscape of the valley ahead more closely resembled Jaiden's imagining of the Abyss than the fields of western Naresgreen. Undulating storm clouds roiled overhead, unnervingly low, creating a dark, living ceiling of gray that threatened to collapse. Three slowly rotating funnel clouds dipped from this ceiling to the ground; cyclones rippling with lighting as they churned across the battlefield.

Countless dead littered the valley already, and the frenzied war hounds of the enemy devoured the fallen as well as attacked the living. More men engaged than Jaiden expected – thousands on either side. Most of the Prince's own army must have come with the Order after their ruler fell. Perhaps they sought vengeance for his assassination.

And yet, Jaiden could not say his side was winning. Pockets of fighting scattered everywhere, but many of the forces from Selamus seemed to have clustered around a small area, and it was not difficult to see why. Another Aasimar – Ellingle, he thought by her burgundy-tipped feathers and hair – rallied and protected the warriors close-by. Sheets of ice lined the earth before her, making approach difficult for her foes, and novas of blue frost erupted from her sword every time it contacted an enemy.

Toward her Palomar flew, and into the valley, Jaiden Luminere charged. A gathering of knights surrounded by black-clad soldiers many times their number, circled their horses in an attempt to hold encroachers at bay. Jaiden figured bringing them aid was as good a place as any to start.

His men reacted quickly to join him, tearing across the field like an avalanche, gaining fury as they fell. So chaotic was the battlefield, the Chelpians did not notice the incoming cavalry until they were plowing through their ranks. Thanks to all his training, Jaiden had matured at fighting from horseback and whipped his sword from side-to-side, using its downward momentum to carry through his upswing. The cluster of soldiers scattered, but that only made it easier for Jaiden's men to spread and pick them off one-by-one.

The knights they rescued seemed invigorated by their change in fortunes and wasted no time rallying with the reinforcements. They turned their attention to a large swath of enemy horsemen who were giving the Order's foot soldiers similar trouble, and headed toward the conflict.

Jaiden spared a moment to scan the field, looking for signs of channeling magic. He knew the sooner he dealt with the King-priest, the better it would be for his side. He heard a crack of thunder from above and recalled Palomar's tale of the re-claiming of Blackthorn – how Ebon Khorel had used the power of the storm against the Aasimar. He looked to where Ellingle and Palomar, now together, hovered over a crowd of enemies, and knew they were in danger. The wind picked up. Most of his knights had left to engage the cavalry, but a handful lingered behind, waiting for their master.

"Sir Luminere, are you hurt?" one of them asked.

Jaiden ignored him, rising up in his saddle, desperately searching for the King-priest. He tried blocking out all distracting sounds surrounding him to focus on his sight. He could hear the echoing *plunk* of raindrops as they landed on his helmet, though all else was muted. Finally, the unusual darkness aided him. As he looked further west, one of the cyclonic clouds of shadow spun past his field of vision, and in its wake, he caught a half-dozen pinpoints of red light flickering.

A circle of black-armored riders guarded a central figure on horseback, away from the other groups engaged in fighting. The ground around them was littered with dead, but no one currently dared to threaten them. The tiny red lights came from the eye-slits of the knights, as well as a larger one from the breast of their leader. It must be the Living Fire – the King-priest and his otherworldly jewel.

All the sounds of the battlefield returned to Jaiden, ushered by another crash of thunder as a surge of lightning danced along the ceiling of clouds. "Come with me!" he yelled to his remaining men before putting his heels to Inferno. His horse bolted in the direction of the black-armored enclave, and Jaiden turned his head just briefly enough to see that his small contingent of knights followed.

From somewhere on his left, a group of archers fired a volley in their direction. One arrow embedded in his shield, another skidded off the top of his helmet, and a third lodged in the saddle beneath his thigh. Inferno did not seem deterred, so he hoped the head hadn't penetrated. As he drew closer to the King-priest's unit, he saw the riders protecting him were not wearing armor at all, but were actually forged from metal. Their horses also lacked flesh and blood, seeming to be creations of shadow and smoke.

"Criesha be with us," Jaiden whispered, tightening his grip on his sword. While the King-priest concentrated on his spell, the uril-chent golems moved to block the approach of the on-comers. Jaiden raised his weapon and let out a howling cry of aggression. The golems wielded barbed spears, and the one headed for Jaiden lowered his like a lance.

Be quick. You have to be quick. They were Jaiden's thoughts, but he heard them in the voice of his father. Trusting in his armor, he left an opening on his right side, his sword side, which the golem pressed. The spear's metal tip, however, veered off-target at the last instant, swerving from his breast to under his arm. Jaiden whipped his arm inward, locking the shaft in his armpit. As Inferno and the ghost horse passed one another, the golem refused to release his grip, snapping the spear in two.

Another uril-chent golem pushed in front to block Jaiden's path, and Inferno reared on his hind legs to avoid colliding with the unearthly enemy. Jaiden held onto the reins with his shield hand, but his right foot slipped from its stirrup and he slid back in his saddle, fearful he would be thrown off. Thankfully, his horse came down quickly, though Jaiden struggled to right himself as the tip of another spear thrust directly toward his clavicle. It also veered aside, but the barbs caught the back of Inferno's neck as the golem pulled back. His mane caught the brunt of it, but Jaiden saw blood splatter onto his steed's shoulder. Inferno, however, kept his poise.

Jaiden stabilized and forced the golem back with two quick strikes. Each one caught the forearm of the creature, his glowing, green blade leaving deep cuts. The momentary separation gave Jaiden an opportunity to check how his comrades were faring. He caught a glimpse of another knight landing an overhand strike to the shoulder of a golem, but sparks flew as the steel simply bounced off the uril-chent body. Two nearby horses bounded away from the conflict, rider-less.

Amazingly, one of his knights made it past the golems to the King-priest, interrupting his incantation with a wild swing that failed to connect. Almost instantly afterward, however, the knight dropped his sword and lifted his visor, as if suddenly stifled and struggling for breath.

Jaiden watched in horror as the skin of his ally's face wrinkled and contracted until it looked like a peach left out in the sun for weeks. He did not have time to see what happened next, another incoming thrust stealing his attention. This one he blocked with his shield, and when he looked back to the King-priest, the attacking knight was slumped over in his saddle, unmoving. His horse then let out a shriek and bolted, its rider falling unceremoniously to the ground as it fled.

The odds were getting worse. Jaiden only had two companions left, and he realized neither of them would be able to harm their enemies. He hoped they could at least hold off the golems while he dealt with Ebon Khorel.

Suddenly, the sound of celestial thunder clapped before him as Palomar's greatsword struck the head of Jaiden's golem from above. The impact toppled the uril-chent abomination from his saddle to the ground. Palomar sang, while his weapon hummed with its own energy.

"The time is now, Jaiden. Even my blade cannot penetrate the King-priest's armor – only Criesha's Gift can."

Jaiden glanced at his sword, glowing like the green moon itself, and knew the truth.

"You must attack, but not until I engage him first. It is the only way to keep you safe."

Palomar had never stopped moving, closing the distance between himself and the King-priest. The remaining uril-chent golems reacted to this new threat to their master, ignoring the Knights of the Order and rallying to protect him.

The Aasimar groaned through clenched teeth as he brought his blade down upon the King-priest. Ebon Khorel was ready, however, parrying the blow with his uril-chent Morningstar, which caused another clap of thunder to ring out. Even as Jaiden raced closer he saw Palomar's arms begin to wither, decaying before his eyes like rotten wood.

"You are safe for now, Jaiden, but must hurry. Criesha told me the curse can only affect one life at a time, but you must finish him before I fall!"

"No, you can't die, Palomar!" Jaiden reached his friend just as a golem drove his spear through one of the Aasimar's wings. A rage overtook him, granting strength beyond normal limits. With a mighty blow he struck the golem's neck and sliced its head clean off.

The King-priest took notice and raised his empty hand in Jaiden's direction. With a few words he could not understand, shards of crackling black energy launched from Ebon Khorel's palm directly toward him. Jaiden raised his shield to no avail. The shards tore through it, past his armor, and into the flesh of Jaiden's arm. A sharp pain stole his attention momentarily, but he pushed through as his vision went red.

Time slowed, and once again the chaotic din of the battlefield receded to the background. He looked left at Palomar, whose once-flawless, pearl skin had turned almost completely gray, even as he struggled to raise his sword. To the right, another golem bore down, raising its spear to impale him. Straight ahead was the King-priest, whose expression was hidden behind a fearsome horned visage of black metal.

"Strike true, my Champion." Criesha's voice was a calm command, and Jaiden didn't know if she actually spoke or if it came from within, but he determined to do just that. Faster than the golem could thrust his spear, faster than the King-priest could raise his weapon in defense, Jaiden brought his sword down upon his foe, just as Inferno brought him within reach. His blade cut through Ebon Khorel's armor at the shoulder, severing his collarbone and continuing until it reached his heart.

Then the world seemed to suddenly catch up. In an instant the smoke of the enemies' horses no longer held shape, flying apart in every direction. The bodies of the King-priest and the uril-chent golems collapsed to the ground, unmoving, the red glow gone from their eye slits.

Jaiden looked over and saw the remaining husk of Palomar on his knees, leaning against his sword, its point stuck in the ground. Jaiden winced as he dismounted, his shredded left arm throbbing as it flexed. He sheathed his sword and unstrapped his shield, letting it fall to the ground. Joining Palomar on his knees, Jaiden lifted his visor and reached out to touch his friend, though his fingers curled inward, afraid to do so.

"Palomar," he said, soft and trembling. "What can I do?" He saw a spear protruding from the Aasimar's left side, shielded from view during the melee.

Palomar did not raise his head, did not move at all, but answered with a voice both weak and calm. *"You have already done it, my friend. You did it long ago, and I will remember you kindly. Tell the Baron and Lady Saffron I am sorry to leave without saying goodbye."*

"Leave?" Jaiden's thought choked off with sob. He tried to smile even as tears betrayed him, "Where are you going?"

Palomar gave no answer, but his body vanished and his sword toppled to the ground. In his place a sphere of white light appeared, not more than a foot across. It floated skyward, passing through the ceiling of low, gray clouds, where it disappeared from view.

Jaiden looked around the battlefield, noticing for the first time that combat had stopped. The disappearance of the cyclones and other traces of the King-priest's magic caught everyone's attention, it appeared, and they were staring in Jaiden's direction, perhaps aware of the vital struggle that had taken place.

With the defeat of their King-priest, the remaining Chelpian forces lost the will to continue fighting, and simply lowered their weapons in mass surrender. Ellingle flew toward Jaiden, though no one else seemed to remember how to move.

"*You did it, Sir Luminere,*" she said, noting the fallen form of the enemy leader as she landed. "*You do not seem happy,*" she said, a puzzled look on her face.

Jaiden simply peered up toward where the ball of light had departed.

"*Do not mourn too much for Palomar, Sir Luminere. He has simply returned to Mount Celestia.*"

He searched her face for some further comfort, and she responded with a gentle smile. Cradling his arm to his body, he took three steps toward the patient Inferno before she interrupted.

"*That is the Living Fire,*" Ellingle said, staring at the ruby pendant lying beside the corpse of the King-priest. "*You should not leave it behind.*"

Jaiden stopped and bent to retrieve the pendant. Holding it at eye level, he watched the inner-light of the gem dance within its facets. "Thank you, Ellingle," he said, turning back to the Aasimar. "I have no doubt you saved many lives today."

She nodded solemnly. "*My service paid a debt.*"

He returned her gesture. "Let us not be idle, for Criesha knows there are many to be cared for, and friends who need us."

Chapter 33

Forging a New Order

Given the circumstances, the idea of returning to the palace at Selamus seemed strange, but Jaiden was weary and did not know where else to go. The people of Dawn's Edge mourned their Prince, but doing so did not keep them from receiving the returning army with the ebullience of those who have been saved.

Travelers along the Dawn Way gladly yielded to let the victorious march proceed past, shouting gratitude and promises to spread word of great deeds. In the capital, the streets of the Eight Hills lined with joyous crowds when Jaiden led the combined troops of the Order and the Province through the city gates.

As a familiar face at the palace, no one questioned him reclaiming residence in the apartments afforded by the now-deceased sovereign of Dawn's Edge. Only a day or two passed before the requests for audience came in from the rest of the Northern Provinces.

The fighting had persisted for another week after the King-priest was vanquished, and thanks once more to Criesha's healing grace, Jaiden was fit to lead the effort. Once the most zealous followers of Ebon Khorel were convinced of his defeat, Chelpian forces rapidly abandoned all holdings north of Halidor. Still, uncertainty hovered across the land like an early morning mist, and with the seats of the Prince and two Dukes empty, the remainder called for a summit to discuss the realms' security.

Of course they chose Selamus as the location for the convergence, and it became Jaiden's duty as resident of the palace to host. In addition to the remaining four dukes, who were shown proper deference, he admitted eight other parties to the council: himself and the Shaper of Selamus, Ellingle, appointed emissaries for the vacant duchies, and heads of the two most powerful regional trade guilds.

Jaiden was unsure of what outcome he even desired, beyond the freedom to spread his devotion of Criesha to others. His father had always been leery of politics, and like so many other ideas, the distrust found its way into Jaiden's point of view. Yet the day had come, and as the mantel of leadership dictated, he joined the other distinguished guests in the Great Council Room.

A herald announced their names and titles, leaving Jaiden to call the meeting to order. He stood at the head of the table. "Each of you are most welcome to Selamus. We have come together because we value the safety of the Northern Provinces, and hopefully realize that threats to any of us can be a threat to all. Following the decorum of court, which I assure you is still mostly a mystery to me..." Jaiden paused while the congregation politely chuckled, "His Grace, Duke Gregor of Crimsonmoon, shall have the honor of introducing the first item of concern." With relief that he remembered more or less all his practiced words, Jaiden sat down and gave way to the Duke.

"Thank you for both your words and deeds, Grandmaster Luminere," the Duke of Crimsonmoon began. "Let us first raise our cups to the brave soldiers who turned back the black tide of Chelpa."

"Hear, hear!" the room echoed as Jaiden received their collective nods. He was about to mention that he was not the only one present who had fought the King-priest, but the Duke continued before he had a chance.

"None of us is venerable enough to remember a time when an Illanese King ruled over all the Northern Provinces. But we remember the stories, and have come to shun the idea of giving governance to one man, lest that man become corrupted. Indeed, we have to look no further than our southern neighbors to see the catastrophe that nearly engulfed us as well."

Duke Preston of Naresgreen leaned forward in his chair and opened his mouth, but a raised finger and glance from Gregor halted him.

"However," the Duke of Crimsonmoon continued, "with our own eyes we have now also seen our lands taken one-by-one, because individually we do not possess the same strength as our united kingdom of old. That is the quandary before us. The empty seats of Halidor, Rosegold, and Dawn's Edge are clear reminders of what can happen when neighbors remain, simply neighbors."

"Are you speaking of a formal alliance, or abdication of our thrones?" asked the Duke of Horizon.

"We need to do something to guarantee safety along the Dawn Way," added the matriarch of the Daylight Trading Company. "Everyone will suffer if we cannot transport goods from one town to the next."

That seemed to be the cue for everyone to begin speaking at once, each pontificating to their neighbor about their particular priorities in the post-war landscape. Jaiden tried listening to four conversations simultaneously, but was quickly overwhelmed.

"Do they not realize how fragile the peace we have won is?" Ellingle's calm, but clear voice separated from the others in his mind. *"Now that the Juda-cai are involved, everything in the world as they know it will change."*

Jaiden made eye contact with her, struck by how flawless her features compared to the rest of the table. Everything from her pearlescent skin to her blazing, wine-colored hair reminded him she was an outsider, but Palomar trusted in her wisdom, and Jaiden couldn't begin to imagine the things she'd seen in her travels to other worlds.

"What I would like to know is," a voice suddenly rose above all others, and the rest shrank away under its authority. It belonged to Duke of Dewfold, who appeared to be of advanced years similar to the Shaper of Selamus, "what are the Grandmaster's plans for the Order of the Rising Moon? You achieved victory over a powerful enemy, and now you are living in the late Prince's palace. Given the current situation, your intentions should be the start of any conversation about our future, though no one else seems to have the courage to ask."

Jaiden felt the weight of nearly a dozen pairs of eyes shift in his direction. He licked his lips while deciding how to respond. "The Order exists both to honor Our Lady, Criesha, and defend those who fall under her protection. Sir Golddrake split the responsibilities of leadership when our ranks swelled beyond one man's capacity. I plan to follow such wisdom, but my vision extends beyond simply providing a mobile fighting force." He swallowed and placed his hands upon the table, leaning forward and growing in confidence as he realized everyone listened to his words with keen interest.

"It is important, as Sir Golddrake knew, for us to be prepared to respond to threats anywhere within the Northern Provinces. I hope for the Dukes' continued support and cooperation toward that end, and I shall appoint a master of our military arm, who reports to me. But it is also imperative that we grow an awareness among the people of the benevolent power of Criesha, without whom these realms would have lost their freedom. So I shall also appoint a master of our devotional arm, to spread the teachings of our patroness."

Finally, after staring from one guild leader to the other, Jaiden concluded his speech. "Such a growing operation demands significant upkeep, so I will appoint a master to overlook the Order's financial concerns as well."

Duke Gregor answered as if he had already taken the measure of the room. "That is all well and good, Sir Luminere, but what I think His Grace is asking is what do you intend to do with the victorious army now under your command? You do, after all, reside in the Royal Palace and have powerful allies behind you." He spared glances at Ellingle and Willem. "Do you intend to rule here in the Prince's place?"

The bluntness of the question struck Jaiden as soundly as an invisible maul. Is that what they thought? He had not asked for this. He did not want Sir Golddrake or Prince Falcionus to die. Yet, everyone was staring at him, holding their collective breaths, waiting for his answer. When it came, it came slowly and calm, and he made sure to meet the eyes of each person at the table.

"I am in Selamus because this is my home. I am in the palace because that is where I was living when I left for war, and didn't know where else to go. I have been chosen by Criesha to be her Champion, and that is what I intend to do. I will carry on Sir Golddrake's work, protect the people of the Provinces, and spread the knowledge that my Goddess has returned to Elisahd. I am not highborn, and my hands will be more than full trying to direct the Order of the Rising Moon. I wouldn't know the first thing about ruling the people."

Duke Preston quickly pounced on the following silence to speak. "And I believe your focused ambition would make you a perfect choice to become 'Protector of the Realm.' Consider it, Your Graces: We, who know the everyday needs of our people best, continue to rule the Provinces in most matters. A small retinue would be maintained to help enforce our laws, of course, but we also pool resources to help support a single fighting force under the leadership of Grandmaster Luminere, who would ensure the security of our entire realm."

Jaiden sat back down, watching carefully as the others absorbed the young Duke of Naresgreen's proposal. He was still considering it himself when the door opened and the controlled cough of Lieutenant Orestes caught his attention.

Jaiden stood. "If you will excuse me for a moment, Your Graces, there is a matter that demands my attention. I should only need a short recess, but please feel free to continue until I return." He waited for their nods before practically bolting for the door, feeling relief at the brief respite from lordly scrutiny.

Orestes spoke softly but clear, "Baron Rogan informed me he wishes to thank you for your hospitality and bid you farewell, and is waiting on the palace steps."

"Thank you. I shall see him off. Would you mind waiting here, Orestes, and being my ears in the room?" The two locked eyes for a full breath – Jaiden still had trouble reading the experienced man-at-arms – before Orestes blinked and nodded.

"Of course, Sir. I will await your return."

Jaiden patted his lieutenant's shoulder, then took purposeful strides toward the front hall, struck by how precisely the architecture of the palace matched that of his dreams of Palomar. Servants swung the heavy doors open at his approach.

"Are you sure you have to leave?" Jaiden teased from the top step of the palace entryway. Given the number of times he genuinely wished Baron Rogan would mysteriously disappear, he was not immune to the irony entwined with asking him to stay. Things had changed in the past few weeks since Naresgreen, however, and with all the uncharted territory ahead, he found himself desiring to hold onto as much of the familiar as possible.

"We do," Rogan responded, wrapping his arm around Dhania's waist. "You may have vanquished Ebon Khorel, but Chelpa still needs helping. That is where I belong, and I am going to start by trying to find my son."

Saffron approached from the paved path, leading a train of three horses.

"Don't tell me you are deserting as well, Lady?" Jaiden took an impromptu step down before regaining control and halting. He knew this day would come, and his fidelity to Criesha demanded he let her go.

"It is time," she said, a tranquil smile creeping to her face. "I have sent a letter to our parents, long overdue, though they will not be pleased to hear neither of their daughters are returning soon."

"And where will you go?" Jaiden asked. "Are you riding to Chelpa as well?" He could not help the pang of jealousy that struck as he imagined himself in Rogan's place.

Saffron shook her head. "I will ride with them as far as Talon Barge, but from there I head west. Willem the Shaper told me of a man in Ifelian who might help me develop my gift further, now that Palomar is gone."

Mention of the Aasimar struck Jaiden with a too-fresh reminder of loss, and a numbness spread through his heart.

She continued, "He also said stories had reached him of innocents being taken for slave-labor in the mines near there, and I intend to look into them as well."

Suddenly, a forgotten thought resurfaced, and Jaiden skipped down the steps past Rogan and Dhania while reaching behind his neck to unfasten the clasp of his gold chain. "I meant to bestow this upon you with more ceremony," he said as he reached Saffron, "but if you are leaving, I suppose a lack of fanfare will have to do." He extended the pendant of Living Fire toward her, its flashing crimson a stark contrast to the summer-blue sky.

Saffron's eyes and mouth formed wide circles. "Jaiden—"

"May I?" He stepped closer, lifting the chain a bit higher.

Without another word, Saffron turned her back as she grasped her ponytail to clear it from her shoulders. With a little awkwardness, he reached the pendant around to rest on her chest and fastened the clasp behind her, letting his hands dwell a moment on the exposed, sepia skin of her neck.

She faced him again while looking down at the jewel. "I don't know what to say; are you sure you want to give this away? To me?"

"It's magical, or so Ellingle tells me. I figure it should belong to someone who is magical as well. I would not be alive without you. And don't worry," he added, "whatever enchantments the King-priest placed upon it vanished with his death."

Saffron looked directly into Jaiden's eyes. "Thank you." She smiled and shook her head slowly. "I can hardly believe how far you have come, *Grandmaster* Luminere."

Jaiden felt his face flush and looked down at his feet. "I know. The Order's behind me, though. Orestes has been great – his support made sure the factions remained united. The remaining Dukes seem serious about formalizing an alliance as well."

"Wonderful news. Are you going to remain in the palace?" she asked.

He nodded. "It looks that way. The people accept me, and Criesha gains more followers every day."

"Congratulations, Jaiden," Baron Rogan said, clasping his shoulder before climbing down the rest of the steps. Dhania followed and they sorted out the reins of their horses. "It will be nice to know you are here if my country needs your help."

"Of course," Jaiden replied. "You are all welcome any time, and will have my aid as long as I am able to give it."

Saffron hugged him, but did not linger in her embrace as long as he would have liked. The three foreigners mounted their horses and waved goodbye, before turning toward the long, downward slope of the Eighth Hill. Jaiden sighed. He realized an ending when he saw one, but that didn't make it any easier to move on.

Epilogue

Izefet looked over the foothills of the Fire-Wall Mountains from his high perch outside the remote Cave of the Crossroads. Treacherous cliffs descended to a dizzying depth below. He wondered how his human father ever found the foreboding location in the first place.

Illicurus suddenly popped into view, rising above the edge of the outcropping. His strong wings flapped furiously as he gained altitude, finally coming to rest as his feet met solid rock. The half-demon waited for the Marshal of the Aasimar to fold his feathery extremities before communicating. The mere presence of the celestial made his skin itch.

"Did you meet with success?" Izefet asked, projecting a calm that came from taking the long-view.

Illicurus sounded much more agitated. *"The King-priest has fallen – it is confirmed."*

Izefet nodded. *"And the Living Fire?"*

"Unaccounted for. My guess is the whelp took it."

"I thought being an Aasimar meant you did not have to guess – you can feel the pull of it."

Illicurus crossed his arms. "That is true, demonspawn. Though the range is not unlimited. We will just have to get closer to pick up the trail."

"Tsk, tsk. No need to get testy, Marshal. We will need more than was in that pendant, though every bit helps. I would think an immortal would show more patience."

The Aasimar's feathers bristled. "I am done serving the needs of lower creatures. Do not make me regret our alliance. If you cannot follow through on your promises—"

Izefet shot him a look that could melt steel. "Be very careful with threats, Illicurus. We are not on Mount Celestia, and I should not have to remind you who my mother is. Bring me the Living Fire, and I will bring so much chaos to this realm its people will beg to serve you in return for stability."

Illicurus stared at him silently, sizing him up. The Aasimar was taller and more physically imposing, but Izefet could taste the uncertainty in his gaze. No matter what scheming led to the celestial's banishment, he could not fathom the underhanded depths that served as daily fare in the Abyss.

Finally, Illicurus uncrossed his arms and took a few, tentative steps toward the cave entrance. "Is there really a Planar Gate inside?"

"There is. But you know it is closed to you. Creatures from our planes must be properly summoned. My human blood grants me an exception, of course. Are you eager to return to your homeland?" Izefet moved to the edge of the cliff and looked down. "That could be arranged quite easily."

"*And fall back under the thumb of Hiruth Jeshu?*" The Aasimar scoffed. "*I think not.*" He looked around the mountainside and threw his arms up to the open air. "*This is my realm now, and I mean to rule it.*"

"*All in due time,*" Izefet practically whispered his thoughts. "*First, I shall spread the Name of the Beast.*"

PHILLIP M. LOCEY

Phillip studied Creative Writing at the University of
North Carolina at Chapel Hill and earned a Master's in
Library and Information Science from the
University of South Florida.
Weaned on the fantasy genre from a young age,
he spent decades creating the imagined world of Elisahd,
where the majority of his tales are now set.

Visit elisahdbooks.com for more stories,
artwork, and news about books to come!